KT-433-700

PENGUIN CLASSICS

CRIME AND PUNISHMENT

FYODOR MIKHAILOVICH DOSTOYEVSKY was born in Moscow in 1821, the second of a physician's seven children. When he left his private boarding school in Moscow he studied from 1838 to 1843 at the Military Engineering College in St Petersburg, graduating with officer's rank. His first story to be published, 'Poor Folk' (1846), was a great success. In 1849 he was arrested and sentenced to death for participating in the 'Petrashevsky circle'; he was reprieved at the last moment but sentenced to penal servitude, and until 1854 he lived in a convict prison at Omsk, Siberia. Out of this experience he wrote *The House of the Dead* (1860). In 1861 he began the review *Vremya* (*Time*) with his brother; in 1862 and 1863 he went abroad, where he strengthened his anti-European outlook, met Mlle Suslova, who was the model for many of his heroines, and gave way to his passion for gambling. In the following years he fell deeply in debt, but in 1867 he married Anna Grigoryevna Snitkina (his second wife), who helped to rescue him from his financial morass. They lived abroad for four years, then in 1873 he was invited to edit *Grazhdanin* (*The Citizen*), to which he contributed his *Diary of a Writer*. From 1876 the latter was issued separately and had a large circulation. In 1880 he delivered his famous address at the unveiling of Pushkin's memorial in Moscow; he died six months later in 1881. Most of his important works were written after 1864: *Notes from Underground* (1864), *Crime and Punishment* (1865–6), *The Gambler* (1866), *The Idiot* (1869), *The Devils* (1871) and *The Brothers Karamazov* (1880).

DAVID McDUFF was born in 1945 and was educated at the University of Edinburgh. His publications comprise a large number of translations of foreign verse and prose, including poems by Joseph Brodsky and Tomas Venclova, as well as contemporary Scandinavian work; *Selected Poems* of Osip Mandelstam; *Complete Poems* of Edith Södergran; and *No I'm Not Afraid* by Irina Ratushinskaya. His first book of verse, *Words in Nature*, appeared in 1972. He has translated a number of nineteenth-century Russian prose works for Penguin Classics. These include Dostoyevsky's *The Brothers Karamazov*, *The House of the Dead*, *Poor Folk and Other Stories* and *Uncle's Dream and Other Stories*, Tolstoy's *The Kreutzer Sonata and Other Stories* and *The Sebastopol Sketches*, and Nikolai Leskov's *Lady Macbeth of Mtsensk*. He has also translated Babel's *Collected Stories* and Bely's *Petersburg* for Penguin Twentieth-Century Classics.

CRIME AND PUNISHMENT

FYODOR DOSTOYEVSKY

TRANSLATED WITH AN
INTRODUCTION AND NOTES BY
DAVID McDUFF

PENGUIN BOOKS

PENGUIN BOOKS

Published by the Penguin Group
Penguin Books Ltd, 27 Wrights Lane, London W8 5TZ, England
Penguin Putnam Inc., 375 Hudson Street, New York, New York 10014, USA
Penguin Books Australia Ltd, Ringwood, Victoria, Australia
Penguin Books Canada Ltd, 10 Alcorn Avenue, Toronto, Ontario, Canada M4V 3B2
Penguin Books (NZ) Ltd, Private Bag 102902, NSMC, Auckland, New Zealand

Penguin Books Ltd, Registered Offices: Harmondsworth, Middlesex, England

This translation first published by Viking 1991
Published in Penguin Classics 1991
15 17 19 20 18 16 14

Translation, introduction and notes copyright © David McDuff, 1991
All rights reserved

The moral right of the translator has been asserted

Printed in England by Clays Ltd, St Ives plc

Except in the United States of America, this book is sold subject
to the condition that it shall not, by way of trade or otherwise, be lent,
re-sold, hired out, or otherwise circulated without the publisher's
prior consent in any form of binding or cover other than that in
which it is published and without a similar condition including this
condition being imposed on the subsequent purchaser

CONTENTS

A NOTE ON THE TEXT

The text used for the present translation is that contained in Volume 6 of F. M. Dostoyevsky: *Polnoye sobranie sochineniy v tridtsati tomakh*, Leningrad, 1973. Use has also been made of the draft material and notes contained in Volume 7.

A NOTE ON MONEY

In 1865, the year in which the action of Dostoyevsky's novel takes place, the most commonly used items of currency were as follows:

the half-copeck piece (*grosh*)
the one-copeck piece (*kopeyka*)
the five-copeck piece (*pyatak*)
the ten-copeck piece (*grivennik*)
the twenty-copeck piece (*dvugrivennyy*)
the fifty-copeck piece (*poltinnik*)
the rouble, usually a yellow banknote (*zholtyy bilet*)

There is some play with this last expression in the novel – in Russian, it also means 'the yellow card' (*la carte jaune*) or 'the yellow ticket', which was a euphemism for the special passport carried by prostitutes. The old woman pawnbroker uses the term *biletiki* (literally, 'little tickets') as slang for 'roubles', something that serves to increase Raskolnikov's irritation.

Mention is also made in the text of paper 'credit bills' (*kreditki*) or banknotes worth five roubles (*sinie bilety*, or 'bluebacks') and ten roubles (*krasnye bilety*, or 'redbacks').

The hundred-rouble note was known as a *raduzhnyy bilet*, or 'rainbow note', from its rainbow colouring.

IOU's ('promissory notes'), Government bonds and lottery tickets were also in circulation, together with regular currency.

Silver roubles had a fluctuating and inconstant value; following the recent devaluation of silver, they were actually worth less than paper roubles.

INTRODUCTION

When in 1866 the first part of *Crime and Punishment* was published in the January and February issues of Mikhail Katkov's journal the *Russian Messenger*, it met with instant public success. The remaining parts of the novel had still to be written, its author was struggling through poverty and debt to meet deadlines that loomed ever closer, yet both he and his readers sensed that this was a work that possessed an inner momentum of its own, one that was linked both to the inexorable processes of outer, social change and to those of an inner, spiritual awakening. 'The novel promises to be one of the most important works of the author of *The House of the Dead*,' an anonymous reviewer wrote.

> The terrible crime that forms the basis of this tale is described with such staggering veracity, in such subtle detail, that one finds oneself involuntarily experiencing the peripeteias of this drama with all its psychic springs and devices, traversing the heart's maze from the first inception within it of the criminal idea to its final development . . . Even the author's subjectivity, from which the characterization of his heroes has on occasion suffered, in this instance produces no harm whatsoever, as it is focused on a single character and is permeated by a typological clarity, artistic in nature.

As the subsequent parts of the novel began to appear it acquired the status of a social and public event. In his memoirs, the critic N. N. Strakhov recalled that in Russia *Crime and Punishment* was the literary sensation of the year, 'the only book the addicts of reading talked about. And when they talked about it they generally complained of its overmastering power and of its having such a distressing effect upon readers that those with strong nerves almost grew ill, while those with weak nerves had to put it aside.' The 'distressing' features of the novel were many. Quite apart from the analysis of social wretchedness and psychological disease, shocking even to readers of Victor Hugo's recently published *Les Misérables*, on which Dostoyevsky had drawn for some of his structural and panoramic inspiration,[1] there was the fact that the book appeared to constitute

[1] All his life Dostoyevsky showed a considerable interest in Victor Hugo's prose

yet another attack on the Russian student body, smearing it with the taint of being allied to the young radicals and nihilists who had placed themselves in violent opposition to the established social and political order. In early reviews, liberal and left-wing critics, who sensed the parallel between the murder of the old woman and the talk of political assassination that was in the air, saw the novel as a particularly virulent contribution to the flood of 'anti-nihilist' literature that had begun to appear in the 1860s, and sprang to the defence of 'the Russian student corporations': 'Has there ever been a case of a student committing murder for the sake of robbery?' asked the critic G. Z. Yeliseyev, writing in the *Contemporary*.

> And even if there had been such a case, what would it prove regarding the general mood of the student corporations? . . . Was it not Belinsky who once drew Dostoyevsky's attention to the fact that the fantastic belonged 'in the madhouse, not in literature'? . . . What would Belinsky have had to say about this new fantasticism of Mr Dostoyevsky, a fantasticism in consequence of which the entire corporation of young men stands accused of a wholesale attempt at robbery with murder?

This cry was taken up by an anonymous reviewer in the newspaper the *Week* (normally reflecting a liberal–conservative viewpoint), who wrote:

> . . . while taking full account of Mr Dostoyevsky's talent, we cannot pass over in silence those melancholy symptoms which in his latest novel manifest themselves with particular force . . . Mr Dostoyevsky is at present displeased with the younger generation. In itself that is not worthy of comment. The generation in question does

---

fiction, and in 1862, during his first visit to western Europe, he read the newly published *Les Misérables* with excitement. *Crime and Punishment* shows the influence of Hugo's novel in respect of plot (a criminal trying to evade a police agent who is shadowing him), background (the sewers of Paris have their counterpart in the canals of St Petersburg) and character (it is possible to draw parallels between Jean Valjean and Raskolnikov, Cosette and Dunya, Marius and Razumikhin, and Thénardier and Svidrigailov, among others). The subject of the many points of coincidence between the two novels has been thoroughly investigated by Nathalie Babel Brown in her valuable study *Hugo and Dostoevsky*, Ardis/Ann Arbor, 1978.

indeed possess defects that merit criticism, and to expose them is most praiseworthy, as long, of course, as it is done in an honourable fashion, without casting stones from round corners. That is the way it was done, for example, by Turgenev when he depicted (rather unsuccessfully, it should be said) the faults of the younger generation in his novel *Father and Sons*; Mr Turgenev, however, conducted the matter cleanly, without having recourse to sordid insinuations . . . That is not the way it has been done by Mr Dostoyevsky in his new novel. While not openly declaring that liberal ideas and the natural sciences lead young men to murder and young women to prostitution, in an oblique fashion he makes us feel that this is so.

The nihilist critic D. I. Pisarev, aware with others of the work's artistic vitality and absolute, undismissible topicality, tried another approach. Basing his critique on a 'social' interpretation of the novel, he argued that Raskolnikov was a product of his environment, and that the radical transformation of society Dostoyevsky seemed to be calling for could be achieved, not by the kind of Christianity Sonya had to offer, but by revolutionary action, the building of a new society. Almost alone, Strakhov attempted to draw his readers' attention to the novel's universal, tragic dimension as a parable of how, after terrible personal sufferings largely caused by society, a gifted young man is ruined by 'nihilistic' ideas, and has to undergo a process of atonement and redemption. Strakhov pointed to Dostoyevsky's compassionate treatment of his hero, and commented: 'This is not mockery of the younger generation, neither a reproach nor an accusation – it is a lament over it.'

Dostoyevsky's well-known response to Strakhov's article – 'You alone have understood me' – has continued to echo down the years; for *Crime and Punishment* has not ceased to present difficulties of interpretation. Even in the second half of the twentieth century critical studies of the novel have been written in which its central, underpinning ideas are either ignored as expressions of ideology which the writer's imaginative art 'overcame', or are distorted into unrecognizable caricatures of themselves. Thus, for example, the American critic Philip Rahv, in an essay that otherwise throws a good deal of light on the sources and background material associated with the novel, maintains that 'Sonya's faith is not one that has been attained through struggle,' and that 'it offers no solution to Raskolnikov, whose spiritual existence is incommensurable with hers,' describing the book's epilogue as 'implausible and out of key with the work as a whole'.[2] While it is true that a *definitive* comprehension of any work of art is impossible, as so much depends upon the possibilities of interpretation, which may be infinite, it is hard in the case of Dostoyevsky not to suspect that in many of the critical analyses of his work the operative factors are of an ideological rather than a purely aesthetic nature. This is hardly surprising, as in the work of Dostoyevsky's maturity thought and image, idea and form are always intertwined. For all this, it may still be useful to recapitulate the original 'idea' of *Crime and Punishment* as it was conceived by its author.

Possibly the clearest explanation of Dostoyevsky's intentions in writing the novel was given by the philosopher Vladimir S. Solovyov (1853–1900), who knew Dostoyevsky as a friend and in the summer of 1878 accompanied him on a pilgrimage to the monastery of Optina Pustyn. In the first of his three commemorative speeches (1881–3, published in 1884), Solovyov states the matter with utter simplicity. In a discussion of *Crime and Punishment* and *The Devils* he writes:

> The meaning of the first of these novels, for all its depth of detail, is very clear and simple, though many have not understood it. Its principal character is a representative of that view of things according to which every strong man is his own master, and all is permitted to him. In the name of his personal superiority, in the name of his belief that he is a *force*, he considers himself entitled to commit murder and does in fact do so. But then suddenly the deed he thought was merely a violation of a senseless outer law and a bold challenge to the prejudice of society turns out, for his own conscience, to be something much more than this – it turns out to be a sin, a violation of inner moral justice. His violation of the outer law meets its lawful retribution from without in exile and penal servitude, but his inward sin of pride that has separated the strong man from humanity and has led him to commit murder – that inward sin of self-idolatry can only be redeemed by an inner moral

[2] Philip Rahv: 'Dostoevsky in *Crime and Punishment*', *Partisan Review*, XXVII (1960).

12

act of self-renunciation. His boundless self-confidence must disappear in the face of that which is greater than *himself*, and his self-fabricated justification must humble itself before the higher justice of God that lives in those very same simple, weak folk whom the strong man viewed as paltry insects.

Solovyov sees the central meaning of Dostoyevsky's early work, which is preoccupied above all with those 'simple, weak folk', as a perception of 'the ancient and eternally new truth that in the established order of things the *best* people (morally) are at the same time the *worst* in the view of society, that they are condemned to be poor folk, the insulted and the injured'. Yet if Dostoyevsky had remained content merely to treat this problem as the subject of fiction, Solovyov maintains, he would have been no more than a glorified journalist. The important point is that Dostoyevsky saw the problem as part of his own life, as an existential question that demanded a satisfactory answer. The answer was an unambiguous one: 'The best people, observing in others and feeling in themselves a social injustice, must unite together, rise up against it and recreate society in their own way.' It was in pursuit of this goal that Dostoyevsky had joined the Petrashevists in their social conspiracy; his first, naïve attempt at a solution to the problem of social injustice led Dostoyevsky to the scaffold and to penal servitude. It was amidst the horrors of the 'House of the Dead' that he began to revise his notions concerning an uprising that was needed, not by the Russian people as a whole, but only by himself and his fellow conspirators.

In penal servitude, Solovyov asserts, Dostoyevsky came consciously face to face for the first time with representatives of true Russian national–popular feeling, in the light of which 'he clearly saw the falsehood of his revolutionary strivings':

Dostoyevsky's companions in the labour camp were, the vast majority of them, members of the common Russian people and were all, with a few striking exceptions, the worst members of that people. But even the worst members of the common people generally retain what members of the intelligentsia usually lose: a faith in God and a consciousness of their sinfulness. Simple criminals, marked out from the popular mass by their evil deeds, are in no way marked out from it in terms of their views and feelings, of their religious world-outlook. In the House of the Dead

13

Dostoyevsky found the real 'poor (or, in the popular expression, "unlucky") folk'. Those earlier ones, whom he had left behind, had still been able to take refuge from social injustice in a sense of their own dignity . . . This was denied to the convicts, but instead they had something more than this. The worst members of the House of the Dead restored to Dostoyevsky what the best members of the intelligentsia had taken from him. If there, among the representatives of enlightenment, a vestige of religious feeling had made him grow pale before the blasphemy of a leading *littérateur*, here, in the House of the Dead, that feeling was bound to revive and be renewed under the influence of the convicts' humble and devout faith.

Solovyov's analysis is doubtless coloured by his theories concerning the Russian Church and people, but even so, in its simplicity and straightforwardness, based on a personal knowledge of Dostoyevsky, it is hard to refute. Far from moving towards a religious dogmatism or alignment with reactionary political views, in the period that followed his incarceration Dostoyevsky began to discover a 'true socialism' – the *sobornost'* ('communion') of the human spirit as it expressed itself in the shared identity of the Russian people and their self-effacing acceptance of God.

The concluding chapters of *The House of the Dead* describe the reawakening of the central character's personality. This personality is not the same as the one that predominates in Dostoyevsky's earlier fiction – its experience of real physical and mental suffering, shared hardship and religious enlightenment lends it a universal dimension. For all its cramped, sardonic wretchedness, the 'I' of *Notes from Underground* inhabits a very different universe from that of Makar Devushkin or Ordynov. In its liberation from a half-asleep, romantic–sentimental vision of the world, in its consciousness of its own consciousness and of the depths of weakness and subterfuge that lie concealed within it, it acquires the status of a 'we': 'As for myself,' the Underground Man declares to his readers, 'all I have really done in my life is to take to an extreme that which you would not dare to take even halfway, interpreting your own cowardice as "good sense" and taking comfort in it, deceiving yourselves.' The first person narrative, far from dividing the narrator from his readers, as it does in some of Dostoyevsky's earlier works (*White Nights*, for example), actually draws him closer to them; by provoking them with a confession that goes to the root of each individual's ultimate helplessness and spiritual bankruptcy – a 'poverty' that can only be surmounted through an acceptance of God's grace – the Underground Man acts as a unifying voice of repentance. 'At any rate,' he writes, 'I have felt ashamed all the time I have been writing this "tale": it is probably not literature at all, but rather a corrective punishment.'

From the drafts and notebooks for *Crime and Punishment* we know that Dostoyevsky originally planned the novel as a confessional work in the same vein as *Notes from Underground*, which was published in 1864. The basis of the novel had already been laid in the *Notes*, where towards the end of Part Two, following the narrator's humiliation at the hotel dinner, his visit to the brothel and cynical manipulation of the prostitute Liza, we come across the following passage:

Towards evening I went out for a walk. My head was still aching and spinning from the previous night. But the further the evening wore on and the thicker the twilight became, the more my impressions, too, grew altered and confused, and after them my thoughts. Something within me, within my heart and my conscience, refused to die away, and burned there with a searing anguish. I loitered my way for the most part through the busiest, most crowded streets, through the Meshchanskayas, Sadovaya, the area near Yusupov Park. I was particularly fond of walking through these streets at dusk, at the very time when the crowd of passersby of all kinds is at its densest, as industrial workers and craftsmen, their faces preoccupied to the point of hatred, return home from their daily employments . . . On the present occasion all this busy street life made me even more irritable. No matter how hard I tried, I could not get a grip on myself, put two and two together. Something was rising, rising within me without cease, causing me pain, and would not quieten down. In a state of complete frustration I returned to my rooms. It was as though some crime lay on my soul.

This could come straight from one of the first drafts of the early chapters of *Crime and Punishment*. Indeed, the two works are in many ways interdependent, the *Notes* constituting a philosophical prologue to the novel. The twenty-three-year-old ex-student who emerges on to the Petersburg street on an evening in early July is a spiritual

15

relative of the Underground Man – we are meant to assume that the weeks of isolation and 'hypochondria' he has spent indoors have been accompanied by the kind of deliberations that fill the pages of the *Notes*. In the early drafts of the novel, the narrative is in the first person, and has the same obsessive, confessional quality familiar from the earlier work. The principal difference is that while the crime of the Underground Man is of an exclusively moral and personal nature, a sin against another human being and against himself, that of Raskolnikov is in the first instance an outright challenge to the fabric of society, though it also involves the moral and personal dimension.

The 'stone wall' that so irks the Underground Man is also present in *Crime and Punishment*. Yet now it stands not only for 'the laws of nature, the conclusions of the natural sciences and mathematics' – it is also a symbol of the laws of society. The walls that surround Raskolnikov and hold him within his coffinlike room are not simply the bounds of 'possibility': they are also society's protection against its own members. In Dostoyevsky's view there is something profoundly wrong with a social order that needs to imprison, impoverish and torture the best people in it. Yet this does not excuse Raskolnikov's crime (the Russian word *prestuplenie* is much more graphic, suggesting the 'stepping across' or 'transgression' that he so desires to make). It is *people* who are responsible for the society in which they live, and whether they are in the grip of 'radical', atheistic ideas like those of Raskolnikov, or 'bourgeois', utilitarian, but also atheistic ideas, like those of Pyotr Petrovich Luzhin, they will abdicate their responsibility to their fellow creatures and destroy them in one way or another. Just as the Underground Man expresses his contempt for the 'antheap', the 'Crystal Palace' of modern 'civilization' which gives rise mostly to 'rivers of blood', so Raskolnikov *acts* out of the same convictions. He also intends, however, to enter the arena of history. It is in this respect above all that *Crime and Punishment* marks a significant development in Dostoyevsky's creative thinking.

The philosopher and literary critic Vasily Rozanov (1856–1919) – another Russian thinker with a close and intuitive understanding of Dostoyevsky – was one of the first to point to this aspect of the writer's art. At the beginning of a 'critical–biographical profile' written in 1893 as an introduction to the publication of Dostoyevsky's complete works in the journal *Niva*, he discusses the function of literature, perceiving it to be the means whereby the individual person is able to withdraw 'from the details of his own life' and to understand his existence in terms of its general significance. History takes its origins in the individual, and man is distinguished from the animals by the fact that he is always a *person*, unique and never-to-be-repeated. This, in Rozanov's view, is why conventional, 'positivist' science and philosophy will never be able to understand 'man, his life and history'. The laws that govern the natural universe do not apply to man. 'Is the most important thing about Julius Caesar, about Peter the Great, about you, dear reader, the way in which we do not differ from other people? In the sense that the most important thing about the planets is not their varying distance from the sun but the shape of their ellipses and the laws according to which they all move equally along them . . .' Unlike science and natural philosophy, art and religion address themselves to the individual person, to his heart and soul. They are concerned with the phases of the inner life, not all of which each individual may experience, but which are characteristic of the history of mankind: a period of primordial serenity, a fall from that serenity and a period of regeneration. The 'fall' is the phase that predominates over the other two – most of history is taken up with 'crime and sin', which is, however, always directed *against* the serenity that went before and also points towards the process of regeneration as the only way towards the recovery of that serenity. In the darkness of history lies the hope of light:

> The darker the night – the brighter the stars,
> The deeper the grief – the closer is God.

'In these two lines of verse,' Rozanov says, 'is the meaning of all history, and the history of the spiritual development of thousandfold souls.' Raskolnikov, with his Napoleon-fixation and muddled, radical ideas, does no more than enter into the historical arena of his times – like Napoleon, he is at once an individual soul and an agent of world history, and as such he is able to draw the reader with him on his exploration of the 'dark night'. The 'power over the antheap' he talks of is in reality the power of Dostoyevsky's own artistic persona over the readers of the novel. As Rozanov points out:

In this novel we are given a depiction of all those conditions which, capturing the human soul, draw it towards crime; we see the crime

17

itself; and at once, in complete clarity, with the criminal's soul we enter into an atmosphere, hitherto unknown to us, of murk and horror in which it is almost as hard for us to breathe as it is for him. The general mood of the novel, elusive, undefinable, is far more remarkable than any of its individual episodes: how this comes to be is the secret of the author, but the fact remains that he really does take us with him and lets us feel criminality with all the inner fibres of our being; after all, we ourselves have committed no crime, and yet, when we finish the book it is as if we emerge into the open air from some cramped tomb in which we have been walled up with a living person who has buried himself in it, and together with him have breathed the poisoned air of dead bones and decomposing entrails . . .

Because of his existence on a historical plane as a psycho-social and moral–intellectual *type*, as a part of the fabric of the time in which he lives, Raskolnikov is able to speak to the collective human reality in all of us. Just as each person contains a tyrant, a Napoleon (or, in a twentieth-century perspective, a Hitler or Stalin), so each contains a suffering victim. The tyrant's crime is punished by that suffering, which alone can redeem it. What Dostoyevsky is pointing to is the possibility, less of social, material change from without than of a transformation of humanity from within. The drafts and notes for the novel speak very clearly of this: the book was originally planned as a novel of 'the Orthodox outlook', expressing 'the essence of Orthodoxy', this being summed up in the notion that 'happiness is bought with suffering', a state of affairs in which 'there is no injustice, for a knowledge of life and an awareness of it (i.e. one spontaneously experienced in body and spirit, i.e. as a part of the integral process of life) are acquired by the experience of pro and contra, which one must carry around with one'.

The experience of pro and contra, the ancient mystery of good and evil dressed in the contemporary costume of the mid-nineteenth century yet none the less terrifying and elemental for that, is what *Crime and Punishment* is 'about'. The novel represents the first act in a gigantic Shakespearian tragedy, the other three acts of which are *The Idiot*, *The Devils* and *The Brothers Karamazov*. In this first act the themes of guilt and punishment are established, the terrain of Hell and Purgatory are mapped out, and the goal of Paradise dimly glimpsed.

Just how intense was the duel of 'for' and 'against' that raged within Dostoyevsky's soul may again be seen in the draft notes and jottings. 'Svidrigailov – despair, the most cynical. Sonya – hope, the most unrealizable. (This must be said by Raskolnikov himself.) He has passionately attached himself to them both,' reads an entry in the notes for the 'Finale of the Novel'. The pages of the notebooks teem with lists of contraries, seeds of conflict, the preliminaries to catastrophe. While many of the episodes and allusions are familiar from one's knowledge of the novel in its final form, there are others which do not appear in it, or appear in a less sharply defined way. Such, for example, is the conflict motif 'socialism–cynicism'. In the final version of the novel, the theme of socialism is kept muted, mostly confined to satirical observations about Fourierist 'phalansteries' and theories of diminished responsibility – it does not emerge in full force until *The Devils*. Yet in Dostoyevsky's notes for *Crime and Punishment* it is well to the fore, and helps us both to establish the link between the Underground Man and Raskolnikov, and to understand the nature of the demonism that drives Raskolnikov to commit his crime. Socialism, in Dostoyevsky's view, suffers from an inherent paradoxical flaw – while professing 'brotherhood' it is in essence cynical, expressing 'the despair of ever setting man on the right road. They, the socialists, are intent on doing it by means of despotism, while claiming that this is freedom!' The Underground Man's confession that 'without power and tyranny over someone else I simply cannot live' is amplified into Raskolnikov's Maratism: the corpses of the old woman moneylender and her sister stand for those of the tyrannized victims on which he will build the new, 'reformed' world.

That these ideological polemics were an integral part of the novel's original conception is amply evidenced by the notebooks. The satire on the nihilists that is worked around the person of Lebezyatnikov is not a superfluous, period-determined ornament to the general flow of the narrative. It is rather a caustic, though humorous, attack on a whole generation, and on human nature itself. In many ways, Yeliseyev's instincts did not deceive him: the novel *is* a work in which 'the entire corporation of young men stands accused of a wholesale attempt at robbery with murder'. What he failed to perceive, however, is that in those nihilists Dostoyevsky saw himself at an earlier phase of his development, and that it is also himself he is satirizing. It is significant that Dostoyevsky's real venom is reserved for the respectable *bourgeois* who laid the groundwork for the theories of the nihilists and made them possible – the utilitarians like Bentham, who inspire the conduct of a Luzhin. In the account of Raskolnikov's dream in the final chapter of the novel, a dream that is in every sense prophetic in its horror, we are made aware of how great are the dangers to mankind that are involved in the abandonment of God:

In his illness he had dreamt that the entire world had fallen victim to some strange, unheard of and unprecedented plague that was spreading from the depths of Asia into Europe. Everyone was to perish, apart from a chosen few, a very few. Some new kind of trichinae had appeared, microscopic creatures that lodged themselves in people's bodies. But these creatures were spirits, gifted with will and intelligence. People who absorbed them into their systems instantly became rabid and insane. But never, never had people considered themselves so intelligent and in unswerving possession of the truth as did those who became infected. Never had they believed so unswervingly in the correctness of their judgements, their scientific deductions, their moral convictions and beliefs. Entire centres of population, entire cities and peoples became smitten and went mad. All were in a state of anxiety and no one could understand anyone else, each person thought that he alone possessed the truth and suffered agony as he looked at the others, beating his breast, weeping and wringing his hands. No one knew who to make the subject of judgement, or how to go about it, no one could agree about what should be considered evil and what good. No one knew who to blame or who to acquit. People killed one another in a kind of senseless anger. Whole armies were ranged against one another, but no sooner had these armies been mobilized than they suddenly began to tear themselves to pieces, their ranks falling apart and their soldiers hurling themselves at one another, gashing and stabbing, biting and eating one another. All day in the cities the alarm was sounded: everyone was being summoned together, but who was calling them and for what reason no one knew, but all were in a state of anxiety. They abandoned the most common trades, because each person wanted to offer his ideas, his improvements, and no agreement could be reached; agriculture came to a halt. In this place and that people would gather into groups, agree on something together, swear to stick together – but would instantly begin doing something completely different from what had been proposed, start blaming one another, fighting and murdering. Fires began, a famine broke out. Everyone and everything perished. The plague grew worse, spreading further and further. Only a few people in the whole world managed to escape: they were the pure and chosen, who had been predestined to begin a new species of mankind and usher in a new life, to renew the earth and render it pure, but no one had seen these people anywhere, no one had heard their words and voices.

In opposition to the nihilists with their pride and *déracinement*, Dostoyevsky introduces the theme of the family. Raskolnikov's fatherless family also serves to de-subjectivize and universalize the image in which he appears to the reader. We can understand, not merely intellectually but also in emotional terms, Raskolnikov's desire to do something in order to secure the fortunes of his mother and sister, to assert the strength that is lacking because of his father's absence. At the same time, we are kept aware of the extent to which Raskolnikov has broken away from the lifelines that bind him to existence. The climate of the family is one of humility, tolerance and mutual acceptance; by his thoughts and actions, Raskolnikov transgresses the laws by which it operates – yet only to a certain extent: as Dunya realizes the *reason* for what he has done, her attitude towards him softens, even though her determination that he should face the consequences of his actions is made resolute. As for Pulkheria Aleksandrovna, his mother, she passes from a state of uncomprehending rejection of her son to one of suffering acceptance. In overcoming his pride and taking upon himself the punishment decreed by the state and society, Raskolnikov re-enters the bosom of his family, which becomes a symbol of *narodnost'* (national and folk identity), and love of neighbour in the Christian sense. This is made abundantly clear in the draft notes, where, for example, Raskolnikov's contempt for the old woman-'louse' is seen as a fatal lapse into the attitude of the nihilists, who really care only about themselves. From a study of the drafts, we can see that the novel's horizons are quite certainly intended to include a vision of a universal family as the longed-for ideal, in opposition to the 'antheap' or the socialist utopia, founded on theoretic abstractions and delusions of 'progress'. In

Raskolnikov's friendship with Razumikhin we can also perceive Dostoyevsky's conception of true brotherhood, as opposed to the 'fraternity' of the student body and the radical movement.

Raskolnikov's family has its counterpart in that of Sonya. The Marmeladov household, with its alcoholic father, consumptive mother and ultimately orphaned children, took its origins in the novel *The Drunkards*, which Dostoyevsky eventually merged with the Raskolnikov tale to produce *Crime and Punishment*, aware of the many parallels of characterization in the two works. For all the disasters that befall it, this ménage is none the less a *family*, an integral unit with its own sacred symbols and objects, such as the green *drap-de-dames* shawl and the travelling-box. It is no coincidence that it should be Sonya, the prostitute from a broken, destroyed home, who raises Raskolnikov from the 'death' of isolation and self-defilement and estrangement into which he has fallen, and restores him to the community of mankind; in order to be thus restored, he must suffer, and his return to humanity must take place in the sign of the Cross and the reality of the Russian earth:

> 'What should you do?' she exclaimed, leaping up from her chair, and her eyes, hitherto filled with tears, suddenly began to flash. 'Get up!' (She gripped him by the shoulder; slowly he began to get up, staring at her in near-amazement.) 'Go immediately, this very moment, go and stand at the crossroads, bow down, first kiss the ground that you've desecrated, and then bow to the whole world, to all four points of the compass and tell everyone, out loud: "I have killed!" Then God will send you life again . . . You must accept suffering and redeem yourself by it, that's what.'

Sonya, who has suffered the loss of her parents, her honour and her dignity, yet has not abandoned her faith, understands the loss sustained by Raskolnikov, who has abandoned his. He has lost God, lost himself, the sanctity of his own personality, and he can recover this only by penal servitude and the living contact it will involve with the Russian people. Here Dostoyevsky explicitly points to his own biography, and to the transition from 'coffin' to regeneration experienced by Goryanchikov, the narrator of *The House of the Dead*. To reduce Sonya to a peripheral character in the way several Western critics have done, usually on philosophical or extra-literary grounds, is to deprive the novel of its central meaning. Sonya is Raskolnikov's good double, just as Svidrigailov is his evil one. Her criminality, which has been forced upon her by the demands of an unjust society, runs parallel to his, but shines with an innocence of which his does not partake. It is because of this that she is able to impart to him a will to believe and a will to live; it is also the reason for her spirituality and 'remoteness' – in a note, Dostoyevsky describes her as following Raskolnikov to Golgotha 'at forty paces'. As she does so, she carries with her both Raskolnikov's past and childhood, and a vision of the man into which he must grow. She is child and mother, family and nation, 'holy fool' and angel. The scene in Part Four, Chapter IV, where she reads aloud the story of the raising of Lazarus to Raskolnikov, is the central point of the novel – a moment of almost unbearable earthly anguish, distress and tension that nevertheless points heavenward, like some Gothic arch.

In the argument of 'pro and contra' (it is significant that this is the title Dostoyevsky later gave to Book V of *The Brothers Karamazov*, which contains Ivan's exposition of the Legend of the Grand Inquisitor), Svidrigailov plays the role of devil's advocate. Joseph Brodsky has likened Dostoyevsky's technique in this respect to the classical dictum that 'before you come forth with your argument, however right or righteous you may feel, you have to list all the arguments of the opposite side'. As he worked at the development of Svidrigailov's personality, Dostoyevsky went to such pains to make it both humanly credible *and* demonic that some readers of the novel have been misled into thinking that Svidrigailov is a mouthpiece for Dostoyevsky's own views. The draft notes, however, make it clear that the character of Svidrigailov is based on that of 'A–v' (Aristov), one of the convicts described in *The House of the Dead*. Aristov, we may remember, is the young nobleman who was 'the most revolting example of the degree to which a man can lower and debase himself and of the degree to which he is capable of killing every moral feeling in himself, without effort or remorse', 'a kind of lump of meat, with teeth and a stomach and an insatiable craving for the coarsest, most bestial physical pleasures', 'an example of what the physical side of man on its own can produce if unrestrained by any inner norms or set of laws'. In the character of Svidrigailov, Aristov's murderous cynicism is clothed in a mantle of 'civilization' – his speech is studded with Gallicisms and French quotations, with learned references and allusions to the latest fashionable ideas and events. Dostoyevsky's draft notebooks are

23

crowded with jottings and sketches for this character, who in many ways represents the essence of criminality, and the mortal danger to which Raskolnikov has exposed himself by his abandonment of faith and surrender to self-will and the *Zeitgeist*. 'Svidrigailov has secret horrors behind him, horrors which he relates to nobody, but which he betrays by the facts of his behaviour and his convulsive, animal need to torture and kill. Coldly impassioned. A wild beast. A tiger.' This predatory sensualist is intended by Dostoyevsky to show what can happen to a Russian who turns his back on his own country, his own roots and origins, as the writer believed the liberal 'Westernizers' had done, with Turgenev at their head. In *Winter Notes on Summer Impressions* (1862), Dostoyevsky had written, under the guise of a travel diary, an energetic attack on Western values and 'civilization', which he saw as a thin and artificial veneer masking an inner chaos and barbarism. In the *Winter Notes'* descriptions of the London brothels and gin-palaces, the gaslit, Poe-like streetscapes with their doomed inhabitants, we are given a foretaste of the street scenes in *Crime and Punishment*, which are presided over by the spirit of the Antichrist in the person of Svidrigailov. The evil of the 'Crystal Palace', the mass industrial society that breeds rootless anonymity and criminal mania, finds its counterpart in the cynical, alienated behaviour of Svidrigailov, to whom all things are possible and permissible, and who therefore suffers from total indifference and a total inability to engage with his own life, to decide what to do with it. Haunted by the ghost of his own wrecked humanity, he tortures, intimidates and murders, he toys with schemes of ballooning and Arctic exploration, of emigration to America (an echo of Balzac's Vautrin) and in the end he commits suicide, for want of any other solution to his boredom. In his conversations with Raskolnikov we hear the surging of this ocean of faithlessness and betrayal from afar as an unsteady scurrying of sudden changes of mood, the meanderings, perhaps, of some tormented political despot, of a Caesar, a Nero, a Napoleon. It is significant that in the early drafts of the novel, both Svidrigailov and Raskolnikov were intended to commit suicide; in the novel's final version, Raskolnikov survives his own evil genius.

Above all, the portrayal of Raskolnikov's character concerns the theme and the problem of *personality*. What is under threat from bourgeois utilitarianism and radical socialism alike is the image of the human self, and its potential for change and transformation. What those ideologies deny to the personality is its freedom, which as Nicholas Berdyaev observed 'is the way of suffering. It is always tempting to free man from suffering after robbing him of his freedom. Dostoyevsky is the defender of freedom. Consequently he exhorts man to take suffering upon himself as an inevitable consequence of freedom.' In itself, freedom is neither good nor evil: it involves a choice of one or the other. Svidrigailov's freedom, the 'liberty' propounded by Western philosophy, political economy and socialist theory as an absolute good, is a false one – in it he reveals himself to be at the mercy of his own animal instincts: without God he is a slave to the impersonal forces of nature, and his personality shrivels and dies. Sonya, on the other hand, who has accepted the necessity and inevitability of suffering, exists in true freedom – she is equally aware of the possibilities for destruction and creation that exist around her, and would concur with Berdyaev's dictum that 'the existence of evil is a proof of God's existence. If the world consisted solely and exclusively of goodness and justice, God would not be necessary, for then the world itself would be God. God exists because evil exists. And this means that God exists because freedom exists.' It is towards this freedom that Raskolnikov makes his way through the pages of *Crime and Punishment* and the swirling alternations of night and day, dream and waking, timelessness and time. His dreams disclose to him the possibilities that hang in the balance: *everything* may be lost, as in the nightmare of the flogged horse, which stands for his own denied self, or *everything* may be gained, as in the fantasy of the Egyptian oasis, where he drinks the water of life:

A caravan was resting, the camels were lying down peacefully; all around there were palm trees, an entire circle of them; everyone was eating their evening meal. He, however, kept drinking water, straight from the spring that flowed murmuring right by his side. It was so cool, and the water was so wonderfully, wonderfully cold and blue, hurrying over various-coloured stones and sand that was so pure, with spangles of gold . . .

Raskolnikov, far from being a madman or psychopathic outcast, is an image of Everyman. His pilgrimage towards salvation is chronicled by Dostoyevsky in terms of the biblical myth of original sin – he has fallen from grace, and must regain it. In his own knowledge of the sacredness of his own person, and of the violation of that sacredness inherent in his crime, he bears within him the seeds of a new life which grows out of the conflict of 'for' and 'against'. The entire 'detective story' form of the novel is intended to simulate the circumstances of an inquisition. Porfiry Petrovich, Zamyotov and the rest of the police apparatus are concerned in the first instance to probe Raskolnikov's soul and to make him aware that the crime he has committed is a sin against the divine presence within himself. Raskolnikov feels little remorse for having killed the old woman, but suffers under a crushing, life-destroying weight of misery at what he has 'done to himself', to use Sonya's words.

One aspect of Raskolnikov's revolt against God that has sometimes been neglected by critics is to be seen in his name: the *Raskol*, or 'Schism', is the term used to describe the split that took place in the Russian Orthodox Church in the mid seventeenth century, when certain liturgical reforms were introduced by Patriarch Nikon. The *raskol 'niki* were sectarians who clung to the old rituals, putting themselves at variance with the civil and ecclesiastical authorities, with whom they came into violent and sometimes bloody conflict. Dostoyevsky had met these 'Old Believers' and their descendants in the labour camp at Omsk, and wrote about them in *The House of the Dead*. In an essay on the Schism, V. S. Solovyov characterized it as a form of 'Russian Protestantism', a disease of true Christianity, diagnosing its central error as a tendency to confuse the human with the divine, the temporal with the eternal, the particular with the universal; denying the supremacy of Christianity's collective principle and reality, the Church, it tended towards a divinization of the individual:

Containing within it a germ of Protestantism, the Russian Schism cultivated it to its limits. Even among the Old Believers, the true preserver of the ancient heritage and tradition is the individual person. This person does not live in the past, but in the present; the adopted tradition, here shorn of an advantage over the individual in terms of living wholeness or catholicity (as in the Universal Church) and being in itself no more than a dead formality, is revitalized and reanimated merely by the faith and devoutness of its true preserver – the individual person. No sooner, however, does a position of this kind start to be aware that the centre of gravity is shifting from the dead past to the living present, than the conventional objects of tradition lose all value, and all significance is transferred to the independent, individual bearer of that tradition; from this there proceeds the direct transition to those free sects which notoriously claim personal inspiration and personal righteousness as the basis of religion.

In *Crime and Punishment* there are clear indications that Dostoyevsky intends the reader to associate Raskolnikov with the religious heresy of *staroobryadchestvo* ('Old Ritualism'), not in any specific sense but rather in a general one. In Chapter II of Part Six the investigator Porfiry Petrovich tells Raskolnikov that Mikolka, who has 'confessed' to the crime, comes from a family in which there are 'Runners' – sectarians who travelled around the country begging, and in search of any chance to humble themselves:

> 'And did you know that he's a Raskolnik – or rather, not so much a Raskolnik as simply a sectarian; there were "Runners" in his family, and it's not so long ago since he himself spent two whole years in the country under the spiritual guidance of some elder or other . . . Have you any conception, Rodion Romanovich, of what the word "suffering" means to some of them? They don't do it for the sake of anyone in particular, but just for its own sake, purely and simply as "suffering"; all that matters is to accept suffering, and if it's from the powers-that-be, that's all to the good . . .'

Porfiry's implication, skilfully presented by means of psychological suggestion and interrogation techniques, is that Raskolnikov, too, has been treading this path – and that he must continue to do so if he is eventually to find salvation. For this is one of the main reasons why Raskolnikov is able to be saved from the error into which he has fallen – his illness is of a specifically Russian kind, caused not only by the influence of 'nihilistic' Western ideas, but also by an inborn *raskol 'nichestvo*, an ancient Russian sympathy for and identification with the strong dissenter who challenges the authority of Church and State alike. The Epilogue to the novel describes the beginning of his journey back to them, a journey that will ultimately involve not only his own personal recovery and transformation, but also the regeneration and renewal of Russian society. It is the persistent tracing of this theme of a 'Russian sickness' of spiritual origin and its cure throughout the book that justifies the author's characterization of it as an 'Orthodox novel'.

*

27

Few works of fiction have attracted so many widely diverging interpretations as *Crime and Punishment*. It has been seen as a detective novel, an attack on radical youth, a study in 'alienation' and criminal psychopathology, a work of prophecy (the attempt on the life of Tsar Alexander II by the nihilist student Dmitry Karakozov took place while the book was at the printer's, and some even saw the Tsar's murder in 1881 as a fulfilment of Dostoyevsky's warning), an indictment of urban social conditions in nineteenth-century Russia, a religious epic and a proto-Nietzschean analysis of the 'will to power'. It is, of course, all these things – but it is more. As the researcher and scholar Helen Muchnic pointed out in 1939,[3] it is hard when reading the critical literature on Dostoyevsky to avoid the feeling that interpretations of his work tend to say more about those who make them than they do about the novelist himself. Even half a century later, this is still largely true of the contributions by Western critics to the study of *Crime and Punishment*: nearly all of them have some special, personal reason for making the kind of statements that they do when writing of the novel. In the case of the British critics, who include J. A. Lloyd, E. H. Carr, Maurice Baring and John Middleton Murry, one receives confirmation of Muchnic's general claim that 'the tone of the English studies has been either aloof or rhapsodic'. The most typical British response to the work was also one of the earliest – that of Robert Louis Stevenson, who after reading the book in French translation wrote to John Addington Symonds in 1886 that while he relished its 'lovely goodness' and admired the power and strength of the action and characterization, he was bewildered by 'the incoherency and incapacity of it all'. Continental European critics proved more deeply perceptive, though for a long time there persisted a fashionable view, first formulated by E.-M. de Vogüé in his *Le Roman russe* (1886), which interpreted *Crime and Punishment* as a work of Hugoesque social and civic 'realism' concerned with 'the religion of suffering', linked to *Poor Folk* and *The House of the Dead*, and thus cut off from the supposedly inferior later novels. Perhaps some of the most telling Western comments on the character of Raskolnikov were made by André Gide in his *Dostoïevski (Articles et causeries)* (1923). It is Gide's celebrated remark – 'humiliation damns, whereas humility sanctifies' – that

[3] Helen Muchnic: 'Dostoevsky's English Reputation (1881–1936)', Smith College Studies in Modern Languages, Vol. 20, Nos. 3/4.

makes us most clearly aware of the depth of hurt pride in which Raskolnikov finds himself at the beginning of the novel, and of the journey towards self-denial that is mapped out across its pages. In his discussion of *Crime and Punishment* Gide also shows the clear links that unite it with Dostoyevsky's later works, and illustrates how it prepares the way for them.

In Russia, as we have seen, criticism of the novel has also been coloured by partisan and ideological interests. In the political climate of nineteenth-century Russia the implications of Dostoyevsky's message were already keenly felt by the book's earliest reviewers, and even today Soviet literary critics tend to write of it as a work of 'moral' and social significance, shying clear of the underlying anti-materialist, anti-revolutionary and anti-humanist elements it contains. Perhaps the most sensitive interpretations apart from those of Rozanov and V. S. Solovyov have come from critics and philosophers of the Christian–existentialist school such as Konstantin Mochulsky and Nicholas Berdyaev, whose thinking and spiritual experience, while not proceeding directly from those of Dostoyevsky, none the less run parallel to them. Berdyaev, who viewed Dostoyevsky not as a psychologist but as a 'pneumatologist', a researcher of souls, probably comes closer than any other critic, Russian or non-Russian, to providing a way towards an inner understanding of the novel for Western readers. The way is to be found in *Dostoievsky – An Interpretation* (1934). There, however, Berdyaev characterizes the Russian soul as being fundamentally different in nature from the Western soul. Berdyaev's study may help Westerners along a part of the route – but in the last result, approached in a non-Russian context, *Crime and Punishment* requires a leap of the spirit and imagination by readers themselves.

PART ONE

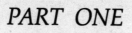

I

At the beginning of July, during a spell of exceptionally hot weather,* towards evening, a certain young man came down on to the street from the little room he rented from some tenants in S— Lane and slowly, almost hesitantly, set off towards K—n Bridge.*

He had succeeded in avoiding an encounter with his landlady on the stairs. His room was situated right under the roof of a tall, five-storey tenement,* and sooner resembled a closet than a place of habitation. His landlady, from whom he rented this room with dinner and a maid, lived on the floor below in a separate apartment, and each time he wanted to go down to the street he had to pass his landlady's kitchen, the door of which was nearly always wide-open on to the stairs. And each time, as he passed it, the young man had a morbid sensation of fear, of which he was ashamed and which caused him to frown. He was heavily in debt to his landlady, and was afraid of running into her.

Not that he was particularly timid or cowed – quite the opposite, indeed; but for some time now he had been in a tense, irritable state of mind that verged upon hypochondria. So absorbed in himself had he grown, so isolated from everyone else, that he was actually afraid of meeting anyone at all, not simply his landlady. He had been crushed by poverty; but even his reduced circumstances had of late ceased to be a burden to him. His vital interests no longer concerned him; he did not even wish to think about them. As a matter of fact, no landlady on earth had the power to make him afraid, whatever she might be plotting against him. But to have to stop on the stairs and listen to all that mediocre rubbish that had nothing whatsoever to do with him, all those pestering demands for payment, those threats and complaints, and be compelled in response to shift his ground, make excuses, tell lies – no, it was better to slink down the stairs like a cat and steal away unseen by anyone.

As he emerged on to the street on this occasion, however, his terror of meeting his creditress shocked even him.

'I plan to attempt a thing like this, yet I allow that kind of rubbish to scare me!' he thought with a strange smile. 'Hm . . . yes . . . Everything lies in a man's hands, and if he lets it all slip past his nose it's purely out of cowardice . . . that's an axiom. It's a curious reflection: what are people most afraid of? Of doing something new, saying a new word of their own that hasn't been said before – that's what scares them most. But I'm rambling. That's why I never do anything – because I ramble on to myself like that. Or perhaps it's the other way round: I ramble because I never do anything. It's during this past month that I've picked up this habit of rambling, lying on my back for whole days and nights on end in my room and thinking . . . about Cloud-cuckoo-land. Well, why am I on my feet now? Am I really capable of *this*? Is *this* a serious matter? Of course it isn't. It's just a fantasy to amuse myself with: it's just pretty pictures! Yes, I do believe that's all it is – pretty pictures!'

Outside the heat was terrible, with humidity to make it worse; and the crowds of people, the slaked lime everywhere, the scaffolding, the bricks, the dust and that distinctive summer aroma, so familiar to every inhabitant of St Petersburg who has not the means to rent a dacha in the country – all these things had a shattering effect on the young man's already jangled nerves. The unbearable stench from the drinking dens, of which there are in this quarter of the city inordinately many, and the drunks he kept running into every moment or two, even though it was still working hours, completed the sad and loathsome colouring of the scene. An emotion of the most profound repugnance flickered for a moment in the young man's features. It may be worth observing that he was remarkably handsome, with beautiful dark eyes and dark, chestnut-coloured hair; he was taller than average, slim and well-built. But soon he appeared to fall into a deep brooding, which might more correctly have been described as a kind of oblivion, and now, as he walked along, he ceased to be aware of his surroundings, nor had he any desire to be aware of them. Only occasionally did he mutter something to himself – a consequence of that addiction to monologues that he himself had so recently acknowledged. At this moment he himself was conscious that every so often his thoughts grew confused, and that he was very weak: for two days now he had had practically nothing at all to eat.

So poorly dressed was he that another man, even one inured to such a style of living, would have been ashamed to go out on the street during the daytime in such rags. However, this particular district was of such a kind that it would have been difficult to surprise anyone by one's manner of dress. The proximity of the Haymarket, the abundance of brothels and the local population which was, for the most part, made up of tradesmen and craftsmen, and huddled together in these streets and lanes of St Petersburg's centre, sometimes enlivened the general panorama with such picturesque subjects that it would have been odd for anyone to be surprised at encountering the occasional freak. But by this time so much vicious contempt had built up in the young man's soul that, in spite of all his sometimes very youthful finickiness, he was least ashamed of his rags while out on the streets. It would have been another matter had he run into people he knew, or any of his erstwhile student colleagues, whom in general he hated meeting at all times . . . And yet when a drunken man, who at that moment was being hauled off down the street, heaven knows where or why, in an enormous waggon drawn by an equally enormous cart-horse, suddenly shouted to him as he rode past: 'Hey, you – German hatter!' and began to bellow at him at the top of his voice, pointing at him – the young man suddenly stopped and grabbed convulsively at his hat. This hat had been one of those tall, round affairs from Zimmerman's,* but was now completely worn out and faded, covered in holes and stains and missing its brim, so that it cocked over to one side at a most outlandish angle. It was not shame that had assailed him, however, but an emotion of quite a different kind, one more akin to terror.

'I might have known it!' he muttered in confusion. 'I thought as much! This is worse than any of it! It is exactly this sort of nonsense, some vulgar little trivial detail, that could ruin the whole plan! Yes, a hat that's too conspicuous . . . It's absurd, and that's why it's conspicuous . . . What I need to go with my rags is a peaked cap – any old flat-top will do, but not this museum-piece. Nobody wears things like this, it would be spotted a mile off, people would remember it . . . the main thing is that it would be remembered afterwards, and bang! – they'd have their evidence. In this sort of business you have to be as inconspicuous as possible . . . The details, it's the details that matter more than anything else! . . . It's that sort of detail that always ruins everything . . .'

He did not have far to go; he even knew how many paces he had to take in order to reach the front entrance of his tenement: seven hundred and thirty exactly. He had somehow managed to count them once, when he had been doing rather a lot of dreaming. At the time he had not yet had much faith in these dreams of his, and had merely irritated himself with their outrageous but seductive daring. Now, a month later, he was beginning to see them differently and, in spite of all his teasing monologues about his own impotence and lack of decision, had even come to view his 'outrageous' dream as a practical undertaking, though he still did not really believe he was capable of carrying it through. What he was actually doing now was going to perform a *rehearsal* of his undertaking, and with every step his excitement mounted higher and higher.

His heart standing still, a nervous tremor running through him, he approached an enormous tenement building that overlooked the Canal* on one side, and — Street on the other. This building consisted entirely of tiny apartments and was inhabited by all kinds of jobbers and people trying to make a living: tailors, locksmiths, cooks, Germans of various descriptions, prostitutes, petty clerks and the like. People kept darting in and out of both entrances and through both courtyards. Here three or four yardkeepers were usually on duty. The young man was most relieved not to run into any of them, and he immediately slipped unnoticed through the front entrance and up a staircase to the right. The staircase was dark and narrow, a 'back stair', but he was already familiar with all this, had studied it, and on the whole the setting appealed to him: in darkness like this even an inquisitive glance would hold no risk. 'If I'm as scared as this now, what would I be like if I were really to *go ahead* with my plan?' he found himself thinking as he reached the fourth floor. Here his way was barred by some loaders in soldiers' uniforms who were carrying the furniture out of one of the apartments. He knew from earlier observation that a German government clerk and his family were living in this apartment: 'This means that that German's moving out now, and it also means that for a while now, on this staircase and this landing, the old woman's apartment is the only one that's going to be occupied. That's just as well . . . you never know . . .' he thought again, and rang the old woman's doorbell. The bell clanked faintly, as though it were made of tin rather than brass. The doorbells of the small apartments in buildings such as this nearly always make that kind of noise. He had forgotten what it sounded like, and the strange clanking suddenly appeared to remind him of something that came to his mind with great clarity . . . He gave a terrible shudder; on this occasion his nerves were simply not up to it. After a while the door opened the merest slit: through it the occupant was scrutinizing the newcomer with evident suspicion, and all that could be seen of her in

36

the darkness was her small, glittering eyes. Observing all the people on the landing, however, she took courage and opened the door the whole way. The young man stepped over the threshold into a dark hallway divided by a partition, behind which there was a tiny kitchen. The old woman stood in front of him, looking at him questioningly. She was a tiny, dried-up little old woman of about sixty, with sharp, hostile eyes, a small, sharp nose and no headcovering. Her whitish hair, which had not much grey in it, was abundantly smeared with oil. Wound round her long, thin neck, which resembled the leg of a chicken, was an old flannel rag of some description, and from her shoulders, the heat notwithstanding, hung an utterly yellowed and motheaten fur jacket. Every moment or so the old woman coughed and groaned. The young man must have glanced at her in some special way, for her eyes suddenly flickered again with their erstwhile suspicion.

'My name's Raskolnikov, I'm a student, I came to see you about a month ago,' the young man muttered hastily, bowing slightly because he had recalled that he must be as courteous as possible.

'I remember, dearie; I remember your visit very well,' the old woman said distinctly, without removing her earlier, questioning gaze from his features.

'So you see . . . I'm here again, about the same thing . . .' Raskolnikov went on, feeling slightly put out, taken off his guard by the old woman's suspicious attitude.

'I suppose she must always be like this, and I simply didn't notice it last time,' he thought, with an unpleasant sensation.

The old woman was silent for a moment, as though she were deliberating; then she moved to one side and said, pointing to the door of a room as she admitted her visitor ahead of her: 'In you go, dearie.'

The little room into which the young man passed, with its yellow wallpaper, its geraniums and its muslin curtains, was at that moment brightly illuminated by the setting sun. 'So the sun will be shining like this *then*, too! . . .' was the thought that flickered almost unexpectedly through Raskolnikov's mind, and with a swift glance he took in everything in the room, in order as far as possible to study and remember its position. But the room contained nothing very much in particular. The furniture, all of it very old and made of yellow wood, consisted of a sofa with an enormous curved back, an oval table that stood in front of it, a mirrored dressing-table standing in between the two windows, chairs along the walls and one or two cheap prints in yellow frames depicting German girls with birds in their hands – and that was all. In one corner a lamp burned in front of a small icon. Everything was very clean; both furniture and floors had been rubbed until they shone. 'That's Lizaveta's work,' the young man thought to himself. There was not a speck of dust to be found in the whole apartment. 'It's the sort of cleanliness you generally find in the homes of sour old widows,' Raskolnikov reflected, continuing his train of thought as he cast a dubious and inquisitive look at the chintz curtain that masked the door into a second tiny room; this accommodated the old woman's bed and chest of drawers, and he had never yet glimpsed its interior. The entire apartment consisted of these two rooms.

'What's your business?' snapped the little old woman, coming into the room and positioning herself in front of him as before, in order to be able to look him straight in the face.

'I've got something I want to pawn. Here, look!' And from his pocket he produced an old, flat, silver watch. Its back bore an engraving of a globe. The chain was of steel.

'But you haven't redeemed the thing you pawned last time, yet. Your time-limit ran out two days ago.'

'I'll pay you another month's interest; be patient.'

'Dearie, it's up to me whether I'm patient or whether I sell what you pawned this very day.'

'How much will you give me for the watch, Alyona Ivanovna?'

'Well, dearie, you come to me with such rubbish, it's practically worthless. I let you have two tickets for that ring last time, and you could buy one new at a jeweller's for a rouble fifty.'

'Let me have four, I promise I'll redeem it – it belonged to my father. I'm expecting some money soon.'

'A rouble fifty, and the interest in advance, that's the best I can do.'

'A rouble fifty?' the young man exclaimed.

'It's up to you.' And the old woman handed his watch back to him. The young man took it, so angry that he nearly stormed out of the apartment; he at once had second thoughts, however, remembering that there was nowhere else he could try, and that in any case he had another purpose for his visit.

'All right, go on then!' he said, roughly.

The old woman reached into her pocket for her keys and went

behind the curtain into the other room. Left alone in the middle of the room, the young man listened curiously, trying to work out what she was doing. He could hear her unlocking the chest of drawers. 'It must be the top drawer,' he thought. 'So she keeps her keys in her right-hand pocket . . . All in one bunch, on a steel ring . . . And there's one key there that's bigger than all the others, three times the size, with a notched bit, it can't be the one to the chest drawers, obviously . . . So there must be some kind of box or chest in there, too . . . That's interesting. Chests often have keys like that . . . God, how dishonourable all this is . . .'

The old woman returned.

'Now then, dearie: the interest's ten per cent a month, so on a rouble fifty you owe me fifteen copecks, payable in advance. You also owe me twenty copecks on the two roubles you had before. That comes to thirty-five copecks. So what you get for your watch is a rouble fifteen. Here you are.'

'What? It's down to a rouble fifteen, now, is it?'

'That's right, dearie.'

The young man did not attempt to argue, and took the money. He looked at the old woman and made no sign of being in a hurry to leave, as though there were something else he wanted to say or do, but did not himself quite know what it was . . .

'I may bring you something else in a day or two, Alyona Ivanovna . . . an item of silver . . . good quality . . . a cigarette-case . . . as soon as I get it back from a friend of mine . . .' He grew confused, and fell silent.

'Right you are then, dearie. We'll talk about it when you come again.'

'Goodbye, then . . . I say, do you spend all the time alone here? Isn't your sister around?' he asked as casually as he could, going out into the hallway.

'And what would you be wanting with her, dearie?'

'Oh, nothing in particular. I was simply asking. I mean, just now, you . . . Goodbye, Alyona Ivanovna!'

Raskolnikov went out feeling decidedly confused. The confusion got worse and worse. As he descended the stairs he even stopped several times, as though he had been struck by some sudden thought. And, at last, when he was out on the street, he exclaimed:

'Oh God! How loathsome all this is! And could I really, could I really . . . No, it's nonsensical, it's absurd!' he added, firmly. 'Could I really ever have contemplated such a monstrous act? It shows what filth my heart is capable of, though! Yes, that's what it is: filthy, mean, vile, vile! . . . And for a whole month I've been . . .'

But he could find neither words nor exclamations with which to give voice to his disturbed state of mind. The sense of infinite loathing that had begun to crush and sicken his heart even while he had only been on his way to the old woman had now attained such dimensions and become so vividly conscious that he was quite simply overwhelmed by his depression. He moved along the pavement like a drunkard, not noticing the passers-by and knocking into them, and only recovered himself when he reached the next street. Looking round, he observed that he was standing beside a drinking den, the entrance to which lay down from the pavement, at the foot of some steps, in the basement. Just at that moment two drunks emerged from the doorway and began to clamber their way up to street-level, supporting each other and cursing. Without so much as a thought, Raskolnikov went down the steps. Never before had he been a visitor to the drinking dens, but now his head was spinning and, what was more, he was parched by a burning thirst. He wanted some cold beer, all the more so since he attributed his sudden state of debility to the fact that he had nothing in his stomach. In a dark and dirty corner he found himself a seat at a sticky little table, asked for some beer and drank his first glass of it with avid greed. The relief he experienced was total and immediate, and his thoughts brightened up. 'This is all a lot of nonsense,' he said to himself with hope. 'There was no need for me to get into such a flap. It was just physical exhaustion! One glass of beer, a *sukhar'** – and in a single moment the mind gains strength, one's thoughts grow lucid and one's intentions firm! Pah! What trivial rubbish all of this is! . . .' But, this contemptuous spit notwithstanding, he already looked cheerful, as if he had suddenly freed himself from some terrible burden, and cast his eyes round at the other people there in a friendly manner. But even as he did so he had a distant sense that all this optimism was also morbid.

At that time there were only a few people left in the drinking den. The two drunk men he had encountered on the steps had been followed out almost immediately by a whole crowd of about five, with one tart and a concertina. After their departure the place seemed quiet and empty. There remained one fellow, a tradesman by the look of him, who was intoxicated, but only slightly, sitting with his beer, and his companion, an enormous, fat, grey-bearded man in a Siberian caftan, thoroughly intoxicated, who had fallen asleep on a bench and who every so often, suddenly, as though in his sleep, snapping his fingers and throwing his arms apart, would begin to make the upper part of his body jerk up and down and, without getting up from the bench, croon some nonsense or other, making an effort to remember the words, which sounded something like:

> One whole year his wife he stroked,
> Onewhole – year – hiswife – hestro-oked . . .

Or, having woken up, again:

> Down the Civil Servants' Road
> There he found his girl of old . . .

But no one shared his happiness; indeed, his silent companion viewed all these sudden explosions with hostility and suspicion. There was yet another man in the den, who by his outward appearance could have been taken for a retired civil servant. He was sitting apart from the other men in front of his jug of vodka, from time to time taking a sip from his glass and looking around him. He also appeared to be in a state of some agitation.

II

Raskolnikov was not accustomed to crowds and, as we have already said, had been avoiding all forms of society, particularly of late. Now, however, he had a sudden longing for company. Something new seemed to be accomplishing itself within him, and one of the things that went with it was a kind of craving for people. So tired was he after a whole month of concentrated depression and gloomy excitement that he wanted, if only for a single moment, to get his breath back in another environment, no matter what it was, and, in spite of all the filth of his surroundings, he was now content to stay on sitting in the drinking den.

The owner of the establishment was in another room, but he frequently entered the main one, coming down into it by way of some steps, whereupon the first thing one saw of him was his dandified blacked boots with their large, red, flapped tops. He was wearing a long-waisted *poddyovka** and a hideously greasy black velvet waistcoat; he wore no cravat, and his entire face looked as though it had been lubricated with oil, like an iron lock. Behind the bar there was a boy of about fourteen, and there was also another, younger boy who took the drinks round when anyone ordered anything. On the bar there were sliced cucumbers, black *sukhari* and some cut-up pieces of fish; all of it smelt very bad. The place was suffocatingly hot, making it almost unbearable to sit there, and so saturated with the fumes of alcohol that the air on its own would have been enough to make a man drunk in five minutes.

There are some encounters, even with people who are complete strangers to us, in which we begin to take an interest right from the very first glance, suddenly, before we have uttered a word. This was precisely the impression made on Raskolnikov by the customer who was sitting some distance away and who looked like a retired civil servant. Several times later on the young man would recall this first impression and would even ascribe it to foreknowledge. He kept glancing at the civil servant incessantly, no doubt because the official was staring persistently at him, and seemed very anxious to get into conversation with him. At the other people in the drinking den, including the owner, however, the official cast a look that seemed in some way habituated and even bored, containing a shade of haughty disdain, as though these were people of inferior social class and education, to whom he had nothing to say. He was a man already on the other side of fifty, of average height and stocky constitution, with hair that was turning grey and a large bald patch. His face had the swollen look that comes of constant drinking, yellow, almost greenish in colour, with puffy eyelids through which his tiny, slitlike eyes shone, reddish and animated. But there was something very strange about him; his gaze displayed an enthusiasm that was positively luminous, and said that here there were most likely both sense and intelligence; but at the same time there was a flicker of something akin to madness. He was wearing an old and completely tattered black dress-coat which had shed all of its buttons except one. This one button was still managing to hang on somehow, and he had it fastened, evidently wishing to observe the proprieties. From under his nankeen waistcoat protruded a white dicky, all crumpled, splashed and stained. He was clean-shaven, in the manner appropriate to government officials, but it must have been a long time since his last shave, for a thick, greyish stubble had begun to appear on his features. There was in his manner, too, something that bespoke the solid, dependable air of the civil servant. He was, however, in a state of agitation; he kept ruffling his hair and from time to time would prop his head in both hands as if in despair, placing his threadbare elbows on the splashed and sticky table. At last he looked straight at Raskolnikov and said, loudly and firmly:

'My dear sir, may I make so bold as to address you with some polite conversation? For although you are not in a condition of eminence, experience tells me that you are a man of education, unhabituated to the beverage. I personally have always respected education united with the feelings of the heart, and am, if I may so inform you, a titular councillor. Marmeladov – such is my name; titular councillor. Dare I inquire whether you yourself have been working in the service?'

'No, I'm studying . . .' the young man answered, rather surprised both at the speaker's peculiarly flowery tone and at being spoken to in such a direct, point-blank manner. In spite of his recent momentary desire for any kind of contact with people, at the first word that was actually addressed to him he suddenly felt his customary irritable and unpleasant sense of revulsion towards any stranger who touched, or merely attempted to touch, his personal individuality.

'So you're a student, or an ex-student!' the civil servant cried. 'I knew it! Experience, dear sir, repeated experience!' And he put a finger to his forehead as a token of bravado. 'You've been a student or have trodden the path of learning! But if you will permit me . . .' He rose to his feet, swayed slightly, picked up his jug and glass, and came over and sat down at the young man's table, slightly to one side of him. He was intoxicated, but he spoke volubly and with eloquence, only on occasion losing his thread slightly and slurring his speech. He pounced upon Raskolnikov avidly, as though he had not spoken to anyone for a whole month, either.

'My dear respected sir,' he began with almost ceremonial formality, 'poverty is not a sin – that is a true saying. I know that drunkenness

43

is not a virtue, either, and that's an even truer saying. But destitution, dear sir, destitution – that is a sin. When a man is poor he may still preserve the nobility of his inborn feelings, but when he's destitute he never ever can. If a man's destitute he isn't even driven out with a stick, he's swept out of human society with a broom, to make it as insulting as possible; and that is as it should be, for I will admit that when I'm destitute I'm the first to insult myself. Hence the beverage! Dear sir, a month ago Mr Lebezyatnikov gave my lady-wife a most unmerciful beating, and that's not quite the same as if he'd given it to me, now, is it? Do you take my meaning, sir? Permit me to ask you another question, sir: have you ever spent the night on the Neva, on the hay barges?'*

'No, I haven't had occasion to,' Raskolnikov replied. 'What are you driving at?'

'Well, sir, that's where I've just come from, this night will be the fifth I've spent there . . .'

He poured himself another glass, drank it, and paused for reflection. The odd wisp of hay could indeed be seen sticking to his clothes; there were even some in his hair. It looked highly probable that for five days he had neither undressed nor washed. His hands, in particular, were filthy – red and oleaginous, with black fingernails.

His conversation seemed to be arousing general, though indolent, attention. The boys behind the bar had begun to snigger. The owner, it appeared, had come down from his upstairs room especially in order to listen to the 'funny man', and had sat down some distance away, yawning languidly but with an air of importance. It was evident that Marmeladov had long been a familiar figure here. Indeed, he had probably acquired his penchant for flowery rhetoric as a consequence of being used to frequent boozy conversations with strangers of various types. This habit becomes a necessity with some drinkers, particularly those who are given rough treatment at home and whose lives are made a misery. It is for this reason that in the company of other drinkers they invariably seem to be doing all they can to justify themselves, and if possible even to gain respect.

'Hey, funny man!' the owner said, loudly. 'Why don't you do any work, why don't you do any serving, if you're a civil servant?'

'You ask why I am not currently engaged in the service, dear sir?' Marmeladov said quickly, addressing himself exclusively to Raskolnikov, as though it were the latter who had asked the question. 'You ask me that? Do you think my reptilian existence doesn't make my heart weep? A month ago, when Mr Lebezyatnikov unmercifully beat my lady-wife and I simply lay there drunk, don't you think I suffered? Permit me to inquire, young man, whether you have ever had occasion to . . . er . . . well, to ask for a loan of some money when it's hopeless?'

'Yes, I have . . . but what do you mean "when it's hopeless"?'

'What I mean, sir, is when it's completely hopeless, when you know beforehand that nothing will come of it. For example, you know in advance with absolute certainty that this man, this most well-intentioned and thoroughly useful citizen, will on no account lend you money, for why, I ask you, should he? I mean, he knows I won't pay it back to him. Out of compassion? But only the other day Mr Lebezyatnikov, who follows the latest ideas,* was explaining that the science of our day has actually declared compassion a social evil, and that this notion is already being put into practice in England, where they have political economy. Why, I ask you, should he lend me anything? And yet, knowing beforehand that he won't, you none the less set off down the high road and . . .'

'But why go to him?' Raskolnikov added.

'But if there is no one, if there is nowhere left to go? I mean, everyone must have at least somewhere to go. For there comes a time in every man's life when he simply must have somewhere he can go! When my only daughter went on the yellow card* for the first time, I went then too . . . (for my daughter lives by the yellow card, sir . . .)' he added in parenthesis, looking at the young man with a certain uneasiness. 'No matter, my dear sir, no matter!' he hastened to add, evidently quite unruffled, as both of the boys snorted with laughter, and even the owner smiled. 'No matter! Such wagging of heads does not confound me, for it is all well known to everyone already, and that which was hid is now revealed;* indeed, my attitude to all that now is one not of contempt but of resignation. So be it! So be it! "Behold the man!" Permit me to ask you, young man, whether you can . . . But no, I must put it more strongly, more figuratively: not *can* you, but *dare* you, as you look upon me in this hour, say beyond all shadow of a doubt that I am not a swine?'

The young man said not a word in reply.

'Well, sir,' the orator continued, in a tone of massive assurance which even had an increased air of dignity about it this time, after he had waited once more for the sniggering that had ensued in the room to die down. 'Well, sir, so be it, I am a swine, but she is a lady! I may possess bestial form, but Katerina Ivanovna, my lady-wife, is a person of education and a field-officer's daughter. So be it, so be it, I am a blackguard, but she has been filled by her upbringing with both lofty spirit and ennobled feelings. And yet . . . oh, if she would only take pity on me! Oh my dear sir, my dear respected sir, I mean, every man must have at least one place where people take pity on him! Even though Katerina Ivanovna is a magnanimous lady, she is also an unjust one . . . And though I am well aware that when she tugs my locks she does it solely out of the kindness of her heart – for, I say it again without embarrassment, she tugs my locks, young man – ' he affirmed with especial dignity, having detected more sniggering, 'but, oh God, if only one single time she would . . . But no! No! All that is in vain, and there's no more to be said, no more to be said! . . . For on more than one occasion I attained that which I desired, and pity was shown me on more than one occasion, but . . . such is my proclivity: I am a born brute!'

'You can say that again,' the owner remarked, yawning.

Marmeladov resolutely hammered his fist down on the table.

'Such is my proclivity! Do you know, do you know, dear sir, that I even bartered her stockings for drink? Not her shoes, sir, for that would have been ever so slightly in the normal way of events, but her stockings – it was her stockings I pawned! She had a little mohair scarf, given to her as a present before our marriage – it was hers, not mine – and I bartered that, too; yet we live in a cold corner of a room, and that winter she caught a chill and began to cough, brought up blood, she did. And we have three little children, and Katerina Ivanovna works from morning to night, scrubbing and washing and bathing the children, for she's been used to cleanliness since an early age, and she has a weak chest and a predisposition to tuberculosis, and I feel that. How could I not feel it? And the more I drink, the more I feel. That's the reason for my drinking. I'm looking for feeling and compassion in it . . . Not revelry do I seek, but pure sorrow . . . I drink, for I desire to suffer doubly!' And, as if in despair, he let his head sink on to the table.

'Young man,' he went on, straightening up. 'In your features I seem to read a certain unhappiness. I saw it as soon as you came in, and that's why I lost no time in appealing to you. For, in communicating to you the story of my life, I seek to avoid exposing myself to the most grotesque ridicule in the eyes of these lovers of idleness, to whom it is all in any case common knowledge, and come to you perceiving you to be a man of sensitivity and education. I may as well tell you that my lady-wife was brought up in a high-class establishment for daughters of the local aristocracy, and that at the ball that was held upon her graduation she danced with the shawl* in the presence of the governor and other notables, for which she received a gold medal and a testimonial of good progress. The medal . . . oh, the medal got sold . . . a long time ago . . . hm . . . but she still keeps the testimonial in her travelling-box, and not so long ago she showed it to our landlady. Even though she exists in a state of the most incessant strife with our landlady, she felt a desire to take a bit of pride in herself in front of someone for a change, and to tell her about her happy bygone days. And I don't condemn her, I don't condemn her, for these memories are all that remain to her now – the rest has all passed to ashes! Yes, yes; she's a hot-tempered, proud and indomitable lady. She scrubs the floors herself, she lives on black bread, but she won't tolerate disrespect towards herself. That's why she made Mr Lebezyatnikov pay for his coarse behaviour, and when Mr Lebezyatnikov gave her a battering in return, she took to her bed not so much because of the beating she'd received as because her feelings had been hurt. She was a widow when I married her, with three children, each smaller than the other. Her first marriage, to an infantry officer, had been an affair of the heart – she'd run away from her parents' house in order to be with him. She loved that husband of hers beyond all bounds, but he took to gambling at cards, got into trouble with the law, and then died. Towards the end he used to beat her; and although she made him pay for it, in terms for which I have irrefutable and documentary evidence, she remembers him to this day with tears in her eyes and uses him in order to reproach me, and I'm glad, I'm glad, for even though it's only in her imaginings, she's able to perceive herself as having once been happy . . . And after his death she was left with three little children in the remote and brutish government district where I happened to be at that time, left in such hopeless destitution, moreover, that although I have experienced a good many various things, I am unable to even describe it. Her relatives had all turned their backs on her, too. And she was proud, far too proud . . . And it was then, dear sir, it was then that I, also in a widowed state, with a fourteen-year-old daughter by my first wife, offered her my hand, for I could not bear to look at such suffering. You may be able to judge the degree of her misfortunes by the fact that she, an educated, well brought-up woman from a family of renown, should have consented to marry a man such as myself! But marry me she did! Weeping and sobbing and wringing her hands – she married me! For she had nowhere left to go. Do you understand, do you understand, dear sir, what it means to have nowhere left to go? No! That you do not yet understand . . . And for a whole year I discharged my duties piously and devoutly and did not touch this (he prodded a finger at his half-*shtof* of vodka*), for I do have feelings. But even that failed to please; and then I lost my job, and that wasn't my fault, either, it was because of a staff reorganization, and then my abstemiousness came to an end. It is now a year and a half since we at last found ourselves, after wanderings and many tribulations, in this magnificent capital city, adorned as it is with numerous monuments. And here I obtained a job . . . Obtained it, and lost it again. Do you understand, sir? This time I lost it through my own fault, for my proclivity started to act up again . . . Now we live in a corner, in the apartment of our landlady, Amalia Ivanovna Lippewechsel, and what we live on and how we manage to pay our rent, I do not know. There are a lot of other people living there besides us . . . It's a Sodom, sir, of the most outrageous kind . . . hm . . . yes . . . And in the meanwhile my daughter, the one from my first marriage, has also grown to woman's estate, and the things she has had to put up with from her stepmother in the process I will not tell you. For although Katerina Ivanovna is full of magnanimous emotions, she is a hot-tempered and irritable lady, and she likes cutting people short . . . Yes, sir! Well, there's no point in raking over all that again. As you may imagine, Sonya has received no education. About four years ago I tried to take her through the elements of geography and world history; but since I myself was never very strong in those branches of knowledge, and there were no suitable textbooks, for the books that we did have . . . hm! Well, we don't even have them any more, those books, and that was the end of the whole attempt at her instruction. We stopped at Cyrus of Persia. Later on, when she'd already attained maturity, she read a few books of a romantic content, and quite recently, through the agency of Mr Lebezyatnikov, she obtained a copy of Lewes' *Physiology** – are you familiar with it, sir? – and read it with great interest; she even communicated extracts from it aloud to us. There you have the full extent of her enlightenment. But now I will address you, my dear respected sir, with a private question on my own account: in your opinion, can a poor but honest girl expect to earn a great deal by honest work?* . . . She'll be lucky to earn fifteen copecks a day, sir, if she's honest and has no particular talents, and even that's only if she never takes a moment off! And what's more, State Councillor Klopstock, Ivan Ivanovich – perhaps you've heard of him? – has not only to this day refused to give her the money he owes her for a half-dozen shirts she made him, but actually turned her out of his house, stamping his foot and calling her indecent names, on the pretext that the shirt collars were the wrong size and not cut straight. And there are the little ones with no food in their bellies . . . And there's Katerina Ivanovna wringing her hands, pacing up and down the room, and saying, with the red spots standing out on her cheeks, as they invariably do in that illness: "You live with us, you female parasite, you eat our food and drink our drink, and take advantage of our heating!" – yet what could she have been eating and drinking when even the little ones hadn't seen a crust of bread for three days? I was lying in bed at the time . . . oh, what the hell, I was drunk, sir, and I heard my Sonya (she's as meek as a lamb, and has such a gentle little voice . . . she has fair hair, and her little face is always pale and thin), I heard my Sonya say: "Oh, no, Katerina Ivanovna, you don't want me to go and do that, do you?" Yet Darya Frantsovna, an ill-intentioned woman who's been in trouble with the police on many occasions, had already two or three times been to make inquiries through the landlady. "So what if I do?" replied Katerina Ivanovna, mockingly. "What's there to protect? Some treasure!" But don't blame her, don't blame her, dear sir, don't blame her! It was something she said when she wasn't in full possession of her faculties, she was ill and agitated, and her children hadn't had anything to eat and were crying; it was said more in order to wound than in any precise sense . . . For that's just the way Katerina Ivanovna is by nature: as soon as the children cry, for example, even if it's because they're hungry, she immediately starts beating them. Well, then I saw Sonechka – this would be at about six o'clock in the evening – get up, put on her shawl and her "burnous" mantlet and leave the apartment, and at nine o'clock she came back again. She came in, went straight up to Katerina Ivanovna, and silently put down thirty roubles on the table in front of her. Not one word did she say as she did this; she didn't even give her a look; she just picked up our big, green *drap-de-dames* shawl* (we have a *drap-de-dames* shawl which we all make use of), completely covered her head and face with it, and lay down on her bed with her face to the wall; only her little shoulders and the rest of her body kept quivering . . . And meanwhile I went on lying there in the state I'd been in all along . . . And then, young man, I saw Katerina Ivanovna go over to Sonechka's bed, also without saying a word; all evening she kneeled before her, kissed her feet, wouldn't get up, and then they both fell asleep together, in each other's arms . . . both of them . . . both of them . . . yes, sir . . . while I . . . lay there drunk.'

Marmeladov fell silent, as though his voice had been cut off by inward emotion. Then he suddenly refilled his glass in haste, drank its contents down and grunted.

'Ever since then, my dear sir,' he continued after a period of silence, 'ever since then, because of a certain inauspicious happening and the fact that some ill-intentioned persons reported the matter to the authorities – something in which Darya Frantsovna played a leading role, apparently in order to get her own back for not having been treated with due respect – ever since then my daughter, Sofya Semyonovna, has been compelled to take the yellow card, and on account of that has been unable to remain with us. For one thing, our landlady, Amalia Ivanovna, would not allow it (though earlier she herself had given Darya Frantsovna a helping hand), and for another, Mr Lebezyatnikov . . . hm . . . Well you see, it was because of Sonya that that entire episode between him and Katerina Ivanovna took place. To start with he'd made the most persistent advances towards Sonechka, but then he went and took umbrage, saying: "How could I, a man of such enlightenment, live in the same apartment as a girl like that?" And Katerina Ivanovna made him pay for that remark, she took her daughter's side . . . well, and then it happened . . . And now Sonechka looks in to see us more towards evening, when it's getting dark, and she tries to make things easier for Katerina Ivanovna and does everything she can to help her. She lodges with Kapernaumov,* the tailor, she rents a bit of floor-space from him; Kapernaumov's lame, and he suffers from a speech disorder, like all the numerous members of his family. His wife has a speech disorder, too

. . . They live in the one room, but Sonya has her own bit of space, partitioned off from the rest . . . Hm . . . yes . . . They're of the very poorest – poor folk who can't speak properly . . . yes. Well, that morning, sir, I girded up my loins, attired myself in my rags, raised my hands to heaven and set off to see His Excellency Ivan Afanasye-vich. Perhaps you're familiar with His Excellency Ivan Afanasyevich? . . . No? Well, in that case you don't know a man of true meekness! He's wax – wax before the countenance of the Lord; for the wax it melteth . . . He even shed a tear or two after he'd heard what I had to tell him. "Well, Marmeladov," he said, "you've already let me down once . . . I'll take you on once again, on my own personal responsibility this time" – those were his very words – "but mind now," he said, "and off you go!" I kissed the dust at his feet, mentally, for in reality he would never have permitted it, being one of the top brass and a man of the very latest ideas with regard to education and public service; I returned home, and when I announced that I'd got my job back and would be receiving my salary again – Lord, what happened then . . .'

Marmeladov again broke off in violent agitation. Just at that moment a whole party of tipplers who were already quite drunk came in off the street, and outside the entrance the sounds of a rented hurdy-gurdy and the small cracked voice of a seven-year-old child singing 'The Little Homestead'* became audible. It grew noisy. The owner and his crew began to attend to the newcomers' requirements. Marmeladov, paying no attention to the new arrivals, began to continue his story. By now he seemed to have grown very weak, but the more the drink went to his head, the more eager he became to talk. The memories of his recent success in the field of work seemed to have enlivened him and were even reflected in his features by a kind of radiance. Raskolnikov listened closely.

'Well, my dear sir, that was five weeks ago. Yes . . . As soon as the two of them, Katerina Ivanovna and Sonechka, heard the news – Lord, it was as though I'd been spirited away to Paradise. Before, I'd lie around like a brute, and get nothing but abuse. But now they went around on tiptoe, keeping the children quiet: "Semyon Zakharych is tired after his work, he's having a rest, shh!" They'd bring me coffee before I went off in the morning, they even boiled cream for me! They began serving me with real cream, can you imagine? And how they managed to scrape together the money to buy me a decent uniform –

eleven roubles and fifty copecks, it cost – I simply do not understand. Boots, calico shirtfronts of the most magnificent quality, a uniform jacket – they got together the whole lot for eleven roubles fifty, and all in the most excellent condition, sir. On the first day I got back from work, I saw that Katerina Ivanovna had made two courses for dinner, soup and salt beef with horseradish sauce, something previously quite unheard-of. She has no dresses . . . I mean none at all, sir, yet now she looked as though she were going out visiting, all dressed up smart, and it wasn't that she'd made do with what she had, she'd quite simply made it all from nothing: she'd done her hair up nicely, put on a clean little collar and over-sleeves, and she looked quite a different person, younger and prettier. My little dove Sonechka had only been helping us out with money, but now she said she didn't think it was a good idea for her to come and see us too often, and she'd only drop in after dark, when no one would see her. Can you imagine, can you imagine? I went to have a nap after dinner, and would you believe it, Katerina Ivanovna hadn't been able to resist temptation: a week earlier she'd quarrelled in the worst kind of way with Amalia Ivanovna, our landlady, yet now she'd asked her in for a cup of coffee. Two hours they sat, whispering all the time: "Semyon Zakharych is working again and drawing his salary; he went to see His Excellency, and His Excellency came out in person, told all the others to wait, and led Semyon Zakharych by the arm past them all into his office." Can you imagine, can you imagine? " 'Well, of course, Semyon Zakharych,' he said, 'bearing in mind the services you have rendered to us in the past, and even though you've been indulging in that frivolous foible of yours, since you're now ready to make a promise, and since moreover things have been going badly for us in your absence (can you imagine, can you imagine?), I now rely upon your word of honour,' he said." In other words, I tell you, she'd gone and made up a whole long story, and not out of silliness but solely because she wanted to do a bit of boasting, sir! No, sir, she believes it all herself, she amuses herself with her own imaginings, I swear to God, sir! And I don't condemn her; no, that I don't condemn! . . . And a week ago, when I brought my first pay-packet – twenty-three roubles and forty copecks – home with me intact, she called me her little minnow: "There, my little minnow!" she said.'

Marmeladov broke off, and was about to smile, but suddenly his chin began to work up and down spasmodically. He managed, however, to bring himself under control. This drinking-house, the man's air of debauchery, his five nights on the hay barges, the jug of vodka, together with his morbid affection for his wife and family, had thrown his listener off balance. Raskolnikov had been listening intently, but with a sense of unhealthy discomfort. He was annoyed at himself for having come here.

'My dear sir, my dear sir!' Marmeladov exclaimed, having recovered himself. 'Oh my dear respected sir, you probably think this is ridiculous, like everyone else, and I'm just upsetting you with the stupidity of all these insignificant details of my domestic life, but they're no laughing matter for me. For I feel it all . . . And I spent the whole of that most heavenly day of my life, and all the evening as well, in transient reveries: of how I would organize everything, buy clothes for the children, give her rest and tranquillity, and turn back my only-begotten daughter from the ways of dishonour unto the bosom of her family . . . And much, much else . . . It's permissible, sir. Well, my dear sir . . .' Marmeladov suddenly seemed to give a start; he raised his head and stared at his listener. 'Well, the very next day after all those reveries (just five days ago, in other words), towards evening, I managed to filch the key to Katerina Ivanovna's travelling-box, took out what was left of the salary I'd brought home, how much it was in all I don't remember, and now here I am, take a look at me, everyone! My fifth day away from home, and they're looking for me, and it's all over with my job, and my uniform jacket's lying in the drinking den next to Egypt Bridge, where I exchanged it for my present apparel . . . and it's all over!'

Marmeladov struck himself on the forehead with his fist, gritted his teeth, closed his eyes and leaned one elbow mightily on the table. But a moment later his features suddenly altered, and with a sort of unnatural cunning and manufactured insolence he looked at Raskolnikov, laughed and said:

'I went over to Sonya's today, to ask her for money so I could treat my hangover. Ha, ha, ha!'

'You don't mean to say she gave it to you?' someone shouted from the direction of the new arrivals, following this up with a roar of laughter.

'This very jug of vodka was purchased with her money,' Marmeladov enunciated, addressing himself solely to Raskolnikov. 'Thirty copecks she gave me, with her own hands, the last money she had, I could see it for myself . . . She didn't say anything, just looked at me in silence . . . That's what it's like, not here upon earth, but up there . . . where people are grieved over and wept for, but not reproached, not reproached! But it hurts even worse, even worse, sir, if one isn't reproached! . . . Thirty copecks, yes, sir. But I mean, she'll be needing them now, won't she, eh? What do you think, my dear, dear sir? After all, she has to keep herself clean nowadays. Cleanliness like that costs money, it's of a particular sort, if you take my meaning. Do you take my meaning? Yes, and she also has to buy face-cream and lipstick, I mean she can't manage without them, sir; starched petti-coats, a certain style of shoe, high-heeled, to show off her foot when she has to step over a puddle. Do you understand, do you under-stand, sir, what cleanliness like that involves? Well, sir, and there I went, her own natural father, and swiped those thirty copecks for my hangover! And I'm drinking them away, sir! I've already drunk them! . . . Well, who would ever take pity on someone like myself? Eh, sir? Do you feel pity for me now, sir? Eh? Ha, ha, ha, ha!'

He tried to pour himself another glass, but the effort was in vain. The half-*shtof* was empty.

'Why would anyone feel pity for you?' shouted the owner, who had once more reappeared to one side of them.

There was a burst of laughter, mixed with swear words. The laughter and abuse came from people who had been listening, but also from those who had not, but were simply staring at the extra-ordinary figure presented by this unemployed civil servant.

'Pity for me? Why should anyone feel pity for me?' Marmeladov suddenly began to wail, rising to his feet with one arm stretched in front of him, in a state of positive inspiration, as though these were precisely the words he had been waiting for. 'Why should anyone feel pity for me, you say? Indeed! There's nothing to pity me for! I ought to be crucified, crucified upon a cross, not pitied! Crucify him, O Heavenly Judge, crucify him and, when it is done, take pity on him! And then I myself will come to thee for mortification, for it is not merrymaking that I seek, but sorrow and tears! . . . Do you think, master publican, that I drank this jug of vodka of yours for the sake of enjoyment? Sorrow, sorrow is what I sought at its bottom, sorrow and tears, and of those have I partaken and those have I found; and the one who will take pity on me is him that hath pity for all men and whose wisdom passeth all understanding, he alone, he is our judge.

He will come this day, and inquire: "And where is the daughter that hath not spared herself for the sake of her harsh-tongued and consumptive stepmother and for young children that are not her own kith and kin? Where is the daughter who took pity on her earthly father, an obscene drunkard, undismayed by his bestial nature?" And he will say unto her: "Come unto me! I have already forgiven thee once . . . Forgiven thee once . . . Thy sins, which are many, are forgiven; for thou lovest much . . ." And he'll forgive my Sonya, he'll forgive her, I know he will . . . I felt that then, when I went to see her, felt it in my heart! . . . And he will judge and forgive everyone, the good and the bad, the wise and the meek . . . And when he is done with all of them, he will raise up his voice to us, saying unto us: "Come out, ye drunkards, come out, O ye that are weak, come out, ye that live in shame!" And we shall come out, and shall not be ashamed, and shall stand before him. And he will say unto us: "Ye are as swine! Made in the image of the Beast, and marked with his brand; but come ye also!" And the wise and the learned will raise up their voices, saying: "Lord! Why dost thou receive them?" And he will say unto them: "Because they none of them ever believed themselves worthy of it . . ." And he will stretch out his hand to us, and we shall fall down . . . and weep . . . and understand everything! Then we will understand everything! . . . everyone will understand . . . even Katerina Ivanovna . . . even she will understand . . . O Lord, thy kingdom come ! . . .'

And he slumped on to the bench, exhausted and enfeebled, not looking at anyone, as though oblivious of his surroundings and sunk in deep thought. His words had made a certain impression: for a moment silence reigned, but soon the laughter and abuse began to ring out again:

'Got it all worked out, he has!'

'What a load of tripe!'

'Quill-driver!'

And so on, and so forth.

'Let us be off, sir,' Marmeladov said, suddenly, raising his head and turning to Raskolnikov. 'Please escort me . . . to Kosel's Tenements, the ones with the courtyard. It's time I went back to . . . Katerina Ivanovna . . .'

Raskolnikov had been wanting to leave for some time now; he himself had thought of helping the other man. Marmeladov proved to be much less assured on his legs than he had been in his speech, and he leaned mightily on the young man. They had about two or three hundred yards to go. Embarrassment and fear began to gain a hold on the drunken man, one which increased the closer they came to the house.

'It's not Katerina Ivanovna I'm scared of now,' he muttered in agitation. 'I'm not scared that she'll start pulling me by the hair. What does my hair matter? . . . It's rubbishy stuff! That's what I say! In fact, it'll be better if she does start pulling it, that's not what I'm scared of . . . It's . . . her eyes that scare me . . . yes . . . her eyes. And the red spots on her cheeks, I'm scared of them, too . . . and also – her breathing . . . Have you ever noticed the way people with that illness breathe . . . when they're excited? I'm also scared of the children's crying . . . Because if Sonya hasn't been feeding them, I . . . I don't know what will have become of them! I don't! But I'm not scared of being beaten . . . I may as well tell you, sir, that not only are such beatings not painful to me – I actually derive pleasure from them . . . For without them I simply can't go on. It's better that way. Let her beat me, it'll help her to unburden her soul . . . it's better that way . . . Well, here are the tenements. The Tenements of Kosel. A locksmith, a German, and a man of wealth . . . Go on, lead the way!'

They entered from the yard and went up to the fourth floor. The further up the staircase they climbed, the darker it grew. It was by now almost eleven o'clock, and although at this time of the year in St Petersburg there is no real night to speak of, at the top of the stairs it was very dark indeed.

A small, soot-grimed door at the point where the staircase ended, at its very summit, stood open. A stub of candle shed its light over a most wretched room about ten yards long; from the passage it could be seen in its entirety. Everything in it was thrown about and in disorder. Particularly noticeable were various ragged items of children's clothing. A sheet, which had holes in it, had been stretched over one of the rear corners. Behind it there was probably a bed. In the room proper there were only two chairs and a very tattered sofa covered in oilcloth, in front of which stood an old pine kitchen table, which had not been painted and bore no covering. On one edge of the table there was a guttering end of tallow candle in an iron candleholder. It turned out that Marmeladov's bed was in a room of his own, and not in the corner, but this room of his was a connecting one, through which everyone else had to pass. The door that led through to the other rooms, or cells, into which Amalia Lippewechsel's apartment had been broken up, had been left ajar. Noise and shouting came from through there. People were roaring with laughter. They appeared to be playing cards and drinking tea. From time to time snippets of the most improper language came drifting through.

Raskolnikov identified Katerina Ivanovna immediately. She had lost a lot of flesh, a thin, rather tall woman, with a good figure and beautiful chestnut-coloured hair; her cheeks really were so flushed that they looked like two scarlet spots. She was pacing to and fro in her little room, her hands clenched against her breast; her lips were parched and her breathing was coming unevenly, in little gasps. Her eyes glittered as if in fever, but her gaze was sharp and fixed, and it was a morbid effect that was produced by this consumptive and excited face, across which the last glimmer of the guttering candle-end trembled and quivered. Raskolnikov thought she looked about thirty, and she did indeed seem an unsuitable sort of wife for a man like Marmeladov to have . . . She had not heard anyone enter, and did not notice them; she seemed to be in a kind of trance, hearing and seeing nothing. The room was suffocatingly hot, but she had not opened the window; a foul odour drifted up from the staircase, but the door that gave on to it was not closed; from the inner rooms, through the door that was ajar, clouds of tobacco smoke floated, but although she was coughing she did not close it, either. The very youngest child, a little girl of about six, was asleep on the floor in a sort of cowering sitting position, her head thrust on to the sofa. A little boy, who must have been about a year older than her, was trembling in a corner, weeping. He looked as though he had just been given a beating. The eldest girl, who must have been about nine, was as tall and slender as a matchstick, and was dressed in nothing but a torn chemise that was covered in holes and, thrown over her bare shoulders, a ragged little *drap-de-dames* 'burnous' mantlet she had probably made for herself a couple of years ago, since it now did not come down even as far as her knees; she stood in the corner beside her little brother with one of her long, withered, matchsticklike arms thrown round his neck. She seemed to be trying to soothe him, and was whispering something to him, doing everything she could to stop him from whimpering again, and following her mother fearfully with her big, big dark eyes, which her frightened, gaunt little face made seem even bigger. Marmeladov did not go into the room, but got down on his knees in the doorway, giving Raskolnikov a shove forwards. At the sight of the stranger, the woman halted abstractedly in front of him and seemed to come to for a moment, as if she were wondering: 'What's he doing in here?' Most likely, however, it at once crossed her mind that he was on his way to one of the other rooms, since theirs was a communicating one. Having decided that this was the case, and paying no further attention to him, she stepped towards the outside door in order to shut it, and then gave a sudden scream upon encountering her husband, who was kneeling on the threshold.

'Aha!' she cried in a frenzy of anger. 'He's back! The sitter in the stocks! The monster! . . . And where's the money? What have you got in your pockets, come on, out with it! And those are not your own clothes you're wearing! What have you done with your clothes? Where's that money? Answer me! . . .'

And she rushed to search him. Marmeladov at once threw his arms wide apart, meekly and obediently, in order to assist her investigation of his pockets. There was not so much as a copeck's worth of small change left in them.

'Where's the money?' she cried. 'Oh Lord, don't say he's gone and drunk the lot! There were twelve silver roubles in the box! . . .' And in a sudden frenzy she grabbed him by the hair and hauled him into the room. Marmeladov himself assisted her exertions by meekly crawling after her on his knees.

'Even this is a pleasure to me! Even this is not painful to me, but is a plea-sure-my-dear-re-spect-ed-sir,' he managed to yelp out as he was shaken by the hair, his forehead actually giving the floor a thump at one point. The child who was asleep on the floor woke up and started to cry. The boy in the corner could no longer hold himself in check; he shuddered and screamed and rushed to his sister in terrible panic, almost in a seizure. The eldest girl was trembling like a leaf, only half awake.

'He's drunk the money! All, all of it – he's drunk it,' the poor woman cried in despair, 'and he's lost his good clothes! And they're hungry, hungry!' (And, wringing her hands, she pointed at the children.) 'Oh, thrice-accursed life! And you, aren't you ashamed?' she said suddenly, turning on Raskolnikov. 'You've been at the drinking den! You've been drinking with him, haven't you. You're another one of them! Go on, get out!'

The young man hurriedly left, without saying a word. What was more, the inner door flew wide open and several curious onlookers peeped round it. Brazen, laughing heads came craning through, with cigarettes, with pipes, in skull-caps. Figures could be seen in dressing-gowns worn completely open, in summer clothes that bordered on the indecent, some with cards in their hands. Their laughter was particularly animated when Marmeladov, as he was being dragged along by his hair, shouted that it was a pleasure to him. People actually started coming into the room; at last the sound of an ominous shrieking made itself heard: this was Amalia Lippewechsel herself forcing her way through in front of everyone else with the intention of restoring order in her own way and for the hundredth time – by terrifying the poor woman with a violently abusive injunction to quit the apartment the very next morning. As he left, Raskolnikov had time to stick his hand in his pocket, scoop out of it the copper change from the rouble he had spent in the drinking den, and place it unobtrusively on the windowsill. A moment or two later, when he was already on the staircase, he almost changed his mind and went back.

'What sort of silly thing to do was that?' he thought. 'They've got Sonya, and I need that money myself.' But, reasoning that he could not possibly take it back now, and that he would not take it back even if such a thing were possible, he waved his arm impatiently and set off on foot for his lodgings. 'After all, Sonya does need to buy face-cream, you know,' he went on, striding along the street and smiling to himself sarcastically. 'Cleanliness like that costs money . . . Hm! And after all, Sonya herself may go bankrupt today, because it's a risky business she's in, as risky as big-game hunting or . . . goldmin-ing, and without my money they may all be on their uppers tomorrow . . . Three cheers for Sonya! They've hit a rich seam there. And they're making the most of it, my, how they're making the most of it. And now they've grown used to it. They've shed a few tears, and are used to it. Man can get used to anything, the villain!'

He began to reflect.

'Well, and what if I'm mistaken?' he suddenly found himself exclaiming. 'What if man – the whole human race in general, I mean – isn't really a *villain* at all? If that's true, it means that all the rest is just a load of superstition, just a lot of fears that have been put into people's heads, and there are no limits, and that's how it's meant to be! . . .'

III

Next morning he woke up late after a troubled sleep that did not refresh him. He awoke feeling bilious, short-tempered and uncharitable, and surveyed his little room with detestation. It was a tiny little cell, about six paces long, and it presented a most pitiful aspect with its grimy, yellow wallpaper that was everywhere coming off the walls; it was so low-ceilinged that to a person of even slightly above-average height it felt claustrophobic, as though one might bang one's head against the plaster at any moment. The furniture was commensurate with its surroundings: there were three old chairs, not in very good condition, and in one corner a painted table on which lay a few books and exercise-books (from the mere fact that they were covered in dust it could be seen that it was a long time since anyone had touched them), and a big, ungainly sofa, which took up practically the whole of one wall and half the width of the room, had at one time had an upholstering of chintz, but was now in rags, and served as Raskolnikov's bed. He often slept on it as he was, without bothering to undress, without a sheet, covering himself with his old, threadbare student's coat and resting his head on a single small pillow beneath which he put all the linen he possessed, clean and soiled, to give some extra height. In front of the sofa there was a little table.

It would have been hard to go much further to seed or to sink to a lower level of personal neglect; but to Raskolnikov, in his present state of mind, this was actually gratifying. He had, in no uncertain terms, withdrawn from everyone, like a tortoise into its shell, and even the face of the maidservant whose task it was to wait upon him and who sometimes peeped into his room irritated him to the point of bile and convulsions. This is often the case with a certain kind of monomaniac who spends all his time thinking too much about something. It was now two weeks since his landlady had stopped supplying him with meals, yet he would never have dreamed of going down to argue with her, even though he went without his dinner. As a matter of fact, Nastasya, the landlady's cook and only servant, was really somewhat pleased by this attitude on the part of the lodger, and had completely given up tidying and sweeping his quarters, except for the odd occasion, roughly once a week, when she poked her broom into them almost by accident. She it had been who just now had woken him up.

'What, are you still sleeping? It's time to get up!' she shouted, standing over him. 'It's nearly gone ten. I've brought you some tea; do you want it? Or are you just going to waste away to nothing?'

The lodger opened his eyes, gave a start and recognized Nastasya.

'What's this? Tea from the landlady?' he asked, slowly and painfully raising himself on the sofa.

'You've got a hope!'

She set before him her own cracked teapot, containing a weak brew of tea made with used leaves, and placed beside it two yellow lumps of sugar.

'Here, Nastasya, take this, please,' he said, fumbling in his pocket (he had been sleeping in his clothes) and pulling from it a small handful of copper change. 'Go out and buy me a roll. And get me a bit of sausage at the sausage-dealer's, the cheapest they have.'

'I'll get you the roll in a minute, but won't you have some cabbage-soup instead of the sausage? It's good stuff, I made it yesterday. I left some for you yesterday, but you were too late. It's good stuff.'

When the cabbage soup had been brought in and he had set to work on it, Nastasya seated herself beside him on the sofa and began to chatter away. She was a country girl, and a very indiscreet one, too.

'Praskovya Pavlovna says she's going to complain about you to the police,' she said.

He frowned hard.

'To the police? What's bothering her?'

'You don't pay your rent but you don't quit the room. It's easy to see what's bothering her.'

'The devil, that's all I needed,' he muttered, gritting his teeth. 'No, this isn't the right time . . . not now . . . She's a fool,' he added, loudly. 'I'll go and see her today, have a word with her.'

'Fool she may be, just the same as me, but what's a clever fellow

61

like you doing lying there like a lump, with never a sound or a sight of you? You said before you used to go and give lessons to children, but now you don't do anything – why?'

'Oh, but I do do something . . .' Raskolnikov said, sternly and reluctantly.

'What?'

'Work . . .'

'What sort of work?'

'Thinking,' he replied seriously, after a brief silence.

Nastasya fairly rolled with laughter. She was a giggly sort of girl, and when anything set her off she would laugh inaudibly, shaking and swaying with her whole body until she began to feel sick.

'Thought up a lot of money, have you?' she managed to get out at last.

'One can't go and give lessons to children if one doesn't have any boots. Oh, in any case, I don't give a spit.'

'Don't spit in the well, will you?'

'They pay one in coppers for giving lessons to children. What can one do with a few copecks?' he went on reluctantly, as if he were trying to find answers to his own thoughts.

'Oh, so you want all the capital at once, do you?'

He gave her a strange look.

'Yes, all the capital,' he replied firmly, after a slight pause.

'Well, take it easy, or you'll end up frightening me; you've made me quite terrified. Do you want me to go and get you that roll, or not?'

'As you wish.'

'Oh, I forgot! There was a letter for you yesterday, it came when you weren't here.'

'A letter? For me? From whom?'

'I don't know. I had to give the postman three copecks out of my own money. Will you give me them back – eh?'

'Oh, go and get it, for God's sake go and get it!' Raskolnikov shouted, thoroughly excited. 'Lord in Heaven!'

A moment later the letter made its appearance. It was as he thought: from his mother, in the province of R—. He actually turned pale as he took it. It was a long time since he had had any letters; now, however, his heart was wrung by some other, quite different emotion.

'Nastasya, in the name of heaven, please go now; here are your three copecks; only, for God's sake, go!'

The letter trembled in his hands; he was reluctant to open it in her presence; he wanted to be left *alone* with this letter. When Nastasya had gone, he quickly brought it to his lips and kissed it; then for a long time he peered closely at the handwriting of the address, at the dear, familiar, fine and slanting script of his mother, who had once upon a time taught him to read and write. He lingered over it; he even seemed to be afraid of something. At last, he broke the seal: the letter was a big, thick one, two *lots* in weight;* the two large sheets of notepaper were entirely covered in microscopic handwriting.

My dear Rodya, (*his mother wrote*)

It is now more than two months since I last spoke to you by letter, and I've suffered on that account, some nights I haven't even been able to sleep for thinking about it. But I know you won't blame me for this unwished-for silence of mine. You know how I love you; you're the only one we think of, Dunya and I, you're everything to us, all our hopes and aspirations rolled into one. How terrible I felt when I learned that a few months ago you dropped out of the university because you couldn't manage to support yourself, and that your lessons and your other means of income had come to a stop! How could I possibly help you when I have only my pension of a hundred and twenty roubles a year? The fifteen roubles I sent you four months ago I borrowed, as you yourself know, on the strength of that pension, from Afanasy Ivanovich Vakhrushin, a local merchant. He's a good, kind man, and he was one of your father's friends. But, having given him the right to receive the pension in my stead, I've had to wait until the debt was paid off, and this has only just happened now, so I've not been able to send you anything all this time. But now, thank God, I think I'll be able to send you a bit more, and indeed in general we can now actually boast of our good fortune, which is what I'm in such a hurry to tell you about. In the first place, dear Rodya, would you believe it if I told you that for the past six weeks your sister has been living here with me, and that we're not going to be parted ever again? Thank the Lord, her torments are at an end, but I shall tell you it all in sequence, so you'll see what's been going on and what it is we've been hiding from you until now. When you wrote

63

about two months ago and told me that you'd heard from someone that Dunya was putting up with a lot of rudeness in the Svidrigailovs' household, and asked me for a detailed explanation – what could I have written you in reply? If I'd given you the whole truth, you would probably have dropped everything and come to see us, on foot even, if you'd had to, because I know your temperament and feelings, and you would have stood up for your sister. I was in despair myself, but what could I do? At that time, not even I knew the whole truth. The main problem was that when Dunya entered their household last year in the capacity of governess, she was given no less than a hundred roubles in advance, but was told that a certain amount would be deducted from her salary each month, thus making it impossible for her to leave her post without having paid off her debt. This sum (now I can explain everything to you, my precious Rodya) she accepted principally in order to be able to send you the sixty roubles you needed so badly at the time and which you got from us last year. We deceived you then, wrote and told you that it was some of the money Dunya had managed to save from her previous job, but that wasn't true; I'm able to tell you the whole truth now because everything has suddenly, by God's will, changed for the better, and I do it also so you will know how much Dunya loves you and what a wonderful warm heart she has. Mr Svidrigailov was indeed rude to her and made various impolite suggestions and sneering remarks to her at table . . . But I don't want to enter into all those distressing details, for they would just upset you for nothing – I mean, it's all over now. To cut a long story short: in spite of the kind and decent treatment she received from Marfa Petrovna (Mr Svidrigailov's wife) and all the rest of the family, Dunya had a very hard time of it, particularly when Mr Svidrigailov, following an old regimental custom of his, happened to be under the influence of Bacchus. But what do you think turned out to be the case later on? Just imagine: that madcap had long had a hankering after Dunya, but had been concealing it beneath a façade of rudeness and contempt towards her. Perhaps he himself was ashamed, and kept falling into a state of horror when he viewed himself, now getting on in years and the father of a family, possessed by such frivolous hopes, and for that reason could not help acting towards Dunya in a hostile manner. It might also have been that his rude behaviour and sneering were an attempt to conceal the truth from others. In the end, however, he could not restrain himself and dared to make Dunya an open and base proposition, holding out various rewards to her and telling her into the bargain that he would give up everything and move with her to another estate or possibly even abroad. You can imagine the suffering she went through! To leave her post at once was impossible, not only because of the money she owed, but also because she wished to spare the feelings of Marfa Petrovna, who might have suddenly had suspicions, and she would consequently end up sowing dissension in the family. Why, it would have been a major scandal for Dunya, too; there would have been no getting out of it. In fact, there were all sorts of reasons why Dunya could on no account expect to be able to escape from that dreadful household. Of course, you know Dunya, you know how clever she is and what a firm character she has. Dunya can put up with all sorts of things, and even in the most extreme situations she's able to find enough generosity of spirit within herself so as not to lose her firmness. She even didn't put it all in her letters in order not to upset me, yet we frequently wrote to each other to exchange news. The dénouement was quite unexpected: Marfa Petrovna chanced to overhear her husband pleading with Dunya in the garden and, misinterpreting it all, accused her of the whole thing, supposing that she was the one who was the cause of it all. In the garden there immediately took place a dreadful scene: Marfa Petrovna actually hit Dunya, wouldn't listen to a word she had to say, spent a whole hour shouting and finally gave orders for her to be taken to me in the town in a simple peasants' cart, into which they hurled all her belongings, her linen and her clothes, all any old how, without any baling or packing. And then it started to pour with rain, and Dunya, insulted and disgraced, had to drive in an open cart, sitting beside a muzhik, all seventeen versts of the way. Think now what sort of letter I could have written you in reply to the one I had from you two months ago! What could I have put in it? I myself was in despair; I didn't dare write you the truth, because you would have been very unhappy, aggrieved and indignant, and what could you have done? You would only have made yourself worse than you already were, and in any case Dunya wouldn't allow it; and I couldn't just fill the letter with rubbish about this, that and the other, when I had such misery in my soul. For all of a month our whole town was rife with rumours concerning this episode, and it came to the point where Dunya and I couldn't even go to church for the contemptuous stares and whispers we received; people even talked about us in our presence. As for our friends, they all shunned us, even stopped saying hallo to us, and I obtained certain knowledge that the merchant's shop-boys and some office clerks were out to do a beastly thing to us – tar the front entrance of the building where we lived, so that our landlords would give us notice to quit our apartment. At the bottom of all this was Marfa Petrovna, who had succeeded in putting the blame on Dunya and blackening her character in every household. She knows everyone in our town, and that month she made visits here practically by the minute; and since she's a bit indiscreet and likes talking about her family matters and, in particular, complaining about her husband to all and sundry, which is a really horrible thing to do, within a short space of time she'd not only spread the whole story all over the town, but over the whole district, too. I fell ill, but Dunya was stronger than I was, and you should have seen the way she bore it all and yet managed to console me and keep my spirits up at the same time! She's an angel! However, by the mercy of God, our torments were cut short: Mr Svidrigailov thought the better of it and repented; probably having taken pity on Dunya, he presented Marfa Petrovna with the complete and tangible proof of Dunya's innocence in the form of a letter which, before Marfa Petrovna had caught them in the garden together, Dunya had been compelled to write and to give to him, in order to put a stop to the personal declarations and secret rendezvous on which he had been insisting, and which, after Dunya's departure, had remained in the hands of Mr Svidrigailov. In this letter she rebuked him in the most fiery manner, full of indignation, for the infamy of his conduct towards Marfa Petrovna, put him reprovingly in mind of the fact that he was a father and a family man and that, moreover, it was vile of him to torment and make even more unhappy a girl whose unhappiness and defencelessness were bad enough. In a word, dear Rodya, this letter was written so nobly and movingly that I sobbed as I read it, and even to this day I can't read it without tears. In addition, Dunya's good name was cleared by the testimony of the servants, who had seen and who knew far more than Mr Svidrigailov had ever supposed, as is always the case in such situations. Marfa Petrovna was utterly shocked and 'destroyed anew', as she herself confessed, but was on the other hand entirely convinced of Dunya's innocence and, on the next day, on the Sunday, coming straight to the church, went down on her knees and in tears begged the Queen of Heaven to give her the strength to endure this new ordeal and to fulfil her duty. Then, fresh from church, without bothering to look in anywhere else, she came straight to us, told us everything, wept bitterly and, in complete repentance, embraced Dunya and begged her to forgive her. That same morning, wasting no time, she went straight from us to all the houses in town, and in every one of them, in terms most flattering to Dunya, shedding floods of tears, re-established Dunya's innocence and the nobility of her emotions and behaviour. Not only that: she showed and read aloud to everyone that letter Dunya had written in her own hand to Mr Svidrigailov, and even allowed people to make copies of it (which I consider is going a bit too far). Thus it was that she had to spend several days going round to everyone in town, as some people began to get offended that others had been shown preference, and thus it was that queues began to form, so that in every house people were waiting for it to be their turn, and everyone knew that on such-and-such a day Marfa Petrovna would be reading that letter in this house or that house, and present at every reading of it would be even those people who had already heard the letter several times in their own homes and those of their friends. It's my opinion that she went far, far too far: but that's the sort of woman Marfa Petrovna is. At any rate, she completely restored Dunya's honour, and the entire vileness of the whole affair has come to rest at the door of her husband, he being the principal culprit, as an indelible disgrace, so that I actually feel sorry for him; they've dealt with that madcap far too harshly. Dunya was immediately invited to go and give lessons in several households, but she refused. In general, everyone started treating her with particular respect. All of this was more than anything else instrumental in bringing about the unexpected circumstance by virtue of which it may be said that our entire fortunes are now changing. I must tell you, dear Rodya, that a bachelor has been seeking Dunya's hand in marriage and that she has now given her consent, a fact of which I hasten to notify you at the earliest possible moment. And although this is something that was done without consulting you, I'm sure you won't bear your sister or myself any grudge, as you will see yourself from the facts of the case that it would have been impossible for us to wait and postpone our decision until we'd had your reply. And you yourself couldn't have formed a proper, detailed judgement without being here. It happened like this. He's already a lieutenant-colonel in the civil service, his name's Pyotr Petrovich Luzhin, and he's a distant relative of Marfa Petrovna, who's had a lot to do with the whole business. It began with him conveying through her his desire to make our acquaintance; we received him in the proper manner, he had coffee with us, and the next day he sent us a letter in which he very politely made his proposal, asking for a swift and definite reply. He's a man of business, he's hard at work and he's now in a hurry to get to St Petersburg, so every moment is precious to him. Of course, at first we were very shocked, as it all happened so suddenly and unexpectedly. We both spent the whole of that day weighing the pros and cons and thinking about the matter. He's a trustworthy and well-to-do man, has two positions and already has capital of his own. It's true that he's already forty-five, but he has a very pleasant appearance and may still be attractive to women, and in general he's a very decent and respectable man, just a bit arrogant and on the gloomy side. But that may just be how he appears at first sight. Now I warn you, dear Rodya, that when you meet him in St Petersburg, which will be very soon now, you mustn't judge him too quickly and hastily, the way you usually do when you don't like something about somebody at first glance. I say this just in case, as I'm certain he'll make a pleasant impression on you. Indeed, in order to get to know anyone at all, it is necessary to approach them cautiously and by stages, so as not to jump to erroneous conclusions which may be very hard to correct and make amends for afterwards. And there are many grounds for believing that Pyotr Petrovich is a highly honourable man. On his first visit to us he told us that he's a positive man, but that he shares, as he himself put it, 'the convictions of our most recent generations', and is an enemy to all forms of prejudice. He said a great many other things, too, because he's a little vain and is rather fond of making other people listen to him, but I mean, that scarcely amounts to a sin. I didn't understand much of it of course, but Dunya explained to me that even though he's not a man of great education, he is none the less intelligent and, it would appear, kind. You know what your sister's like, Rodya. She's a steadfast, sensible, patient and magnanimous girl, though she has a fiery heart – something I've come to know very well. Of course, neither on his side nor on hers is there any great love, but Dunya, quite apart from being a clever girl, is at the same time a being as noble as an angel, and she will make it her duty to constitute the happiness of her husband, who in his turn will care about hers; of this last we have as yet no major reason to doubt, though I must admit that the whole thing has happened a bit quickly. What's more, he's a very prudent man, and he naturally sees that his own conjugal bliss will be that bit more secure the happier Dunya is being married to him. And as for a few roughnesses of character, old habits and even a certain lack of harmony with regard to ideas (something that is impossible to avoid even in the most happy of marriages), on that score Dunya herself has told me that she has faith in herself, that there is no reason to worry and that she will be able to put up with a great deal just as long as their future relationship is an honest and fair one. I also found him a bit hard-mannered at first; but I mean it could just be that he's a straightforward sort of man, and I'm sure that's what it is. For example, on his second visit, when he'd had Dunya's consent, he said during the course of the conversation that even in the days before he had met Dunya he had decided to marry an honest girl, but one without a dowry, and she must be the kind of girl who already knew what poverty was like; because, as he explained, a husband must in no way be beholden to his wife, and it's always far better if the wife views the husband as her benefactor. I should add that he put it in terms that were somewhat gentler and more affectionate than the ones I have used, I'm afraid I've forgotten his actual words and remember only the general sense; what's more, he didn't say it in any carefully thought-out sort of way, it was obviously something he blurted out in the heat of the conversation, as afterwards he even tried to correct and soften what he'd said; but even so, it did sound a bit on the harsh side to me, and I said so to Dunya later on. But Dunya came back at me with a fair amount of irritation, saying that 'words aren't deeds', which is, of course, true. During the night before she made up her mind, Dunya suffered from insomnia, and, assuming me to be already asleep, got up from her bed and spent the hours walking up and down the room; at last, she got down on her knees and prayed fervently in front of the icon. In the morning she told me that she'd taken her decision.

I have already mentioned that Pyotr Petrovich is now on his way to St Petersburg. He has an important case to attend to there, and he wants to open a public lawyer's office in the capital. For a long time now he's been engaged in the pursuance of various actions and lawsuits, and only the other day he actually won an important suit. It is essential for him to go to St Petersburg now, as he has an important case in the Senate Court. So, dear Rodya, he may be extremely useful to you, in all sorts of ways, and in fact Dunya and I have already come to the conclusion that it would be perfectly possible for you, starting this very day, to begin putting a career together for yourself, and that you could consider your future already clearly marked out. Oh, just think if that were really to be so! That would be such a wonderful thing that we should have to consider it as nothing less than a direct act of charity to us from the Almighty. Dunya dreams of nothing else. We've already taken the risk of saying a few words about it to Pyotr Petrovich. He expressed himself cautiously and said that, naturally, since he won't be able to do without a secretary, it would of course make more sense to pay the salary to a relative rather than a stranger, as long as he turns out to have an aptitude for the post (as though in your case there could be any doubt of that!), but then he voiced some doubts as to whether your university studies would leave you time to keep office hours with him. That was as far as the matter went on that occasion, but now Dunya can't keep her mind on anything else. For several days now she's simply been in a kind of fever and she's already dreamed up a whole scheme whereby you'll eventually become Pyotr Petrovich's friend and even his partner in his legal business, especially since you're in the Faculty of Law. I must say, Rodya, that I'm completely in agreement with her, and share all her hopes and plans, as they seem to be perfectly capable of realization; and in spite of Pyotr Petrovich's present unwillingness to be pinned down (which stems from the fact that he doesn't know you yet), Dunya is firmly convinced that she'll achieve it all by the good influence that she'll have on her future husband, and of that there is no dissuading her. Of course we have been careful not to say anything to Pyotr Petrovich about any of these long-term dreams of ours, particularly the one about you becoming his partner. He's a positive man and I think he would take it rather amiss, as it would all seem to him just a lot of fancies. By the same lights, neither Dunya nor I have as yet said so much as a word to him on the subject of our fervent hope that he'll help us to supply you with money while you're still in university; we didn't mention it in the first place because it's something that will come of its own accord later on, and he'll probably offer something of the kind himself without being asked (I'd like to see him refuse Dunya that), all the more so because you yourself may be able to become his right-hand man in the office, and receive this assistance not as charity, but as the salary that you have earned. That's the way Dunya wants to arrange it, and I'm in complete agreement with her. In the second place, we didn't say anything about it because when you meet him now I particularly want to set you off on an equal footing with him. When Dunya spoke of you to him with warm enthusiasm, he replied that in order to be able to judge someone it's necessary to examine him for oneself, and at close quarters, and that he would reserve the privilege of forming an opinion about you until he had had a chance of getting to know you a bit. Do you know, my precious Rodya, I think that, for various reasons (which, I hasten to add, have nothing whatsoever to do with Pyotr Petrovich, but are just a result of my own personal and possibly even old-womanish, female whims) – I think that I may possibly do better if after the marriage I continue to live on my own, as I do at present, and not together with them. I'm quite certain that he'll have the decency and sensitivity to invite me to live with them, and propose that I not be parted from my daughter any more, and that, even though he hasn't said anything about it so far, that's just because I'm supposed to take it for granted without being asked; but I shall refuse. Several times in my life I have noticed that mothers-in-law are not much to men's liking, and not only do I not want to be even the least little bit of a burden to anyone – I want to be completely independent for as long as I have my own crust of bread to eat and children such as Dunya and yourself. If I can, I'll find somewhere to live that's not too far from you both, because, Rodya, I've been saving the best bit of my letter for the end: let me tell you, my dear friend, that soon, possibly very soon indeed, we shall all meet again and put our arms round one another, all three of us, not having seen one another for three years!

It's quite *definitely* been decided that Dunya and I are to travel to St Petersburg – exactly when, I don't know, but at any rate it will be very, very soon, even possibly within the week. Everything depends on the instructions we receive from Pyotr Petrovich, who will let us know as soon as he's had a chance to get his bearings in St Petersburg. Because of certain special considerations, he wants to get the wedding ceremony over with as soon as possible, and hold the reception in the days remaining before Shrovetide, or if that should not prove to be possible, as time is so short, then immediately after the *gospozhinki*.* Oh, with what happiness I shall press you to my heart! Dunya is wild with excitement and joy about the prospect of seeing you again, and she once said in jest that that alone made it worthwhile to marry Pyotr Petrovich. She's an angel! She isn't writing you anything for the moment, but she's told me to write and say that there are many things she wants to talk about with you, so many things that her hand won't lift to grasp the pen, because one can't write everything in a few lines, and just ends by upsetting oneself; she told me to send you a big hug and kisses without number. But, in spite of the fact that we may very soon be meeting face to face, I shall still send you as much money as I can in a few days' time. Now that everyone knows that Dunya is going to marry Pyotr Petrovich my credit has suddenly shot up, and I know for a fact that Afanasy Ivanovich will now let me have as much as seventy-five roubles on account of my pension, so I may be able to send you twenty-five or even thirty. I would have sent even more, but I'm afraid of how much our travel costs may come to; and although Pyotr Petrovich was so kind as to fund a part of the expenses for our journey to the capital out of his own pocket, and has in fact offered to forward our luggage and big trunk for us (they'll be sent via some friends of his), but even so we'll still have to keep enough for our arrival in St Petersburg, where one can't show one's face if one is penniless, not in the early days, at least. Actually, however, Dunya and I have already worked it all out exactly, and it seems that in fact the journey itself won't cost very much. Where we live is only ninety versts from the railway, and we've already come to an arrangement with a muzhik waggon-driver we know, just in case; and when we get to the train, Dunya and I will be quite happy to travel third class. So perhaps I'll manage to send you thirty roubles, not twenty-five – in fact, I'm sure I will. But that's enough; I've covered both sides of two whole sheets with writing, and there's no room left for any more; there you have our whole story; goodness, what a lot of things to happen at once! And now, my precious Rodya, I embrace you until our imminent meeting, and send you my maternal blessing. Rodya, love Dunya, that sister of yours; love her as she loves you, and realize that she loves you infinitely, more than she does herself. She's an angel, and you, Rodya, you're everything to us – all our hopes and aspirations rolled into one. If only you were happy, so should we be. Do you say your prayers, Rodya, the way you used to, and do you believe in the mercy of the Creator and Our Redeemer? I fear in my heart that you may have been affected by this latest fashion of unbelief. If that's the case, then I pray for you. Remember, my darling, how when you were still only a child, in the days when your father was still alive, you used to babble your prayers on my knees, and how happy we all were then! Goodbye, or, rather, *until we meet*! I hug you tight as tight, and send you kisses without number.

Yours to the tomb
Pulkheria Raskolnikova

For almost the whole time it took him to read the letter, right from its very beginning, Raskolnikov's face was wet with tears; but when he had finished, it was pale and distorted with a nervous twitch, and a nasty, lugubrious, jaundiced smile snaked across his lips. He put his head on his thin, threadbare pillow and thought and thought for a long time. His heart was beating violently, and his thoughts were violently agitated. At last he began to feel suffocated and claustrophobic in this little yellow room that was more like a cupboard or a trunk. His eyes and his brain craved space. He grabbed his hat and went out, this time without fear of running into anyone on the stairs; he had forgotten about that. His path lay in the direction of Vasily Island by way of V— Prospect,* and he looked as though he were hurrying there on business; he walked, however, in his customary manner, without noticing where he was going, whispering to himself and even talking aloud to himself, something that was a great source of wonder to passers-by. Many of them thought he was drunk.

IV

His mother's letter had exhausted him. With regard to its principal, capital point, however, he had not been in a moment's doubt, not even as he read the letter. The principal essence of the matter had been resolved within his head, and resolved decisively: 'That marriage will not take place while I am alive, and to hell with Mr Luzhin!

'Because the whole thing's perfectly clear,' he muttered to himself with a little smirk, maliciously exulting over the victory of his decision in advance. 'No, mother, no, Dunya, you won't fool me! . . . And they even apologize for not having asked my advice and for having decided the matter in my absence! I should hope so! They think it's too late to undo it now, but we shall see about that! What a capital excuse: it's as if they were saying that Pyotr Petrovich is such a busy man that he can only get married in a post-chaise, or on the train, practically. No, Dunechka, I see it all and I know what the "many things" are that you want to discuss with me; I know, too, what you thought about all night as you walked up and down your room, and what you were praying about in front of the Kazan Virgin that stands in mother's bedroom. It's hard work, the ascent to Golgotha. Hm . . . So, then, it's finally been decided: you're going to marry a man of business and reason, Avdotya Romanovna, one who has capital of his own (who *already* has capital of his own – that's more solid and impressive-sounding), who has two positions and who, "*it would appear*, is kind", as Dunechka herself observes. That *it would appear* is the most wonderful bit of all! It's because of that that Dunechka, *it would appear*, is going to get married! . . . Wonderful! Wonderful! . . .

'. . . I'm intrigued though, as to why mother should have written me that bit about "our most recent generations". Was it simply a character reference, or did she have some ulterior motive: to coax me into taking a favourable view of Mr Luzhin? Oh, those cunning women! I'm curious to have some light shed on another matter, too: to what extent were they both frank with each other that day and night and during all the time that followed? Did they put it all straight into *words*, or did they both realize that they had the same thing in their hearts and minds, so that there was no point in saying it all out loud and needlessly letting the cat out of the bag? There was probably an element of that; it's clear from her letter: mother thought he seemed *a bit* harsh-mannered at first, and poor, naïve mother went trotting off to Dunya with her comments and observations. And Dunya, of course, lost her temper and "came back at her with a fair amount of irritation". I'm not surprised! Who wouldn't get frantic when the whole matter was perfectly clear without naïve questions, and when it had already been decided that even to talk about it was spurious? And what's this she writes to me? "Rodya, love Dunya, she loves you more than she does herself"; isn't that her conscience secretly giving her trouble for having agreed to sacrifice her daughter for the sake of her son? "You're all our hopes and aspirations rolled into one, you're our everything!" Oh, mother! . . .' Malice was boiling up inside him more and more violently, and if he had happened to meet Mr Luzhin at that moment he would probably have murdered him!

'Hm, that's true,' he went on, following the vortex of thoughts that was whirling inside his head. 'It is true that "in order to get to know anyone, it is necessary to approach them cautiously and by stages"; but Mr Luzhin doesn't take much figuring out. The main thing is that "he's a man of business, and, *it would appear*, kind"; it's no small matter that he should have taken responsibility for their luggage, forwarding that big trunk at his own expense! How could he be anything but kind? And the two of them, the mother and the *bride-to-be*, are hiring a muzhik and a cart with a hood made of bast-matting. (Why, I've ridden in just such a cart myself!) Oh, it's nothing! Only ninety versts, "and we'll be quite happy to travel third class", a thousand versts, if need be. And sensible, too: one must cut one's coat according to the cloth; but I say, Mr Luzhin – what can you be thinking of? After all, you're the one whose bride she's going to be . . . surely you must know that mother is borrowing money on the strength of her pension in order to pay for the journey? Of course, you've a common commercial interest here, something undertaken to mutual advantage and in equal shares, the expenses split fifty-fifty, in other words; "some bread and salt together but a pinch of snuff apart," as the saying goes. And the man of business has managed to pull the wool over their eyes a little in this instance: paying to have their luggage moved is less expensive than paying for their journey, and it may even go for nothing. Why can't they both see that? Or don't they want to see it? I mean, they're pleased, they're actually pleased! And to think that this is just the blossom on the boughs, and the real fruits have still to come! I mean, what's important here? It's not the meanness and the miserliness, but the *tone* of all this. I mean, it's setting the tone for the whole marriage, it's a prophecy . . . And why is mother being so extravagant, anyway? What's she going to have left by the time she shows up in St Petersburg? Three silver roubles, or two "tickets", as she . . . the old woman . . . calls them . . . hm! What does she think she's going to live on in St Petersburg afterwards? I mean, she must surely realize by now that it'll be *impossible* for her and Dunya to go on living together after the marriage, even just initially? The charming fellow has doubtless *let the cat out of the bag* on that score, too, and showed himself in his true colours, even though mother is warding the invitations off with both hands, saying, "I shall refuse." What does she think she's up to? What's she got to rely on? Her hundred and twenty roubles' pension, with deductions in order to pay off her debt to Afanasy Ivanovich? She knits her little scarves and sews her little armlets, ruining her old eyes. And I mean, the scarves only bring in about twenty-five roubles a year to add to her hundred and twenty, I know that for a fact. So one must conclude that she's relying on the nobility of Mr Luzhin's feelings: "He'll make the offer himself, he'll beg me." Don't bank on it! That's the way it always is with these Schillerean *"Schöne Seelen"** – right up until the last possible moment they'll deck a man out in peacock feathers, hoping for the good and refusing to believe in the bad, and although they have a sense that there may be another side to the coin, nothing will induce them to utter so much as one word of truth before they absolutely have to; the very thought gives them the shivers, they ward off the truth with both hands right up to the moment when the man they've adorned with all those virtues makes a fool of them. I wonder if Mr Luzhin has any medals? I bet he has a St Anne's Ribbon* and puts it in his lapel when he goes out to dine with contractors and merchants. He'll probably wear it at his wedding, too. But the devil take him! . . .

'. . . Well, mother I can understand, there's nothing to be done there, that's just the way she is, but I'm surprised at Dunya. Dear Dunechka, I mean, I know you! . . . Why, the last time we saw each other you were just about to be twenty; but I already understood your temperament. Mother writes that "Dunechka can put up with a great deal". I could have told her that! I already knew that two and a half years ago, and I've spent the past two and a half years thinking about it, about that very fact that "Dunechka can put up with a great deal". After all, if she can put up with Mr Svidrigailov, and all the consequences of that, she really must be able to put up with a great deal. And now they've decided that she can put up with Mr Luzhin as well; who expounds the theory of the superiority of wives who have been plucked from poverty and are the recipients of charity from their husbands, and expounds it practically at their first meeting, what's more. Well, all right, suppose he "unintentionally let it slip", even though he's a man of reason (which means, perhaps, that he didn't let it slip unintentionally at all, but was simply anxious to make the situation plain as soon as possible), but what of Dunya, what of her? I mean, the man must be an open book to her, yet she's going to live with him. I mean, she'd live on black bread and water rather than sell her soul, she wouldn't give up her inner freedom for the sake of a bit of comfort; she wouldn't give it up for the whole of Schleswig-Holstein, never mind about Mr Luzhin. No, Dunya wasn't like that when I knew her, and . . . well, she hasn't changed, that's all! . . . There's no use denying it, the Svidrigailovs are hard work! It's hard work trailing around in the provinces all your life as a governess on two hundred roubles a year, but I know all the same that my sister would rather go and work with the Negroes on some plantation-owner's estate or with the Latvian peasants of some Baltic German than defile her spirit and her moral sensibility by a liaison – forever – with a man whom she doesn't respect and to whom she has nothing to say, solely for her own personal gain! And even if Mr Luzhin had been made of the purest gold or sheer unadulterated diamond, not even then would she have agreed to become the legal concubine of Mr Luzhin! Why is she agreeing to it now? What's the game? What's the clue? It's not hard to see: she won't sell herself for the sake of her own comfort, not even in order to save herself from death, but she'll do it for someone else! She'll sell herself for those who are dear to her, those she looks up to! That's what the whole business is all about: she's selling herself for her brother, for her mother! Selling everything! Oh, in cases like that we suppress our moral sensibilities; our freedom, our peace of mind, even our conscience, all of it, all of it goes to the secondhand market. Let my life go to hang, we say, just as long as those dear, beloved creatures of mine are happy. Not only that: we invent our own casuistry, too, we study with the Jesuits for a time, perhaps, and put our minds at rest, convince ourselves that

77

this is how it has to be, that it really must be like this if the good object is to be attained. That's just the way we are, and it's all as plain as daylight. It's plain that it's Rodion Romanovich Raskolnikov and no one else who is at stake here and who has pride of place. Yes, of course, she can see to it that he's happy, support him while he's at the university, make him a partner in an office, provide a whole future for him; perhaps he'll be a rich man one day, and end his days honoured, respected, even famous! And mother? Oh, but it's Rodya, her precious Rodya, her first-born! How could she not sacrifice even such a daughter as this for such an important son? Oh loving and inequitable hearts! And what of that? In this case we wouldn't even refuse the lot of Sonechka, Sonechka Marmeladova, eternal Sonechka, for as long as the world lasts! Are you completely aware of the size of the sacrifice you're making? Is it right? Is it being made under duress? Will it do any good? Is it sensible? Do you realize, Dunechka, that Sonechka's fate is in no way any uglier than the one you're contemplating with Mr Luzhin? "There can't be any love between them," mother writes. But what if it's not only love, but also respect that there can't be; what if, instead, there's revulsion, contempt, loathing, what then? And what if it then turns out that once again it's necessary to *"keep oneself clean"*? Am I right? Do you realize, do you realize what that kind of cleanliness involves? Do you realize that the Luzhin kind of cleanliness is just the same as Sonechka's cleanliness, and perhaps even worse, even more filthy and more vile, because you, Dunechka, can still count on a surplus of comfort, while over there it's quite simply a question of staving off death by starvation! "It's expensive, expensive, that kind of cleanliness, Dunechka!" Well, and what if your strength isn't up to it, what if you wish you'd never done it? Think of the hurt, the sadness, the cursing, the tears, hidden from everyone, because you're not Marfa Petrovna, are you? And what do you think mother will feel like then? I mean, even now she's uneasy, she's worried; but what about when she sees it all clearly for what it is? And what do you think I'll feel like? . . . Have the two of you ever really stopped to think about me? I don't want your sacrifice, Dunechka, I don't want it, mother! It won't take place while I'm alive, it won't, it won't! I won't accept it!'

He suddenly came to himself, and paused.

'Won't take place? And what are you going to do to stop it? Forbid it? By what right? What can you promise them instead, in order to possess such a right? To devote your whole life, your whole future to them, *when you finish your course and get a job*? We've heard that one before, that's just maybe – what about *now*? I mean, you've got to do something right now, do you realize that? And what are you doing? Robbing them. I mean, the only money they've got is what they can raise on the strength of a hundred-rouble pension and the patronage of the Svidrigailovs! How are you going to protect them from the Svidrigailovs, from Afanasy Ivanovich Vakhrushin, you millionaire-to-be, you Zeus, disposer of their fortunes? You'll do it in ten years' time? But in ten years' time mother's eyesight will have gone, from all those scarves she's made, and doubtless from shedding too many tears as well; she'll have wasted away from hunger; and your sister? Well, just think what may have happened to your sister in ten years' time, or even during them? Got it?'

With these questions he teased and tormented himself, even deriving a certain amount of enjoyment from them. Actually, none of them were new or unexpected questions; they were all old, painful ones of long standing. It was a long time since they had begun to lacerate his heart, and it was positively an age since his present sense of anguish and depression had come into being, having grown, accumulated and, of late, matured and taken concentrated form, assuming the guise of a terrible, monstrous and fantastic question that had begun to torture his heart and mind and inexorably demanded resolution. Only now his mother's letter suddenly struck him like a thunderbolt. It was clear that now was not the time to feel miserable, to suffer passively with the thought that the questions were not capable of resolution; no, instead he must do something, and at once, as quickly as possible. Whatever happened, he must take some action, or else . . .

'Or else turn my back on life altogether!' he suddenly cried in a frenzy. 'Obediently accept my fate, such as it is, once and for all, and stifle all my aspirations, renouncing every right to action, life and love!'

'Do you understand, do you understand, dear sir, what it means to have nowhere left to go?' The question Marmeladov had asked the day before suddenly came back to him. 'For every man must have at least somewhere he can go . . .'

Suddenly he gave a start: a certain thought, another from yesterday, had flashed through his head. But that was not what had made him start. After all, he had *known in advance* that it was about to 'flash through', and he had been waiting for it; and in fact it was not really a thought from yesterday at all. The difference was that a month ago, and even yesterday, it had been only a dream, while now . . . now it was suddenly no longer a dream, but had acquired a new, menacing and completely unfamiliar aspect, and it had been that which he had suddenly realized . . . There was a hammering in his head, and everything went dark before his eyes.

Quickly, he glanced around. He was looking for something. He wanted to sit down, and he was looking for a bench; at that moment he was walking along K— Boulevard.* A bench was visible some hundred yards ahead of him. He began to walk towards it as quickly as he could; on the way, however, he had a little adventure which for a few minutes took up all his attention.

In spying out the bench he had noticed a woman who was walking along some twenty yards in front of him, but at first had not let his attention dwell upon her, any more than it had dwelt on any of the other objects that had flitted before his gaze until that moment. Many had been the occasions on which he had arrived home quite without remembering the route he had taken, and he was used to this kind of walking. There was, however, something strange about this woman who was making her way along, something that was immediately striking – at first sight – so that little by little his attention began to fasten itself on her – at first reluctantly and almost with annoyance, and then with increasing intensity. He suddenly wanted to find out just what it was that was so strange about this woman. For one thing, she could only have been a girl, and quite a young one at that; she was walking along in that blazing heat with no headwear, parasol or gloves, swinging her arms in an absurd sort of way. She was wearing a little silk dress of thin material ('silk stuff'), but she had it on in a very odd manner, with hardly any of its fasteners done, and in behind, just where the skirt began, at her waist, it was torn; a whole piece of material had come away and hung loose. She had a little triangular scarf thrown over her exposed neck, but it protruded sideways, and was not on straight. To complete it all, the girl was walking unsteadily, stumbling and even reeling in all directions. This encounter finally aroused all of Raskolnikov's attention. He drew level with the girl as they approached the bench, but as soon as she reached it she fairly flopped down on it, in one corner, threw her head back against the rear support and closed her eyes, plainly in extreme exhaustion. Taking a close look at her, he at once realized that she was completely drunk. It made a strange and preposterous sight. He even wondered whether he might not be mistaken. Before him was an extremely young little face, that of a girl of about sixteen or even perhaps a year younger – a face that was small, framed by fair hair, pretty but flushed all over and somehow swollen-looking. By now the girl appeared to be taking in very little; she had crossed one of her legs over the other, advancing it out far more than was decent, and looked by all the signs as though she had only the dimmest awareness that she was out on the street.

Raskolnikov did not sit down, but was reluctant to go away, standing before her in perplexity. This boulevard is always deserted, but now, at two o'clock in the afternoon, and in heat like this, there was almost no one about at all. Yet, to one side of them, on the edge of the pavement, some fifteen paces away, a certain gentleman had stopped; by the look of him he would also very much have liked to approach the girl with certain intentions in view. He had probably spied her from a distance and caught her up, but Raskolnikov had spoiled his plans. He was giving Raskolnikov malevolent looks, trying, however, not to make them too obvious, and impatiently awaiting his turn, which would come after the bothersome fellow in rags had gone. It was obvious what the gentleman was after. He was about thirty years old, plump and thick-set, with a milk-and-blood complexion, pink lips, a little moustache and a very modish style of dress. Raskolnikov was filled with a terrible anger; he suddenly wanted to do something to insult this plump man-about-town. Leaving the girl for a moment, he went up to the gentleman.

'Hey, you! Svidrigailov!* What do you want here?' he shouted, clenching his fists and laughing through lips that had begun to froth with rage.

'What's the meaning of this?' the gentleman asked sternly, frowning and expressing supercilious astonishment.

'Clear off, that's what!'

'How dare you, you riff-raff!'

And he brandished his riding whip. Raskolnikov rushed at him with his bare fists, not even pausing to consider that the thick-set gentleman could easily dispose of two men such as himself. Just then, however, someone seized hold of him from behind: between them stood a policeman.

'That'll do now, gentlemen, no scrapping in public places, if you don't mind. What do you want? Who are you?' he said to Raskolnikov sternly, observing his rags.

Raskolnikov gave him an attentive look. This was a gallant soldier's face, with a long, grey moustache and side-whiskers; its expression was an intelligent one.

'You're the very man I want,' Raskolnikov shouted, seizing him by the arm. 'I'm Raskolnikov, ex-university student . . . It wouldn't do you any harm to take note of that, either,' he said, turning to the gentleman. 'And as for you, please come with me – I want to show you something . . .'

And, seizing the policeman by the arm, he drew him towards the bench.

'There, look, she's completely drunk; she was walking down the boulevard just now: God knows who her people are, but she doesn't look like one of the profession. Most likely somebody gave her too much to drink and made her the victim of foul play . . . for the first time . . . – do you get my meaning? – and then just let her wander off down the street. Look how her dress is torn, look at the way she's got it on: I mean, somebody put it on for her, she didn't do it herself – and whoever it was had clumsy hands, the hands of a man. That's obvious. And now look over there: that man-about-town I was just about to get into a brawl with – I don't know him, never seen him before; but he also saw her walking along just now, drunk and not really aware of where she was, and he's just raring to go up to her now and intercept her – since she's in that state – so he can drive her off somewhere . . . I'm certain that's so; believe me, I'm not mistaken. I saw the way he was watching her, spying on her, but I got there before him, and now he's waiting till I'm gone. Look, there he is over there now, he's moved away a little, I think he's rolling himself a cigarette* . . . Are we just going to let him get his hands on her? Aren't we going to try to fetch her home? Think about it!'

In an instant the policeman had taken it all in and sized up the situation. The stout gentleman was easy enough to make out, but there remained the girl. The old soldier bent down to take a closer look at her, and sincere compassion showed itself in his features.

'Ah, what a shame!' he said, shaking his head. 'She's still just a child. She's been the victim of foul play, there's no doubt about that. Listen, young lady,' he said, trying to get her to sit up. 'Where do you live?' The girl opened her tired, bleary eyes, looked dully at her interrogators and waved them away with one arm.

'Listen,' Raskolnikov said. 'Here' – he felt in his pocket and drew out twenty copecks; he could spare them – 'Look, hire a cab and tell the driver to take her to her home address. Only we'll have to find out what it is, first!'

'Young lady – er, young lady!' the policeman began again, taking the money. 'I'm about to get you a cab and I'll come with you in it myself. Where have we to go? Eh? Where do you have your quarters?'

'G'way! . . . Shtop peshtering me,' the girl muttered, and again gave a defensive wave of her arm.

'Ah, ah, how terrible! Ah, how shameful, young lady, how shameful!' Again he began to shake his head in embarrassment, compassion and indignation. 'Why, there's a poser for you, sir!' he said, turning to Raskolnikov; as he did so, he once again quickly looked him up and down from head to foot. No doubt he thought the young man strange: dressed in such rags, yet parting with money!

'Was it far from here that you found her, sir?' he asked.

'I tell you, she was walking along ahead of me, staggering to and fro, right here on the boulevard. As soon as she reached the bench she just flopped down on it.'

'Oh, what shameful things happen in the world nowadays, Lord in Heaven! A simple little thing like that, and she's drunk! She's been the victim of foul play, that's for sure! Look, her little dress is torn . . . Ah, the depravity there is nowadays! . . . And she's probably from a good family, one that's not got much money . . . There's a lot of those now. You can tell by the look of her that she's one of the delicate kind, sort of ladylike,' – and again he bent down over her.

Perhaps he himself had daughters like this – 'the delicate kind, sort of ladylike', with well brought-up manners and all the latest fashions already thoroughly assimilated . . .

'The main thing,' Raskolnikov said anxiously, 'is to stop that villain getting his hands on her! I mean, he's just going to commit another outrage on her. It's perfectly obvious what he wants; look at him, the villain, he's still standing there!'

Raskolnikov spoke these words in a loud voice, pointing straight at the person whom they concerned. He heard them, and seemed on the point of flying into a rage again, but thought the better of it and confined himself to a single contemptuous glance. Then he slowly withdrew another ten paces or so, and once again came to a halt.

'We can stop him doing that, sir,' the old NCO replied thoughtfully. 'All she has to do is tell us where to drop her off, and . . . Young lady! Er, young lady!' he said, bending forward again.

The girl suddenly opened her eyes wide, looked attentively at them, as though she had just realized something, got up from the bench and set off back in the direction from which she had come.

'Ugh, you shameless brutes, shtop peshtering me!' she said, with the same defensive wave of her arm. She was walking quickly, but staggering badly, as she had been before. The man-about-town began to follow her, but along the other side of the boulevard, keeping his eyes trained on her.

'Don't worry, sir, I won't let him get away with it,' said the man with the long moustache in a firm voice, and he set off in pursuit of them. 'Ah, the depravity there is nowadays,' he said again, out loud, sighing.

At that moment Raskolnikov reacted as though he had been stung by something; in a single instant he seemed utterly transformed.

'Listen, hey!' he shouted after the man with the long moustache.

The latter turned round.

'Stop it! What's it to you? Forget about it! Let him have his bit of fun.' (He pointed at the man-about-town.) 'What's it to you?'

The policeman failed to comprehend, and stared at him. Raskolnikov burst out laughing.

'A-ach!' the old soldier said, and with a wave of his arm set off in pursuit of the girl and the man-about-town, doubtless of the opinion that Raskolnikov was either a madman or something even worse.

'He's walked off with my twenty copecks,' Raskolnikov said with vicious irritation when he was left alone. 'Well, I hope the other fellow gives him the same to let him get his hands on the girl, and then that'll be the end of it . . . Why did I poke my nose in, trying to help? Is it for me to do that? Do I have any right to? Oh, they can swallow each other alive for all I care! And how could I ever have gone and given away those twenty copecks? Were they mine?'

In spite of these strange remarks, he felt really terrible. He sat down on the abandoned bench. His thoughts were distracted ones . . . In general at that moment he felt terrible trying to think of anything at all. He would have liked to sink all his troubles in oblivion, forget everything and then wake up and begin completely anew . . .

'Poor girl!' he said, looking at the empty corner of the bench. 'She'll come out of it, cry a bit, and then her mother will get to know . . . First she'll box her ears, then she'll give her a thrashing, a hard, painful and ignominious one, and then she'll probably turn her out of the house . . . And even if she doesn't, the Darya Frantsovnas will get wind of it, and soon my little girl will start trotting about from one port of call to another . . . Then it'll be straight to hospital (it's always the ones who live very proper lives at home with their mothers and get up to mischief on the sly who end up there), well, and then . . . and then hospital again . . . vodka . . . the drinking dens . . . and again the hospital . . . and in two or three years' time she'll be a paralysed cripple, and the sum-total of her years will be nineteen, or perhaps only eighteen . . . Haven't I seen girls like that before? And how did they get to be like that? That's how they got to be like that . . . Pah! So be it! It has to be like that, they say. They say that each year a certain percentage has to go off down that road* . . . to the devil, I suppose, in order to give the others fresh hope and not get in their way. A percentage! Nice little words they use, to be sure: they're so reassuring, so scientific. Just say: "percentage", and all your troubles are over. Now if one were to choose another word, well, then . . . then things might look a little less reassuring . . . And what if Dunechka ends up in the percentage? . . . If not this year's, then perhaps that of another?

'But where am I going?' he thought suddenly. 'That's funny. I mean, I came out for something. As soon as I'd finished reading the letter, I came out . . . I set off for Vasily Island to see Razumikhin, yes, that's right . . . I remember, now. But the only thing is – why? And how did the idea of going to see Razumikhin happen to enter my head just now, of all times? It's extraordinary!'

He marvelled at himself. Razumikhin was one of his old university friends. It was a point worthy of note that during his time at the university, Raskolnikov had had practically no friends, had avoided all the other students, never gone to see any of them and received their visits with reluctance. But in any case, they all quickly turned away from him. He somehow failed to take any part in their communal gatherings, their discussions and their amusements, and he had no share in any other aspect of their lives. He studied intensely, not sparing himself, and for this he was respected; nobody liked him, however. He was very poor and at the same time somehow haughtily arrogant and uncommunicative: as though he were keeping something to himself. Some of his fellow students had the impression that he looked down on them all from a certain height, as though they were children, as though he had outstripped them all in terms of education, knowledge and convictions, and that he viewed their convictions and interests as something inferior.

For some reason, on the other hand, he had got along with Razumikhin; or, if that were putting it too strongly, had at least been on more communicative, more plain-talking terms with him. It was, in fact, impossible to be on any other kind of terms with Razumikhin. He was an uncommonly cheerful and talkative fellow, good-natured to the point of naïveté. Beneath this outward simplicity of manner there lay, however, both depth of character and a certain dignity. The better of his companions understood this, and everyone liked him. He was very far from being stupid, though on occasion he really could be a little naïve. His appearance said a lot about him – tall, thin, always ill-shaven, black-haired. He occasionally got into brawls, and had the reputation of being a bit of an athlete. One night, when out with some others, he had with a single blow brought down a certain pillar of the law about six and a half feet tall. His capacity for alcohol was limitless, but he could equally well go without it altogether; sometimes he indulged in pranks to an impermissible degree, but he often went for long periods without indulging in them at all. Razumikhin was also remarkable for the fact that none of his failures ever upset him, and it appeared that there were no adverse circumstances capable of weighing him down. He could make his lodgings anywhere, even on the roof, put up with the most terrible hunger and the severest cold. He was very poor and was decidedly his own sole supporter, scraping together what money he could from various odd employments. He knew a million ways of getting hold of money, always in the form of earnings, of course. For the whole of one winter he did not heat his room at all, and he asserted that it was even more comfortable that way, as one slept better in the cold. At the present time he, too, had been compelled to give up the university, but it was not to be for long, and he was hurrying with all his might to improve his circumstances, so as to be able to resume classes as soon as possible. It was some four months since Raskolnikov had been to see him, and Razumikhin did not even know where he lived. Once, a couple of months back, they had met in the street, but Raskolnikov had turned away and even crossed over to the other side, hoping that the other would not notice him. And Razumikhin, though he had noticed him, walked on by, not wishing to bother his *friend*.

V

'It's true, I did think of asking Razumikhin to help me find some work recently, I was going to ask him if he couldn't get me some private teaching, or something of that sort.' The recollection suddenly dawned upon Raskolnikov. 'But how can he help me now? Supposing he is able to get me some teaching, supposing he does have a copeck to spare, so I can even buy a pair of boots and have my clothes mended, to be able to go and give lessons . . . hm . . . Well, and what then? What will I be able to do on a few *pyataks*? Is that what I require? It's really rather silly of me to have come to see Razumikhin . . .'

The question of why he had now come to see Razumikhin was troubling him even more than he himself was aware; he kept searching uneasily for some ill-omened significance in this apparently most ordinary of actions.

'Wait a moment: did I really think I could put everything right just by going to see Razumikhin, find a way out in the person of Razumikhin?' he wondered to himself in astonishment.

He thought and rubbed his forehead, and it was a strange thing that, after a long spell of reflection, there suddenly occurred to him, almost without being prompted, a certain very peculiar idea.

'Hm . . . Razumikhin,' he suddenly said very calmly, as though he had reached some final decision. 'I'm going to see Razumikhin, of course I am . . . only – not right now . . . I'll go and see him the day after *it*, when *it's* all over and everything's begun anew . . .'

And suddenly he came to his senses.

'After *that*?' he exclaimed, leaping up from the bench. 'Is *that* going to happen? Is it really going to happen?'

He abandoned the bench and set off, almost at a run: his original intention had been to turn back and go home, but the thought of going home suddenly seemed a horribly repulsive one: there, in his corner, in that horrible cupboard of his, all *this* had been fermenting within him for more than a month now, and he moved wherever his eyes led him.

His nervous trembling had become slightly feverish; he thought he might possibly be catching a chill, for even in this heat he felt cold. Almost unconsciously, prompted by a kind of inner necessity, he began with a kind of effort to scrutinize every object he encountered, as though in desperate quest of some diversion, but this failed to work, and he kept sinking back into his state of brooding. But when, with a sudden start, he raised his head again and looked around him, he immediately forgot what he had been thinking about a moment ago and even what part of town he had been walking through. In this fashion he traversed the whole of Vasily Island, came out on to the Little Neva, crossed the bridge and turned in the direction of the Islands. At first his tired eyes found the leafy coolness agreeable,* used as they were to the dust and slaked lime of the city, and to its enormous, constricting and oppressive buildings. Here there was neither humidity, nor stench, nor drinking dens. But soon even these new, agreeable sensations gave way to ones that were morbid and irritating. Sometimes he would stop in front of some dacha lavishly adorned with verdure, look through the fence and see, far away on the balconies and terraces, finely dressed women and, in the garden, children running about. He was particularly caught by the flowers; he looked at them longer than at anything else. He also encountered sumptuous carriages, horsemen and horsewomen; he followed them with an inquisitive gaze and forgot about them before they had even disappeared from view. Once he stopped in order to count his money; he turned out to have thirty copecks. 'Twenty to the policeman, three to Nastasya for the letter – that means I must have given the Marmeladovs forty-seven or fifty copecks yesterday,' he thought, for some reason totalling it up, but he had soon even forgotten the reason he had pulled the money from his pocket in the first place. As he was passing some sort of eating establishment that looked like a cookshop, it came back to him, and he suddenly felt hungry. Entering the cookshop, he drank a glass of vodka and had a pie with some kind of filling. He finished it as he went on his way. It was a very long time since he had drunk vodka, and it had an instant effect on him, even though he had only had one glass. His legs suddenly grew heavy, and he began to feel a powerful inclination to sleep. He turned back in a homeward direction; but when he reached Petrovsky Island he stopped in complete exhaustion, wandered off the road into the bushes, collapsed into the grass and fell asleep that very same instant.

When one is in a morbid state of health, one's dreams are often characterized by an unusual vividness and brilliance, and also by an extremely lifelike quality. Sometimes the scene that is conjured up is a monstrous one, yet the setting and the entire process of its representation are so lifelike and executed with details that are so subtle, astonishing, yet correspond in an artistic sense to the integral nature of the whole, that the dreamer himself could never invent them while awake, not even if he were an artist of the order of Pushkin or Turgenev. Dreams such as these – the morbid ones – invariably remain in the memory long afterwards, and have a powerful effect on the individual's deranged and already overstimulated organism.

Raskolnikov had a terrible dream. It was a dream about his childhood, back in the little town where they had lived. He was about seven years old and he was taking a walk, on a holiday, towards evening, somewhere beyond the outskirts with his father. It was a grey sort of day, overcast and humid, and the locality looked exactly the way it had survived in his memory; even in his memory it had become far more indistinct than it was now in his dream. The little town stood in an exposed position, as on the palm of someone's hand, with not a willow in sight; somewhere very far away, right on the edge of the horizon, a patch of forest showed up black. At a few yards' remove from the town's last kitchen garden stood a drinking-house, a very large drinking-house that had always produced in him the most unpleasant sensations, amounting almost to fear, whenever he walked past it on those outings with his father. There was always such a crowd in there, there was so much yelling, laughter and foul language, so much hoarse and ugly singing, and such frequent fighting; there were always so many drunken and frightening charac-ters lounging about outside . . . When they encountered them, he would always press up close against his father, trembling all over. The road passed close to the drinking-house; it was a country road, always dusty, and its dust was always so black. On it went, winding and twisting, and after some three hundred yards or so it veered off to the right, skirting the town cemetery. In the middle of the cemetery stood a stone church with a green onion dome; a couple of times a year he would visit the church with his father and mother for mass, when burial rites were performed in memory of his grandmother, who had died long ago, and whom he had never seen. On these occasions they always took with them some *kut'ya** on a white dish wrapped in a napkin, and the *kut'ya* was the sugary sort, made of rice, with raisins pressed into it in the form of a cross. He loved this church with its old icons, most of them without mountings, and the old priest with his trembling head. Beside his grandmother's tomb, on which there lay a funerary slab, was the little grave of his younger brother who had died at the age of six months, whom he also had never known at all and of whom he had no memory; he had, however, been told that he had had a younger brother, and every time he visited the cemetery he would cross himself above the little grave in religious awe, bowing down to it and kissing it. And this was what he dreamt: he and his father were walking along the road to the cemetery, and passing the drinking-house; he was holding his father's hand, and looking over at the drinking-house with fear. Something special was going on, and it drew his attention: on this occasion, too, there seemed to be the sound of festive merrymaking, a dressed-up crowd of artisans' wives and peasant women, their husbands and all kinds of riff-raff. They were all drunk and singing songs, and by the entrance to the drinking-house stood a cart – but it was a strange sort of cart. It was one of those big ones that are usually drawn by great cart-horses, and are used for transporting goods and wine-barrels. He had always liked watching those enormous cart-horses with their long manes and brawny legs, moving at a tranquil, measured pace as they hauled along an entire mountain of goods with not a shadow of strain, as though they actually found it easier to move when they had such a load to haul than when they did not. It was a strange thing, however, that in the present instance one of these massive carts had been harnessed up to a small, thin, greyish peasant jade, one of the kind which – he had often seen this – sometimes overstrain themselves when hauling a tall load of hay or firewood, particularly if the cart gets bogged down in the mire or in a rut, and which the muzhiks always beat so viciously, so viciously with their knouts, sometimes even about the muzzle and the eyes, and the sight of this would always make him feel so sorry, so sorry that he would almost burst

90

into tears, and his mother would take him away from the window. But all of a sudden it had started to get very noisy: out from the drinking-house, drunk as lords, shouting, singing, brandishing bala-laikas, came some big muzhiks in red and blue shirts, their *armyaks** thrown over their shoulders. 'Come on, get in, the lot of you!' one of them shouted – a man still young, with a fat neck and a meaty face that was as red as a carrot. 'I'll take you all, get in!' Instantly, however, there was a burst of laughter and exclamations.

'That old jade'll never make it!'

'Come off it, Mikolka, have you lost your brains, or what? Harness-ing that little filly to that great cart!'

'That little grey mare must be all of twenty by now, lads!'

'Get in, I'm going to take you all!' Mikolka said, leaping into the cart first, taking the reins and standing up at full height on the front-board. 'Matvey went off with the bay this morning,' he shouted from the cart, 'and this little filly's fair breaking my heart; I feel like doing her in, she eats her oats and gives nothing back. Get in, I say! I'll fly there at the gallop! I'll *make* her gallop!' And he picked up his knout, preparing with satisfaction to flog the little grey mare.

'Go on, get in, why don't you?' people laughed in the crowd. 'You heard him – he's going to fly there at the gallop!'

'I'll bet that mare hasn't galloped in ten years.'

'Well, she's going to now!'

'Don't spare her, lads, take knouts, all of you, have them ready!'

'That's right! Flog her!'

Roaring with laughter and cracking jokes, they all piled into Mikolka's cart. Six of them got in, and there was room for even more. They took a fat, red-cheeked peasant woman with them. She was dressed in bright red calico, with a *kichka* and beads, and *koty** on her feet; she was cracking nuts and laughing softly to herself. The people in the crowd that surrounded them were also laughing, and indeed, how could they fail to laugh? A wretched little mare like that going to pull such a load at a gallop? Two of the lads in the cart at once picked up knouts in order to lend Mikolka a hand. At the cry of 'Gee-up!' the little jade began to tug with all her might, but not only was she unable to set off at a gallop – she could barely manage to move forward at all; her legs skittered about underneath her as she whinnied and cowered under the blows from the three knouts that rained down on her to no effect whatsoever. The laughter in the cart and among the crowd

91

doubled in intensity, but Mikolka lost his temper and began to flog the little mare even harder, as though he really believed he could make her gallop.

'Let me have a go, lads!' a young fellow who had now got a taste for the thing shouted from the crowd.

'Get in! All of you, get in!' Mikolka shouted. 'She'll take us all. I'll flog her!' And he lashed her and lashed her until he hardly knew what he was doing in his frenzy.

'Papa, Papa!' he cried to his father. 'Papa, what are they doing? Papa, they're beating the poor little horse!'

'Come along, come along!' said his father. 'They're drunk, playing mischief, the fools; come along, don't look!' And he tried to draw him away, but he broke loose from his father's arms and, beside himself, ran over to the little horse. But by this time the little horse was in a bad way. It would gasp, stop moving, start tugging again, and then nearly fall down.

'Flog her to death!' cried Mikolka. 'It's come to that. I'll do it myself!'

'What's the matter, wood-devil? Not got a Christian heart in you?' an old man called from the crowd.

'Have you ever seen a little jade like that pull such a load?' another man added.

'You'll do her in!' shouted a third.

'Leave me alone! She belongs to me! I'll do as I like with her. More of you get in! All of you! I'll damn well make her gallop! . . .'

Suddenly a loud volley of laughter rang out, drowning everything: the little mare, unable to endure the intensified rain of blows, had begun an ineffectual kicking of her hindlegs. The old man could not repress a bitter smile. It was true enough: a wretched little mare like that, yet she could still kick!

Two more lads in the crowd each took another knout and ran over to the little horse in order to whip its flanks. One lad ran to either side.

'Whip her on the muzzle, on the eyes, on the eyes!' Mikolka shouted.

'A song, lads!' someone shouted from the cart, and everybody in the cart joined in. A song with dubious words rang out, a tambourine rattled, and there was whistling during the refrains. The woman went on cracking nuts and laughing softly to herself.

. . . He was running alongside the little horse, now he was a few steps ahead of it, he could see it being whipped across the eyes, right across the eyes! He was crying. His heart rose up within him, his tears flowed. One of the lads who were doing the whipping caught him on the face with his knout; he felt nothing; screaming, his hands working convulsively, he rushed towards the grey-haired old man with the grey beard who was shaking his head and condemning the whole scene. One of the peasant women took him by the arm and tried to lead him away; but he tore himself free and ran back to the little horse once more. Even though by this time it was at its last gasp, it was beginning to kick again.

'What the hell's the matter with you?' Mikolka shrieked in a fury. He threw down the knout, leaned over and hauled from the bottom of the cart a long, thick cart-shaft, took hold of one end of it in both hands, and with an effort proceeded to brandish it over the little grey mare.

'He's going to kill her!' the shout went round.

'He's going to do her in!'

'She belongs to me!' Mikolka shouted, and swung the shaft down at full force. There was the sound of a heavy blow.

'Take the whip, take the whip to her! Why have you stopped?' voices shouted from the crowd.

But Mikolka was brandishing the cart-shaft for a second time, and another blow landed with full force on the back of the unfortunate jade. She sank right back on to her hindquarters, but then leapt up again and started tugging, tugging with all the strength she had left in various directions, in order to get going with her load; but whichever way she moved she was greeted by six knouts, and the cart-shaft rose and fell a third time, and then a fourth, in measured rhythm, with all its wielder's might. Mikolka was in a frenzy of rage because he was unable to kill her with one blow.

'She's certainly got some life in her!' the shout went round.

'She'll fall down in a minute, lads, it's all over with her now!' one versed in such matters called from the crowd.

'Take an axe to her, for God's sake! Get it over with quickly!' cried a third.

'Ach, I'll make you eat those flies! Let me through!' Mikolka shrieked violently. Throwing down the shaft, he leaned inside the cart once more and hauled out an iron crowbar. 'Watch out!' he cried, and with all his might he swung it down on his poor little beast. The blow thudded down; the little mare began to totter, sank down, tried to give another tug, but the crowbar again came down on her back, and she fell to the ground, as if all her four legs had been cut away from under her at once.

'Finish her off!' Mikolka shouted, leaping out of the cart as though he no longer knew what he was doing. A few of the lads, who were also red-faced and drunken, seized hold of whatever they could lay their hands on – knouts, sticks, the cart-shaft – and ran over to the dying mare. Mikolka stood to one side and began to beat her on the spine with the crowbar at random. The jade stretched her muzzle forwards, uttered a heavy sigh, and died.

'That's the end of her!' people shouted in the crowd.

'She ought to have galloped.'

'She belongs to me!' Mikolka shouted, holding the crowbar, his eyes bloodshot. He stood there looking as though he were sorry there was no creature left to beat.

'It's right enough: anyone can see you haven't got a Christian heart in you!' many voices were now shouting from the crowd.

But the poor boy was now beside himself. With a howl he forced his way through the crowds towards the little grey mare, flung his arms round her dead, bloodied muzzle and kissed it, kissed her on the eyes, on the lips . . . then he suddenly leapt up and rushed at Mikolka, hammering at him with his little fists. At that point his father, who had been chasing after him for a long time, finally seized hold of him and carried him away from the crowd.

'Come along, come along!' his father said to him. 'We're going home!'

'Papa! The poor little horse . . . Why did they . . . kill it?' he sobbed, but his breathing was choked, and again those howls escaped from his constricted chest.

'They're drunk, they're up to mischief, it's none of our business, come on!' his father said. He flung his arms round his father, but his chest felt so tight, so tight. He felt he wanted to draw breath, to scream, and woke up.

He awoke panting, drenched in sweat, even his hair sweat-soaked, and sat up in horror.

'Thank God, it was only a dream!' he said, settling down under a tree and taking a deep breath. 'But what is this? I must be catching a fever: what an ugly dream!'

His entire body felt paralysed; his soul was dark and troubled. He put his elbows on his knees and supported his head in both hands.

'Oh God!' he exclaimed. 'Will I really do it, will I really take an axe and hit her on the head with it, smash her skull in? . . . Will I slip on her warm, sticky blood, break open the lock, steal the money and tremble; then hide myself, covered in blood . . . with the axe . . . Oh Lord, will I really?'

As he said this, he was trembling like a leaf.

'But what's got into me?' he went on, hunching up again, as if in deep amazement. 'I mean, I did know that I'd never have the endurance for this, so why have I been torturing myself all this time? I mean, even yesterday, yesterday when I went to do that . . . *rehearsal*, I knew yesterday for certain that I'd never be able to go through with it . . . So what am I doing now? Why can I still not make up my mind about it? I mean, yesterday, when I was coming down the staircase, I told myself it was vile, loathsome, base, base . . . I mean, the very thought of it made me feel sick and gave me the horrors *in real life* . . .

'No, I couldn't go through with it, I couldn't! Not even, not even if there were no uncertainties in all those calculations, not if everything I've determined to do this past month were as clear as daylight, as plain as arithmetic – Lord! Why, not even then could I do it! I mean, I simply couldn't go through with it, I couldn't, and that's it! . . . So why, why, even now . . .'

He rose to his feet, looked around him in astonishment as though he were wondering how he had got there, and set off towards T—v Bridge. He was pale, his eyes were burning, he was suffering from exhaustion in every limb, but suddenly his breathing seemed to grow easier. He felt now that he had thrown off that terrible burden which had been weighing him down for so long, and his soul began suddenly to experience a sense of lightness and peace. 'O Lord,' he prayed, 'show me my path, and I will renounce this accursed . . . dream of mine!'

As he crossed the bridge, he looked quietly and calmly at the Neva, at the brilliant going-down of the brilliant red sun. In spite of his debilitated condition he did not even feel tired. It was as though the abscess on his heart, which had been gathering to a head all month, had suddenly burst. Freedom, freedom! Now he was free from that sorcery, that witchcraft, that fascination, that infatuation!

Later on, when he remembered that time and all that had happened to him during those days, minute by minute, point by point, detail by detail, there was always one thing that struck him with an almost superstitious wonder, even though it was something that was in essence not really all that unusual; to him, however, it always seemed like some preordained announcement of his fate. Namely: he could not for the life of him understand or explain to himself why in his tired, exhausted state, when the best thing he could have done was to take the very shortest and most direct route home, he should have gone home by way of the Haymarket, which did not lie on his route at all. Even though it was a small detour, it was nevertheless an obvious and quite unnecessary one. Of course, it was true that he had gone home dozens of times without taking note of the streets he was walking along. But then why, he always wondered afterwards, why should he have had an encounter which was at one and the same time of such important, decisive consequence for him, and of such an extremely fortuitous nature in the Haymarket of all places (where he had not even any reason to be), and why should it have occurred at precisely that hour, that minute of his life, coinciding with precisely that colouring of his mood and with precisely those circumstances which made it quite inevitable that it, that encounter, should produce the most devastating and lasting influence on his entire personal fate? As though it had been waiting for him there on purpose!

By the time he crossed the Haymarket, it was about nine o'clock. All the tradesmen with tables, trays, stalls and benches were closing up their establishments or taking down and clearing away their wares and dispersing to their homes, in the same way as their customers were doing. Next to the cookshops that occupied the lower floors of the Haymarket buildings, in the dirty and stinking courtyards, and most of all outside the drinking dens, there were jostling crowds of small manufacturers and ragpickers of every sort. Raskolnikov preferred these haunts, along with all the neighbouring lanes and alleyways, to any other part of town, whenever he went out walking with no purpose. Here his rags drew no snooty attention, and it was possible for him to go about looking any way he chose without scandalizing anyone. Right at the corner of K— Lane,* an artisan and a peasant woman, his wife, were selling goods at two tables: thread, braid, cotton headscarves and the like. They were also clearing up and making ready to go home, but were being rather slow about it, talking with an acquaintance of theirs who had approached them. This acquaintance was Lizaveta Ivanovna, or simply, as everyone called her, Lizaveta, the younger sister of that very same old woman Alyona Ivanovna, the collegiate registrar's widow and pawnbroker in whose home Raskolnikov had been the day before when he had gone there in order to pawn his watch and perform his *rehearsal* . . . He already knew all about Lizaveta, and she even knew him a little. She was a tall, ungainly, timid and submissive female of about thirty-five, practically an idiot, who lived in complete slavery to her sister and drudged for her day and night, going in fear of her and even enduring beatings from her. She was standing reflectively face to face with the artisan and the peasant woman, holding a bundle and listening to them attentively. They were explaining something to her with peculiar animation. When Raskolnikov suddenly caught sight of her, a strange sensation resembling the most profound amazement took hold of him, even though there was nothing extraordinary about this encounter.

'You'd do best to settle the matter yourself, Lizaveta Ivanovna,' the artisan said loudly. 'Come and see us tomorrow, at about seven. Those folk will be coming here then, too.'

'Tomorrow?' Lizaveta said in a slow, reflective voice, as though unable to make her mind up about something.

'My, that Alyona Ivanovna's fairly got the wind up you!' the tradesman's wife, a no-nonsense sort of woman, began to prattle. 'Look at you, you're just like a little infant. She's not even your own kith and kin, just a half-sister, and look at the power she has over you!'

'Oh, don't you say anything to Alyona Ivanovna about it this time, miss,' said her husband, interrupting, 'that's my advice – just come by and see us without asking. It's a good bargain you'll be getting. Your sister will be able to work it out for herself later on.'

'You want me to come by?'

'Tomorrow at seven; and there'll be some of those folk here, too, miss; you'll be able to settle the matter for yourself.'

'And we'll have the samovar ready,' his wife added.

'Very well, I'll come,' Lizaveta said, still reflecting, and slowly she began to move off down the street.

By this time Raskolnikov had passed where they were standing and heard no more. He had made his passage quietly, unobtrusively, trying not to miss a single word. His initial amazement had little by little given way to horror, as a cold chill ran down his spine. He had learned, he had suddenly, at a stroke, and quite unexpectedly learned that at seven o'clock tomorrow evening Lizaveta, the old woman's sister and her sole living-companion, would not be at home and that consequently at seven o'clock tomorrow evening the old woman *would be at home completely alone.*

He only had a few paces left to go to the entrance to his lodgings. He went up to his room like a man who has been condemned to death. His mind was completely empty, and he was quite incapable of filling it with anything; but with his whole being he suddenly felt that he no longer possessed any freedom of thought or of will, and that everything had suddenly been decided once and for all.

It went without saying that even had he spent years on end waiting for a suitable occasion, not even then, assuming that he had still had the same plan, could he have counted on a more obvious step towards the successful realization of that plan than the one that had suddenly presented itself just then. At any rate, it would have been difficult to ascertain yesterday, with the greatest degree of exactitude and the smallest amount of risk, circumventing the need for all dangerous questions and inquiries, that tomorrow, at that particular time, that particular old woman, the one on whose life he was preparing to make an attempt, would be at home all on her very own.

VI

Raskolnikov chanced subsequently to learn why the artisan and the peasant woman had invited Lizaveta to their home. The matter was of the most ordinary kind, and involved nothing particularly remarkable. A family from out of town who had landed in poverty were selling some of their belongings, clothes and the like, all of it women's stuff. Since selling things in the market never brought much profit, they were looking for a woman to do the selling for them elsewhere.

This was the occupation Lizaveta had found for herself: she took commission, went here and there on business, and did a thriving trade as she was very honest and always asked the lowest price: whatever price she named, that was the one at which she sold. As a rule she said little and, as has already been remarked, was submissive and easily frightened . . .

Recently, however, Raskolnikov had become superstitious. The traces of superstition were to remain in him for a long time afterwards, and he never really got rid of them. Indeed, in this whole affair he was always subsequently inclined to perceive a certain strangeness and mystery, as if it involved the working of certain peculiar influences and coincidences. Back in the winter a certain student he knew, by the name of Pokorev, had at one point during a conversation they had had as the latter was about to depart for Kiev slipped him Alyona Ivanovna's – the old woman's – address, in case he should need to pawn anything. For a long time he had held off from going to see her, as he had had his teaching and was managing to get by somehow. Some six weeks ago he had remembered about the address; he had two personal possessions that were suitable for pawning: one was the old silver watch he had inherited from his father, and the other was a small golden ring with three red stones of some description which his sister had given him at their parting as a keepsake. He decided to take the ring; having tracked the old woman down, he felt towards her, at first glance, without as yet knowing anything in particular about her, an unmasterable sense of revulsion, took two 'tickets' from her, and on his way looked in at a certain rather inferior little eating-house. He ordered tea, sat down and began to think very hard. A strange idea had popped up in his head, like a chicken broken from an egg, and he was finding it very, very absorbing.

Sitting almost side by side with him, at another table, were a student whom he did not know at all and whose face he did not remember, and a young officer. They had been playing billiards, and were now drinking tea. Suddenly he heard the student telling the officer about 'the pawnbroker, Alyona Ivanovna, the collegiate secretary's widow' and giving him her address. This alone seemed somehow strange to Raskolnikov: there he was, having just come from there, and now the first people he met were talking about her. It was merely a coincidence, of course, but even so he was now unable to get rid of a certain very peculiar feeling, and now it was as if someone were doing his best to worm himself into his favour: the student had suddenly begun to tell his companion all sorts of details about this Alyona Ivanovna.

'She's amazing,' he was saying. 'You can always get money out of her. She's as wealthy as a Jew, she could let you have five thousand straight off, yet she won't turn her nose up even at a rouble pledge. A lot of us have been to see her. Only she's a horrible old cow . . .'

And he began to relate how mean and capricious she was, how one needed only to be one day late in redeeming one's pledge for the thing to be lost. She would give one a quarter of the item's value, and take monthly interest of five and even seven per cent, and so on. The student got carried away and informed his companion, moreover, that the old woman had a sister called Lizaveta whom she, small and repulsive, beat every minute of the day and kept in total bondage, like a little child, while Lizaveta, at least six feet tall . . .

'I mean, it's a real phenomenon!' the student exclaimed, and burst into laughter.

They began to discuss Lizaveta. The student talked about her with a peculiar satisfaction, and kept laughing, while the officer listened with great interest and asked the student to send this Lizaveta over to mend some linen for him. Raskolnikov did not miss a single word and learned everything in one go: Lizaveta was the old woman's younger half-sister (they had had different mothers), and she was thirty-five years old. She worked for her sister day and night, performed the functions of cook and washerwoman in the household, and, in addition, did sewing which she sold, and even hired herself out to scrub floors, giving all that she earned to her sister. She did not dare to take a single order or accept a single job of work without the old woman's consent. Another thing was that the old woman had already made her will, a fact that was known to Lizaveta, who did not stand to inherit a single copeck, just the old woman's personal effects, some chairs and so forth; all the money had been earmarked for distribution to a certain monastery in the province of N—, in return for the eternal remembrance of her soul. Lizaveta had retained her petty-bourgeois origins, unlike her sister, who had married into the civil service; she had not married, and was terribly awkward, of remarkable height, with great long, almost bandy-looking legs, always with down-at-heel goatskin shoes on her feet, and she paid especial attention to her personal cleanliness. The thing that the student found astonishing and that made him laugh, however, was that Lizaveta was constantly pregnant . . .

'But I thought you said she was a freak?'

'Well, she's sort of swarthy, like a soldier dressed up, pretending to be a woman, but you know she's not at all a freak. She has such a kind face, such kind eyes. Yes, really, she has. And the proof of it is that a lot of men find her attractive. She's a quiet sort, meek, mild, compliant, she'll go along with anything. And she has a really nice smile.'

'I say, do you find her attractive, too?' the officer laughed.

'Oh, only because she's so strange. No, but I'll tell you this: I'd murder that old woman and rob her of all her money, and I swear to you, I'd do it without the slightest twinge of conscience,' the student added with heat.

The officer burst out laughing again, and Raskolnikov started. How strange this was!

'If you'll permit me, I'd like to ask you a serious question,' the student said, growing excited. 'I was joking just now, of course, but look: on the one hand you have a nasty, stupid, worthless, meaningless, sick old woman who's no use to anyone and is, indeed, actually harmful to people, who doesn't even know herself why she's alive, and who's going to kick the bucket of her own accord tomorrow. Do you get my meaning? Do you?'

'Yes, I think I do,' the officer replied, fixing his eyes on his excited companion.

'Listen to this, then. There, on the other hand you have young, fresh energies that are going to waste for want of backing – thousands of people are involved, and it's happening everywhere! A hundred, a thousand good deeds and undertakings that could be arranged and expedited with that old woman's money, which is doomed to go to a monastery! Hundreds, possibly even thousands of lives that could be set on the right road; dozens of families saved from poverty, break-up, ruin, depravity, the venereal hospitals – and all of that with her money. If one were to kill her and take her money, in order with its help to devote oneself to the service of all mankind and the common cause: what do you think – wouldn't one petty little crime like that be atoned for by all those thousands of good deeds? Instead of one life – thousands of lives rescued from corruption and decay. One death to a hundred lives – I mean, there's arithmetic for you! And anyway, what does the life of that horrible, stupid, consumptive old woman count for when weighed in the common balance? No more than the life of a louse, a cockroach, and it's not even worth that, because the old woman is harmful. She's wearing another person's life out: she's mean: she bit Lizaveta's finger out of meanness the other day; she very nearly severed it!'

'Of course she doesn't deserve to live,' the officer observed. 'But then that's nature.'

'Ah, but it's possible to correct and channel nature, you know, old man – otherwise we would all just drown in a sea of prejudice. If it weren't for that, there would never have been a single great man. People say: "duty, conscience" – well, I won't say a word against duty and conscience – but after all, what do we mean by them? Wait, I want to ask you another question. Listen!'

'No, I want to ask you a question, first. *You* listen!'

'Well?'

'Well, here you are talking and holding forth in that oratorical way of yours, but tell me: are *you* going to kill the old woman?'

'Of course not! I merely thought it would be her just deserts . . . It's no business of mine . . .'

'Well, the way I see it is that there are no just deserts in it at all unless you're prepared to do it yourself. Let's go and have another game.'

Raskolnikov was in a state of extreme excitement. All this was, of course, the most commonplace and the most frequently encountered kind of conversation; many times before he had heard the same ideas expressed by young people in other forms and in relation to other subjects. But why had he chanced to hit upon such talk and such ideas precisely now, when inside his own head there had just been engendered . . . *precisely those very same thoughts*? And why precisely now, when he had only just come away from the old woman with the embryo of his idea, should he immediately have happened upon a conversation about her? . . . This coincidence always seemed to him a strange one. This trivial, eating-house conversation had an extremely strong influence on him during the subsequent development of the affair: as though here some form of predestination, of augury had been at work . . .

* * *

Returning from the Haymarket, he threw himself on the sofa and sa there for a whole hour with no movement. Meanwhile it grew dark; he had no candle, and indeed the notion of lighting one never entered his head. Later, he could never remember whether he had been thinking about anything during that time. At last he felt a return of his earlier fever and shivering, and realized with pleasure that it was possible to lie down on the sofa, too. Before long a sound, leaden sleep descended on him, seeming to press him down.

He slept for an unusually long time, and had no dreams. Nastasya, when she came into his room at ten o'clock the next morning, was hardly able to rouse him. She had brought him tea and bread. The tea was again weak stuff, made with used leaves, and was again served in her own teapot.

'Ugh, the way he sleeps!' she exclaimed indignantly. 'He does nothing *but* sleep, either!'

With an effort, he raised himself. His head was aching; he got to his feet, turned round once in his room, and fell back on the sofa again.

'Sleeping again!' Nastasya exclaimed. 'Are you ill, or what?'

He made no reply.

'Do you want your tea?'

'Later,' he said with an effort, closing his eyes again and turning his face to the wall. Nastasya went on standing over him for a bit.

'Maybe he really is ill,' she said, turned away and went out of the room.

She came back again at two o'clock with some soup. He was lying as he had been earlier. The tea stood untouched. Nastasya actually took offence, and began to push him and shove him with spite.

'What are you snoozing away there for?' she exclaimed, looking at him with revulsion. He raised himself on one elbow and sat up, but said nothing to her and merely looked at the floor.

'Are you ill or aren't you?' Nastasya asked, but again she received no reply. 'You want to get out for a bit,' she said, after a pause. 'It would do you good to get some fresh air. Are you going to have this food, or what?'

'Later,' he said weakly. 'Go away!' And he made a motion with his hand.

She stood there a bit longer, looked at him compassionately, and then went out.

103

A few moments later he raised his eyes and gave the tea and the soup a long stare. Then he took the bread, and the spoon, and began to eat.

He hardly touched the food, had no appetite, took only three or four spoonfuls, in an absent-minded sort of way. His head was aching less now. Having had all he wanted, he stretched out on the sofa again, but was unable to get back to sleep, and lay there without moving, on his front, with his face thrust into the pillow. He kept having waking fantasies, and they were all such strange ones: most frequently of all he fancied he was somewhere in Africa, in some kind of Egyptian oasis. A caravan was resting, the camels were lying down peacefully; all around there were palm trees, an entire circle of them; everyone was eating their evening meal. He, however, kept drinking water, straight from the spring that flowed murmuring right by his side. It was so cool, and the water was so wonderfully, wonderfully cold and blue, hurrying over various-coloured stones, and sand that was so pure, with spangles of gold . . . Suddenly he distinctly heard the sound of a clock striking. He started, snapped out of his trance, raised his head, looked out of the window, figured what time it was and suddenly leapt up, in full possession of his senses now, as though someone had hauled him off the sofa. He went over to the door on tiptoe, softly opened it a little way, and began to listen on the stairs. His heart was beating terribly. But on the staircase all was quiet, as if everyone were asleep . . . It seemed wild and improbable to him that he could have spent since yesterday in such oblivion, without yet having done anything or made any preparations . . . And that might have been six o'clock striking just now . . . And suddenly an extraordinary, feverish and somehow helpless turmoil seized hold of him, in place of his slumber and torpor. There were, in fact, few preparations to be made. He strained all his energies in order to think of everything and leave nothing out; but his heart kept beating and beating, thumping so badly that he began to find it difficult to breathe. The first thing he had to do was make a loop and sew it to his coat – the work of a moment. He felt under his pillow and retrieved from the pile of linen he had stuffed underneath it one of his shirts, which was practically falling apart, old and unwashed. From its rags he tore off a ribbon-like strip about two inches wide and sixteen inches long. He folded this strip in two, took off his wide, tough-fabric summer coat (the only outdoor garment he possessed) and began to sew both ends of the strip to the inside of its left armpit. His hands shook as he sewed, but he managed to do it, and in such a way that from the outside nothing was visible when he put the coat back on. The needle and thread he had procured long ago, and he kept them in his bedside table, wrapped up in a piece of paper. As for the loop, this was a very ingenious device of his own design; the loop was intended to hold an axe. It was out of the question to go around in the streets with an axe in one's hand. Even if one were to hide it under one's coat, one would still have to keep it in place with one's arm, which would be noticeable. Now, with the loop, however, all he had to do was to put the head of the axe through it and it would hang conveniently under his arm, on the inside of the coat, all the way there. And, by putting his hand in one of the side pockets, he could hold on to the handle of the axe to stop it from dangling about; and since, too, the coat was a very roomy one, a veritable sack, no one would be able to see from the outside that he was holding on to something through the lining of his pocket. This loop was also something he had devised earlier, some two weeks previously.

Having finished with this, he thrust his fingers into the narrow slit between his 'Turkish' sofa and the floor, felt about in the left-hand corner and pulled out the 'pledge' he had manufactured and hidden there a long time ago. This 'pledge' was in fact not really a pledge at all, just a smoothly planed piece of wood no larger or thicker than the average silver cigarette-case. He had found this piece of wood on one of his walks, in a certain courtyard, one wing of which housed some workshop or other. Later he had added a thin, smooth iron plate – it had probably broken off something else – which he had also found in the street that same day. Fitting the two objects together (the iron one was smaller than the wooden one), he bound them firmly to each other, crosswise, by means of a length of thread; then he wrapped them neatly and presentably in a sheet of clean, white paper and tied the parcel with a slender ribbon, also crosswise, adjusting the knot in such a manner that it would be rather difficult to undo. This was so that the old woman's attention would be distracted for a time; while she was fiddling with the knot he would seize the moment. He had added the iron plate for the sake of extra weight, so that the old woman would not at once guess that the 'item' was made of wood. All this he had been keeping under his sofa until the time came. No sooner had he retrieved the thing than he suddenly heard a shout down in the yard somewhere:

'It struck six long ago!'

'Long ago! Oh my God!'

He rushed to the door, listened, snatched up his hat and began to descend his thirteen steps, cautiously, inaudibly, like a cat. A most important part of the business still lay ahead – he had to steal an axe from the kitchen. That the deed had to be done with an axe was something he had decided long ago. He also had a folding garden knife; but he had no confidence in the knife, and still less in his own strength – that was why he had finally decided that he must use an axe. It may, incidentally, be worth noting here one peculiar feature of all the final decisions he had so far taken in this affair. They all had one strange characteristic: the more final they had grown, the more monstrous and absurd they at once became to his eyes. In spite of the entire agonizing inner struggle he went through, never for one instant was he able to believe in the feasibility of his intentions, during that whole time.

And even if it were somehow to come to pass that he managed to work everything out, make all his decisions watertight, down to the last detail, leaving no room for a single doubt – even then he would have turned his back on the whole thing as on something absurd, outrageous and impossible. There remained, however, a whole host of unresolved points and questions that still had to be dealt with. As for how he was to get hold of an axe, that trivial question did not trouble him in the slightest, because there was nothing easier. The fact was that Nastasya was hardly ever at home, and this was especially true in the evenings: she was either going off to see the neighbours or running down to the corner shop, and she always left the door wide open. That was the very thing the landlady kept having those quarrels with her about. So, all he had to do when the time came was to go quietly into the kitchen and take the axe, and then, an hour later (when it was all over), come in once more and put it back. There were, however, certain imponderables: supposing he were to return an hour later in order to put the axe back, only to find that Nastasya, too, had returned? Then, of course, he would have to go past and wait until she had gone out again. But what if she were to notice that the axe had gone, and begin to look for it, raise a hue and cry? Then there would be suspicion, or at least grounds for suspicion.

But these were merely trivial considerations to which he did not even begin to give any thought, and indeed he had not the time to do so. He was thinking about what was most important – the detail could wait until *he was satisfied with everything*. This latter condition really did seem unrealizable, however. At least, that was how it appeared to him. There was no way, for example, that he could ever imagine bringing his ratiocinations to an end, getting up and simply going there . . . Even his recent *rehearsal* (the visit he had made with the intention of making a final survey of the place) had only been an *attempt* at a rehearsal, not a real one, much as if he had said: 'Come on, I'll go and test it out, what's the point of lying here dreaming?' – and had at once been unable to go through with it, had shrugged his shoulders and run away in bitter rage at himself. Yet at the same time he had the feeling that, so far as the moral aspects of the question were concerned, his analysis was now complete: his casuistry had been whetted sharp as a razor, and he was unable to find any more conscious objections within himself. In the last resort, however, he simply had no faith in himself and obstinately, slavishly, sought objections right, left and centre, fumbling around for them as though someone were compelling him and drawing him to it. But now this latest day, which had dawned so unexpectedly and had decided everything, acted on him in an almost entirely mechanical fashion: as though someone had taken him by the hand and pulled him along behind him, inexorably, blindly, with unnatural force, countenancing no objections. As though a corner of his clothing had got caught in the flywheel of a machine, and he was beginning to be drawn into it.

At first – this had actually been a long time earlier – a certain question had preoccupied him: why were nearly all crimes so easily tracked down and found out, and why did the traces of nearly all criminals show up so clearly? Little by little he had arrived at certain diverse and interesting conclusions and, in his opinion, the principal cause was to be found less in the criminal's lack of ability to conceal the material evidence of his crime than it was in the criminal himself; it was the criminal himself who, in almost every case, became subject at the moment of his crime to a kind of failure of will and reason, which were replaced by a childish and phenomenal frivolity, and this right at the very moment when the things that were needed most of all were reason and caution. According to the way he saw it, this eclipse of reason and failure of will attacked human beings like an illness, developing slowly and reaching their crisis not long before the enactment of the crime; they continued to manifest themselves in the same critical fashion at the moment of the crime itself and also for a short time thereafter, depending on the individual; then they passed, in the same way that every illness passes. On the other hand, the question of whether it was an illness that gave rise to the crime, or whether the crime itself was, by its own peculiar nature, invariably accompanied by something resembling an illness, was one that he did not yet feel able to determine.

Arriving at such conclusions, he decided that where he personally was concerned, in his own undertaking, there could be no such morbid upheavals, and that his reason and his will would remain inalienably with him throughout the entire enactment of what he had planned, for the sole reason that what he had planned was – 'not a crime' . . . We shall omit the lengthy process by which he had arrived at this last conclusion; we have run too far ahead even as it is . . . We shall merely add that in general the factual, purely material difficulties of the undertaking played a decidedly secondary role within his mind. 'As long as I can manage to preserve my will and my reason and exercise them over them to the fullest extent, then they in their turn will all be vanquished when it becomes necessary for them to acquaint themselves with every last, microscopic detail of the affair . . .' But the affair was not making any progress. He continued to have not the slightest faith in his final decisions, and when the fatal hour struck, everything turned out not that way at all, but somehow unexpectedly – even, one might almost say, astonishingly.

A circumstance of the most trivial kind landed him in an impasse even before he had got to the bottom of the stairs. As he drew level with his landlady's kitchen, the door to which as always stood wide open, he directed a cautious, disapproving look inside, in order to find out in advance whether, Nastasya being absent, the landlady was there, or, if she was not, whether the door to her room was properly shut – he did not want her peeping out of there when he went in for the axe. Great, however, was his amazement when he suddenly saw that not only was Nastasya at home and in her kitchen, but she was actually doing some work: she was taking the laundry out of its basket and hanging it on the clothes-line! At the sight of him she stopped what she was doing, turned towards him and continued to stare at him steadily all the time he was passing. He averted his eyes and continued his descent as though he had not noticed anything. But the whole affair was at an end: he had no axe! He was horribly shaken.

'Now where did I get that idea?' he thought, as he was going through the entrance-way. 'Where did I get the idea that she'd be bound to be out just then? Why was I so certain of it – why, why?' He felt crushed, even in some way humiliated. He wanted to jeer at himself with malicious spite . . . A slow-witted, animal rage seethed up inside him.

He paused in the entrance-way in order to reflect. To go out on to the street like this, for show, as if he were taking a walk, was a prospect he found repugnant; the thought of going back to his room was one still more repugnant. 'What a chance I've lost forever!' he muttered as he stood, shorn of purpose, in the entrance-way, right opposite the yardkeeper's dark little cubicle, the door to which also stood open. Suddenly he gave a start. From the little room, which was only two yards away from him, his eyes had caught the glint of something underneath a bench on the right . . . He looked around him – no one. On tiptoe he approached the yardkeeper's room, went down the two little steps and called the yardkeeper in a faint voice. 'As I thought, he's not at home! But he must be somewhere nearby in the yard, because the door is wide open.' He pounced headlong on the axe (it was an axe), dragging it out from under the bench where it lay in between two logs and, right there and then, while he was still inside, fastened it to his loop, stuck both hands in his pockets and stepped out of the cubicle again; no one had noticed anything! 'If reason won't, the devil will!' he thought, smiling a strange, ironic smile. This stroke of fortune had thoroughly revived his spirits.

He continued on his way quietly and *sedately*, without hurry, in order not to give rise to any suspicion. He paid little attention to the passers-by, making a great effort not to look them in the face at all, and to be as inconspicuous as possible. Then he remembered he was wearing his hat. 'For God's sake! I even had some money the day before yesterday, yet I didn't go and buy a cap instead!' A curse erupted from his soul.

Glancing casually out of one eye into a little shop, he saw that the clock on the wall inside said ten past seven. He would have to hurry, and at the same time make a detour: approach the house by a roundabout route, from the other side . . .

Previously, whenever he had had occasion to picture all this to himself in his imagination, he had sometimes thought that he would be very afraid. But he was not particularly afraid now – indeed, he was not afraid at all. At the present moment he was actually preoccupied by some totally irrelevant thoughts, though they did not last for long. On his way past Yusupov Park* he even began to be thoroughly taken up with an imaginary project of his own devising: the construction of tall fountains, and the way in which they would properly refresh the air on all the city's squares. Little by little he moved on to the conviction that if the Summer Garden were to be extended the entire length of the Field of Mars and even possibly connected with the gardens of the Mikhailovsky Palace, this would be an attractive improvement that would also be of benefit to the city. At this point he suddenly began to develop an interest in the question of why it was that in all great cities people seemed to be especially inclined to live and settle in precisely those parts of town where there were no gardens or fountains, where there were dirt and foul smells and all kinds of filth, and that this was not really caused by material necessity. Here he recalled his own walks in the Haymarket, and for a moment he snapped out of his trance. 'What a load of nonsense!' he thought. 'God, I'd do better not to think at all!'

'I suppose this must be how men who are being led to the scaffold cling with their thoughts to all the things they meet along the way.'* This notion flashed across his mind, but it was only a flash, like lightning; he suppressed it as quickly as possible . . . But now he was close – here was the house, here were the gates. Somewhere a clock beat a single chime. 'What, is it really half-past seven? That's impossible, it must be fast!'

To his good fortune, everything went without incident at the gates again. Not only that, but at that very moment, as if by design, a cart carrying an enormous load of hay was in the process of entering the gate in front of him, completely shielding him from view during the whole time he was walking through the entrance-way; the instant the cart had succeeded in manoeuvring through the gate into the yard, he slipped through to the right. Over there, on the other side of the haycart, several voices could be heard shouting and talking, but no one observed him and he encountered no one, either. Many of the windows that looked on to this enormous quadrangular courtyard were open at that moment, but he did not raise his head – he had not the strength. The staircase that led up to the old woman's apartment was close by, just inside the gateway, to the right. He was already on the stairs . . .

Pausing for breath and pressing one hand against his thumping heart, then feeling about for the axe and setting it straight again, he began carefully and quietly to ascend the staircase, straining his ears every moment. But at that particular time the staircase was quite deserted; all the doors were shut; no one was about. True, the door to one empty apartment on the second floor was wide open, and some decorators were at work inside, painting, but they paid him no attention. He stood still for a moment, thought, and then continued his ascent. 'Of course it would have been better if there'd been nobody here at all, but . . . there are two more floors above them.'

Now here was the fourth floor, here was the door, and there was the apartment opposite: the empty one. To judge by all the signs, the apartment on the third floor, the one right underneath the old woman's, was also empty: the visiting card that had been fixed to the door with nails had been taken down – the other people had moved out! . . . He was panting. For a single instant there passed through his head the thought: 'Shouldn't I just go away?' But he left his own question unanswered and began listening at the old woman's door: dead silence. Then he listened on the stairs again, listened long and carefully . . . After that, he looked round one last time, pulled himself together, straightened himself up and again tested the axe in its loop. 'Don't I look terribly . . . pale?' he thought. 'Don't I look awfully agitated? She's suspicious . . . Shouldn't I wait a bit more . . . until my heart has quietened down? . . .'

But his heart did not quieten down. On the contrary, as if by design, it proceeded to beat harder and harder and harder . . . He could not endure it; slowly he stretched out his hand to the bell and rang it. Half a minute later he rang it again, slightly louder this time.

No reply. It was pointless to go on ringing to no purpose, and besides, it might attract attention. The old woman was at home, of course, but she was suspicious and alone. He knew something of her habits . . . and again he put his ear firmly to the door. Whether it was that his senses were extraordinarily keen (which on the whole was unlikely) or whether each sound really was very audible, he suddenly thought he could make out the cautious whisper of a hand on the latch and the rustle of a dress immediately on the other side of the door. Someone was standing imperceptibly right by the lock and listening, just as he was out here, keeping quiet inside and, apparently, also putting an ear to the door . . .

He purposely made a movement and muttered something in rather a loud voice, so as not to make it seem that he was acting furtively; then he rang a third time, but quietly, sedately, and without any hint of impatience. When he remembered it later, in clear and vivid detail, this moment was chiselled within him forever; he could not think where he had got so much cunning from, all the more so as his mind had been subject to momentary blackouts, and he had hardly been conscious of his body at all . . . A moment later the sound of someone undoing the bolt was heard.

VII

As on the previous occasion, the door opened the merest slit, and again two sharp, suspicious eyes fastened him with their gaze out of the darkness. At that point Raskolnikov lost his head and almost made a fatal blunder.

Apprehensive lest the old woman be alarmed at the fact that they were alone, and lacking confidence that the sight of him would put her at her ease, he grabbed hold of the door and pulled it towards him, so that the old woman would not get the idea of locking herself in again. Aware of what he was doing, she did not jerk the door back towards herself, but did not let go of the lock either, with the result that he very nearly hauled her out on to the staircase along with the door. When he saw that she was standing in the doorway to block his entrance, he walked straight towards her. She jumped to one side in alarm, tried to say something but could not seem to manage it, and stared at him round-eyed.

'Hello, Alyona Ivanovna,' he began as familiarly as he could, though his voice would not obey him and kept breaking and trembling. 'I've . . . brought you something . . . but look, we'd better go over there . . . where it's light . . .' And, turning his back on her, without waiting for permission, he walked straight into the room. The old woman came running after him; she had found her tongue at last.

'Good Lord! What do you want? . . . Who are you? What's your business?'

'For heaven's sake, Alyona Ivanovna . . . You know me . . . Raskolnikov . . . Look, I've brought something to pawn, the thing I said I'd bring the other day . . .' And he held out the pledge to her.

The old woman glanced at it briefly, but immediately fastened her eyes on those of her uninvited guest. It was a nasty, attentive, suspicious look. About a minute passed: he even thought he could see in her eyes something akin to a mocking smile, as though she had already guessed everything. He felt he was losing his head, that he was almost on the point of terror, terror such that were she to have gone on looking at him like that without saying a word for another thirty seconds he would have run away from her.

'What are you staring at me like that for, as if you didn't recognize me?' he suddenly said, with malicious spite. 'If you want it, take it, and if not – I'll go to someone else. I haven't the time for this.'

He had not meant to say this, it had suddenly escaped from him, somehow of its own accord.

The old woman came back to herself, her guest's resolute tone having evidently reassured her. 'But why did you suddenly fly off the handle like that, dearie? . . . What have you got there?' she asked, looking at the pledge.

'A silver cigarette-case: you know – the one I told you about last time.'

She stretched out her hand.

'But why are you so pale? Look, your hands are shaking! Have you come out of a bath, dearie?'

'It's fever,' he replied abruptly. 'One can't help looking pale . . . if one doesn't get anything to eat,' he added, barely able to get the words out. His strength was failing him again. But the reply had sounded convincing; the old woman took the pledge from him.

'What is it?' she asked, looking Raskolnikov up and down with her fixed stare and weighing the pledge in her hand.

'Something I want to pawn . . . a cigarette-case . . . a silver one . . . take a look.'

113

'Funny-shaped thing. Doesn't feel like silver to me, either . . . Wrapped it up well, haven't you?'

As she attempted to untie the ribbon she turned towards the window in search of more light (all the windows in her apartment were closed, in spite of the stifling heat), and for a few seconds she moved right away and stood with her back to him. He undid his coat and freed the axe from its loop, but did not take it right out, merely held it in place with his right hand under the garment. His hands were horribly weak; with each moment that passed he could feel them grow ever more numb and wooden. He was scared he would lose his grip on the axe and drop it . . . suddenly his head started to go round.

'Why on earth has he wrapped it up like this?' the old woman exclaimed in annoyance, and she moved a little way towards him.

There was not another second to be lost. He took the axe right out, swung it up in both hands, barely conscious of what he was doing, and almost without effort, almost mechanically, brought the butt of it down on the old woman's head. At that moment he had had practically no strength left. But as soon as he brought the axe down, new strength was born within him.

The old woman was bareheaded, as always. Her scanty, light-coloured, greying hair, smeared thickly all over with oil as it always was, had been plaited into a rat's tail and gathered together under the remains of a horn comb which jutted out at the nape of her neck. The blow landed smack on the crown of her head, something made easy by her smallness. She cried out, but very faintly, and suddenly sank in a heap to the floor, though even then she managed to raise both arms to her head. In one hand she was still holding the 'pledge'. At that point, with all his might, he landed her another blow, and another, each time with the butt and each time on the crown of the head. The blood gushed out as from an upturned glass, and her body collapsed backwards. He stepped back, allowed her to fall and at once bent down over her face: she was dead. Her eyes were goggling out of her head as though they might burst from it, while her forehead and all the rest of her features were crumpled and distorted in a convulsive spasm.

He put the axe on the floor beside the dead woman, and at once began to feel inside her pocket, trying not to get the welling blood on his hand – the same right pocket from which she had taken her keys

114

the last time he had been there. He was in full possession of his faculties, he had no blackouts or dizziness now, but his hands were still shaking. Later, he remembered that he had actually been very careful and thorough, doing his utmost not to get any blood on himself . . . He took the keys out at once; as on the previous occasion, they were all in one bunch, all on a single steel ring. He ran at once into the bedroom with them. It was a very small room, which contained an enormous case full of icons. Against a second wall there was a large bed, which looked extremely clean, with a quilted silk coverlet made up of patchwork. Against the third wall there was a chest of drawers. It was a strange thing: hardly had he begun to fit the keys to the lock of the chest of drawers, hardly had he heard their clinking, than a convulsive shiver seemed to run through him. Once again he suddenly felt like abandoning the whole undertaking and going away. But this only lasted for a moment: it was too late for him to go. He even smiled an ironic smile at himself; but then suddenly another, anxious thought hit him with the force of a blow. The notion had suddenly occurred to him that the old woman might still be alive, and that she might yet regain consciousness. Abandoning the keys and the chest of drawers, he ran back to the body, grabbed hold of the axe and swung it up yet again above the old woman, but did not bring it down. There could be no doubt that she was dead. Bending down and examining her again at close quarters, he saw quite clearly that her skull had been smashed, and was even dislocated slightly to one side. He moved as though to touch it with one finger, but then withdrew his hand quickly; he did not need to do that in order to see what was what. In the meantime a whole puddle of blood had come welling out. Suddenly he noticed that there was a thin piece of cord around her neck. He tugged at it, but it was strong and did not break; it was, moreover, soaked in blood. He tried to pull it straight off her body, but something was holding it, preventing him from doing so. In his impatience he again swung the axe up in order to bring it down and cut the cord right there and then, on her body, but had not the courage to do it, and with difficulty, after some two minutes of fiddling about, in the course of which he got blood both on his hands and on the axe, he managed to sever the cord without touching the body with the axe, and pulled it out; he had not been mistaken – it was her purse. On the cord there were two crucifixes, one made of cypress and the other of copper, with, in addition, a small enamel

115

icon; and right there together with them hung a small, grease-stained chamois-leather purse with a steel rim and ring. The purse was filled very tightly; without examining it, Raskolnikov stuffed it in his pocket, flung the crucifixes on to the old woman's breast and, grabbing the axe this time, rushed back into the bedroom.

He was in a frantic hurry. He grabbed the keys and again began to fuss with them. But for some reason he met with no success: none of them would fit in any of the locks. It was not that his hands were shaking all that badly now, but rather that he kept making the wrong decisions: for example, he would see that a key was the wrong one and would not fit, yet would keep thrusting it in. Suddenly, doing some quick thinking, he remembered that this large key, the one with the serrated bit, which was dangling there along with all the smaller ones, could not possibly belong to the chest of drawers (the same thought had occurred to him on his previous visit) but must fit some small trunk or chest, and that possibly in that everything lay hidden. He abandoned the chest of drawers and got down under the bed, since he was aware that in old women's dwellings that is the place where such boxes are usually kept. So it was: he found a chest of considerable dimensions, nearly a yard in length, with a bulging lid, upholstered in red morocco and inlaid with steel studs. The serrated key fit perfectly and opened it. On top, under a white sheet, lay a hare-skin coat covered with red packing material; underneath it was a silk dress, then a shawl, and finally, underneath that, there seemed to be nothing but rags. The first thing he did was to start to rub his hands on the red-silk packing material. 'It's red, so it won't show the blood so much,' he found himself thinking, and then realized what he was about. 'Good God! Am I going crazy, or what?' he thought in fright.

As soon as he moved the pile of rags, however, a gold watch slipped out from under the hare-skin coat. He fell upon the things in a rush to turn them over. It really was so: intermingled with the rags there were objects made of gold, which were doubtless all the pledges, both redeemed and unredeemed – bracelets, chains, earrings, hatpins and the like. Some of them were in cases, others had merely been wrapped in newspaper, but neatly and carefully, in double thick-nesses, and tied round with cloth tape. Wasting no time, he began to stuff them into the pockets of his trousers and overcoat, without investigating or opening any of the parcels and cases, but he did not manage to take many . . .

Suddenly, from the room where the old woman lay, came the sound of footsteps. He stopped what he was doing, and went as still as a corpse. But all was quiet, he must have imagined it. Then, without warning, there was a barely audible cry, or a sound like someone uttering a quiet, abrupt moan, and then breaking off. There followed another dead silence, which lasted a minute or two. He sat squatting by the chest and waited, scarcely breathing. Then he leapt up, grabbed the axe and ran from the bedroom.

In the middle of the room stood Lizaveta, with a large bundle in her hands, staring in rigid horror at her murdered sister; her face was as white as a handkerchief, and she was apparently unable to utter a sound. As she saw him run out she began to quiver like a leaf, with a mild shudder, and her features worked spasmodically; she raised one arm, began to open her mouth, but still could not get out a scream and began slowly to back away from him into the corner, staring at him fixedly, but still without uttering a sound, as though she had not sufficient breath to do so. He rushed at her with the axe; her lips grew contorted in the pitiful manner common to very young children when they begin to be afraid of something, stare fixedly at the thing that is frightening them and prepare to cry out loud. Moreover, this unhappy Lizaveta was so simple, downtrodden and utterly intimidated that she did not even raise her hands to protect herself, even though this would have been a most natural, lifesaving gesture for her to make at that moment, as the axe was raised right above her face. She merely raised her unengaged left arm the tiniest distance, a long way from her face, and slowly extended it towards the axe, as though in an attempt to ward it off. The blow landed right on her skull, blade-first, and instantly split open the whole upper part of her forehead, almost to the crown of her head. She fairly crashed to the floor. Raskolnikov began to lose his nerve completely; he seized hold of her bundle, threw it down again and ran into the hallway.

Terror was gaining an increasing hold on him, particularly after this second, quite unpremeditated murder. He felt that he wanted to escape from this place as quickly as possible. And if at that moment he had been capable of seeing things in better proportion and of making decisions, if he had been able to perceive all the difficulties of his situation, in all its desperate, monstrous absurdity, and to realize just how many problems he would have to overcome and how much villainy he might have to perform in order to get out of this place and arrive back home again, he might very well have abandoned the whole undertaking and gone at once to give himself up – not out of fear for himself, but from a simple feeling of horror and revulsion at what he had done. The sense of revulsion in particular kept rising up and growing inside him with each moment that passed. Not for anything in the world would he have gone back to the chest now, nor even to the rooms of the apartment.

Little by little, however, he had begun to fall into a kind of absent-minded, even reflective condition; at some moments he seemed to forget himself, or rather forget what was important and cling to trivial things instead. Even so, when he took a look in the kitchen and caught sight of a half-full pail of water on a bench, he hit upon the notion of giving his hands and the axe a good wash. His hands were covered in blood and his fingers were stuck together. He lowered the axe straight into the water, blade-first, grabbed a small piece of soap that was lying in a broken saucer on the windowsill and began to wash his hands right there, in the pail. When they were clean, he pulled out the axe, gave the iron part of it a thorough rinsing, and spent a long time – about three minutes – cleaning the wooden shaft, on which a great deal of blood had gathered, using the soap to get rid of it. After that he wiped everything down with some of the washing that was hanging up to dry on the clothes-line that had been strung up across the kitchen, and then made a long and attentive examination of the axe over by the window. Not a vestige remained; the shaft was still damp, that was all. Carefully he put the axe back into the loop inside his coat. Then, as far as the dim light of the kitchen would allow, he examined the coat, his trousers and boots. On a first, superficial glance there appeared to be nothing to worry about; only the boots showed some stains. He soaked his rag in the water and rubbed the boots down. He was, however, aware that he was not examining everything properly, that there might be something immediately obvious which he had not noticed. He stood in the middle of the room, reflecting. A dark, tormenting thought was rising up inside him – the thought that he was behaving like a madman and that he was not at that moment in a position either to think properly or to protect himself, that what he was doing now was not at all what he ought to be doing . . . 'Oh my God! I must flee, flee!' he muttered to himself, and he rushed into the entrance-hall. But here there awaited him a shock of horror the like of which he had never once yet experienced.

He stood, looked, and was unable to believe his eyes: the door, the outer door which led from the hallway on to the staircase, the very same door at which he had rung earlier and through which he had walked, was open by a distance easily as wide as a man's hand; no lock, no bolt, for the whole time, for all this time! The old woman had not locked the door after him when he had come in, possibly out of caution. But for God's sake! After all, he had seen Lizaveta later on! How, how could he not have realized that she must have got in somehow? She hadn't come through the wall, had she?

He flung himself at the door and fastened the bolt.

'No, that's not the right thing to do, either! I must go, go . . .'

He undid the bolt, opened the door and began to listen on the stairs.

He listened for a long time. Somewhere far away, down at the foot of the stairs, probably somewhere in the entrance-way, two voices were shouting loudly and shrilly, arguing and exchanging abuse. 'What's up with them? . . .' Patiently, he waited. At last the hubbub stopped without warning, as though cut short; they had gone their separate ways. He was on the point of making his exit when suddenly a door opened with a noise on the floor below, and someone began to go downstairs humming some tune or other. 'What a noise they're all making!' was the thought that flashed across his mind. He closed the door again, and waited. At last all sounds had died away, there was not a soul about. He was just about to put his foot on the staircase when he suddenly heard more footsteps, someone else's this time.

These footsteps were very far away, right at the bottom of the stairs, but he later recalled very well and distinctly that right from the very first sound of them he began to suspect that for some reason whoever it was was coming *here*, to the fourth floor, to the old woman's apartment. Why had that been? Was there anything particularly special or portentous about those sounds? The steps were heavy, regular, unhurried. There – now *he* had passed the first floor, now he was coming up further; there, louder and louder! The heavy breathing of the man who had entered the building was now audible. Now he had started his climb to the third floor . . . He was coming here! And suddenly he felt that he had gone stiff and numb, that this was like something in a dream, the sort of dream where one is being hunted down by pursuers who are close on one's heels and have the intention of killing, while one seems to have become rooted to the spot and is unable to move a limb.

Then, as the visitor was beginning his ascent to the fourth floor, only then did he suddenly rouse himself and manage to slip back quickly and deftly out of the passage and into the apartment again, closing the door behind him. Then he gripped the bolt and quietly, soundlessly slid it into its fastening. Some instinct helped him. When he had finished these preparations he hid, scarcely breathing, right behind the door. The unbidden visitor was now also next to the door. They were standing opposite each other, just as earlier he and the old woman had stood, when the door had separated them, and he had listened.

The visitor gasped heavily several times, recovering his breath. 'He must be a big, stout fellow,' Raskolnikov thought, as he clutched the axe in his hand. This really was all like a dream. The visitor grabbed at the bell-pull and rang it loudly.

No sooner had the tinny sound of the bell clanked out than he suddenly fancied there was movement in the room. For a few seconds he actually gave the matter some serious attention. The stranger, whoever he was, clanked the bell again, waited a little longer and then suddenly, in impatience, began to tug at the door handle for all he was worth. Raskolnikov watched the tongue of the bolt leap in its fastening, and waited in dull terror for it to come flying out. That really did seem possible, so violent was the tugging. He thought of holding the bolt in place with his hand, but then reflected that *he* would guess what was happening. His head had started to go round again. 'I'm going to fall!' flashed across his mind, but the stranger began to speak, and he at once recovered his balance.

'What's wrong with them in there, are they asleep or has somebody strangled them? The cursed wr-r-etches!' he roared, in a voice that seemed to come from a barrel. 'Hey, Alyona Ivanovna, you old witch! Lizaveta Ivanovna, my fabled beauty! Open up! Ach, the cursed wretches, are they sleeping or what?'

And again, in a frenzy of rage, he pulled at the bell a dozen times in succession with all his strength. This must certainly be some intimate frequenter of the household, who possessed authority over it.

Just at that moment light, hurried footsteps were heard somewhere on the stairs, not far away. Someone else was coming, too. Raskolnikov could not catch what they were saying at first.

'Is there really no one in?' one of the men who had come upstairs shouted in a resonant, cheerful voice, addressing the original visitor, who was still continuing to pull at the bell. 'Hallo, Koch!'

'If his voice is anything to go by, he must be very young,' Raskolnikov thought suddenly.

'The devil only knows what they're up to in there, I've practically smashed the lock to bits,' Koch replied. 'May I inquire how you know my name?'

'I like that! Hey, I beat you at billiards three times in a row at the Gambrinus* the day before yesterday.'

'Aha-a-a . . .'

'So they're not in? Funny. It's damn silly, in fact. Where would an old woman like her be off to? I've got business with her.'

'I too, my dear fellow – I too have business with her.'

'Well, what's to be done? Go back again, I suppose. Damn! And there was I thinking I'd get some money!' the young man exclaimed.

'That's right, there's no point hanging around here. But why go and fix an appointment? She herself actually fixed an appointment with me. I mean, it's not exactly on my usual route. Where the devil can she have gone gadding off to? That's what I don't understand. All year round she sticks at home moping, the old witch, telling you how her legs ache, and now suddenly she's off for a walk!'

'Couldn't we ask the yardkeeper?'

'Ask him what?'

'Where she's gone and what time she'll be back.'

'Hm . . . the devil . . . having to ask . . . I mean, she never goes anywhere . . .' And again he pulled at the bell-handle. 'The devil, there's nothing to be done! Let's go!'

'Wait!' the young man shouted, suddenly. 'Look: do you see the way the door catches when you pull it?'

'So?'

'That means it isn't locked, but only bolted – on the hook, in other words. Listen, can't you hear the bolt clinking?'

'So?'

'So what's your problem? It means that one of them's at home. If they'd both gone out, they'd have locked the door from the outside, using the key, not bolted it from inside. There – you hear the bolt clinking? For the bolt to be fastened inside like that there would have to be somebody in there. They must be there, but they're not opening up! Do you see what I mean?'

'Well, I never! Now that you come to mention it, I do!' Koch exclaimed in astonishment. 'Then what are they up to in there?' And he began to rattle the door violently.

'Wait!' the young man shouted again. 'Don't do that! There's something fishy here . . . I mean, you've rung the bell, you've rattled the door, yet they don't open up; that means either they've fainted, or . . .'

'What?'

'I tell you what: let's go and find the yardkeeper; let him winkle them out.'

'It's a deal.' They both started off down the stairs.

'Wait! You stay here, and I'll run down and get the yardkeeper.'

'Why do I have to stay?'

'Don't you think one of us ought to? . . .'

'I suppose so . . .'

'I mean, I'm studying to be a state investigator! There's obviously, *ob*-vi-ous-ly something fishy here!' the young man heatedly exclaimed, before rushing off down the stairs at full gallop.

Koch stayed behind, and gently moved the bell-pull once again; the bell gave a single clank. Then quietly, as though he were musing and conducting an exploration, he began to move the door-handle, pulling it out and drawing it downwards in order to convince himself again that it was secured by the bolt alone. Then, breathing heavily, he bent down and began to look through the keyhole; but the key had been inserted into it from the other side and, consequently, nothing was visible.

Raskolnikov stood clutching the axe. He was in a kind of delirium. He had even been preparing to fight them when they came in. While they were knocking and discussing what they ought to do, he had several times had a sudden urge to get it all over with and shout to them from his side of the door. At times he had felt like cursing and taunting them, until they forced the door open. 'Hurry up!' flashed across his mind.

'To devil with it, what's keeping him . . .'

Time passed, one minute, then another – no one came. Koch began to get restless.

'To the devil with this! . . .' he suddenly exclaimed, and in impatience, abandoning his vigil, set off down to the bottom as well, hurrying along and making a noise with his boots on the stairs. His footsteps died away.

'O Lord, what shall I do?'

Raskolnikov undid the bolt, opened the door a little way, heard nothing, and suddenly, quite without thinking now, went outside, closed the door as tightly as he could and rushed off downwards.

He had gone three floors when there was a sudden, violent noise below – what was to become of him? There was nowhere to hide. He started to run back upwards to the apartment again.

'Hey, damn it, you devil! Stop!'

With a yell someone burst out of an apartment on the floor below and, not so much running as falling down the stairs, shouted at the top of his voice:

'Mitka! Mitka! Mitka! Mitka! Mitka! The deuce have your hide!'

The shout ended on a high-pitched, yelping note. These last sounds came from outside; everything grew quiet. But at that same instant several men, talking loudly and quickly, began to make their way upstairs with a good deal of noise. There were three or four of them. He made out the young man's resonant voice. 'It's them!'

In complete despair he went straight towards them: what must be, must be! If they stopped him it would all be over, if they let him past, it would all be over, too: they would remember. They were now practically on top of one another: between them there was only one flight of stairs – and suddenly salvation! Only a few steps away from him, to the right, was an empty apartment whose door stood wide open, the very same second-floor apartment that the workmen had been decorating, and which now, as if by special design, they had abandoned. They it must have been who had come rushing out with such a noise a moment ago. The floors had just been painted, in the middle of the room were a small tub and a crock of paint with a paintbrush in it. In a single instant he slipped through the open door and hid himself behind the wall, not before time – they were already on the landing. At that point they turned, passing him, and went on up towards the fourth floor, exchanging loud conversation with one another. He bided his time, then emerged on tiptoe and ran downstairs.

There was no one on the staircase! Nor anyone in the entrance, either. He walked through it and turned left along the street.

He knew very well, he knew abundantly well that at that very second they were already inside the apartment, that they had been much astonished to find it unlocked, when only just a short time ago it had been locked, that they were looking at the bodies and that it would take them no more than a moment to put two and two together and figure out beyond all question that the murderer had just been there and had managed to hide somewhere, to slip away past them, to flee; they would doubtless also guess that he had been in the empty apartment as they were making their way upstairs. Yet meanwhile he did not dare on any account to quicken his step, even though there were still a hundred yards to go before the first turning. 'Couldn't I just slip through some gateway and wait on the stairs of some building until it's all clear? No, that would be disastrous. Couldn't I throw the axe away somewhere? Couldn't I hire a cab? Disastrous, disastrous!'

Here at last was the side-street; he lurched along it, more dead than alive; now he was halfway out of danger, and he knew it: he was under less suspicion; what was more, there were a great many people scurrying about, and he was obliterated among them like a grain of sand. But all the torments he had been through had drained him of so much energy that he was scarcely able to move. The sweat was rolling off him in drops; his neck was running with moisture. 'Look at you – cut to the teeth!' someone shouted to him when he came out on to the Canal.

He was now in a bad state of diminished consciousness; the further he walked, the worse it became. He did remember, however, that as he came out on to the Canal he was suddenly afraid that there were not enough people about and that he would be more conspicuous here, and nearly turned back into the side-street again. In spite of the fact that he was almost at the point of collapse, he made a detour and went back to his lodgings by a totally different route.

Not fully conscious, he walked through the gateway of the building where he lived; at least, not until he had begun to climb the stairs did he remember about the axe. He had forgotten a certain vital task: he had to put it back, and in as inconspicuous a manner as possible. It went without saying that by this time he was no longer capable of realizing that possibly by far the best thing he could do was not to put the axe back in its old place at all, but to leave it by stealth, not now but later on perhaps, in some part of another courtyard.

But it all went off without a hitch. The door of the yardkeeper's room was set ajar, but not fixed with the lock, which meant that most probably the yardkeeper was at home. To such a degree had he lost his ability to think straight, however, that he went directly up to the yardkeeper's door and opened it. If the yardkeeper were to have asked him: 'What do you want?' he would probably have simply handed him the axe. But the yardkeeper was once again absent, and he managed to put the axe back in its former place under the bench, even screening it with the log as before. No one, not a single soul, did he meet after that on his way up to his room; the landlady's door was closed. Entering his quarters, he threw himself on the sofa, without taking his coat off, just as he was. He did not sleep, but lay in a kind of oblivion. If anyone had come into the room, he would have leapt up instantly with a yell. The rags and tatters of vague thoughts swarmed in his head; but he could not seize hold of a single one of them, could not focus on a single one of them, even though he tried to force himself to . . .

PART TWO

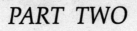

In this fashion he lay for a very long time. Occasionally he seemed to wake up, and at such moments he would realize that it had been night for a long time now; yet the idea of getting up never entered his head. At last he saw it was light – as good as daylight. He was lying flat-out on the sofa, still paralysed by his recent loss of consciousness. What had reached him were the terrible, desperate cries from the street that he heard regularly every night under his window some time after two o'clock. These it had been that had woken him up just now. 'Ah! That'll be the drunks coming out of the dens,' he thought. 'It's gone two a.m.' And suddenly he leapt up, as though someone had pulled him off the sofa. 'What? It's gone two?' He sat down on the sofa – and then it all came back to him. Suddenly, in a single flash, it all came back.

For that initial second he thought he was going insane. A terrible coldness had seized him; but the coldness was also due to the fever which had begun in him a long time ago, while he had been asleep. Now he was suddenly attacked by an ague so violent that his teeth nearly leapt from his mouth, so violently did they chatter, and his entire body started to shake. He opened the door and began to listen: everyone in the building was fast asleep. In amazement he examined first himself, and then every aspect of the room, unable to comprehend how he could possibly have come in the evening before and not have set the door on its hook, but simply thrown himself on the sofa with all his clothes on – even his hat: it had rolled to the floor, where it lay near his pillow. 'If anyone had come in, what would they have thought? That I was drunk, but . . .' He rushed to the window. There was quite a lot of light now, and he quickly began to examine himself all over, from head to toe, all his clothes, to see if there were any marks. But he could not do it like that: shaking with ague, he began to take off all his things and examine them thoroughly. He ransacked everything, everything, right down to the last thread, the last scrap of cloth and, lacking confidence in himself, repeated the examination some three times. But it was all right, there seemed not to be any marks; only his trouser-ends, in the place where they hung down and rubbed the ground, retained some thick traces of coagulated blood. He grabbed hold of his large folding knife and pared the rubbed ends.

There seemed not to be anything else that required attention. Suddenly he remembered that the purse and the objects he had stolen from the old woman's chest were all of them still in his pockets, and had been there all this time! It had taken him until now to think of removing them and hiding them away! He had not even remembered about them just then, as he had been examining his clothes! What was wrong with him? In an instant he fell on them, taking them out and hurling them on to the table. When he had removed them all, even turning the pockets inside out in order to make sure there was nothing left in them, he carried the whole pile to the far corner of the room. There, right in the very corner, down at the bottom, the wallpaper was torn in one place where it had peeled away from the wall: he immediately began to cram everything into this hole, under the paper – in it went! 'All hidden from sight, the purse as well!' he thought with relief, getting up on his knees and looking stupidly at the corner, with its hole that was now bulging out more than ever. Suddenly he recoiled in horror. 'Good God!' he whispered in despair. 'What's the matter with me? Do you call that hidden? Are those things anywhere near hidden?' As a matter of fact, the discovery of those objects had not been a part of his calculations; he had supposed there would be only money, and for that reason had not prepared a hiding-place in advance. 'But now, now what have I got to laugh about?' he thought. 'My sanity really is deserting me!' In a state of utter exhaustion he sat down on the sofa, and instantly an unbearable ague began to make him shake and shiver once more. Mechanically he pulled towards him the old winter overcoat that was lying beside him on the chair; it was the overcoat he had had as a student, a warm one, but by this time it was in rags. He covered himself with it, and was at once embraced by sleep and delirium. He lost consciousness.

Not more than about five minutes later he leapt up again and once more, in an instantaneous, sudden frenzy, rushed over to his clothes. 'How could I have fallen asleep again, when nothing's been done! I knew it, I knew it: I haven't even taken the loop out from under the armpit yet! I forgot it, I could forget a thing like that! A piece of incriminating evidence like that!' He tugged the loop out and quickly began to tear it into shreds, stuffing them into the linen under his pillow. 'Some bits of torn canvas can't possibly arouse any suspicion; surely not, surely not!' he repeated, standing in the middle of the room and beginning to look around him again with a focus of attention that was intensified to the point of pain, surveying the floor and all the other parts of the room, in an agony lest he had forgotten something. A certainty that everything, even his memory, even the simple faculty of reason, was deserting him had begun to torment him unendurably. 'What, is it really beginning now, is this the punishment beginning? Yes, yes, I knew it!' It was true: the parings of his trouser-ends which he had cut away were strewn all over the floor, in the middle of the room, for the first person who walked in to observe! 'What on earth's the matter with me?' he exclaimed again, like a lost soul.

A strange thought suddenly came into his head: what if all his clothes were covered in blood, what if there were many stains, only he could not see them, could not find out where they were, because his reason had grown feeble, broken apart . . . his mind grown darkened . . . Suddenly he remembered that there had been blood on the purse, too. 'Ah! That means there must be blood in my pocket, too, because I shoved the purse into it while it was still wet!' In a flash he turned out the pocket, and in its lining discovered, as he had known he would – traces of blood, whole stains! 'That means my reason hasn't yet deserted me entirely, if I could remember and think of it on my own it means I still have my wits about me and my memory intact!' he reflected in triumph, breathing a deep, joyful sigh with the whole of his lungs. 'It's just weakness brought on by my fever, the delirium of a moment,' he told himself, as he ripped the lining away in its entirety from the left pocket of the trousers. At that moment a ray of sunlight illuminated his left boot; on the sock that was peeping out through the crack at the front of the boot he thought he saw marks. He kicked off his boots: 'Yes, there are marks! The whole toe of the sock is saturated in blood.' He must have stepped in that puddle without noticing at the time . . . 'But now what can I do about it? Where am I going to put this sock, the bits of my trouser-ends, the pocket lining?'

He raked them all together in one hand and stood in the middle of the room. 'Should I hide them in the stove? But the stove's the first place they'll start rummaging about in. Burn them? But what with? I don't even have any matches. No, I'd better take them somewhere outside and throw them away. Yes, the best thing to do is throw them away!' he repeated, sitting down on the sofa again. 'And right now, this minute, without delay! . . .' Instead, however, his head sank back on the pillow again; again the unendurable ague sent its icy chill through him; again he pulled the overcoat about him. And for a long time, several hours, he kept telling himself in his dreams: 'Come on, you must take the stuff right now and throw it all away out of sight somewhere, quickly, quickly!' Several times he tried to get off the sofa and stand up, but was unable to. At last a loud knock at the door woke him.

'Come on, open up – are you alive or dead? He's still snoozing!' Nastasya shouted, beating her fist against the door. 'Whole days on end he snoozes, like a hound-dog! That's what he is – a hound-dog! Open up, can't you? It's nearly eleven o'clock!'

'Perhaps he's not in,' a man's voice said.

'Ah! That's the yardkeeper's voice . . . What does he want?'

He leapt up into a sitting position on the sofa. His heart was beating so violently that it actually hurt him.

'Here – who's been setting the door on the hook?' Nastasya said in an affronted tone of voice. 'Would you believe it – he's started locking himself in now! Is he scared they'll come and take him away, or something? Open up, stupid-head, wakey-wakey!'

'What do they want? Why is the yardkeeper there? They know everything. Should I put up a fight or open the door? I'd better open the door! I may as well take a chance . . .'

He raised himself on one elbow, leaned forward and took the door off the hook.

The entire room was of such dimensions that it was possible to take the door off the hook without getting out of bed.

It was as he had supposed: Nastasya and the yardkeeper were standing there.

For some reason he thought Nastasya was looking him over in a strange sort of way. He glanced at the yardkeeper with a challenging and desperate air. The yardkeeper silently extended towards him a grey, double-folded document sealed with bottle-green sealing-wax.

'It's a summons, from the bureau,' he said, handing him the document.

'What bureau? . . .'

'It means the police want to see you, in their bureau. You know what bureau I mean.'

'The police! . . . Why? . . .'

'Don't ask me. If they want you, you go.' The yardkeeper gave him an attentive look, cast his eyes about and turned on his heel to go.

'I think you're quite ill, aren't you?' Nastasya observed, not taking her eyes off him. The yardkeeper also turned his head round for a moment. 'He's had a fever since yesterday,' she added.

He made no reply and continued to hold the document without unsealing it.

'No, don't you get up,' Nastasya went on, moved to pity, and seeing that he was lowering his legs off the sofa. 'If you're ill, don't go; there's no hurry. What's that in your hand?'

He looked: in his right hand he was holding the pared-off bits of trouser-end, the sock and the remnants of the lining he had torn out of his pocket. Yes, he had slept with them like that. Thinking about this later on, he remembered that, half regaining consciousness in his fever, he had squeezed all these things in his hand as tightly as he could, and then fallen back to sleep again.

'Look at him – been out rag-collecting, and now he sleeps with his rags as though they were treasure.' And Nastasya went off into fits of her morbidly nervous laughter. In a flash he shoved everything under the overcoat and fixed the coat intently with his gaze. Even though he was very far from being able to think coherently at that moment, he nevertheless sensed that this was not the way people behave with someone who is about to be arrested. 'But . . . the police?'

'What about some tea? Do you want some? I'll bring it for you; there's still some left . . .'

'No . . . I shall go; I'll go there right now,' he muttered, getting to his feet.

'You don't look to me as though you could get downstairs.'

'I'll go . . .'

'It's up to you . . .'

She followed the yardkeeper out of the room. Immediately he rushed to the light in order to examine the sock and the trouser-ends: 'There are some stains, but they're not very noticeable; the blood's all covered in dirt and grime, it's got discoloured. If one didn't know in advance, one would never see it. That means that Nastasya can't have noticed anything – she was too far away, thank God!' Then with trepidation he broke the seal on the summons and began to read it; it took him a long, long time to do so, and at last he understood. It was an ordinary summons from the local police authority, requesting him to report to the district superintendent's bureau that very same morning at nine-thirty.

'When has this ever happened before? I never have any dealings with the police! And why today all of a sudden?' he thought in tormented wonderment. 'O Lord, let it be over quickly!' He nearly dropped to his knees in order to pray, but then burst out laughing – not at the notion of praying, but at himself. He quickly began to dress. 'If the game's up, it's up, and there's nothing I can do about it. Why don't I put the sock on?' he thought, suddenly. 'It'll get even more dirt on it that way, and the marks will disappear.' As soon as he put it on, however, he tore it off again in revulsion and horror. But, having done so, he remembered that he had no others, and he picked it up and put it back on – and burst out laughing once more. 'This is the way it is in story-books, it's all relative, all just for form's sake,' he thought fleetingly, in some remote periphery of his mind, and he trembled in every limb. 'I mean, look, I've put it on! That's what it has come to – I've put it on!' His laughter was, however, instantly replaced by despair. 'No, I'm not strong enough . . .' he thought. His legs were trembling. 'With terror,' he muttered to himself. His head was spinning and aching with fever. 'It's a ruse! They're using cunning in order to lure me there, and then they'll knock me for six,' he went on to himself, as he started to go downstairs. 'The worst of it is that I'm almost delirious . . . I may go and say something stupid . . .'

As he was going downstairs he remembered that he had left all the gold objects in the hole behind the wallpaper. 'They may easily make a search of the place while I'm gone,' he reflected, and came to a halt. But he was suddenly overcome by such despair and by such cynicism with regard to his own downfall, if one may use such an expression, that he waved his hand in impatience and continued his descent.

'Just let it be over quickly! . . .'

Outside the heat was once again unbearable; not a single drop of rain all these days. Again the dust, brick and lime, again the stench from the little shops and drinking dens, again at every moment the drunks, the Finnish pedlars and the cabs that were practically falling to bits. The sun was glaring brightly into his eyes, making them hurt, and his head had begun to go round with a will – the usual sensation of a person in a fever who suddenly comes out to the street on a bright, sunny day.

134

When he reached the turning into *yesterday's* street, he glanced along it in an agony of anxiety, to *that* house . . . and immediately looked away.

'If they ask me about it I may tell them,' he thought, as he approached the building that housed the bureau.

The bureau was only about a quarter of a verst from where he lived. It had recently been transferred to new quarters on the fourth floor of a new building. He had once been briefly in the old quarters, but that had been a very long time ago. As he walked in through the entrance-way he saw a staircase to the right, down which a muzhik was coming with a book in his hand. 'That'll be a yardkeeper; that means the bureau's up there,' and he began to climb the staircase on the off-chance that this was the right one. He did not want to have to ask anyone the way.

'I shall go in, get down on my knees and tell them everything,' he thought as he went on up to the fourth floor.

The staircase was small, narrow, steep and awash with dirty water. All the doors of all the kitchens of all the apartments on all four floors were open on to this staircase and remained so all day. This produced a terrible, airless heat. Coming up and down the stairs were yard-keepers with house-books under their arms, police clerks and various tradespeople of both sexes – the callers. The door into the bureau itself was also open wide. He went in and halted in the vestibule. Some muzhiks were standing around there, waiting. Here too the airless heat was extreme and, in addition, from the newly decorated rooms there was a nauseating stink of paint that had not yet dried, and had been ground in rotten drying-oil. Having waited for a bit, he decided to move on, into the next room. All the rooms were tiny and low-ceilinged. A terrible impatience kept drawing him further and further. No one paid any attention to him. In the second room some scribes sat copying, dressed only slightly better than he was himself, a strange-looking bunch. He turned to one of them.

'What do you want?'

He held up the summons he had received from the bureau.

'Are you a student?' asked the scribe, glancing at the summons.

'Yes, an ex-student.'

The scribe let his eyes pass over him, but without a flicker of curiosity. He was an extremely rumpled-looking man, with some fixed idea in his gaze.

'It's no good asking him, because he couldn't care less,' Raskolnikov thought.

'Go in there and see the clerk,' said the scribe, pointing ahead to the very furthest room.

He went into this room (the fourth in sequence), which was cramped and full to overflowing with members of the public – people dressed slightly better than those in the other rooms. Among these callers were two ladies. One was in mourning; dressed in widow's weeds, she sat on the other side of the clerk's desk, facing him, while she wrote down something he was dictating to her. The other lady, who was very plump and had a reddish-purple, blotched complexion, a stately woman, most opulently attired, with a brooch at her bosom the size of a saucer, stood to one side and was waiting for something. Raskolnikov thrust his summons towards the clerk. The clerk gave it a fleeting glance, told him to wait and continued his business with the lady in mourning.

His breath came more easily now. 'It's definitely not about the other!' Gradually his spirits began to revive, and he inwardly exhorted himself to have courage and gather his thoughts.

'The slightest stupid mistake, the slightest little indiscretion and I may easily give myself away entirely! Hm . . . it's a pity there's no air in here,' he went on. 'It's so stuffy . . . My head is getting even dizzier . . . and my mind, too . . .'

He was experiencing a terrible sense of disorder that affected his whole being. He was afraid he would lose control of himself. He tried to fasten his attention on something, think about something – anything at all – that had nothing whatever to do with all this, but failed completely. The clerk, on the other hand, he found intensely interesting: he wanted to guess everything by his features, penetrate the very heart of his being. This clerk was a young man of about twenty-two; he had a swarthy, mobile physiognomy that made him look older than his years, and he was fashionably, even foppishly dressed: his hair was parted at the back of his head, thoroughly combed and pomaded, and there were a large number of rings and . signets on his white, scrubbed fingers, and gold chains on his waistcoat. With one of the foreign visitors to his room he had even exchanged a word or two in French, and quite passably at that.

'Luiza Ivanovna, you'd better sit down,' he said cursorily to the overdressed reddish-purple lady, who was still standing as if she did not dare to sit down, even though there was a chair beside her.

'*Ich danke,*' she said quietly, lowering herself on to the chair with a silken, swishing sound. Her light-blue dress with its white lace trimmings spread around the chair like a balloon, taking up practically half the room. There was a smell of perfume. But the lady was plainly abashed at taking up half the room and at smelling so strongly of perfume, in spite of the fact that she was smiling in a way that was timorous and brazen at the same time, though with obvious uneasiness.

The lady in mourning finally completed what she was doing and began to get up. Suddenly, with a certain amount of clamour, an officer made an extremely dashing entrance, swinging his shoulders in a peculiar way with every step he took, threw his cap with its cockade on to the desk and sat down in one of the armchairs. The opulent lady fairly leapt up from her chair at the sight of him, and began to drop curtsies with a singular enthusiasm; but the officer paid her not the slightest attention, and she did not dare to sit down again while he was there. He was a lieutenant, the superintendent's auxiliary, with a horizontal reddish moustache that jutted out in both directions and a face that was extremely small-featured and expressed nothing much except a certain insolence. He gave Raskolnikov a sidelong glance that was tinged with indignation: those clothes he was wearing were really in a shocking state, yet in spite of his humiliating position his bearing was not in keeping with his clothes; Raskolnikov, caught off his guard, had cast too long and direct a look at him, so that the officer had taken offence.

'What's your business?' he bawled, doubtless astonished that a ragged fellow such as this had not been reduced to nothing by his lightning-charged gaze.

'I was told to report . . . I got a summons . . .' Raskolnikov managed to reply.

'It's about the exaction proceedings for the recovery of funds from him, from the *student*,' the clerk said, beginning to bustle about as he stopped working on his document. 'Here!' And he threw Raskolnikov the book, pointing out the relevant place. 'Read that!'

'Funds? What funds?' thought Raskolnikov. 'But that means it's definitely not about the other!' And he shuddered with relief. He suddenly began to feel terribly, inexpressibly lighthearted. All his cares seemed to lift from his shoulders.

'And what time does it say you were supposed to be here, my dear sir?' the lieutenant bawled, for some unknown reason growing more and more outraged. 'You're down for nine, but it's after eleven now!'

'I was only served the summons a quarter of an hour ago,' Raskolnikov answered loudly over his shoulder, suddenly also losing his temper in spite of himself and even taking a certain pleasure in it. 'It ought to be enough that I've come at all, since I'm ill and have a fever.'

'Be so good as not to shout, will you?'

'I'm not shouting, I'm talking quite softly; it's you who are shouting at me – but I'm a student and won't allow people to shout at me.'

This made the assistant so livid that for a moment he was incapable of speech, and all that happened was that some spittle came flying from his lips. He leapt up from his seat.

'Be si-i-i-lent! You're in a government bureau. None of your r-r-rudeness, sir!'

'You're in a government bureau, too,' Raskolnikov exclaimed, 'and what's more, by shouting and by smoking that cigarette you're letting us all down.' Having said this, he felt an inexpressible sense of enjoyment.

The clerk looked at them with a smile. The quick-tempered lieutenant was visibly taken aback.

'That's not your concern, sir!' he cried, at last, in an unnaturally loud voice. 'And now kindly be so good as to make the statement that's required of you. Show him, Aleksandr Grigoryevich. We've had complaints about you! You don't pay your bills. Crikey, a fine, upstanding young fellow you are, and no mistake!'

But Raskolnikov was no longer listening; he had greedily snatched up the document, in search of a speedy resolution of the problem. He read it through once, and then a second time, but understood nothing.

'What's this?' he asked the clerk.

'It's a document demanding funds from you in acknowledgement of debt – an exaction note. You must either pay it in full with all due penalties, including those for late payment, or else file a written statement saying when you will be able to pay it, and you must also undertake not to leave the capital nor to sell or conceal any property you may possess. The creditor, on the other hand, is empowered to sell your property, and to take proceedings against you in accordance with the law.'

'But I . . . don't owe anyone anything!'

'That's no concern of ours. All we know is we've received an overdue and legally protested acknowledgement of debt in the sum of a hundred and fifteen roubles, issued by you some nine months ago to the collegiate assessor's widow Zarnitsyna, and discharged by her in transfer to the court councillor Chebarov, and we've called you in so you can file your statement.'

'But, I mean, she's my landlady!'

'So, what if she is?'

The clerk smiled at him with a look of pitying condescension which was accompanied by one of a certain triumph, as if this were some new conscript who had only just begun to face life under fire, and as though to say: 'Well, what do you feel like now?' But what, what did he care now about acknowledgements of debt and exaction notes? Did all that warrant even a moment's anxiety now, even a moment's attention? He stood, read, listened, answered, even asked questions himself, but did it all mechanically. An exultant sense of self-preservation, of having escaped from the danger that had been crushing him – that was what filled the whole of his being at that moment, and it contained no predictions, no analysis, no plans or guesses about the future, no doubts and no questions. It was a moment of total, spontaneous, purely animal joy. But at that very moment there occurred in the bureau something akin to thunder and lightning. The lieutenant, still in a state of complete shock from the lack of respect he had been shown, burning with anger, and evidently wishing to bolster up his damaged self-esteem, descended like all the gods of war upon the unfortunate 'opulent lady' who had been looking at him, ever since he had come in, with a thoroughly stupid smile.

'And as for you, Madam this-that-and-the-other,' he suddenly shouted at the top of his voice (the lady in mourning had gone by this time), 'what was happening at your place last night? Eh? More shameful goings-on, involving the whole street in your debauchery? More fighting and drunkenness? Got your sights on the house of correction, have you? Look here, I've warned you, I've told you a dozen times this will happen once too often. And now you've gone and done it again – again, Madam this-that-and-the-other!'

The document actually fell out of Raskolnikov's hands, and he stared wildly at the opulent lady who had been given such an unceremonious dressing-down; soon, however, he had fathomed what all this was about, and immediately the whole episode took on a positively appealing aspect. He listened with enjoyment, and even felt like laughing, laughing, laughing . . . All his nerves were dancing on edge.

'Ilya Petrovich!' the clerk began with a note of concern in his voice, but thought the better of it and decided to wait until the storm had passed, as there was no way to restrain the lieutenant when he was in a rage except by force – something he knew from personal experience.

As for the opulent lady, at first the thunder and lightning nearly made her jump out of her skin; but it was a strange thing: the more numerous the oaths became and the greater their violence, the more affectionate and charming was the smile that she turned upon the fierce lieutenant. She minced about on the spot and kept up a ceaseless curtsying, waiting with impatience to be allowed to put her side of the argument, until her chance finally came.

'There was no trouble or fighting on my premises, *Herr Kapitän*,' she suddenly rattled out in a voice that was like the scattering of dried peas, in a strong German accent, though her Russian was fluent. 'And there was no, no scandal, but they were drunk when they arrived, that's all there is to it, *Herr Kapitän*, and I'm not to blame . . . I keep a decent house, *Herr Kapitän*, and a decent vay of life, and I have always, always avoided any kind of scandal. But they arrived completely drunk and then they asked for another three bottles, and then one of them put his legs up and started to play the piano vith his foot, and that is not the vay to behave in a decent house, and he ruined the piano – *ganz* – and had completely no, no manners, I told him so. But he picked up a bottle and began poking everyone in the back with it. At that point I called the yardkeeper, quick, and Karl came up, he took hold of Karl and gave him the black eye, and also one to Henriette, and he hit me in the face five times. Oh, that vas so unmannered in a decent house, *Herr Kapitän*, and I shouted. And he opened the vindow on to the Canal and he stood there sqvealing out of it like a little pig, and that was disgraceful. How could he do it, squeal like a little pig out of the window for everyone in the street to hear? *Pfui-pfui-pfui!* And Karl pulled him back from the window by his coat-tails, and tore *sein Rock* in *zwei*, that is true, *Herr Kapitän*. And then he shouted, *man muss* fine of fifteen roubles pay. And I, *Herr Kapitän*, paid him five roubles for *sein Rock*. Oh, what a rude guest he vas, *Herr Kapitän*, and what a scandal he did make! He said "I'll have a big lampoon about you *gedruckt*, for I can write whatever I like about you and get it in all the newspapers."'*

'He's a writer, then?'

'Yes, *Herr Kapitän*, and what a rude guest, *Herr Kapitän*, in a decent house to . . .'

'All right, all right! That's enough! I've told you and told you, I mean, I've told you . . .'

'Ilya Petrovich!' the clerk said again, meaningfully. The lieutenant gave him a quick glance; the clerk nodded his head slightly.

'. . . So that, my most estimable *Laviza* Ivanovna, is the long and the short of my tale, and this is the last time I'm going to tell you it,' the lieutenant went on. 'If there's so much as one more scandalous scene in that decent house of yours, I shall give you the *zu Hundert* treatment,* as they say in polite circles. Do you hear? So a literary gentleman, one of those writers, got five roubles in a "decent house" for a coat-tail, did he? There's one of them standing right there!' he said, throwing a contemptuous glance in Raskolnikov's direction. 'There was some trouble with another of them in an inn the day before yesterday: the fellow had eaten a meal but didn't want to pay for it. "I'll write a lampoon about you if you try to make me," he said. And there was yet another on board a steamer last week, who flung the vilest abuse at the distinguished family of a state councillor, wife and daughter. One was kicked out of a pastry shop the other day. That's the sort of fellows they are, those writers, those literary gents, those students, those messengers of doom . . . Pah! Now you be off! I'll be popping in to see you myself one of these days . . . then you'd better watch out! Do you hear?'

With hurried good manners Luiza Ivanovna began to curtsy in all directions, backing towards the door as she did so; but in the doorway her posterior collided with a handsome officer who had a fresh, open face and a magnificent pair of the very thickest blond side-whiskers. This was none other than Nikodim Fomich himself,* the district superintendent. Luiza Ivanovna made haste to curtsy very nearly to the floor, and then, jumping up and down with her quick little steps, she rushed out of the bureau.

'More crashing and banging, more thunder and lightning, more tornadoes and hurricanes,' Nikodim Fomich said to Ilya Petrovich in an amiable, friendly tone of voice. 'They've upset you again, you've lost your temper again! I could hear it from the stairs.'

'So what?' Ilya Petrovich said with well-bred casualness (indeed, it sounded more like 'suh wut' than 'so what') as he took some documents over to the other desk, waggling his shoulders picturesquely as he did so – one waggle to each step. 'Here we are, sir, if you'll be so good as to take a look: a certain Mr Writer, alias Student – ex, that is. Doesn't pay his bills, been fobbing people off with promissory notes, won't quit his lodgings, we've had a ceaseless flow of complaints about him, yet he nearly filed a claim against me for lighting a cigarette in front of him! He acts like a mean b-b-bastard and, if you'll be so good as to take a look at him now, sir: here he is being his most attractive self!'

'Poverty's no crime, old chap; now what was the trouble? I bet it's that gunpowder temper of yours, you must have taken offence. You must have been insulted by something he said and not been able to restrain yourself,' Nikodim Fomich went on, turning to Raskolnikov politely. 'But there was really no need for you to: he's the most extra-ord-inar-ily well-bred chap, but powder, powder! He catches fire, sizzles up and burns away in a flash – and that's it! It's all over! And as a result he has a heart of pure gold! That's what they used to call him in that regiment of his: "Lieutenant Gunpowder" . . .'

'And what a r-r-regiment it was!' Ilya Petrovich exclaimed, thoroughly pleased at having his vanity tickled in such an agreeable manner, but still sulking nevertheless.

Raskolnikov suddenly felt like being very nice to them.

'Look, for heaven's sake, captain,' he began in a thoroughly familiar tone of voice, suddenly turning to Nikodim Fomich. 'Put yourself in my position . . . I'm even prepared to apologize to him if I've said something wrong. I'm a poor, sick student, oppressed (he actually said: "oppressed") by poverty. The reason I'm an ex-student is that I can't support myself now, but I'll be getting some money . . . I have a mother and a sister in the Province of — . . . They'll be sending me some money, and then I'll . . . pay up. My landlady's a kindhearted woman, but she got so angry at me for having lost my private teaching and being more than three months behind with the rent that she doesn't even send any meals up to me now . . . And I really don't know what this promissory note is that you keep talking about! Here she is demanding payment by means of an acknowledgement of debt, and how can I possibly make it, judge for yourselves! . . .'

'Well, I'm afraid that's not our business . . .' the clerk observed.

'Quite, quite, I couldn't agree with you more, but please let me explain,' Raskolnikov said, taking the initiative, and addressing his words not to the clerk but still to Nikodim Fomich, though also endeavouring with all his might to include Ilya Petrovich as well, in spite of the fact that the latter was pretending to rummage about in his papers, scornfully ignoring him. 'Let me explain my side of the argument: I've been living in her place for about three years now, ever since I arrived from the provinces, and some time ago . . . some time ago . . . oh well, why shouldn't I make a clean breast of it? Right from the time I moved in I promised her that I'd marry her daughter, it was only a promise by word of mouth and I was completely free to change my mind . . . She was just a girl . . . I actually found her rather appealing . . . though I wasn't in love with her . . . in short, you could put it down to my youth, that is, I mean to say, my landlady let me have a lot of credit and I also led a life that was rather . . . I was very frivolous . . .'

'We're not at all interested in matters of an intimate nature, sir, and anyway we haven't the time,' Ilya Petrovich said, starting to interrupt him rudely and with triumph, but Raskolnikov heatedly prevented him from going any further, even though he was suddenly finding it very difficult to speak.

'Quite, quite, but just let me tell you . . . what happened . . . even though I agree with you that it's not really relevant – but a year ago this girl died of typhus, I remained as a lodger as before, and when my landlady moved into her present apartment she told me . . . and told me quite cordially . . . that she had every confidence in me . . . but please would I give her an acknowledgement of debt, the one you see before you now, in the sum of a hundred and fifteen roubles, this being all she considered I owed her. I must point out, sirs, that she specifically said that as long as I gave her that document she would let me have as much credit as I liked and that as far as she was concerned never, never – those were her very own words – would she turn that document to account until I was able to pay her . . .

And yet now, when I've lost my private teaching and have nothing to eat, she serves me with an exaction note . . . What more can I say?'

'All these sentimental details are no concern of ours, my dear sir,' said Ilya Petrovich, brazenly cutting him short. 'You must file a statement and sign a treaty of obligation, but as for the fact of your falling in love and all the rest of these tragic episodes, they are quite simply no business of ours.'

'Now you're being a bit . . . hard . . .' muttered Nikodim Fomich, sitting down at his desk and also beginning to do some signing. He was feeling a little embarrassed.

'Well, get on with it,' the clerk said to Raskolnikov.

'What do you want me to write?' the latter asked, somehow especially coarsely.

'I'll dictate it to you.'

Raskolnikov had a feeling that the clerk had started to treat him with even less respect and even greater contempt since he had made his confession. But it was a strange thing – he suddenly felt he really did not give a damn about what anyone thought, and this change took place in the interval of a single flash, a single moment. If he had taken the trouble to do a little thinking, he would doubtless have been astonished that he could have spoken to these men the way he had just done, even bothering them with his emotions, wherever those emotions had come from. On the other hand, if now the room were suddenly to have filled up not with policemen but with his dearest and most cherished friends, he would not have had a single kind word to say to them, so desolate had his heart become. His soul had suddenly and consciously been affected by a gloomy sense of alienation, compounded with one of an agonizing, infinite solitariness. It was not the cheapness of his emotional outpourings to Ilya Petrovich, nor the cheapness of the lieutenant's triumph at his expense that had suddenly capsized his mood. Oh, what did he care now about his own baseness, about all these sensitive *amours-propres*, these lieutenants, German ladies, exaction notes, bureaux, and so on and so forth? Even if he had been sentenced to be burned alive just then, he would not have moved a muscle, nor for that matter paid much attention.

Something was happening to him that was completely unfamiliar to him, something new, unannounced and unprecedented. Less did he understand than clearly sense with all the power of sensation that not only was it impossible for him to address these people in the superintendent's bureau with the sentimental expansiveness he had lately employed – he could address them on no other terms, either, and even if they had all been his very own brothers and sisters, and not police lieutenants at all, even then he would have had absolutely no reason to address them about any circumstances of his life that he could possibly imagine; never until that moment had he experienced such a strange and terrible sensation. And what made it all the more tormentingly painful was that it was more a sensation than a perception, an idea; a direct, unmediated, sensation, the most tormenting of all the sensations he had ever experienced in the whole of his life.

The clerk began to dictate a statement to him in the form that was usually adopted in such cases, which said that he was unable to pay, that he would pay by such-and-such a date, that he would not leave town, or sell any property he owned or give it to anyone, etc., etc.

'But, I say, you can't write properly, the pen's falling out of your hand,' the clerk observed with curiosity, peering at Raskolnikov. 'Are you all right?'

'No . . . I feel dizzy . . . continue!'

'There isn't any more, that's it. Please sign it.'

The clerk took the document away and busied himself with some others.

Raskolnikov handed back the pen, but instead of getting up and leaving, he put both elbows on the desk and clutched his head with his hands. He felt as though a nail were being driven through its crown. A strange idea suddenly came to him: that of standing up right now, going over to Nikodim Fomich and telling him everything that had happened the day before, down to the last detail, and then taking him to his lodgings and showing him the gold objects in the corner, inside the hole. The urge was so strong that he actually stood up in order to put in into action. 'Shouldn't I think about it for a moment?' flashed through his head. 'No, it's better to do it without thinking, and get it off my chest!' But suddenly he stood still like one thunderstruck: Nikodim Fomich was talking heatedly to Ilya Petrovich, and he could hear what they were saying:

'It is impossible, they'll both be set free! For one thing, none of it makes any sense; judge for yourself: why would they go and fetch the yardkeeper if they were the ones who had done it? In order to give themselves up, or what? Or because they were trying to be clever? No, that would be a bit too clever! And then there's the fact

145

that the student Pestryakov was seen by both yardkeepers and an artisan woman in the entrance-way as he was going in: he was with three companions and he left them outside while he went in and asked the yardkeepers if there was any accommodation to be had, though his companions saw him doing it. Well, would he have been asking about accommodation if he'd had a plan like that in his head? And as for Koch, well, he spent half an hour talking to the silversmith first, and went up to the old woman's apartment at exactly a quarter to eight. Now figure it out from that . . .'

'Well, if you don't mind my saying so, sir, how is it that there's the same contradiction in both their statements? They say that they knocked and that the door was closed, and yet three minutes later, when they came back up again with the yardkeeper, the door turned out to be open?'

'That's precisely it: there's no doubt at all that the murderer was in the apartment and had bolted himself inside; and there's no doubt, either, that he'd have been caught there, if only Koch hadn't been stupid and gone to look for the yardkeeper as well. Our fellow must have taken advantage of that breathing-space in order to get down the stairs and somehow sneak past them. Koch eagerly swears that if he had stayed there, the fellow would have jumped out at him and killed him with the axe. He's going to offer up thanksgiving prayers, Russian-style, ha-ha!'

'And no one caught sight of the murderer?'

'How could they, in such a place? That building's a Noah's Ark!' the clerk, who had been listening from his seat, observed.

'The man's right, you know – the matter's perfectly clear,' Nikodim Fomich said, heatedly.

'No, sir, on the contrary. The matter's most unclear,' Ilya Petrovich affirmed.

Raskolnikov picked up his hat and walked towards the door, but did not get that far . . .

When he recovered consciousness, he realized he was sitting on a chair, being supported by a man on his right, that there was another man on his left holding a yellow tumbler full of yellow water, and that Nikodim Fomich was standing before him, staring at him fixedly; he had risen from his seat.

'What's this – are you ill?' Nikodim Fomich asked, rather sharply.

'When he was signing he could hardly get the pen across the

146

paper,' the clerk commented, sitting down in his place and busying himself with his papers again.

'How long have you been ill?' Ilya Petrovich shouted from his seat, also in the process of sorting through his papers. He had, needless to say, also been examining the sick man as he had lain unconscious, but had moved away the instant he had come to.

'Since yesterday . . .' Raskolnikov muttered in reply.

'Did you go out yesterday?'

'Yes.'

'Even though you were ill?'

'Even though I was ill.'

'At what time?'

'About eight p.m.'

'And where did you go, may I ask?'

'Down the street.'

'Don't waste words, do you?'

Raskolnikov had delivered his replies abruptly, jerkily, pale as a square of white cloth, and without letting his black, inflamed eyes fall away from Ilya Petrovich's gaze.

'He can hardly stay standing, yet you . . .' Nikodim Fomich began to protest.

'It's – quite – all – right!' Ilya Petrovich said in an odd tone of voice. Nikodim Fomich was on the point of adding something, but, glancing at the clerk, who was now looking fixedly at him, too, changed his mind. Everyone suddenly fell silent. There was something strange about it.

'All right, sir,' Ilya Petrovich said, winding up the proceedings. 'We won't detain you any further.'

Raskolnikov went out. After he had left he distinctly heard a sudden burst of heated conversation, in which the questioning voice of Nikodim Fomich was raised high, above all the others . . . On reaching the street, he came wide awake.

'A search, a search, there'll be a search without delay!' he said to himself, hurrying to get back to his room. 'The crafty devils! They suspect!' Again he was seized by his former sense of terror, all over, from top to toe.

II

'And what if there's already been a search? What if I actually find them in my room?'

But here was his room. There was nothing, no one; no one had called to visit him. Not even Nastasya had been in. But, oh Lord! How could he have left all those goods in that hole earlier on?

He rushed to the corner, thrust his hand under the wallpaper and began to haul them out, stuffing his pockets with them. There were eight items in all: two small boxes containing earrings or something of the kind – he did not pause to look; then four small morocco-leather cases; a chain, wrapped in nothing but newspaper; and something else, also wrapped in newspaper, he thought it might be a medal . . .

He put everything into various pockets, those of his coat and the one still empty in the right-hand side of his trousers, trying to make it all look as inconspicuous as possible. He took the purse along with all the other items. Then he left the room, this time leaving the door wide open.

He walked with a quick, firm step, and even though he felt that he ached all over, he still had his wits about him. He was afraid of his pursuers, afraid that in a quarter or half an hour's time the instruction would be given for him to be followed; and if that were so, then at all costs he must get rid of all the evidence in time. He must succeed in this, while he still had some strength and powers of reasoning at his disposal . . . Where should he go?

This he had decided a long time earlier: 'I must throw it all in the Canal; no one will be any the wiser, and that'll be the end of it.' He had arrived at this decision during the night, in his delirium, at the moments when he had made his repeated attempts to get to his feet and be off: 'Quick, quick, go and throw it all away.' But throwing it all away turned out to be not that easy.

He had now been walking along an embankment of the Yekateri-ninsky Canal for something like half an hour, or possibly even longer, several times pausing to take a look at the flights of steps leading down to the Canal whenever he came across them. But it was out of the question for him to carry out his plan: either there were rafts at the foot of the steps, with washerwomen on them washing linen, or there were boats tied up – and people swarmed everywhere; worse still, he would be fully visible from both embankments in all directions, and people would notice what he was doing and think it suspicious that someone should have gone down to the water's edge especially in order to throw something in. And what if the leather cases didn't sink, but floated? Of course, that would be what would happen. Everyone would see them, and him. People were already eyeing him enough as it was when they met him, staring him over as though they could think of nothing else. 'I wonder why that is? Or is it just my imagination?' he thought to himself.

At last it occurred to him that he might be better off going to some spot along the Neva. There were fewer people there, he would be less conspicuous, might at least get a chance to do what he had to do, and, most importantly, he would be further away from the part of town he was in at present. And he was suddenly filled with astonishment: how was it that he had been wandering around for a whole half an hour in despair and anguish, in a place that held such risk for him, and yet had not thought of this before? He had wasted a whole half hour on a demented plan for the simple reason that he had thought it up in his delirium! He was becoming thoroughly absent-minded and forgetful, and he knew it. He really must pull himself together!

He set off towards the Neva along V— Prospect; but on the way there another thought suddenly came to him: 'Why the Neva? Why throw the stuff in the water? Wouldn't it be better to go somewhere very far away, perhaps out to the Islands again, find some solitary place in the woods, under a bush somewhere, perhaps – and bury it there, perhaps remembering the spot by observing the look of one of the trees?' And although he sensed that he was in no condition just then to make clear and sensible decisions, he could see no flaws in this plan.

But he was not fated to go to the Islands, either; instead, something else happened: as he was emerging from V— Prospect on to the square,* he suddenly saw on his left the entrance to a yard that was surrounded by completely blank walls. To the right, immediately inside the gate, the vacant, blank wall of a neighbouring four-storey building stretched far into this yard. To the left, running parallel to the blank wall and also just inside the gate, there was a wooden fence that extended some twenty yards into the interior of the yard and

149

then made a sudden turning to the left. It was a dead, fenced-off spot where there were some kind of building materials lying around. Further away, in a hollow of the yard, the corner of a low, soot-grimed stone shed peeped from behind the fence, evidently forming part of some workshop or other. Here there were probably some trade premises – a coachmaker's or a metal works, or something of that kind; the entire area, right from the gateway, was blackened with a large quantity of coal dust. 'This is the sort of place where I can throw it all away and run,' he thought suddenly. Observing no one about inside, he strode through the gateway and at once saw, just inside it, a long gutter that had been fitted to the fence (the sort of arrangement that is often found in buildings where there are a lot of factory hands, artel workers, draymen and the like); on the fence above the gutter someone had scrawled in chalk the witticism usual in such cases: 'STOPPING OF CARTS PROHIBBITED.' This was all to the good, as his having gone in and stopped here would arouse no suspicion. 'I must throw it all away somewhere and get out of here!'

As he cast another look round, he was already putting his hand into one of his pockets when he suddenly noticed, right up by the outer wall, between the gateway and the gutter, which stood at a distance of just over two feet from each other, a large, unhewn building block, which might have weighed fifty pounds and was resting close against the stone street wall. Behind this wall lay the street and the pavement, he could hear passers-by, of whom there were invariably not a few in this part of town, shuffling past; but he could not be seen behind the gate, except if someone came in off the street, which was quite likely, and was why he had to hurry.

He stooped down to the block, seized the top of it firmly in both hands, and, mustering all his strength, succeeded in turning it over. Underneath it there was a small hollow; into this he began to throw the entire contents of his pockets. The purse went on the very top of the pile, yet there still remained room in the hollow. Then he again seized hold of the block, heaved it back with one push into its former position, and there it sat, just as it had been, except that it looked possibly a shade higher. But he raked some earth round it, pressing it into place with his foot. Nothing could be seen.

After that he left the yard and made his way towards the square. Again an intense, scarcely endurable feeling of joy, like the one he had earlier experienced in the police bureau, took mastery of him for a moment. 'The evidence is buried! And who would ever think of looking under that block? It has probably been lying there ever since the building was put up, and it will go on lying there just as long. And even if the things are found: who would ever think of me? It's finished! There's no evidence.' And he laughed. Yes, he remembered later that he laughed a long, faint, nervous, inaudible laugh, and that he continued to laugh during the whole time he was crossing the square. But when he set foot on K— Boulevard, where the day before yesterday he had had that encounter with the young girl, his laughter suddenly evaporated. Other thoughts came creeping into his mind. He also suddenly felt that he would find it horribly repugnant to walk past that bench, on which, after the girl had gone, he had sat and reflected; it would also, he thought, be horribly unpleasant to meet the man with the long moustache to whom he had given the twenty-copeck piece. 'The devil take him!'

He walked, looking around him in absent-minded hostility. Now all his thoughts were whirling around a single central point – and he felt that this central point really did exist and that now, only now, was he alone face to face with it – and for the first time since these two months had elapsed.

'And the devil take *all* of this!' he suddenly thought in a fit of inexhaustible rancour. 'If it's begun, it's begun, and to the devil with her, and the new life! Lord, how stupid all that was! . . . And how much lying and baseness I've sunk to today! How vilely I cringed and fawned back there in front of that cretin Ilya Petrovich! And in fact that's all a lot of rubbish, too! I don't give a spit for any of them or any of it, not even for my having cringed and fawned! That has nothing to do with it, nothing to do with it at all! . . .'

Suddenly, he stopped in his tracks; a new, quite unexpected question of extreme simplicity threw him off balance in a flash and bitterly amazed him:

'If you really did that with all your wits about you and not like some fool in a trance, if you really had a firm and definite goal before you, then how is it you still haven't even looked in the purse to see what you've got, the prize for which you've taken all those torments upon yourself and intentionally done such a base, vile, loathsome thing? I mean, you were going to throw the purse into the water just now along with all the other things, which you haven't examined, either, just now, weren't you? . . . What's the meaning of that?'

Yes, it was true; every bit of it was true. He had, in fact, been conscious of it all along, and it was not a new question in any way; in deciding to throw everything into the water he had done so without the slightest hesitation or demur, but straight out, as though that was the way he had planned it, and no other way could possibly be imagined . . . Yes, he had known it all and borne it all in his mind; indeed, it had all been decided yesterday, at the very moment when he had sat over the chest and pulled the leather cases from it . . . Oh, it was true all right! . . .

'It's because my health's not at all good,' he decided morosely, at last. 'I've worn myself out with all this worry, I don't know what I'm about . . . I was doing it yesterday, and the day before yesterday, and I've been doing it all these weeks – wearing myself out with worry . . . If I get better, I'll . . . stop doing it . . . But what if I don't get better at all? Lord, how sick of all this I am . . . !' He continued to talk, never stopping once. He had a terrible desire to get his mind off the whole business altogether, but did not know how to go about it. A certain new, unmasterable sensation was gaining a stronger and stronger hold of him with practically every minute that passed; it was an infinite, almost physical revulsion to everything he encountered and everything that surrounded him, an emotion that was insistent, hostile and full of hatred. He found all the people he met repulsive – their faces, their manner of walking, their movements were repulsive to him. He reflected that if anyone had said anything to him he would quite simply have spat at that person, or bitten him . . .

Suddenly, as he emerged on to the embankment of the Malaya Neva, on Vasily Island, beside the bridge, he stopped in his tracks. 'This is where he lives, right here, in this building,' he thought. 'What on earth? I would never have come to see Razumikhin of my own accord! It's the same story as last time . . . But it really is very curious: did I come here of my own accord, or did I simply walk around and end up here? It doesn't make any difference: I said . . . the day before yesterday . . . that I'd go and see him the day after *it* – well, and so I shall! I can't really very well not go up and see him now, in any case . . .'

He climbed the stairs to the fifth floor, where Razumikhin lived.

His friend was at home, in his little room. At that moment he was at work, writing, and he let Raskolnikov in himself. It was some four months since they had seen each other. Razumikhin sat in his room

152

wearing a dressing-gown that was worn to rags, with slippers on his bare feet, tousled, unshaven and unwashed. His face expressed astonishment.

'Never!' he cried, examining his newly arrived companion from head to toe; then he fell silent, and let out a whistle. 'Are things really as bad as that? Well, brother, you've gone one better than I,' he added, looking at Raskolnikov's rags. 'Oh, sit down – you must be tired!' he said. And at those words Raskolnikov subsided on to the oilcloth Turkish sofa, which was in an even worse state than his own. Razumikhin suddenly perceived that his visitor was ill.

'I say, you're seriously ill, do you know that?' He began to feel his pulse; Raskolnikov tore his hand free.

'Stop it,' he said. 'I've come . . . look: I've got no teaching . . . I was going to . . . actually, I don't need any teaching at all . . .'

'You know something? You're delirious!' Razumikhin observed, studying him with fixed attention.

'No, I'm not . . .' Raskolnikov got up from the sofa. When he had been climbing the stairs to Razumikhin's room, it had not occurred to him that he might have to confront him face to face. Now, however, in a single instant, he knew from experience that what he felt least of all like doing just then was to confront anyone face to face, anyone in the whole wide world. All his spleen rose up within him. Hardly had he stepped across the threshold of Razumikhin's room than he nearly choked with venom at himself.

'Goodbye!' he said suddenly, and walked to the door.

'What's this, you're off again? Wait, you strange fellow!'

'Stop it . . .' Raskolnikov said again, once more tugging his hand free.

'What the devil did you come for, then? Have you gone crazy, or what? I mean, it's . . . almost insulting. I won't let you go just like that.'

'Oh, listen: I came to you because I don't know anyone else who could have helped me . . . to get started . . . because you're kinder than all the rest of them, more intelligent, I mean, and you're able to take an objective view of things . . . But now I realize that I don't need anything, do you hear, nothing at all . . . need no help or sympathy from anyone . . . I'll manage by myself . . . on my own . . . Well, I've said enough! Now leave me alone!'

'Wait a minute, chimney-sweep! You're completely mad! I mean, as

153

far as I'm concerned you can do as you please. You see, I haven't any teaching worth a spit, but down at the fleamarket there's a bookseller by the name of Kheruvimov who's a whole lesson in himself. I wouldn't exchange him now for five hours' teaching in a merchant's house. He does these special editions and publishes miserable little books on natural science – but my, don't they sell! The titles alone are worth something! You always used to say I was stupid, but my God, brother, there are folk more stupid than I am! Now he's started going in for the radical stuff, too; not that he has an ounce of sympathy for the cause himself, but I encourage him all the same. Look, here are two and a bit printer's sheets of some German text – if you ask me, it's the most inane charlatanry: what it discusses, in short, is the question of whether a woman is a human being or not.* Well, needless to say, the author solemnly manages to prove that she is. Kheruvimov's going to bring it out as one of those woman-question books; I'm the translator: he'll spin out these two and a bit sheets into six, we'll dream up the most lavish title you've ever seen, half a page long, and put it on the market at fifty copecks a throw. It'll do very nicely. I'm being paid six roubles a sheet, that means I'll get about fifteen roubles for the whole thing, and I've taken six in advance. When we've finished this one, we'll start translating a thing about whales, and then there are some really boring spicy bits from the second part of the *Confessions* that we've marked out, we'll translate them, too; someone told Kheruvimov that Rousseau was a sort of Radishchev.* Who am I to argue? Let him go to the devil. Well, how would you like to translate the second sheet of *Is Woman Human?* If you like, you can take the text with you right now, take some pens and paper – it's all government stuff – and have three roubles: since my advance was for the whole translation, for the first sheet and the second sheet, three roubles is about right for your share. And when you finish the sheet, you'll get another three roubles. And there's one other thing: please don't think I'm doing you a favour. On the contrary – as soon as you walked in, I figured you could be of use to me. For one thing, my spelling is terrible, and for another my German is quite simply *schwach*, so what I write is mostly just my own invention, and I like to think it's even better than the original. Well, but who knows, perhaps it isn't, perhaps it's worse . . . Will you do it, or won't you?'

Raskolnikov silently took the sheets containing the German text of the article, accepted the three roubles and went out, not saying a word. Razumikhin stared after him in astonishment. Having got as far as the First Line,* however, Raskolnikov suddenly turned back, went back up to Razumikhin's room, placed both sheets and money on the table and left again, still without saying a word.

'I think you must have the DTs!' Razumikhin roared at last, frantic with rage. 'What kind of playacting is this? You've got me so I don't know whether I'm coming or going . . . What did you come here for, damn it?'

'I don't need any . . . translations . . .' Raskolnikov muttered, already on his way downstairs.

'Well, what *do* you need then, damn it?' Razumikhin shouted from above. Raskolnikov silently continued his descent.

'Hey! Where are you living?'

There was no answer.

'Well, then, to the de-e-evil with you! . . .'

But by this time Raskolnikov was already out on the street. At the Nicholas Bridge he was once again forced wide awake by something extremely unpleasant that happened to him. The driver of a carriage gave him a solid blow across the back with his knout for having very nearly ended up under the horses' hooves, even though the driver had shouted to him some three or four times. This blow made Raskolnikov so angry that, having darted aside to the railings (for some reason he had been walking along the very middle part of the bridge, which is used by vehicles, not pedestrians), he began to gnash and grind his teeth in envenomed fury. It went without saying that laughter arose all around him:

'Got what he deserved!'

'Must be some kind of clever dick!'

'That's an old one: they pretend to be drunk and fall under the wheels on purpose; and then you're responsible for them.'

'That's how they make their living, my dear fellow, that's how they make their living.'

At that moment, however, as he was standing by the railings, still staring vacantly and in fury after the receding carriage, and rubbing his back, he suddenly felt someone shove a coin into his hand. He looked: it was an elderly merchant's wife, in a *golovka** and goat-skin shoes, accompanied by a girl, probably her daughter, in a bonnet, holding a green parasol. 'Take it, dearie, for the love of Christ,' the woman said. He took it, and they walked on by. It was a twenty-copeck piece. From his clothes and general appearance they might very well have concluded that he was a beggar, a genuine street-gatherer of small change, but this donation of a whole twenty-copeck piece was more likely due to the blow he had received from the knout, which had moved them to pity.

Clutching the twenty-copeck piece in his hand, he walked on about ten paces and turned round to face the Neva, looking towards the Palace. There was not the least trace of cloud in the sky, and the water was almost blue – something very rare for the Neva. The dome of the cathedral, which is in no other spot so clearly delineated as when viewed from here on the bridge, not twenty paces from the chapel, was fairly gleaming, and through the pure air it was possible to discern clearly each one of its adornments. The pain of the knout had died away, and Raskolnikov had forgotten about the blow; a certain restless and not quite limpid thought was preoccupying him now to the exclusion of all else. He stood looking into the distance fixedly, and for a long time; this place was particularly familiar to him. When he had been going to university, he had been in the habit – most often as he was returning home – of stopping (he must have done it at least a hundred times) at this very spot, peering fixedly at this indeed magnificent panorama and each time being almost aston-ished by a certain vague and enigmatic feeling it aroused in him. He always felt an inexplicable coldness drifting towards him from this magnificent panorama; for him, this lavish tableau was full of a tongueless, hollow spirit . . . Each time he had marvelled at his gloomy and mysterious emotion and had postponed its fathoming until some future date, not trusting his judgement. Now he suddenly had a vivid recollection of his earlier sense of wonder and bewilder-ment, and he thought it no accident that he should have remembered it now. The mere fact that he had stopped at the same place as before seemed to him amazing and outlandish, as though he actually imagined that he could think about the same things as before, and be carried away by the same ideas and images that had carried him away before . . . only such a short time ago. It very nearly made him laugh, but at the same time his chest felt constricted to the point of pain. In some deep space below him, scarcely visible beneath his feet, he now beheld the whole of his earlier past – his old thoughts, old problems, old preoccupations and old feelings, and this whole panorama, and himself, and everything, everything . . . He seemed to be flying somewhere into the heights, and everything seemed to vanish before his eyes . . . Making an automatic movement with his hand, he suddenly felt the twenty-copeck piece that was clutched in it. He unclenched his fist, stared fixedly at the little coin and, with a swing of his arm, hurled it into the water; then he turned on his heel and went home. At that moment he felt as though, with a pair of scissors, he had cut himself off from everyone and everything.

It was getting on towards evening when he arrived back at his room; that meant he had been walking for some six hours altogether. By what route and in what manner he had returned – of that he had no memory. Taking off his coat and shivering all over like a horse that has been driven too hard, he lay down on the sofa, pulled the overcoat on top of him and sank into instant oblivion . . .

He awoke in deep twilight to the sound of a terrible clamour. God, what a clamour it was! Never had he heard or witnessed such unnatural sounds, such a wailing, such a howling, such a gnashing of teeth, such weeping, beating and cursing. He could not even imagine such savagery, such frenzy. In horror he raised himself on one elbow and sat on his bed, rigid, tormented with anxiety. But the fighting, the howling and cursing were getting louder and louder. And then, to his most profound amazement, he suddenly caught the voice of his landlady. She was howling, screeching and wailing, her words coming out in a hurried stream, so that it was impossible to decipher what she was pleading for – probably for whoever it was to stop beating her, for someone was mercilessly beating her on the staircase. The voice of the man who was doing the beating had become so terrible with spite and rabid fury that it was now little more than a wheeze, but even so he was also saying something, and also quickly, indecipherably, in a hurry, and choking. Suddenly Raskolnikov began to tremble like a leaf: he had recognized that voice – it belonged to Ilya Petrovich. Ilya Petrovich was beating his landlady! He was kicking her, drubbing her head against the steps – there was no doubt of it, one could tell it by the sounds, by the howls, by the blows! What was this? Had the world turned upside-down, or what? On every floor, all the length of the staircase, a crowd could be heard gathering, there were voices, exclamations, people coming up the stairs, knocking at doors, banging them, grouping together. 'But why, why . . . and how is it possible?' he kept repeating, seriously believing that he had gone completely insane. But no – he could hear it all only too clearly! . . . And, if that were the case, they would be coming up to his room now, 'because . . . all this is probably . . . connected with what happened yesterday . . . Oh Lord!' He wanted to lock himself in by setting the door on the hook, but his arm would not lift . . . and anyway, it was no good! Fear enveloped his soul like ice, torturing him and turning him stiff and numb . . . But then, at last, all this commotion, which must have lasted all of ten minutes, began gradually to die away. His landlady continued to moan and groan, Ilya Petrovich still threatened and shouted abuse . . . But finally his voice, too, died away; there, he could be heard no longer. 'Has he really gone? Oh Lord!' Yes, there was his landlady going, too, still moaning and weeping . . . there was her door banging shut . . . There were the people who formed the crowd dispersing on the stairs and going back to their apartments – exclaiming, arguing, crying out to one another, now raising their voices to a shout, now lowering them to a whisper. There must have been a lot of them; practically the whole building had taken part. 'Oh God, is this really possible?' he thought. 'And why, why did he come here?'

Raskolnikov fell on to the sofa in helpless exhaustion, but was now unable to close his eyes; for half an hour he lay in such suffering, such an unendurable sense of limitless horror, as he had never in his life experienced. Suddenly his room was lit by a bright light: Nastasya had come in with a candle and a plate of soup. Giving him an attentive look and perceiving that he was not asleep, she put the candle down on the table and began to lay out the things she had brought: bread, salt, the plate, a spoon.

'I do believe he hasn't eaten a thing since yesterday. Been gadding about all day, he has, and all the time he's got the fever on him.'

'Nastasya . . . why was the landlady being beaten?'

She gave him a fixed look.

'Who was beating the landlady?'

'Just now . . . half an hour ago. Ilya Petrovich, the assistant superintendent, on the stairs . . . Why did he give her such a terrible beating? And . . . why did he come here?'

Without saying a word, Nastasya studied him, frowning, and continued to look at him for a long time like that. This intent scrutiny began to make him feel very uncomfortable, and even afraid.

'Nastasya, why don't you say anything?' he said at last, timidly, in a faint voice.

'That's blood,' she replied, at last, quietly and as though she were talking to herself.

'Blood? What blood? . . .' he muttered, turning pale and backing away against the wall. Nastasya continued to stare at him in silence.

'No one's been beating the landlady,' she said, in a firm, stern voice. He looked at her, scarcely breathing.

'I heard it with my own ears . . . I wasn't asleep . . . I was sitting up,' he said even more timidly. 'I spent a long time listening . . . The assistant superintendent came here . . . Everyone came out on to the stairs, from all the apartments . . .'

'No one's been here. That's your own blood, making a noise inside you. It's when it can't get out and begins clotting in your liver, you start seeing things . . . Are you going to have some of this, or aren't you?'

He did not answer. Nastasya went on standing over him, staring fixedly at him and making no sign of being about to depart.

'Nastasyushka . . . I'm so thirsty.'

She went downstairs and a couple of minutes later returned with a white clay jug of water; but he did not remember what happened next. All he could remember was taking one sip of cold water and spilling some of the jugful on his chest. Thereupon, unconsciousness ensued.

III

Not that he was completely unconscious during the whole period of his illness: it was rather a state of fever, with delirium and semi-wakefulness. He remembered much of it afterwards. Now it seemed to him that a large number of people had gathered round him with the intention of seizing him and carrying him off somewhere, arguing and quarrelling fiercely over him. Now he was suddenly alone in the room, everyone had gone away in fear of him, and only now and then would they open the door ever so slightly in order to look at

159

him; they would threaten him, make arrangements about something between themselves, laugh at him and tease him. He remembered Nastasya being frequently beside him; he could also discern another person whom he thought seemed very familiar, but who this was he could not for the life of him determine – and this made him miserable, so that he even cried. Sometimes he would fancy that he had been lying there for a month; at other times, that it was still the same day. As far as *that* was concerned, however – *that* he had forgotten about altogether; though every minute or so he would remember that he had forgotten about something it was out of the question for him to forget about, and as it came back to him he would be racked with torment and anguish – groaning as he sank into rabid fury or fearful, unbearable terror. Then he would endeavour to get up, to flee, but someone always stopped him by force, and he would fall back helpless, unconscious. At last he came back to himself completely.

This happened in the morning, at ten o'clock. At that hour, on clear days, the sun sent a long band of light over the right-hand wall of his room, illuminating the corner beside the door. By his bed stood Nastasya and another person who was examining him very curiously and was totally unfamiliar to him. This was a young lad in a caftan, with a beard, who was probably a money messenger by the look of him. Through the half-open door peeped the landlady. Raskolnikov raised himself on one elbow.

'Who's this, Nastasya?' he asked, pointing to the lad.

'Would you look at him, why, he's woken up!' she said.

'So the gentleman has,' the money messenger replied. Realizing that this was so, the landlady ceased her observation through the doorway, closed the door and disappeared from view. She was invariably shy, and found conversations and arguments irksome; she was about forty, and was plump and oily, black-eyebrowed and black-haired, with the good nature that goes along with plumpness and laziness; actually, she was quite a comely woman. More bashful than she needed to be.

'You . . . who are you?' he went on, continuing his inquiry, and addressing the money messenger himself. But at that moment the door again opened wide, and, stooping slightly because of his height, Razumikhin came in.

'It's a regular ship's cabin,' he exclaimed, as he entered. 'I always bang my head; and they call these lodgings! So you've woken up, have you, brother? I heard it just now from Pashenka.'

'He only woke up a second ago,' said Nastasya.

'That's right, only a second ago,' the money messenger echoed with a smile.

'And who might you be, sir?' Razumikhin asked, suddenly turning to him. 'I'd like to make it clear to you that my name's Vrazumikhin; not Razumikhin, as everyone calls me,* but Vrazumikhin – a student and gentleman's son, and he's my chum. Well, sir – and who are you?'

'I'm the money messenger in our office, I've been sent from the merchant Shelopayev's, sir, and I'm here on business.'

'Will you be so good as to sit down on this chair, please?' Razumikhin sat down on another, at the opposite side of the table. 'It's just as well you've woken up, brother,' he went on, addressing Raskolnikov. 'You've hardly had a bite to eat or a drop to drink for four days. Really – we've been giving you tea in spoonfuls. Twice I brought Zosimov to see you. Do you remember Zosimov? He examined you carefully and immediately said it was all a lot of nonsense – you'd had some kind of stroke in your head, or something. Some nervous rubbish, poor diet, he said, not enough beer and horseradish, that was why you'd got ill, but it was nothing, it would pass. Good old Zosimov! He set about tending to you nobly! Well, sir, I mustn't keep you any longer,' he said turning to the money messenger again. 'Please be so good as to tell us what you want. I may as well let you know, Rodya, that this is the second time someone's come from that office of theirs; only last time it wasn't this fellow, but another, and he and I had a bit of a talking-to. Who was that fellow who came here before you?'

'I think that sounds as though it must have been the day before yesterday, sir. It must have been Aleksey Semyonovich; he works in our office too, sir.'

'Would you say he was a bit more intelligent than you? What's your opinion?'

'Yes, sir; he's sort of – a bit more solid, sir.'

'Spot on. Well, sir: continue.'

'Well you see, sir, there's a money order come to our office for you through Afanasy Ivanovich Vakhrushin, of whom you've heard a few times before, I believe, at the request of your mother, sir,' the money messenger went on, addressing Raskolnikov directly. 'In the event of your being in possession of your faculties, sir, I'm to entrust thirty-five roubles to you, sir, as Semyon Semyonovich has received instructions to that effect from Afanasy Ivanovich, in the same manner as on the previous occasion, at your mother's request. Would you be knowing Afanasy Ivanovich, sir?'

'Yes . . . I remember . . . someone called Vakhrushin,' Raskolnikov said, meditatively.

'Do you hear that? He knows the merchant Vakhrushin!'* Razumikhin exclaimed. 'How could he possibly not be in possession of his faculties? As a matter of fact, I'm beginning to notice now that you're an intelligent chap, too. I say, sir! It's nice to do business with a man who can talk with some wit.'

'It's the same Vakhrushin, sir, Afanasy Ivanovich Vakhrushin, and at the request of your mother, who has already sent some money through him in the same manner, he's agreed to do it again on this occasion, sir, and a day or two ago sent instructions from his domicile that you were to be paid thirty-five roubles, in expectation of better days to come, sir.'

' "Better days to come"? That's your best crack yet; though the one about "your mother" wasn't bad, either. Well, tell me, in your opinion: is he or isn't he in full possession of his faculties – eh?'

'It's all right with me, sir. Only he ought to sign for it, sir.'

'He'll scratch his name, never fear! What's the form? Do you have a book, or something?'

'Yes, sir, here it is, sir.'

'Give it here. Now, Rodya, sit up. I'll support you; just scribble Raskolnikov for him; take the pen, brother, for money is sweeter than sugar to us right now.'

'I don't want it,' Raskolnikov said, pushing the pen away.

'What on earth are you talking about?'

'I won't sign.'

'The devil, man, but you've got to!'

'I don't want . . . the money . . .'

'So it's: "I don't want the money", is it? Well, brother, you're singing the wrong tune there, I have my ears as a witness! Please don't worry, he's off on his . . . travels again. It happens to him even when he's wide awake . . . You're a sensible chap, and we'll provide

162

him with a bit of guidance, that's to say, we'll simply guide his hand, and he'll sign. Well, let's get on with it . . .'

'Oh, I think perhaps I'll look in some other time . . .'

'No, no; there's no reason for you to put yourself out. You're a sensible chap . . . Now, Rodya – don't delay our visitor any longer . . . he's waiting, you see.' And he earnestly prepared to guide Raskolnikov's hand.

'Leave me, I'll do it . . . myself . . .' Raskolnikov said, took the pen and signed his name in the book. The money messenger laid out the cash and beat a retreat.

'Bravo! Now, brother, are you hungry?'

'Yes,' Raskolnikov replied.

'Have you any soup?'

'There's some of yesterday's left,' Nastasya, who had been standing there all this time, replied.

'Rice-flour and potato?'

'That's right.'

'I know it off by heart. Bring on your soup, and let us have some tea while you're about it.'

'All right, then.'

Raskolnikov was looking at everything with deep amazement and a vacant, senseless terror. He decided to say nothing and wait for what might happen next. 'I don't appear to be delirious,' he thought. 'This must all be real . . .'

Two minutes later Nastasya returned with the soup and announced that the tea would be along in a moment. To accompany the soup, two spoons and two plates put in an appearance, together with a complete dinner-set: a salt-cellar, a pepperpot, mustard for the beef and so on, the like of which had not been seen for a long time. There was even a clean tablecloth.

'It might not be a bad idea, Nastasyushka, if Praskovya Pavlovna were to send us up a couple of bottles of beer. We could do with a drop of something.'

'Quick on your toes, aren't you?' Nastasya muttered, and went off to fulfil his command.

Raskolnikov continued to stare at everything wildly and with strained attention. In the meantime Razumikhin moved over and sat beside him on the sofa, and with the clumsiness of a bear placed his left arm around his head, even though Raskolnikov could quite easily

163

have raised himself, and with his right hand brought a spoonful of soup to his mouth, first having blown on it as a precaution, so that he should not burn his tongue. The soup, however, was only barely warm. Raskolnikov greedily gulped down one spoonful, then another, then yet another. But then, having given him a few spoonfuls, Razumikhin suddenly stopped and announced that before letting him have any more he would have to consult Zosimov.

Nastasya came in with two bottles of beer.

'What about that tea, do you want it?'

'Yes.'

'Run and get the tea, Nastasya, there's a good girl – I think we may safely indulge in tea without consulting the medical faculty. But now we have beer, too!' He moved back to his own chair, drew the soup and the beef towards him, and began to eat with such appetite that one might have thought he had had nothing to eat for three days.

'You know, brother Rodya, I eat like this at your place every day now,' he muttered as clearly as he was able with his mouth stuffed full of beef. 'That wonderful landlady of yours, Pashenka, sees to everything – she makes these feasts in my honour and really puts her heart into them. Of course, it's not at my insistence, but then I don't exactly protest either. And now here's Nastasya with the tea. Quick, wasn't she? Nastenka, would you like some beer?'

'Oh, you and your mischief!'

'Some tea, then?'

'Yes, I'd quite like some.'

'Go on then, pour it out. Wait, I'll do it; sit down at the table.'

He at once took over from her, poured one cup, then another, abandoned his lunch and sat down on the sofa again. As before, he put his left arm around the patient's head, lifted him up and began to spoon tea into him with a teaspoon, again blowing on it constantly with especial zeal, as though this process of sufflation contained within it the element that was central and crucial to Raskolnikov's recovery. Raskolnikov said nothing and offered no resistance, in spite of the fact that he felt he had quite enough strength to raise himself and sit on the sofa without anyone's help; not only did he feel he could keep sufficient control of his hands in order to hold a spoon or a cup – he could even, he felt, have walked. But the workings of some strange, almost animal cunning suddenly prompted him to conceal his strength until the right moment, to lie low, pretend to be not yet quite conscious, if need be, while all the while listening and pricking up his ears to find out what was going on. He was, however, unable to master his revulsion: having gulped down about a dozen spoonfuls of tea, he suddenly jerked his head free, pushed the teaspoon away fretfully, and collapsed once again on the pillows. There were actually proper pillows under his head now – feather ones with clean slips; this, too, he observed and took into account.

'We must get Pashenka to send us up some raspberry jam today, so we can make him a drink,' said Razumikhin, sitting down on his own chair and once again resuming work on the soup and the beer.

'And where's she going to get raspberries?' Nastasya asked, holding her saucer on five splayed fingers and sucking her tea 'through the sugar', peasant-fashion.

'She can buy them at the corner shop, my dear. You see, Rodya, a whole mass of events has taken place while you've been away on your travels. When you ran away from me in that knavish way of yours, without even telling me where your lodgings were, I was suddenly seized by such a temper that I decided to track you down and punish you. I set to work that very same day. Oh, I walked and walked, asked questions here, asked questions there! I'd forgotten about this place where you are now; actually, it never occurred to me, because I didn't know you were here. Well, and as for your old lodgings, all I could remember was that they were at Five Corners, in Kharlamov's Tenements. I searched and searched for those Kharlamov Tenements – and then of course it turned out that it wasn't the Kharlamov Tenements at all, but the Buch ones* – you know the way one gets the names of things mixed up! Well, then I began to lose my temper. I lost my temper and the next day I thought "here goes", and I went to the address bureau, and would you believe it? Within two minutes they'd found you for me. You're on their books!'

'On their books?'

'Of course. Yet while I was there there was someone looking for a General Kobelev, and they couldn't find him to save themselves. Well, old chap, it's rather a long story. But as soon as I popped up here, I immediately got acquainted with all your doings – all of them, brother, all of them, I know about the lot. I made the acquaintance of Nikodim Fomich, had Ilya Petrovich pointed out to me, met the yardkeeper and Mr Zamyotov, met Aleksandr Grigoryevich, met the

165

clerk at the local police bureau, and finally met Pashenka – that crowned everything. And now she knows, too . . .'

'He's sugared her up,' Nastasya murmured, smiling a mischievous, ironic smile.

'And you ought to put yours down in the cup where it belongs, Nastasya Nikiforovna.'

'Oh, you rotten pig!' Nastasya exclaimed suddenly, and burst out laughing. 'Anyway, here – my name's Petrova, not Nikiforovna,' she added suddenly, when she had stopped.

'I shall take it to heart, madam. Well now, brother, to cut a long story short, at first I wanted to wire the whole place up with electric current, in order to get rid of all the prejudices there are around here in one go; but Pashenka won the day. You know, brother, I had no idea she was such a . . . dish . . . eh? What do you think?'

Raskolnikov said nothing, though never for one moment had he taken his troubled gaze off his friend, and was now continuing to stare intently at him.

'And you might even say,' Razumikhin went on, not in the slightest put out by the silence, and as if in confirmation of some reply he had received, 'you might even say that she's got all that it takes, and in all the right places, too.'

'You dirty beast!' Nastasya screamed again, plainly finding this conversation a source of the most unutterable delight.

'You see, brother, what you did wrong was not to get stuck in there right at the beginning. She needed to be handled in a different sort of way. I mean, she really is a most surprising character! Well, more about her character later . . . Only how could you have let things get to such a pass that she didn't even dare to send your dinner up to you? And then that promissory note? Had you taken leave of your senses, to go signing a thing like that? And then what about this business of you promising to marry her daughter, when Natalya Yegorovna was still alive, that is . . . I know everything! However, I can see that I've touched a delicate chord, and that I'm an ass; you must forgive me. But while we're on the subject of stupidity: what do you think – I mean, Praskovya Pavlovna's not at all as stupid as one might suppose at first glance, is she, eh?'

'No,' Raskolnikov said through his teeth, looking to one side, but realizing that it would be more to his advantage to pursue the conversation.

'Don't you think so?' Razumikhin exclaimed, evidently delighted to have received a reply. 'But then she's not exactly clever, either, is she, eh? A truly, truly surprising character! You know, brother, I'm sometimes at my wits' end, to tell you the truth . . . She must be all of forty. She says she's thirty-six, and she has every right to do so. Actually, to be quite honest, I approach her more on an intellectual level, a purely metaphysical one; we've got a sort of secret code between us that's worse than algebra! I don't understand any of it! Oh, but that's all a lot of nonsense. The thing is that when she saw you'd stopped being a student, that you'd lost your private teaching and your decent suit of clothes, and that after her daughter's death there was no reason for her to treat you as one of her family any more, she suddenly got frightened; and since you were hiding yourself away in your room and had dropped your previous friendly relations with her, she decided to kick you out. She'd been cherishing that plan for a long time, but was loath to say goodbye to the promissory note. What was more, you'd been telling her that your mother would pay it . . .'

'I was a bastard to say that . . . my mother's practically begging on the streets . . . I lied to her so she'd let me stay in my lodgings and . . . provide me with meals,' Raskolnikov said, loudly and distinctly.

'Yes, and that was a wise thing to do. Only the trouble was that who should turn up just then but Mr Chebarov,* court councillor and man of legal business. If he hadn't been there Pashenka would never have thought of any of it, she's far too shy; well, men of business aren't shy, and of course the first thing he asked her was: Question – was there any hope of payment on the promissory note? Answer – yes, because there was a mother who actually sent her Rodenka money out of her 125-rouble pension, even though it meant she would have to go without food, and a sister who would sell herself into bondage for her brother's sake. It was on this that he based his course of action . . . What are you moving about like that for? I know all your precious secrets now. It wasn't in vain that you indulged in those confidences with Pashenka when you were still part of her family, and here I speak as a friend . . . But that's how it is: a man of honesty and sensitivity indulges in confidences, while a man of business listens, but goes on licking up the cream. So the next thing she did was to give the said promissory note to the said Chebarov in lieu of payment, and he had no qualms about formally demanding the amortization of the debt. When I found out about all this I felt like giving him a dose of electric current too, to clean out his conscience, but at that time Pashenka and I were getting along swimmingly, and I told her to stop the whole thing, right at the source, as it were, vouching to see to it that you paid up. I vouched for you, brother, do you hear that? We summoned Chebarov, stuck ten roubles under his nose and got the document back; I now have the honour of presenting it to you – they'll believe what you tell them now – here, take it, I've even torn it slightly in the way one is supposed to.'

Razumikhin spread the acknowledgement of debt out on the table. Raskolnikov glanced at it and, without saying a word, turned his face to the wall. Razumikhin fairly winced.

'I can see, brother,' he said after a while, 'that I've made a fool of myself again. I thought I'd cheer you up and take your mind off things with a bit of chatter, but I think I've merely annoyed you.'

'Were you the person I didn't recognize when I was delirious?' Raskolnikov asked, having also remained silent for a while, and without turning his head round.

'That's right. And a fair old frenzy you got into about it, too, especially when I brought Zamyotov with me one day.'

'Zamyotov?. . . The police clerk? . . . Why?' Raskolnikov quickly turned round and stared at Razumikhin.

'What the devil . . . Why are you upset? He wanted to make your acquaintance; it was his own idea, because he and I had been talking so much about you . . . How would I know so much about you unless I'd been talking to him? He's a splendid fellow, brother, a most wonderful chap . . . in his own way, naturally. We're buddies now; we see each other practically every day. I mean, I've even moved into this bit of town now. Didn't you know? I've only just moved. He and I have been to Laviza's place a couple of times. Do you remember Laviza? Laviza Ivanovna?'

'Did I rave a lot?'

'You bet! You weren't your own man!'

'What did I rave about?'

'Heavens, man, what did you rave about? People rave about all sort of things . . . Well, brother, we mustn't waste time, there's business to see to.'

He rose from his chair and grabbed hold of his cap.

'What did I rave about?'

'Oh, how you keep on! Is it some secret you're afraid of having given away? Don't worry: you said nothing about any countesses. But you said a great deal about a bulldog, some earrings and chains or other, Krestovsky Island, some yardkeeper fellow, and Nikodim Fomich and Ilya Petrovich, his assistant. Oh yes, and you were particularly interested in one of your own socks! You kept moaning: "Give it to me," over and over again. Zamyotov himself went looking around for your socks and with his very own hands, bathed in scent and bedizened with rings, put the whole rubbishy lot into your grasp. Only then did you calm down, and you held on to that rubbish for days on end: it was impossible to get it away from you. It must be somewhere under your quilt even now. And then you asked for the ends of your trousers, and my, how tearful you were about it! We tried to find out what sort of ends they were, but we couldn't make it out, it was a mystery . . . Well, now I really must be off! Look, here are your thirty-five roubles; I'll take ten of them, and in a couple of hours' time I'll be back here and show you what use I've made of them. At the same time I'll let Zosimov know how you are, though he really ought to have been here long ago – it's getting on for twelve o'clock. And Nastenka, while I'm gone please look in often and find out if he wants anything to drink or whatever . . . As for Pashenka, I'll tell her what she needs to know right now. Goodbye!'

'Calling her "Pashenka" like that! Listen to old crafty-lips!' Nastasya said as he went out; then she opened the door and began to eavesdrop, but lost patience and ran downstairs. She was extremely interested to know what Razumikhin was talking about down there with the landlady; indeed, it was in general obvious that she was quite taken with him.

No sooner had the door closed behind her than the patient threw off his quilt and leapt up from the bed like a man half crazy. With burning, convulsive impatience he waited for them to go, so he could begin his task. But what was it, what was the task? Now, as though by design, it seemed to have gone clean out of his head. 'O Lord! Just tell me one thing: do they know about it all, or haven't they found out yet? Or is it that they've simply been pretending, playing cat-and-mouse with me while I was still laid up in bed, and will suddenly come in and tell me that they've long known everything and have merely been . . . Then what am I to do now? I've gone and forgotten

– that would have to happen; one moment it was in my head, and the next it went out of it! . . .'

He stood in the centre of the room and looked around him in agonized bewilderment; he went over to the door, opened it, listened; but that was not it. Suddenly, as though it had come back to him, he rushed to the corner where the hole in the wallpaper was, began to examine everything, put his hand through the hole, felt about, but that was not it, either. He went to the stove, opened it and began to feel around in the ashes: the fragments of his trouser-ends and the shreds of his torn-out pocket-lining were scattered about where he had thrown them earlier; that meant that no one had seen them! At that point he remembered the sock that Razumikhin had told him about just then. True enough, there it was lying on the sofa, under the quilt; but it was now so dirty and unnoticeable that Zamyotov could not possibly have spotted it.

'That's it – Zamyotov! . . . the bureau! . . . But why do they want me at the bureau? . . . Where's that summons? Wait a minute! I'm getting mixed up: that was back then! And back then I examined my sock, too, but now . . . now I've been ill. But why did Zamyotov come to see me? Why did Razumikhin bring him here?' he muttered helplessly, sitting down on the sofa again. 'What is all this? Is it still my delirium playing up, or is it real? It seems to be real . . . Yes! I remember: I must flee! I must take to my heels right now, I have absolutely, absolutely no choice! But . . . where am I to run to? And where are my clothes? My boots aren't here! They've cleared them away! Hidden them! It's all too clear! But here's my coat – they must have missed it! And here's my money on the table, thank God! Here's the note, too . . . I'll take the money and leave, and I'll rent new lodgings, they'll never find me! . . . Yes, but what about the address bureau? They'll find me. Razumikhin will. I'd better flee entirely . . . go far away . . . to America, and let them go to hang! I'll take the note, too . . . it'll come in handy over there. What else should I take? They think I'm ill! They don't even know I can walk, ha, ha, ha! All I need to do is get down to the bottom of those stairs! But what if they've put people on watch down there, policemen? What's this – tea? Ah, there's some beer left, too, half a bottleful, and it's cold!'

He seized hold of the bottle, in which there was enough beer left to fill a whole tumbler, and drank it down with pleasure in one draught, as though he were extinguishing a fire within himself. But hardly had a moment gone by than the beer went to his head, and along his spine passed a gentle and even welcome shiver. He lay down and pulled the quilt over him. His thoughts, which were already morbid and incoherent as it was, began increasingly to merge with one another, and before long slumber, light and welcome, held him in its grasp. With pleasure he sought a place for his head on the pillow, wrapped himself more tightly in the soft quilt which now lay on top of him in place of the tattered overcoat he had been used to before, uttered a quiet sigh and fell into a deep, sound, restorative sleep.

What woke him up was the sound of someone coming up to his room. Opening his eyes, he saw Razumikhin, who had opened the door wide and was standing in the threshold, wondering whether to go in or not. Raskolnikov quickly sat up on the sofa and looked at him, as though making an effort to remember something.

'Ah, you're awake! Well, here I am! Nastasya, bring the bundle up here!' Razumikhin shouted down the staircase. 'In a second or two I'll show you how I spent the money . . .'

'What time is it?' asked Raskolnikov, looking round him uneasily.

'Why, you've slept in grand style, brother; it's evening outside, it must be about six o'clock. You've been asleep for about six hours and a bit . . .'

'Good Lord! What's wrong with me? . . .'

'What's wrong with you? It'll have done you good. Where's the hurry? Off to a rendezvous, or something? Now all our time's our own. I've already been waiting for you for about three hours; I looked in a couple of times, but you were asleep. I went to call on Zosimov twice: nothing doing – he wasn't in! But don't worry, he'll be along! . . . I also took a bit of time off to see to my own paltry affairs. You see, I moved today, moved completely, together with my uncle. I've got an uncle living with me now, you see . . . But to hell with that – to our task! . . . Give me the bundle over here, Nastenka. Now, we'll just . . . Er, how are you feeling, brother?'

'I'm all right. I'm not ill . . . Razumikhin, have you been here long?'

'I told you, I've been waiting for three hours.'

'No, but before that.'

'What do you mean, before?'

'How long is it since you began these visits to the house?'

'But, I mean – I told you all that this morning; or have you forgotten?'

171

Raskolnikov began to reflect. The events of that morning flitted before him as in a dream. He was unable to recall them single-handed, and looked questioningly at Razumikhin.

'Hm!' Razumikhin said. 'You have forgotten! Why, even just this morning I thought you weren't yet in your . . . Yet now your sleep has made you recover . . . You really do look a lot better. Good for you, lad! But now to business! You'll remember it all in a jiffy. Look what I have here, my dear fellow.'

He began to undo the bundle, on which he had obviously lavished a good deal of care.

'Believe me, brother, this is something that lies particularly close to my heart. For we must make a proper human being of you. Let's get on with it; we'll start at the top. Do you see this little casquette?' he began, producing from the bundle a fairly decent but at the same time very ordinary and cheap-quality peaked cap. 'Would you like to try it on?'

'Later, afterwards,' Raskolnikov said, brushing it aside peevishly.

'No, brother Rodya, don't be quarrelsome – afterwards it'll be too late; and besides, I shan't be able to get a wink of sleep all night, because I don't know your size, I bought it on a guess. Perfect!' he exclaimed triumphantly, having tried it on Raskolnikov's head. 'It fits perfectly! What a man wears on his head, brother, is the most important item of his costume – it's a kind of introduction, in a way. Every time my friend Tolstyakov goes into one of those public places, he sees that all the other gents standing there are wearing caps and hats, and he finds himself compelled to remove his own humble lid. Everyone thinks he does it because he has servile feelings, but it's really because he's ashamed of that birds' nest of his: he's a man with a sense of shame! Well now, Miss Nastenka, here are two items of headdress for you: this grand old Palmerston' (he produced from the corner Raskolnikov's mangled round hat, which for some unknown reason he had given the name Palmerston), 'or this intricate little knick-knack. What's your guess, Rodya – how much do you think I paid for it? How about you, Nastasyushka?' he said, turning to her, observing that Raskolnikov was not going to say anything.

'I should think it cost you twenty copecks,' Nastasya replied.

'Twenty copecks, you brainless girl?' he exclaimed, taking offence. 'Why, one couldn't even buy you for twenty copecks these days – it cost eighty! And that was only because it's been worn. But then, it

172

carries a guarantee: if you wear it out this year, they'll give you another next year for nothing, so they will! Now, let us proceed to the United American States, as they used to be called in the gymnasium I attended. I must warn you that I'm rather proud of the breeches!' And in front of Raskolnikov he stretched out a pair of grey trousers, made of a light summer woollen material. 'They bear not a hole nor a stain, and they're not bad at all, even though they are a bit worn, and there's a waistcoat to go with them, the same colour, as fashion requires. Actually, the fact that the stuff's been worn is a positive advantage: it's softer, more comfortable . . . You see, Rodya, it's my opinion that in order for a man to make his way in the world, it's sufficent for him always to observe the seasons; if one doesn't demand asparagus in January one may keep a few roubles in one's purse, and the same thing applies to the purchase before you now. At present it is summer, so I have made a summer purchase, because for autumn you'll need things made of warmer material, and you'll have to throw these ones away . . . all the more so since by that time this stuff will have fallen to bits, if not because of its increased splendour, then because of certain inner defects. Well, give me your guess! How much, do you suppose? Two roubles and twenty-five copecks! And remember, again there's the same guarantee: if you wear these out this year, you may take some others next year for nothing! Those are the only terms of trade at Fedyayev's shop: you pay your money once and you get goods to last all your life, because otherwise you'd never go near the place again. Well, now, let's proceed to the boots – what do you think? I mean, it's easy to see they've been worn, yet they'll answer perfectly for a month or two, as they're foreign craftsmanship and foreign manufacture: the secretary of the British Embassy sold them at the fleamarket last week; he'd only been wearing them for six days, but he needed the money badly. The price was one rouble fifty copecks. All right?'

'But they may not fit!' Nastasya observed.

'Not fit? What do you think this is?' And from his pocket he hauled one of Raskolnikov's old, stiffened boots, caked all over with dried mud and full of holes. 'I took this monster along in reserve, and by measuring it they were able to determine his size. The whole business was conducted in a most cordial fashion. And as for his linen, I've had a word with the landlady. Here, to start with, are three shirts, coarse-cloth ones, but fashionably styled on the outside . . . Well, so:

eighty copecks for the cap, two roubles twenty-five for the rest of the clothes, that makes three roubles and five copecks; a rouble fifty for the boots – because they're very nice ones – so that comes to four fifty-five, and five roubles inclusive for the linen – they were bought wholesale – so the whole lot comes to nine roubles and fifty-five copecks exactly. There's forty-five copecks change, in copper fives, here, please take them – and so Rodya, now your wardrobe is completely renewed, as in my opinion your coat is not merely still serviceable, but actually possesses an air of a certain nobility: that's what one gets when one orders one's clothes from Sharmer's!* As for socks and the rest, I'll leave that up to you; we've twenty-five roubles left, and you don't need to worry about Pashenka and paying the rent; I told you: I've got the most unlimited credit with her. And now, brother, you must please let me change your linen for you, or else your germs will probably just go on lingering in your shirt . . .'

'Stop it! I don't want all this!' Raskolnikov protested, warding him off, having listened with revulsion to Razumikhin's strained efforts at humour in his account of how he had bought the clothes.

'It's no good making a fuss, brother; I haven't worn my boot-leather out for nothing!' Razumikhin insisted. 'Nastasyushka, don't be so embarrassed, come and help me, that's right!' And in spite of Raskolnikov's protests, he none the less managed to change his linen. Raskolnikov fell back on the pillows and for a couple of minutes did not say a word.

'They're not going to leave me alone for a long time yet!' he thought. 'Out of whose money did you buy all this?' he asked, at last, looking at the wall.

'Whose money? What questions you do ask! Why, your own, of course. That money messenger was here this morning, from Vakhrushin's, your mother sent it; or have you forgotten?'

'I remember now . . .' said Raskolnikov, after a long and morose bout of reflection. Frowning, Razumikhin kept glancing at him uneasily.

The door opened, and there entered a tall, thick-set man, whom Raskolnikov also thought looked somewhat familiar.

'Zosimov! At last!' Razumikhin exclaimed, in relief.

IV

Zosimov was a big, fat man with a puffy, colourlessly pale and smooth-shaven face, and straight, very fair hair. He wore spectacles, and on one of his fat-swollen fingers there was a large gold ring. He must have been about twenty-seven. He was dressed in a light, capacious and stylish paletot, light-coloured summer trousers, and in general everything about him was ample, stylish and brand-new; his linen was immaculate, his watch-chain massive. His manner was slow, giving an impression of being at once languid and at the same time studiedly familiar; although he did his utmost to conceal them, his pretensions to superiority showed through at every moment. Everyone who had anything to do with him found him a hard man to get along with, but said that he knew his job.

'I've been to your place twice today, brother . . . You see? He's woken up!' cried Razumikhin.

'I see, I see; well, so what are we feeling like now, eh?' Zosimov said as he turned to Raskolnikov, peering at him fixedly and coming to sit at his feet on the sofa, where he immediately sprawled into a lounging position, as far as was possible.

'Oh, he's in a constant fit of spleen,' Razumikhin went on. 'We changed his linen just now, and he practically burst into tears.'

'That's natural; you could have left the linen until later, if he didn't want it changed . . . His pulse is first-rate. I expect you've still got a bit of a headache, eh?'

'I'm all right, I'm perfectly all right!' Raskolnikov said, insistently and with irritation. Suddenly he sat up on the sofa, his eyes flashing, but immediately collapsed back on to the pillow and turned his face to the wall. Zosimov was observing him fixedly.

'Very good . . . all's as it should be,' he said, languidly. 'Has he had anything to eat?'

They told him, and asked him what sort of food should be given.

'Oh, he can have anything he wants . . . Soup, tea . . . No mushrooms or cucumbers, of course – oh yes, and beef's not a good idea, either, and . . . but what's the point of my sitting here chattering away like this? . . .' He exchanged glances with Razumikhin. 'No medicine, and no nothing. And tomorrow I'll look in again . . . Perhaps even later on today . . . Yes, why not . . .'

'Tomorrow evening I shall take him out for a walk!' Razumikhin said, decisively. 'We'll go to Yusupov Park, and then look in at the "Palais de Cristal".'*

'I wouldn't have him up and about tomorrow, although . . . a little . . . well, we'll see later on.'

'Oh, what a pity, I'm giving a housewarming party this evening, it's just a couple of yards from here; I wish he could come too. He could lie in our midst on the sofa! You'll come, won't you?' Razumikhin said suddenly, turning to Zosimov. 'Don't forget, now – you've promised.'

'I may look in a bit later on. What do you have planned?'

'Oh, nothing – tea, vodka, herring. There's to be a pie: just some friends getting together.'

'Who, exactly?'

'Well, they're all from round about here and they're most of them new acquaintances, to tell you the truth – except perhaps for old Uncle, and he's new, too: he only arrived in St Petersburg yesterday, on some wretched business or other; I see him about once in every five years.'

'Who is he?'

'Oh, he's been vegetating all his life as a district postmaster . . . He draws a miserable little pension, sixty-five a year, it's hardly worth talking about . . . I'm actually rather fond of him. Porfiry Petrovich will be coming: he's the head of our local criminal investigation department . . . a trained lawyer. Oh, you know him . . .'

'Is he some kind of relative of yours, too?'

'Only of the most distant kind; but why are you frowning? You mean to say that just because the two of you once had a swearing match, you may not come?'

'I don't give a spit about him . . .'

'So much the better, then. Well, and then there'll be some students, a teacher, a certain government clerk, a certain musician, an officer, Zamyotov . . .'

'I say, would you mind telling me what you or he' – Zosimov nodded at Raskolnikov – 'can possibly have in common with a fellow like that Zamyotov?'

'Oh these fussy folk! Principles! . . . You operate on principles as though they were mechanical springs; you don't even dare to turn round of your own accord; in my view, the man's all right – that's the only principle I go on, and I won't hear another word against him. Zamyotov's a splendid chap.'

'He's got an itchy palm.'

'So what if he has – I don't give a spit! What of it, anyway?' Razumikhin exclaimed suddenly, getting inordinately worked up. 'Did I praise him to you for having an itchy palm? All I said was that he's all right in his own way! To be quite honest, if one goes into all the ins and outs of everyone, are there really going to be all that many good people left? I mean, I'm certain that no one would give so much as one baked onion for me, entrails and all, and even then only if you were thrown in as well! . . .'

'That's not enough. I'd give two for you . . .'

'Well, I'd only give one for you! Zamyotov's still a little boy, and I'll give his hair another pull, because he must be drawn along, not pushed away. If you push a man away you'll never set him on the right path, and the same is even truer of a boy. With a boy you have to be twice as careful. Oh, you progressive blockheads, you don't know a thing! You've no respect for others, and you've no respect for yourselves . . . But since you're asking – yes, we may very well have a certain matter in common.'

'I'd be most interested to hear about it.'

'It's all to do with that case about the painter – the decorator, that is . . . Oh, we'll get him out of trouble! Actually, he's not in any danger now. The whole thing's quite, quite obvious! All we need is some more steam.'

'What decorator is this?'

'What, didn't I tell you about him? I didn't? No, that's right, I only told you the beginning . . . You see, it's about this murder there's been, of the old woman pawnbroker, the civil servant's widow . . . Well, now there's a decorator mixed up in it . . .'

'Oh, I heard about that murder before you did, and I'm actually rather interested in the case . . . partly . . . because of a certain circumstance . . . and I've been reading about it in the newspapers! And now . . .'

'Lizaveta was murdered, too!' Nastasya blurted out suddenly, turning to Raskolnikov. She had remained in the room all the time, huddled up beside the door, listening.

'Lizaveta?' Raskolnikov murmured, in a barely audible voice.

177

'Yes, the market-woman, you know who I mean, don't you? She used to come in downstairs. Mended a shirt for you once, too.'

Raskolnikov turned to the wall, where on the dirty yellow wallpaper with its little white flowers he selected one clumsy white flower in particular which had small brown lines on it, and began to examine it to see how many leaves it had, how many serrations there were on each leaf and how many lines. He felt that his hands and feet had gone numb, as though he had lost the use of them, but he did not even try to move and stared persistently at the flower instead.

'Well, what about the decorator?' Zosimov said, interrupting Nastasya's chatter with a peculiarly marked displeasure. Nastasya sighed and fell silent.

'They've got him on the list of suspects, too!' Razumikhin went on, animatedly.

'On what evidence?'

'They don't need evidence! But as a matter of fact, it's the evidence that won't stand up, and what we've got to prove is that it's not evidence at all! It's exactly how they behaved at the beginning when they arrested those other two fellows and put them on the list of suspects – what are their names, again . . . oh yes, Koch and Pestryakov. Pah! What a stupid way it's all being handled, it gives one a nasty feeling even though one's not involved. The Pestryakov chap may be looking in at my place this evening . . . Actually, Rodya, you already know about this business, it happened before you got ill, just the evening before you fainted in the bureau, when people were talking about it there . . .'

Zosimov gave Raskolnikov an inquisitive look; Raskolnikov did not move.

'Do you know something, Razumikhin? I've been keeping an eye on you: you're a busybody,' Zosimov observed.

'That's as may be, but we'll get him out of it all the same!' Razumikhin exclaimed, banging his fist on the table. 'I mean, what is it that's so offensive about the whole thing? I mean, it's not the fact that they're lying; one can always forgive a man for telling lies; lying's a harmless activity, because it leads to the truth. No – what's offensive is that they're lying and making a fetish out of their own inventions! I've a lot of respect for Porfiry, but . . . I mean, for example, what set them off on the wrong foot to start with? The door was closed, but when they got there with the yardkeeper it was open: right, they said, Koch and Pestryakov must have done it! That's the sort of logic they follow, you see.'

'Oh, don't get so worked up; they've simply been detained, that's all; it's inevitable . . . Actually, I've met that Koch; why, he turned out to have been buying up unredeemed pledges from the old woman, didn't he? Eh?'

'Yes, he's some kind of swindler. He buys up promissory notes as well. A professional. Oh, to the devil with him! No, what I'm trying to say is, there's something about it that makes me angry – know what I mean? It's that rotten, stinking, fossilized routine of theirs that makes me angry . . . Yet here, in this one case alone, one might open up a whole new approach. From the psychological information alone it would be possible to show how to get on to the right track. "We've got facts," they say. But facts aren't everything; at least half the battle consists in how one makes use of them!'

'And that's what you're able to do?'

'Well, I mean, one can't just stay silent when one feels, knows instinctively, that one could be of assistance on the case, if . . . Oh damn it! . . . Look, are you familiar with the details of the case?'

'I'm waiting to hear about the decorator.'

'Oh yes, that's right. Well, then, listen; here's the story. Just three days after the murder, in the morning, when they were still wasting time with Koch and Pestryakov – even though those fellows had accounted for every single move they'd made: it's so obvious, it's crying out loud! – a most unexpected fact popped up. A certain peasant named Dushkin, the landlord of a drinking den opposite the building in question, appeared at the bureau with a jewel-case containing some gold earrings, and launched into a long tale: "This fellow came running into my place," he said, "two days ago, just after eight o'clock in the evening" – the day and the hour! You get the point? – "a decorator he was by trade, and he'd been into my establishment earlier on, in the afternoon, Mikolai,* they call him; he'd brought me this box with some gold earrings and precious stones, and he wanted me to give him two roubles on account for them, but when I asked him where he'd got them from he said he'd found them on the pavement. I didn't inquire any further" – this was Dushkin speaking – "but let him have a ticket (a rouble, that is), because I figured that if he didn't pawn it with me, he'd find someone else to pawn it with, it would all be the same – he'd drink the money

179

away, and the things would be better with me: the further away you put it, the closer it is to hand, as they say, and I thought, if anything turns up, or I hear any rumours, I'll take it in to the bureau." Well, of course, this was all a load of moonshine, he was lying like a horse, for I know this Dushkin, he's a pawnbroker himself and hides stolen goods, and he wouldn't go diddling Mikolai out of an article worth thirty roubles merely in order to "take it in". He was just scared, that's all. But to the devil with that; listen! Dushkin went on: "Now I've known this peasant, Mikolai Dementyev, since he was little, we come from the same province, Ryazan, and the same district, Zaraisk. And although Mikolai's no drunkard, he likes a drop now and again, and I knew he was working in that building, doing the place up, together with Mitrei* – they're both from the same village. Once he'd got the ticket, he immediately had it changed into coins, drank two glasses of vodka straight off, took his change and made off – I didn't see Mitrei with him at the time. Well, the next day we heard that Alyona Ivanovna and her sister, Lizaveta Ivanovna, had been murdered with an axe; I knew them, sir, and it was then that I suddenly had my suspicions about the earrings – because I knew that the old woman used to pay out money on pledged items. I went to their house and began to make cautious inquiries, softly-softly, and the first thing I asked was whether Mikolai was there. Mitrei told me that Mikolai had gone off on a binge and had come home at dawn, drunk, had spent about ten minutes there and then gone out again, and that he, Mitrei, hadn't seen him again after that and was finishing the work by himself. The place they've been doing up is on the same staircase as the murdered women's apartment, on the second floor. When I heard all that, I didn't let on to anyone about it at the time," – this was still Dushkin speaking – "but I found out everything I could about the murders and came home still with the same suspicions. Then at eight o'clock this morning," – he's talking about the third day after the murder, you understand – "lo and behold, I saw Mikolai coming into my place. He wasn't sober, but he wasn't particularly drunk either, and he was able to understand what you said to him. He sat down on one of the benches and didn't say anything. Now, apart from him in the place at that time there was only one customer, and a fellow I knew, a friend of mine, who was asleep on a bench, and our two boys, sir. 'Have you seen Mitrei?' I asked. 'No,' he said, 'I haven't.' 'And you've not been here?' 'I've not been here,' he said, 'since the day before yesterday.' 'And where did you spend last night?' 'At Peski, with some friends in Kolomna.' 'And where did you get those earrings?' 'I found them on the pavement.' It sounded fishy, the way he said it – he didn't look at me. 'Have you heard what happened that very same evening, at that same time, on that same staircase?' 'No,' he said, 'I haven't.' But he was listening, his eyes were staring out of his head, and he suddenly turned as white as chalk. As I was telling him about it, I saw him reach for his hat and start to get up. At that point I tried to keep him from going: 'Wait, Mikolai,' I said. 'What about a quick one?' And I winked to one of my boys as a sign for him to hold the door, and came out from behind the bar: then he shot out of my place, ran off down the street and disappeared into a side-lane – I haven't seen him since. By that time my suspicions were confirmed, because you could tell a mile off he'd got something to hide . . ."'

'I bet he had,' Zosimov said.

'Wait! You haven't heard the end of it. It goes without saying that they were immediately off at the double, hunting for Mikolai: Dushkin was put in detention, and his premises searched. Mitrei got the same treatment. The friends in Kolomna were cleaned out, too – but then suddenly, the day before yesterday, Mikolai was brought in: they'd arrested him in a roadhouse near the — Gate. He'd turned up there, taken off the crucifix he wore, a silver one it was, and asked for a glass of vodka in exchange for it. They gave him it. A few minutes later, the woman went out to the cowshed and looked through a crack in the wall: in the barn next door he'd tied his sash to one of the beams, and had made a noose; he'd got up on a chopping-block and was trying to put the noose around his neck; the woman screamed at the top of her voice and people came running: "So that's the sort of fellow you are!" "Take me to a police station," he said, "and I'll confess to the lot." Well, they took him to a police station – the one here, that is – with all the appropriate honours. Well, they asked him this and they asked him that, who he was, what he did, how old he was – "Twenty-two" – and so on, and so forth. To the question: "When you and Mitrei were working together, did you see anyone on the staircase at such-and-such and such-and-such a time?" he replied: "Well, all sorts of people must have been going up and down, but we never paid any attention to them." "Didn't you hear anything, any noises, for example?" "No, we didn't hear anything unusual."

181

"Well, were you aware, Mikolai, that on that very day, at such-and-such an hour, a certain widow and her sister were robbed and murdered?" "I didn't know anything about it. The first I heard of it was from Afanasy Pavlych, the day before yesterday, in the drinking den." "And where did you get the earrings?" "I found them on the pavement." "Why didn't you show up for work with Mitrei the next day?" "Because I was off on a binge." "Where did you have your binge?" "Oh, at this place and that place." "Why did you run away from Dushkin?" "Because I was dead scared." "What were you scared of?" "That they'd think I did it." "Why were you scared of that, if you don't feel guilty of having done anything wrong? . . ." Believe it or not, Zosimov, that question was put to him literally in those words, I know it for a fact, I was given a reliable account of it! What do you say to that, eh?'

'Yes, well, they do have some evidence, after all.'

'It's not the evidence I'm talking about – it's that question, and the whole way they perceive their role! Oh, to the devil with it! . . . Well, so they kept on and on at him, piling up the pressure, and finally he confessed: "I didn't find it on the pavement, I found it in the place Mitrei and I were decorating." "Be more explicit." "Well, Mitrei and I had been painting that place all day; it was now eight o'clock in the evening, and we were getting ready to go home, when Mitrei picked up a paintbrush and daubed some paint on my face with it; then he ran away, and I went after him, shouting fit to burst; and as I was coming off the staircase and turning into the gateway I ran smack into a yardkeeper and some other gentlemen who were with him, I don't remember how many of them there were. The yardkeeper yelled at me, and so did another yardkeeper, and the wife of one of them came out and started yelling at us, too, and then a gentleman and a lady came in through the gateway, and he yelled at us too, because Mitka and I were lying in the way; I grabbed Mitka by the hair and knocked him down and began pummelling him, and Mitka did the same to me – but we weren't doing it in a nasty sort of way, more like two friends having a playful scrap. Then Mitka got away from me and ran off down the street, and I set off after him, but I couldn't catch him up, so I went back on my own to the place we'd been decorating – there was some clearing-up that needed to be done. I began to get on with it, waiting all the while in case Mitrei came back. Well, by the door in the passageway, in the corner behind the wall, I stepped on this little box. I looked, and saw it was wrapped up in paper. I took off the paper, there were these teeny-little hooks, I unfastened them – and in the box were the earrings . . ."'

'Behind the door? It was lying behind the door? Behind the door?' Raskolnikov suddenly shouted, looking at Razumikhin with a dull, frightened stare, raising himself on the sofa slowly, with one arm.

'Yes . . . what is it? What's wrong with you? Why are you acting like that?' Razumikhin said, also getting up.

'Never mind! . . .' Raskolnikov answered, in a voice that was barely audible, sinking back on the pillow and turning round again to face the wall. For a while no one said anything.

'He must have nodded off and had a dream,' Razumikhin said at last, directing an inquiring gaze at Zosimov, who gave a slight, negative move of his head.

'Well, go on then,' said Zosimov. 'What happened after that?'

'After that? As soon as he saw the earrings, he forgot all about the apartment and Mitka, ran off to Dushkin's establishment and, as you know, got a rouble out of him, lying to him that he'd found the rings on the pavement, and immediately went off on a binge. As for the murder, all he would do was keep on repeating what he'd said before: "I don't know a thing about it, the first I heard of it was the day before yesterday." "And why didn't you report here earlier?" "I was scared." "Why did you want to hang yourself?" "Because of the thought." "What thought?" "That they'd think I'd done it." Well, that's the whole story. Now, what do you suppose they made of that?'

'There's no need to suppose: there's a trail, of sorts. A piece of incriminating evidence. They can't very well let your decorator go free now, can they?'

'But I mean, they've practically identified him as the murderer! They haven't the shadow of a doubt! . . .'

'Nonsense; you're just getting yourself worked up. What about the earrings? You must admit that if those earrings from the old woman's trunk fell into Nikolai's hands on the very day of the murder, at the very hour it took place, they must have got there somehow! That means quite a lot in an investigation like this one.'

'You ask how they got there? How they got there?' Razumikhin exclaimed. 'Can it really be that you, a doctor, who has as his principal obligation the study of man and who possesses more opportunity than anyone else of studying human nature – are really unable to see, with all this information before you, what kind of a man this Nikolai is? Can you really not see, at a first glance, that all the evidence he gave during his interrogation is the most sacred truth? Those earrings fell into his hands exactly as he swore they did. He stepped on the box and picked it up.'

'The most sacred truth? But he himself confessed that he'd been lying right from the word go.'

'Listen to me. Listen carefully: all of them – the yardkeeper, Koch, Pestryakov, the other yardkeeper, the wife of the first yardkeeper, the artisan's wife who'd been sitting in the yardkeeper's room at the time, the court councillor Kryukov, who at that very moment had alighted from a cab and was walking in through the gateway arm-in-arm with a lady – they all of them, eight or nine witnesses, that is, swear unanimously that Nikolai had forced Dmitry down to the ground, was lying on top of him pummelling him, while Dmitry had seized hold of Nikolai by the hair and was pummelling him back. They were lying across the road, blocking the way; people were shouting and cursing at them from every side, while they, "like little children" (that was actually the expression used by those who were present), lay on top of each other, yelping, scuffling and laughing, each of them laughing to make the other laugh, with the most ridiculous faces, and then they ran away down the street, chasing each other like kids. Got it? Now take careful note: the bodies in the apartment were still warm, do you hear, warm, when they found them! If those two, or even just Nikolai on his own, had killed anyone and broken open any chests, or had merely taken part in some robbery or other, permit me to ask you one simple question: would a state of mind like that, characterized as it was by yelping, laughter and childish scrapping in the entrance-way, fit in with axes, blood, villainous cunning, deliberation, robbery? Imagine the scene: they've only just committed the murders, some five or ten minutes previously – because it turns out that the bodies were still warm – and suddenly, leaving the bodies in the apartment with the door open, and knowing that people had just passed that way, they go out and sprawl around in the roadway like little children, laughing and drawing everyone's attention to themselves, for there are ten unanimous witnesses who say that they did!'

184

'Well, there's no denying it's a bit odd . . . I suppose it's impossible, but . . .'

'No, brother, no buts. If the earrings, which turned up in Nikolai's hands at the very day and hour the murder took place, really constitute such an important piece of evidence against him – though it can be directly explained by his testimony, and is thus *contestable evidence* – then we must also take into consideration the *exonerating* evidence, since it is also *irrefutable*. Now, being familiar with the character of our jurisprudence, what do you suppose: is it willing to accept, is it even capable of accepting a piece of evidence of this kind – one founded purely on a simple psychological impossibility, on a simple state of mind – as being irrefutable and having the effect of demolishing all the incriminating and circumstantial evidence, whatever it may be? No, it is not. It is not willing to do so on any account, for a box was found, and a man tried to hang himself, "something he would never have done if he had not felt himself to be guilty"! There is the capital question, there is what makes me get so worked up! Perhaps now you will understand!'

'Yes, I can see that you're worked up. Wait, though, I forgot to ask: what proof is there that the box containing the earrings really did come from the old woman's chest?'

'It's been proved,' Razumikhin answered, frowning, and almost reluctantly. 'Koch recognized the earrings and was able to identify the man who had pawned them, and he positively confirmed that they'd belonged to him.'

'That's not so good. Now something else: did anyone see Nikolai during the time that Koch and Pestryakov were going upstairs? Can't that be proved somehow?'

'That's just it. Nobody saw him,' Razumikhin replied with vexation. 'That's the very devil of it. Not even Koch and Pestryakov noticed him when they were going upstairs, though their testimony wouldn't carry much weight now in any case. "We saw that the door to the apartment was open," they said, "and that work must be going on there, but we continued on our way up and didn't pay attention, and we don't remember whether there were actually workmen inside at that moment or not."'

'Hm. So the only exonerating evidence is that the two men had been pummelling each other and laughing. I suppose that's firm enough proof, but . . . let me ask you now: how do you account for

185

the whole sequence of events? How do you explain his finding the earrings, if he really did find them in the way he says he did?'

'How do I explain it? There's nothing to explain: the matter is quite clear! At any rate, the path of inquiry that ought to be followed is clear and proven, and it's the box that has done the proving for us. It was the real murderer who dropped those earrings. The murderer was inside the apartment when Koch and Pestryakov knocked at the door, and had fastened the bolt. Koch was stupid, and went downstairs; at that point the murderer left the apartment and went downstairs, too, because he had no other means of exit. On his way down he hid from Koch, Pestryakov and the yardkeeper by ducking into the empty apartment, the instant after Dmitry and Nikolai had gone running out of it. He waited behind the door while the yardkeeper and the others were going upstairs, waited until their footsteps had died away, and then took himself off downstairs as calm as you please, at the very moment Dmitry and Nikolai were running out into the street; everyone had gone their separate ways, and there was no one left in the gateway. He may have been seen, but no one paid him any attention, as there are always so many people going in and out. As for the box, it fell out of his pocket as he was standing behind the door, and he didn't notice, as he had other things on his mind. But the box offers clear proof that it was precisely there that he stood. There you have it!'

'Clever! Yes, brother, but it won't do. It's just a little too clever!'

'Why do you say that?'

'Because it all fits together too well . . . it's too neat . . . like something out of a play.'

'You really are the most . . .' Razumikhin began to exclaim, but at that moment the door opened, and there entered a new *dramatis persona* who was not familiar to a single one of those present.

V

This was a gentleman who could no longer be described as young. There was an imposing, stand-offish air about him, and he had a face that expressed peevishness and caution. The first thing he did was to stand still in the doorway and look around him with unconcealed and sour astonishment, as though he were wondering: 'Where's this I've ended up?' Suspiciously, and with the affectation of a certain alarm, of offence, even, he viewed Raskolnikov's cramped and low-ceilinged 'ship's cabin'. With the same look of astonishment he transferred his gaze and fixed it upon Raskolnikov himself, undressed, unkempt and unwashed, lying on his dirty little sofa, and considering him with a similarly motionless stare. Then, with the same slow look he began to examine the dishevelled, uncombed and unshaven person of Razumi-khin, who in his turn looked him cheekily and questioningly straight in the eye, without moving from the spot. The strained silence lasted for about a minute, and then finally, as one might have expected, a slight alteration took place in this dramatic tableau. Having come to the conclusion – assisted, doubtless, by certain decidedly uncompro-mising features of the situation – that in this 'ship's cabin' nothing whatever was to be attained by a mien of such exaggerated severity, the newly arrived gentlemen softened his manner somewhat and politely, though not without sternness, turned to Zosimov, and, rapping out each syllable of his question, enunciated:

'Rodion Romanovich Raskolnikov, student or ex-student?'

Zosimov slowly stirred, and might even have ventured a reply, had not Razumikhin, who was not part of the proceedings at all, at once got in before him:

'That's him lying there on the sofa. And what might you be after?'

This familiar 'And what might you be after?' fairly brought the stand-offish gentleman up short; he even turned slightly in Razumi-khin's direction, but managed to restrain himself in time and moved back quickly to face Zosimov.

'This is Raskolnikov,' Zosimov drawled, casting a nod in the patient's direction; then he yawned, opening his mouth inordinately wide as he did so, and keeping it that way for an inordinately long time. After that, he slowly felt around in the pocket of his waistcoat, took out a most enormous, bulging, solid-gold watch, opened its cover, glanced at its dial and slowly and lazily put the thing back in his pocket again.

As for Raskolnikov, during all this time he lay on his back, not saying a word, staring intently, though without any reason that was particularly apparent, at the man who had come in. His face, which he had now turned away from the interesting flower on the wallpaper, was extremely pale and displayed an expression of uncommon suffering, as though he had just undergone a painful operation or had, only a moment ago, been released from torture. Gradually, however, the newly arrived gentleman began to occupy more and more of his attention; this state of attention changed to bewilderment, then suspicion and finally something that resembled fear. Indeed, when Zosimov, pointing at him, said: 'This is Raskolnikov,' he suddenly roused himself in a hurry, leapt upright, sat on the edge of the sofa and in a voice which was almost challenging, but none the less faint and broken, articulated:

'Yes! I'm Raskolnikov. What do you want?'

The visitor gave him a careful look and announced imposingly:

'Pyotr Petrovich Luzhin. I hope and presume that my name is not wholly unknown to you.'

But Raskolnikov, who had been expecting something quite different, looked at him dully and reflectively and made no reply, as though this were the first time he had ever heard the name Pyotr Petrovich.

'What? Have you really not been told the news yet?' Pyotr Petrovich inquired, making a slightly wry grimace.

In response to this, Raskolnikov slowly sank back on his pillow, threw his arms behind his head and began to look at the ceiling. Consternation was now discernible in Luzhin's features. Zosimov and Razumikhin began to survey him with even greater curiosity, and he was finally unable to disguise his complete embarrassment.

'I had assumed and was counting on the probability,' he mumbled, 'that a letter which was entrusted to the mail more than ten days, practically two weeks ago . . .'

'Listen, what are you hanging about in the doorway for?' Razumikhin suddenly said, interrupting. 'If you have something to tell us, please sit down, it's getting a bit crowded over there, what with you and Nastasya as well. Nastasyushka, do stand aside and let the gentleman through! Come along, sir, here's a chair for you, this way! That's right, squeeze your way through!'

He drew his chair back from the table, made some space between the table and his knees, and waited in a slightly tense position for the visitor to 'squeeze his way' through the small gap. The moment was chosen in such a way as to make refusal out of the question, and the visitor hurriedly squeezed his way through the narrow space, stumbling as he went. Upon reaching the chair, he sat down and gave Razumikhin a mistrustful look.

'Please don't feel embarrassed,' Razumikhin said carelessly. 'Rodya's been ill for the past five days and was delirious for three, but now he's recovered, and he's even been eating with some appetite. That's his doctor sitting there, he's just been examining him, and I'm one of old Rodka's friends, an ex-student like him, and I'm here making a fuss over him. So don't bother about us and don't feel awkward – go right ahead and say what it is you want.'

'I thank you. But do you not suppose that I may disturb the patient by my presence and discourse?' Pyotr Petrovich said, turning to Zosimov.

'Oh no,' Zosimov drawled. 'You may even provide him with some diversion.' And again he yawned.

'Oh, he came round a long time ago – this morning, actually!' Razumikhin went on, his excessive familiarity taking the form of such artless good nature that, on thinking about it, Pyotr Petrovich found his spirits reviving, possibly to a certain extent because this insolent ragamuffin had, after all, introduced himself as having had something to do with the university.'

'Your mother . . .' Luzhin began.

'Ahem!' Razumikhin said loudly. Luzhin gave him a questioning look.

'It's all right, I was just clearing my throat; do go on . . .'

Luzhin shrugged his shoulders.

'. . . Your mother, during my sojourn in her vicinity, began a letter to you. Upon my arrival in St Petersburg I purposely deferred my visit to you for a few days, in order to make quite sure that you would have been informed about the whole matter; but now, to my astonishment . . .'

'I know, I know!' Raskolnikov said with an expression of the most impatient vexation. 'You're the fellow, aren't you? The fiancé. Oh, I know all about you . . . you've said enough.'

This time Pyotr Petrovich decidedly took offence, but he said nothing. He had lost no time in energetically seeking an answer to what the significance of all this could possibly be. A silence ensued, lasting all of a minute.

Meanwhile Raskolnikov, who had turned slightly in Pyotr Petrovich's direction as the latter had made his reply, suddenly began to study him fixedly again, and with a peculiar inquisitiveness, as though he had not so far managed to get a proper look at him, or had been struck by some new aspect of him; he even raised himself from his pillow especially in order to do this. There was, indeed, something singularly striking about Pyotr Petrovich's general appearance, something which, as it were, justified the designation of 'fiancé' that had been so unceremoniously conferred upon him only a few moments earlier. For one thing, it was obvious, too much so, even, that Pyotr Petrovich had lost no time in making energetic use of his few days in the capital in order to smarten himself up and acquire some embellishments pending the arrival of his bride – an activity that was, after all, perfectly blameless and within the bounds of decent behaviour. Even his own possibly too self-complacent awareness of his own gratifying change for the better might be forgiven in such an instance, for Pyotr Petrovich had entered upon the career of fiancé. All his clothes were newly procured from the tailor's, and they were all of them excellent, leaving aside the fact that they were too new and were too divulgent of a certain purpose. Even his stylish, brand-new round hat bore witness to that purpose: Pyotr Petrovich treated it too reverentially and held it with too much caution in his grasp. His charming pair of lilac gloves, of real Jouvain manufacture,* bore similar testimony, if only because he did not wear them, but merely carried them around for show. Pyotr Petrovich's other garments were, on the other hand, of predominantly light and youthful colours. He wore a handsome summer jacket of a light brown hue, light-coloured, lightweight trousers, a waistcoat of the same material, fine linen that had just been purchased, the very lightest of pink-striped cambric cravats – and what crowned it all was that the whole ensemble actually suited Pyotr Petrovich to a T. Even as it was, his face, which was very fresh-complexioned and even handsome, looked younger than its forty-five years. On either side it was pleasantly overshadowed by a pair of dark side-whiskers, shaped in the form of two mutton-chops, and becoming rather elegantly bushy in the region of his smooth-shaven chin, which shone to the point of glossiness. Even his hair, which contained only the merest traces of grey, combed and curled at the barber's, did not thereby impart to him a comical or stupid aspect, as is generally the case with hair that has been curled, since it gives one's face the inevitable look of a German going to the altar. No, if in this rather personable and commanding physiognomy there was anything unpleasant or alienating to be found, it proceeded from other causes. Having examined Mr Luzhin without ceremony, Raskolnikov smiled a poisonous smile, sank back on his pillow and began to look at the ceiling again. Mr Luzhin, however, restrained himself, having apparently decided to ignore all these eccentricities for the present.

'I am most, most sorry to find you in such a plight,' he began again, breaking the silence with an effort. 'Had I known that you were unwell, I would have called earlier. But business, you understand . . . I have, what is more, a very important matter at the Senate, in my capacity as lawyer. Not to mention certain other concerns, at which you may be able to guess. I expect the arrival of your family – of your mother and sister, that is – at any moment . . .'

Raskolnikov began to stir and appeared to be on the point of saying something; his face expressed a certain agitation. Pyotr Petrovich paused in expectancy, but as nothing was forthcoming, he continued:

'. . . any moment. I have found them lodgings for their earliest convenience . . .'

'Where?' Raskolnikov said weakly.

'Rather far from here – Bakaleyev's Tenements . . .'

'That's on Voznesensky,' Razumikhin said, chipping in. 'There are two floors of rented rooms; it's run by a merchant named Yushin.* I've been there.'

'Yes, quite so – rented rooms . . .'

'It's the most abominable place: dirty, smelly and of doubtful character, too; there have been incidents; the devil only knows who lives there! . . . I looked in there once myself after some scandal or other. It's cheap, though . . .'

'Well, of course, I did not have so much information at my disposal, as I am myself new in town,' Pyotr Petrovich retorted delicately. 'But I must say they are two most, most clean little rooms, and since it is

only for a most brief space of time . . . I have already found a proper
apartment, that is to say, our future one,' he said, turning to
Raskolnikov, 'and it is now being decorated; and meanwhile I myself
have squeezed into rented quarters in the apartment of Mrs Lippewechsel – the abode of a certain young friend of mine, Andrei
Semyonych Lebezyatnikov; it was he who directed me to Bakaleyev's
Tenements . . .'

'Lebezyatnikov?' Raskolnikov said slowly, as though he were
remembering something.

'Yes, Andrei Semyonych Lebezyatnikov, an official at the Ministry.
Is he known to you?'

'Yes . . . no . . .' Raskolnikov answered.

'Forgive me, your question led me to believe that he was. I was at
one time his tutor . . . a very likeable young man . . . well-informed,
too . . . I like meeting young people: it is from them that one learns
what is new.' Pyotr Petrovich examined everyone who was present
with a look of hope.

'In what sense do you mean?' Razumikhin asked.

'In a most serious one – in, as it were, the very essence of the
matter,' Pyotr Petrovich said, following on, as though well pleased by
the question. 'You see, it is ten years since last I visited St Petersburg.
All these innovations, reforms and ideas of ours – all these things
have touched us in the provinces, too; but in order to obtain a clearer
view and one that is more comprehensive, it is necessary to be in St
Petersburg. Well, sir, and the opinion I have formed is that one
notices and learns most by observing our younger generation. And I
will confess: I have been encouraged . . .'

'By what, exactly?'

'Your question would take some considerable time to answer. I may
be in error, but I have the impression of discerning a clearer view –
more, as it were, criticism; more efficiency . . .'

'That's true,' Zosimov said through his teeth.

'Nonsense, there's no efficiency,' Razumikhin said, seizing the bait.
'Efficiency's acquired with some effort, it doesn't just fall from the
skies. And we've spent practically the last two hundred years getting
out of the habit of all effective action . . . Oh, it's true that there's a
ferment of ideas,' he said, turning to Pyotr Petrovich, 'and a desire
for good, though it's a childish one; there's even some honesty to be
found, in spite of the fact that crooks have been arriving here in their

droves; but efficiency, that there isn't! Efficiency requires a pair of boots.'

'I do not agree with you,' Pyotr Petrovich replied, with visible pleasure. 'There are, of course, enthusiasms and eccentricities, but one must be lenient: those enthusiasms bespeak zeal for action and the unfavourable outer environment in which that action must take place. If little has been done, then one must remember that there has not been much time, either. To say nothing of means and remedies. If you desire my own personal opinion, quite a great deal has already been achieved: new, wholesome ideas have been disseminated, several new, wholesome literary works have received circulation in place of the old, dreamy, romantic ones; literature is assuming a more mature inflection; many harmful prejudices have been uprooted and put to scorn . . . In a word, we have irrevocably cut our ties with the past, and that, in my opinion, sir, amounts to effective action . . .'

'He learned all that by rote! He's showing off!' Raskolnikov articulated suddenly.

'What did you say, sir?' Pyotr Petrovich, who had not heard him properly, inquired, but received no answer.

'It's all true enough,' Zosimov hastened to interject.

'Do you not think so?' Pyotr Petrovich went on, beaming agreeably at Zosimov. 'You must agree,' he continued, addressing Razumikhin again, but this time with a certain note of triumph and superiority, and nearly adding: 'young man', 'that there is at least prosperity, or, as is said nowadays, progress, in the fields of science and economic justice . . .'

'That's a cliché!'

'No, sir, it is not! Until now, if I were told, for example: "love", and I obeyed, what came of it?' Pyotr Petrovich went on, with just a little too much haste. 'What came of it was that I rent my caftan in twain, shared it with my neighbour, and we both ended up half-naked – as the Russian proverb puts it: "Go in pursuit of several hares at once, and you will not secure a single one."* Science, however, tells us: "Love yourself before all others, for everything in the world is founded upon self-interest."* If you love only yourself, you will conduct your enterprises in a proper manner and your caftan will remain whole. Economic justice adds, moreover, that the more privately organized enterprise there is in society, and the more, as it were, whole caftans there are, the more firmly it is founded and the better the public cause is organized, too. From this it follows that in acquiring wealth solely and exclusively for myself, I am by virtue of that very same fact acquiring it for all and am contributing to a situation whereby my neighbour may receive slightly more than a rent caftan, and this not because of any private, individual acts of generosity, but as a consequence of the resulting universal prosperity. A simple thought, but one that has unfortunately taken a long time to arrive, overshadowed as it has been by enthusiasm and proneness to dreaming; yet no great wit would seem to be required in order to surmise it . . .'

'Well, you'll have to forgive me, I'm afraid I'm another of those witless folk,' Razumikhin said, sharply, 'so perhaps we should forget it. I opened my mouth with a purpose, but all these self-indulgent bits of chatter, all these constant, incessant clichés, the same thing over and over again, have become so obnoxious to me during the past three years, that I swear to God I blush when other people, let alone myself, utter them in my presence. You were, of course, in a hurry to show off your knowledge, and that is very excusable, I don't condemn it. All I was trying to do just now was find out what sort of man you are, because, you see, so many professional manipulators have battened on to the public cause and have bent all that they touched to their own interest to such a degree that they've brought the whole cause into disrepute. Well, that's enough of that!'

'Sir,' Mr Luzhin began, wincing with extreme dignity, 'surely you do not mean to imply in this unceremonious manner that I, too . . .'

'Oh, come, come, sir! What do you think I am? That's enough!' Razumikhin snapped, turning suddenly in Zosimov's direction in order to resume their earlier conversation.

Pyotr Petrovich had enough sense to accept this response in good faith. He had, in any case, decided to leave in a minute or two.

'I hope that the acquaintance we have now begun,' he said, turning to Raskolnikov, 'may, after you have recovered and in view of certain circumstances with which you are familiar, consolidate itself even further . . . I particularly wish you good health . . .'

Raskolnikov did not so much as turn his head. Pyotr Petrovich began to get up from his chair.

'It was quite certainly one of her clients who murdered her,' Zosimov said, affirmatively.

'That's right!' Razumikhin replied, in an approving tone of voice.

'Porfiry's not giving anything away, but he's questioning the clients all the same . . .'

'He's questioning the clients?' Raskolnikov asked, loudly.

'Yes – what of it?'

'Oh, nothing.'

'How is he tracking them down?' Zosimov inquired.

'Some of them were pointed out to him by Koch; others had their names written on the paper in which their goods were wrapped, and there were yet others who came in of their own free will when they heard . . .'

'Well, he must have been a skilled and experienced blackguard, then! What audacity! What resolve!'

'That's exactly what it wasn't!' said Razumikhin, interrupting. 'That's what's been throwing you all off the scent. No, in my opinion he's neither skilled nor experienced, and he's probably a first-timer. If you assume that calculation was involved, and that he's a clever bastard, it all looks rather improbable. If, on the other hand, you assume he was inexperienced, it looks as though it was only chance that saved him from disaster, and what doesn't chance get up to? For heaven's sake, he may not even have had any idea of the problems he might encounter! And how does he go about doing it? He takes some items worth ten to twenty roubles each, stuffs his pocket with them, digs around in the old woman's chestful of rags – yet all the while, in a cash-box in the top drawer of the chest of drawers there's a good clear fifteen hundred roubles in gold, never mind all the banknotes! He didn't even know how to conduct a robbery, all he knew was the business of killing! It was his first time, I tell you, his first time; he lost his nerve! And it wasn't calculation but chance that got him out of it!'

'I believe you are referring to the recent murder of the civil servant's widow?' Pyotr Petrovich said, breaking into the conversation and addressing Zosimov; he now had his hat and gloves in his hand, preliminary to his departure, but wished to throw in a few more intelligent remarks before leaving. He was evidently concerned to make a favourable impression, and vanity had got the better of good sense.

'Yes. You've heard about it?'

'I could hardly have failed to, sir . . . It happened in the vicinity . . .'

'Are you familiar with the details?'

'That I cannot pretend; but what interests me about the case is another aspect of it – one that relates to the whole question, as it were. It is not simply that during the past five years crime has been on the increase among the lower classes of society; it is not simply the high and unbroken incidence of fires and burglaries; what I find strangest of all is that crime is similarly on the increase even among the upper classes, running, as it were, in a parallel direction. Here there is news of an ex-student robbing the mail on the open road; here men who, by their social position, occupy a leading place in society are found guilty of forging banknotes; in Moscow they have caught an entire gang who forged the tickets of the last lottery loan – and among the principal culprits was a university lecturer in world history; abroad, the secretary of one of our embassies was murdered for some obscure, financial reason* . . . And now, if this old woman pawnbroker was murdered by one of her clients, it was doubtless a man of the more elevated classes, for muzhiks do not pawn gold articles, and how is one to explain this immoral behaviour on the part of the civilized portion of our society?'

'There have been a lot of economic changes . . .' Zosimov commented.

'How is one to explain it?' Razumikhin said, rallying to the attack. 'Why, it may quite readily be explained by the all too deep-rooted lack of effective activity.'

'Explain yourself more clearly, sir.'

'Well, it's what your lecturer in world history replied when he was asked why he'd been forging lottery tickets: "Everyone's making themselves better-off by various means, so I wanted to do the same in as short a time as possible." I don't remember his exact words, but the gist of it was that he wanted it all for nothing, as quickly as possible, without any effort. People have grown accustomed to having everything ready-made for them, they're used to depending on the guidance of others, having everything chewed up for them first. Well, and when the great hour finally struck, they all showed themselves at face value . . .'

'But do you not consider that morality is involved? And, as it were, the rules of . . .'

'What have you got to worry about?' Raskolnikov said, unexpectedly intervening. 'Why, it's all turned out according to your theory!'

'What theory?'

'Well, if you take those ideas you were advocating just now to their ultimate conclusion, the end result would be that it's all right to go around killing people . . .'

'For goodness' sake!' Luzhin exclaimed.

'No, that's not right,' was Zosimov's comment.

Raskolnikov lay pale, his upper lip quivering and his breath coming with difficulty.

'Everything has its limits,' Luzhin went on, in a haughty, superior tone. 'An economic concept is not yet tantamount to an invitation to murder, and one has only to suppose . . .'

'Is it true,' Raskolnikov interrupted again in a voice that trembled with malevolent hostility, betraying a kind of pleasure in being offensive, 'is it true that you told your fiancée . . . at the very moment you received her consent, that what appealed to you most about her was the fact . . . that she is destitute . . . because a man does better to take a wife from a poor background so he can have mastery over her later on . . . and be able to wield the constant reproach over her that he's done her a favour? . . .'

'Sir!' Luzhin exclaimed in vicious irritation, flushing scarlet and thrown completely off balance. 'Sir . . . to distort my purpose in this manner! Forgive me, but I must tell you that the rumours that have reached you, or, to be more precise, which have been brought to you, contain not a shred of solid foundation, and I . . . have my suspicions as to who . . . to put it briefly . . . this arrow . . . to put it briefly, your mother . . . Indeed, I had already noticed that, for all her excellent qualities, her ideas are somewhat sentimental and romantic in nature . . . But even so, I was a thousand versts from the supposition that she could possibly have construed and represented the matter in a form such as this, perverted by her imagination . . . And moreover . . . moreover . . .'

'Do you want to know something?' Raskolnikov exclaimed, raising himself on his pillow and fixing him with a penetrating, glittering stare. 'Do you?'

'Well, sir?' Luzhin stood still and waited with an offended, challenging look on his face. The silence lasted for several seconds.

'If you so much as dare . . . to say another single word . . . about my mother . . . I'll knock you head over heels downstairs!'

'Hey, what's got into you?' cried Razumikhin.

'Ah, so that's the way it is!' Luzhin turned pale and bit his lip. 'Now listen to me, my good fellow,' he began in measured tones, doing his utmost to restrain himself, but breathing fiercely none the less. 'From the very outset, as soon as I arrived here, I observed your hostility, but remained here on purpose in order to learn more. There is much that I am willing to forgive a man who is ill and a relative of mine, but now . . . I will never . . .'

'I'm not ill!' Raskolnikov shouted.

'What a pity! . . .'

'Oh, go to the devil!'

But Luzhin was already on his way out, not bothering to finish what he had been saying, squeezing his way once again between table and chair; this time Razumikhin stood up in order to let him through. Without giving anyone a glance, and without even nodding to Zosimov, who had for a long time been motioning to him to leave the sick man in peace, Luzhin went out, cautiously raising his hat to shoulder-height as he bent down in order to pass through the doorway. And even the curve of his spine seemed on this occasion to say that he was carrying away with him a terrible personal insult.

'We can't just let him go like that, can we?' said a perplexed Razumikhin, shaking his head.

'Leave me, leave me alone, all of you!' Raskolnikov shouted in a frenzy. 'Will you leave me alone now, you torturers! I'm not afraid of you! I'm not afraid of anyone, anyone now! Go away! I want to be alone, alone, alone!'

'Come on,' Zosimov said, motioning to Razumikhin.

'For pity's sake, we can't just leave him like that.'

'Come on!' Zosimov said again, insistently, and went out. Razumikhin thought for a moment and then ran to catch him up.

'It might have made him worse if we hadn't done as he wanted,' Zosimov said, on his way down the staircase now. 'He mustn't be made irritable . . .'

'What is it that's wrong with him?'

'If only he could be given some kind of beneficial shock, that's what he needs! He was all right just a while ago . . . He's got something on his mind, you know. Some fixed idea that's hanging over him . . . I'm very much afraid that that's the case . . . there's no doubt of it!'

'Perhaps it's that gentleman, that Pyotr Petrovich fellow! From what they were saying it appears he's getting married to Rodya's sister, and that Rodya had had a letter about it just before he fell ill . . .'

'Yes; the devil must have brought him just now; he may have upset the whole process of recovery. By the way, have you noticed that he's indifferent to everything, doesn't say a word about anything except the one subject, that sends him into a frenzy: that murder . . .'

'Yes, yes!' Razumikhin said, following his train of thought. 'I've noticed that a lot! It interests him, he gets scared about it. He got scared about it on the day he fell ill, in the superintendent's bureau; he passed out.'

'You can let me know some more about that this evening, and I'll tell you a few things afterwards. He interests me, very much! In half an hour's time I'll look in to see how he is . . . He won't catch pneumonia, anyway . . .'

'I'm most grateful to you! I'll wait downstairs with Pashenka in the meantime and Nastasya can keep an eye on him for me . . .'

When they had gone, Raskolnikov gave Nastasya a look of anguished impatience: but she seemed to be in no hurry to leave.

'Would you like some tea now?' she asked.

'Later! I want to sleep! Leave me alone . . .'

With a cramped, convulsive movement he turned to the wall; Nastasya went out.

VI

As soon as she had gone, however, he got up, set the door on the hook, untied the bundle of clothes which Razumikhin had brought earlier and done up again, and began to put them on. It was a strange thing: he suddenly seemed to have become completely calm; now he was affected neither by the mad delirium that had plagued him earlier, nor the panic fear from which he had suffered all the time thereafter. This was his first moment of a strange, abrupt calm. His movements were precise and clearly focused, they contained a hint of a firm resolve. 'Today, it must be today! . . .' he muttered to himself. Though he knew he was still weak, a most powerful emotional tension which had attained the pitch of a state of calm, a fixed and obsessive idea, had given him strength and self-confidence; even so, he hoped he would not fall down in the street. Completely attired in his new suit of clothes, he looked at the money that lay on the table, thought for a moment, and put it in his pocket. It amounted to twenty-five roubles. He also took all the copper five-copeck coins, the change from the ten roubles Razumikhin had spent on the clothes. Then he quietly undid the hook, emerged from the room and descended the staircase, glancing in through the wide-open door of the kitchen as he went: Nastasya stood there with her back to him, bending down as she blew on the coals in the landlady's samovar. She did not sense his presence. And indeed, who would ever have supposed that he might simply leave? A moment later, and he was out on the street.

It was about eight o'clock, the sun was going down. There was still the same breathless heat as before; but it was with greed that he inhaled this stinking, dust-laden, town-infected air. His head began to go round a little; a kind of wild energy suddenly shone in his inflamed eyes and pale yellow, emaciated features. He did not know where he should go, and was not even thinking of it; all he knew was that 'all *this* must be brought to an end today, in one go, right now; otherwise I can't go home, because *I don't want to go on living like this*'. How was he to bring it to an end? With what means? He had not the slightest idea, and he did not want to think about it, either. He drove the thought away: thought tormented him. All he could do was feel, knowing that, whatever else happened, the situation must be changed, 'by whatever means possible', he kept repeating with a desperate, obsessive self-confidence and resolve.

Following his old habit, and taking the customary route of his previous walks, he set off straight for the Haymarket. Some distance before he got there, in the roadway in front of a chandler's shop, he encountered a young man with black hair who was playing the hurdy-gurdy, churning out a thoroughly poignant romance. He was accompanying a girl of about fifteen who stood before him on the pavement, dressed like a young lady of the aristocracy in a crinoline, mantilla, gloves and a straw hat with a bright orange feather in it; all of these were old and shabby. In a nasal street voice that was none the less strong and appealing she was singing the romance to its end in the expectation of receiving a two-copeck piece from the shop.

Raskolnikov paused, side by side with two or three other members of the audience, listened for a while, took out a five-copeck coin and placed it in the girl's hand. Quite suddenly she interrupted her singing on the very highest and most poignant note, as though she had cut it off with a knife, called sharply to the hurdy-gurdy player: 'That's enough!', and they both dragged themselves off to the next little shop.

'Do you like street-singing?' Raskolnikov suddenly inquired, addressing himself to the elderly passer-by who had been standing next to him listening to the hurdy-gurdy and who had the appearance of a *flâneur*. The man looked at him in timid astonishment. 'I do,' Raskolnikov went on, but with an air that suggested he was talking about some subject quite remote from that of street-singing. 'I like to hear singing to the accompaniment of a hurdy-gurdy on a cold, dark and damp autumn evening, it must be a damp one, when the faces of all the passers-by are pale green and sickly-looking; or, even better, when wet snow is falling, quite vertically, with no wind, do you know? And through it the gas-lamps gleaming . . .'

'No, sir, I don't know . . . Excuse me . . .' the gentleman muttered, frightened both by Raskolnikov's question and by his strange appearance, and crossed over to the other side of the street.

Raskolnikov walked straight on and emerged at the corner of the Haymarket where the artisan and the peasant woman had been talking to Lizaveta that day; but now they were nowhere to be seen. Recognizing the spot, he stopped, looked around and turned to a young lad in a red shirt who was standing outside the entrance to a flour-dealer's shop* and staring with vacant curiosity:

'There's an artisan who has a stall on this corner, with a peasant woman, his wife, isn't there?'

'There's all kinds of folk have stalls here,' the lad replied, giving Raskolnikov a measuring look from above.

'What's his name?'

'Whatever he was christened.'

'You're from Zaraisk, too, aren't you? Which province?'

The lad again surveyed Raskolnikov.

'What we have, your excellency, is not a province but a district, and since my brother's the one who did the travelling, while I stayed at home, I don't rightly know, sir . . . Perhaps your excellency will forgive me out of the greatness of his soul.'

'Is that an eating-house up there?'

'It's an inn. They've got billiards, too; and you'll find some of those princesses there . . . Couldn't be better.'

Raskolnikov walked across the square. At this corner there was a dense crowd of people – muzhiks, all of them. He squeezed his way into the very thick of them, peering into their faces. For some reason he felt a longing to talk to them all. But the muzhiks paid no attention to him, and somehow kept on making a tremendous din, bunched up into little groups. He stood for a bit, reflected, and then turned right along the pavement in the direction of V—. Leaving the square behind, he found himself in a side-lane* . . .

He had walked down this lane many times before. It made a bend, and led from the square to Sadovaya Street. During his recent weeks of wretchedness he had actually felt a longing to loaf around in all these places, 'so as to get even more wretched'. Now he entered the lane, thinking of nothing. There was a large building here which was entirely taken up with drinking dens and other food-and-drink establishments; every moment or so women came running out of them, attired 'for the neighbourhood' – bareheaded and wearing only their dresses. In two or three places they were huddled together on the pavement in groups, mostly at the top of the descents to the lower floor, where by way of a couple of steps it was possible to enter various establishments of a highly recreational nature. Coming from one of these at that moment was enough noise and uproar to fill the whole street, the strum of a guitar, the singing of songs, and the sound of people enjoying themselves to the full. A large group of women was gathered outside the entrance; some of them sat on the steps, others on the pavement, and yet others stood talking together. Beside them, in the roadway, loudly swearing, a drunken soldier was wandering around aimlessly with a cigarette in his hand, apparently looking for some place he wanted to go to, but unable to remember where it was. One ragged man was exchanging abuse with another ragged man, and someone else who was dead drunk lay sprawled across the street. Raskolnikov stopped beside the large group of women. They were talking in hoarse voices; they were all wearing cotton dresses and goat-skin shoes, and their heads were uncovered. Some of them were over forty, but there were others who were not much more than seventeen, and nearly all of them had black bruise-marks round their eyes.

For some reason the singing interested him – all that noise and uproar down there . . . From inside, through shrieks and bursts of laughter, came the sound of a reedy, falsetto voice singing an impetuous melody to a guitar accompaniment; someone was dancing desperately to it, beating out the rhythm with his heels. He listened with an attention that was fixed, sombre and reflective, bent forward as he stood at the entrance looking curiously down from the pavement into the passage below.

> Oh you handsome duty policeman,
> Please don't beat me for no reason! –

the singer's reedy voice spilled out. Raskolnikov felt a terrible desire to find out what this song was, as though everything were bound up in that.

'Why don't I just go in?' he thought. 'They're laughing. Drunk. Well, what if they are: why don't I get drunk, too?'

'Why don't you go in, dear master?' one of the women asked in a somewhat resonant voice that was not yet completely hoarse. She was young and even not bad-looking – the only one in the whole group.

'Not likely, pretty-face!' he replied, coming out of his stooping position and giving her a look.

She smiled: the compliment was thoroughly to her liking.

'You're rather pretty yourself,' she said.

'Look how skinny he is!' another woman observed in a bass voice. 'Have you just come out of hospital, or something?'

'You could almost believe they were generals' daughters if it weren't for those snub noses of theirs!' a muzhik who had just approached suddenly said, interrupting in a tipsy fashion; his *armyak* was hanging wide open, and his ugly horse-face bore a crafty grin. 'Cor, what a party!'

'In you go, since you've come!'

'I will, too! Yum-yum!'

And he fell down the steps, head over heels.

Raskolnikov began to move on.

'Oh, master, listen!' the girl called after him.

'What is it?'

She began to show signs of confusion.

'Well, you see, dear master, normally I'd be glad to spend some time with you, but right now you've got my conscience going so I don't know where to look. O charming chevalier, please give me six copecks for a drink!'

Raskolnikov took out what came into his hand: three five-copeck pieces.

'Oh, what a kind master!'

'What's your name?'

'You just ask for Duklida, sir.'

'Have you ever seen anything like it?' one of the women in the group observed suddenly, shaking her head at Duklida. 'Begging like that – I don't know what things are coming to. If it were me, I'd drop dead from sheer embarrassment!'

Raskolnikov looked with curiosity at the woman who had spoken. She was a pockmarked prostitute of about thirty, covered in bruises, with a swollen upper lip. She had delivered her condemnation in quiet, serious tones.

'Where was it,' thought Raskolnikov, as he walked onward, 'where was it I read about a man who's been sentenced to die,* saying or thinking, the hour before his death, that even if he had to live somewhere high up on a rock, and in such a tiny area that he could only just stand on it, with all around precipices, an ocean, endless murk, endless solitude and endless storms – and had to stand there, on those two feet of space, all his life, for a thousand years, eternity – that it would be better to live like that, than to die so very soon! If only he could live, live and live! Never mind what that life was like! As long as he could live! . . . What truth there is in that! Lord, what truth! Man is a villain. And whoever calls him a villain because of it is one himself!' he added a moment later.

He came out at another street. 'Ah – the "Crystal Palace"! This is the place Razumikhin was talking about earlier on. But why would I want to go in there just now? Oh yes: to catch up on my reading! . . . Zosimov said he'd seen something in the newspapers . . .'

'Do you keep newspapers?' he asked, going into the extremely spacious and well-kept inn premises which stretched for several rooms and were, moreover, rather empty. Two or three visitors were drinking tea, and in one distant room sat a group of what looked like four men drinking champagne. Raskolnikov thought one of them might be Zamyotov. It was, however, impossible to be sure from so far away.

'Oh well, if it is, it is,' he thought.

'Ordering vodka, sir?' the waiter asked.

'Some tea, please. And if you'll bring me some newspapers, the old ones, for five days back, I'll give you something for your own vodka.'

'Very well, sir. These are today's. And you'll order some vodka, too?'

The old newspapers appeared, together with the tea. Raskolnikov settled down and began to hunt through them: 'Izler* . . . Izler . . . Aztecs . . . Aztecs . . . Izler . . . Bartola . . . Massimo . . . Aztecs* . . . Izler . . . God, what revolting rubbish! Ah, here's the chronicle: woman falls down staircase . . . artisan dies, drunk, in fire . . . fire at Peski . . . fire at St Petersburg Side* . . . Izler . . . Izler . . . Izler . . . Izler . . . Massimo . . . Ah, here it is . . .'

At last he found what he had been looking for, and began to read. The lines jumped before his eyes, but he read the entire item of 'news' to the end and then began to hunt avidly through the subsequent issues for later additions. His hands trembled as they turned over the pages, in convulsive impatience. Suddenly someone sat down beside him, at the table. He took a quick glance: it was Zamyotov, the same Zamyotov, looking just as he had done before, with his rings and chains, the parting in his black, curly and pomaded hair, in his flashy waistcoat, his somewhat shabby frock-coat and his stale linen. He was in a good mood, or at any rate was smiling a very good-natured smile, which appeared to imply that this was so. His swarthy features were slightly flushed from the champagne he had drunk.

'I say, are you here?' he began, taken aback, and in a tone of voice that suggested a lifetime's acquaintance. 'Yet Razumikhin was telling me only yesterday that you were still unconscious. There's a strange thing! I mean, I was at your place . . .'

Raskolnikov had known he would come up to him. He set his newspapers aside and turned to face Zamyotov. There was an ironical smile on his lips, and in this smile there was a touch of some new element, a kind of irritable impatience.

'I know you were,' he replied. 'I heard you. You were looking for my sock . . . You know, Razumikhin's simply wild about you, he says you and he went to see Laviza Ivanovna – you know, the woman you were trying to get off with that time, the one you kept winking to "Lieutenant Gunpowder" about, but he didn't get it – remember?

Though how he could ever have been in the dark about it beats me . . . it was as plain as daylight . . . eh?'

'What a rowdy chap he is!'

'Who, "Gunpowder"?'

'No, your friend. Razumikhin . . .'

'You live a good life, don't you, Mr Zamyotov? Free entry to all the best establishments! Who was that filling you up with champagne just now?'

'Oh, we were just . . . having a drink or two . . . Do you call that filling up?'

'An honorarium! You never let an opportunity slip!' Raskolnikov began to laugh. 'It's all right, my chubby little man, it's all right!' he added, slapping Zamyotov on the shoulder. 'I don't mean it in a nasty way, "more like two friends having a playful scrap", as that decorator fellow of yours said after he'd been having a go at Mitka – you know, in the case about the old woman.'

'How do you know about that?'

'Perhaps I know more about it than you do.'

'I say, it strikes me there's something strange about you . . . I think you're still very ill. You should never have come out . . .'

'Something strange about me?'

'Yes. What are you doing, reading the newspapers?'

'That's right.'

'There's a lot about fires in them.'

'No, I haven't been reading about the fires.' Just then he gave Zamyotov a mysterious look; the mocking smile distorted his lips once more. 'No, not about the fires,' he went on, winking at Zamyotov. 'Come on, dear young man, own up: you're just dying to know what I've been reading about, aren't you?'

'No, I'm not; I just asked, that's all. What's wrong with that? Why do you keep . . .'

'Listen: you're a well-read, educated man, aren't you?'

'I did six years at the gymnasium,' Zamyotov replied with a certain amount of dignity.

'Six! A real little man of the world! With a parting, and rings – a wealthy individual! Goodness me, what a charming little fellow!' At this point Raskolnikov dissolved into nervous laughter, right in Zamyotov's face. Zamyotov started back, not so much offended as thoroughly astonished.

'I say, you really are behaving most strangely!' Zamyotov said again in a very serious tone of voice. 'If you ask me, you're still delirious.'

'Delirious? You're wrong there, my little man of the world! . . . So you think I'm strange, do you? Curious, are you? Eh?'

'Yes, I am.'

'Curious to know what I was reading about, what I was looking for? Goodness, how many back numbers I asked them to bring me! Looks suspicious, eh?'

'Well, tell me then.'

'All ears upstairs?'

'What do you mean – upstairs?'

'I'll tell you afterwards what stairs I have in mind, but right now, my dear, beloved little fellow, I'm going to make you a declaration . . . No, a "confession" . . . No, that's not right, either: "I shall make a deposition, and you shall take it down" – that's it! My deposition is as follows: I was reading, I'd got interested . . . was looking . . . searching . . .' Raskolnikov screwed up his eyes and waited. 'Searching – and so I dropped in here – to find out about the murder of the civil servant's widow – ' he articulated at last, almost in a whisper, bringing his face extremely close to Zamyotov's. Zamyotov was looking steadily at him, not moving a muscle and never once turning his face away. Later on, Zamyotov thought that the strangest thing of all had been the fact that their silence had lasted a whole minute, and that they had spent its entirety staring at each other.

'Well, so what if you have been reading about it?' he shouted suddenly, in bewilderment and impatience. 'What business is it of mine? What does it matter?'

'It's the same old woman,' Raskolnikov went on, still in a whisper and without batting an eyelid at Zamyotov's outburst, 'the same old woman you'd started to talk about in the bureau that time when I passed out, if you remember. Well, now do you understand?'

'What do you mean? What should I . . . understand?' Zamyotov managed to get out, almost in a state of panic.

For a single instant, Raskolnikov's impassive and serious face was transformed, and he suddenly dissolved again into the same nervous laughter as before, as though unable to control himself. And in a single flash he remembered with extreme clarity of sensation a certain moment, not long past, when he had stood behind the door with the axe, when the bolt had leapt up and down, when those men had been cursing and trying to break their way in, and he had suddenly felt like shouting to them, returning their abuse, sticking his tongue out at them, teasing them, laughing, laughing, laughing, laughing!

'You're either crazy, or . . .' Zamyotov said – and stopped, as though a thought had suddenly struck him, having flickered without warning through his brain.

'Or? What do you mean "or"? Well, explain yourself!'

'Never mind!' Zamyotov replied, angrily. 'It's all rubbish!'

They both fell silent. In the wake of his abrupt, paroxysmic explosion of laughter Raskolnikov grew suddenly reflective and sad. He leaned his elbows on the table and propped his head in his hand. One might have thought he had completely forgotten about Zamyotov. The silence lasted rather a long time.

'Why aren't you drinking your tea? It'll get cold,' Zamyotov said.

'Eh? What? Tea? . . . Yes, I suppose so . . .' Raskolnikov took a swallow from his glass, put a piece of bread in his mouth and suddenly, as he looked at Zamyotov, remembered everything and seemed to brighten up: at the same moment his features re-acquired their previous mocking expression. He continued to drink the tea.

'There's a lot of this crookery going on just now,' Zamyotov said. 'Not so long ago I read in the *Moscow Gazette* that they'd caught a whole gang of forgers. It was a regular business. They were forging lottery tickets.'

'Oh, that's history! I read about it a month ago,' Raskolnikov replied calmly. 'So you think they're crooks, do you?' he added with an ironic smile.

'What else?'

'Those men? Those men are just children – *blancs-becs*, not crooks! Fifty of them joined forces on that racket! Is it possible? Three would be too many, and each of them would have to be more sure of the others than he was of himself! And if just one of them got drunk and spilled the beans, the whole thing would go up in smoke! *Blancs-becs!* They hired unreliable people to cash the forged tickets at the banks: is that the kind of thing you'd entrust to the first person who walked along? All right, let's suppose it worked, even with *blancs-becs*, each man succeeds in cashing a million's worth – all right, what about afterwards? The whole of the rest of their lives? Each of them depending on the others for the whole of the rest of his life! A man would do better to hang himself! But these fellows didn't even know

208

how to go about cashing the things: one of them walked into a bank, got five thousand, and his hands started to tremble. He managed to count four, but took the fifth without counting, on trust, in a hurry just to get the loot into his pocket and make off as quickly as possible. Well, of course he aroused suspicion. And the whole thing went bang just because of one simpleton! Is it possible?'

'That his hands shook?' Zamyotov said, catching on to his train of thought. 'Oh yes, sir, it's possible. Indeed, I'm quite sure that it's possible. Sometimes they just can't go through with it.'

'A thing like that?'

'Well, I mean – would you be able to? I know I wouldn't! To endure such horrors just for the sake of a hundred-rouble pay-off? Take forged lottery tickets – where? – to a bank, where they know that kind of thing inside out? No, I'd lose my nerve. Wouldn't you?'

Raskolnikov suddenly had a terrible urge to stick out his tongue. At moments a feverish chill ran up and down his spine.

'I wouldn't do it like that,' he said from far away. 'This is how I'd go about it: I'd count the first thousand about three or four times from each end, examining every note, and then I'd move on to the second thousand; I'd start counting it, wait until I got to the middle and then take out a fifty-rouble note, say, hold it up to the light, turn it round, hold it up to the light again – what if it were a fake? "I've learned to be wary," I'd say. "My aunt lost twenty-five roubles the other day like that"; and I'd tell the whole story right there and then. And after I'd started counting the third thousand, "No," I'd say – "I'm sorry, I think I made a mistake when I was counting the seventh hundred of the second thousand." I'd be seized by doubt, give up counting the third thousand, and go back to counting the second again – and go on like that until I'd counted all five. And when I'd finished, I'd take a note from the fifth and a note from the second, and hold them up to the light, as before, and again with a dubious look, "change those two, please" – and by then the sweat would be streaming down the cashier's face so badly that he'd do anything to be free of me! When I was finally through, I'd walk off, open the door, but then say, "No, I'm sorry," go back to the counter again, ask some question or other, request an explanation, perhaps – that's the way I'd go about it!'

'Good Lord, those are terrible things you're saying!' Zamyotov remarked, laughing. 'But that's all just words, and in real life I bet you'd come to grief. Indeed, I'll go so far as to say that not only you or I, but even a hardened, desperate man wouldn't be able to rely on his powers. And one doesn't have to look far for an example – here's one: in our district an old woman's been murdered. I mean, this fellow must really have been a desperate sort of chap, he did it in broad daylight, ran every risk he could possibly have taken, got away with it by some miracle – but even *his* hands shook: he didn't manage to get his hands on the money, he couldn't go through with it; the facts of the case are quite plain . . .'

Raskolnikov almost took offence.

'Plain? Well, off you go right now and catch him, then!'

'What's the point? He'll be caught.'

'By whom? You? Who are you to catch him? You'll have your work cut out! I mean, what's the thing one always looks for first? It's whether a man's spending money or not, isn't it? One moment he doesn't have a bean, and the next he's suddenly splashing out everywhere – so it stands to reason it must be him! Any schoolboy could fool you that way, if he felt like it!'

'The fact remains that they all do it,' Zamyotov replied. 'A man will commit some cunning murder, risk his own life, and then go shooting off to a pot-house. It's the spending that catches them out. They're not all cunning chaps like you. You'd never go to a drinking-house, I imagine?'

Raskolnikov knit his brows and gave Zamyotov a fixed look.

'I suppose by this time you're getting into the swing of it, and want to know how I'd have acted in this case?' he asked with a disgruntled air.

'I would,' Zamyotov replied seriously and firmly. His words and appearance were becoming just a little too serious.

'Really?'

'Really.'

'Very well. This is how I'd have acted,' Raskolnikov began, once again suddenly bringing his face close to Zamyotov's, again looking steadily at him, and again speaking in a whisper, so that this time Zamyotov actually flinched. 'This is what I'd have done: I'd have taken the money and the valuables and once I'd got away I wouldn't have looked in anywhere but would have immediately gone to some remote place where there were just a lot of fences, and practically nobody about – a kitchen garden, or somewhere like that. In this yard I'd have picked out beforehand some heavy building block of a pood or more in weight, somewhere in a corner, by the fence, a block that had lain there since the time the house was built, perhaps; I'd have lifted up that block – underneath it there'd be bound to be a hole – and into the hole I'd have put all the valuables and money. Then I'd have replaced the block in the position it had lain in before, pressed it down with my foot, and gone away. And I wouldn't have taken the stuff for a year, not for two years, or even three – they could look as hard as they liked! They'd never find it!'

'You're crazy,' Zamyotov said, also practically in a whisper, and for some reason he suddenly moved away from Raskolnikov. Raskolnikov's eyes had begun to glitter; he had gone terribly pale; his upper lip was trembling and twitching. He leaned as close to Zamyotov as he could and began to move his lips without saying anything; he knew what he was doing, but could not control himself. The terrible words, like the door bolt that day, were leaping up and down on his lips: in a moment they would break loose; in a moment he would let them out, in a moment he would say them aloud!

'What if it were I who murdered Lizaveta and the old woman?' he said suddenly and – recovered his grip.

Zamyotov stared at him wildly for an instant and turned as pale as a sheet. His face was distorted by a smile.

'Is this really possible?' he said in a voice that could scarcely be heard.

Raskolnikov gave him a look of malicious hostility.

'Admit that you believed me! You did, didn't you?'

'Of course I didn't! And now I believe you even less!' Zamyotov said, hastily.

'Caught you at last! The man of the world's been stymied! You must have believed me before if now you "believe me even less".'

'I didn't, I tell you!' Zamyotov exclaimed, obviously embarrassed. 'Is that why you've been trying to frighten me – to lead me up to this?'

'So you don't believe me? Then what were you talking about in my absence, after I'd left the bureau that day? And why did "Lieutenant Gunpowder" question me after I'd recovered from my faint? Hey, you!' he shouted to the waiter, getting up and taking his cap. 'How much does mine come to?'

'Thirty copecks in all, sir,' the waiter replied, hurrying across.

'Here's twenty copecks extra for your vodka. Good heavens, what a lot of money!' he said, stretching out a trembling hand full of banknotes in Zamyotov's direction. 'Redbacks, bluebacks, twenty-five roubles! Where did they come from? And where did my new clothes come from? I mean, you know I hadn't a copeck! I expect you've already interrogated my landlady . . . Well, that's enough! *Assez causé!** Goodbye . . . Delighted to have met you! . . .'

He went out, trembling all over with a kind of wild hysteria, in which there was at the same time an element of unendurable pleasure – he was, however, morose and horribly tired. His features were distorted, as after a fit of some kind. Quickly, his exhaustion grew greater. His energies would suddenly be aroused and spring into life at the very first impulse, at the first stimulating sensation, and would ebb away just as quickly, as the sensation itself ebbed away.

Meanwhile, Zamyotov, now left alone, sat for a long time in the same spot, pondering things in his mind. Without intending to, Raskolnikov had upset all his calculations with regard to a certain point, and had definitively confirmed his opinion.

'That Ilya Petrovich is a numskull,' he decided at last.

No sooner had Raskolnikov opened the door on to the street than suddenly, right there on the forecourt, he collided with Razumikhin, who was on his way in. Neither observed the other, even a single step away, with the result that they almost banged their heads together. For a moment or two they gave each other a measuring look. Razumikhin was utterly dumbfounded, but suddenly anger, real anger, flashed threateningly in his eyes.

'So this is where you've got to!' he shouted at the top of his voice. 'You've absconded from your sickbed! And there was I looking for him under the sofa! We even went up to the attic! I nearly gave Nastasya a dusting because of you . . . And this is where he is! Rodya, my lad, what's the meaning of it? Tell me the truth – all of it! Confess, do you hear?'

'The meaning of it is that I'm heartily sick of the lot of you, and I want to be on my own,' Raskolnikov answered calmly.

'On your own? When you can't even walk yet, when your face is as white as a sheet and you're out of breath? You fool! . . . What have you been doing in the "Crystal Palace"? Confess this instant!'

'Leave me alone!' Raskolnikov said, and tried to walk past. This drove Razumikhin into frenzy; he seized Raskolnikov firmly by the shoulder.

'Leave you alone? You dare to tell me to leave you alone? Do you know what I'm going to do with you now? I'm going to pick you up, put you under my arm, take you home and place you under lock and key!'

'Listen, Razumikhin,' Raskolnikov began quietly and, it appeared, in a state of total calm. 'Are you really unable to see that I don't want your good deeds? And what is this desire of yours to do good deeds for people who . . . spit upon them? Who, if the truth be told, find them a serious burden on their endurance? I mean, why did you bother to track me down when I first fell ill? What if I'd been only too happy to die? After all, surely I've made it plain enough to you today that you've been tormenting me . . . that I'm fed up with you! You seem to have a positive desire to torment people! I do assure you that all this is seriously getting in the way of my recovery, because it's a constant irritation to me. I mean, Zosimov actually left earlier on today so as not to irritate me. So for God's sake leave me alone, too! In any case, what right do you have to keep me there by force? Surely you can't possibly fail to see that I'm speaking with all my wits about me now? Tell me, what, what can I do to stop you pestering me and doing good deeds for me? I'm willing to admit that I'm mean and ungrateful, only leave off, all of you, for God's sake, leave off, leave off, leave off!'

He had begun calmly, savouring the mass of venom he was about to unleash, but ended in a state of frenzy, gasping for breath, as he had done earlier, with Luzhin.

Razumikhin stood still, thought for a moment, and then released his hand.

'Then clear off and go to the devil,' he said quietly, and almost reflectively. 'Wait!' he roared suddenly, as Raskolnikov was about to move off. 'Listen to what I've got to say. I hereby declare to you that you're all, every last one of you, a crowd of windbags and show-offs! As soon as you come up against some pathetic little bit of suffering you fuss over it like a hen with an egg! And even then you steal from other authors. There's not a spark of independent life in you! You're made of spermacetic ointment, and you've got whey in your veins instead of blood! I wouldn't trust a single one of you! The first thing you do in every circumstance is to find out how *not* to behave like a human being! Wa-it!' he shouted with redoubled fury, noticing that Raskolnikov was once again preparing to move off. 'Hear me through!

You know, I'm having a housewarming party tonight, in fact, some of the guests may already have arrived, and I've left my uncle there – I just dashed round here just now – to let people in. So look, if you're not a fool, a vulgar fool, an arrant fool, not some translation from a foreign original . . . you see, Rodya, I admit you're a clever fellow, but you're a fool! – so look here, if you don't want to be a fool, you'd better come over to my place this evening and sit at my party table instead of wearing your boots out for nothing. Now that you're up and about you've no alternative! I'd wheel up a nice soft armchair for you, the landlords have one . . . A sip of tea, some company . . . No, I know – I'll put you on the couch – you'll be able to lie down, but still be in our midst . . . And Zosimov will be there. What do you say – will you come?'

'No.'

'R-r-rubbish!' Razumikhin exclaimed in impatience. 'What do you know about it? You can't answer for yourself. And you're totally unaware of it . . . I've spat and fought with people a thousand times exactly like that, but I've always gone running back to them again afterwards . . . You get ashamed – and go back to the person! So remember: Pochinkov's Tenements, third floor . . .'

'You know, Mr Razumikhin, I do believe you'd let a man beat you up just for the satisfaction of doing him a favour.'

'Who? Me? I'd put his nose out of joint at the mere suggestion! Pochinkov's Tenements, number forty-seven, the apartment of civil servant Babushkin . . .'

'I shan't come, Razumikhin!' Raskolnikov turned round and walked away.

'I bet you do!' Razumikhin shouted after him. 'Otherwise you . . . Otherwise I don't want to know you. Hey! Wait! Is Zamyotov in there?'

'Yes.'

'Did you meet him?'

'Yes, I did.'

'And did you speak to him?'

'Yes.'

'What about? Oh, to the devil with you, don't tell me, then. Pochinkov's, number forty-seven, Babushkin's place – remember, now!'

Raskolnikov walked along to Sadovaya Street, and then turned the corner. Meditatively, Razumikhin watched him go. At last, with a wave of his hand, he went inside the building, but stopped halfway up the stairs.

'The devil take it!' he thought, almost aloud. 'He talks rationally enough, but it's as if . . . Why, I'm a fool, too! Don't madmen talk rationally? This was what Zosimov said he was afraid of, if I'm not mistaken!' He tapped his head with his forefinger. 'I mean, what if . . . Oh, how could I have let him go off on his own like that? He may drown himself . . . Damn it, how stupid I was . . . This will never do!'

And back he went running in order to catch Raskolnikov up, but by now the scent had grown cold. He spat, and with rapid steps returned to the 'Crystal Palace' in order to ask Zamyotov some questions.

Raskolnikov had gone straight to —sky Bridge. He stood in the middle of it, by the railing, leaning on it with both elbows, and began to look far into the distance. After he had taken his leave of Razumikhin he had grown so weak that he had hardly been able to drag himself here. He felt like sitting or lying down somewhere, out in the street. As he leaned over the water, he gazed absent-mindedly at the last pink reflection of the sunset, at the row of buildings that loomed darkly in the thickening twilight, at one far-off window in an attic somewhere on the left bank, gleaming as though aflame from the sun's last ray which had struck it for a moment, at the darkening water of the Canal – and seemed to be staring at that water with attention. At last red circles began to spin in his eyes, the buildings began to move, passers-by, embankments, carriages – all began to revolve and dance in a circle. Suddenly he gave a shudder, possibly saved once more from fainting by a wild, outlandish apparition. He sensed that someone was standing beside him, to the right of him; he glanced round – and saw a woman, tall, with a kerchief on her head, her face oblong, yellow and haggard and her eyes reddish and sunken. She was looking straight at him, but was obviously aware of nothing and unable to tell if anyone was there. Suddenly she leaned her right elbow on the railing, raised her right leg and let it flop over the edge, then got her left leg across and threw herself into the Canal. The dirty water sagged, and swallowed up its victim in a trice, but a moment later the drowning woman floated up again, and was carried off slowly downstream, her head and legs in the water, and her back

215

out of it, with her skirt whipped up and ballooning on the surface like a pillow.

'She's drowned herself! She's drowned herself!' dozens of voices clamoured; people came running, both embankments were crawling with spectators, and all around Raskolnikov on the bridge people crowded together, pressing him and pushing him from behind.

'Oh for God's sake, that's our Afrosinyushka!' a woman's voice wailed somewhere close by. 'For God's sake, rescue her! Kind friends and fathers, pull her out of there!'

'A boat! A boat!' people shouted from the crowd.

But now a boat was no longer required: a policeman ran down the steps of one of the descents to the Canal, threw off his overcoat and boots, and hurled himself into the water. There was not much that needed to be done: the water had carried the drowning woman to a point just a couple of yards from the descent; with his right hand he seized her by her clothes, while with his left he succeeded in catching hold of a pole which his mate held out to him, and the woman was hauled out. They laid her on the granite slabs of the descent. She soon came to, raised herself, sat up, and began to sniff and sneeze, vacantly wiping her wet dress with her hands. She did not say anything.

'She's drunk herself crazy, friends, drunk herself crazy,' the same female voice wailed, from beside Afrosinyushka now. 'And the other day she tried to hang herself, too, we had to take her down from the rope. I went out to the corner shop, left my little girl to keep an eye on her – and look what a terrible thing happened! She's from round these parts, dearie, from round these parts, we live next door to her, the second building from the end, right here . . .'

The crowd dispersed, the policemen continued to hover around the woman who had tried to drown herself, someone shouted something about the bureau . . . Raskolnikov looked at everything with a strange sense of indifference and lack of involvement. He had begun to feel revolted. 'No, that's vile . . . the water . . . it's not worth it,' he muttered to himself. 'Nothing's going to happen,' he added. 'There's no point in waiting around. What was that about the bureau? . . . And why isn't Zamyotov at the bureau? It doesn't close until ten . . .' He turned his back to the railing and looked around him.

'Well, so what, then? Perhaps I will,' he said, resolutely, left the bridge and set off in the direction of the bureau. His heart felt empty and hollow. He did not want to think. Even his depression had gone, and he possessed not a trace of the energy he had felt earlier when, leaving his quarters, he had told himself he was going to 'bring it all to an end'. It had been replaced by a state of complete apathy.

'After all, this is a way out, too!' he thought, as he walked slowly and languidly along the embankment of the Canal. 'I *will* bring it all to an end, because I want to . . . But will it be a proper way out? Oh, it's all the same! There'll be a couple of feet to turn round in – ha! But what an end! Will it really be the end? Will I tell them, or won't I? Oh . . . the devil. I'm tired; I want to sit or lie down as soon as possible! The most embarrassing thing about it is that it's so stupid. Oh, I don't give a spit. God, what stupid things come into one's head . . .'

In order to reach the bureau he had to keep straight on and take the second turning to the left: it was hardly any distance at all. When he came to the first turning, however, he stopped, thought for a moment, then walked down the alley and made a detour by way of two other streets – perhaps without any particular purpose in view, but perhaps, also, in order to spin out the moment and gain some time. As he walked, he looked at the ground. Suddenly it was as if someone had whispered something in his ear. He lifted his head and saw he was standing outside *that* building, right by its front entrance. He had not been here since *that* evening, had not so much as passed it by.

An irresistible and inexplicable desire drew him onwards. He went into the building, walked right through the entrance-way, then entered the first door on the right and began to climb the familiar staircase up to the fourth floor. The steep, narrow stairs were very dark. He stopped at each landing and looked around with curiosity. The frame of the window on the first-floor landing had been completely removed. 'This wasn't like that then,' he thought. Here, too, was the apartment on the second floor where friends Nikolai and Mitya had been working: 'The door's shut, and it's been freshly painted, too; that means the place is up for rent.' Here was the third floor . . . and the fourth . . . 'Here!' He was gripped with bewilderment: the door of the apartment was wide open.

It was also being redecorated; there were workmen in it, and this seemed to make a particular impression on him. For some reason he had imagined that he would find everything exactly as he had left it that day, that even the dead bodies might still be lying in the same positions on the floor. But now he found: bare walls, no furniture. There was something strange about it. He walked over to a window and sat down on its ledge.

There were only two workmen, both young fellows, one with a senior look about him, and the other very decidedly his junior. They were covering the walls with new wallpaper which was white with lilac-coloured flowers, replacing the old yellow paper which was frayed and torn. For some reason Raskolnikov did not like this one little bit; he viewed the new wallpaper with hostility, as though he regretted their having changed everything in this way.

The workmen had obviously been taking their time over the job; now it was late, however, and they were hurrying to roll up their paper and be off home. To Raskolnikov's appearance they paid only the merest attention. They were talking together about something. Raskolnikov folded his arms and began to listen carefully.

'This one comes up to me this morning,' the older workman was telling the younger, 'the crack of dawn it was, and she was all dressed up to kill. "What are you an-orangeing-and-a-lemoning* with me like that for?" I said. "Oh, Tit Vasilyich," she said, "I want to be in your complete control from this day forth." How do you like that? And boy, was she dressed to kill: a *journal*, a proper *journal*.'

'What's a *journal*, uncle?' the young workman asked. He evidently looked up to his 'uncle' as a source of instruction.

'A *journal*, my lad, is a lot of pictures, coloured ones, which arrive by post at the tailors' establishments here in town from abroad every Saturday to show everyone how to dress, the male sex, that is, every bit as much as the female sex. It's drawings, see. The male sex is drawn mostly in waisted coats with gathers, but in the women's section there's tarts the likes of which you could never get enough of!'

'Here, they've got everything in this St Petersburg place!' the younger workman exclaimed enthusiastically. 'Apart from mum and dad, they've got the lot!'

'Apart from them, my lad, they have,' the older workman affirmed, in the tone of a mentor.

Raskolnikov got up and went through to the other room, which had contained the trunk, the bed and the chest of drawers; without its furniture he thought the room looked terribly small. The wallpaper was still unchanged; in one corner it clearly showed the spot where the icon-case had stood. Having cast a glance round, he returned to his window. The older workman peered at him sideways.

'What do you want, sir?' he asked, suddenly, turning towards him.

Instead of replying, Raskolnikov stood up, went out into the passage, took hold of the bell-pull and gave it a tug. It was the same bell, the same tinny sound! He tugged it again, then yet again, listening attentively, and remembering. The tormentingly fear-ridden, outrageous sensation he had had then was beginning to return to him with greater and greater vividness and clarity, with each ring he shuddered, and started to enjoy it more and more.

'Well, what do you want? Who are you?' the workman cried, coming out after him. Raskolnikov went back in through the doorway.

'I want to rent some lodgings,' he said. 'I'm taking a look round.'

'They don't rent lodgings at night; and anyway, you're supposed to come up with the yardkeeper.'

'The floor's been washed; is it going to be painted?' Raskolnikov went on. 'Has the blood all gone?'

'What blood?'

'Oh, an old woman and her sister were murdered here. There was a whole pool of blood in this room.'

'Here, what sort of a bloke are you?' the workman cried, with uneasiness in his voice.

'Me?'

'Yes.'

'Would you really like to know? . . . Then let's go down to the bureau, I'll tell you there.'

The workmen looked at him bewilderedly.

'It's time we were off, we're late. Come on, Alyosha, my lad. We've got to lock up,' the older workman said.

'All right, let's go,' Raskolnikov replied with indifference, going out ahead of them, and moving off slowly down the stairs. 'Hey, yardkeeper!' he shouted, as he was going out through the gate.

A few people were standing just outside the street entrance to the building, gaping at the passers-by: the two yardkeepers, a peasant woman, an artisan in a dressing-gown, and someone else. Raskolnikov walked straight up to them.

'What do you want?' one of the yardkeepers responded.

'Have you been to the bureau?'

'Yes, I've just come back from it. What's it to you?'

'Are they still at their desks?'

'Yes.'

'Is the assistant superintendent there, too?'

'He was for a while. What's it to you?'

Raskolnikov did not reply and stood beside him, thinking.

'He came to have a look at the apartment,' the older workman said, coming over.

'Which apartment?'

'The one where we're working. "Why have you washed the blood away?" he says. "There was a murder here," he says, "and I've come to rent the place." He started ringing the bell, too, just about pulled it off. "Let's go down to the bureau," he says, "I'll tell you all about it there." Pestering us, he was.'

The yardkeeper was viewing Raskolnikov with bewilderment, a frown on his face.

'And who might you be?' he shouted, threateningly.

'I'm Rodion Romanych Raskolnikov, ex-student, and I live in Schiel's Tenements,* in the alley just round from here, apartment no. 14. Ask the yardkeeper . . . he knows me.' Raskolnikov said all this in a lazy, reflective voice, without turning round, staring fixedly at the darkening street.

'Why did you go up to that apartment?'

'To take a look.'

'What's there to take a look at in it?'

'Why don't we just take him down to the bureau?' said the artisan, intervening suddenly, and then falling silent.

Raskolnikov cocked an eye at him over his shoulder, took a good look, and said, quietly and lazily as before:

'Very well, come on, then!'

'Yes, we ought to take him down there!' the artisan resumed, encouraged by this remark. 'What led him to talk about *that*? What's he got on his mind, eh?'

'Maybe he's drunk, or maybe he isn't – God only knows!' the workman muttered.

'What it's got to do with you, anyway?' the yardkeeper shouted again, growing angry in earnest now. 'Why have you come poking your nose in?'

'Are you scared of going to the bureau?' Raskolnikov said to him with a mocking smile.

220

'Who said anything about being scared? Why have you come bothering us?'

'Sly-boots!' the peasant woman shouted.

'Come on, what's the point in talking to him?' exclaimed the other yardkeeper, an enormous muzhik in an open caftan with a key stuck in his belt. 'Send him on his way! . . . A sly-boots, that's what he is . . . Send him on his way!'

And, seizing Raskolnikov by the shoulder, he hurled him into the street. Raskolnikov almost turned head over heels, but managed to keep his balance, straightened himself up, looked silently at all the spectators and then went on his way.

'That's a peculiar chap,' the workman commented.

'The whole country's peculiar these days, if you ask me,' the peasant woman said.

'I still say we ought to take him down to the bureau,' the artisan put in.

'It's better not to have anything to do with him,' the big yardkeeper said, firmly. 'He was a sly-boots, believe you me! Making a nuisance of himself with a purpose in view, he was; it's an old ploy – once you get mixed up with them you can never get away . . . I know his sort!'

'Well, shall I go there or shan't I?' Raskolnikov wondered, coming to a standstill in the midst of the roadway at the intersection and looking around him, as though he expected someone to supply the final word. But there was no response from any quarter; everything was dull and dead as the stones on which he trod, dead to him, and only to him . . . Suddenly, in the distance, some two hundred yards away from him at the end of the street, in the thickening darkness his eyes distinguished a crowd, and he heard talking, shouting . . . Amidst the crowd there was some carriage or other . . . A light was gleaming in the middle of the street. 'What's that?' Raskolnikov turned right and walked towards the crowd. It was as if he were clutching at straws, and he smiled ironically as this thought occurred to him, because he had now taken a firm decision regarding the bureau and knew for a certainty that it would all very soon be over.

VII

In the middle of the street stood a barouche, a grand and elegant one, harnessed to a pair of fiery grey horses; there was no one in it, and its coachman had climbed down from the box and was standing along-side; he was holding the horses by the bridle. All around jostled a throng of people, with policemen at the front. One of the policemen was holding a lighted lantern which he was using in order to illuminate something that was lying in the roadway, right underneath the wheels. Everyone was talking, shouting, sighing; the coachman seemed to be in a state of bewilderment, and every so often he would say:

'Oh, what a sin! Lord, what a terrible sin!'

Raskolnikov squeezed his way through as best he could, and at last saw the object of all this fuss and curiosity. On the ground lay a man who had just been run down by the horses, unconscious by the look of it, very poorly dressed, but in 'respectable' clothes, and covered in blood. Blood streamed from his face and head; his face was battered, torn and mutilated. He had clearly been run down in earnest.

'Sainted fathers!' the coachman was wailing. 'What could I have done? If I had been going fast, or if I hadn't shouted to him – but I was driving slow and even. Everybody saw it: I'm only human. A drunk man doesn't stop to light a candle – it's a well-known fact! . . . I saw him crossing the street, he was staggering about, nearly falling down . . . I shouted once, I shouted again and then a third time, and I reined the horses in; but he just fell straight under their hooves! I don't know whether he did it on purpose or whether he was just very drunk . . . These horses are young ones, easily frightened – they jerked, and he screamed – then they jerked even worse . . . that's what the trouble was.'

'That's right, that's the way it happened!' the voice of someone who had witnessed the accident called from the crowd.

'And he did shout, it's true – he shouted three times,' another voice responded.

'That's right, three times, we all heard him!' called a third.

The coachman was not, however, particularly downhearted or upset. It was plain that the carriage had a rich and important owner who was somewhere awaiting its arrival; the policemen were, of course, taking considerable pains to see that this did, in fact, take place. All that remained was for the man who had been run down to be taken to the police station, and from there to the hospital. No one knew his name.

Meanwhile Raskolnikov had managed to squeeze his way through, and he bent down even closer. Suddenly the lantern brightly illuminated the face of the unfortunate man; Raskolnikov recognized him.

'I know him, I know him!' he shouted, forcing his way right to the front. 'He's a retired civil servant, a titular councillor – his name's Marmeladov! He lives in this part of town, just along there, in Kosel's Tenements . . . Quick, send for a doctor, I'll pay, look!' He pulled the money out of his pocket and showed it to the policeman. He was in a state of violent excitement.

The policemen were pleased that someone had recognized the victim of the accident. Raskolnikov told them his own name, too, gave them his address, and with all his might, as though it were his very own father who lay there, set about persuading them to carry the unconscious Marmeladov up to his lodgings.

'He lives right here, just three buildings along,' he said, pleading with them. 'In Kosel's Tenements, the place that belongs to that German, the one with all the money . . . This man must be drunk, and was on his way home. I know him . . . He drinks . . . Along there he has a family – a wife and children, there's a daughter. We'll have to wait a long time before they cart him off to hospital, but there's bound to be a doctor in one of the apartment houses here! I'll pay, I'll pay! . . . At least he'll get some private attention; otherwise he'll die before he ever gets to the hospital . . .'

He even went to the length of discreetly slipping something into the policeman's hand; but the whole thing was without snags and above board, and in any case help was more readily available here. The injured man was lifted up and carried: helpers had come forward. Kosel's Tenements were situated some thirty yards away. Raskolnikov brought up the rear, carefully supporting the man's head and pointing out the way.

'In here, in here! We'll have to carry him up the stairs head first. Turn him round . . . that's right! I'll pay for everything, I'll make it worth your while,' he muttered.

As always whenever she had a spare moment, Katerina Ivanovna had lost no time in beginning to pace up and down her little room, from the window to the stove and back again, her arms firmly folded in front of her as she talked to herself and coughed. Recently she had begun to hold ever more frequent conversations with her elder daughter, the ten-year-old Polenka, who, although there was much that she did not as yet understand, was none the less well aware that her mother needed her, and for this reason always followed her with her large, intelligent eyes and did her utmost to appear all-comprehending. On this occasion Polya was undressing her little brother, who had been unwell all day, in order to put him to bed. As he waited while she removed his shirt, which was to be washed overnight, the boy sat on the chair in silence, his expression serious, direct and unmoving, his little legs extended forwards, pressed tight together, the heels of his stockinged feet held up to his audience, and the toes turned outwards. He was listening to what his mother and sister were saying, his lips blown out, his eyes opened wide, without moving, in exactly the way that all intelligent young boys sit while they are being undressed in order to go to bed. A little girl even younger and smaller than he, in utter rags, stood behind the screen, awaiting her turn. The door on to the staircase was open, in order to afford at least some relief from the waves of tobacco smoke that were escaping from the other rooms and which every now and again made the poor consumptive woman cough long and agonizingly. During this last week Katerina Ivanovna seemed to have grown even thinner, and the red spots on her cheeks burned even more vividly than before.

'You would never believe, you never would imagine, Polenka,' she was saying as she paced about the room, 'what a splendid, cheerful life we led in the house of my Papa, and how this drunken man has ruined me and will ruin you all! My Papa was a civil service colonel, and very nearly a governor; he only had one more step to climb up the ladder, and everyone used to come from miles around to see him and they'd say: "We all consider you our governor, Ivan Mikhail-ovich." When I . . . ca-huh! . . . when I . . . ca-huh, ca-huh, ca-huh . . . Oh, curse this existence!' she screamed, coughing up phlegm and clutching her chest. ' – When I . . . no, when Princess Bezzemelnaya saw me . . . at the Marshal's . . . last ball – she gave me her blessing when I married your father, Polya – she asked me at once: "Are you not the charming young lady who danced with the shawl at the Graduation Ball?" (That tear must be mended; you'd better get a needle and sew it up at once, the way I taught you, or tomorrow . . . ca-huh! . . . tomorrow . . . ca-huh, ca-huh, ca-huh! . . . it'll get even bigger!' she shouted, overstraining herself) . . . 'Then there was Prince Shchegolskoy, a Gentleman of the Royal Bedchamber, who had just arrived from St Petersburg . . . he danced the mazurka with me and declared his intention of coming to me the following day with a proposal of marriage; but I thanked him in flattering language and told him that my heart belonged to another, and had done so for a long time. That other was your father, Polya; Papa was horribly angry . . . Is the water ready? Right, hand me that shirt; and what about his socks? . . . Lida,' she said, turning to the little younger daughter, 'you'll have to sleep as you are tonight, without your chemise; yes, you'll manage . . . and lay your socks out beside it . . . I'll wash the whole lot together . . . What's keeping that drunken vagabond? He's worn his shirt out like some floorcloth, it's full of holes . . . I want to do the whole lot together, so as not to have this torture two nights running! Good God! Ca-huh-ca-huh, ca-huh, ca-huh! What's this?' she screamed, taking a glance at the crowd in the passage and at the men who were squeezing their way through with some sort of burden into her room. 'What's this? What are they carrying? For the love of God!'

'Where do you want him?' the policeman asked, taking a look round now that the blood-covered, senseless figure of Marmeladov had been hauled into the room.

'On the sofa! Put him right there on the sofa with his head pointing this way,' Raskolnikov said, showing him.

'He was run down in the street! Drunk!' someone shouted from the passage.

Katerina Ivanovna stood utterly pale, her breath coming with difficulty. The children were frightened. Little Lida gave a scream, rushed over to Polya, threw her arms round her and began to tremble all over.

Having found Marmeladov a place to lie, Raskolnikov rushed over to Katerina Ivanovna.

'For heaven's sake calm down, don't be so fright !' he said in a fast patter. 'He was crossing the street, a barouche ran him down, don't worry, he'll come round, I told them to bring him here . . . I came to see you, don't you remember? . . . He'll come round, I'll pay for everything!'

225

'He's got what he wanted!' Katerina Ivanovna screamed in despair, and rushed over to her husband.

Raskolnikov quickly perceived that this woman was not one of those who collapse in a faint on the slightest pretext. In a flash a pillow appeared beneath the head of the unfortunate man – something no one had though of until now; Katerina Ivanovna began to undress him, examine him and fuss over him without losing her nerve, as she had forgotten about herself, was biting her trembling lips and suppressing the screams that were ready to burst from her bosom.

Meanwhile, Raskolnikov had managed to persuade someone to go and get a doctor. It turned out that a doctor lived in the next building but one.

'I've sent someone to fetch a doctor,' he kept saying to Katerina Ivanovna again and again. 'Don't worry, I'll pay for everything! Have you some water? . . . And bring me a napkin or a towel or something, quickly; we don't yet know how badly hurt he is . . . He's been injured, but he's not dead, you may be assured of that . . . The doctor will give us his opinion . . .'

Katerina Ivanovna rushed over to the window; there, on a broken chair in a corner, stood a large earthenware basin containing the water for the nocturnal washing of her children's and husband's clothes. This nocturnal laundering was performed by Katerina Ivanovna herself with her own hands at least twice a week, and sometimes even more often, for they had reached the point where there were almost no relief items of linen left, and each member of the family possessed only one copy of anything; but Katerina Ivanovna could not abide uncleanliness, and, sooner than tolerate the presence of dirt in her home, preferred to submit herself to this exhausting labour, which was beyond her strength, at night when everyone was asleep, so that the wet things would have time to dry on the indoor clothes-line and so that when morning came she would be able to present her family with clean linen. She seized hold of the basin in order to bring it over as Raskolnikov had requested, but almost fell to the floor under the burden. By now, however, Raskolnikov had managed to find a towel; he soaked it in the water and with it began to wash Marmeladov's bloodied face. Katerina Ivanovna stood beside him, drawing her breath painfully and holding her hands to her chest. She was herself in need of medical attention.

Raskolnikov began to realize that he might have done the wrong thing in having persuaded the police to allow the injured man to be brought here. The policeman was also looking somewhat at a loss.

'Polya!' Katerina Ivanovna shouted. 'Run and get Sonya, quickly. If you don't find her in it doesn't matter, just tell them that her father's been run down by the horses and that she's to come here as soon . . . as she gets back. Quickly, Polya! Here, cover yourself with the shawl!'

'Run like billy-o!' the boy in the chair cried suddenly, and, having said this, immersed himself once more in his earlier silent, upright position, his eyes protruding, his heels stuck forward and his toes turned out.

Meanwhile the room had become so full of people that there was hardly room to move an elbow. The policemen had all gone, apart from one who remained for a time and tried to drive the audience that had come gathering in from the staircase back out down the stairs again. These spectators were, however, replaced by very nearly all the lodgers in Mrs Lippewechsel's apartment, who came pouring through from the inner rooms, at first merely jostling together in the doorway, but then trooping in their cohorts into the room itself. Katerina Ivanovna was in a frenzy.

'You might at least let him die in peace!' she shouted at the multitude. 'Come to watch the performance! With cigarettes in your mouths! Ca-huh, ca-huh, ca-huh! That's right, come in with your hats on, I don't mind! . . . Yes, there's one wearing his hat . . . Get out of here! At least show some respect for a dead man!'

She choked with coughing, but her remonstrances had had the desired effect. It was clear that the lodgers were even somewhat afraid of Katerina Ivanovna; one by one, they squeezed their way back to the door with that strange sense of inner satisfaction that may unfailingly be observed even in those closest to one another, in the event of some sudden misfortune affecting one of their number, and to which, without exception, not a single person is immune, no matter how sincere his or her feelings of compassion and concern may be.

Now, moreover, voices could be heard outside the door with talk of hospital and how they ought not to bother these people unnecessarily.

'A man oughtn't to die unnecessarily, you mean!' shouted Katerina Ivanovna, and she rushed to open the door in order to release upon them the full fury of her wrath; in the doorway, however, she collided with none other than Mrs Lippewechsel herself, who had only just been informed of the accident and had come running to establish order. She was an extremely silly and quarrelsome German woman.

'Ach, my God!' she cried, raising her hands in horror. 'Your husband has been trampled drunk by a horse. To the hospital with him! I am the landlady round here!'

'Amalia Lyudvigovna! I must ask you to mind your manners,' Katerina Ivanovna began haughtily (she always adopted a haughty tone when speaking to the landlady, in order to make her 'remember her place', and was unable even now to deny herself this satisfaction). 'Amalia Lyudvigovna . . .'

'I have told you once and for all that you must never dare to call me Amalia Lyudvigovna; my name is Amalia Ivanovna.'

'No it's not, it's Amalia Lyudvigovna, and since I'm not one of those base flatterers of yours, unlike Mr Lebezyatnikov, who is laughing outside the door at this very moment – ' (there was indeed the sound of laughter outside the door, and a cry of 'They're fighting!') ' – I shall go on calling you Amalia Lyudvigovna, though I truly cannot understand why you dislike that name. You can see for yourself what has happened to Semyon Zakharovich; he's dying. I must ask you now to bolt that door and not to let anyone in. At least let him die in peace! If you do not, I wish to make it clear that your behaviour will be reported tomorrow to the governor-general himself. The Prince knew me before I was married and has a very clear memory of Semyon Zakharovich, to whom on many occasions he was a benefactor. Everyone knows that Semyon Zakharovich had many friends and patrons whom he himself relinquished out of decent pride, aware of his unhappy weakness; but now (she pointed to Raskolnikov) we are being helped by a certain magnanimous young man who is possessed of means and connections, and whom Semyon Zakharovich knew as a boy, and I may assure you, Amalia Lyudvigovna . . .'

All this was delivered in an extremely fast patter that grew even faster as it continued; suddenly, however, Katerina Ivanovna's eloquence was abruptly cut short by her coughing. At that moment the dying man recovered consciousness and gave a groan, and she ran over to him. He opened his eyes and, still unable to recognize anyone or take in anything, began to peer at Raskolnikov, who was standing over him. The injured man was breathing heavily, deeply and at long intervals; blood was seeping from the corners of his mouth; a sweat had broken out on his forehead. Not recognizing Raskolnikov, he began to stare uneasily about him. Katerina Ivanovna was looking at him with a gaze that was sad but stern, and tears streamed from her eyes.

'Oh my God! The whole of his chest's been trampled in! Look at the blood, the blood!' she said in desperation. 'We must take off all his upper garments! Turn round a bit if you can, Semyon Zakharovich,' she shouted to him.

Marmeladov recognized her.

'A priest!' he said in a hoarse voice.

Katerina Ivanovna walked over to the window, leant her forehead against the windowframe and in despair exclaimed:

'Oh, curse this existence!'

'A priest!' the dying man said again, after a moment's silence.

'They've *go-one* for one!' Katerina Ivanovna shouted at him; in obedience to her cry, he fell silent. With a timid, melancholy gaze his eyes searched for her; again she came back to him and stood by the head of the sofa. He grew slightly calmer, but not for long. Soon his gaze came to rest on little Lida (his favourite among the children), who was trembling in a corner as though in a fit, staring at him fixedly with her astonished child's eyes.

'But . . . but . . .' he said, pointing at the child with concern. He was trying to say something.

'What is it now?' screamed Katerina Ivanovna.

'There's nothing on her feet! Nothing on her feet!' he muttered, indicating the little girl's bare feet with a wild look.

'Be *qui-et*!' Katerina Ivanovna cried irritably. 'You know very well why there's nothing on her feet!'

'Thank God, the doctor!' Raskolnikov exclaimed in relief.

The doctor came in, a punctilious little old man, a German, looking about him with an air of suspicion; he went over to the patient, took his pulse, carefully felt his head and with Katerina Ivanovna's help unbuttoned his utterly blood-soaked shirt, exposing his chest. The whole of the chest was mutilated, crushed and battered out of shape: several ribs on the right-hand side were broken. On the left-hand side, right on the place of the heart, there was a large, ominous, yellowish-black bruise – a savage kick-mark made by a hoof. The doctor frowned. The policeman told him that the patient had been caught in the wheel and dragged along, turning round with it for some thirty yards along the roadway.

'It's amazing he's come round at all,' the doctor whispered to Raskolnikov quietly.

'What do you think?' Raskolnikov asked.

'He's going to die any moment.'

'Is there really no hope?'

'Not the slightest! He's at his last gasp . . . What's more, he has very bad head injuries . . . Hm. If you like, I can let some blood . . . but . . . that won't do any good. In five or ten minutes he'll most certainly be dead.'

'Do it all the same! . . .'

'If you like . . . But I warn you, it will be quite useless.'

At that moment there was the sound of more footsteps, the crowd in the passage made way, and a priest, a little grey-haired old man, appeared on the threshold bearing the holy gifts. The policeman had gone to get him while they had all still been down on the street. The doctor at once ceded his place to him and they exchanged meaningful glances. Raskolnikov prevailed upon the doctor to wait just a little longer before going. The doctor shrugged his shoulders and remained.

Everyone drew away. The confession lasted only a very short time. It was doubtful whether the dying man took in much of what was said; he could only articulate jagged, unclear sounds. Katerina Ivanovna picked up little Lida, took the boy down from the chair and, moving away into the corner where the stove was, got down on her knees and made the children kneel in front of her. The little girl could do nothing but tremble; but the boy, poised on his bare little knees, kept raising his hand with a rhythmical motion, crossing himself at all four points of the cross and bowing down to the floor, knocking his forehead against it, something it was evident he particularly enjoyed doing. Katerina Ivanovna was biting her lips and holding back her tears; she was also praying, from time to time straightening the boy's shirt and managing to throw over the too-exposed shoulders of the little girl a triangular headscarf which she took from the chest of drawers while still continuing to kneel and pray. Meanwhile the door that led in from the inner rooms began to be opened once more by the inquisitive crowd. In the passage an ever denser throng of spectators, residents from the whole staircase, was gathering; none of them, however, stepped over the threshold. A single candle-end illumined the entire spectacle.

At that moment, in through the crowd from the passage rushed Polenka, who had run to get her sister. She came in, hardly able to draw her breath from having run so fast, took off the shawl, sent a searching gaze round in quest of her mother, went over to her and said: 'She's coming! I met her in the street!' Her mother pushed her down into a kneeling position, and stationed her next to her. Timidly and silently squeezing her way through, a girl emerged from the crowd, and strange was her sudden appearance in that room amidst poverty, rags, death and despair. She was also in rags; her clothes were of the cheapest, but tarted up in the manner of the streets, in accordance with tastes and conventions that have developed in a peculiar world of their own, with a gaudy and shameful purpose that is all too obvious. Sonya stopped out in the passage right on the threshold, but did not cross it, and peered in like one who is embarrassed, seemingly unaware of everything, oblivious to the fact that she was wearing her coloured silk dress, bought at fourth hand, and quite out of place here, with its ridiculous long train and vast, bulging crinoline that took up practically the whole doorway, her light-coloured boots, her parasol, superfluous at night, but which she had brought with her all the same, and her absurd round straw hat with its bright orange feather. From under the tilted hat there peeped a thin, pale and frightened little face with an open mouth and eyes that were motionless with horror. Sonya was small of stature, about eighteen years old, a thin but rather good-looking blonde, with wonderful blue eyes. She was staring fixedly at the bed, at the priest; she, too, was out of breath from having walked so fast. At last the whispering, some of the things being said by the people in the crowd, must have reached her attention, for she lowered her gaze, took a step over the threshold and stood in the room, though still only right by the doorway.

Confession and communion were over. Katerina Ivanovna again went over to her husband's bed. The priest withdrew and, as he left, began to say a few parting words of consolation to her.

'And what am I supposed to do with these?' she said, interrupting him sharply and irritably, pointing at her urchins.

'God is merciful; trust in the help of the Almighty,' the priest began.

'Oh, go away! Merciful He may be, but not to us He isn't!'

'It's a sin, a sin, to say such things, dear lady,' the priest said, shaking his head.

'And what about that – isn't that a sin?' Katerina Ivanovna shouted, pointing to the dying man.

'It may be that those who were the involuntary cause of it will agree to compensate you, if only in the matter of lost income . . .'

'Oh, you don't know what I'm talking about!' Katerina Ivanovna cried irritably, with a wave of her arm. 'Anyway, why would they compensate me? I mean, it was him – he was drunk, he walked under those horses himself! What income? He's never brought in any income, just a lot of trouble. He's a drunkard, you know, he's drunk everything we owned. He stole our things and took them to that drinking-house, used up their lives and my own in that place, he did. Thank God he's dying! We'll be a bit better off!'

'One must forgive at the hour of death; it's a sin to talk that way, dear lady, such sentiments are a grievous sin!'

Katerina Ivanovna had been bustling around the dying man, giving him water, wiping the sweat and blood from his head, straightening his pillows, and passing the odd comment to the priest now and then, turning to him each time as she did so, in the midst of her labours. Now, however, she suddenly rushed at him, almost in a frenzy:

'Oh, father! All that's just words, and nothing but words! Forgive? Look, if he hadn't been run over today he'd have come home drunk as usual, still wearing that one and only shirt of his, all worn to threads and in tatters; he'd have tumbled into bed and slept like a pig, and I'd have had to swill around in water until daybreak washing his rags and the children's, then hang them out to dry outside the window, and then as soon as daybreak came sit mending them – and there'd be my night gone! . . . So what point is there in talking about forgiveness? I've done enough forgiving already!'

A terrible, deep-seated cough brought her words to a halt. She spat into a handkerchief and demonstratively shoved it under the priest's eyes, with her other hand clutching her bosom in pain. The handkerchief was covered in blood . . .

The priest lowered his head and said nothing.

232

Marmeladov was in his final death agony; his eyes were fixed on the face of Katerina Ivanovna, who was now leaning over him again. There was still something he wanted to say to her; and indeed he began to speak, moving his tongue with difficulty and getting the words out unclearly. But Katerina Ivanovna, realizing that he was trying to beg her forgiveness, at once shouted at him in a commanding tone:

'Be *quiet*! I don't want to hear it! . . . I know what you're trying to say! . . .' And the injured man fell silent; at that same moment, however, his wandering gaze alighted on the doorway, and he saw Sonya.

Until now he had not noticed her: she was standing in the corner, in the shadow.

'Who's this? Who's this?' he suddenly articulated in a hoarse, gasping voice that was filled with consternation, motioning in horror with his eyes towards the doorway where his daughter stood, and making an effort to sit up.

'Lie down! Lie *down*!' Katerina Ivanovna began to shout.

But with a superhuman effort he managed to support himself on one arm. Wildly and fixedly he stared for a time at his daughter as though he did not know who she was. And indeed, this was the first time he had ever seen her dressed in clothes like these. Suddenly he recognized her – humiliated, in total despair, dressed up to the nines and covered in shame and embarrassment, meekly awaiting her turn to say farewell to her dying father. Infinite suffering showed itself in his features.

'Sonya! Daughter! Forgive me!' he cried, and made to reach out his hand to her, but, losing his support, came crashing down from the sofa, face to the floor; they rushed to lift him up, put him back, but he was already breathing his last. Sonya uttered a faint scream, ran over to him, embraced him and froze hard in that embrace. He died in her arms.

'Got what he wanted!' Katerina Ivanovna cried, at the sight of her husband's dead body. 'Well, what am I going to do now? Where am I going to get the money to bury him? And what about them, what am I going to feed them on tomorrow?'

Raskolnikov went up to Katerina Ivanovna.

'Katerina Ivanovna,' he said to her. 'Last week your deceased husband told me all about your life and its attendant circumstances.

Please let me assure you that he spoke of you with rapturous esteem. From the very evening on which I learned how devoted he was to you all, and what especial love and respect he nurtured towards you, Katerina Ivanovna, in spite of his unfortunate weakness – from that evening we became friends . . . Please permit me now . . . to effect . . . the repayment of my debt to my deceased friend. Look, here are . . . twenty roubles, I think – if they will be of any assistance to you, then . . . I . . . in short, I shall be back again – I shall most certainly be back . . . I may even be back tomorrow . . . Goodbye!'

And he quickly walked out of the room, hurriedly squeezing his way through the crowd onto the staircase; in the mêlée, however, he suddenly collided with Nikodim Fomich, who had heard about the accident and wished to take a personal hand in dealing with the situation. They had not seen each other since the time of the scene at the bureau, but Nikodim Fomich recognized him instantly.

'Ah, what are you doing here?' he inquired.

'He's dead,' Raskolnikov answered. 'The doctor was here, the priest has been, everything's in order. Please don't go bothering the destitute wife, she's got consumption as it is. Try to give her some courage, if you can . . . I mean, you're a good man, I know you are . . .' he added with an ironic smile, looking him straight in the eye.

'I say, you're fairly covered in blood, aren't you?' Nikodim Fomich commented, having discerned by the light of his lantern several fresh bloodstains on Raskolnikov's waistcoat.

'Yes, I am . . . I'm covered in blood all over!' Raskolnikov said with a peculiar look, then smiled, gave a nod of his head, and walked off down the staircase.

He made his descent slowly, not hurrying, in a state of total fever, and, without being aware of it, charged with a certain new and boundless sensation of full and powerful life that had suddenly swept in upon him. This sensation might be compared to that experienced by a man who has been sentenced to death and is suddenly and unexpectedly told he has been reprieved. Halfway down, he was overtaken by the priest, who was on his way home; Raskolnikov silently let him pass, exchanging a wordless bow with him. As he was treading the last few steps, however, he suddenly heard some hurried footsteps behind him. Someone was trying to catch him up. It was Polenka; she was running after him, calling: 'Listen! Listen!'

He turned round to face her. She ran down the last flight of stairs and stopped right in front of him, one step above. A dim light was filtering up from the courtyard. Raskolnikov could make out the thin but pleasant face of the little girl, who was smiling to him and looking at him in a lively, childish way. She had been sent to him with a message, something which she was evidently very pleased about.

'Listen – what's your name? . . . and also: where do you live?' she asked in a hurried little out-of-breath voice.

He put both his hands on her shoulders and looked at her with a kind of happiness. He took such pleasure in looking at her – he himself did not know why.

'Who sent you?'

'My sister Sonya,' the little girl replied, her smile even livelier now.

'I somehow knew it was your sister Sonya.'

'Mother sent me, too. When my sister Sonya started sending me, Mother came over, too, and said: "Run as fast as you can, Polya!"'

'Do you love your sister Sonya?'

'I love her more than anyone else!' Polenka said with a peculiar firmness, and her smile suddenly became more serious.

'And will you love me, too?'

In lieu of a reply, he saw the little girl's face with its pouting lips naïvely extended in order to give him a kiss. Suddenly her matchstick-thin arms seized him in the tightest of embraces, her head inclined towards his shoulder, and the little girl began quietly to weep, pressing her face harder and harder against him.

'I want my Papa!' she said a moment later, raising that face, now stained with tears which she wiped away with her hand. 'We've had such a lot of bad luck recently,' she added unexpectedly, with that peculiar air of solid strength children adopt with such intensity whenever they suddenly try to talk like 'grown-ups'.

'And did your papa love you?'

'Of us all, he loved Lidochka the best,' she went on very earnestly, without smiling, this time speaking exactly in the way grown-ups do. 'He loved her because she's little, and also because she's ill – he was always bringing her sweets. And as for us, he taught us to read, and he taught me grammar and holy Scripture,' she added with dignity. 'And Mama never said anything, but we knew she liked that, and Papa knew it too, and Mama wants to teach me French, because it's time I was getting some education.'

'And do you know your prayers?'

'Oh, goodness – of course we do! We've known them for ages; I say my prayers to myself, because I'm big now, but Kolya and Lidochka say theirs out loud with Mama; first they recite the "Mother of God", and then they say another prayer that goes, "O Lord, forgive and bless our sister Sonya," and then another one that goes, "O Lord, forgive and bless our other Papa," because our old Papa's dead now, and this is our other one, you see, but we say a prayer for our old one, too.'

'Polechka: my name's Rodion; please say a prayer for me, too, sometime: "and thy servant Rodion" – that'll do.'

'I'll pray for you all the rest of my life,' the little girl said passionately, and again she suddenly laughed, rushed to him and embraced him tightly.

Raskolnikov told her his name, gave her his address and promised to come and see them again the next day without fail. The little girl went back upstairs completely enraptured by him. It was already getting on for eleven by the time he emerged on to the street. Five minutes later he was standing on the bridge at the very spot where the woman had thrown herself over the day before.

'That's enough!' he said, solemnly and decisively. 'Begone, mirages, begone, affected terrors, begone, apparitions! . . . There's a life to be lived! I was alive just now, after all, wasn't I? My life didn't die along with the old woman! May she attain the heavenly kingdom – enough, old lady, it's time you retired! Now is the kingdom of reason and light, and . . . freedom and strength . . . and now we shall see! Now we shall measure swords!' he added, self-conceitedly, as though addressing some dark power and challenging it. 'And there was I consenting to live in one *arshin* of space!

'. . . I'm very weak at the moment, but . . . I think my illness has finally passed. I knew it would when I left my apartment earlier today. Come of think of it: Pochinkov's Tenements – that's just a couple of steps from here. Oh, I must go to Razumikhin's place, I'd have to go there even if it weren't so close . . . let him win his wager! . . . even let him make fun of me if he wants to – it doesn't matter, let him! . . . Strength, strength is what I need: one can't get anything without strength; and strength has to be acquired by means of strength – that's what they don't understand,' he added with pride and self-assurance, and continued his way across to the other side of the bridge, hardly able to shift his legs. His pride and self-assurance were increasing with each moment that passed; from one moment to the next he was not the same person. But what had happened that was so special, that had caused this transformation in him? He himself did not know; like a man clutching at a straw, he had suddenly conceived the notion that for him, too, 'life was possible', that there was 'still a life to be lived', that his life 'hadn't died along with the old woman'. This was, perhaps, a somewhat hasty inference to draw, but he spent no time thinking about it.

'I asked her to say a prayer for "thy servant Rodion", didn't I?' – the thought flashed suddenly through his head. 'Oh well, that was . . . just in case!' he added, and immediately laughed at his childish behaviour. He was in a most marvellous frame of mind.

He did not have much difficulty in finding Razumikhin; the new tenant was already familiar at the Pochinkov building, and the yardkeeper was able to show him the way at once. Even halfway up the staircase one could hear the noise and animated conversation of a large gathering. The door of the apartment was wide open; shouting and arguments could be heard. Razumikhin's room was quite a large one, and some fifteen people were gathered in it. Raskolnikov stopped in the entrance hall. There, behind a partition, two of the landlord's serving maids were fussing over two large samovars, and over bottles and plates and dishes holding pies and *zakuski*, all of which had been brought up from the landlord's kitchen. Raskolnikov sent one of them in to tell Razumikhin he was there. Razumikhin came running in delight. At first glance one could tell he had had rather a lot to drink, and although Razumikhin almost never got drunk, on this occasion his condition was somewhat noticeable.

'Listen,' Raskolnikov said hurriedly. 'I just came to tell you that you've won your wager and that it really is true that no one can tell what may happen to him. I can't come in and join you: I'm so weak that I'd just fall down. So, greetings and farewell! But come and see me tomorrow . . .'

'Do you know what? I'm going to take you home! I mean, if you yourself are complaining of being weak, then . . .'

'But what about your guests? I say, who's that curly-haired chap who was looking this way just now?'

'Him? God only knows! He must be some friend of my uncle's, or perhaps he just walked in . . . I'll leave Uncle with them; he's a most valuable fellow; it's a pity I can't introduce you to him now. But to hell with them all! They're not interested in me just now, and I need some fresh air – so you've come at the right time, brother; to be quite honest, another two minutes in there and I'd have started a fight with someone! They're talking such a load of rubbish . . . You can't imagine the crazy things people will say! Though actually, perhaps you can. Don't we say a lot of silly things ourselves? Well, let them talk nonsense: perhaps then they'll talk sense later . . . Look, sit here for a minute while I go and get Zosimov.'

Zosimov pounced on Raskolnikov with something approaching greed; one could observe in him a peculiar kind of inquisitiveness; soon his face brightened up.

'You must go to bed at once and sleep,' he pronounced, having examined the patient as well as he could under the circumstances, 'and take a certain little something for the night. Will you take one? I prepared it earlier on . . . it's a type of powder.'

'I'll take two if you like,' Raskolnikov answered.

The powder was taken there and then.

'It's a very good idea for you to take him home,' Zosimov commented to Razumikhin. 'We'll see how he is tomorrow, but today at any rate he doesn't seem too bad at all: a remarkable change from earlier on. One lives and learns . . .'

'Do you know what Zosimov whispered to me just now as we were on our way out?' Razumikhin let drop as soon as they were out in the street. 'I may as well tell you it all straight, because they're such idiots. Zosimov said I was to talk to you a lot on the way and get you to talk a lot, too, and then to tell him what you'd said, because he's got the idea . . . that you're . . . insane, or something like it. Can you imagine? For one thing, you're three times cleverer than he is, for another, if you're not insane you shouldn't give a damn that he's got such rubbish in his head, and for yet another, that lump of brawn, who's a surgeon by training, has now got a craze about mental illness, and what convinced him in your case was the conversation you had with Zamyotov earlier on today.'

'Has Zamyotov told you everything?'

'Yes, and it's just as well he did, too. I've got all the ins and outs of it now, and so has Zamyotov . . . Well, you see, Rodya, to put it bluntly . . . the fact is . . . I'm a bit drunk now . . . But it doesn't matter . . . the fact is that this idea . . . you know what I'm talking about? . . . really has popped up in their brains . . . do you know what I mean? That's to say, they didn't dare to say it out loud, because it's the most absurd rubbish, especially since the arrest of that housepainter, the whole thing just burst and vanished forever. Oh, why are they such idiots? Actually, at that point I gave Zamyotov a bit of a dusting – that's between ourselves, brother; please don't give the slightest hint that you know anything about it; I've noticed that he's a bit sensitive about things like that; it happened at Laviza's place – but today, today all has become clear. It's all that Ilya Petrovich fellow's fault! He took advantage of your fainting-fit at the bureau, and he himself was ashamed afterwards; I mean, I know he was . . .'

Raskolnikov listened avidly. Razumikhin was drunkenly blabbing.

'I passed out that time because it was so stuffy, and there was a smell of oil-paint,' Raskolnikov said.

'There's yet another explaining factor! And it wasn't just the paint, either: that fever of yours had been coming on for a whole month; Zasimov testifies to it! And as for that over-zealous greenhorn, he's really had the wind taken out of his sails, you simply can't imagine! "I'm not worth that man's little finger!" he says. Yours, he means. He's sometimes capable of having good feelings, brother. But the lesson, the lesson he got today in the "Crystal Palace", that beat everything! I mean, you really frightened the daylights out of him at first, nearly gave the poor chap a fit! You actually made him half believe all that outrageous nonsense and then suddenly – stuck your tongue out at him as if to say: "There, what do you make of that?" Perfect! Now he's shattered, destroyed! Why, you're a master, I do declare – that's the way to handle them. Oh, how I wish I'd been there! He was dying to meet you just now. Porfiry wants to get to know you, too . . .'

'Ah . . . him too, now . . . And why have they decided I'm insane?'

'Oh, not really insane. I think I've been saying too many things to you, brother . . . You see, what struck him was that you only seemed to be interested in that one point . . . Now it's clear why you found it interesting; knowing all the circumstances . . . and how that irritated you then and got mixed up with your illness . . . I'm a bit drunk, brother – it's just that, heaven only knows why, he's got some idea of his own about it . . . I tell you, he's got a craze about mental illness. But if I were you, I wouldn't give a damn . . .'

For some thirty seconds neither of them said anything.

'Listen, Razumikhin,' Raskolnikov said. 'I want to tell you this straight: I've just been at the home of a man who's died, he was a civil servant . . . I gave all my money away there . . . and, what's more, I've just been kissed by a certain creature, who even if I'd killed someone would still have . . . and, to be brief, when I was there I saw yet another creature . . . with a bright orange feather . . . but actually, I'm talking a lot of nonsense; I'm very weak, please help me to stay upright . . . I mean, we'll soon be at the staircase . . .'

'What's the matter with you? What is it?' Razumikhin asked with alarm.

'My head's going round a bit, but that's not what it is. It's that I feel so sad, so sad! Like a woman, really . . . Look, what's that? Look! Look!'

'What on earth?'

'Don't you see? There's a light in my room! Look, through the gap in the door . . .'

Now they stood facing the last flight of stairs, beside the landlady's door, and it really was true: from down there it was plainly evident that there was a light in Raskolnikov's room.

'That's strange! Perhaps it's Nastasya,' Razumikhin observed.

'She never comes up to my room at this time of night, and anyway, she'll have gone to bed long ago, but . . . it's all the same to me! Goodbye!'

'Don't be silly, we're going in there together. I'm seeing you home, remember?'

'I know we're going in together, but I want to say goodbye to you out here. Well, give me your hand. Goodbye!'

'What's the matter with you, Rodya?'

'Nothing; come on up, then; you can be a witness . . .'

They began to climb the flight of stairs, and for a moment Razumikhin had a fleeting suspicion that Zosimov might be right. 'Damn! I've gone and upset him with my chatter!' he muttered to himself. Suddenly, as they approached the door, they heard voices from inside the room.

'What on earth's going on in there?' Razumikhin exclaimed.

Raskolnikov got to the door first and opened it wide. He stood on the threshold, transfixed.

His mother and sister were sitting on his sofa, where they had been awaiting him for the past hour and a half. Why was it that they were the very last people he had expected to meet, the very last people who had been on his mind, in spite of the fact that even that day he had had repeated confirmation of the news that they had left home, were on their way, would arrive at any time now? All during that hour and a half they had vied with each other in interrogating Nastasya, who even now was standing in front of them, having by this time managed to tell them the whole involved story. They had been out of their minds with fear on learning that he had 'run away today', not yet recovered from his illness and, as was evident from the story, still in delirium! 'Oh God, what's wrong with him?' Both had wept, and both had endured the torments of the cross during those one and a half hours of waiting.

Raskolnikov's appearance was greeted by joyful, ecstatic cries. Both women rushed towards him. But he stood there like a corpse; a sudden and intolerable realization had struck him like a thunderbolt. His arms would not even leave his sides in order to embrace them: they could not. His mother and sister were hugging him, kissing him, laughing, crying . . . He took one step, staggered, and collapsed on the floor in a dead faint.

Consternation ensued, cries of horror, moans . . . Razumikhin, who was standing in the doorway, came bounding into the room, seized Raskolnikov in his powerful arms, and in a flash the sick man found himself on the sofa.

'It's nothing, nothing!' Razumikhin cried to Raskolnikov's mother and sister. 'He's fainted, that's all, it's not serious! The doctor's just said he's much better, that he's completely recovered! Bring some water! Look, he's coming round already, he's all right again now . . . !'

And, grabbing Dunya's arm so hard that he very nearly wrenched it off, he forced her down in order to make her see that Raskolnikov was 'all right again now' . . . Both mother and sister gazed at Razumikhin as at some emanation of Providence, with gratitude and tender emotion; they had already heard from Nastasya what had been done for their Rodya, during his illness, by this 'prompt young man' – the expression that had been used about him that very evening in the course of her intimate conversation with Dunya by Pulkheria Aleksandrovna Raskolnikova herself.

PART THREE

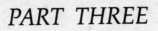

PART THREE

Raskolnikov lifted himself on one elbow, and sat up on the sofa.

He made a weak gesture to Razumikhin in order to bring to a stop the veritable deluge of incoherent and impassioned consolation that was being directed upon his mother and sister, took them both by the hand and spent a couple of minutes studying them closely, looking now from the one to the other. His mother was alarmed by his gaze. In that gaze there was visible an emotion that held the intensity of suffering, but at the same time there was something fixed and even reckless about it. Pulkheria Aleksandrovna began to weep.

Avdotya Romanovna was pale; her hand trembled in that of her brother.

'Go home . . . with him,' he said in an unsteady voice, pointing to Razumikhin. 'Tomorrow . . . let's leave it all till tomorrow . . . Have you been in town long?'

'Since this evening, Rodya,' Pulkheria Aleksandrovna replied. 'The train was terribly late. But Rodya, I absolutely refuse to leave you like this. I'm going to spend the night here beside you . . .'

'Stop harassing me!' he said, making an irritable gesture with his hand.

'I'll stay with him!' Razumikhin exclaimed. 'I shan't turn my back on him for a second, and to hell with all those guests of mine, let them climb up and down the walls if they want to! My uncle's in charge of them now.'

'Oh, how, how can I ever thank you!' Pulkheria Aleksandrovna began, pressing Razumikhin's hands again, but Raskolnikov cut her short once more:

'I can't cope with this, I really can't!' he said irritably. 'Stop harassing me! That's enough, now, go away . . . I can't cope with it!'

'Come on, mother, let's at least get out of the room for a minute,' Dunya whispered in alarm. 'We're having a bad effect on him, anyone can see that.'

'What's the matter, can't I look at him? It's three years since I've seen him, you know!' Pulkheria Aleksandrovna wept.

'Wait!' he cried, stopping them again. 'You keep interrupting me and my thoughts are getting muddled . . . Have you met up with Luzhin?'

'No, Rodya, but he already knows we've arrived. We've heard that Pyotr Petrovich was so kind as to come and see you today,' Pulkheria Aleksandrovna added with a certain timidity.

'Yes . . . he was so kind as to do that . . . Dunya, I told Luzhin earlier on today that I'd kick him downstairs, and I told him to go to the devil . . .'

'Rodya, what's got into you? I suppose you . . . You don't mean to say that . . .' Pulkheria Aleksandrovna began in alarm, but stopped, looking at Dunya.

Avdotya Romanovna was staring fixedly at her brother, waiting for him to go on. Both women had already been forewarned about the quarrel by Nastasya, to the extent that she had been able to comprehend and describe it, and they had worn themselves out with worry, bewilderment and foreboding.

'Dunya,' Raskolnikov went on with an effort. 'I don't want you to go ahead with this marriage, and so first thing tomorrow you must tell Luzhin that you've refused his offer, and that he must never come near us again!'

'Oh my God!' Pulkheria Aleksandrovna exclaimed.

'Think what you're saying, brother!' Avdotya Romanovna began, hot-temperedly, but at once restrained herself. 'But I suppose you're in no state to think about it now, you're too tired,' she said, meekly.

'Because I'm delirious? No . . . You're marrying Luzhin *for my sake*. And I won't accept your sacrifice. That's why you must write a letter that will reach him tomorrow . . . refusing his offer . . . You must show it to me in the morning, and then that will be the end of the matter!'

'I can't do that!' the offended girl exclaimed. 'By what right . . .'

'Dunechka, you're too worked up, stop it now, tomorrow . . . Can't you see? . . .' her mother said in a frightened tone of voice, rushing to her side. 'Oh, we'd better go away!'

'He's raving!' cried Razumikhin, who was still feeling the effects of the drink he had consumed. 'He must be, otherwise he'd never dare! All this nonsense will have popped out of his head by tomorrow . . . But he really did throw that fellow out earlier today. It really did happen that way. Well, and the fellow got angry . . . Started making speeches here, showing off his knowledge, and then went away with his tail between his legs . . .'

'So it's true, then?' Pulkheria Aleksandrovna exclaimed.

'Until tomorrow, brother,' Dunya said with compassion. 'Come on, mother . . . Goodbye, Rodya!'

'Look here, sister,' he said as they went out, gathering the last of his energies. 'I'm not delirious; this marriage you're planning is a vile business. I may be a villain, but you mustn't . . . some jumped-up nobody . . . and although I'm a villain, I refuse to accept any sister who does such a thing as a sister of mine! It's either Luzhin or me! Now go . . .'

'Hey, you're out of your mind! Despot!' bawled Razumikhin, but Raskolnikov made no reply, nor, in all likelihood, would he have been able to. He lay down on the sofa and turned to the wall in complete exhaustion. Avdotya Romanovna gave Razumikhin an inquisitive look; her black eyes flashed: Razumikhin actually shuddered beneath their gaze. Pulkheria Aleksandrovna stood as though stricken.

'I cannot possibly go!' she whispered to Razumikhin, practically in despair. 'I shall find somewhere to stay here . . . please take Dunya home.'

'And you'll ruin everything!' Razumikhin said, also in a whisper, beside himself. 'Let's at least go out to the staircase. Nastasya, bring us some light! I swear to you,' he went on in a semi-whisper, out on the staircase now, 'that earlier on he very nearly gave the doctor and me a thrashing! Do you understand? The doctor himself! And the doctor let him have his own way, so as not to irritate him, and left; I stayed downstairs on guard, meanwhile, but he put his clothes on and sneaked out. He'll do it again if you get him all worked up like that, and it'll be at night this time, and he may go and do something silly to himself . . .'

'Oh, what are you saying!'

'And in any case it's quite out of the question for Avdotya Romanovna to be left alone in those rooms without you! Just think where it is you're staying! I mean, surely that villain Pyotr Petrovich could have found you some better accommodation . . . But you know, I'm a bit drunk and that's why I'm . . . shouting; don't pay any . . .'

'Oh, but I shall go and see the landlady here,' Pulkheria Aleksandrovna insisted. 'I shall implore her to give Dunya and myself a room for the night. I can't leave him like this, I can't!'

All this was said on the staircase, on the landing right outside the landlady's door. Nastasya was shining a lantern on them from the bottom step. Razumikhin was in a state of excitement unusual even for him. Half an hour earlier, escorting Raskolnikov home, he might have been somewhat too talkative – something he himself admitted – but completely bright and cheerful and almost fresh, in spite of the terrible quantity of vodka he had drunk that evening. Now, however, his condition resembled some trancelike state, and at the same time it was as if all the vodka he had drunk, instantly and with redoubled strength, had rushed back up to his head. He stood with both ladies, holding them both by the hands, talking them round and presenting his arguments with astonishing frankness; doubtless for the sake of added persuasion, with practically each word he uttered, hard as hard, as in a vice, he squeezed their hands until they hurt, appearing to devour Avdotya Romanovna with his eyes as he did so, without the slightest inhibition. Because of the pain he was causing them they would from time to time pull their hands out of his enormous, bony paw, but not only did he fail to observe what was going on – he drew them even more tightly towards him. If just then, as a favour, they had requested him to throw himself down the stairs head first, he would have done it instantly, without a moment's hesitation or reflection. Pulkheria Aleksandrovna felt that the young man was very eccentric and was squeezing her hand far too hard; because of the state of utter anxiety she was in concerning her Rodya, however, she none the less tended to view him as having been sent by Providence, and tried not to notice all these eccentric details. But, in spite of sharing this anxiety, Avdotya Romanovna, though by nature not easily frightened, encountered the wildfire-glittering stares of her brother's friend with astonishment and even alarm, and it was only the limitless confidence inspired by Nastasya's stories about this strange man that held her back from the temptation of running away from him and hauling her mother off with her. She had also, perhaps, realized that it was now impossible for them to run away from him. For all that, after some ten minutes had elapsed she grew considerably calmer: Razumikhin had a way of saying all he had to say on any particular subject in a single flash, no matter what his frame of mind, so that it was very easy for people to discover whom they were dealing with.

'It's no good your going to see the landlady – it's the most terrible, nonsensical idea!' he exclaimed, trying to make Pulkheria Aleksandrovna see reason. 'Even though you are his mother, if you stay you'll drive him into a frenzy, and then the devil knows what may happen! Look here, this is what I'll do: Nastasya will sit with him now, and I'll take you both back to your lodgings, because you simply can't go out in the streets alone; here in St Petersburg on that score we . . . Oh, to hell with it! . . . Then, when I've seen you safely home, I'll return here at the double and a quarter of an hour later, so cross my heart, I'll bring you a report on how he is, on whether he's asleep or not, and all the rest of it. Then – no, listen! – then from your place I'll set off like a flash to my own quarters – I've guests there, they're all drunk – I'll go in and get Zosimov – he's the doctor who's looking after him, he's at my place now, he's not drunk; *he'll* not be drunk, he's never drunk! I'll haul him off to see Rodya and then come back to you immediately, that way you'll get two reports on him – and this one will be from the doctor, you understand, from the doctor himself; that's a bit different from getting one from me! If he's in a bad way, I swear to you I'll bring you here myself, but if he's all right you can go to bed. I'll spend the night out here in the passage, he won't know I'm there, and I'll tell Zosimov to spend the night in the landlady's apartment, so he'll be near at hand. Think about it: who does he need more just now – yourselves or the doctor? The doctor, of course – the doctor's of far more use to him. Well, so off you go home! But it's no good your going to see the landlady; I can get somewhere with her, but you couldn't – she won't let you stay there, because . . . oh, because she's an idiot! If you really must know, she'd be jealous of Avdotya Romanovna, and of my knowing you, too . . . She's a most, most peculiar character! But I'm an idiot, too . . . But to hell with it! Come on! Do you trust me? Well, do you, or don't you?'

'Come on, mother,' said Avdotya Romanovna. 'I expect he'll do as he says. He's already revived my brother, and if it's true that the doctor will agree to spend the night here, what could be better?'

'There! You . . . you . . . you understand me, because you're an – angel!' Razumikhin exclaimed in ecstasy. 'Let us be on our way! Nastasya! Go up there this instant and sit there with him, take your lantern; I'll be back in quarter of an hour . . .'

Even though Pulkheria Aleksandrovna was not really quite convinced, she offered no further resistance. Razumikhin took them both by the arm and drew them down the stairs. But he, too, made her uneasy: 'even though he's prompt and kind, is he really in a condition to carry out what he's promising to do? I mean, he's in a certain state! . . .'

'Ah, I've got it: you think I'm in a certain state!' Razumikhin said, intercepting her thoughts, having guessed them as he loped along the pavement with the most enormous strides, so that the ladies were scarcely able to keep up with him – something he failed, however, to notice. 'Nonsense! That's to say . . . I'm as drunk as a village oaf, but not that way; I'm drunk, but not from drinking alcohol. When I first caught sight of you, everything rushed to my head . . . But to hell with me! Don't pay any attention: I'm talking nonsense; I'm unworthy of you . . . I'm in the highest degree unworthy! . . . And as soon as I've taken you home, I'm going to go straight down to the Canal and empty two pails of water over my head, and be done with it . . . If only you knew how I love you both! . . . Don't laugh, and don't be angry . . . You can be angry with anyone else, but not with me! I'm his friend, so that means I'm your friend, too. I so much want . . . I had a premonition of this . . . last year, there was a moment like this . . . But it wasn't really a premonition at all, because the two of you have quite simply fallen from heaven. Oh, I probably shan't be able to sleep all night . . . Old Zosimov was afraid earlier on that he might go mad . . . That's why he mustn't be excited . . .'

'What are you telling me?' Raskolnikov's mother exclaimed.

'Did the doctor really say that?' asked Avdotya Romanovna, in fear.

'Yes, he did. But he's wrong, quite wrong. He gave him some medicine, a powder, I saw it, and then you arrived. Damn! . . . You'd have done better to arrive tomorrow! It's just as well we left. But in an hour's time Zosimov himself will provide you with a report on him. *He's* never drunk! And I won't be drunk by then, either . . . Why did I ever go and get myself so smashed? Oh, it was because I was led into an argument by those accursed fellows! I mean, I swore an oath that I wouldn't get involved in any arguments . . . ! Such nonsense they talk! I very nearly gave them a dusting! I've left my uncle there in charge of them . . . I mean, would you believe it: they demand complete impersonality, and find in that the very pith of the matter! How to avoid being themselves, how to resemble themselves as little as possible! That's what they consider to be the highest degree of progress. I mean, if at least it was their own nonsense, but this is simply . . .'

'Listen now,' Pulkheria Aleksandrovna interrupted timidly, but this only increased the temperature.

'What do you suppose?' Razumikhin shouted, raising his voice even louder. 'Do you suppose I'm going on like this because they talk nonsense? Rubbish! I like it when they talk nonsense! Talking nonsense is the sole privilege mankind possesses over the other organisms. It's by talking nonsense that one gets to the truth! I talk nonsense, therefore I'm human. Not one single truth has ever been arrived at without people first having talked a dozen reams of nonsense, even ten dozen reams of it, and that's an honourable thing in its own way; well, but we can't even talk nonsense with our own brains! Talk nonsense to me, by all means, but do it with your own brain, and I shall love you for it. To talk nonsense in one's own way is almost better than to talk a truth that's someone else's; in the first instance you behave like a human being, while in the second you are merely being a parrot! The truth won't go away, but life can be knocked on the head and done in. I can think of some examples. Well, and what's our position now? We're all of us, every one of us without exception, when it comes to the fields of learning, development, thought, invention, ideals, ambition, liberalism, reason, experience, and every, every, every other field you can think of, in the very lowest preparatory form of the gymnasium! We've got accustomed to making do with other people's intelligence – we're soaked in it! It's true, isn't it? Isn't what I'm saying true?' cried Razumikhin, trembling all over and squeezing the hands of both ladies. 'Isn't it?'

'Oh, my goodness, I really don't know,' said poor Pulkheria Aleksandrovna.

'Yes, it is, it is . . . only I don't agree with all of what you've been saying,' Avdotya Romanovna added seriously, and then let out a cry, so painfully did he squeeze her hand this time.

'It is? You say it is? Well, if you can say that, you . . . you . . .' he shouted in ecstasy, 'you're the fount of goodness, purity, reason and . . . perfection! Give me your hand, give it me . . . and please give me yours as well, I want to kiss your hands here and now, on my knees!'

And he knelt down in the middle of the pavement, which at this time was fortunately deserted.

'Stop it, I beg of you – what are you doing?' cried Pulkheria Aleksandrovna, extremely alarmed.

'Get up, get up!' Dunya laughed, also somewhat anxiously.

'Certainly not – not until you give me your hands! There we are! That's enough, up I get, and on we go! I'm a miserable oaf, I'm drunk and unworthy of you, and I'm ashamed of myself . . . I'm not worthy to love you, but to kneel before you is the duty of every man, unless he's a complete brute. And so I too have knelt . . . Ah, here are your rooms. Rodion was right to kick Pyotr Petrovich out just for this reason alone! How dare he put you in such a place! It's outrageous! Do you know what sort of people they allow in here? I mean, you're going to be married! You are, aren't you? Well, let me tell you that if he can do a thing like this your fiancé is a villain!'

'Look here, Mr Razumikhin, you seem to have forgotten . . .' Pulkheria Aleksandrovna began.

'Yes, yes, you're right, I've forgotten myself, and I'm ashamed of it!' Razumikhin said, suddenly remembering where he was, 'but . . . but . . . you can't be angry at me for speaking as I have done! Because I'm speaking sincerely, and not because I . . . ahem! That would be a cheap thing to do; oh, all right then, let's leave it there, I shan't say why, I don't dare to! . . . But we all knew when that fellow walked in earlier on today that he wasn't one of us. Not because he'd been to the barber's to have his hair curled, not because he was in such a hurry to show off his intelligence, but because he's a spy and a speculator; because he's a Jew and an ingratiating hypocrite, and you can tell it a mile off. Do you suppose he's got brains? No, he's a fool, a fool! Well, is he any sort of a man for you? Oh my God! You see, ladies,' he said, coming suddenly to a halt as they were climbing the staircase to the rented rooms, 'even though those people at my place are all drunk, they're all honest, too, and even though we talk a lot of nonsense, for I too am talking nonsense, we'll finally talk our way to the truth, because we tread the path of decency, while Pyotr Petrovich . . . does not. Although I may have called them the most terrible names just now, but in the last analysis I respect them all; and even though I may not respect Zamyotov, I like him because he's a – puppy! I even like that brute Zosimov, because he's a decent fellow and he knows his job . . . But enough, all is said and forgiven. It is forgiven, isn't it? Well, let's go on, then. I know this corridor, I've been here before; in the third room, here, there was a scandal . . . Well, which number are you? Eight? Once you've locked yourselves in for the night, don't let anyone in. In a quarter of an hour I shall be back with news, and then a quarter of an hour after that I'll be back again with Zosimov, you'll see! Goodbye now, I must run!'

'Oh Lord, Dunechka, what's going to happen?' said Pulkheria Aleksandrovna, turning to her daughter in fear and alarm.

'Calm down, mother,' Dunya replied, taking off her hat and cape. 'This gentleman has been sent by God himself, even though he's come straight from a drinking-bout. We may rely on him, I do assure you we may. And after all the things he's done for my brother . . .'

'Oh, Dunechka, the Lord only knows whether he'll come back! And how could I ever have brought myself to leave Rodya! . . . I never, never imagined I should find him like that! How stern he was, as though he wasn't even glad to see us . . .'

Tears came to her eyes.

'No, mother, that's not how it was. You didn't look at him properly, you kept crying all the time. He's very unsettled because he's been seriously ill. That's the reason for all of it.'

'Oh, this illness! Something bad will happen, it will, I know it will! And the way he spoke to you, Dunya!' said her mother, looking timidly into her daughter's eyes in order to find out what she was thinking, and already half consoled because Dunya was defending Rodya, and must therefore have forgiven him. 'I'm sure he'll see it differently tomorrow,' she added, trying to find out everything that was there.

'And I'm sure that tomorrow he'll still be talking the same way . . . about that,' Avdotya Romanovna said abruptly. There, of course, the matter rested, as this was the very point about which Pulkheria Aleksandrovna was now too afraid to open her mouth. Dunya went over to her mother and kissed her. Her mother embraced her tightly, saying nothing. Then she sat down in the anxious expectation of Razumikhin's return, and began timidly to follow the movements of her daughter, who, her arms folded, also in expectation, had begun to walk up and down the room, meditating to herself. This habit of walking up and down a room from one end to the other while meditating was a constant one of Avdotya Romanovna's, and at such moments her mother was always afraid of disturbing the privacy of her thoughts.

Razumikhin had, of course, been making a fool of himself with his sudden and drunkenly conceived passion for Avdotya Romanovna; but had they taken one look at Avdotya Romanovna, particularly just then, as she walked up and down the room, sadly and meditatively, with her arms folded, it is possible that many people would have forgiven him, his eccentric condition apart, that is. Avdotya Romanovna was remarkably attractive: tall, with a wonderful figure, strong and self-confident, something that was expressed in her every gesture and yet in no way detracted from the softness and gracefulness of her movements. She bore a facial likeness to her brother, but in her these features were almost those of a beauty. Her hair was of a dark chestnut colour, a little lighter than that of her brother; her eyes were nearly black – flashing, proud, and yet at moments extraordinarily kind. She was pale, but not morbidly so; her face shone with freshness and health. Her mouth was a little too small, and her lower lip, fresh and scarlet, jutted ever so slightly forward, together with her chin – the only irregularity in this beautiful countenance, endowing it, however, with an especial characteristic distinctiveness and, it should be said, a certain hauteur. Her expression was generally more serious and thoughtful than it was lively; yet how well her smile suited that face of hers, how well it was adapted to laughter – young, lively, wholehearted! It was understandable that the hot-blooded, outspoken, simple-hearted, honest, Herculean-strong and drunken Razumikhin, who had never seen anything similar before, should have lost his head at first sight. As though on purpose, moreover, chance had given him his first sight of Dunya at the beautiful moment of her love for her brother, and of her joy at seeing him again. Thereafter he had seen how her lower lip had trembled in response to her brother's rudely delivered and cruelly ungrateful injunctions – and had been unable to restrain himself.

He had, however, not been mistaken when, drunk on the staircase earlier, he had unintentionally let it slip that Raskolnikov's eccentric landlady, Praskovya Pavlovna, would be jealous not only of Avdotya Romanovna but also possibly of Pulkheria Aleksandrovna herself. In spite of the fact that Pulkheria Aleksandrovna was now forty-three, her face still retained the traces of her former beauty, and indeed she looked much younger than her years, something that nearly always happens to women who keep the lucidity of their spirit, the freshness of their perceptions, and an honest, pure warmth of heart until old age. Let us observe in parenthesis that the retention of all these things is the only means by which one may avoid losing one's looks even when one is old. Her hair was already beginning to turn grey and grow thin, small, radiating wrinkles had long ago started to appear around her eyes, her cheeks had become sunken and wasted from worry and grief, yet even so this face was beautiful. It was a portrait of Dunya, only twenty years later, and without that expression of the lower lip, which in her did not jut forward. Pulkheria Aleksandrovna was emotional, but not in a sickly-sweet way, timid and compliant, but only up to a certain point: there was much that she was capable of letting pass, much to which she would give her agreement, even that which ran counter to her convictions, but there was always a certain point of uprightness, good conduct and last principles beyond which no eventuality could induce her to go.

Exactly twenty minutes after Razumikhin's departure there were two low but hurried knocks at the door; he was back.

'I won't come in, there's no time,' he began to fuss as the door was opened to him. 'He's sleeping like a log, soundly and peacefully, and may God see to it that he sleeps for ten hours. Nastasya's in his room; I told her not to leave it until I get back. Now I shall go and fish out Zosimov, he'll provide you with a report, and then you'd better turn in, too; I can see that you're plain worn out.'

And he set off along the corridor, away from them.

'What a prompt and . . . devoted young man!' Pulkheria Aleksandrovna exclaimed, thoroughly overjoyed.

'He seems to be a wonderful character!' Avdotya Romanovna replied with a certain ardour, starting to walk up and down the room again.

Almost an hour later there was the sound of footsteps in the corridor and another knock at the door. Both women had been waiting, this time entirely believing Razumikhin's promise; and indeed, he had managed to fish out Zosimov. Zosimov had at once agreed to leave the banquet and take a look at Raskolnikov, though he had come to the rooms of the ladies reluctantly and with great suspicion, unsure whether to believe the drunken Razumikhin. His vanity was, however, at once assuaged, and even somewhat flattered: he realized that he was actually being awaited as an oracle. He stayed precisely ten minutes, and completely succeeded in convincing Pulkheria Aleksandrovna and putting her fears to rest. He spoke with emphatic solicitude, but in a restrained manner and with the kind of intense seriousness entirely proper to a twenty-seven-year-old doctor at an important consultation, never once saying anything that was not relevant to the matter at hand and without displaying the slightest desire to enter into more personal and private relations with the two ladies. Having noted upon entering how dazzlingly beautiful Avdotya Romanovna was, he at once endeavoured not to pay any attention to her at all, throughout the entire duration of his visit, addressing himself exclusively to Pulkheria Aleksandrovna. All this afforded him great inward satisfaction. With regard to the patient, he declared that at the present time he considered him to be in a thoroughly satisfactory condition. As far as he could determine, the patient's illness had, beyond the negative effect of the material environment in which he had been living for the last few months, certain mental causes: 'It is, so to speak, the product of many complex mental and material influences – of anxieties, apprehensions, worries, of certain ideas . . . and the like.' Having noticed in passing that Avdotya Romanovna had begun to listen attentively, Zosimov allowed himself to expand a little more on this theme. In response to Pulkheria Aleksandrovna's worried and timid inquiry regarding 'certain suspicions of insanity', however, he replied with a calm, open and ironic smile that he had been exaggerating; that, to be sure, the patient displayed a certain *idée fixe*, something that suggested monomania – the fact was that he, Zosimov, was at present conducting a special study of this extremely interesting branch of medicine – but, after all, it must be borne in mind that almost right up until today the patient had been in delirium, and . . . and, of course, the arrival of his family would strengthen him, take his mind off things and have a salutary effect on him, 'as long as it is possible to avoid any more shocks of a particular kind,' he added significantly. Then he got up, bowed solidly and affably, was escorted to the door with blessings, expressions of ardent gratitude, entreaties and even the hand of Avdotya Romanovna, which was extended towards him for him to shake without his asking, and he emerged thoroughly satisfied with his visit and even more so with himself.

'We'll talk tomorrow; now you must go off to bed, immediately!' Razumikhin said, to round things off, as he left together with Zosimov. 'I shall be back with my report as early as I can tomorrow morning.'

'I say, that Avdotya Romanovna's a delicious little kiddy,' Zosimov commented, practically licking his lips, as both men emerged on to the street.

'Delicious? Did you say delicious?' Razumikhin roared, and he suddenly rushed at Zosimov and grabbed him by the throat. 'If you ever dare . . . Got it? Got it?' he shouted, shaking him by the collar and forcing him against the wall. 'Got it?'

'Oh, let me go, you drunken sod!' said Zosimov, beating off the attack; then, when Razumikhin had let him go, Zosimov looked at him fixedly and suddenly went off into peals of laughter. Razumikhin stood before him, his arms lowered, in gloomy and serious reflection.

'Of course, I'm an ass,' he said, looking as gloomy as a thunder-cloud. 'But I mean . . . so are you.'

'No I'm not, brother, I'm not one at all. I don't spend my time dreaming about stupid things.'

They walked on without saying anything, and it was only when they were approaching Raskolnikov's lodgings that Razumikhin, intensely preoccupied, broke the silence.

'Listen,' he said to Zosimov. 'You're a wonderful chap, but in addition to all your other rotten qualities you're a lecher, I know you are, and one of the filthiest. You're a weak, nerve-ridden scoundrel, you're unstable, you've run to fat and can't deny yourself anything – and I call that filth, because it leads straight down into the filth. You've grown so soft that I must confess I find it hard to understand how you can still be a good, or even a selfless doctor. You sleep on a feather bed all day (a doctor!), and only get up at night to attend to the odd patient! In three years' time you won't even be doing that . . . Well, to hell with that, that's not what I was going to say; what I want to say is: you'll be spending the night in the landlady's apartment (I had some job persuading her!), and I'll be in the kitchen: there's your chance to get better acquainted with her! No, it's not what you're thinking! There's not a shadow of that kind of thing there, brother . . .'

'But I wasn't thinking anything of the sort.'

'What you have there, brother, is shyness, reticence, bashfulness, fierce chastity, and yet at the same time – sighs, and she melts like wax, ah, how she melts! You've got to save me from her, for the sake of all the devils in the world! She's a dish! . . . I'll earn it, I'll do my damndest to earn it!'

Zosimov began to chortle even more loudly than before.

'Really in the grip of it, aren't you? But what would I want with her?'

'I assure you that there's not much trouble involved; all you have to do is talk any kind of wish-wash you like, just sit beside her and talk. What's more, you're a doctor – you could start treating her for something. I swear you won't be sorry. She has an old piano; well, you know, I tinkle on it a bit now and then; there's a song I like to play there, a real Russian one, called "I'll drown in burning tears . . ." She likes the real ones. Well, it all started with that song; but I mean, you're a virtuoso on the piano, a *maître*, a Rubinstein* . . . I assure you, you won't be sorry!'

'What have you been doing – making her promises? Signed a note, have you? Perhaps you've promised to marry her . . .'

'No, no, there's been absolutely nothing like that! Anyway, she's not that kind; Chebarov tried approaching her . . .'

'Well, drop her, then!'

'It's not as easy as that!'

'Why not?'

'It's just not, that's all! You see, it involves the principle of induction, brother.'

'Then why did you lead her astray?'

'I didn't. Perhaps I allowed myself to be led astray, out of stupidity, but it'll really be all the same to her whether it's me or you, all she wants is for there to be someone sitting there next to her, sighing. You see, brother . . . I can't put it into words . . . well, and I mean, you're good at mathematics, you're still studying it, I know . . . well, you could start teaching her integral calculus – no, I'm not joking, I mean it seriously, it really will all be the same to her: she'll look at you and sigh, and it'll go on like that for a whole year. Actually, I spent two whole days telling her about the Prussian Assembly of Nobles (because I couldn't think of anything else to tell her) – and she just sat there sighing and sweating! Only don't mention the word "love" – she's so shy it nearly gives her a seizure; but pretend you can't leave her side, either – that'll be sufficient. It's incredibly comfortable; you can make yourself completely at home – read, sit, lie on the sofa, write . . . You can even kiss her, if you're careful about it . . .'

'But what do I want with her?'

'Damn it, I can't seem to explain it to you at all! Look: you're both completely suited to each other! This isn't the first time I've thought of you . . . I mean, this is how you're going to end up eventually, anyway! So isn't it all the same to you whether it's sooner or later? You see, brother, it involves the feather-bed principle – damn it, and not just the feather-bed one, either! It's a process of induction; it means the end of the world, an anchor, a quiet haven, the hub of the universe, the tri-ichthyic foundation of the earth, the essence of *blinis*, of juicy *kulebiakis*,* of the evening samovar, of quiet lamentations and snug, fur-trimmed jackets, of warm stove-couches – yes, as if you had died, but were still alive, with the simultaneous advantages of both! Well, brother, the devil, I'm talking through my hat, it's time to go to bed! Listen: I sometimes wake up at night, so I'll probably go in and take a look at him. Only there's nothing the matter with him, it's nonsense, everything's all right. So don't you worry either, and look in too just once, if you can. But if you should notice anything, delirium or fever, for example, wake me up at once. But I don't think you'll need to . . .'

II

It was a serious and preoccupied Razumikhin who awoke at eight o'clock the following morning. Many were the new and unforeseen perplexities that suddenly came to visit him that morning. He himself had never imagined that some day he might wake up feeling like this. He recalled, down to the last detail, everything that had happened the day before and understood that something far from commonplace had happened to him, that he had been the host to a certain experience which was quite unfamiliar to him, and which resembled nothing he had encountered previously. At the same time he had a clear awareness that the dream that had caught light within his head was in the highest degree incapable of realization – so much so, indeed, that he was now ashamed of it, and quickly moved on to the other, more urgent concerns and perplexities which were the legacy bequeathed to him by that 'damned, bloody last night'.

The memory that horrified him most was the way in which he had proved himself 'base and despicable', not simply by being drunk, but by having abused the fiancé of a young girl out of stupid and hasty jealousy, taking advantage of her position and ignorant not only of their mutual relationship and commitment to each other, but also of the man himself, with whom he had no proper acquaintance. What right did he have to make such hasty and precipitate judgements about him? And who had asked him to make such judgements in the first place? Would a creature such as Avdotya Romanovna give herself to a man unworthy of her just for the sake of money? No, he must possess certain merits. The rooms? But how could he have known that the rooms were of that kind? After all, he was preparing an apartment . . . Ugh, how despicable it all was! And what sort of an excuse was it that he had been drunk? It was a stupid pretext, which made him even more despicable! *In vino veritas* – and the *veritas* had well and truly manifested itself, 'that's to say, the utter filth of my loutish, envious heart!' And in any case, was such a dream permissible to him, Razumikhin? Who was he compared to a girl like that – he, a drunken ruffian and boaster of the exploits of the night before? 'Is such a cynical and absurd comparison even thinkable?' Razumikhin blushed desperately at the very thought, and suddenly, as though by some design, he was at that very moment visited by the clear memory of how, standing on the stairs the evening before, he had told them that the landlady would be jealous of Avdotya Romanovna on his account . . . that was the final straw! With all his might he struck his fist against the kitchen stove, hurting his hand and dislodging one of the bricks.

'One thing's certain,' he muttered to himself a moment later, with a certain feeling of self-humiliation, 'and that's that there's no question of my being able to mask or smooth over that ugly behaviour either now or ever in the future . . . and so there's no point in even thinking about it. I must present myself to them in silence and . . . carry out my obligations . . . also in silence, and . . . and not ask to be forgiven, and say not a word, and . . . and I may be certain that all is now lost!'

All the same, as he got dressed he examined his suit more carefully than usual. These were the only clothes he possessed; had he any others, he would probably not have worn them – 'I'd make a special point of not wearing them.' But, when all was said and done, it would not do for him to go around like a cynic and a dirty slob: he had no right to offend the sensibilities of others, even less so as those others were themselves in need of him and were summoning him to their assistance. He cleaned his suit thoroughly, employing the use of a brush. As for his linen, it was always in a tolerable state; on that account he observed a particular cleanliness.

That morning he washed himself zealously – Nastasya happened to have some soap – scrubbing his hair, his neck and especially his hands. When, however, it came to the question of whether he should shave off his stubble, or not (in Praskovya Pavlovna's apartment there were some excellent razors which had been preserved from the days of the deceased Mr Zarnitsyn), the dilemma was resolved, not without a certain desperation, in negative fashion: 'Let it remain as it is! Well, otherwise they'll think I've shaved myself for . . . they're bound to think that! Not for anything in the world!'

No . . . no, the worst of it was that he was such a dirty, loutish fellow, he had behaved as though he'd been brought up in a tavern; no . . . no, even supposing he knew that he, too, if ever so slightly, was a decent human being . . . well, what was there to be proud of about that? Everyone ought to be a decent human being, and a clean one, too, and . . . and even so (this he remembered) in his time he had done some nasty things . . . not exactly dishonest ones, but all the same . . . And the thoughts he had had! Hm . . . And for him to go and try to present all that to Avdotya Romanovna! Oh well, to hell with it. That was just the way it was. He would make a point of continuing to be that dirty, greasy, tavern-bred oaf, and to blazes. He'd do it even more . . .

It was in monologues such as these that he was discovered by Zosimov, who had spent the night in Praskovya Pavlovna's front parlour.

Zosimov was about to leave for home, but before going wanted to take a quick look at his patient. Razumikhin informed him that Raskolnikov was sleeping like a log. Zosimov gave instructions that the patient not be roused until he awoke of his own accord, and promised to look in at about eleven o'clock.

'That is, if he's still here by then,' he added. 'My God! I don't even have any control over my own patient, so how on earth am I supposed to cure him? I don't suppose you know whether *he* is going to them, or *they* are coming here?'

'They're coming here, I think,' Razumikhin replied, having grasped the purpose of the question, 'and they'll doubtless spend all the time talking about their family business. I'll go out. As a doctor, you have more right to be here than I have, of course.'

'I'm not a priest, though. I'll come and then go away again. I've enough to do as it is.'

'There's just one thing that's worrying me,' Razumikhin said, interrupting him with a frown. 'When I was drunk last night and was taking him home, I told him about various stupid things . . . about various . . . among other things, that you were afraid he . . . might have a tendency towards madness . . .'

'Yes, you were telling the ladies about that last night, too.'

'I know it was a stupid thing to do! I just couldn't help it! But tell me – did you really have such a definite opinion?'

'It's nonsense, I tell you; what definite opinion? You yourself described him as a monomaniac when you brought me to him . . . Well, and we raised his temperature even further yesterday with those stories . . . about the painter; a fine kind of thing to talk about when that was the very thing that had probably driven him out of his mind in the first place! If I'd known what exactly had happened in the bureau that day and had been told that some rascal had . . . insulted him by treating him as a suspect in that case! Hm . . . I'd never have allowed you to say those things to him yesterday. I tell you, these monomaniacs will make mountains out of molehills, they see their own cock-and-bull fantasies walking around in real life . . . As far as I can remember, what Zamyotov told me yesterday cleared half the business up, in any case. My God! I know of one case where a certain hypochondriac, a man of forty, couldn't stand the daily jeering of his eight-year-old urchin of a son and cut his throat! And here you have a fellow all in rags, an insolent jackanapes of a policeman, an incipient illness and a suspicion of that kind! All that, and the chap's a crazed hypochondriac! With fantastic, extraordinary vanity! Oh well, to hell with it! . . . Actually, you know, that Zamyotov is quite a pleasant little guttersnipe; if only . . . hm . . . he hadn't gone and given everything away like that yesterday. He's a terrible chatterbox!'

'But who did he tell? Just you and me, wasn't it?'

'And Porfiry.'

'Oh, Porfiry doesn't matter!'

'Come to think of it, do you have any sort of influence with those two, the mother and the sister, I mean? They ought to go easy on him today . . .'

'They'll come to some arrangement,' was Razumikhin's unwilling response to this.

'And why does he keep going on against this Luzhin fellow? He's got money, she apparently doesn't find him too unattractive . . . and I mean, they haven't got a bean, have they? Eh?'

'Oh, why do you keep trying to get things out of me?' Razumikhin cried irritably. 'How should I know whether they have or they haven't? Ask them yourself, and perhaps you'll find out . . .'

'God, how stupid you are sometimes! You've still got that vodka in you . . . Goodbye, then; thank Praskovya Pavlovna for letting me spend the night here. She locked herself in and didn't say anything in reply when I shouted "*bonjour*" this morning. But she got up at seven and had the samovar brought to her room across the passage from the kitchen . . . I had the honour of setting eyes on her.'

At exactly nine o'clock Razumikhin presented himself at Bakaleyev's Tenements. Both ladies had been long awaiting him in hysterical impatience. They had risen at seven, or even earlier. He entered with a gloom like that of the night and paid his compliments in a clumsy fashion, whereupon he at once lost his temper – at himself, of course. He had bargained without the mistress of the chamber: Pulkheria Aleksandrovna fairly hurled herself at him; she seized him by both hands and very nearly kissed them. He cast a timid glance at Avdotya Romanovna; at the present moment, however, that haughty countenance displayed an expression of such gratitude and benevolence, such complete and unanticipated respect for him (in place of those mocking looks and automatic, ill-disguised contempt!), that he would have found it easier had they greeted him with abuse – as it was, the whole situation confused him utterly. Luckily there was a ready subject of conversation, and he lost no time in grasping hold of it.

On hearing that he had not woken up yet, but that 'everything was fine', Pulkheria Aleksandrovna declared that this was just as well, 'because I very, very, very much want to talk things over with you first'. This was followed by an inquiry about whether he would like tea, and an invitation to have some with them; they themselves had not yet had any, in expectation of his arrival. Avdotya Romanovna rang the bell. At her summons a dirty, ragged fellow appeared, and was instructed to bring tea, which was eventually served, but in so dirty and improper a manner as to make the ladies feel ashamed. Razumikhin began to deliver some energetic criticism of the establishment, but, remembering Luzhin, fell silent, grew embarrassed, and was thoroughly relieved when at last Pulkheria Aleksandrovna's questions began to rain down in a ceaseless shower.

In replying to them, he talked for three-quarters of an hour, being constantly interrupted and asked to repeat, and managed to convey to them all the major and essential facts concerning the most recent year of Raskolnikov's life, concluding with a detailed account of his illness. There was, however, much that for obvious reasons he left out, such as the scene at the bureau, with all its consequences. His story was listened to with eagerness; but just when he thought he had finished and had satisfied the demands of his listeners, it proved that as far as they were concerned he had hardly begun.

'Look, you must tell me, you must tell me what you think . . . Oh, I'm sorry, I still don't know your first names,' Pulkheria Aleksandrovna said hastily.

'Dmitry Prokofich.'

'Well, then, Dmitry Prokofich, I should very, very much like to know . . . the way he . . . sees things now, or rather, you understand, how can I explain to you, let me put it this way: what are his preferences and aversions? Is he always so irritable? What does he want, or better still, what does he dream about? What is it that's having such a peculiar effect on him just now? In short, I'd like to . . .'

'Oh, mother, how can he possibly answer all those questions at once?' Dunya commented.

'Good heavens – you see I really never, never expected to find him like this, Dmitry Prokofich.'

'That's perfectly natural, madam,' Dmitry Prokofich replied. 'My mother's dead, but well, my uncle comes up to town every year and on each occasion he fails to recognize me, even outwardly, and he's an intelligent man; well, and during the three years you've been apart a lot of water has passed under the bridge. What can I say? I've known Rodion for one and a half years: he's a morose sort of chap – gloomy, stand-offish and proud; recently (and for all I know not so recently, as well) he's been over-anxious, with a tendency to hypochondria. But sometimes it's not hypochondria at all that he's suffering from, he's simply cold and unfeeling to the point of inhumanity, it's really just as though there were two opposing characters alternating within him. He's sometimes unconscionably short on conversation! It's all: "I've no time, stop bothering me", yet he just lies there not doing anything. He doesn't mock, yet it's not because he doesn't have enough wit, but rather as though he didn't have enough time for such trivial matters. He doesn't listen to what people say to him. He's never interested in what everyone else is interested in at any given moment. He has a fearfully high opinion of himself, and perhaps not entirely without justification. Well, what else? . . . I think your arrival will have a most salutary effect on him.'

'Oh my God, I do hope so!' Pulkheria Aleksandrovna exclaimed, worried to death by this character report of Razumikhin's on her Rodya.

And at last Razumikhin directed a more cheerful look at Avdotya Romanovna. During the course of his account he had frequently glanced at her, but fleetingly, just for an instant, immediately averting his gaze. Some of the time Avdotya Romanovna would sit down at the table, listening attentively; every so often, however, she would get up again and begin to walk, as was her habit, from one corner of the room to another, her arms folded, her lips pressed tight, from time to time inserting a question of her own, but without ceasing her walk, and lost in reflection. She was also in the habit of not listening to what anyone said. She was wearing a dark-coloured dress made of some thin material, and a white, transparent scarf was tied at her throat. By many signs Razumikhin had at once been able to tell that the two women were in extremely impoverished straits. Had Avdotya Romanovna been dressed like a queen, he would not have been afraid of her in the slightest; but now, perhaps precisely because she was so poorly dressed and because he had taken cognizance of the niggardly means at their disposal, fear became implanted in his heart, and he began to worry about the effect of his every word, his every gesture – something which was, to say the least, inconvenient for a man who already felt unsure of himself.

'You have told us many interesting things about the character of my brother, and . . . have told them dispassionately. That is good; I believed you went rather in awe of him,' Avdotya Romanovna commented with a smile. 'I also think it's true what you said: that he needs a woman to look after him,' she added, in reflection.

'I didn't say that, but perhaps you're right about that – only . . .'

'Yes?'

'Well, I mean, there's no one he loves; there probably never will be,' Razumikhin said, abruptly.

'You mean he's incapable of loving anyone?'

'You know, Avdotya Romanovna, you're extraordinarily like your brother in every respect!' he suddenly blurted out, unexpectedly even to himself, but at once, remembering the things he had just told her about her brother, blushed like a beetroot and grew terribly confused.

'I think you may both be wrong about Rodya,' Pulkheria Aleksandrovna interjected, somewhat piqued. 'I'm not talking about the way he's behaving at present, Dunechka. The things Pyotr Petrovich writes in this letter . . . and the things you and I have assumed . . . may be untrue, but you cannot imagine, Dmitry Prokofich, what a fantastical imagination Rodya has and – how shall I put it? – how capricious he is. I was never able to trust his character, not even when he was only fifteen years old. I am certain that even now he may go and do something to himself that no one else would ever think of doing . . . And one doesn't have to look far: have you any idea of how he shocked, amazed and very nearly killed me that time a year and a half ago when he decided to marry that girl, what was her name – the daughter of that Zarnitsyna woman, his landlady?'

'Are you familiar with any of the details of that episode?' Avdotya Romanovna inquired.

'Do you suppose,' Pulkheria Aleksandrovna went on heatedly, 'that anything would have stopped him – even though I cried bitter tears, got down on my knees to him, even though I was ill, might have died of grief, even though we were destitute? As calm as you please, he would have stepped over every obstacle. Oh, does he really, really not love us?'

'He's never ever told me about that episode,' Razumikhin answered cautiously, 'though I heard a few bits here and there from Mrs Zarnitsyna herself, who is not, it must be said, one of nature's storytellers, and the things I heard were, as a matter of fact, rather strange . . .'

'What, what did you hear?' both women asked at once.

'Oh, nothing much in particular. All I found out was that this marriage, which had been arranged in every particular and only failed to take place because of the death of the bride, did not at all carry Mrs Zarnitsyna's approval . . . It was said, moreover, that the bride was

266

not at all good-looking, that she was, indeed, very ugly . . . terribly ailing . . . and strange . . . yet I think she must have had certain merits; otherwise it's impossible to understand . . . There was no dowry, either, and he would never have expected one, anyway . . . As a rule it's difficult to make judgements in cases like that.'

'I'm sure she was a decent girl,' Avdotya Romanovna said, crisply.

'God forgive me, I was so relieved when she died, even though I don't know which of them would have been worse for the other: would he have destroyed her, or would she have destroyed him?' Pulkheria Aleksandrovna said in conclusion; then cautiously, with hesitations in her speech and constant glances at Dunya, which Dunya obviously found annoying, she began once more to ask questions about the scene that had taken place the day before between Rodya and Luzhin. It was clear that this event was what had unsettled her most of all, to the point of fear and trembling. Once again Razumikhin went over the whole story in detail, this time, however, adding an ending of his own: he directly accused Raskolnikov of a calculated plan to insult Pyotr Petrovich, and this time he made little reference to the excuse of illness.

'He thought that up before he fell ill,' he added.

'That's what I think, too,' Pulkheria Aleksandrovna said, with a depressed look. She was, however, particularly struck that on this occasion Razumikhin spoke of Pyotr Petrovich in such cautious terms, even, she thought, displaying a certain respect. Avdotya Romanovna was also struck by this.

'So that is your opinion of Pyotr Petrovich, is it?' Pulkheria Aleksandrovna could not restrain herself from asking.

'Where the future husband of your daughter is concerned, I can't be of any other opinion,' Razmukhin replied firmly and with heat, 'and I don't say that out of mere vulgar politeness, but because . . . because . . . well if you like for the simple reason that Avdotya Romanovna herself, of her own free will, has conferred her choice upon this man. My berating him the way I did last night you may attribute to the fact that I was filthy drunk and also . . . reckless; yes, reckless, taken leave of my senses, mad, completely mad . . . and this morning I'm ashamed of it!' His face reddened, and he fell silent. Avdotya Romanovna flushed, but did not break her silence. She had not uttered a single word from the moment they had begun to talk about Luzhin.

Meanwhile, in the absence of her support, Pulkheria Aleksandrovna was clearly in a state of indecision. At last, hesitantly, and constantly looking at her daughter, she announced that there was something which at present was causing her extreme worry.

'You see, Dmitry Prokofich,' she began. 'May I be completely frank with Dmitry Prokofich, Dunechka?'

'Of course, mother,' Avdotya Romanovna said, encouragingly.

'It's like this,' her mother began in a hurry, as though this permission to communicate her grief had removed a mountain from her heart. 'Very early this morning we received a note from Pyotr Petrovich, replying to the one we sent him yesterday announcing our arrival. He was supposed to meet us at the station yesterday, you see, the way he'd promised. But instead he sent some manservant to meet us, with the address of these rooms and instructions on how to find our way here, and the message that he would come here himself this morning. But instead this note arrived from him this morning . . . the best thing would be for you to read it yourself; it contains a point that causes me great concern . . . you'll see what it is yourself in a moment, and I want you to . . . give me your honest opinion, Dmitry Prokofich. You know Rodya better than anyone, and you're the best person to advise us. I should warn you that Dunechka made her mind up as soon as she read it, but I – well, I'm still not sure what to do, and . . . and I've been waiting for you . . .'

Razumikhin unfolded the note, which was marked with the previous day's date and read the following:

Dear Madam, Pulkheria Aleksandrovna,

It is my honourable duty to inform you that, because of certain sudden and unavoidable delays, I have been unable to meet you on the platform, sending to that purpose a man well capable of the task. I shall also forgo the honour of meeting you tomorrow morning, on account of certain business at the Senate which will brook no postponement, and also for the reason that I do not wish to intrude upon your reunion with your son and on that of Avdotya Romanovna with her brother. I shall not have the honour of visiting you and greeting you in your accommodation until tomorrow evening at eight o'clock precisely. In this regard I must venture to append the earnest and, I would add, urgent request that Rodion Romanovich not be present at our joint meeting, as in the course of my sick-visit to him yesterday he insulted me in an unprecedented and discourteous manner, and as, moreover, I am anxious to have an urgent personal discussion with you in respect of a certain point, your own interpretation of which I am desirous to learn. I have the honourable duty to warn you in advance that if, contrary to my request, I encounter Rodion Romanovich, I shall have no option but to leave without further ado, and for that you will have only yourselves to blame. I write, moreover, in the supposition that Rodion Romanovich, who at the time of my visit to him yesterday appeared so ill, two hours later suddenly recovered, and that, since he is able to go out of doors, he may arrive at your address. I received confirmation of this with my own eyes yesterday, at the lodgings of a certain drunkard who was run down by horses and has since died of his injuries; to the daughter of this man, an unmarried woman of immoral conduct, he gave a sum amounting to twenty-five roubles, on the pretext of funeral expenses, an action that surprised me greatly, knowing as I do the difficulty you had in raising the said amount. In spite of all this, however, and in testimony to my especial esteem for your respected daughter, Avdotya Romanovna, I beg you to accept the sentiments of respectful devotion on the part of

your obedient servant,
P. Luzhin

'What am I to do now, Dmitry Prokofich?' said Pulkheria Aleksandrovna, almost in tears. 'I mean, how can I tell Rodya not to come? He was so adamant yesterday about demanding that we say no to Pyotr Petrovich, and now we're being told not to let Rodya in, either! And I mean, he'll be sure to come when he finds out, and . . . what will happen then?'

'You should do whatever Avdotya Romanovna wants to do,' Razumikhin answered calmly and without hesitation.

'Oh, good heavens! She says . . . Heaven knows the things she's been saying, and she doesn't tell me what the point of it all is, either! She says it's best – that's to say, not best, but for some reason absolutely essential that Rodya should also make a special effort to come here at eight o'clock this evening, and that it's essential for the two of them to meet each other . . . And there I was unwilling even to show him the letter – I'd planned to make some cunning arrangement through you, to stop him coming . . . because he's so irritable

. . . And in any case I've absolutely no idea who this drunkard is who has died, or who the daughter is, or how he could have given away all of that last lot of money . . . which . . .'

'Which cost you such a lot to get hold of, mother,' Avdotya Romanovna added.

'He wasn't himself yesterday,' Razumikhin said, meditatively. 'If you knew what he got up to in a restaurant yesterday, even if it was clever . . . hm! Yes, it's true, he did tell me about some woman or other as we were walking home, but I couldn't make head nor tail of it . . . In any case, last night I too . . .'

'Mother, the best thing would be for us to go and see him ourselves; I'm certain that once we're there we'll realize at once what to do. And anyway, it's time . . . Oh good heavens! It's after ten!' she exclaimed, glancing at the magnificent gold-enamelled watch that hung around her neck on a slender little Venetian chain and clashed terribly with the rest of her attire. 'A gift from the bridegroom,' Razumikhin thought.

'Oh, it's time we were gone! Come along, Dunechka, come along!' Pulkheria Aleksandrovna began to fuss. 'He'll think our taking so long to arrive means we're still angry with him about yesterday. Oh good heavens!'

So saying, she agitatedly threw her cape around her and put her hat on; Dunechka also got ready. The gloves she was wearing were not only threadbare, but actually torn in several places, something that Razumikhin noticed, and yet this manifest poverty of costume actually lent both ladies a kind of peculiar dignity, which is always the case with people who know how to wear poor clothes. Razumikhin looked at Dunechka with veneration and felt proud that he was to escort her. 'It is of course certain,' he thought to himself, 'that the queen who mended her stockings in prison looked like a real queen as she did it, and even more so than at the time of her most lavish triumphs and entrances.'*

'Oh my goodness!' Pulkheria Aleksandrovna exclaimed, 'I never imagined I would be as afraid of meeting my own son, my own dear, dear Rodya, as I am now! . . . I'm frightened, Dmitry Prokofich!' she added, giving him a timid glance.

'Don't be, mother,' Dunya said, kissing her. 'You ought to trust him. I do.'

'Oh, my goodness! I *do* trust him, but I wasn't able to sleep all night!' the poor woman exclaimed.

They emerged on to the street.

'You know, Dunechka, when towards morning I finally fell asleep, I suddenly had a dream about poor dead Marfa Petrovna . . . and she was all in white . . . she came up to me, took me by the hand, and shook her head at me, so sternly, so sternly, as though she were condemning me . . . Do you think that's a bad sign? Oh, good heavens, didn't you know, Dmitry Prokofich: Marfa Petrovna is dead!'

'No, I didn't; which Marfa Petrovna is that?'

'It was so sudden! And just imagine . . .'

'Later, mother,' Dunya interposed. 'I mean, he doesn't even know who Marfa Petrovna is yet.'

'Oh, don't you? And I thought you knew everything. You must forgive me, Dmitry Prokofich – my mind can't keep up with my reason these days. To be sure, I look upon you as our Providence, and so was quite convinced that you knew everything. I look upon you as one of my own kin . . . Please don't be angry with me for talking like this. Oh, good heavens, what happened to your hand? The right one. Did you hurt it?'

'Yes, I did,' muttered the gratified Razumikhin.

'Sometimes I talk too much from the heart – Dunya tells me off for it . . . But, good heavens, what a little cupboard that is he's living in! Do you suppose he'll have woken up yet, by the way? Does this woman, this landlady of his, really call that a room? Listen – you say he doesn't like to show his feelings, so perhaps I'll get on his nerves with my . . . weaknesses? Please be my guide, Dmitry Prokofich! How should I behave with him? I'm going around every bit like a lost soul, you know.'

'Don't ask him too many questions, especially if you see him frowning; in particular, you mustn't ask him about his health: he doesn't like it.'

'Oh, Dmitry Prokofich, how hard it is to be a mother! But here's that staircase . . . What a dreadful staircase!'

'Why, mother, you're terribly pale, calm down, my little dove,' said Dunya, fondling her. 'He ought to be happy to see you, and here are you, tormenting yourself,' she added, with a flash of her eyes.

'Wait, I'll go on up and see if he's awake yet.'

The ladies slowly made their way up the stairs behind Razumikhin, who had set off ahead of them, and as on the fourth floor they drew level with the door of the landlady's apartment, they noticed that it was open a tiny slit, and that two quick black eyes were examining them both out of the darkness. When they met the gaze of these eyes, however, the door suddenly banged shut with such a loud noise that Pulkheria Aleksandrovna almost cried out in fright.

III

'He's recovered, he's recovered!' Zosimov cried merrily as he greeted the newcomers. He had arrived some ten minutes before and was sitting in the corner of the room he had occupied the previous day, on the sofa. Raskolnikov was sitting in the corner opposite with all his clothes on, having washed himself thoroughly and combed his hair, things he had not done for a long time. The room filled up at once, but even so Nastasya succeeded in following the visitors in, and began to listen.

It was true: Raskolnikov had almost recovered, particularly by comparison with the day before, though he was still very pale, distracted and morose. Outwardly he looked like a man who has been wounded or is in severe pain: his eyebrows were drawn together, his lips pressed tight, his gaze inflamed. He spoke little and reluctantly, as though he were having to make an effort or were discharging some obligation, and every so often a vague unease appeared in his movements.

With a sling or a taffeta bandage he would have entirely resembled a man with a bruised arm or a very painful finger abscess, or something of that sort.

None the less, even this pale and morose countenance brightened up for a moment, as if with a ray of light, when mother and sister made their entrance but this merely lent the sufferer's expression an additional element of concentrated agony, replacing his previous melancholy absent-mindedness. The light soon faded, but the look of agony remained, and Zosimov, who was observing and studying his patient with all the youthful fervour of a doctor only just at the beginning of his career, noted with surprise that instead of displaying joy at the arrival of his nearest and dearest, Raskolnikov seemed to show a grim, concealed determination to endure another hour or two of torture which could not now be avoided. He subsequently observed how almost every word of the conversation that now began seemed to touch some wound in his patient and irritate it; but at the same time he found himself wondering somewhat at the way in which yesterday's monomaniac, whom the slightest word had plunged into a state bordering upon frenzy, was today able to master himself and conceal his emotions.

'Yes, now even I realize that I've almost recovered,' said Raskolnikov, kissing his mother and sister affectionately, which at once made Pulkheria Aleksandrovna beam with joy, 'and I'm not saying that *the way I did yesterday*,' he added, turning to Razumikhin and squeezing his arm in friendly fashion.

'I'm really amazed at him today,' Zosimov began, thoroughly relieved at the newcomers' arrival, as in the course of ten minutes he had already succeeded in losing the thread of his conversation with the patient. 'If he goes on like this, in another three or four days he'll be quite his old self again, just the way he was a month, or two . . . or, possibly three . . . ago. I mean, all this began and was on the cards a long time ago, wasn't it . . . eh? Will you admit now that you yourself were probably to blame?' he added with a cautious smile, as though he were still afraid of saying something that might irritate him.

'It's very likely,' Raskolnikov answered coldly.

'I say this,' Zosimov went on, acquiring a taste for his new role, 'because by and large your complete recovery now depends solely on yourself. Now that it's possible to talk to you, I would like to impress on you how essential it is that the original, as it were, root causes which gave rise to your morbid condition be eliminated; if they are, you'll be cured. If not, it will come back, only worse. You're an intelligent man, and I'm sure you've been keeping an eye on yourself. I think the beginning of your disorder coincided to some extent with your leaving the university. It's essential that you not be left at a loose end, and that's why I believe that hard work and a firmly fixed goal would be of great assistance to you.'

'Yes, yes, you're quite right . . . Look, I'll be returning to university soon, and then everything will go . . . like clockwork . . .'

Zosimov, who had begun delivering this sensible advice partly in order to make an impression on the ladies, was naturally somewhat perplexed when, upon concluding his remarks, he glanced at his hearer and observed on the latter's face an expression of undisguised mockery. This only lasted an instant, however. Pulkheria Aleksandrovna at once began to thank Zosimov, in particular for having made his visit to their hotel the night before.

'What, he was with you at night as well, was he?' Raskolnikov asked, seemingly in alarm. 'I suppose that means you didn't get any sleep after your journey?'

'Oh, Rodya, it was only until two o'clock. Even at home Dunya and I never go to bed before two.'

'I don't know how to thank him, either,' Raskolnikov went on, suddenly frowning, and lowering his gaze. 'Even disregarding the money side of it – excuse me for mentioning that,' he said, turning to Zosimov, 'I really don't know why I've deserved such special attention from you! I just don't understand . . . and . . . because of that, I actually find it rather hard to accept: I tell you that in all openness.'

'Now don't get annoyed,' Zosimov laughed, forcedly. 'Just suppose you're my best patient. Well, you know, some of us who are only just beginning to practise medicine love our best patients as if they were our own children, and indeed there are some fellows who practically fall in love with them. And I mean, I don't exactly have very many patients.'

'To say nothing of him,' Raskolnikov added, pointing at Razumikhin. 'Even though he's had nothing from me but trouble and insults.'

'God, what rot he's talking! In a sentimental mood today, are we?' Razumikhin exclaimed.

If he had looked a little more searchingly he would have seen that here no sentimental mood but something quite the opposite was involved. Avdotya Romanovna had, however, noticed this. She was keeping a fixed and uneasy gaze trained on her brother.

'And as for you, mother, I don't even dare to say what I think,' he went on, as though he were repeating some lesson he had learned by rote that morning. 'Only today have I begun to have any inkling of what torments you must have been through here last night as you waited for me to arrive.' Having said this, he suddenly, without a word, held out his hand to his sister, smiling. This time, however, the smile contained a genuine, unfeigned emotion. Dunya at once

274

caught and pressed the hand extended towards her, relieved and grateful. It was the first time he had said anything to her since their disagreement of the previous day. His mother's face lit up with delight and happiness at the sight of this conclusive and wordless reconciliation of brother with sister.

'There – that's what I love him for!' whispered the forever-exaggerating Razumikhin, energetically turning round in his seat. 'He has these – gestures . . .'

'And how well he does it all,' thought the mother to herself. 'What noble impulses he has and how simply and with what tact he put an end to that misunderstanding with his sister yesterday – just by stretching out his hand at the right moment and giving her the right kind of look . . . What beautiful eyes he has, and how handsome his face is! . . . But, good heavens, look at that suit he's wearing – how dreadfully badly he's dressed! Afanasy Ivanovich's shop-boy Vasya has better clothes! . . . Oh, I could just rush up to him and throw my arms round him, and . . . cry – but I'm afraid, afraid . . . Lord, what's got into him? . . . I mean, even when he talks kindly I'm afraid! But what am I afraid of? . . .'

'Oh, Rodya,' she said suddenly, entering into the conversation, in a hurry to respond to the remark he had just made, 'you could never imagine how . . . unhappy Dunechka and I were yesterday! Now that it's over and we're all happy again it won't matter if I tell you. Imagine, we came running here in order to embrace you, straight off the train, practically, and this woman – yes, there she is! Hallo, Nastasya! . . . suddenly told us that you had delirium tremens and had just given the doctor the slip and gone gibbering out into the street, and that people had set off to look for you. Can you imagine what we felt? I immediately thought of the tragic death of Lieutenant Potanchikov, whom we knew – he was a friend of your father's – you wouldn't remember him, Rodya – and who also ran off like that with delirium tremens and fell down a well in the yard outside, it wasn't until the next day that they were able to pull him out. And we, of course, thought it was even worse than that. We were going to rush away and look for Pyotr Petrovich, in order to enlist his help . . . because I mean we were alone, completely alone,' she wailed in a piteous voice, and then suddenly stopped short, remembering that it was still rather risky to mention Pyotr Petrovich, even though they were 'all completely happy again' . . .

'Yes, yes . . . of course, that's all a great shame . . .' Raskolnikov muttered in reply, but with such a distracted, inattentive air that Dunya looked at him in amazement.

'Now what was the other thing I wanted to say?' he continued, making an effort to remember. 'Yes: please, mother – and you, too, Dunechka – don't get the idea that I didn't want to come and see you today, but was waiting for you to come to me.'

'What *are* you talking about, Rodya?' Pulkheria Aleksandrovna exclaimed, also in surprise.

'What's he doing, talking to us out of duty?' Dunya wondered. 'He's making it up and asking to be forgiven as though he were performing a ritual or reciting some lesson or other.'

'I'd just woken up and I was going to come and see you, but my clothes held me up; I forgot to tell her . . . Nastasya . . . to clean that blood off yesterday . . . It was only a moment ago that I managed to get dressed.'

'Blood? What blood?' Pulkheria Aleksandrovna said, in alarm.

'Yes . . . don't be upset. It was blood I got on myself yesterday when I was roaming around in a bit of a delirium – I stumbled across a man who'd been run down in the street . . . a civil servant . . .'

'In a delirium? But I mean, you can remember it all,' Razumikhin said, interrupting.

'That's true,' Raskolnikov replied to this, with a kind of especial thoughtfulness. 'I can remember it all, right down to the very last detail, and yet if you were to ask me why I did it, where I was going, or what I said, I wouldn't be able to explain it now.'

'That's a very common phenomenon,' Zosimov chipped in. 'The execution of the deed is sometimes masterfully done, in the most ingenious fashion, yet the control of the individual actions that comprise it, the origin of those actions, is diffuse and is associated with various morbid sensations. Rather like a dream.'

'I must say, it's probably just as well he thinks I'm practically a madman,' Raskolnikov thought.

'But surely that's true of normal people as well,' Dunya commented, looking at Zosimov with unease.

'An observation not far off the mark,' Zosimov replied. 'It is perfectly true that in that sense we all of us, very often, conduct ourselves like mad folk, with the slight distinction that the "mentally ill" are a little crazier than we are, and so there it is necessary to draw a line. The harmonious individual, it needs to be said, hardly exists at all; out of many tens, even hundreds of thousands perhaps one or two at most are encountered, and even then in rather feeble versions . . .'

At the word 'crazy', which had carelessly escaped Zosimov's lips as he became immersed in chattering on about his favourite subject, everyone winced. Raskolnikov seemed to pay no attention; he sat brooding, a strange smile on his pale lips. He continued to weigh something over.

'Well, what about this man who was run down in the street? I interrupted you!' Razumikhin asked, quickly.

'What?' said Raskolnikov, seeming to wake up. 'Yes . . . well, I got some of his blood on myself when I was helping to carry him up to his apartment . . . Incidentally, mother, I did an unforgivable thing yesterday; I must have been quite out of my mind. I gave all that money you sent me . . . to his wife . . . for the funeral. She's a widow now, a pitiful, consumptive woman . . . she has three little fatherless children who are hungry . . . there's no food in the house . . . and there's another daughter, too . . . I think you yourself might have given them that money if you'd seen them . . . Of course, I realize that I had no right to part with it, especially since I knew how you'd got hold of it. In order to help anyone, one must first have a right to do so, for if one hasn't: *"Crevez chiens, si vous n'êtes pas contents!"*' He burst out laughing. 'Isn't that so, Dunya?'

'No, it isn't!' Dunya replied, firmly.

'Aha! So you, too, have . . . good intentions! . . .' he muttered, giving her a look almost of hatred, and smiling with derision. 'I might have guessed . . . Well, it does you credit, I suppose; good for you . . . if you reach a point where you can't go on, you'll be miserable, yet if you do manage to go on you'll be even more miserable . . . But that's all nonsense!' he added irritably, annoyed at having got carried away without meaning to. 'All I wanted to say was that of you, mother, I ask forgiveness,' he concluded sharply and abruptly.

'Enough, Rodya. I'm sure that everything you do is wonderful,' his mother said in relief.

'Don't be,' he replied, twisting his mouth into a smile. A silence ensued. Running through the whole of this conversation there had been a strained tenseness; it had affected silence, reconciliation and absolution in equal measure, and they had all felt it.

'Why, it's as if they were afraid of me,' Raskolnikov thought to himself as he gave his mother and sister a suspicious look. And it really was the case that the longer Pulkheria Aleksandrovna kept silent, the more frightened she felt.

'I seemed to love them so much when they weren't here,' flashed through his head.

'You know, Rodya, Marfa Petrovna has died,' Pulkheria Aleksandrovna suddenly twittered out.

'Which Marfa Petrovna is that?'

'Oh, good heavens, Marfa Petrovna – Svidrigailov's wife! I wrote so much to you about her.'

'Yes, yes, yes, I remember . . . so she's died? Oh, she hasn't really, has she?' he said suddenly, starting as though he had woken up. 'Died? What of?'

'Can you imagine? It was so sudden!' Pulkheria Aleksandrovna got in quickly, encouraged by his curiosity. 'It happened just at the time I posted that letter to you, that very same day! Imagine, that horrible man was apparently the cause of her death. They say he gave her a terrible beating!'

'Did they really live that kind of a life together?' he asked, turning to his sister.

'No, quite the reverse, actually. He was always very patient with her – polite, even. There were a lot of times when he made too many concessions to the kind of woman she was, throughout all the seven years they were married . . . In the end he must simply have lost patience.'

'You mean he can't have been all that bad, if he lasted out for seven years? You seem to be trying to find an excuse for him, Dunya!'

'No, no, he's a horrible man! I can't imagine anyone or anything more horrible,' Dunya replied with something approaching a shudder, knitting her brows and beginning to reflect.

'That took place in the morning,' Pulkheria Aleksandrovna went on, hurriedly. 'Afterwards, she immediately ordered the horses to be harnessed, so she could drive straight to town after dinner, as that was what she always did in such situations; they say she ate her dinner with a good appetite . . .'

'After she'd been beaten?'

'. . . Well, you see, that was always one of her . . . customs, and no sooner had she finished than, so as not to be late in setting off, she went straight off to the bath-house . . . You see, she was apparently taking baths as part of some treatment; they have a cold spring there and she used to bathe in it regularly every day, and no sooner had she entered the water than she suddenly had a stroke!'

'I bet she did!' Zosimov said.

'And had he beat her badly?'

'Oh come, that's neither here nor there,' Dunya retorted.

'Hm! Actually, mother, I don't know why you're bothering to tell me all this nonsense,' Raskolnikov said suddenly in an irritable tone, almost as if without meaning to.

'Well, my dear, I didn't know what to talk about,' burst from Pulkheria Aleksandrovna.

'What is it – are you all afraid of me, or something?' he said with a distorted smile.

'It really is true,' said Dunya, looking sternly and directly at her brother. 'When we were coming up the staircase, mother was actually crossing herself from fear.'

His face was wrenched by a kind of convulsion.

'Oh, what's got into you, Dunya? Please don't be angry, Rodya . . . Why did you say that, Dunya?' Pulkheria Aleksandrovna said in embarrassment. 'It's true that all the way here in the train I kept dreaming of how we were going to see each other again, how we would tell each other everything . . . and I was so happy that I didn't notice anything of the journey! But what am I going on about? I'm happy now . . . You really shouldn't say such things, Dunya! I'm happy just to see you, Rodya . . .'

'Yes, yes, mother,' he muttered, embarrassed, avoiding her with his eyes and giving her hand a squeeze. 'There'll be time for us to have a good talk!'

Having said this, he suddenly grew confused and turned pale: again a certain recent sensation traversed his soul with a deadly chill; again it suddenly became quite clear and self-evident to him that he had just told a horrible lie, that not only now would there not be time for him to have a good talk – it was now out of the question for him to *speak* to anyone about anything ever again. The effect on him of this tormenting thought was so powerful that for a split second he almost lost consciousness altogether; he got up from his seat and, without looking at anyone, began to march out of the room.

'What's up with you?' Razumikhin exclaimed, catching him by the arm.

He sat down again and began to look around him in silence; they were all looking at him in bewilderment.

'Why are you all looking so glum?' he cried suddenly, without any warning. 'Come on, say something! You can't go on sitting like that! Well, let's hear you talk! Let's have a conversation . . . Here we are, all gathered together, yet we haven't a word to say for ourselves . . . Come on, there must be something!'

'Oh, thank God! For a moment I thought he was going to start behaving like yesterday,' Pulkheria Aleksandrovna said, crossing herself.

'What's wrong, Rodya?' Avdotya Romanovna asked, suspiciously.

'Oh, it's nothing – I just remembered something silly, that's all,' he replied, and at once gave a laugh.

'Oh well, if it was something silly, that's all right! Just for a moment there I also began to think . . .' Zosimov muttered, getting up from the sofa. 'But it's time I was going; I may look in again . . . if I find you at home . . .'

He bowed to each of them in farewell and went out.

'What a wonderful man!' Pulkheria Aleksandrovna observed.

'Yes, he's wonderful, first-rate, educated, intelligent . . .' Raskolnikov suddenly said in an astonishing patter of words, and with an animation hitherto almost unprecedented. 'I can't remember where I first met him . . . it was some time before I fell ill . . . I think I met him somewhere . . . This is a fine chap, too!' he said, nodding at Razumikhin. 'How do you like him, Dunya?' he asked her, and suddenly, for no apparent reason, burst out laughing.

'Very much,' Dunya answered.

'Oh, really, Rodya, what an old . . . swine you are!' a terribly embarrassed and blushing Razumikhin managed to articulate, getting up from his chair. Pulkheria Aleksandrovna gave a slight smile, and Raskolnikov crowed with loud laughter.

'Where are you going?'

'I've also got . . . things to do.'

'No, you haven't. You stay here! Just because Zosimov's gone, it doesn't mean you have to go, too . . . What time is it? Is it twelve yet? What a pretty watch that is, Dunya! But why have you gone quiet again? I'm doing all the talking . . .'

'It was a present from Marfa Petrovna,' Dunya replied.

'And a very expensive one, too,' Pulkheria Aleksandrovna added.

'I say! It's so big, it's almost not like a ladies' watch at all.'

'I like watches like this,' said Dunya.

'So it's not a present from the bridegroom,' Razumikhin thought, and for some unknown reason felt relieved.

'I thought it was from Luzhin,' Raskolnikov observed.

'No, he hasn't given Dunechka any presents yet.'

'Oh, I say! I expect you remember, mother, the time when I, too, was in love and was going to get married,' he said suddenly, looking at his mother, who was struck by the strange manner and tone of voice in which he had begun to talk about this.

'Yes, yes, dear, I remember.' Pulkheria Aleksandrovna exchanged looks with Dunya and Razumikhin.

'Hm. Yes. What else is there to say? I can't even remember much about it now. She was a sickly sort of girl,' he went on, suddenly seeming to reflect, and lowering his eyes. 'Really not at all well: she was fond of giving to the poor, and she was always dreaming about joining a nunnery – she once actually burst into tears when she started to tell me about it; yes, yes . . . I remember . . . I remember very well. She was such a . . . plain little thing. I don't really know why I got so attached to her at the time, I think it must have been because she was always ill . . . If she'd been lame or a hunchback I'd have probably have fallen in love with her even more . . . (He smiled, reflectively.) Yes . . . It was a sort of spring fever . . .'

'No, it wasn't just spring fever,' Dunya said, animatedly.

He gave his sister a hard, intent look, but seemed not to catch what she had said, or possibly not to understand it. Then, in deep reflection, he got up, went over to his mother, gave her a kiss, returned to his place and sat down.

'You love her even now,' Pulkheria Aleksandrovna said, touched.

'Her? Now? Oh yes . . . you're talking about her! No. Now it's as if it had all happened in another world . . . and so long ago. And it's as if everything around me were happening somewhere else . . .'

He gave them a considering look.

'There you are, too . . . it's as if I were looking at you from a thousand miles away . . . But the devil knows why we're talking about this! Why ask me about it, in any case?' he added with annoyance, and fell silent, biting his fingernails and lapsing into reflection once more.

'What a horrible room you've got, Rodya – it's like a coffin,' Pulkheria Aleksandrovna said suddenly, breaking her painful silence. 'I'm convinced it's half because of this room that you've become such a melancholic.'

'This room? . . .' he replied, absent-mindedly. 'Yes, this room is responsible for quite a lot of things . . . I've also thought that . . . Oh, but if you only knew what a strange thing you said just now, mother,' he added suddenly, with a peculiar, ironic grin.

If this had gone on much longer, the company he was now in, with these members of his family whom he had not seen for three years, the family tone of the conversation coupled with the utter impossibility of actually discussing anything would have ended by becoming quite intolerable to him. There was, however, one urgent practical matter that he must decide today, one way or the other – so he had determined earlier, on awakening. Now he felt relief in the *practical*, as a way out of the situation.

'Look, Dunya,' he began seriously and coldly. 'Of course I'm sorry about the way I said goodbye to you yesterday, but I feel it's my duty to remind you again that I meant what I said. It's either me or Luzhin. I may be a villain, but you mustn't go down that road. That jumped-up nobody. If you marry Luzhin I'll stop regarding you as my sister.'

'Rodya, Rodya! Oh no, now you're acting the way you did yesterday!' Pulkheria Aleksandrovna wailed piteously. 'And why do you keep calling yourself a villain, I can't bear it! You said the same thing yesterday . . .'

'Brother,' Dunya replied firmly and also coldly, 'somewhere in all this there is an error on your part. I thought about it all last night, and I believe I know what that error is. The whole trouble with you is that you seem to believe I'm sacrificing myself to someone for someone else's sake. That really is not the case. I'm simply getting married for my own sake, because things are not going well for me; later on, of course, I shall be pleased if I can succeed in being of assistance to my family, but that is not the principal element in my determination . . .'

'She's lying!' he thought to himself, biting his fingernails in fury. 'The proud bitch. She doesn't want to admit that she has an ambition to be a benefactress . . . What arrogance! Oh, these base characters!

Even when they love it's as if they hated . . . Oh, how I . . . hate them all!'

'In other words,' Dunya continued, 'I am marrying Pyotr Petrovich because I consider that to be the lesser of two evils. I intend to fulfil decently all the expectations he has of me, and thus I am not deceiving him . . . Why did you smile like that just now?'

She flushed, and in her eyes there was a momentary gleam of anger.

'Ah, so you're going to fulfil them all, are you?' he asked, with a poisonous smile.

'Within certain limits. Both the manner and the form of Pyotr Petrovich's proposal showed me at once what he requires. Of course, it's probably true that he has rather too high an opinion of himself, but I hope that he has a high opinion of me, too . . . Why are you laughing again?'

'Why are you blushing again? You're lying, sister, you're lying for the sake of it, out of sheer female cussedness, just in order to have your own way with me . . . You can't possibly respect Luzhin: I've met him and talked to him. So what you're doing is selling yourself for money, or at any rate acting basely, and I'm glad you can at least blush about it!'

'It's not true, I'm not lying! . . .' Dunya exclaimed, losing all her sang-froid. 'I won't marry him unless I'm convinced that he has a high opinion of me and will look after me; I won't marry him unless I'm firmly persuaded that I can respect him. Fortunately, I am so persuaded, and have actually received certain confirmation of that today. And a marriage of this kind is not a "vile business", as you call it. Even if you were right, even if I really had decided to do something vile – wouldn't it be cruel of you to say a thing like that to me? Why do you demand of me a heroism you yourself probably don't possess? That's despotism! It's coercion! If I ruin anyone's life, it will only be my own . . . I haven't killed anyone yet! . . . Why are you looking at me like that? Why have you gone so pale? Rodya, what's the matter with you? Rodya, dear . . .'

'Oh, good Lord! You've given him a fainting-fit!' Pulkheria Aleksandrovna exclaimed.

'No, no . . . it's not serious . . . it's nothing . . . My head started to go round, that's all. It's not a fainting-fit! You've got fainting-fits on the brain . . . Hm . . . Yes . . . Now what was I going to say? Yes:

283

what is this "certain confirmation" you received today that makes you able to respect him and know that he . . . has a high opinion of you, as you said? You did say today, didn't you? Or did I mishear you?'

'Mother, show Rodya Pyotr Petrovich's letter,' Dunya said.

With trembling hands Pulkheria Aleksandrovna gave him the letter. He took it with great curiosity. But, before unfolding it, he suddenly looked at Dunya with vague astonishment.

'It's funny,' he said slowly, as though a new idea had suddenly occurred to him. 'Why am I getting so worked up? What's all the fuss about? Go and marry anyone you like!'

He said it almost to himself, but spoke the words out loud and looked at his sister for a moment or two, seemingly perplexed.

At last he unfolded the letter, still retaining an air of strange and vague astonishment; then slowly and attentively he began to read it, and read it through twice. Pulkheria Aleksandrovna was in a state of peculiar anxiety; and indeed they were all waiting for something peculiar to happen.

'I find this surprising,' he began after some reflection, handing the letter back to his mother, but not addressing anyone in particular. 'I mean, he's a man of business, a lawyer, and he even talks in that special way . . . with a bit of a flourish; yet he writes like an illiterate.'

They all shifted uneasily; this was not at all what they had been expecting.

'Oh, they all write like that,' Razumikhin observed, curtly.

'You've read it, too, have you?'

'Yes.'

'We showed it to him, Rodya, we . . . asked for his advice earlier,' an embarrassed Pulkheria Aleksandrovna began.

'It's actually written in a judicial style,' Razumikhin cut in. 'Judicial documents are still written like that.'

'Judicial? Yes, that's right – a judicial, business style . . . Not exactly illiterate, but not what you might call literary, either; a business style!'

'Pyotr Petrovich makes no attempt to conceal the fact that he was brought up on a shoestring, and actually boasts of having made his own way in the world,' Avdotya Romanovna observed, slightly offended by her brother's new tone.

'Well, if he boasts of it, there must be something in it. Don't let me contradict him. If you ask me, sister, you're offended because after reading the whole letter I could only find such a frivolous comment to make, and think I've started talking about such trifles in order to upset you because I'm annoyed with you. On the contrary: with regard to the style there occurred to me an observation that is not at all out of place in the present context. There's a certain expression there: "you will have only yourself to thank", which puts it all very clearly and succinctly, and there's also his threat to walk out if I show up. That threat is nothing more nor less than a threat to abandon you both if you don't obey him, and do it to you now, when he's brought you all the way to St Petersburg. Well, what's your opinion? Don't you think one ought to be offended at such an expression from Luzhin every bit as much as if he had used it (he pointed to Razumikhin), or Zosimov, or any of the rest of us?'

'N-no,' Dunya replied, growing animated. 'I realized very well that that bit was put too clumsily and that perhaps he's not all that gifted at writing . . . It was clever of you to spot that, Rodya. I actually didn't expect . . .'

'It's put in judicial language, and in judicial language that's the sort of thing they say, and I daresay it came out more crudely than he'd intended. But I'm afraid I'm going to have to disillusion you a bit; there's another expression in that letter, a certain slanderous remark about myself, and a pretty vile one, too. I gave that money yesterday to a consumptive and broken widow, and not "on the pretext of funeral expenses", but precisely in order to help her to cover them, and I didn't put the money in the hands of her daughter – an unmarried woman, as he writes, "of immoral behaviour" (and one, incidentally, whom I saw yesterday for the first time in my life), but gave it straight to the widow. In all this I see an over-hasty desire to blacken my name and make me quarrel with you. It's again expressed in judicial language, that's to say with an all too obvious disclosure of the intended aim, and with a haste that's thoroughly inept. He's a clever man, but in order to act cleverly, cleverness alone is not enough. It all bespeaks the man and . . . I don't really think he has a high opinion of you. I'm telling you this solely for your own edification, because I sincerely wish you well . . .'

Dunya made no reply; her decision had been made long ago, and she was simply waiting for it to be evening.

'So what have you decided, Rodya?' Pulkheria Aleksandrovna asked, disturbed even more than she had been the previous day, the source of her fresh anxiety being his new and suddenly adopted 'business-like' tone of voice.

'What do you mean – decided?'

'Well, Pyotr Petrovich says in his letter that he doesn't want you to be present this evening and that he'll leave . . . if you come. So – will you?'

'I must say I think that's not for me to decide, but for you, if Pyotr Petrovich's demand doesn't seem offensive to you; and secondly for Dunya, if she's also not offended by it. As for myself, I will do what you prefer,' he added coldly.

'Dunya has already decided, and I agree with her completely,' Pulkheria Aleksandrovna hurried to insert.

'Rodya, I've decided to ask you most urgently to be present at this meeting of ours,' Dunya said. 'Will you come?'

'I will.'

'I'd like to ask you to come and join us at eight o'clock, too,' she said, turning to Razumikhin. 'Mother, I'm inviting him, too.'

'That's excellent, Dunya. Well, since you're all decided now, let that be the way it's to be,' Pulkheria Aleksandrovna added. 'Why, I feel better now; I don't like all that pretence and lying; I'd rather we spoke the whole truth . . . whether it makes Pyotr Petrovich angry or not!'

IV

Just then the door opened quietly, and a certain young girl entered the room, looking timidly around her. They all turned towards her in surprise and curiosity. It took Raskolnikov a glance or two before he recognized her. This was Sofya Semyonovna Marmeladova. He had seen her the evening before, but such had been the moment, the surroundings and her manner of dress that his memory had retained the image of someone very different. Now she was modestly and even poorly dressed, and she looked very young, almost like a little girl, with a modest and demure manner and a clear but rather frightened-looking face. She was wearing a very plain little house-dress, and on her head there was an old-fashioned bonnet of a kind that is no longer worn; the only item of yesterday's costume was the parasol, which she held in one hand. Having suddenly realized that the room was full of people, she was less embarrassed than completely at a loss, as intimidated as a small child, and she even made a movement as if to go away again.

'Oh . . . it's you!' Raskolnikov said, extremely surprised, and was suddenly himself thrown off-balance.

It immediately occurred to him that his mother and sister must already have picked up some knowledge in passing from Luzhin's letter about an unmarried woman 'of immoral conduct'. Only just now he had been protesting against Luzhin's slanderous remarks, mentioning that he had seen the woman for the first time on the day in question, and now here she was. He remembered, too, that he had raised no protest against Luzhin's use of the expression 'of immoral conduct'. All this slipped through his head obscurely, in an instant. Giving her a closer look, however, he suddenly perceived that this humiliated creature was so humble that he felt sorry for her. And when she made that movement to flee in terror – something in him seemed to turn over.

'I wasn't expecting you at all,' he said hurriedly, stopping her with his gaze. 'Please be so good as to sit down. I expect you've come from Katerina Ivanovna. No, not over here, please sit there . . .'

When Sonya had come in, Razumikhin, who was sitting on one of Raskolnikov's three chairs, right beside the door, had got up in order to allow her into the room. At first Raskolnikov had been about to ask her to sit down in the corner of the sofa where Zosimov had sat, but reflecting that this sofa was rather too 'familiar' a spot, as it served him as a bed, he hastily directed her to Razumikhin's chair.

'And you sit here,' he said to Razumikhin, motioning to him to sit down in the corner Zosimov had occupied.

Sonya sat down, almost shivering with terror, and gave the two ladies a timid look. It was evident that she herself had not the faintest idea of how she could possibly have sat down beside them. Having pondered this, she grew so frightened that she suddenly got up again and, in complete confusion, turned to Raskolnikov.

'I . . . I've . . . only dropped in for a moment, forgive me for

287

disturbing you,' she said, falteringly. 'I've come from Katerina Iva-novna, there was no one else she could send . . . she told me to say that she would be very glad if you would come to the funeral tomorrow morning . . . for the service . . . at the Mitrofaniyev Cemetery,* and then . . . to our home . . . to her home . . . after-wards, to take some food . . . You would be doing her an honour . . . She told me to ask you.'

Sonya faltered and was silent.

'I'll certainly . . . see if I can . . . certainly . . .' Raskolnikov replied, who had also got up and was also faltering, his sentence unfinished . . . 'Look, do me the favour of sitting down,' he said suddenly. 'I want to talk to you. Please – I know you're probably in a hurry – but do me this favour and give me two minutes of your time . . .'

And he moved up a chair for her. Sonya again sat down, again gave the two ladies a quick look of timid embarrassment, and suddenly lowered her gaze.

Raskolnikov's pale face flushed; he seemed to convulse all over; his eyes caught fire.

'Mother,' he said firmly and insistently. 'This is Sofya Semyonovna Marmeladova, the daughter of poor Mr Marmeladov, the man whom I saw run down by the horses yesterday and whom I've already told you about . . .'

Pulkheria Aleksandrovna glanced at Sonya and narrowed her eyes at her slightly. In spite of all her confusion before Rodya's insistent and challenging stare, she could on no account deny herself this satisfaction. Dunya had battened her gaze earnestly and directly on the poor girl's face, and was examining her with perplexity. On hearing the introduction, Sonya looked up again, but this time grew even more embarrassed.

'What I wanted to ask you,' Raskolnikov said, turning to her, 'is how you've managed to cope with things today? Have you had any trouble? . . . from the police, for example?'

'No, sir, it all went . . . I mean, it's only too plain to see what caused his death; no one's given us any trouble; except the other lodgers – they're angry with us.'

'Why?'

'Because the body's lying out too long . . . I mean, it's so hot just now, there's a smell . . . so they're taking it to the cemetery today,

288

before vespers, to lie in the chapel until tomorrow. Katerina Ivanovna didn't want them to at first, but now she sees herself it won't do . . .'

'So they're moving it today, are they?'

'Yes, and she wants you to do us the honour of coming to the funeral service in the church tomorrow, and then attending the funeral repast at her home.'

'She's arranging the funeral repast?'

'Yes, sir – some *zakuski*; she told me to thank you very much for coming to our assistance yesterday . . . If it hadn't been for you we'd never ever have been able to find the money to bury him.' Both her lips and her chin suddenly began to dance, but she mastered and restrained herself, quickly lowering her eyes to the ground again.

During the course of their conversation, Raskolnikov studied her fixedly. This was a thin, very thin and pale little face, rather irregular and sharp, with a sharp, small nose and chin. One could certainly not have called her pretty, but on the other hand her blue eyes were so clear, and when they grew animated the expression of her face became so kind and open-hearted that one felt oneself involuntarily drawn to her. There was about her face, moreover, as about all the rest of her, one peculiar distinguishing feature: in spite of her eighteen years, she still looked more or less like a little girl, far younger than she was, almost a complete child, and occasionally, in some of her movements, this made itself almost absurdly evident.

'But can Katerina Ivanovna really manage all this on such limited means? She's even planning *zakuski*? . . .' Raskolnikov asked, insistently continuing the conversation.

'Well, the coffin's to be a simple one, sir . . . and the whole thing will be simple, so it won't cost much . . . Katerina Ivanovna and I worked it all out earlier on so that there would be enough left for a meal in his memory . . . and Katerina Ivanovna very much wants there to be one. I mean one can't . . . her that consolation . . . I mean, that's the way she is, sir, you know her . . .'

'I understand, I understand . . . of course . . . Why are you staring at my room like that? You know, my mother says *it* looks like a coffin!'

'You gave us all the money you had yesterday!' Sonya said suddenly by way of reply, in a kind of loud, hurried whisper, and then with equal suddenness lowered her eyes as far as she could. Her lips and chin began to dance again. Ever since she had come in she had been struck by Raskolnikov's impoverished surroundings, and now these words broke from her suddenly of their own accord. A silence ensued. Dunya's eyes brightened a little, and Pulkheria Aleksandrovna even gave Sonya a friendly look.

'Rodya,' she said, getting up, 'it goes without saying that we'll have dinner together. Come along, Dunya . . . And you ought to go out for a bit of a walk, Rodya; after that, have a rest, lie down for a while, and then come to us as soon as you can . . . Otherwise I'm afraid we'll have tired you out . . .'

'Yes, yes, I'll come,' he replied, getting up and starting to bustle about. 'Actually, there's some business I have to attend to . . .'

'I say, you're not going to have dinner on your own, are you?' Razumikhin exclaimed, looking at Raskolnikov in astonishment. 'What *are* you up to?'

'Yes, yes, I'll come, don't worry, don't worry . . . Anyway, I want you to stay for a minute. After all, you don't need him right now, do you, mother? Or am I perhaps depriving you of him?'

'Oh no, no! Now then, Dmitry Prokofich, you will come and dine with us, too, won't you?'

'Please do,' Dunya said entreatingly.

Razumikhin bowed, beaming all over. For a moment they all suddenly grew strangely embarrassed.

'Goodbye, Rodya, or rather *until we meet*; I don't like saying "goodbye". Goodbye, Nastasya . . . Oh, there, I said it again . . . !'

Pulkheria Aleksandrovna intended to bow to Sonya as well, but somehow failed to get round to it and made a bustled exit from the room.

Avdotya Romanovna, on the other hand, had evidently been awaiting her turn and, as she walked past Sonya in the wake of her mother, made her an attentive, polite and completely formed bow. Sonya grew flustered, bowed back in a hurried, frightened sort of way, and a look of pain appeared in her features, as though she found Avdotya Romanovna's politeness and attention distressful and tormenting.

'Goodbye, Dunya!' Raskolnikov shouted, when they were already out on the stairs. 'Give me your hand!'

'But I've already given it to you, remember?' Dunya replied, turning round to face him, affectionately and awkwardly.

'Never mind, let me take it again!'

And he squeezed her fingers tightly. Dunya smiled at him, blushed, quickly extricated her hand from his and followed her mother downstairs, also for some reason thoroughly happy.

'Well, there's a glorious thought!' he said to Sonya as he came back to his room, giving her a bright look. 'May the Lord grant rest to the souls of the dead, and let life be the realm of the living! That's right, isn't it? Isn't it? Don't you think so!'

Sonya looked at his suddenly brightened features with positive wonderment; for a few split seconds he stared at her silently and fixedly: at that moment all the things her dead father had told him about her suddenly passed through his memory . . .

'Oh good heavens, Dunechka!' Pulkheria Aleksandrovna said, as soon as they were out in the street. 'Why, I mean, I really think I'm glad we left; I feel easier somehow. Well, I must say that as I sat in the train I never dreamt I would feel this sort of relief.'

'I tell you again, mother – he's still very ill. Can't you see it? It may be that worrying about us has upset him. We must try to be tolerant, and then we'll be able to forgive him a great, great many things.'

'Well, you haven't been doing very well at being tolerant, have you?' Pulkheria Aleksandrovna at once interrupted with fervid jealousy. 'You know, Dunya, I was watching you both just now, you're the complete likeness of him, not so much in your features as in your soul: you're both melancholics, both gloomy and liable to flare up, both overweening and both generous . . . I mean, it couldn't just be that he's an egoist, Dunechka? Eh? . . . Oh, when I think of what may happen at our lodgings this evening, my heart stops beating!'

'Don't worry yourself, mother; what will be, will be.'

'Dunechka! But just think of the situation we're in now! I mean, what if Pyotr Petrovich withdraws his suit?' poor Pulkheria Aleksandrovna suddenly said, incautiously.

'And what would he be worth after that?' Dunya replied sharply and contemptuously.

'We did the right thing in leaving just now,' Pulkheria Aleksandrovna broke in at once, quickly. 'He was hurrying off somewhere on business; let him get out and do some walking, breathe some air . . . it's horribly stuffy in that place of his . . . though where's he going to find air here? These streets are just like rooms without ventilators. God, what a town! . . . Wait, look out, you'll be crushed, those people are carrying something! Why, it's a piano they're carrying, I do believe . . . How they're pushing one another . . . That young lady makes me very frightened . . .'

'What young lady, mother?'

'That one, that Sofya Semyonovna who was with us just now . . .'

'Why?'

'I have a sort of premonition, Dunya. Believe it or not, as soon as she walked in just then I thought: "She's at the bottom of it all . . ."'

'She's not at the bottom of anything!' Dunya exclaimed in vexation. 'Oh, you and your premonitions, mother! He only met her yesterday, and when she walked in just now he didn't even recognize her.'

'Well, you wait and see! . . . She worries me; you'll see, you'll see! And what a fright she gave me – looking at me with those eyes of hers, I could hardly stay in my chair, do you remember, when he started to introduce her? And I find it strange that Pyotr Petrovich should have written the way he did about her in his letter, yet he introduced her to us, and to you, as well! That means he must be attached to her!'

'Oh, he writes all sorts of things! He said them about us, too, and put them in his letters to people, or have you forgotten? I'm sure she's . . . perfectly all right, and that all these things you're saying are nonsense!'

'I hope to God you're right!'

'And Pyotr Petrovich is a worthless gossip-monger,' Dunya suddenly snapped out.

Pulkheria Aleksandrovna fairly wilted. The conversation broke off.

'Look, this is what I want to talk to you about . . .' Raskolnikov said, drawing Razumikhin over to the window . . .

'So I'll tell Katerina Ivanovna you're coming . . .' Sonya said quickly, bowing in order to leave.

'Just one moment, Sofya Semyonovna, we have no secrets, you're not intruding on us . . . There are a couple of other things I'd like to say to you . . . Look,' he said suddenly, not finishing his sentence, and turning back to Razumikhin as though tearing himself away. 'You know that fellow . . . what's his name . . . Povfiry Petrovich?'

'I should think I do! He's a relative of mine. Why do you ask about him?' Razumikhin added with a small explosion of curiosity.

'Well, yesterday you said that he's . . . in charge of this case . . . you know, this murder business . . .'

'Yes . . . And? . . .'

'You said he'd been questioning the people who'd pawned things with the old woman. Well, I pawned some stuff with her, too – oh, just rubbish, but there was a ring of my sister's which she gave me as a keepsake when I left for St Petersburg, and a silver watch that belonged to my father. They're worth no more than five or six roubles in all, but they're precious to me for the memories they contain. So now what am I to do? I don't want to lose the objects, particularly the watch. I was terribly afraid that mother might ask to have a look at it when we began talking about Dunechka's watch. It's the only thing of father's that's left in the family. She'll make herself ill if it gets lost! Women! So what am I to do, tell me! I know I ought to go to the police station. But wouldn't it be better if I just went to see Porfiry? Eh? What do you think? I want to get the matter sorted out quickly. You'll see – mother will ask me for that watch before dinner!'

'On no account go to the police station, and by all means go and see Porfiry!' Razumikhin exclaimed in a state of uncommon excitement. 'Oh, what a relief! Hang it all, let's go there now, it's only a couple of yards away, we're sure to find him in!'

'Very likely . . . yes, let's . . .'

'And he'll be very, very, very pleased to meet you! I've told him a lot of things about you at various times . . . I was talking to him about you just yesterday. Come on! . . . So you knew the old woman, did you. Aha! . . . This is all turning out most mar-vel-lous-ly! . . . Ah yes . . . Sofya Ivanovna . . .'

'Sofya Semyonovna,' Raskolnikov said, correcting him. 'Sofya Semyonovna, this is my friend Razumikhin, and he's a good man . . .'

'If you have to go now . . .' Sonya began, not looking at Razumikhin at all, and becoming even more embarrassed as a result . . .

'Come on, let's be off!' Raskolnikov said, decisively. 'I shall come and see you today, Sofya Semyonovna, only you'll have to tell me where you live.'

He was less disconcerted than in a kind of hurry, and he avoided her gaze. Sonya gave him her address, blushing as she did so. They all went out together.

'Don't you bother to lock your door?' asked Razumikhin, coming down the stairs after them.

'Never! . . . Actually, I've been meaning to buy a lock these past two years,' he added casually. 'The people who have nothing to lock up are the happy ones, aren't they?' he said, turning to Sonya, and laughing.

When they got outside they stopped at the gates.

'Is it off to the right you go, Sofya Semyonovna? Incidentally, how did you manage to find me?' he asked, in a way that suggested he really wanted to say something quite different to her. He kept wanting to look into her clear, quiet eyes, and this aim somehow kept eluding him.

'Oh, you gave Polechka your address yesterday.'

'Polya! Ah yes . . . Polechka! That . . . little girl . . . she's your sister? So I gave her my address, did I?'

'Do you really not remember?'

'Yes . . . I do . . .'

'And I heard about you from my poor dead father that time . . . Only I didn't know your name then, and neither did he . . . I came here today . . . and since I'd found out your name yesterday . . . I asked: "Does Mr Raskolnikov live here?" . . . Not knowing that you were a lodger, too . . . Goodbye, sir . . . I'll tell Katerina Ivanovna . . .'

She was immensely relieved to have finally got away; she hurried off with her eyes lowered, anxious to get out of their sight, to cover those twenty yards as quickly as possible and then turn along the street to the right and be at last on her own, and then, as she walked on her way, making haste, not looking at anyone, paying no attention to anything, to think, remembering, considering each word that had been spoken, each circumstance of the situation. Never, never had she experienced anything like this before. An entire new world had settled, mysteriously and dimly, on her soul. She suddenly remembered that Raskolnikov had said he would come to see her today, perhaps this very morning, perhaps right now!

'Oh, not today, please not today!' she murmured with a trembling of her heart, as if she were imploring someone, like a child that is frightened. 'Oh merciful Lord! To my lodgings . . . to that room . . . he'll see . . . Oh merciful Lord!'

And so it was hardly surprising that she failed to notice a certain gentleman, not of her acquaintance, who at that moment had his gaze assiduously fixed upon her and was following close on her heels. He had been following her ever since she had emerged from the gateway. Just as all three of them, Razumikhin, Raskolnikov and herself, had stopped for a couple of words on the pavement, this passer-by had suddenly seemed to give a start as he made his way round them and, in so doing, unexpectedly caught Sonya's words: 'I asked: "Does Mr Raskolnikov live here?"' Quickly, but attentively, he examined all three, in particular Raskolnikov, to whom Sonya had been speaking; then he looked at the building and seemed to make a note of it. All this had happened within the space of instant, on the move, and the passer-by, desirous of remaining unnoticed, had walked on, slowing his pace and apparently waiting for something. What he was waiting for was Sonya; he had realized that they were saying goodbye to one another and that Sonya was just about to return to wherever it was she lived.

'I wonder where that is? I'm sure I've seen that face before,' he thought, as he recalled Sonya's features . . . 'I must find out.'

When he reached the turning he crossed to the other side of the street, swung round and observed that Sonya was now coming along the same way he had come, oblivious to everything. Sure enough, upon reaching the same turning, she entered the street in which he stood. He set off after her, keeping his eyes fixed on her from the opposite pavement; having gone some fifty yards or so, he crossed back to the side of the street along which Sonya was making her way. caught her up and began to walk behind her at a distance of about five paces.

He was a man of around fifty, of somewhat above average height, with broad, perpendicular shoulders that gave him a slightly stooping appearance. He was dressed in stylish comfort, and looked like a portly aristocrat. In one of his hands he held an elegant walking-stick which he tapped on the pavement with each step he took, and those hands wore freshly laundered gloves. His broad, high-cheekboned face was pleasant enough, and its complexion was a fresh one of a kind one does not often encounter in St Petersburg. His hair, still very thick, was entirely blond, with the merest hint of grey here and there, and his wide, thick beard, which descended in a square, shovel-shape, was even fairer than the hair of his head. His eyes were blue and had a cold, fixed and reflective look; his lips were bright red. All in all, he was a remarkably well-preserved man, who looked much younger than his years.

When Sonya came out on to the Canal, they found themselves together on the pavement. As he watched her, he had time to note her pensive, distracted air. On reaching the building where she lived, Sonya turned in at the gates, and he walked in after her, somewhat surprised. Entering the courtyard, she turned right towards that corner of it which housed the entrance of the staircase that led up to her lodgings. 'Aha!' muttered the unknown aristocrat, and began to make his way up the stairs behind her. Only then did Sonya notice him. She reached the third floor, turned off down the connecting passage and rang the doorbell of apartment number nine, on the door of which was chalked 'Kapernaumov, Tailor'. 'Aha!' the stranger said again, surprised by the odd coincidence, and rang the bell of apartment number eight, next door. The two doors were some six yards distant from each other.

'You live at Kapernaumov's!' he said, looking at Sonya and laughing. 'He altered a waistcoat for me yesterday. Well, I live here, next door to you, in the home of Madam Resslich, Gertruda Karlovna, you know. Such is fate!'

Sonya gave him a close look.

'We're neighbours,' he went on, in a voice that was for some reason particularly cheerful. 'I mean, I've been in town for three days. Well, goodbye for now.'

Sonya did not reply; the door opened, and she slipped through to her room. For some reason she felt ashamed, and she even looked frightened . . .

As they made their way to Porfiry's, Razumikhin was in an especially excited frame of mind.

'This is marvellous, brother,' he said several times. 'How relieved, how relieved I am!'

'What are you so relieved at?' Raskolnikov wondered to himself.

'I mean, I had no idea you'd also pawned things with the old woman. And . . . and . . . how long ago was this? I mean, how long ago was it that you went to see her?'

'What a naïve fool!' Raskolnikov thought.

'Now when was it? . . .' he said out loud, pausing as he tried to remember. 'Yes, I think I went to see her about three days before she died. By the way, I'm not going there in order to redeem the objects now,' he interposed with a special kind of hurried concern about the objects. 'I mean, I've only got one rouble in silver to my name . . . all because of that damned delirium I had yesterday!'

As he mentioned the delirium he made his voice sound particularly emphatic.

'Yes, yes, yes,' Razumikhin agreed hurriedly, and for no apparent reason. 'And that's why you were so . . . taken aback, so to speak . . . and you know, even in your delirium you kept going on about some rings and chains and things! . . . Yes, yes . . . It all makes sense, it all makes sense now.'

'So that's it!' Raskolnikov thought. 'That's how far that idea has worked its way among them! I mean, this man would go to Calvary for my sake, yet even he's thoroughly relieved that it's been *cleared up* why I kept mentioning those rings when I was delirious! That's the kind of hold it's got on them all! . . .'

'But will he be in?' he asked, suddenly.

'He will, he will,' Razumikhin hurried to reassure him. 'He's a marvellous fellow, brother, you'll see! He's a bit clumsy – oh, he's a man of the world all right, but I mean clumsy in another sense. He's a clever chap, with a lot of common sense, even, only he has a rather peculiar cast of mind . . . He's suspicious, a sceptic, a cynic . . . he likes to hoodwink people – oh, I don't really mean hoodwink, it's more that he likes to make fools of them . . . You know, the old material method . . . And he knows his job, oh, he knows it, all right . . . There was one case he cleared up last year, concerning a murder, in which nearly all the clues had been lost! He's very, very, very anxious to make your acquaintance!'

'Why all the "very"s?'

'Oh, it's not that he . . . Just recently, you see, when you were ill, I often and repeatedly found myself mentioning you . . . Well, he used to listen . . . and when he found out that you're in the law faculty and are unable to finish your course because of your financial circumstances, he said: "What a pity!" And I concluded . . . well, taking it all together, I mean, it wasn't just that, there's something else as well: yesterday Zamyotov . . . Look, Rodya, I said a lot of silly things to you when I was drunk yesterday and we were going home . . . and well, brother, I'm scared you may have blown them up out of all proportion, you see . . .'

'What's all this about? You mean this business about them thinking

I'm insane? Well, perhaps they're right.' He smiled a thin, ironic smile.

'Yes . . . yes . . . dammit, I mean, no! . . . Well, everything I said (including whatever I said about that other business) was all nonsense and the result of my hangover.'

'Oh, why do you keep apologizing? I'm getting really fed up with all this!' Raskolnikov shouted with exaggerated irritability. He was, indeed, to a certain extent pretending.

'I know, I know, I understand. Please believe me, I understand. I'm even ashamed to talk about it . . .'

'Well, don't then!'

They both fell silent. Razumikhin was in a state bordering upon ecstasy, and Raskolnikov sensed this with disgust. He was also alarmed by the things Razumikhin had just said about Porfiry.

'I'll have to complain about my lot to this fellow, too,' he thought, turning pale, his heart thumping. 'And make it sound natural. The most natural thing would be to say nothing at all along those lines. Make damned sure I don't say anything! No, but that would *also* be unnatural . . . Well, we'll soon see . . . how things turn out . . . when we get there . . . is it a good thing I'm going there or isn't it? The moth flies to the candle-flame of its own accord. My heart's thumping, that's the worst of it!'

'It's this grey building,' Razumikhin said.

'What matters most of all is whether Porfiry knows I went to that old witch's apartment yesterday . . . and asked about the blood. I must find that out immediately, right at the start, as soon as I go in, find it out by the expression on his face; o-ther-wise . . . I'm done for!'

'You know what, brother?' he said suddenly, turning to Razumikhin with a mischievous smile. 'I've noticed that ever since this morning you've been in a state of extraordinary excitement. True?'

'What do you mean? I don't know what you're talking about,' Razumikhin winced.

'No, brother, that's no good, it's too obvious. You were sitting on your chair back there just now in a way you never normally do, you were sitting right on the edge of it, and you kept having minor convulsions. You'd jump to your feet for no apparent reason. One minute you were angry and the next your ugly mug would mysteriously turn as sweet as toffee. You even blushed; especially when they asked you to dinner, you turned horribly red.'

'I never did; that's nonsense! . . . What are you driving at, anyway?'

'For heaven's sake, you're cringing like a schoolboy! My God, there he is, blushing again!'

'Oh, you are a swine!'

'What are you so embarrassed about? Romeo! You just wait, I'll tell a few people about this today, ha-ha-ha! I'll make mother laugh, and someone else as well . . .'

'Listen, listen, listen, I mean, this is serious, I mean, this is . . . What are you trying to say, you devil?' Razumikhin said in confusion, turning cold with horror. '*What* will you tell them? You know, brother, I . . . Ugh, what a swine you are!'

'Like a rose in springtime! And how it suits you, if only you knew; a Romeo seven feet tall! I say, you *have* washed yourself nicely today, cleaned your fingernails, eh? I've never known you do that before! My God, you've even pomaded your hair! Come on, let me see, bend down!'

'*Swine!*'

Raskolnikov was laughing so hard that it seemed he would never stop, and thus it was with laughter that they entered Porfiry Petrovich's apartment. That was what Raskolnikov had wanted: from the rooms within it could be heard that they had been laughing as they came in and were still guffawing as they stood in the entrance hall.

'Not another word in here, or I'll . . . smash your skull!' Razumikhin whispered in fury, seizing Raskolnikov by the shoulder.

V

Raskolnikov was already on his way into the interior of the apartment. He had gone in looking as though he were doing all he possibly could in order not to burst with laughter. Behind him, as red as a peony, with a countenance that displayed rage and frustration, lanky of limb and clumsy of hand and foot, came the embarrassed Razumikhin. At that moment the expression of his face and figure really was absurd, and fully justified Raskolnikov's laughter. Raskolnikov, who had not yet been introduced, bowed to the master of the premises, who stood in the middle of the room and was looking at them inquiringly, extended his hand and shook that of his host, still making an extreme and visible effort to choke back his merriment and get out at least a couple of words of self-introduction. Scarcely, however, had he succeeded in assuming a serious air than suddenly, as though unable to help himself, he glanced at Razumikhin again and this time failed to restrain himself: the smothered laughter burst forth all the more uncontainably for having been held back until now.

The extraordinary rage with which Razumikhin greeted this 'sincere' laughter gave the whole of this scene an air of the most unfeigned joviality and – most importantly – naturalness. Razumikhin, as though on purpose, did his bit to help things along.

'You horrible devil!' he roared, gesturing with one arm, and immediately bringing it down on a small, round table on which stood an empty tea-glass. Everything went flying and splintering.

'I say, why break the chairs, gentlemen? It's a drain on the exchequer,'* Porfiry exclaimed merrily.

The scene unrolled in the following manner: Raskolnikov continued to laugh, his hand forgotten in that of his host, but, knowing when enough was enough, began to look for an opportunity of bringing his mirth to as swift and natural a conclusion as possible. Razumikhin, brought at last to the point of total disorientation by the falling of the table and the smashing of the glass, cast a gloomy eye at the splinters, made a mock spitting gesture, and turned abruptly towards the window, where he stood with his back to his audience, his face like thunder, looking outside and seeing nothing. Porfiry Petrovich was laughing, and quite prepared to go on laughing, but it was plain that he wanted an explanation. Zamyotov, who had been sitting on a chair in one corner, had risen to his feet at the entrance of the visitors and was standing expectantly, his mouth turned up in a smile, but in a state of bewilderment and even incredulity as he observed the entire scene, viewing Raskolnikov with downright embarrassment. Zamyotov's unexpected presence came as an unpleasant shock to Raskolnikov.

'I'll have to get to the bottom of this,' he thought.

'Please, you must forgive me,' he began, thrown badly off balance. 'Raskolnikov's the name.'

'Oh, for goodness' sake, sir, it's pleasant to meet you, and very pleasantly you came in, too . . . What about him, doesn't he want to say hallo?' Porfiry Petrovich said, nodding to Razumikhin.

'I honestly don't know why he got into such a rage at me. All I did was to tell him on the way here that he was a Romeo, and . . . and backed it up with evidence. I don't think I said anything else.'

'Swine!' Razumikhin answered, without turning round.

'Well, there must be something very serious behind it if he lost his temper at one little word,' Porfiry burst out, laughing.

'Oh you – investigator! . . . Oh, to the devil with the lot of you,' Razumikhin snapped, and then suddenly, himself bursting into laughter, his face cheerful now, went over to Porfiry Petrovich as though nothing had happened, and said:

'That's enough of that! We're all behaving like fools. Let's get down to business: this is my friend, Rodion Romanovich Raskolnikov. In the first place, he's heard a lot about you, and wanted to meet you, and in the second place, he's got a certain small item of business he'd like to talk to you about. Aha! Zamyotov! What are you doing here? I didn't know you knew each other. Known each other long, have you?'

'What's this, now?' Raskolnikov thought with alarm.

Zamyotov seemed a bit put out, but not very badly.

'I met him at your place last night,' he said casually.

'God must be looking after me: last week this fellow kept pestering me to introduce him to you, Porfiry Petrovich, and now you've sniffed each other out independently . . . That reminds me – where's your snuff?'

Porfiry Petrovich was dressed for a day at home, in a dressing-gown, a spotlessly clean shirt and a pair of down-at-heel slippers. He was a man of about thirty-five, slightly below average in height, well-fed, with even a slight paunch, clean-shaven, with neither moustache nor side-whiskers, the hair closely cropped on his large, round head, which somehow bulged with especial prominence at the rear. His round, puffy and slightly snub-nosed face had an unhealthy dark yellow hue, but it was cheerful enough, and even quizzical. It would even have been good-natured, were it not for the expression of his eyes, which had a kind of watery, liquid sheen, and were almost concealed by white, blinking eyelashes that seemed almost to be winking at someone. The look of those eyes was somehow strangely out of harmony with the rest of his figure, which had about it

301

something that could only be described as feminine, and lent it a far more serious air than one might have expected at first sight.

As soon as Porfiry Petrovich heard that his guest had a 'small item of business' to discuss with him, he lost no time in asking him to sit down on the sofa, himself sat down at its other end, and fixed his eyes upon him in eager anticipation of hearing the nature of the business, with that exaggerated and all-too-serious attention which actually has the effect of irking and embarrassing the other person right from the word go, particularly if he is a stranger and particularly if what he has to tell is, in his own opinion, quite unmeriting of such extraordinarily serious attention. Even so, in a few brief, coherent words Raskolnikov gave a clear and precise explanation of the matter, and was so pleased with himself that he even managed to take a good look at Porfiry. Porfiry Petrovich likewise did not remove his eyes from him during all the time he talked. Razumikhin, who had taken a seat opposite them, at the same table, hotly and impatiently followed Raskolnikov's account of the matter, every moment or so transferring his gaze from one to the other, until it began to get a little out of hand.

'Fool!' Raskolnikov cursed silently to himself.

'What you should do, sir, is make a statement to the police,' Porfiry replied with a thoroughly businesslike air. 'What you say is that having learned of such-and-such an occurrence – this murder in other words – you in your turn wish to inform the investigator in charge of the case that such-and-such objects are items of your possession and that you wish to redeem them . . . something of that sort . . . as a matter of fact, they'll write it for you.'

'You see, er, the thing is that just at this moment,' Raskolnikov said, trying to sound as embarrassed as possible, 'I'm right out of cash . . . and I can't even find the small change that would be necessary . . . what I'd like to do, you see, is simply make a declaration that these objects are mine, and that when I have the money . . .'

'That doesn't make any difference, sir,' Porfiry Petrovich replied, greeting this explanation of Raskolnikov's finances with coldness. 'But if you like you can simply write directly to me, saying something to the same effect, namely that having learned of such-and-such and wishing to make a declaration concerning such-and-such items of your possession, you request . . .'

'Can I write it on ordinary paper?' Raskolnikov hurriedly interrupted, again displaying an interest in the financial side of things.

'Oh, on the most ordinary you wish, sir!' And suddenly Porfiry Petrovich gave him an almost openly mocking look, narrowing his eyes and practically winking at him. This was, perhaps, only how it seemed to Raskolnikov, as it lasted no more than a split second. At least, something of the kind happened. Raskolnikov could have sworn that Porfiry had winked, the devil knew for what reason.

'He knows!' The thought flashed through him like lightning.

'You must forgive me for bothering you with such a trivial matter,' he went on, slightly thrown off his balance. 'Those things of mine aren't worth more than five roubles altogether, but they're particularly dear to me as a memory of those from whom I received them, and I must confess that when I found out about it I felt very alarmed . . .'

'You fairly flew up in the air yesterday when I happened to mention to Zosimov that Porfiry was questioning the people who'd pawned things with the old woman!' Razumikhin put in with evident intention.

This was now beyond endurance. Raskolnikov lost his self-control and glared at him viciously with black eyes that burned with anger. He at once pulled himself together.

'What's this, brother, are you making fun of me?' he said, addressing him with skilfully manufactured irritation. 'I can see that I'm possibly getting far too worked up about what to your eyes is simply old junk; but you can't call me either an egoist or greedy for that, and in my eyes those two worthless little objects aren't junk at all. I've only just finished telling you that that silver watch, which is only worth a few copecks, is the only thing of my father's we have left. You may laugh if you wish, but my mother came to see me,' he said, turning suddenly to Porfiry, 'and if she were to find out that the watch has been lost,' he went on, turning quickly to Razumikhin this time, exerting a special effort to make his voice tremble, 'she'd be in despair! Women!'

'You've got it all wrong! I didn't mean it that way at all! Just the other way about!' cried an aggrieved Razumikhin.

'I wonder if that was the right thing to do?' Raskolnikov thought to himself, with an inward tremor. 'Did it sound natural? Did I exaggerate too much? Why did I say "Women!" like that?'

'So your mother came to see you, did she?' Porfiry Petrovich wanted to know, for some reason.

'Yes.'

'When would that be, now, sir?'

'Yesterday evening.'

Porfiry said nothing, as though lost in thought.

'Your things can't possibly have got lost,' he went on, calmly and coldly. 'I've been waiting for you to get here for ages.'

And as though nothing were particularly the matter, he carefully began to push the ashtray towards Razumikhin, who was relentlessly scattering cigarette-ash on the carpet. Raskolnikov started, but Porfiry seemed not to notice, still worried about Razumikhin's cigarette.

'Wha-at? Waiting? You mean you knew he'd pawned stuff *there*?' Razumikhin exclaimed.

Porfiry Petrovich addressed Raskolnikov directly:

'Both of your articles, the ring and the watch, were found in *her* apartment wrapped up in the same piece of paper, with your name clearly marked in pencil on it, together with the date she received them from you . . .'

'How come you're so observant?' Raskolnikov smiled awkwardly, making a special effort to look him straight in the eye; but he could not control himself and suddenly added: 'I said that just now because there must have been an awful lot of people who'd pawned things . . . so many that it must have been hard for you to remember who they all were . . . Yet you seem to remember them all quite clearly, and . . . and . . .

'Stupid! Clumsy! Why did I put that in?'

'Practically all of those who'd pawned anything are now known to us, and you're the only one who hasn't been so good as to oblige,' Porfiry replied with a barely perceptible hint of mockery.

'I've not been entirely well.'

'I've heard about that too, sir. I also heard that you've been very upset about something. Why, even now you look pale.'

'I'm not pale at all . . . there's absolutely nothing the matter with me!' Raskolnikov snapped, rudely and aggressively, suddenly altering his tone. The aggression was seething up in him, and he was unable to check it. 'But if I behave aggressively I'll give myself away!' passed, again like a flash, through his head. 'Oh, why are they tormenting me? . . .'

'Not entirely well!' Razumikhin chipped in. 'Listen to the man! Up until yesterday he was practically unconscious, and raving . . . Would you believe it, Porfiry? He could scarcely stand upright, yet as soon as Zosimov and I had turned our backs yesterday he got his clothes on, took to his heels and went off playing silly pranks somewhere almost until midnight, and all of this, I tell you, in a state of the most complete delirium – can you imagine? Quite extraordinary!'

'You don't say? And in a *state of the most complete delirium*, too! Do tell me more!' Porfiry said, shaking his head with a womanish gesture.

'Oh, rot! Don't believe him! Well, you don't believe him anyway,' Raskolnikov blurted out, far too aggressively. But Porfiry Petrovich seemed not to hear these strange words.

'Well, if you weren't delirious, why did you go out then?' Razumikhin suddenly cried in angry vexation. 'Why did you? What was your purpose . . . And why did it have to be in secret? Were you in your right mind? Now that it's all over, I think I ought to be frank with you!'

'I got really fed up with everyone yesterday,' Raskolnikov said suddenly, turning to Porfiry with an insolently provocative smile, 'so I ran away from them in order to rent another room, where they wouldn't be able to find me, and I took a lot of money with me. Mr Zamyotov here saw the money. Well, Mr Zamyotov, was I in my right mind yesterday, or was I delirious? Please resolve our dispute for us!'

He looked as though he would have liked to strangle Zamyotov at that moment. Zamyotov's silence, and the way he was staring at him, were very decidedly not to his taste.

'Oh, in my opinion you were talking very sensibly, even cleverly, sir – though I must say you did seem rather irritable,' Zamyotov remarked, thinly.

'You know, Nikodim Fomich was telling me,' Porfiry Petrovich inserted, 'that he met you very late last night in the lodgings of some civil servant who'd been run down in the street . . .'

'Yes, what about that civil servant?' Razumikhin chimed in. 'Weren't you carrying on like a madman at his home? You gave all the money you had to his widow for funeral expenses! Well, if you'd wanted to help, I'd have understood if you'd given her fifteen, or even twenty or so, and left three for yourself, but you went and lavished the whole twenty-five on her!'

'And what if I'd found some hidden treasure that you don't know about? What if that's why I was so generous? . . . Ask Mr Zamyotov: he knows I've found some hidden treasure! Please forgive us,' he said, turning to Porfiry Petrovich, his lips quivering. 'It's really inexcusable of us to bother you for a whole half an hour with such a mundane recitation. You must be sick of us by now, eh?'

'For heaven's sake, sir, not at all, not at all! If you only knew the interest you arouse in me! It's so fascinating to watch and listen . . . indeed, I must confess I'm delighted you've been so good as to do me the honour at last.'

'What about some tea? My throat's as dry as a whistle!' Razumikhin exclaimed.

'A splendid idea! Perhaps we'll all join you. But wouldn't you like something a little more . . . essential first?'

'Spare us the hospitality!'

Porfiry Petrovich went off to order tea.

The thoughts were spinning round in Raskolnikov's head like a whirlwind. He was horribly over-stimulated.

'What's clear above all is that they're not bothering to cover anything up or stand upon ceremony! If he doesn't know me, why was he talking about me to Nikodim Fomich? It can only mean that they don't even want to conceal the fact that they're following me like a pack of dogs! They're prepared to spit in my face quite openly!' he thought, quivering with fury. 'Go on, why don't you just hit me straight out? Stop playing this cat-and-mouse game. I mean, it's offensive, Porfiry Petrovich, and in any case I may not let you go on with it! . . . I'll get up and blurt out the whole truth to the lot of you, right in your ugly mugs; and then you'll see what contempt I have for you! . . .' With effort he took a new breath. 'But what if it only seems this way to me? What if it's a mirage and I'm wrong about everything, what if I'm simply getting aggressive because of my inexperience, my inability to sustain the shabby role I'm acting? Perhaps they don't mean anything by all these remarks? All the things they're saying are perfectly ordinary, yet there's something else there, too . . . They're all the kind of things one may say at any time, yet there's more to it. Why did he say "in *her* apartment" like that? Why did Zamyotov say I'd spoken *with cunning*? Why are they using that tone? Yes, that's what it is . . . a tone . . . Razumikhin's been sitting here, too – why hasn't he noticed anything? That innocent blockhead never notices anything! It's my fever again . . . Did Porfiry wink at me just then, or didn't he? Oh, it's probably rubbish; why would he wink at me? What are they trying to do – get on my nerves, or are they teasing me? Either it's all a mirage, or else they *know*! . . . Even Zamyotov's being insolent . . . Or is he? He's done some thinking overnight. I had a feeling he would! He's behaving as if he were at home, yet this is the first time he's been here. Porfiry isn't even treating him like a guest, he's sitting with his back to him. They're in league with each other! And it's *because of me* that they're in league! It's quite obvious that they were talking about me before we arrived . . . Do they know I went back to the apartment? Oh, I wish they'd hurry up and get it all over with! . . . When I said I'd run away last night in order to rent another room he let it pass, didn't raise any . . . It was clever of me to put in that bit about a room: it'll come in handy later on! . . . "In a state of delirium," he said . . . Ha, ha, ha! He knows all about yesterday evening! But he didn't know that my mother had come to town . . . And the old witch had even written the date on the things in pencil! . . . You're wrong, I won't let myself be caught! I mean, those aren't facts, they're just a mirage! Come on, let's see some facts! Even the apartment's not a fact, it's just a feverish hallucination; I know what to say to them . . . Do they know about the apartment? I shan't leave until I've found out! Why did I come here? Well, I certainly am aggressive now, and that *is* a fact! God, how irritable I feel! Perhaps that's just as well; the role of the invalid . . . He's testing me. He'll try to throw me off balance. Why did I come here?'

All this passed through his head like lightning.

Porfiry Petrovich returned almost instantly. He seemed suddenly to have become more cheerful.

'You know, cousin, I've still got a sore head after your party last night . . . In fact, I've come a bit unstuck all over,' he began in a completely different tone, addressing his remark to Razumikhin, and laughing as he did so.

'Well, was it interesting? I mean, I left you just when it was starting to get interesting, didn't I? Who came out on top?'

'Oh, no one, of course. They alighted on the eternal questions, but went up on a gust of hot air.'

'Would you believe it, Rodya? Last night they got on to the question of whether there's such a thing as crime or not! I told you they were talking a devil of a lot of nonsense!'

'What's so extraordinary about it? It's a social problem you hear discussed all the time,' Raskolnikov answered, his thoughts elsewhere.

'Not in the terms in which they were formulating it,' Porfiry observed.

'You can say that again,' Razumikhin hastened to agree, beginning to get worked up, as was his custom. 'I say, Rodion: listen and give me your opinion. I want to hear it. I nearly burst a blood-vessel arguing with them last night before you arrived, I couldn't wait for you to get there; I'd told them you were coming . . . What sparked it off was when we started talking about the view of the socialists. It's a view that is well-known: crime is a protest against the craziness of the social system – and that's all there is to it, no more than that, and no other reasons conceded – so it doesn't matter! . . .'

'Here comes the nonsense again!' Porfiry Petrovich exclaimed. He was growing visibly animated, and kept laughing as he watched Razumikhin, which set the latter still further ablaze.

'N-no other reasons are conceded!' Razumikhin came back at him with fervour. 'It's not nonsense! . . . I can show you the books they have: they put it all down to being "a prey to one's surroundings"* – and that's it! It's their favourite expression! From that it follows directly that if only society were to be organized sanely, crime would simply disappear, as there would be nothing to protest about and everyone would become virtuous, just like that. Nature isn't taken into consideration, nature is banished, nature is not supposed to exist. The way they see it, it's not mankind which, moving along a historical, *living* path of development, will finally transmute itself into a sane society, but rather a social system which, having emanated from some mathematical head, will at once reorganize the whole of mankind and in a single instant make it virtuous and free from sin, more speedily than any living process, bypassing any historical or living path! That is why they have such an instinctive dislike of history: "It's nothing but a catalogue of outrages and follies," they say – and it can all be explained as the result of stupidity! That's why they have such distaste for the *living* process of life: they don't want the *living soul*! The living soul demands to live, the living soul isn't obedient to the laws of mechanics, the living soul is suspicious, the living soul is reactionary! No, what they prefer are souls which can be made out of rubber, even if they do have a smell of corpse-flesh – but

308

at any rate they're not alive, they have no will of their own, they're servile, won't rebel! And as a result they've reduced everything to brickwork and the disposition of the rooms and corridors inside a phalanstery!* Their phalansteries may be ready, but the human nature that would fit them is not yet ready, it wants to live, it hasn't yet completed the vital process, it's not ready for the burial-ground! It's impossible to leap over nature solely by means of logic! Logic may predict three eventualities, but there are a million of them! Snip off the entire million and reduce everything to the question of comfort – that's a very easy solution to the problem! Temptingly obvious, and one needn't even think about it! That's the main thing – that one shouldn't need to think! The whole of life's mystery can be accommodated within two printer's sheets!'

'There he is off again, beating his drum! He needs to be kept in hand,' Porfiry laughed. 'Just imagine,' he said, turning to Raskolnikov, 'there were six of them all carrying on like that in one room last night, and he'd filled them up with punch beforehand – can you credit it? No, cousin, you're wrong: "one's surroundings" have a great deal to do with crime, I can assure you.'

'Oh, you don't need to tell me that, but look – tell me this: a man of forty rapes a girl of ten: is it his surroundings that have compelled him to it?'

'You know, in the strictest sense that may very possibly be true,' Porfiry observed with an unexpectedly serious air. 'Crimes against young girls may indeed very often be explained by reference to "surroundings".'

Razumikhin was by this time practically frothing at the mouth.

'All right,' he roared, 'shall I *prove* to you that you've got white eyelashes for the sole, exclusive reason that the Church of Ivan the Great is thirty-five sagenes* high, and prove it clearly, in exact detail, in a progressive manner with even a bit of liberal bias thrown in? If you're willing, I'm game! Is it a wager?'

'I accept! Let him have our attention, if you please! I must say I shall be interested to hear his proof.'

'Oh, the devil, he's always play-acting, damn him!' Razumikhin exclaimed, leaping up and waving an arm. 'It's not worth talking to you! I mean, he does it on purpose, you don't know him, Rodion! He did this last night, took their side, merely in order to make fools of us all! And my God, the things he was saying! And they were so pleased!

. . . I mean, he can go on for two weeks in that fashion. Last year for some reason he took it into his head to persuade us that he was going to join a monastery: for two months he stuck to his story! It's not so long ago since he kept telling us that he'd decided to get married, that everything was ready for the wedding. He'd even had new clothes made for himself. We'd all begun to congratulate him, but there was no bride, no nothing – it was all a mirage!'

'You've got it wrong again! I had the clothes made earlier. It was the new clothes that gave me the idea of leading you all up the garden path.'

'So you're really quite a play-actor?' Raskolnikov asked, casually.

'Why? Don't I look like one? Just you wait, I'll lead you up there, too – ha, ha, ha! No, look, sir, I'll be perfectly frank with you. The fact is that while we were talking about all that stuff just now, crime, one's surroundings, young girls, I suddenly remembered a certain little article – it's been of constant interest to me, actually – you wrote, "On Crime", or something, it was called . . . I can't remember the title now. I had the pleasure of reading it two months ago in the *Periodical Leader*.'

'An article by me? In the *Periodical Leader*?' Raskolnikov asked in surprise. 'It's true, I did write one about six months ago, after I left the university. It was a review of a book, but I wrote it for the newspaper *The Weekly Leader*, not for the *Periodical*.'

'Well, the *Periodical* is where it ended up.'

'But I mean, the *Weekly Leader* went out of circulation, that's why it was never printed . . .'

'That's true, sir; but when it went out of circulation, the *Weekly Leader* was incorporated into the *Periodical Leader*, and so two months ago your article appeared in the *Periodical Leader*. Didn't you know?'

Raskolnikov really did know nothing about it.

'For goodness' sake, why, you can request payment for that article! What a peculiar character you are! You live such a cloistered existence that you don't have the faintest notion about matters that concern you personally. I mean, it's a fact, sir.'

'Bravo, Rodya! I didn't know about it either!' Razumikhin exclaimed. 'I'm going to go down to the reading-room today and ask for the issue! Two months ago, you say? What date? Oh, it doesn't matter, I'll find out! There's a nice thing! He won't even tell me!'

'But how did you know the article was by me? There was nothing but an initial at the bottom of it.'

'Oh, I found out by chance, just the other day, actually. Through the editor; he's an acquaintance of mine . . . I was *very* interested.'

'Let's see now, my article was about the psychological state of a criminal's mind throughout the entire process of committing his crime, wasn't it?'

'Yes, sir, and you insisted that the enactment of a crime is invariably accompanied by illness. Most, most original, but . . . that wasn't actually the part of your little article that interested me so much, it was rather a certain idea that you introduced at the end of the piece, but which you unfortunately alluded to only in passing, obscurely . . . In short, if you remember, you make a certain allusion to the idea that there may exist in the world certain persons who are able . . . or rather, who are not only able, but have a perfect right to commit all sorts of atrocities and crimes, and that it's as if the law did not apply to them.'

Raskolnikov smiled ironically at this crass and intentional distortion of his idea.

'What? What on earth? A right to crime? Not because of "the influence of one's surroundings", I hope?' Razumikhin inquired with a certain alarm.

'No, no, it has nothing to do with that,' Porfiry replied. 'The whole point of his article is that the human race is divided into the "ordinary" and the "extraordinary". The ordinary must live in obedience and do not have the right to break the law, because, well, because they're ordinary, you see. The extraordinary, on the other hand, have the right to commit all sorts of crimes and break the law in all sorts of ways precisely because they're extraordinary. That's more or less what you wrote, isn't it, if I'm not mistaken?'

'What the devil! This can't be right!' Razumikhin muttered in bewilderment.

Raskolnikov gave his ironic smile again. He had at once realized what was going on and towards what he was being pushed; he went over the article in his mind. He decided to accept the challenge.

'No, that's not quite what I wrote,' he began in a modest, unassuming tone. 'Actually, I will admit that you've given an almost correct account of my idea, even a completely correct one, if you like . . . (He seemed to take pleasure in agreeing that it was completely correct.)

311

The only point of difference is that I don't at all insist that extraordinary people are in all circumstances unfailingly bound and obliged to commit "all sorts of atrocities", as you put it. Indeed, I don't even think that an article which said that would be allowed into print. No, all I did was quite simply to allude to the fact that an "extraordinary" person has a right . . . not an official right, of course, but a private one, to allow his conscience to step across* certain . . . obstacles, and then only if the execution of his idea (which may occasionally be the salvation of all mankind) requires it. You say that my article is obscure; I am prepared to explain it to you, to the best of my ability. I think I may not be mistaken in supposing that that is what you would like me to do; by all means, sir. It is my view that if the discoveries of Kepler and Newton could not on any account, as a result of certain complex factors, have become known to people other than by means of sacrificing the life of one person, the lives of ten, a hundred or even more persons, who were trying to interfere with those discoveries or stand as an obstacle in their path, then Newton would have had the right, and would even have been obliged . . . to *get rid of* those ten or a hundred persons, in order to make his discoveries known to all mankind. From this it does not, of course, follow that Newton had the right to kill anyone and everyone he wanted to, or go stealing at the market every day. Furthermore, as I remember it, I went on to develop the idea that all the . . . well, for example, all the law-makers and guiding spirits of mankind, starting with the most ancient ones, and continuing with the Lycurguses, the Solons, the Mahomets, the Napoleons and so on, were all every one of them criminals, if only by the fact that, in propounding a new law, they were thereby violating an old one that was held in sacred esteem by society and had been inherited from the ancestors; and, of course, they did not shrink from bloodshed, if blood (sometimes entirely innocent and shed in valour for the ancient law) was something that could in any way help them. It is in fact worth noting that the majority of those benefactors and guiding spirits of mankind were particularly fearsome blood-letters. In short, I argued that all people – not only the great, but even those who deviate only marginally from the common rut, that's to say who are only marginally capable of saying something new, are bound, by their very nature, to be criminals – to a greater or lesser degree, of course. Otherwise they would find it hard to get out of the rut, and it goes without saying that, again because of their nature, they could not possibly agree to remain in it, and indeed, in my view, they have a positive duty not to agree to remain in it. As you will perceive, there's nothing particularly new in my argument so far. All this has been printed and read a thousand times. As for my division of people into the ordinary and the extraordinary, I agree that it is somewhat arbitrary, but after all, I don't insist on precise figures. It's only my central idea that I place my faith in. That idea consists in the notion that, by the law of their nature, human beings *in general* may be divided into two categories: a lower one (that of the ordinary), that is to say raw material which serves exclusively to bring into being more like itself, and another group of people who possess a gift or a talent for saying *something new*, in their own milieu. There are within these categories infinite subdivisions, of course, but the distinguishing features of each are quite clearly marked: the people of the first category, the raw material, that is, are in general conservative by nature, sedate, live lives of obedience and like to be obeyed. In my view, they have a duty to be obedient, as that is their function, and there is really nothing about this that is degrading to them. The second category all break the law, are destroyers, or have a tendency that way, depending on their abilities. The crimes of these people are, of course, relative and multifarious; for the most part what they are demanding, in highly varied forms, is the destruction of the present reality in the name of one that is better. But if such a person finds it necessary, for the sake of his idea, to step over a dead body, over a pool of blood, then he is able within his own conscience to give himself permission to do so – always having regard to the nature of the idea and its dimensions – note that. It's in this sense alone that I speak in my article of their right to crime. (You'll remember that we started off with the discussion of a legal question.) Actually, there's no need to get particularly alarmed about this, you know: the masses are almost never prepared to acknowledge them this right, they flog them or hang them (more or less), thereby quite correctly exercising their conservative function, the only slightly odd thing being that in subsequent generations those same masses put on a pedestal the people they've flogged or executed and pay homage to them (more or less). Those of the first category are always the lords of the present, while those of the second category are the lords of the future. The first conserve the world and increase its population; the second move the world and lead it towards a goal.

Both the one and the other have a completely equal right to exist. In short, the way I see it, everyone possesses equal rights, and – *vive la guerre éternelle* – until the New Jerusalem, of course!'

'So you still believe in the New Jerusalem,* do you?'

'Yes, I do,' Raskolnikov answered firmly; as he said this he looked at the floor, as he had done throughout the whole of his long tirade, choosing a particular point on the carpet to fix his eyes on.

'And – and – and do you believe in God? Forgive me for being so inquisitive.'

'Yes, I do,' Raskolnikov said again, raising his eyes to Porfiry.

'And – and do you believe in the resurrection of Lazarus?'

'Y-yes. Why are you asking all this?'

'Do you believe in it literally?'

'Yes.'

'Really, sir . . . I was simply curious. Please forgive me. But there's just one thing – I'm going back to what you were saying just now – I mean, they don't always flog them or hang them; in fact, some of them . . .'

'Come out on top in their own lifetime? Oh yes, some of them get what they want while they're still alive, and then . . .'

'They themselves start flogging and executing people?'

'If they have to, and you know, that's exactly what most of them do. On the whole your remark is rather a witty one.'

'Thank you, sir. But now tell me this: how do you distinguish these extraordinary people from the ordinary ones? Do they have some sort of special birthmarks? What I mean is, we need a bit more precision there, a bit more external focus, as it were: you must forgive in me the natural anxiety of a practical and well-intentioned man, but might it not be possible to give them some sort of special clothing to wear, for example, or perhaps they could be branded? . . . For I think you'd agree that if there were to be a mix-up and a person from one of the categories thought he belonged to the other, and started to clear away all the "obstacles", as you so neatly called them, I mean . . .'

'Oh, that happens all the time! That remark was even wittier than your last one . . .'

'Thank you, sir . . .'

'Not at all, sir; but please bear in mind that mistakes are only possible on the part of the first category – that is, of the "ordinary" people (as I perhaps quite unsuitably called them). In spite of their

314

inborn tendency towards obedience, a certain capriciousness of temperament, which is not denied even to the cow, leads rather a large number of them to fondly suppose they're progressive individuals, and in the guise of "destroyers" to appropriate the "new word" for themselves – and this in all sincerity, sir. Often, however, they fail to notice the genuinely *new* people and even look down on them as being persons of backward and degrading views. But I do not believe that they represent any significant threat, and you really need not be anxious, as they never get very far. Of course, it would do them no harm to give them a thrashing now and then, to punish them for getting carried away and to remind them of their rightful place, but no more than that; one doesn't even need a whip-master for the job – they'll whip themselves, because they're very well-behaved; some of them will perform this service for one another, while others do it for themselves with their own hands . . . Moreover, they impose various public acts of penitence on themselves – the effect is both splendid and edifying and, in short, you have nothing to worry about . . . It's a kind of law.'

'Well, you've set my mind at rest a little on that score, at least; but, you know, there are other things that trouble me, sir. Please tell me: are there many of these people who have the right to murder others, of these "extraordinary" folk, I mean? I'm prepared to treat them with the respect they merit, of course, but you must admit it would be a bit terrifying if there were a great many of them, sir, eh?'

'Oh, you needn't worry about that, either,' Raskolnikov went on in the same tone of voice. 'On the whole there are extremely few people with new ideas, or who are even the merest bit capable of saying something *new* – so few that it's almost strange. The only thing that's clear is that the order that governs the way in which people come into the world and creates all these categories and subdivisions must be very accurately and precisely determined by some law of nature. This law is, of course, at present unknown to us, but I believe in its existence and think that one day we shall know what it is. The vast mass of people, the human material, exists in the world solely in order at last, by means of a kind of effort, a process that so far remains a mystery to us, involving some strange crossing of generations and races, to muster its strength and bring into the world the one person out of a thousand who is even slightly independent. One person out of ten thousand (I'm talking approximately, by way of illustration) is, perhaps, born with a somewhat higher degree of independence. One out of a hundred thousand, with even more. People of genius are born one out of millions, while the great geniuses, the achievers of humanity, only come into being after many thousands of millions of people have passed through the earth. In a word, I haven't seen inside the retort where all this takes place. But there is quite certainly and is bound to be a law of some kind; all this cannot be the result of chance.'

'What are you both doing – playing jokes, or something?' Razumikhin exclaimed, at last. 'Are you pulling each other's legs, or aren't you? There they sit, chaffing each other! Are you being serious, Rodya?'

Raskolnikov silently raised his pale and almost mournful face to him, and made no reply. And, beside this quiet, mournful countenance, Razumikhin thought strange the irritable, obtrusive, unconcealed and *uncivil* causticity of Porfiry.

'Well, brother, if this really is serious, then . . . Of course you're right when you say that this is nothing new and resembles all the things we've read and heard a thousand times; but what is really *original* about all this – and this really is your own exclusive property, much to my horror – is that you condone the shedding of blood *on grounds of conscience*, and, if you'll forgive me, with such fanaticism . . . That's what your article is really all about. I mean, to condone the shedding of blood *on grounds of conscience* is . . . is in my opinion more terrible than if it were to be permitted officially, by law . . .'

'Perfectly true – it is more terrible, sir,' Porfiry remarked.

'No, you must have got carried away! There's some mistake here. I'll read it . . . You got carried way! You can't possibly think that . . . I'll read it.'

'None of that's actually in the article, it's merely alluded to,' Raskolnikov said.

'Quite so, sir, quite so,' Porfiry said, unable to keep still in his seat. 'I think I've almost grasped the way in which you choose to view crime, sir, but . . . please forgive me for being so insistent (I really am putting you to a lot of trouble, I feel quite guilty!) – you see, sir, it's like this: you set my mind at rest just now with regard to erroneous instances of confusion between the two categories, but . . . well, there are certain practical possibilities that still bother me! Oh, take some man or some young chap who imagines he's a Lycurgus or a Mahomet

316

. . . a budding one, of course – well, off he goes to clear away all the obstacles . . . and he says to himself: "I've a long way ahead of me, and I'll need some money for the road . . ." Well, and so he starts going about getting his hands on that money . . . you know what I mean?'

Zamyotov gave a sudden snort from the corner in which he was sitting. Raskolnikov did not even raise his eyes to look at him.

'I must admit,' he replied calmly, 'that cases of that kind are indeed bound to occur. Those who are stupid and vain are particularly liable to swallow that hook – especially the young.'

'Well, sir, you take my point, then. I mean, how can that be allowed, sir?'

'Oh, that's just the way things are, I'm afraid,' Raskolnikov said, with an ironic smile. 'It's not my fault they're like that. That's the way things are and that's how they'll always be. Take what he' – he nodded at Razumikhin – 'said just now about my condoning blood-shed. So what if I do? I mean, society's all too well provided with such phenomena as exile, prison, legal investigators and penal servitude – so what's there to worry about? All you have to do is catch your thief!'

'All right, say we do catch him – what then?'

'He's got what he deserves!'

'One can't say you're not logical. Well, sir, and what about his conscience?'

'Why should you care about that?'

'Oh, for humanitarian reasons, sir.'

'If he has one, he'll suffer when he realizes the error of his ways. That's his punishment – that, in addition to penal servitude.'

'Yes, but what about the really gifted ones?' Razumikhin asked, frowning. 'I mean, the ones who have been granted the right to murder – are they not obliged to suffer at all, not even for the blood they've shed?'

'Why do you use the word *obliged*? There's no permission or prohibition involved in all this. Let him suffer if he's sorry for his victim . . . Pain and suffering are inevitable for persons of broad awareness and depth of heart. The truly great are, in my view, always bound to feel a great sense of sadness during their time upon earth,'* he suddenly added in a reflective tone that was hardly that of a conversation.

317

He raised his eyes, looked at them all thoughtfully, smiled and picked up his cap. He was very calm now, compared to the way he had been when he had walked in just now, and he could feel this. They all got up.

'Well, sir, you'll no doubt curse me for this, and it'll probably make you angry, but I simply cannot restrain myself,' Porfiry Petrovich said, resuming his argument again. 'Please permit me to give expression to just one more little question (I know I'm causing you the most dreadful bother, sir!), one more little idea, simply so I don't forget it . . .'

'Very well, tell me your little idea,' Raskolnikov said, standing before him in pale and serious anticipation.

'What I mean is, sir . . . goodness, I don't even know how to find the right words for it . . . it's such a playful little idea . . . a psychological one, sir . . . What I mean is, sir, that when you were writing your article, it couldn't just possibly have been, could it – ha, ha! – that you too considered yourself – oh, just the merest bit – to be one of the "extraordinary" people who can say *a new word* – in the sense you've explained . . . I mean, is that the case, sir?'

'I wouldn't rule it out,' Raskolnikov answered, contemptuously.

Razumikhin made a movement.

'And if that *is* the case, sir, then is it really possible that you might also have decided – oh, because of some everyday setback or financial difficulty, let's say, or because you wanted to further the interests of all humanity in some way – to step across an obstacle? . . . Well, by robbing and murdering someone, for example? . . .'

And again he suddenly winked at him with his left eye and shook with silent laughter, in exact repetition of his behaviour a few minutes earlier.

'If I had, I certainly wouldn't tell you,' Raskolnikov replied with a challenging, haughty contempt.

'Oh, but I mean, sir, you must understand, my interest stems solely from a desire to understand your article, and is of a purely literary nature . . .'

'Ugh! How brazen and obvious this is!' Raskolnikov thought with disgust.

'Please let me make it perfectly clear,' he replied coldly, 'that I consider myself neither a Mahomet nor a Napoleon . . . nor any of those other persons of that kind, and, not being one of them, am

318

consequently unable to give you a satisfactory account of how I might have behaved.'

'Oh, for heaven's sake! Who doesn't think he's a Napoleon among us in Russia these days?' Porfiry suddenly articulated with breathtaking familiarity. This time even the intonation of his voice contained an extraordinarily clear hint.

'Perhaps it was some budding Napoleon who did in old Alyona Ivanovna with an axe last week,' Zamyotov suddenly barked out from his corner.

Raskolnikov said nothing, and looked at Porfiry with a firm, fixed gaze. Razumikhin frowned gloomily. Even before this, he had begun to sense that something was wrong. Angrily, he looked about him. A moment of gloomy silence elapsed. Raskolnikov turned to go.

'Off already?' Porfiry said sweetly, extending his hand in a thoroughly amiable manner. 'Most, most glad to have made your acquaintance. Oh, and about your application, don't let anyone put you off. Just write it the way I told you. In fact, the best thing would be if you looked in to see me there . . . in a day or two . . . or why not tomorrow? You can be sure of finding me there at around eleven. We'll sort it all out . . . have a bit of a talk . . . As one of the last people to have been *there*, you may be able to tell us a few things . . .' he added with the most good-natured air.

'You want to question me officially, with all the trappings?' Raskolnikov asked, sharply.

'Now why would I want to do that, sir? That's not at all required for the time being. You took what I said the wrong way. You see, I never miss a chance and . . . and since I've already talked to all the people who had pawned things . . . taken statements from some of them . . . and you, as the last person . . . Oh, but listen, by the way!' he exclaimed, suddenly brightening up at some recollection. 'I've just remembered, what could I have been thinking of . . .?' he said, turning to Razumikhin. 'I mean, you know that Nikolashka you were giving me an earache about the other day? . . . Well, I mean, I know, I know perfectly well,' he continued, addressing Raskolnikov, 'that the fellow's got clean hands, but what was I to do, after all, I had to inconvenience Mitka as well . . . that's where the heart of the matter lies, sir, its very essence: now permit me to ask . . . when you made your way up that staircase . . . well, would it have been some time between seven and eight, sir?'

'Yes, that's right,' Raskolnikov replied, at that very second experiencing a nasty feeling that it might have been better not to say this.

'Well, between seven and eight that evening, as you were making your way . . . up that staircase . . . didn't you see, in the apartment on the second floor . . . the one that was unlocked and had its door open – remember? – two workmen, or at any rate one of them? They were decorating in there, didn't you notice? Now this is very, very important for them! . . .'

'Decorators? No, I didn't see them,' Raskolnikov replied slowly and as though he were digging about in his memory, at the same instant straining the whole of his being and shivering with the torment of trying to perceive as quickly as possible where the trap was, and not to miss anything. 'No, I didn't see any decorators, and I don't think I noticed an unlocked apartment of that kind, either . . . but on the fourth floor, now,' – he had already worked out where the trap was, and felt triumphant – 'I do remember there was a government clerk moving out of the apartment . . . opposite Alyona Ivanovna's . . . I remember . . . I distinctly remember . . . that some soldiers were carrying some sort of sofa outside and I remember being squeezed against the wall as they passed . . . but decorators – no, I don't remember there being any decorators . . . and I'm sure there were no unlocked apartments, either. Yes, I'm quite sure . . .'

'Wait a minute!' Razumikhin exclaimed, suddenly, as though coming to his senses and realizing what was happening. 'I mean, the decorators were painting there on the day of the murder itself, and he was there three days earlier! What are you trying to get him to say?'

'Damn! I've got confused!' Porfiry said, clapping his hand to his forehead. 'The devil take it, this case is too much for my poor brain!' he went on, turning to Raskolnikov, almost as if in apology. 'The thing is, you see, it's so important we should find someone who saw them between seven and eight, in that apartment, that I went and imagined just now that you could tell us . . . I got completely confused!'

'Well, you ought to be a little more careful,' Razumikhin observed sourly.

These last words were spoken in the entrance hall. Porfiry Petrovich ushered them right to the door with the utmost affability. When they emerged on to the street they were both sullen and gloomy, and they walked several yards without saying a word. Raskolnikov took a deep breath . . .

VI

'. . . I don't believe it! I can't possibly believe it!' a puzzled Razumikhin kept repeating, doing everything within his power to refute Raskolnikov's arguments. They were by this time drawing near to Bakaleyev's Tenements, where Pulkheria Aleksandrovna and Dunya had long been awaiting them. Every moment or so Razumikhin would stop in his tracks in the heat of the conversation, excited and confused by the simple fact that for the first time they had begun to talk about *it* – without any equivocation.

'Well, don't then!' Raskolnikov replied sardonically, with a cold and casual smile. 'As usual, you didn't notice anything, but I was weighing up every word.'

'That's because you don't trust anyone . . . Hm . . . I agree that Porfiry's tone was a bit strange, though – and what did you make of that shabby character Zamyotov? – You're right, there was something peculiar about the way he was carrying on – but what was it all about? Eh?'

'He's done a bit of thinking overnight.'

'I don't agree! I don't agree! If they had that idiot notion in their heads they'd do all in their power to try to hide it, they'd try to play their cards close to their chests, in order to be able to pounce later on . . . No, what they were doing just now was brazen and ill-advised.'

'If they had some facts, real facts, that is, or at least some well-founded suspicions, then they really would try to play a cat-and-mouse game in the hope of making an even bigger haul (and they'd have searched my place long ago, too!). But they've no facts, not one – it's all a mirage, a conjecture, just a fleeting idea – they're trying to make me lose my nerve by means of effrontery. Or perhaps he was annoyed about not having any facts, and burst out with all that because he's so irritated. But there may have been some intention behind it . . . I think he's a clever man . . . Perhaps he was trying to frighten me by showing me that he knows . . . There's a peculiar kind of psychology involved there, brother . . . Oh, but all that doesn't bear thinking about. Don't remind me of it!'

'I know, it's insulting, it's insulting! I understand the way you feel. But . . . now that we've begun to talk straight (and I'm so glad that we have) – I'll admit to you now that I've noticed they've had it for ages, this idea, during all this time, oh, only in the most tenuous form, of course, as the merest creeping suspicion – but why even that? How do they dare? Where, where are the roots of these suspicions of theirs? Oh, if you only knew what a furious rage I've been in! Good Lord: just because a poor student, crippled by poverty and hypochondria, on the brink of a severe illness and delirium which may have already begun at the time in question (take note of that!), suspicious because of the poor state of his health, proud, conscious of his own worth, who has been in his room without seeing anyone for six months, and is dressed in rags and tatters and boots with no soles – appears before some wretched local policemen and puts up with their assaults upon his dignity; whereupon they wave an unexpected debt under his nose, the overdue promissory note of court councillor Chebarov, there's a stink of rotten paint, the thermometer reads thirty degrees Réaumur, there's no air in the place, the room is jammed with people, they're talking about the murder of someone he had visited not long before, and all this on an empty stomach! How could he have failed to pass out? And to make that the basis of the whole thing! The devil take it, I understand how annoyed you must feel, but if I'd been in your place, Rodya, I'd have laughed in their faces or, even better: I'd have s-spat in the ugly mugs of the whole lot of them, with a good gobbet of spit, too, and let fly a couple more dozen gobbets in the proper direction, and left it at that. Go on, spit on them! Keep your spirits up! They ought to be ashamed of themselves!'

'I say, he put that rather well,' Raskolnikov thought.

'Spit on them? But he's going to question me again tomorrow!' he said with bitterness. 'How can I have a showdown with them? I feel bad enough about having lowered myself to Zamyotov's level in the restaurant yesterday . . .'

'The devil take it, I'll go and see Porfiry myself! I'll exert some *family* pressure on him; I'll make him tell me everything – the whole story! And as for Zamyotov . . .'

'At last, he's guessed!' thought Raskolnikov.

'Wait!' Razumikhin shouted, suddenly grabbing him by the shoulder. 'Wait! You're wrong! I've just realized: you're wrong! What kind of trap was that? You say that the question about the workmen was a trap? Look, this is what it's all about: I mean, if you'd done *that*, how could you possibly let on that you'd seen the apartment was being painted . . . and that you'd seen the workmen? Oh, no: you'd have said you saw nothing, even if you had seen them! Who's going to make an admission like that, against his own interests?'

'If I had done that *deed*, I would most certainly have said I'd seen the workmen in the apartment,' Raskolnikov said, continuing his reply unwillingly and with evident disgust.

'But why say a thing that harmed you?'

'Because only muzhiks and the most inexperienced novices deny everything outright when they're being questioned. If a man has even the slightest bit of intelligence and worldly wisdom, he'll try as far as possible to admit to all the external and undeniable circumstances; only he'll try to find other reasons for them, will introduce some special and unexpected feature of his own, one which gives them a totally different significance and puts them in a new light. Porfiry may easily have reckoned that I would give that sort of reply and say I'd seen the workmen for the sake of plausibility, and then insert something by way of an explanation . . .'

'But I mean, he'd have told you at once that there couldn't possibly have been any workmen there two days earlier and that consequently you must have been there on the evening of the murder, between seven and eight. He'd have caught you out over a trivial thing like that.'

'Yes, that's what he was counting on – that I wouldn't have time to consider and would hurriedly make the most plausible reply I could think of, forgetting that two days earlier there wouldn't have been any workmen there.'

'But how could you forget something like that?'

'The easiest thing in the world! It's over utterly trivial things like that that clever people are caught. The cleverer a person is, the less he suspects he'll be caught out over some ordinary thing like that. In fact, the way to catch a clever person is to use the most ordinary thing you can think of. Porfiry's not at all as stupid as you might suppose.'

'If what you say is true, he's a bastard!'

Raskolnikov could not help laughing. At that same moment, however, his own animation and the eagerness with which he had made this last explanatory remark seemed strange to him, bearing in mind the fact that during the whole of the preceding conversation he had maintained a sullen air of disgust, apparently for ends of his own, and from necessity.

'I'm getting a taste for certain aspects of this!' he thought to himself.

But almost at that very same moment he suddenly grew agitated, as though an unexpected and disturbing thought had occurred to him. His agitation increased. They had now reached the entrance to Bakaleyev's Tenements.

'You go in alone,' Raskolnikov said suddenly. 'I'll be back soon.'

'Where are you off to? I mean, after all, we're here!'

'I must, I must, some business . . . I'll be back in half an hour. Tell them when you get up there.'

'Well, it's as you please, but I'm coming with you!'

'Oh, so you want to make my life a misery too, do you?' Raskolnikov exclaimed, with such bitter irritation, such despair in his gaze that Razumikhin lost heart. For a while he stood on the front steps and gloomily watched Raskolnikov striding rapidly away in the direction of the lane in which he lived. At last, gritting his teeth and clenching his fists, he swore to himself that this very day he would squeeze Porfiry till the pips burst, and went upstairs to soothe the mind of Pulkheria Aleksandrovna, who was by this time in a state of alarm at their long absence.

When Raskolnikov arrived at the building where he lived, his temples were soaked with sweat, and he was breathing heavily. He hurried up the staircase, went into his unlocked room and immediately shut the door and set it on its hook. Then, in a kind of mad fear, he rushed to the corner, to that same hole in the wallpaper where the objects had lain that day, thrust his hand into it and for a few moments probed it thoroughly, fingering every nook and cranny and every fold in the wallpaper. Not finding anything, he got up and took a deep breath. As he had been approaching the front steps of Bakaleyev's Tenements just then, he had suddenly had the notion that some object, one of the little chains, or a cufflink, perhaps, or even just a scrap of the paper in which they had been wrapped, with the old woman's handwriting on it, might somehow have slipped away and got caught in some little crack, in order suddenly to glare before him as a piece of unexpected and irrefutable evidence.

He stood still, seeming to muse, and an odd, self-disparaging, almost vacant smile fleeted across his lips. At last he took his cap and quietly went out of the room. His thoughts were jumbled. Musing, he walked out through the entrance gate.

'There he is, that's him!' a loud voice shouted; he raised his head.

The yardkeeper was standing by the doorway of his little cubicle, pointing straight at him for the benefit of a short man who had the air of an artisan, and was dressed in a waistcoat and something resembling a dressing-gown; from a distance he looked very like a woman. His head, in a soiled peaked cap, hung limply forward towards the ground, and indeed the whole of him seemed bent and hunched. His flabby, wrinkled face set him the other side of fifty; his small, bloated eyes stared sullenly, sourly and with resentment.

'What's going on?' Raskolnikov asked, going up to the yardkeeper.

The artisan gave him a surly, oblique glare, looking him over with close, fixed attention, taking his time; then he slowly turned away and, without saying a word, walked through the gateway out to the street.

'What's going *on*?' Raskolnikov exclaimed.

'Oh, that fellow was asking if there was a student who lived here, he gave your name, and wanted to know whose apartment you lived in. You came down here, I pointed you out to him, and off he went. Whatever next?'

The yardkeeper was also somewhat bewildered, but not greatly so, and, having thought for a little while longer, turned and went back inside his cubicle.

Raskolnikov rushed off in pursuit of the artisan and immediately caught sight of him walking down the other side of the street, still with the same unhurried, even gait, his eyes fixed on the ground, as though he were thinking about something. He quickly caught him up, but kept behind him for a bit; at last he drew even with him and looked into his face from the side. The artisan noticed him immediately, looked him over quickly, but then lowered his eyes again, and thus they continued for about a minute, side by side and not saying a word.

'Were you asking the yardkeeper . . . about me?' Raskolnikov got out, at last, but in a voice that was somehow rather faint.

325

The artisan made no reply and did not even look at him. Again they said nothing for a while.

'But why did you . . . come and ask for me . . . and then not say anything . . . What's the matter?' Raskolnikov's voice petered out; somehow he had difficulty in articulating his words clearly.

This time the artisan raised his eyes and gave Raskolnikov a black, menacing look.

'Murderer!' he said suddenly, in a voice which, though quiet, was clear and distinct . . .

Raskolnikov continued to walk at his side. His legs suddenly went horribly weak, a chill ran down his spine, and for a moment his heart almost froze; then it suddenly began to beat as though it had been released from a catch. In this manner they walked for about a hundred yards, side by side, and again without saying one word.

The artisan did not look at him.

'What are you talking about? . . . Eh? . . . Who's a murderer?' Raskolnikov muttered, barely audibly.

'*You* are a murderer,' the artisan said, even more distinctly and reprovingly, with a smile that expressed something akin to hate-filled triumph, and again he looked straight into Raskolnikov's pale face and rigid, staring eyes. At that moment they both arrived at the intersection. The artisan turned off down the street to the left, and went on his way without a look to either side. Raskolnikov stayed where he was, following the man with his gaze for a long time. When the artisan had gone about fifty yards, he saw him turn round and look at him where he stood, motionless, at the same spot. It was impossible at that distance to be sure, but Raskolnikov fancied that once again the man smiled his cold, hate-filled and triumphant smile.

With slow, dragging steps, his knees trembling, and for some reason feeling terribly cold, Raskolnikov went back and climbed the stairs to his closet-like room. He took off his cap and put it on the table, and for about ten minutes stood next to it, motionless. Then, in exhaustion, he lay down on the sofa and stretched out on it painfully, uttering a weak moan; his eyes were closed. Thus he lay for about half an hour.

He thought about nothing. To be sure, there were a few vague thoughts or fragments of thoughts, vague notions, without order or coherence – the faces of people whom he had seen back in his childhood or whom he had met somewhere on only one occasion and had forgotten all about; the belltower of the V. Church; the billiard table of a certain inn, and an officer playing billiards, the smell of cigars in some basement tobacco shop, a drinking den, a back staircase, completely dark, running with slop-water and scattered with eggshells, and from somewhere the ringing of Sunday bells . . . Objects spun round, changing place with one another, like a whirlwind. Some of them even caught his fancy, and he clutched at them, but they faded, and in general he felt a sense of some heavy weight within him, but it was not excessive. At times it even felt good . . . He was still affected by a slight shivering, and this too almost felt good.

He heard Razumikhin's voice and hurried footsteps, closed his eyes and pretended he was asleep. Razumikhin opened the door and stood in the threshold for a while as though he were pondering something. Then he quietly stepped into the room and cautiously approached the sofa. Nastasya's whisper was heard:

'Don't bother him! Let him have his sleep! He can eat later.'

'Indeed so,' Razumikhin replied.

Cautiously they both went out and closed the door. About another half hour went by. Raskolnikov opened his eyes and again threw himself back, clasping his hands behind his head . . .

'Who is he? Who is this man who's come up from under the ground? Where was he, and what did he see? He saw it all, there's no doubt of it. But where was he standing that day, and where was he looking from? Why has he only surfaced now? And how could he have seen – is that possible? . . . Hm . . .' Raskolnikov went on, quivering, his blood running cold. 'And the jewel-case Nikolai found behind the door: is that possible, too? Evidence? You miss the one hundred-thousandth hyphen in the text – and there's a piece of evidence the size of an Egyptian pyramid! The fly was on the wall, and it saw! Is that really possible?'

And with loathing he suddenly felt how weak, how physically weak he had grown.

'I should have thought of this,' he reflected, with a bitter, ironic smile. 'How could I have dared, knowing the person I am, knowing *what it would do to me*, to take an axe and bloody my hands? I should have thought it out in advance . . . Ah, but I did! . . .' he whispered in despair.

At times he would stop dead in the face of some thought:

'No, those men aren't made like that; the real *overlord*, to whom all things are permitted, ransacks Toulon, commits a massacre in Paris, *forgets* an army in Egypt, *throws away* half a million men in his Moscow campaign and talks his way out at Vilna with a clever remark; and after his death they put up statues to him – and that means that *everything* is permitted to him. No! Men like that don't have bodies but lumps of bronze!'

There was one sudden and extraneous thought which almost set him laughing. 'Napoleon, the Pyramids, Waterloo – and the disgusting, emaciated widow of a registering clerk, an old crone who lends money and keeps a special trunk under her bed – how could Porfiry Petrovich ever digest that? . . . How could any of them digest it? . . . Their sense of aesthetics would get in the way: "Would a Napoleon go crawling under an old woman's bed?" they'd ask. "Go on, don't be so stupid! . . ."'

At moments he felt he might be delirious: he would lapse into a mood of feverish entrancement.

'The old woman is rubbish!' he thought, heatedly and with violence. 'It's possible that the old woman was a mistake, but she's not what it's all about, in any case! The old woman was just an illness . . . I wanted to get my stepping-over done as quickly as possible . . . It wasn't a person but a principle that I killed! I killed the principle, but I didn't step over it, I remained on this side of it . . . All I was able to do was to kill. And the way it's turning out, it seems I didn't even manage to do that . . . The principle? Why was that imbecile Razumikhin calling the socialists such rude names just now? They're hard-working, businesslike people; they occupy themselves with the "common happiness" . . . No, life has been given me once and it won't come along again: I don't want to wait for "universal happiness". I want to live my own life, too, otherwise I'd do better not to live at all. I mean, look, all I want is not to have to walk past a hungry mother, clutching my rouble in my pocket as I await the advent of "universal happiness", as though to say: "*J'apporte ma pierre à l'édifice nouveau** of 'universal happiness', and that gives me peace of mind!" Ha, ha! Why have you let me slip past? I mean, I'm only going to live once, and I also want to . . . Oh, I'm an aesthetic louse, that's what!' he added suddenly, bursting into laughter like a crazy man. 'Yes, that's what I am, a louse,' he continued, battening on to the idea with malicious joy, rummaging about in it, playing with it and amusing himself with it, 'if only because of the fact that, for one thing, I'm now arguing that I'm a louse; and because, for another, throughout the whole of the past month I've been pestering all-beneficent Providence by asking it to be a witness that I wasn't undertaking my project in order to gratify my own fleshly lust, but that I had in mind a splendid and agreeable aim – ha, ha! And because, for yet another, that I proposed to observe the greatest possible degree of fairness in its execution – weighing, measuring and employing all the operations of arithmetic: of all the lice I could find I selected the most useless one and, having squashed it, proposed to take from it exactly as much as I needed in order to make my first step, no more and no less (and consequently what was left would have gone to a monastery, according to the terms of her will – ha, ha!) . . . And finally I'm a louse because, because,' he added, grinding his teeth, 'because I myself am possibly even more loathsome and disgusting than a squashed louse, and *knew in advance* that I'd tell myself this only *after* I'd squashed it! Is there anything that will stand comparison with a monstrous plan such as that? Oh, the vulgarity of it! Oh, the baseness! . . . Oh, how well I understand "the prophet", with his sword, on horseback: Allah commands and "trembling" mortals must obey!* He's right, he's right, "the prophet", when he mounts a d-decent-sized battery across some street somewhere and blasts away at righteous and sinners alike, without even bothering to explain! "Obey, trembling creatures, and – *do not desire*, because that is no business of yours!" . . . Oh, never, never will I forgive that old woman!'

His hair was soaked with sweat, his lips, which had been quivering, were parched, his motionless gaze was fixed upon the ceiling:

'My mother, my sister – how I have loved them! Why now do I hate them? Yes, I hate them, physically hate them, cannot endure their presence close to myself . . . Just a while ago I went up to my mother and gave her a kiss, I remember . . . That I could have embraced her, thinking that if she found out, then . . . could I really have told her then? I'm capable of it . . . Hm! *She* must be the same as I am,' he added, thinking with an effort, as though he were struggling with the delirium that was enveloping him. 'Oh, how I hate that old woman now! If she came back to life, I think I'd kill her again! Poor Lizaveta! Why did she have to go and turn up when she did? . . . I say, that's strange, I wonder why I hardly even think about her, as though I'd never even killed her? . . . Lizaveta! Sonya! Poor, meek

329

souls with meek eyes . . . Dear souls! . . . Why aren't they crying? Why aren't they moaning? . . . They're sacrificing everything . . . their gaze is so meek and quiet . . . Sonya, Sonya! Tranquil Sonya! . . .'

He dozed off; he thought it strange that he could not remember how he had ended up in the street. It was already late in the evening. The twilight was thickening, the full moon was shining brighter and brighter; but the air was somehow particularly suffocating. Crowds of people were passing through the streets; artisans and people who had been on business were going home, others were loitering about at a loose end, there was a smell of dust, slaked lime and stagnant water. Raskolnikov walked along, sad and preoccupied: he was very well aware of having come out with some plan, of there being something he had to do and do quickly, but what it was he had forgotten. Suddenly he stopped, and saw that on the opposite pavement a man stood, waving to him. He crossed the street towards him, but suddenly the man swung round and walked on as though nothing had happened, his head lowered, not turning round and showing no sign of having beckoned to him. 'Steady on – was he beckoning to me?' Raskolnikov wondered, and began to catch the man up in any case. Before he had gone ten paces, he suddenly realized who it was – and felt a shock of fear: it was the artisan from earlier in the day, still wearing the same dressing-gown, and still as bent and hunched as ever. Raskolnikov walked behind him at a distance; his heart was thumping: they turned off into a lane – still the man did not turn round. 'Does he know I'm walking behind him?' Raskolnikov wondered. The artisan walked in through the gateway of a certain large apartment building. Raskolnikov quickly approached the gateway and began to stare in, wondering if the man would turn round and beckon to him. Sure enough, having passed through the archway and emerged into the courtyard, he suddenly turned round and again seemed to wave to him. Raskolnikov immediately walked through the archway, but when he reached the courtyard the artisan was no longer there. That could only mean he had gone up the first staircase. Raskolnikov leapt after him. Sure enough, two flights further up someone's regular, unhurried footsteps could be heard. It was strange – the staircase looked somehow familiar. There was the window on the first floor; sadly and mysteriously the moonlight shone through its panes; here was the second floor. Aha! This was the apartment where the workmen had been painting . . . How had he not recognized it at once? The footsteps of the man walking up ahead of him died away: 'He must have stopped, or hidden somewhere.' Here, now, was the third floor; ought he to go any further? What silence there was in here – it was terrifying . . . But on he went. The noise of his own footsteps frightened and disturbed him. God, how dark it was! The artisan was doubtless lurking in a corner somewhere up here. Ah! There was the apartment with its door open on to the landing; he thought for a moment, then went inside. In the hallway it was very dark and empty, not a living soul, as though everything had been moved out of it; quietly, on tiptoe, he moved on into the sitting room: the whole room was brightly lit by moonlight; everything was as it had been before: the chairs, the mirror, the yellow sofa and the pictures in their frames. An enormous, round, copper-red moon was looking straight in through the windows. 'It's the moon that's making this silence,' Raskolnikov thought. 'What it's doing just now is trying to obtain the answer to a riddle.' He stood and waited, waited for a long time, and the more silent the moon, the more violently his heart thumped, until it actually started to become painful. And all the while the silence deepened. Suddenly there was a momentary, dry crack, like the sound of a breaking splinter, and then everything sank into stillness again. A fly that had woken up suddenly swooped and beat against the windowpane, buzzing plaintively. Just then, hanging on the wall in the corner, between the little cupboard and the window, he caught sight of what looked like a woman's housecoat. 'What's that housecoat doing there?' he thought. 'I mean, it wasn't there before . . .' He crept up to it and realized that there was apparently someone hidden behind it. Cautiously, with one hand, he moved the housecoat out of the way and saw there was a chair in the corner there, and that on the chair the old woman was sitting, all doubled up and her head hanging down, so that, no matter how hard he looked, he could not see her face – but it was her. He stood over her: 'She's scared!' he thought, stealthily freed the axe from its loop and struck the old woman across the crown of the head with it, once, twice. But it was strange: she did not move at all at the blows, as though she were made of wood. In fear he stooped closer to her, began to examine her, but she inclined her head even lower. Then he bent right down to the floor and began to look up at her from below, looked and froze: the old woman was laughing – fairly shaking with quiet, inaudible laughter, exerting the utmost control in order that he would not hear. He suddenly fancied that the bedroom door opened the merest slit, and that in there there were more people laughing and whispering. He was overcome by rabid fury: with all his might he began to hack the old woman about the head, but with each blow of the axe the laughter and whispering from the bedroom was getting louder and louder and the old woman was swaying about all over with silent cackling. He rushed to escape, but the hallway was now full of people, the doors of the other apartments on that flight were wide open, and on the landing, on the staircase and wherever one gazed below there were people, their heads pressed together, all looking – but all of them keeping out of the way and waiting, uttering no word . . . His heart contracted, his legs would not move, they were rooted fast . . . He attempted to scream and – woke up.

He took a deep, hard breath. But it was strange – the dream did not yet appear to be over: the door of his room was wide open, and on the threshold a man who was a complete stranger to him stood examining him fixedly.

Raskolnikov had not yet managed to get his eyes completely open, and for a moment he closed them again. He lay on his back and did not move. 'Is this still my dream, or isn't it?' he wondered, and once again imperceptibly opened his eyelids the merest fraction in order to take a look: the stranger was still standing there, continuing his intent scrutiny of him. Suddenly, he stepped cautiously over the threshold, closed the door carefully after him, waited for a moment – never once taking his eyes off Raskolnikov – and quietly, without fuss, sat down on the chair next to the sofa; he placed his hat by his side, on the floor, leaned on his cane with both hands, and lowered his chin on to them. It was clear that he was prepared to wait for a long time. As far as Raskolnikov could make out through the blinking of his eyelashes, this man was of advancing years, square-built and with a thick, light-coloured, almost white beard . . .

Some ten minutes went by. It was still light, but the day was drawing to a close. In the room there was complete silence. Not even from the staircase came a single sound. There was only the buzzing and struggling of some large fly as it swooped and beat against the windowpane. At last it became intolerable: Raskolnikov suddenly raised himself on one elbow and sat up on the sofa.

'All right, what do you want?'

'You know, I had a feeling you weren't asleep, but were just pretending,' the stranger replied in a peculiar tone of voice, laughing easily. 'Arkady Ivanovich Svidrigailov. Permit me to introduce myself . . .'

PART FOUR

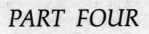

PART FOUR

'Can this really still be my dream?' Raskolnikov wondered again. Cautiously and with suspicion he peered closely at his unexpected guest.

'Svidrigailov? Rubbish! I don't believe it!' he finally said out loud, in a puzzled voice.

His guest seemed to find this exclamation not at all astonishing.

'I've looked in to see you on account of two reasons: for one thing, I felt like making your personal acquaintance, as I've long been hearing things about you that put you in a curious and favourable light; and for another, I cherish the fond hope that you may not refuse to assist me in a certain undertaking that directly affects your sister, Avdotya Romanovna. Alone and without introduction, she would probably not admit me to her chambers just now, because of prejudice, but, well, now, with your assistance, I expect to . . .'

'You expect too much,' Raskolnikov said, interrupting.

'They only arrived in town yesterday, if I'm not mistaken?'

Raskolnikov made no reply.

'It was yesterday, I know. Why, I myself arrived only the day before. Well now, Rodion Romanovich, sir, this is what I want to say to you on that account: while I consider it superfluous to embark upon self-justifications, I should be grateful if you would tell me what was so particularly criminal about my part in that matter, viewing it without prejudice, that is, and from a common-sense point of view?'

Raskolnikov continued to study him in silence.

'The fact that I went chasing after a defenceless young girl in my own home and "outraged her honour with my infamous proposals"? Is that it, sir? (Thus do I anticipate your reply!) But I mean to say, if you will only bear in mind that I am a human being, *et nihil humanum* . . . in a word, that I am capable of being attracted and falling in love (something which, needless to say, takes place without deference to our wishes), then everything may be explained in the most natural fashion. The point at issue here is as follows: am I a monster or am I myself a victim? What if the latter be true? I mean, in suggesting to the object of my desires that she elope to America or Switzerland with me, I may have entertained the most respectful feelings towards her, and may even have intended to usher in our future happiness! . . .

Reason is, after all, the servant of passion; I may have been harming myself even more, for heaven's sake!'

'That's not what's at issue at all,' Raskolnikov interrupted, with disgust. 'The simple fact is that, quite apart from the question of whether you're right or wrong, you're an obnoxious character – well, and so people don't want to have anything to do with you, they show you the door, and out you go! . . .'

Svidrigailov suddenly roared with laughter.

'I say . . . I say, there's no putting you off the mark, is there?' he said, laughing in the frankest possible manner. 'I thought I could pull the wool over your eyes, but no, you've gone straight to the heart of it all!'

'You're still trying to pull the wool over my eyes at this very moment.'

'What if I am? What if I am?' Svidrigailov replied, with a gaping laugh. 'I mean, it's what they call *bonne guerre*, and it's the most permissible form of wool-pulling there is! . . . But you interrupted me just now, you know; and one way or the other, I shall say it again: there would have been no unpleasantness if it hadn't been for the incident in the garden. Marfa Petrovna . . .'

'Did you wear her out, as well, the way they say you did?' Raskolnikov interrupted, rudely.

'Oh, you've heard about that, too, have you? Though you couldn't really have failed to, I suppose . . . Well, with regard to your question, I must admit that I really don't know what to say, though my own conscience is perfectly clear on the matter. What I mean is, please don't get the idea that I had any misgivings about it – it all took place quite in accordance with the natural order of events and in precisely the manner common to such cases: the medical inquiry established apoplexy as the cause of death, brought on by bathing immediately after a large meal accompanied by nearly a whole bottle of wine, and there is no way in which it could possibly have discovered anything else . . . You know, sir, for a while I thought about it, particularly as I sat in the train on my way here, wondering whether I might not have helped to bring about this whole . . . misfortune, oh, by causing her some inner upset, or something of that sort? But I have come to the conclusion that of that, too, there can have been absolutely no question.'

Raskolnikov began to laugh.

'I wonder you let it bother you!'

'Now what are you laughing at? Look at it like this: I only hit her with that little horsewhip twice, there weren't even any marks . . . Please don't think me a cynic; I mean, I have a precise awareness of just what an infamous thing it was to do, and so on, and so forth; but you see, I also know for a fact that Marfa Petrovna actually derived pleasure from my, as it were, enthusiasm. The story of the episode concerning your sister had been squeezed of its last dregs of interest. It was the third day running that Marfa Petrovna had been compelled to stay at home; she had no pretext for showing her nose in town, and she'd bored everyone to death with that letter of hers (you've heard about the letter-reading, I expect?). And suddenly these two smacks of a horsewhip land on her out of the blue! She ordered that carriage like a shot! . . . And all this quite apart from the fact that there are certain occasions when women take an inordinate degree of enjoyment in being trampled on, all their surface indignation to the contrary. They all have them, those occasions; and indeed, human beings in general are fond, even inordinately fond, of being trampled on, have you noticed that? But of women it's especially true. One might even say that they can't get along without it.'

At one particular time Raskolnikov thought of getting up and leaving, thereby terminating the interview. But a certain curiosity, not unmixed with circumspection, held him back for a moment.

'So you like a good fight, do you?' he asked, absent-mindedly.

'No, not terribly,' Svidrigailov replied, unruffled. 'But Marfa Petrovna and I hardly ever came to blows. We lived in harmony most of the time, and she never seemed to grumble at me. As for the horsewhip, I think that, during the whole of our seven years together, I used it on her only twice (that's if one doesn't count a certain third occasion, which was, I may add, highly ambiguous, to say the least): the first time was two months after our marriage, just after we arrived at the estate, and the second time is the one there's just been. What did you think: that I was a monster, a reactionary, a feudalist? Hee-hee! . . . By the way, Rodion Romanovich, I wonder if you remember how a few years ago, when we were still in the era of beneficent *glasnost*,* a certain member of our gentry – I've forgotten his name! – was publicly disgraced in all the organs of the press for having horsewhipped a German woman in a train – remember? I believe it was the year of "The Indecent Act of *The Age*".* (Oh, you remember –

the reading from *Egyptian Nights*, the public one! The "black eyes",
and "Oh, where art thou, golden springtime of our youth?"!) Well,
sir, if you want my opinion, I am deeply out of sympathy with the
gentleman who horsewhipped the German woman, because . . .
there's really not much to sympathize with, is there? But at the same
time I can't help adding that one occasionally encounters "German
women" of such an inflammatory nature that I doubt if there's a
single progressive who would be able to entirely answer for himself.
No one saw the matter from that point of view at the time, yet it's the
only genuinely humane one, I do assure you, sir!'

Having delivered himself of this remark, Svidrigailov once again
went off into roars of laughter. It was evident to Raskolnikov that this
was a man who had firmly made up his mind to do something, and
who had all his wits about him.

'It sounds as though it must be several days since you spoke to
anyone,' he said.

'Just about. Why? Are you surprised that I'm such an adaptable
man?'

'No, what surprises me is that you're too much of one.'

'Because I didn't take offence at the rudeness of your questions? Is
that what you mean? Yes, well . . . why take offence? As I was asked,
so did I reply,' he added, with an astonishingly ingenuous look.
'After all, to be quite honest with you, there's practically nothing that
interests me,' he went on, reflectively. 'Particularly just now – I've
nothing on my hands . . . Actually, you're quite entitled to suppose
that I'm sucking up to you with some ulterior motive, all the more so
since I have some business with your sister, as I told you. But I tell
you quite frankly: I've been bored stiff! Particularly these last three
days, so I'm actually rather glad to see you . . . Don't be angry,
Rodion Romanovich, but for some reason you seem terribly strange
to me. Say what you like, but there's something funny about you;
and particularly now . . . that's to say, not precisely at this very
moment, but now in general . . . There, there, it's all right, I won't, I
won't, don't be dismayed! After all, I'm not such a boor as you think.'

Raskolnikov gave him a gloomy look. 'Actually, I think you're
probably very far from being a boor,' he said. 'I even think that you
may be a man of very good society, or that at any rate you can on
occasion behave like a decent human being.'

'Oh, I'm not really interested in what anyone thinks of me,'

Svidrigailov replied coldly, and even with a touch of superciliousness, 'and so why shouldn't I go around like a vulgar parvenu when those clothes fit so comfortably in our climate and . . . and particularly if one has a natural inclination that way,' he added, starting to laugh again.

'I've heard you have a lot of acquaintances here, though. I mean, you're what's known as "not without connections". So it stands to reason you wouldn't be coming to see me unless you had ulterior motives.'

'What you say is true, I do indeed have acquaintances,' Svidrigailov said, following on without replying to the main thrust of the question. 'I've started running into them already; after all, this is the third day I've been loitering about; either I recognize them, or they apparently recognize me. Oh, it's perfectly true, I'm dressed quite well and am not thought poor; the peasant reforms didn't affect us, you see: the place is just woods and water-meadows, so the money keeps on coming in; but . . . I shan't go to call on them; I was sick of their company even in the old days; this is the third day I've been at large, and I haven't declared myself to anyone . . . My, what a town it is! I mean, who on earth ever dreamed it up? A town of red-tapists, and seminarists of every description! You know, I must say there are a lot of things I never noticed in the old days, eight years or so ago, when I used to hang around here . . . I tell you quite frankly, I put all my faith in anatomy now!'

'What sort of anatomy might that be?'

'And as for those clubs, those evenings at Dussot's,* those outdoor fêtes on the *pointe*,* or even, dare I say it, that progress of theirs – well, they don't need yours truly for any of that,' he went on, again ignoring the question. 'What's so wonderful about being a card-sharper, anyway?'

'So you've been a card-sharper too, have you?'

'How could I have failed to be? There was a whole set of us, a most respectable bunch we were, eight or so years ago; we used to pass the time together; and you know, we all had excellent manners, we were poets, capitalists. In fact, as a general rule in Russian society the best manners are found among those who've been horsewhipped – have you noticed that? Oh, nowadays I've lost the knack down there in the country. But even so, I did go to prison for debt one time, some trouble with a filthy Greek from Nezhin. At that point Marfa Petrovna turned up, she did some haggling and bought me out for thirty thousand silver roubles. (I owed seventy thousand altogether.) We were united in lawful wedlock, and she carried me straight off to her country estate as though I were some treasure trove. I mean, she was five years older than me, you know. *Very* fond of me, she was. For seven years I never left the place. And please observe that she had a document she was going to keep for the rest of her life, signed in someone else's name, which said I was beholden to the tune of those thirty thousand roubles, so if I'd once taken it into my head to rebel she'd have banged the lid shut on me, like that! Oh, she'd have done it! In women all those things co-exist together, you know.'

'And if she hadn't had the document, you'd have taken to your heels?'

'I don't know what to say to you. That document troubled me hardly at all. I didn't feel like going anywhere, and on a couple of occasions Marfa Petrovna even invited me to go abroad with her, when she saw I was bored. But, well, I'd been abroad before, and the place always made me feel sick. I don't know why it is, but the dawn arrives, there's the Bay of Naples, the sea, one looks at it, and feels somehow sad. What makes it even worse is that one really does have something to feel sad about! No, it's better in Russia: here, at least, one can blame other people for everything, and find excuses for oneself. I may go on an expedition to the North Pole now,* as *j'ai le vin mauvais* and loathe drinking, yet drink's about all there is left. I've tried the lot. I say, is it true that Berg* is to make an ascent in a giant balloon in Yusupov Park this Sunday, and that he's willing to take passengers with him for a fee?'

'Don't tell me you want to go up with him?'

'Me? No . . . yes . . .' Svidrigailov murmured, as though he really were pondering something.

'What on earth's got into him?' Raskolnikov wondered.

'No, the document didn't trouble me,' Svidrigailov went on, ruminatively. 'It was I who didn't want to leave the estate. It's almost a year now since Marfa Petrovna returned the document to me on my name-day, together with a remarkably generous sum which she said was a present. All the capital was hers, you know. "You see how I trust you, Arkady Ivanovich," she said – I do assure you, she actually used those words. You don't believe it, do you? Yet I mean, I'd become a respected master on that estate, you know; they know me

342

in the neighbourhood. I used to order books, too. At first Marfa Petrovna approved of that, but later she kept worrying that I'd study too hard.'

'Am I right in thinking that you miss Marfa Petrovna quite a lot?'

'Me? Possibly. Yes, quite possibly. By the way, do you believe in ghosts?'

'What sort of ghosts?'

'Oh, just ordinary ones – that sort.'

'Do you?'

'Well, perhaps not, *pour vous plaire* . . . I'm not so sure, though . . .'

'Do you see them, then?'

Svidrigailov gave him a rather strange look.

'Marfa Petrovna considers it expedient to visit me,' he said, contorting his mouth into a strange smile.

'What do you mean?'

'Well, she's been to see me three times now. The first time I saw her was on the very day of her funeral, an hour after we'd put her in the ground. That was the day before my departure for St Petersburg. The second time was the day before yesterday, as I was sitting in the train at Malaya Vishera Station; and the third time was two hours ago, in my room at the apartment where I'm staying; I was alone.'

'Was this when you were awake?'

'Absolutely. I was awake on all three occasions. She comes in, speaks for a moment, and then walks out of the door; it's always the door. I even seem to hear it.'

'How did I know that something of that kind was happening to you?' Raskolnikov said suddenly, at the same moment taken aback at having said this. He was in a violent state of agitation.

'Good Lord! You knew, did you?' Svidrigailov said in astonishment. 'Did you really? Well, didn't I say we had certain points in common, eh?'

'You certainly did not!' Raskolnikov replied sharply, losing his self-control.

'I didn't?'

'No!'

'It's funny, I thought I did. Just now, when I came in and saw you lying there with your eyes closed, pretending – I instantly said to myself: "That's the fellow!"'

'*What* did you say? What are you getting at?' Raskolnikov shouted.

'Getting at? I really don't know what I'm getting at . . .' Svidrigailov muttered candidly, as though he himself were somewhat confused.

For a moment they said nothing. They both stared at each other.

'It's a lot of nonsense!' Raskolnikov exclaimed, angrily. 'What does she say to you when she visits you?'

'Her? Would you believe it, it's always the pettiest, most trivial things, things that really make you wonder; I mean, that's just what I find so annoying. The first time she came in (you know how it is, I was tired: there'd been the funeral service, with the prayers for the repose of her soul, followed by the *litiya*,* and then the funeral meal – well, at last I was alone in my study, I'd lit a cigar, had started to brood about things), she walked in at the door: "Oh, Arkady Ivanovich," she said, "with all this fuss, you've forgotten to wind up the dining-room clock." And you know, I really had wound up that clock every week for the past seven years, and if ever I forgot, she'd always be sure to remind me. By the following day I was on my way here. At dawn I got out at a station – I'd been dozing overnight, I was shattered, all bleary-eyed – and had some coffee; I looked – and Marfa Petrovna suddenly sat down beside me; she had a pack of cards in her hand: "Wouldn't you like me to tell your fortune for the journey, Arkady Ivanovich?" she said. And you know, she was very skilled at telling fortunes. Oh, I'll never forgive myself for not having let her! I got scared and ran away, and in any case the bell was ringing for the train to leave. Then today, as I was sitting with a heavy stomach after a most wretched meal I'd ordered from a cookshop – I was having a cigarette – Marfa Petrovna suddenly came in again, all dressed up in a new green silk dress with the very longest of trains: "Hallo, Arkady Ivanovich," she said, "what do you think of my dress? Aniska could never have made something like this!" (Aniska's a seamstress on our estate, one of our former serf girls who went to train in Moscow – rather a pretty girl, actually.) There she stood, turning this way and that in front of me. I inspected the dress, and then looked her closely, closely in the eye, and said: "I wonder you come to bother me with such trivial matters, Marfa Petrovna." "Oh, good heavens, dear, you're well beyond my reach now!" she replied. Well, just to tease her, I said to her: "You know, Marfa Petrovna, I think I'm going to get married again." "That's just what I'd expect of you, Arkady Ivanovich; but it won't look very good if you go and take another wife no sooner than you've buried your previous one. And even if you

344

make a good choice, I can tell you now – it won't provide either you or her with much amusement, but only the public at large." At that point she went out, and I swear I heard her train rustle. I mean, what sort of nonsense was that, eh?'

'What if you're still lying?' was Raskolnikov's response to this.

'I seldom lie,' Svidrigailov replied meditatively, seeming not to notice the question's rudeness.

'And previously – before this, I mean – you never saw any ghosts?'

'Er . . . yes, I did, only once in my life, six years ago. I used to have a manservant called Filka; we'd only just buried him, and one day I shouted, forgetting he was dead: "Filka, my pipe!" He came in and went straight over to the cabinet where I keep my pipes. I sat there, thinking: "This is him taking his revenge" – because just before his death we'd had a terrible quarrel. "How dare you come in here with your elbow in tatters like that – be off with you, good-for-nothing!" He turned, went out and didn't come back. I said nothing to Marfa Petrovna about it at the time. I'd been going to have a requiem sung for him, but I was too ashamed of myself.'

'You ought to see a doctor.'

'Oh, I don't need you to tell me I'm ill, though I must say I honestly can't imagine what it can be; I should think I'm about five times healthier than you are. I didn't ask you whether you believe that ghosts are seen by people – I asked you whether you believe there are such things as ghosts?'

'No, I most certainly do not!' Raskolnikov exclaimed with more than a touch of aggressiveness.

'I mean, what do people usually say?' Svidrigailov murmured, as though to himself, looking to one side and inclining his head slightly. 'They say: "You're ill, so the things you see are just a non-existent hallucination." But that's woolly thinking, you know. I agree that ghosts are only seen by people who are ill; but I mean, that only proves that ghosts can only be perceived by people who are ill – not that they don't exist.'

'It proves nothing of the kind!' Raskolnikov insisted, irritably.

'Oh? That's your opinion, is it?' Svidrigailov went on, giving him a long, slow look. 'Well, but what if one were to put the argument this way (come along, now, give me a hand): "Ghosts are, so to speak, shreds and fragments of other worlds, their source and origin. Of course, the man who is healthy doesn't need to see them, because the healthy man is the most earthly sort of person, and so is bound, for the sake of gaining an all-round and orderly view of things, to live exclusively the life of this world. Well, but he has only to fall ill, to suffer a disruption of the normal, earthly order of things within his organism, and the possibility of there being another world begins to exert its influence; the iller he gets, the more numerous are his contacts with the other world, the result being that, when he finally dies, he goes straight there." I've been thinking this out for a long time. If you believe in a life to come, you ought to be able to believe in that argument, too.'

'I don't believe in a life to come,' Raskolnikov said.

Svidrigailov sat looking pensive.

'And what if there's nothing there except spiders, or something of that kind?' he said suddenly.

'This is a madman,' Raskolnikov thought.

'You see, we always think of eternity as an idea that can't be comprehended, as something enormous, gigantic! But why does it have to be so very large? I mean, instead of thinking of it that way, try supposing that all there will be is one little room, something akin to a country bath-house, with soot on the walls and spiders in every corner, and there's your eternity for you. You know, I sometimes see it that way.'

'Can you really, really not imagine anything more just and consoling than that?' Raskolnikov exclaimed with a feeling of pain.

'Just? But who knows, perhaps that's exactly what it is – just, and you know, if I'd been given the job, I'd most certainly have designed things that way!'

Raskolnikov was suddenly gripped by a kind of chill at this outrageous reply. Svidrigailov lifted his head, gave him a fixed look and suddenly roared with laughter.

'But don't you see?' he began to shout. 'Only half an hour ago we hadn't yet clapped eyes on each other, we thought we were enemies, with some unfinished business to settle, but here we are, we've chucked the business out of the window and got ourselves into all this literary stuff! Well, I was speaking the truth, wasn't I, when I said we were birds of a feather?'

'Look, do me a favour,' Raskolnikov said, irritably. 'Please spare me the explanations and tell me why you've honoured me with this visit . . . and . . . well . . . I'm in a hurry, I've no time, I want to go out . . .'

'Why, certainly, certainly. Your sister, Avdotya Romanovna, is to marry Mr Luzhin – Pyotr Petrovich – isn't she?'

'Will you kindly not talk about my sister, and refrain from mentioning her name. I quite honestly don't know how you can dare to utter it in my presence, if you really are Svidrigailov!'

'But I mean, it's about her that I've come to talk to you – how can I avoid mentioning her name?'

'Very well; speak, but make it quick!'

'I'm certain that by now you will have formed your own opinion of this Mr Luzhin, who is a cousin of mine on my wife's side of the family, if you've so much as spent half an hour with him or even just heard a few of the hard and unquestionable facts about him. He's not a suitable match for Avdotya Romanovna. In the way I view this matter, Avdotya Romanovna is sacrificing herself in an utterly magnanimous and reckless fashion for the sake of . . . for the sake of her family. It struck me, after all I've heard about you, that you, too, might be glad if this marriage could be stopped from going ahead without your interests being harmed. Indeed, now that I've made your personal acquaintance, I feel positively confident of it.'

'You know, you're being very innocent about all this; I'm sorry, I nearly said insolent,' Raskolnikov said.

'In other words, you mean I'm worried about my own pocket. Have no fear, Rodion Romanovich, if it was my own best interests I was worried about, I wouldn't be bringing all this out in the open with you so directly, I'm not a complete fool, after all. On that score, allow me to reveal to you a certain psychological curiosity of mine. While justifying my love for Avdotya Romanovna to you a few moments ago, I said I myself was a victim. You may as well know that I don't feel any love at all now, n-none whatever, so that it actually seems strange to me now, as I mean I really did have certain feelings . . .'

'Caused by idleness and lechery,' Raskolnikov interrupted.

'Yes, it's true, I'm a lecherous and an idle man. But actually, your sister possesses so many virtues that not even I could help succumbing to a certain – influence. But that was all nonsense, as now I myself realize.'

'Have you realized it long?'

'It's been with me for some time, the realization, but I finally made

347

up my mind the day before yesterday, almost at the very moment I arrived in St Petersburg. Though even when I was in Moscow, I still thought I was making my journey with the object of winning the hand of Avdotya Romanovna, and saw Mr Luzhin as my rival.'

'Look, excuse me interrupting you, but you'd really be doing me a favour if you'd cut the detail and get to the point about the purpose of your visit. I'm in a hurry, I must go out . . .'

'With the greatest of pleasure. Since I'm now in town and have decided to undertake a certain . . . *voyage*, I am anxious to make a few essential arrangements in advance of my departure. My children have stayed behind with an aunt of theirs; they are not short of money; and I myself am not necessary to them. What kind of a father am I, in any case? For myself I have taken only what Marfa Petrovna gave me a year ago. That is sufficient for me. Please bear with me, I shall come to the point right away. Before my *voyage*, which may very well take place, I want to have done with Mr Luzhin. It's not that I find him so very unendurable, but rather that he was the cause of my quarrel with Marfa Petrovna, when I discovered she'd cooked up this marriage. What I want to do now is meet with Avdotya Romanovna, through your good agencies and even possibly in your presence, and explain to her that, in the first place, not only will she fail to obtain from Mr Luzhin the slightest advantage – she will most certainly suffer manifest harm. Then, after I have asked her forgiveness for these recent disagreeable happenings, I should like to request her permission to offer her ten thousand roubles and thereby lessen the inconvenience of her break with Mr Luzhin, a break to which I am convinced she would not be averse, were but the opportunity to present itself.'

'But you really *are* mad!' Raskolnikov exclaimed, less in anger than surprise. 'How dare you talk like that!'

'I knew you'd hit the ceiling; but the first point to note here is that even though I'm not a wealthy man, I do have that ten thousand to spare, I mean, it's quite, quite superfluous to me. If Avdotya Romanovna won't accept it, I shall probably put it to some even more stupid use. That's point number one. Point number two is that my conscience is completely at rest; I make this offer without calculation of any kind. You may believe it or not, as you choose; all I can tell you is that sooner or later both you and Avdotya Romanovna will realize that it is so. The fact of the matter is that I really did cause your greatly respected sister a certain amount of trouble and unpleasantness; and thus, in the throes of sincere repentance, I genuinely wish – oh, not to buy myself out, to pay for the unpleasantness, but quite simply do something that is to her advantage, on the grounds that, well, I haven't assumed for myself the privilege of doing her nothing but harm. If there were in my offer even the millionth part of calculation, I should not be offering a mere ten thousand, when only five weeks ago I offered her more than that. There is, in addition, the possibility that in the very, very near future I shall marry a certain young lady, and if that does indeed come to pass then consequently all suspicion as to my making approaches to Avdotya Romanovna must inevitably be destroyed. In conclusion I would point out that by marrying Mr Luzhin, Avdotya Romanovna will be taking that same money, only from another side of the family . . . So don't be angry, Rodion Romanovich, think about it calmly and with composure.'

As he said this, Svidrigailov was the very model of calm and composure.

'I think you'd better stop,' Raskolnikov said. 'What you're saying is outrageously insolent.'

'Not in the least. If that were so, people would be able to do one another nothing but harm in this world, and not even possess the right to do a single crumb of good, merely because of some empty accepted convention. That's absurd. I mean, suppose I were to die, and left that sum to your sister in my will, do you really think she'd refuse it then?'

'It's highly probable.'

'Well, I suppose that means she would, sir. Oh well, if she would, she would, so be it. Only ten thousand is not a bad thing to have, it can come in handy. All the same, I'd be obliged if you would pass on to Avdotya Romanovna what I've said to you.'

'No, I won't.'

'In that case, Rodion Romanovich, I shall be compelled to try to obtain a personal interview with her myself, and may consequently upset her.'

'And if I do pass on to her what you said, you won't try to see her in person – is that it?'

'I really don't know what to say to you. I'd very much like to see her just once.'

349

'Don't rely on it.'

'Pity. But then, you don't really know me, do you? Perhaps we shall come to be on closer terms with each other.'

'You think that's likely, do you?'

'Why ever not?' Svidrigailov said, smiling. He got up and took his hat. 'I mean, after all, I really didn't mean to trouble you very much by coming here, and didn't even have any particularly clear idea in my head of what it was I expected to gain by it, though I must say, the look on your face this morning did startle me somewhat . . .'

'Where did you see me this morning?' Raskolnikov asked, uneasily.

'Oh, somewhere or other, I don't remember now, sir . . . I still keep thinking there's something about you that resembles myself . . . And I mean, don't worry, I'm not an utter bore; I used to get along all right with the card-sharpers; Prince Svirbey, who's an important fellow and a distant relative of mine, didn't find my company boring; I was able to write a few lines about Raphael's Madonna in Mrs Prilukova's visiting album; I lived with Marfa Petrovna for seven years quite literally without a break; I've even spent nights in the Vyazemsky* down on the Haymarket; and I may go up in Berg's balloon.'

'Very well, then. May I ask if you're planning to make your journey soon?'

'What journey?'

'Oh, the *voyage*, or whatever it was you were talking about . . . You know what I mean.'

'The *voyage*? Ah, yes! . . . Quite so, I did indeed mention my *voyage* to you . . . Well, that's rather a long story . . . And I mean, if you only knew what you're asking me about!' he added, and suddenly gave a short, loud burst of laughter. 'Actually, I may get married instead of going on my *voyage*; I'm in the process of finding a wife.'

'Here?'

'Yes.'

'Whenever did you get time?'

'But even so, I would very much like to see Avdotya Romanovna just once. I do implore you most seriously. Well, *au revoir* . . . Ah, yes! I know what it was I forgot! Rodion Romanovich, please tell your sister that Marfa Petrovna has left her three thousand roubles in her will. It's absolutely true. Marfa Petrovna made the stipulation a week before her death, and I helped her to sign the particulars. Avdotya

Romanovna may even receive the money in two or three weeks' time.'

'Are you telling the truth?'

'The truth. Convey it to her. Well, sir – your servant. Why, I reside not far from you at all.'

On his way out through the doorway, Svidrigailov collided with Razumikhin.

II

It was almost eight o'clock; they were both hurrying to Bakaleyev's Tenements, in order to get there before Luzhin.

'I say, who was that?' Razumikhin asked, as soon as they were out in the street.

'Oh, that was Svidrigailov, the landowner I told you about in whose home my sister was ill-treated when she worked as a governess there. It was because of his amorous attentions that she had to give up that post – Marfa Petrovna turned her out. This Marfa Petrovna subsequently asked Dunya to forgive her, but now she's suddenly died. She's the woman we were talking about earlier today. I don't know why, but that man really gives me the creeps. He has arrived in town having only just buried his wife. He's a very strange character, and has some sort of desperate plan . . . It's as if he knows something . . . Dunya must be protected from him . . . that's what I wanted to tell you – are you listening?'

'Protected? What can he possibly do to Avdotya Romanovna? Well, if you say so, Rodya – thank you for keeping me informed . . . Yes, by all means let's protect her! . . . Where's he staying?'

'I don't know.'

'Why didn't you ask him? Damn, that's a pity! But don't worry, I'll find out.'

'Did you see him?' Raskolnikov asked, after a short silence.

'Oh yes, I made a note of him; a firm, mental note.'

'You're sure you saw him? Actually saw him?' Raskolnikov said, insistently.

'Yes, I'd remember him anywhere; I've got a good memory for faces.'

Again they said nothing for a while.

'Hm . . . there we are, then . . .' Raskolnikov muttered. 'But you know . . . at the time I thought . . . indeed I still do . . . that what I saw there might have been some kind of fantasy.'

'What on earth are you talking about? I don't think I quite understand.'

'Well,' Raskolnikov went on, contorting his mouth into a smile, 'you all say that I'm crazy; so just now I even thought it might be true, and I'd merely seen a ghost!'

'What?'

'I mean – who knows? Perhaps I really am crazy, and all the things that have happened these last few days have simply been in my imagination . . .'

'Oh, Rodya! We've upset you again! . . . But what was he saying, why had he come to see you?'

Raskolnikov made no reply. Razumikhin thought for a moment.

'Well, then, listen to what I've got to tell you,' he began. 'I came up to see you, but you were asleep. Then we ate dinner, and after that I went back to see Porfiry. Zamyotov was still with him. I started to try to talk to them, but I couldn't get anywhere. I couldn't communicate with them properly. It's as if they don't understand and are incapable of understanding, yet it doesn't seem to bother them one bit. I drew Porfiry over to the window and began to talk to him, but again I couldn't get anywhere: he kept looking away, and so did I. In the end I brought my fist up to his ugly mug and told him, as one relative to another, that I'd smash his skull. He just looked at me. I spat and went out, and that was it. Really silly. I didn't exchange a word with Zamyotov. But there's one thing you should note: I thought I'd gone and ruined everything, but as I was on my way down the staircase a certain thought occurred to me, one that fairly made me think: what are we making all the fuss about? I mean, if you were in some danger, or something of that sort, I could understand it. But I mean, why should you worry? None of this has anything to do with you, so my advice is – spit on them; we'll laugh at them later on, when it's all over, but if I were in your shoes I'd start mystifying them a bit, too. I mean, how ashamed of themselves they'll be later on! Spit on them;

later on we'll give them a beating, too, too, but in the meanwhile let's just have a good laugh to ourselves!'

'Yes, it stands to reason,' Raskolnikov answered. 'But what will you be saying tomorrow?' he thought to himself. Strangely enough, he had not yet once been visited by the notion: 'What will Razumikhin say when he finds out?' With it now in his mind, Raskolnikov gave him a close look. The account Razumikhin had just given of his visit to Porfiry's had been of very little interest to him: so much water had flowed under the bridge since then! . . .

In the corridor they bumped into Luzhin; he had turned up punctually at eight o'clock and was now searching for the room, with the result that all three of them made their entrance together, but without looking at one another and without saying hallo. The young men went in ahead, while Pyotr Petrovich, for the sake of common decency, hung around in the vestibule for a while, taking off his coat. Pulkheria Aleksandrovna at once came out to greet him in the doorway. Dunya said hallo to her brother.

Pyotr Petrovich came in and exchanged greetings with the ladies politely enough, though with redoubled sedateness. He looked, however, as though he had been slightly put off his guard and had not yet quite recovered it. Pulkheria Aleksandrovna, who also seemed rather shy, made haste to allot places to everyone at the round table, on which a samovar was bubbling. Dunya and Luzhin were given seats opposite each other on either side of the table. Razumikhin and Raskolnikov ended up opposite Pulkheria Aleksandrovna – Razumikhin next to Luzhin and Raskolnikov beside his sister.

A momentary silence ensued. Pyotr Petrovich unhurriedly took out a lawn handkerchief that smelt of scent and blew his nose with the air of a man who, although virtuous, had none the less received a certain affront to his dignity, and was, moreover, firmly resolved to obtain an explanation. Out in the hallway he had wondered whether it might be better not to take his coat off at all, but to leave and to go away, thereby visiting upon both ladies a severe and damning punishment, such as would instantly make them aware of the whole depth of his feelings. This, however, he did not quite dare to do. What was more, this was a man who could not abide uncertainty: if his instructions had so flagrantly been violated, that meant something must be going on, and whatever it was he had better find out before it led anywhere; there would, after all, be plenty of time for punishments later on, and it lay in his power to administer them.

'Your journey was satisfactory, I trust?' he said, addressing Pulkheria Aleksandrovna in an official-sounding tone.

'Yes, Pyotr Petrovich – thanks be to God.'

'I am unconscionably pleased to hear it, madam. I trust Avdotya Romanovna did not find it too tiring, either?'

'Oh, I'm young and strong, but mother had a dreadful time,' Dunya answered.

'What is one to do, madam; our national railroads are unconscionably long. The so-called "Mother Russia" is great in more senses than one . . . I am afraid that, all my wishes to the contrary, I was totally unable to be at the station to meet you yesterday. I trust, however, that everything went off without too much bother?'

'Well as a matter of fact, Pyotr Petrovich, we were very dismayed,' Pulkheria Aleksandrovna said quickly, in a peculiar tone of voice, 'and if God Himself had not sent us Dmitry Prokofich yesterday, we would quite simply have been lost. Here he is, Dmitry Prokofich Razumikhin,' she added, introducing him to Luzhin.

'Ah yes, I had the pleasure . . . yesterday,' Luzhin muttered; he gave Razumikhin a hostile, sideways look, then frowned and fell silent. On the whole, Pyotr Petrovich belonged to that category of men who, when observed in society, appear extremely amiable and make a special virtue of their amiability, but who, as soon as anything is not quite to their liking, at once lose all their inner resources and become more reminiscent of sacks of flour than easy-going cavaliers whose task it is to enliven the company. Again they all fell silent: Raskolnikov kept resolutely taciturn, Avdotya Romanovna did not want to break the silence prematurely, Razumikhin could think of nothing to say, with the result that Pulkheria Aleksandrovna flew into another flap.

'Marfa Petrovna died, I expect you've heard,' she began, resorting to her capital fund of conversational material.

'Indeed, madam, I have. I was informed at the first rumour thereof, and have in fact come here now in order to tell you that immediately after his wife's funeral Arkady Ivanovich Svidrigailov set off in a hurry for St Petersburg. Such, at any rate, would appear to be the case according to the most precise information I have been able to obtain.'

'To St Petersburg? Here, you mean?' Dunya asked anxiously, exchanging a glance with her mother.

'Precisely so, madam, and, needless to say, not without certain ulterior motives, if the speed of his departure and the nature of the preceding circumstances are anything to go by.'

'Oh good Lord! Will he really not leave Dunya in peace even here?' Pulkheria Aleksandrovna exclaimed.

'I do not believe that either you or Avdotya Romanovna need have any particular concern – assuming, of course, that you wish to have nothing whatever to do with him. As for myself, I am even now investigating the whereabouts of the address at which he is residing . . .'

'Oh, Pyotr Petrovich, you have no idea how you frightened me just now!' Pulkheria Aleksandrovna went on. 'I've only ever seen him twice, and I thought he was horrible, horrible! I'm convinced he was responsible for Marfa Petrovna's death!'

'With regard to that, one must not jump to conclusions. I have precise information. I will not dispute that he may have contributed to the accelerated tempo of events by the – as it were – psychological influence of the outrage he perpetrated on her; but as for the conduct and the general moral characteristics of the person concerned, I am in agreement with you. I do not know whether he is rich now, or what exactly Marfa Petrovna may have left him; I shall have information concerning this in the very nearest future; if I know anything of the man, however, being possessed of even only a few financial resources, he will at once, here in St Petersburg, revert to his old customs. He is one of the most depraved and lost examples of all that category of men! I have considerable grounds for supposing that Marfa Petrovna, having had the misfortune, eight years ago, to fall in love with him and redeem his debts, performed a service to him in another respect, too: it was exclusively thanks to her efforts and sacrifices that a criminal charge, which involved more than a dash of bestial, nay, fantastic, murderousness, was nipped in the bud at the very outset, a charge which, had he had to answer it in court, could most, most easily have landed him in Siberia. That is the kind of man he is, if you wish to know.'

'Oh, good Lord!' Pulkheria Aleksandrovna exclaimed. Raskolnikov was listening intently.

'And you're not making it up when you say you have precise information about this?' Dunya asked, sternly and imposingly.

'All I can tell you is what I myself heard, in confidence, from the deceased Marfa Petrovna. It is worth observing that, from a legal point of view, this case was somewhat unsubstantiated. There lived – and indeed still lives – in this part of town a certain foreign woman by the name of Resslich, who is, moreover, a small-time moneylender, and also undertakes certain other kinds of business. Mr Svidrigailov had for a long time maintained certain close and mysterious contacts with this Resslich woman. She had a distant relative – a niece, I think it was – living with her; this was a girl of about fifteen, or possibly even only fourteen, a deaf-mute, and the Resslich woman had a boundless hatred for her and grudged her every bite; she even used to beat her in a quite inhuman fashion. One day the girl was found hanging in the attic. Her death was adjudged to be suicide. After the usual legal proceedings the matter was dropped, but later on someone made a statement to the police that the child had been . . . brutally raped by Svidrigailov. True, all this was unsubstantiated, the information came from another German woman, a prostitute whose testimony could not be relied on; in the end there was not even an official statement, thanks to the efforts and financial resources of Marfa Petrovna; it all remained a rumour. On the other hand, it is a rumour that tells us a great deal. Avdotya Romanovna, I am sure that during the time you spent in their house you also heard about what happened to their manservant Filipp, who some six years ago died of the tortures that were inflicted on him back in the days of serfdom.'

'Oh, but what I heard was that Filipp hanged himself.'

'Precisely so, madam, but it was the system of incessant victimizations and punishments devised and put into execution by Mr Svidrigailov that compelled, or rather predisposed him to seek a violent death at his own hand.'

'I don't know anything about that,' Dunya replied coldly. 'All I heard was a very strange story to the effect that Filipp was a hypochondriac, a kind of domestic philosopher of whom the servants used to say that he'd "read too much", and that he'd hanged himself more because of the taunts of Mr Svidrigailov than because of his beatings. During my time there he treated the servants well, and one could even have said that they liked him, though it's true that they also blamed him for Filipp's death.'

'I observe, Avdotya Romanovna, that you seem suddenly to have developed an inclination to defend him,' Luzhin remarked, contorting his mouth into an ambiguous smile. 'Indeed, he is a man of cunning and seductive charm where ladies are concerned, as witness the deplorable example of Marfa Petrovna, who died so strangely. I simply wished to serve your mother and yourself with my advice, in view of his renewed and doubtless impending efforts. As for myself, I am firmly convinced that this man is going to disappear into a debtors' prison again. Marfa Petrovna certainly never had any intention of allotting any substantial sum to him, with his children in mind, and if she did leave him something, then it was only that which was most essential, of little value and ephemeral duration, and which would not last a man of his habits even a year.'

'Pyotr Petrovich, please, I beg of you, do let us stop talking about Mr Svidrigailov. It's making me feel depressed.'

'He came to see me just now,' Raskolnikov said suddenly, for the first time breaking the silence.

There were gasps all around, everyone turned to look at him. Even Pyotr Petrovich looked worried.

'About an hour and a half ago, while I was asleep, he came in, woke me up and introduced himself,' Raskolnikov continued. 'He was rather jovial and relaxed, and seems fully to expect that I'll strike up some sort of friendship with him. By the way, Dunya, he seems to be absolutely desperate to have a meeting with you, and he asked me to arrange it. He has a proposition to make to you, and he told me what it was. Moreover, he informed me quite definitely that a week before her death Marfa Petrovna left you three thousand roubles in her will, and you may receive this money in the very nearest future.'

'Thank God!' Pulkheria Aleksandrovna exclaimed, crossing herself. 'Pray for her, Dunya, pray for her!'

'It is indeed true,' broke from Luzhin.

'Yes, yes – what else did he say?' Dunya said, hurrying her brother.

'Then he said that he himself was not a rich man and that the whole of the estate was to go to his children, who are at present living with an aunt. Then he told me he was staying somewhere not far from me, but as to exactly where it is I don't know, I didn't ask . . .'

'But what is it, what is this proposition he wants to make Dunya?' Pulkheria Aleksandrovna asked in fear. 'Did he tell you?'

'Yes, he did.'

'Tell us, then.'

'I'll tell you later.' Raskolnikov fell silent and addressed himself to his tea.

Pyotr Petrovich took out his watch and glanced at it.

'There is some business I must attend to, and so I shall not intrude any longer,' he added with a slight air of pique, and began to get up from his seat.

'Oh, don't go, Pyotr Petrovich,' Dunya said. 'After all, you intended to come for the whole evening. What's more, in your letter you said there was something you wanted to discuss with mother.'

'Precisely so, Avdotya Romanovna,' Pyotr Petrovich said, imposingly, sitting down on his chair again, but still with his hat in his hands. 'I did indeed wish to discuss some most important points with both you and your mother. But just as there are certain proposals of Mr Svidrigailov which your brother appears unable to talk about in my presence, so there are certain most, most important matters I, too, do not wish to discuss . . . in the presence of others . . . What is more, my fundamental and most urgent request has not been obeyed . . .'

Luzhin made a sour face, and lapsed into sedate silence.

'Your request that my brother not be present at our meeting was disregarded at my insistence,' said Dunya. 'You wrote in your letter that you had received an insult from him; I think that ought to be cleared up at once, and the two of you ought to settle your differences. And if Rodya really did insult you, then he *must* and *will* apologize to you.'

Pyotr Petrovich at once began to bully.

'There are certain insults, Avdotya Romanovna, which with all the good will in the world it is impossible to forget. There are certain limits beyond which it is inadvisable to go as, once having crossed them, there may be no going back.'

'That's not really what I was talking about, Pyotr Petrovich,' Dunya broke in with some impatience. 'What you must understand is that the whole of our future now hangs on the question of whether all this can be cleared up and settled, and as soon as possible. I will tell you right now that I cannot view the matter in any other light, and that if you value me at all then, even though it may be hard, all this nonsense must end today. I repeat: if my brother has wronged you, he will ask your forgiveness.'

'It surprises me that you should put the matter in those terms, Avdotya Romanovna,' Luzhin said, getting more and more irritated. 'While I think highly of you and, as it were, adore you, at the same time I think I should make it perfectly plain that there may very well be a member of your family for whom I have not the slightest affection. In proffering my claim to the favour of your hand, I cannot at the same time assume obligations which may be incompatible . . .'

'Oh, stop being so touchy, Pyotr Petrovich!' Dunya interrupted with feeling. 'Please try to behave like the intelligent and noble-spirited man I have always considered you, and should like to go on considering you. I have given you the great promise: I am your betrothed; please trust me, and have confidence in my power of dispassionate judgement in this matter. My taking upon myself the role of a judge is as much of a surprise to my brother as it is to you. When, after receiving your letter today, I asked him to be present at our meeting, I told him nothing of my intentions. It's like this, you see: if the two of you don't settle your differences, I shall have to choose – either you or him. That is how matters stand with regard to you both. I don't want to make the wrong choice. If I choose you, then I must break with my brother; if I choose my brother, I must break with you. Now I want to discover beyond any shadow of doubt whether he is a true brother to me or not. And as for you, what I want to find out is whether you value me, think highly of me; whether you will be a true husband to me.'

'Avdotya Romanovna,' Luzhin said, wincing, 'your words are all too clear to me, and I must say that I find them positively offensive, bearing in mind the position I have the honour to hold in your regard. Quite apart from the strange and offensive comparison you have made, setting me on a par with an . . . arrogant youth, you imply by your remarks the possibility of breaking the promise you gave me. "Either you or him," you say, thereby demonstrating to me how little I mean to you . . . I find this more than I can tolerate, in view of the relations and . . . commitments that exist between us.'

'What?' Dunya exclaimed, blazing up. 'I put your interests on the same level as all that has hitherto been precious to me in life, that has constituted the *integrity* of my life, and you suddenly take offence because you think I value you *too little*?'

Raskolnikov smiled a silent, caustic smile, and Razumikhin was seized with inward mirth; but Pyotr Petrovich did not accept Dunya's reply; on the contrary, with every word she spoke he was growing more and more quarrelsome and irritable, as though he were acquiring a taste for it.

'The love you feel for your future companion in life, for your husband, must come before your love for your brother,' he pronounced sententiously. 'But however that may be, it is out of the question for me to be placed on an equal level with him . . . Even though I insisted earlier that I would not and could not explain in the presence of your brother the reasons for my coming here, I now intend to address your esteemed mother in respect of a certain salient point that affects my honour. Your son,' he said, turning to Pulkheria Aleksandrovna, 'yesterday, in the presence of Mr Rassudkin (er . . . that's right, isn't it? I'm sorry, your name has slipped my memory),' he said, bowing amiably to Razumikhin, 'insulted me by misrepresenting a remark I made to you in the course of a private conversation as we were having coffee together one day – namely, that there is more conjugal advantage to be obtained from marrying a girl from a poor family who has already experienced some of life's woes than there is in marrying one from a well-off background, because the former will be more likely to behave in a moral fashion. Your son deliberately exaggerated the import of my words to the point of absurdity, accusing me of evil intentions and, in my opinion, founded his attack on material drawn from your own correspondence with him. I shall consider myself fortunate, Pulkheria Aleksandrovna, if you can succeed in assuring me that the contrary is the case, thus doing much to set my mind at rest. Will you be so good as to tell me in exactly what terms you conveyed my words in your letter to Rodion Romanovich?'

'I don't remember,' Pulkheria Aleksandrovna said, getting confused. 'I conveyed them in the sense in which I'd understood them. I don't know what Rodya told you . . . perhaps he did exaggerate.'

'He could not have done so without your influence.'

'Pyotr Petrovich,' Pulkheria Aleksandrovna said with dignity, 'the proof that Dunya and I did not take your words in too negative a sense is that we are *here*.'

'Bravo, mother!' Dunya said, approvingly.

'So I'm to blame there too, am I?' Luzhin said in an offended tone.

'Look, Pyotr Petrovich: you're forever blaming Rodion, but you yourself said something that wasn't true about him in that letter you wrote,' Pulkheria Aleksandrovna added, gaining some courage.

'I do not recall having written anything untrue, madam.'

'What you wrote in your letter,' Raskolnikov said abruptly, without turning to face Luzhin, 'was that I gave that money yesterday not to the widow of the man who had been trampled to death, as was actually the case, but to his daughter (whom I hadn't ever met until yesterday). You wrote that in order to stir up unpleasantness between me and my family, and to that purpose you added some filthy remarks about the behaviour of a girl you don't even know. It's all base lies and slander.'

'Pardon me, sir,' Luzhin replied, quivering with vindictive rage. 'In my letter I expatiated on your qualities and actions solely in response to the request of your mother and sister that I describe them, as they wished to know in what state I had found you and what sort of an impression you had made on me. As for the comments you refer to, I defy you to quote one line of them that is not true – in other words, prove to me that you were not wasting your money and that that family, though unfortunate, did not contain unworthy persons.'

'Well, if you want my opinion, you, with all your attributes of worthiness, are not worth the little finger of the unhappy girl at whom you cast your stone.'

'So you would allow her into the company of your mother and sister, would you?'

'I have already done it, if you really want to know. I made her sit down with mother and Dunya when she came to visit me today.'

'Rodya!' Pulkheria Aleksandrovna exclaimed.

Dunya blushed; Razumikhin knit his eyebrows. Luzhin gave a superior, caustic smile.

'I think you may judge for yourself, Avdotya Romanovna,' he said. 'What agreement is possible here? I hope that this matter is now concluded and fully explained, once and for all. Now, however, I shall betake myself elsewhere, in order not to disturb the continued pleasantness of this family reunion and the divulging of confidences.' (He rose from his chair and picked up his hat.) 'As I leave, however, I venture to suggest that in future I be spared such meetings and, as it were, compromising situations. I address a particular request to you in this regard, my dear Pulkheria Aleksandrovna, all the more so since my letter was addressed to yourself, and not to anyone else.'

Pulkheria Aleksandrovna was somewhat offended.

'Anyone might think you were trying to take us completely in your power, Pyotr Petrovich. Dunya has told you the reason for your request not being obeyed: she acted with the best of intentions. You know, your letter to me reads as though you were giving me orders. Are we really to consider your every request a command? I for my part would like to say to you that you ought to be extremely tactful and considerate to us now, because we've given up everything and, trusting you, have come here – practically in your power already just for having done that.'

'That is not entirely just, Pulkheria Aleksandrovna, especially not at the present moment, when tidings have arrived concerning the three thousand roubles bequeathed by Marfa Petrovna, tidings most opportune, it would appear, given the new tone in which you have begun to address me,' he added, bitingly.

'If that remark is anything to go by, one can really only suppose that you've been calculating on our helplessness,' Dunya observed in irritation.

'Well, now at any rate I can make no such calculations, and I am particularly anxious not to impede the divulging of the confidential proposals emanating from the person of Arkady Ivanovich Svidrigailov, proposals he has entrusted to your brother and which, I see, may be of fundamental and possibly agreeable significance to you.'

'Oh, good heavens!' Pulkheria Aleksandrovna exclaimed.

Razumikhin could not keep still on his chair.

'Don't you feel ashamed now, sister?' Raskolnikov asked.

'Yes I do, Rodya,' Dunya said. 'Pyotr Petrovich, get out of here!' she said to him, pale with anger.

Pyotr Petrovich, it seemed, had not at all expected such an ending to the scene. He had too much self-confidence, too much belief in his own power and in the helplessness of his victims. Even now he could not quite believe it. He turned pale, and his lips began to quiver.

'Avdotya Romanovna, if I go out of that door now, with parting words like those, then – of this you may be certain – I shall never return. Think about it carefully! My word is my bond.'

'What effrontery!' Dunya exclaimed, getting up quickly. 'Why, I don't want you to return!'

'What? So tha-a-at's it!' Luzhin shouted, right up to the last moment unable to believe in the possibility of such a dénouement, and therefore now totally at a loss. 'So *that*'s it! But you know, Avdotya Romanovna, I may fight this in court.'

'What right do you have to speak to her like that?' Pulkheria Aleksandrovna said, heatedly intervening. 'What case can you possibly have against her? And what rights do you have, anyway? Do you think I would give my Dunya to a man like you? Go away, leave us alone! We ourselves are to blame for having agreed to a bad arrangement, and I am the one who bears the most guilt . . .'

'You don't say, Pulkheria Aleksandrovna!' Luzhin cried in a rabid turmoil of fury. 'But you know, you have bound me by your word, which you are now breaking . . . and, what is more, what is more, I have, as it were, been involved in certain expenses . . .'

This final complaint was so characteristic of Pyotr Petrovich that Raskolnikov, pale with anger and the effort of repressing it, suddenly could contain himself no longer and – burst out laughing. Pulkheria Aleksandrovna, however, lost her temper entirely:

'Expenses? What expenses? I suppose you mean our trunk? But you know very well that the guard took it on the train for nothing. Good Lord, you say we've bound you! I think you ought to bear in mind, Pyotr Petrovich, that it's you who have bound us hand and foot – not the other way round!'

'That's enough, mother – please, that's enough!' Avdotya Romanovna implored her. 'Pyotr Petrovich – be so kind as to leave!'

'Very well, madam – but one last word before I do!' he said, no longer quite in control of himself. 'Your mother would appear to have completely forgotten that I ventured to take you, as it were, in the face of the rumours that were being passed around town and had spread over the entire neighbourhood concerning your reputation. By thus spurning public opinion for your sake and by re-establishing your good name, I believe I might most, most possibly be within my rights in expecting something in return from you, and even in demanding your gratitude . . . Only now my eyes have been opened! I myself see that I may have acted most, most unwisely in neglecting the public voice . . .'

'Does he want his head broken, or what?' Razumikhin shouted, leaping up from his chair and already preparing to administer retribution.

'You're a base and wicked man!' said Dunya.

'That will do now! No more gestures!' Raskolnikov exclaimed, holding Razumikhin back; then he went right up to Luzhin, so that their faces almost touched.

'Be so good as to get out of here!' he said, quietly and distinctly. 'And not another word, otherwise . . .'

For a few seconds Luzhin stared at him with features that were pale and twisted with hostile rage. Then he turned and went out, and it is possible that no man ever bore within his heart so much violent hatred for another human being as this man did for Raskolnikov. It was Raskolnikov, and Raskolnikov alone, whom he blamed for everything. It is worth noting that, even as he made his way downstairs, he still fancied that his cause might not yet be entirely lost, and that, in the case of the ladies, at least, might 'most, most possibly' be capable of rectification.

III

The truth of the matter was that right up to the last moment he had never even dreamt that such a dénouement might be possible. He had bullied his way to the very limit, and it had never once entered his head that two impoverished and defenceless women might be able to escape from his power. His certainty on this account had been much assisted by vanity and a degree of self-confidence that might better be termed self-conceit. Pyotr Petrovich, who had fought his way up from nowhere, was in the morbid habit of admiring himself, had a high opinion of his own intelligence and ability, and would even on occasion, when alone, admire his own face in the mirror. What he cherished and valued more highly than anything else in the world, however, was his money, which he had acquired by hard work and by all kinds of means: it put him on an equal footing with all that was above him.

In recalling to Dunya with bitterness just then that he had ventured to take her in spite of the negative rumours there had been about her, Pyotr Petrovich had been speaking perfectly seriously, and had experienced a deep sense of indignation at such 'flagrant ingratitude'. As a matter of fact, however, at the time of making his proposal to

Dunya he had been fully convinced of the absurdity of all these rumours, which had been publicly refuted by Marfa Petrovna and had long been forgotten by all the inhabitants of the unpleasant little town, who had come out warmly on Dunya's side. He himself would not now have denied that he had known all that even at the time. Nevertheless, he had set a high price on his determination to raise Dunya to his own exalted level, viewing it as a noble deed. In mentioning it to her just then he had been expressing a most secret, cherished thought of his, one that he had several times admired in private to himself; he was unable to comprehend how others could fail to admire it, too. On presenting his visiting credentials to Raskolnikov the day before he had made his entrance with the sense of being a benefactor, preparing to harvest the fruits of his endeavour and to receive the very sweetest of compliments. And so it was natural that now, as he descended the staircase, he considered himself to have been spurned and insulted in the very highest degree.

The plain fact was that Dunya was essential to him; he found it unthinkable that he should forgo her. For a long time, several years now, he had been entertaining voluptuous dreams of marriage, but had kept piling up his money and waiting. He had thought with rapture in deepest secret of a chaste and poor young girl (she must be poor), very young, very pretty, well-mannered and well brought up, very intimidated, who had experienced a great many misfortunes and would now be wholly at his bidding, the kind of girl who all her life would consider him her salvation, go in awe of him, subordinate herself to him, wonder at him, at him and him alone. How many scenes, how many delightful episodes had he created in his imagination on this alluring and whimsical theme as he rested quietly from his business affairs! And then suddenly the dream of all those years had almost come true: Avdotya Romanovna's beauty and education had impressed him; her helpless situation had excited him beyond all measure. Here there was even more than he had dreamed of: the girl who had appeared was proud, full of character, virtuous, superior to him in education and upbringing (he sensed this), and yet this creature would view him with servile gratitude all her life for his noble deed, reverentially effacing herself before him, and he would have unlimited and exclusive power over her! . . . Almost as if in accordance with some plan, not long before, after lengthy deliberations and calculations, he had finally decided to change his career and to enter upon a wider arena of activity, while at the same time little by little making his way into a higher echelon of society, something he had been thinking voluptuous thoughts about for a long time . . . He had, in short, decided to 'have a stab at St Petersburg'. He knew that with women it was 'most, most possible' to gain a great deal. The charm of a lovely, virtuous and educated woman could gild his path in the most remarkable fashion, draw people to him, create an aura around him . . . and now all that had collapsed about his ears! The sudden, outrageous severing of bonds that had just taken place had an effect on him like a clap of thunder. This was some monstrous joke, an absurdity! He had done the merest amount of bullying; he had not even managed to say all he had intended to say; all he had done was make a few jests, follow the spirit of the moment – and it had all ended so seriously! Then there was the fact that he did, after all, love Dunya in his own way, he already had power over her in his dreams – and now suddenly! . . . No! Tomorrow, tomorrow all this would have to be repaired, remedied, put right, and above all – that overgrown urchin, that arrogant milksop whose fault it all was would have to be annihilated once and for all. With a sensation of pain he remembered, somehow in spite of himself, Razumikhin . . . but he soon put his mind at rest on that account: 'He can go down the drain together with him!' But the person he was really afraid of was – Svidrigailov . . . In short, much trouble lay ahead . . .

* * *

'No, I'm the one who's most to blame!' Dunya said, embracing her mother and kissing her. 'I was tempted by his money, but I swear to you, brother – I had no idea he was such an unworthy man. If I had seen him for what he was earlier I should not have been tempted for anything in the world! Please don't hold it against me, brother!'

'God has spared us! God has spared us!' Pulkheria Aleksandrovna muttered, but almost unconsciously, as though she had not quite realized the full extent of what had happened.

They all felt a sense of relief, and after five minutes had passed were even laughing. Only occasionally did Dunya turn pale and frown as she remembered what had taken place. Pulkheria Aleksandrovna, too, had never imagined that she would feel like this; only that morning the prospect of a break with Luzhin had seemed to her a terrible misfortune. But Razumikhin was in ecstasy. Although he was not yet fully able to express it, he was trembling all over as if he were in a fever, and as if a ton weight had been lifted from his heart. Now he possessed the right to devote the whole of his life to them, to serve them . . . All kinds of things were possible now! As yet, however, he shyly drove away any further thoughts as to what these might be, and felt afraid of his own imagination. Only Raskolnikov was still sitting where he had been earlier, looking sullen and even absent-minded. He, who had raised the greatest demand that Luzhin be sent away, now seemed less interested than any of them in what had just happened. Dunya could not help feeling that he was still very angry with her, and Pulkheria Aleksandrovna kept peering fearfully at him.

'What did Svidrigailov say to you?' Dunya said, going over to him.

'Oh yes, tell us, tell us!' Pulkheria Aleksandrovna exclaimed.

Raskolnikov lifted his head:

'He's absolutely set on giving you ten thousand roubles, and he also wants to have a meeting with you in my presence.'

'A meeting? Not for anything in the world!' exclaimed Pulkheria Aleksandrovna. 'And how dare he offer her money!'

Then Raskolnikov recounted (in somewhat dry terms) his conversation with Svidrigailov, leaving out the part about Marfa Petrovna's ghosts so as not to clutter his narrative with excessive detail, and because he did not feel like saying any more than was strictly essential.

'What did you reply?' Dunya asked.

'At first what I said wouldn't convey any message to you. Then he announced that he would do everything within his power to obtain an interview with you. He said his passion for you had been a freakish fancy, and that now feels nothing for you . . . He doesn't want you to marry Luzhin . . . In general the things he said were rather confused.'

'How do you account for his behaviour, Rodya? What sort of an impression did he make on you?'

'To tell you the truth, I'm really not sure. He offers you ten thousand, yet he himself says he's not rich. He announces his intention of going off on a journey somewhere, and ten minutes later he's forgotten he even told me about it. Then he suddenly tells me that he wants to get married, and that a bride is already being found for him . . . But then again, it's a bit strange to suppose that he'd go about things so stupidly if he had evil designs on you . . . I naturally refused the money, on your behalf, once and for all. In general, the impression he made on me was a very strange one, in fact . . . I'd even say . . . he showed signs of insanity. But I may be wrong; it may simply be a case of some kind of showing-off. I think Marfa Petrovna's death is having a certain effect on him . . .'

'May the Lord grant her soul rest!' cried Pulkheria Aleksandrovna. 'I shall pray for her ceaselessly, ceaselessly! Oh, Dunya, what would we have done without that three thousand roubles? Lord, it's as though it had fallen from heaven! Oh, Rodya, I mean, all we had left this morning was three roubles, and the only thought Dunya and I had in our heads was how we could pawn her watch somewhere as quickly as possible so we wouldn't have to ask that man to lend us money before he'd realized what our situation was.'

For some reason Svidrigailov's proposition had startled Dunya greatly. She stood there, pondering.

'He's going to do something horrible!' she said, almost in a whisper to herself, and shuddering slightly.

Raskolnikov noticed this excessive fear.

'I don't think this is the last I've seen of him,' he said to her.

'We'll watch him! I'll spy on him!' Razumikhin exclaimed, energetically. 'I won't let him out of my sight! Rodya's given me permission. That's what he told me earlier – "Look after my sister," he said. Do I have your permission, too, Avdotya Romanovna?'

Dunya smiled, and she extended her hand to him; but the worried look stayed on her features. Pulkheria Aleksandrovna kept giving her timid glances; but the three thousand roubles had obviously put her mind at rest.

A quarter of an hour later they were all deep in lively conversation. Even Raskolnikov, though he was not taking part, had been listening attentively for some time. Razumikhin was delivering a harangue.

'Why, why should you leave?' he was saying in a rapture of expansive enthusiasm. 'What will you do in that nasty little town? The point is that you're all together here, and you're going to need one another – oh, you're going to need one another, believe me! Well, for a while, anyway . . . Take me along as a friend, a companion, and I promise you we'll make an excellent business team. Listen! I'll set it all before you in detail – the entire project! It started to occur to me this morning, before any of this had happened . . . This is what I have in mind: I have an uncle (I'll introduce you; he's a well-built and most respectable old chap!), and this uncle has a capital of a thousand roubles, but he lives on a pension and has no use for the money. For two years now he's been on at me to borrow the thousand from him and pay him an interest of six per cent. I can see what he's trying to do, of course: he simply wants to help me; well, last year I didn't need the money, but this year I decided I'd take up his offer as soon as he arrived in town. Now, if you'll put in another thousand, out of your three, that will be enough to start with, and we'll combine forces. And what do you think we're going to do?'

At this point Razumikhin began to outline his project, talking a great deal about how practically none of Russia's booksellers and publishers knew the first thing about the merchandise in which they traded, and were for that reason bad at their trade, and about how decent editions of books generally paid for themselves and made a profit, sometimes a sizeable one. It was of starting up business as a publisher that Razumikhin had been dreaming; for the past two years he had been working for other publishers, and he possessed quite a reasonable knowledge of three European languages, in spite of the fact that some six days earlier he had told Raskolnikov he was '*schwach*' in German, with the aim of trying to persuade him to take a half of the translation against a three-rouble advance: he had been lying then, and Raskolnikov knew it.

'Why, why should we miss our opportunity when we have one of the principal means for its realization – our own money?' Razumikhin said, getting excited. 'Of course, a lot of work will be necessary, but we shall work, you, Avdotya Romanovna, Rodion and I . . . There are certain types of edition that yield a handsome profit nowadays! And the rock-solid basis of our enterprise will be that we know just what requires translating. We shall translate, and publish, and study, all at the same time.* I can make myself useful now, because I've got some experience. After all, I'll soon have been hanging around publishers for about two years now, and I know all their most cherished secrets: they're no saints, believe me! Why, why let a tasty morsel like that get away? I mean, I myself can think of two or three books of which I have copies and which I've never told anyone about, which would be worth a hundred roubles each just for the idea of translating and publishing them, and indeed there's one that I wouldn't take less than five hundred for. Yet what do you suppose?

Even if I'd told one of those publishers about them, he'd probably still be humming and hawing, the dunderhead! And as far as all the business about typesetting, paper, sales is concerned, you can leave that to me! I know all the ins and outs! We'll start from humble beginnings and attain great things – or at any rate we'll have enough to live on, and whatever happens we'll cover our losses.'

Dunya's eyes were shining. 'What you say appeals to me very much, Dmitry Prokofich,' she said.

'Well, of course, I don't know anything about such things,' Pulkheria Aleksandrovna responded. 'It may be a good idea – but then again, God only knows. It sounds new and unfamiliar. It's true that we shall have to remain here, at least for a certain time . . .' She looked at Rodya.

'What do you think, brother?' Dunya said.

'I think he has a very good idea,' he answered. 'Of course, one shouldn't think about founding a firm this far ahead, but it really would be possible to publish five or six books with unquestionable success. I myself can think of one book that would be certain to do well. And as for the question of whether he'd know how to manage the business, of that I have no doubts either: he knows his way around . . . Anyway, there'll be time for you to arrange things later . . .'

'Hurrah!' Razumikhin shouted. 'Now just a moment! There's an apartment here, in this very same building, rented out by the same landlords. It's separate and on its own, and it doesn't connect with these rooms – it's furnished, too, and it's available at a moderate rent, three rooms. I think you ought to take it to begin with. I'll pawn your watch tomorrow and bring you the money, and then everything else will sort itself out later. The main thing is that all three of you can live together, and Rodya needn't be apart . . . I say, where are you going, Rodya?'

'What is it Rodya? Are you leaving so soon?' Pulkheria Aleksandrovna asked with a note of alarm.

'At a moment like this?' Razumikhin bawled.

Dunya looked at her brother with suspicious astonishment. He had his cap in his hands; he was preparing to go outside.

'Somehow it's as if you were burying me or saying farewell to me forever,' he said in a strange kind of way.

He gave what looked like a smile, though it might not have been anything of the sort.

'I mean, who knows – perhaps this is the last time we'll ever see one another,' he added involuntarily.

He had thought this to himself, but it had somehow been spoken aloud.

'What's got into you?' his mother exclaimed.

'Where are you going, Rodya?' Dunya asked, in a strange voice.

'Oh, I've really got to go,' he replied vaguely, as though hesitant as to what he was trying to say. But in his pale features there was a kind of sharp determination.

'I wanted to tell you . . . as I was on my way here . . . I wanted to tell you, mother . . . and you, Dunya, that I think it would be better if we parted company for a while. I'm not feeling very well, I'm not at ease . . . I'll come and see you later, I'll come of my own accord, when . . . I can. I keep you in my thoughts and I love you . . . Now leave me! Leave me alone! I took this decision some time ago, before you arrived . . . It's a firm decision . . . Whatever happens to me, whether I perish or not, I want to be alone. Please forget about me altogether. It will be better that way . . . Don't try to find out about me. When the time is right, I'll come and see you myself, or . . . I'll summon you. Perhaps everything will be all right! . . . But now, if you love me, say goodbye to me . . . Otherwise I shall start to hate you, I can feel it . . . Goodbye!'

'Merciful Lord!' Pulkheria Aleksandrovna exclaimed.

Both mother and sister were in a terrible state of fright; so was Razumikhin.

'Rodya, Rodya! Make it up with us, let's go back to how we were before!' cried the poor mother.

Slowly he turned towards the door and slowly he left the room. Dunya ran and caught him up.

'Brother! What are you doing to our mother?' her gaze whispered, as it burned with indignation.

He looked at her heavily.

'It's all right, I'll be back, I'll come back and see you!' he muttered in an undertone, as though he were not completely conscious of what he was trying to say, and went out of the room.

'He's in-*sane*, not callous! He's mad! Can't you see it? If you can't

371

you're the one who's callous! . . .' Razumikhin whispered hotly, right into her ear, and gripping her arm tightly.

'I'll be back in a moment!' he shouted, turning to the rigid Pulkheria Aleksandrovna, and ran out of the room.

Raskolnikov was waiting for him at the end of the corridor.

'I knew you'd come out after me,' he said. 'Go back to them and stay with them . . . Come and see them tomorrow, too . . . and for ever after. I . . . may come back . . . if I can. Goodbye!'

And without offering his hand, he walked away.

'But where are you off to? What is it? What's got into you? You can't do this! . . .' Razumikhin muttered, completely taken aback.

Raskolnikov stopped a second time.

'Look, once and for all: don't ask me about any of this, ever. There's nothing I can tell you . . . Don't come to see me. I may come back here . . . Now abandon me . . . but *don't abandon them*. Do you understand?'

In the corridor it was dark; they were standing beside a lamp. For a moment they looked at each other without saying anything. Razumikhin was to remember that moment for the rest of his life. Raskolnikov's fixed and burning gaze seemed to gather in strength at each instant, penetrating Razumikhin's soul, his awareness. Razumikhin gave a shudder. Something strange seemed to have taken place between them . . . Some kind of idea had slipped out, a kind of hint; something horrible, monstrous and suddenly comprehensible to them both . . . Razumikhin turned as white as a corpse.

'Now do you understand?' Raskolnikov said suddenly, his features painfully twisted. 'Go on, get back in there with them,' he added and, turning quickly, walked out of the building . . .

I shall not attempt now to describe what took place that evening in the lodgings of Pulkheria Aleksandrovna, how Razumikhin went back to the two women, how he calmed them down, how he tried to impress upon them that Rodya's illness demanded that he have rest, tried to reassure them that Rodya would quite certainly come and see them every day, that he was very, very upset, that he must not be over-excited; how he, Razumikhin, was going to watch over him, get him a good doctor, the best, a whole council of doctors . . . In short, from that evening on Razumikhin became to them a son and a brother.

But Raskolnikov had gone straight to the house on the Canal where Sonya lived.* It was a three-storey building, old and green-coloured. He tracked the yardkeeper down and received from him some imprecise directions as to where Kapernaumov the tailor lived. Having discovered in one corner of the courtyard the entrance to a dark, narrow flight of stairs, he went up to the second floor and came out on to a gallery that ran right round the building, overlooking the courtyard. While he was wandering about in the darkness, puzzled as to where the entrance to Kapernaumov's apartment might be, only two or three paces away from him a door suddenly opened; without thinking, he seized at it.

'Who is it?' a female voice asked, uneasily.

'It's me . . . I . . . came to see you,' Raskolnikov answered, and he entered the tiny hallway. There, on a chair with a broken seat, in a crooked brass candlestick, stood a candle.

'It's you! Oh, merciful Lord!' Sonya said with a faint scream, and she froze, petrified.

'Which way's your room? In here?'

And Raskolnikov, trying to avoid her eyes, quickly went into her room.

A moment later Sonya herself came in, set up the candle and stood facing him, completely taken aback, in a state of inexpressible agitation and all too plainly alarmed by his unexpected visit. The colour suddenly rushed to her pale features, and tears fairly flooded to her eyes . . . She felt sick, embarrassed and gratified . . . Raskolnikov quickly turned away and sat down on a chair at the table. He managed to take in the room with a cursory glance.

It was a large room, but very low-ceilinged, the only one rented out by the Kapernaumovs, the locked door to whose apartment was situated in the wall on the left. On the other side of the room, in the wall on the right, there was another door, which was always kept tightly bolted. This led to another apartment, the one next door, which had a different number. Sonya's room resembled some sort of barn, possessing the form of a highly irregular rectangle, and this gave it a misshapen appearance. A wall with three windows that looked out onto the Canal somehow cut the room transversely, so that one of its corners, forming a horribly acute angle, ran off into the depths somewhere, and in the faint light one could not even make it out properly; the angle of the other corner was, on the other hand, quite hideously obtuse. The whole of this large room contained hardly any furniture. In the right-hand corner was the bed; beside it, closer to the door, was a chair. Against the same wall where the bed was, right by the door into the next-door apartment, stood a plain, wooden table that was covered with a blue tablecloth; at the table stood two wicker chairs. Finally, against the other wall, near the acute-angled corner, was a small chest of drawers made of simple timber, practically lost in the emptiness. That was all there was in the room. The yellow-ish, shabby, peeling wallpaper had turned black in all the corners; the air must have been damp and fume-ridden here in the winter. The signs of poverty were everywhere; there were not even any curtains over the bed.

Without saying anything, Sonya looked at this guest of hers who had studied her room so closely and with so little ceremony, and at last she began to tremble with fear, as though she were standing before the judge and arbiter of her destiny.

'I'm sorry, it's late . . . It must be after eleven, isn't it?' he asked, still without raising his eyes to her.

'Yes,' Sonya murmured. 'Oh, yes, it is!' she said, suddenly, in a hurry, as though this were for her the end of the matter. 'The landlord's clock chimed just now . . . I heard it . . . It is past eleven.'

'This is the last time I shall be visiting you,' Raskolnikov went on, darkly, although this was actually the first time he had ever called on her. 'I may not see you again . . .'

'Are you . . . going somewhere?'

'I don't know . . . I'll find out everything tomorrow . . .'

'So you won't be at Katerina Ivanovna's tomorrow?' Sonya said, with a quiver in her voice.

'I don't know. I'll know it all tomorrow morning . . . That's not why I'm here; I've come to tell you something . . .'

He brought his thoughtful gaze up to meet hers and suddenly noticed that he was seated, while she continued to stand facing him.

'Why are you standing up? Sit down,' he said in a voice that had swiftly altered, a quiet, caressing voice.

She sat down. For a moment he gave her a friendly look that was almost one of compassion.

'How thin you are! Look at that hand of yours! One can see right through it! Your fingers are like a corpse's.'

He took her hand. Sonya smiled faintly.

'I've always been like this,' she said.

'Even when you lived at home?'

'Yes.'

'Yes, I suppose you have!' he said abruptly, and his facial expression and tone of voice again swiftly altered. Again, he looked round him.

'You rent this place from Kapernaumov?'

'Yes, sir . . .'

'What about the people through the door, do they rent from him, too?'

'Yes . . . They have a room like this one.'

'All of them in the same room?'

'Yes, sir.'

'I'd be scared in here at nights,' he observed, darkly.

'The landlord and landlady are very good, very affectionate to me,' Sonya replied, still somehow not quite with all her wits about her, and still unsure of the situation. 'All the furniture, everything . . . it all belongs to them. Oh, they're very kind, and their children often come to see me . . .'

'Are they the ones who can't speak properly?'

'That's right, sir . . . He has a stammer, and he's lame, too. His wife's that way, as well . . . She hasn't actually got a stammer, but she can't get her words out properly. She's kind, very. And he's a former house-serf. They've got seven children . . . Only the eldest one has a stammer, and the others are simply ill . . . and they don't stammer . . . But how do you know about them?' she added with some astonishment.

'Your father told me all about them before he died. He told me all about you . . . About how you'd go out at six and come back at nine, and about how Katerina Ivanovna used to kneel beside your bed.'

Sonya was covered in embarrassment.

'I thought I saw him today,' she whispered, uncertainly.

'Who?'

'My father. I was walking along the street, down there, near this building, on the corner, and he seemed to be walking ahead of me. It really did look like him. I was just about to call on Katerina Ivanovna . . .'

'You were off duty?'

'Yes,' Sonya whispered abruptly, again covered in embarrassment, and with her eyes lowered.

'Katerina Ivanovna used to beat you when you lived with the family, didn't she?'

'No! Why do you say that, why do you say that, no!' Sonya said, looking at him with fright.

'So you love her, do you?'

'Love her? Of co-u-rse!' Sonya said, drawing the word out piteously, and suddenly clasping her hands in suffering. 'Oh, you don't know her . . . If only you knew her. I mean, she's just like a child . . . I mean, she's nearly gone insane . . . with unhappiness. And how clever she used to be . . . how magnanimous . . . how kind! You don't know anything, anything . . . oh-h!'

Sonya had said this as though she were in despair – frantic with suffering, and wringing her hands. Her pale cheeks had flared with colour again, and her eyes expressed torment. It was clear that a terrible number of things had been stirred up in her, that there was something she terribly wanted to express, to say out loud, to plead for. A kind of *voracious* compassion, if it might be put that way, was suddenly displayed in every feature of her face.

'Beat me? But why do you say that? Beat me? Oh, merciful Lord! And what if she did beat me – what then? What does it matter? You don't know anything, anything . . . She's so unhappy, oh, so unhappy! And ill . . . She's looking for justice and truth . . . She's so pure . . . She believes there must be justice in everything, and she demands it . . . And even if you were to torture her, she wouldn't do something that was unjust. She herself simply isn't aware that it's impossible for there to be justice and truth among people, and she gets upset. Like a child, like a child! She's so, so truthful!'

'And what's going to become of you?'

Sonya gave him a questioning look.

'I mean, you're their main support, now. You were their support before, too, and your father used to come and ask you for money so he could treat his hangover. Well, what's going to happen now?'

'I don't know,' Sonya said sadly.

'Will they stay where they are?'

'I don't know. They're behind with the rent on that place; but apparently the landlady told them today that she's going to banish them from the doorstep, and Katerina Ivanovna herself says she doesn't want to stay there another minute.'

'Why the pretence of bravery? Is she putting her hope in you?'

'Oh, don't say such things! . . . We live as one, in harmony,' Sonya said, growing frantic again, and even showing signs of irritation, for all the world in the way a canary or some other small bird might lose its temper, if it could. 'I mean what, what is she to do?' she asked, growing angry and excited. 'And how she wept today, oh, how she wept! Her mind's growing confused, haven't you noticed? She's growing confused; at one moment she's worrying like a little girl about everything being just right tomorrow, with the proper snacks and everything . . . at the next she's wringing her hands, spitting blood and weeping, and suddenly she starts beating her head against the wall, as though she were in despair. And then she gets over it again, she puts all her hope in you: she says you're her helping hand now, and that she's going to borrow some money from somewhere and take me back to her home town with her, and start a boarding-school for girls from good families and hire me as one of the teachers, and a completely new and wonderful life will open up for us, and she kisses me, embraces me, consoles me, and, I mean, she really believes it! She really believes those fantasies of hers! Well, how can one contradict her? And all day today she's been washing, cleaning and mending; she dragged the wash-trough into the room herself, with her feeble energies, and collapsed on the bed, gasping for breath; and she and I went to the Row* this morning to buy shoes for Lena and Polechka, because their old ones are falling to pieces, only we'd underestimated the amount they would cost, underestimated it by a very long way, and she'd had her eye on such a lovely little pair of shoes, because she has taste, you simply don't know . . . She burst into tears right there in the shop, in front of the owners, because she didn't have enough . . . Oh, how pitiful it was to see her!'

'Well now you've told me that, I can understand why you live like . . . this,' Raskolnikov said with a bitter, ironic smile.

'But don't you feel sorry for her? Don't you?' Sonya said, hurling herself towards him again. 'I mean, I know you gave her the last money you had, but you hadn't seen anything. If you had – oh, merciful Lord! Oh, how many, many times I've brought her to tears!

And that evening last week, too! Oh, what could I have been thinking of? Only a week before his death. How cruelly I behaved! And how many, many times that has happened. Oh, and then, just as now, I would go through the agony of thinking about it all day!'

As she spoke, Sonya actually wrung her hands at the pain of the recollection.

'You mean you're the one who was cruel?'

'Yes, I was, I was! That evening, when I arrived,' she continued, weeping, 'my father said: "Read to me, Sonya, my head's aching, read to me . . . here, I've a book." He had some book or other, he must have got it from Andrei Semyonych – that's Mr Lebezyatnikov who lives near here, he was always getting hold of such amusing books. But I told him it was late, I had to be going, so I couldn't read to him, I'd only dropped in to show Katerina Ivanovna some lace collars; Lizaveta, the market-woman, had brought me some lace collars and armlets at a low price, good ones they were, new, with patterns. Katerina Ivanovna thought they were marvellous, she put them on and looked at herself in the mirror, oh, she thought they were quite, quite wonderful: "Please let me have them, Sonya," she said. She even said "please" – that's how much she wanted them. But what would she have done with them? It was simply that they reminded her of her earlier, happier days! She looked at herself in the mirror, admiring herself, and I mean, she doesn't have one single dress, not a single one, she hasn't had anything of her own for heaven knows how many years! And she'd never ask anyone for anything; she's proud, she'd rather give away the last she owned, and here she was asking – so wonderful did she think they were! But I was sorry to part with them – "What would you be doing with those, Katerina Ivanovna?" I asked. That was how I said it – "What would you be doing with those?" I shouldn't have said that to her! She gave me a terrible look, because it had really, really hurt her that I'd said no to her, and it was so pitiful to see . . . I mean, it wasn't the collars she was hurt about, but the fact that I'd said no, I could see it. Oh, if only I could, I think I'd take it all back, undo it all, all of what I said that evening . . . Oh, what a miserable person I am! . . . But what's the use? . . . I mean, why should you care?'

'Did you know that Lizaveta woman – the one who ran the market stall?'

'Yes, I did . . . Did you?' Sonya asked with a certain degree of surprise.

'Katerina Ivanovna has incurable consumption: she's going to die soon,' Raskolnikov said, after a moment's silence, and without answering her question.

'Oh, no, no, no!' Sonya cried, and with an unconscious gesture she seized him by both hands, as though begging him to say it was not true.

'But I mean, it's better if she dies,' he said.

'No it's not, it's not better, it's not better at all!' she kept repeating, frightened and without any control.

'But what about the children? Where will you take them if not here, with you?'

'Oh, I don't know!' Sonya screamed, almost in despair, and she clutched at her head. It was evident that this thought had fleetingly occurred to her on many, many occasions, and that he had startled it to life again.

'Well, and what if you were to fall ill even now, while Katerina Ivanovna is still alive, and you were taken to hospital, what would happen then?' he said, pressing on without mercy.

'Oh, stop it, stop it! That's not possible!' Sonya shrieked, and her face was twisted with a terrible panic.

'What do you mean, not possible?' Raskolnikov continued with a hard, ironic smile. 'You're not insured, are you? So what would happen to them? You'd all be out in the street, the whole gang of you, she'd be coughing and begging and beating her head against a wall somewhere, as she did today, and the children would be crying . . . And then she'd collapse, and be taken to the police station, the hospital, she'd die, and the children . . .'

'No! . . . God won't let it happen!' were the words that finally broke from Sonya's constricted chest. She was listening, looking at him in supplication, looking at him and clasping her hands in a speechless plea, as though all depended on him.

Raskolnikov got up and began to pace about the room. About a minute went by. Sonya stood with her arms dropped and her head lowered, in terrible anguish.

'Can't you save some money? Put something by for when you need it?' he asked, stopping suddenly in front of her.

'No,' Sonya whispered.

'I dare say not. But have you tried?' he added, with something very close to mockery.

'Yes, I have.'

'And it didn't work out! Well, that's that, I suppose. There's no point in my even asking, is there?'

And again he began to pace about the room. About another minute went by.

'You don't earn every day, I hope?'

Sonya grew even more embarrassed than she had been previously, and the colour again rushed to her face.

'No,' she whispered with an agonized effort.

'I expect the same thing will happen to Polya,' he said, suddenly.

'No! No! It's not possible! No!' Sonya screamed, like a soul in despair, or as though someone had just stuck a knife into her. 'God, God wouldn't let anything so dreadful happen! . . .'

'He lets it happen to other people.'

'No, no! God will look after her, he will!' she said, beside herself.

'But there may not be any God,' Raskolnikov replied with a kind of malicious satisfaction, gave a laugh and looked at her.

Sonya's face suddenly changed in a most terrible manner; it was crossed by convulsive spasms. She glanced at him with a look of inexpressible reproach, made as if to say something, but could not get the words out, and instead suddenly began to sob with the utmost bitterness, covering her face with her hands.

'You say that Katerina Ivanovna's mind's growing confused; it's your own that is,' he said after a pause.

Some five minutes passed. He kept pacing to and fro, not saying a word and not looking at her. At last, he went over to her; his eyes were glittering. He took her by the shoulders with both hands and looked straight into her weeping face. His gaze was dry, inflamed and sharp, his lips were quivering violently . . . With sudden rapidity he stooped and, getting down on the floor, kissed her foot. Sonya jerked back from him in horror, as from a madman. And indeed, he really did look like a man who was wholly insane.

'Why are you doing that? Why are you doing it? In front of me!' she muttered, her face now pale, and suddenly her heart was wrung with utter agony.

He immediately got up.

'It wasn't you I was bowing to, but the whole of human suffering,' he said almost savagely, and went over to the window. 'Listen,' he added, coming back to her after a moment or two, 'I told an insulting fellow earlier today that he wasn't worth your little finger . . . and that I'd done my sister an honour by making her sit next to you.'

'Oh, why did you tell him that? And in her presence, too!' Sonya exclaimed in fear. 'Sitting with me? An honour? But I mean . . . I don't have any honour . . . Oh, why did you say that?'

'I said it about you not because of your sin or your dishonour, but because of your great suffering. And as for your being a great sinner, that's simply a fact,' he added, almost beside himself, 'and you're even more of a sinner because you've mortified and betrayed yourself *for nothing*. Isn't that monstrous? Isn't it monstrous that you're living in this filth which you hate and loathe, while all the time you know (you have only to open your eyes) that you're neither helping nor saving anyone by it? And, I mean, tell me,' he said, in a near frenzy, 'how such turpitude and vileness can exist in you alongside these other, opposing and holy emotions? I mean, it would be more just, a thousand times more just, and more reasonable to throw yourself head first in the water and have done with it!'

'But what would become of them?' Sonya asked faintly, giving him a look of suffering, but at the same time apparently not at all taken aback by what he had suggested. Raskolnikov looked at her strangely.

From her gaze alone he surmised everything. So it was true: she really had had that idea. It was quite possible that she had seriously many times considered the best way of having done with it, so seriously that now she was not really astonished at his suggestion. She had not even noticed how cruel were the things he had been saying to her (neither, of course, had she realized the true meaning of his reproaches and of the peculiar view he took of her turpitude, and this was plain to him). But he fully understood the degree of monstrous agony with which, for a long time now, the thought of her dishonoured and shameful position had tormented her. What was it, he wondered, what was it that had until now reined in her determination to have done with it? And only now did he fully comprehend what those poor little orphaned children meant to her, and that pitiful, half-insane Katerina Ivanovna, with her consumption and her beating of her head against the wall.

Even so, it was obvious to him that Sonya, possessing the character she did, and with the education which, in spite of everything, she had managed to obtain, could not possibly stay like this. Yet the question would not go away: how could she have stayed in this untenable position for so very long without going mad, since she was unable to throw herself in the water? Of course, he was aware that the social position Sonya found herself in was one that depended on factors of chance, although, unfortunately, it was far from being unique or exceptional. He felt, however, that it was this very element of chance, this, together with a certain degree of education and the kind of life she had led in the past, which one might have supposed would have crushed her at the very first step she had taken along this loathsome road. What had preserved her? Not lust, surely? It was quite evident that all this turpitude affected her only mechanically; not one drop of genuine lust had as yet penetrated her heart: he could see this; she stood before him exposed in her reality . . .

'There are three ways open to her,' he thought: 'she can either jump in the Canal, end up in a madhouse or . . . or throw herself at last into a life of depravity, which will stultify her mind and turn her heart to stone.' He found this last notion the most repugnant of the three; but by now he was a sceptic, he was young, detached and, therefore, cruel, and so he could not avoid concluding that the last way out – depravity, in other words – was the most probable one.

'But can it really be true?' he exclaimed to himself. 'Can it really be that this creature, who still retains her purity of spirit, will at last be consciously drawn into that loathsome, stinking pit? Can it be that the process of induction has already begun, and can it also be that the only reason she has been able to hold out so long is because vice no longer seems repugnant to her? No, no, that's not possible!' he exclaimed, as Sonya had done just then. 'No, what has held her back from the Canal so long is her consciousness of sin, and *them, the others* . . . If for so long she has prevented herself from going mad . . . But who can be sure that she hasn't gone mad? Is she really in her right mind? Do people in their right minds talk the way she does? Do people in their right minds produce the kind of arguments she does? Is it acceptable for her to sit on the brink of ruin the way she does, right on the edge of the stinking pit into which she is already being drawn, fending one off and shutting her ears when one warns her of the danger she's in? What is she up to? Is it a miracle she's waiting for? Yes, that's probably what it is. Are these not the signs of madness?'

He seized stubbornly on this thought. It was the explanation that appealed to him more than any other. He began to study her more fixedly.

'So you say a lot of prayers to God, do you, Sonya?' he asked her.

Sonya said nothing. He stood next to her, waiting for a reply.

'What would I be without God?' she whispered quickly, with energy, hurling the gaze of her suddenly flashing eyes at him, and she gripped his hand tightly in her own.

'Yes, I was right!' he thought.

'And what does God do for you in return?' he asked, probing further.

For a long time Sonya said nothing, as if she were unable to reply. Her feeble chest was heaving with excitement.

'That's enough! Don't ask such questions! You don't deserve an answer!' she exclaimed suddenly, looking at him severely and angrily.

'Yes, I was right, I was right,' he said emphatically to himself.

'He does everything!' she whispered quickly, lowering her eyes again.

'So that's the way out she's chosen. And there's the explanation for it, too!' he decided to himself, examining her with avid curiosity.

It was with a new, strange, almost morbid sensation that he studied this pale, thin and irregularly angular little face, these meek blue eyes that were able to flash with such fire, such severe energy and emotion, this little body that was still shivering with indignation and anger, and it all began to seem stranger and stranger to him, almost impossible. 'She's a holy fool! A holy fool!' he kept saying to himself over and over again.

On the chest of drawers lay a book. Each time he had paced up and down the room it had caught his attention; now he picked it up and looked at it. It was a New Testament, in Russian translation. The book was an old one, secondhand, in a leather binding.

'And where did that come from?' he called to her across the room. She was still standing in the same spot, some three paces from the table.

'It was brought to me,' she replied with seeming reluctance, not looking at him.

'By whom?'

'Lizaveta; I asked her to.'

'Lizaveta! That's peculiar!' he thought. He was beginning to find everything about Sonya more peculiar and more wonderful with every minute that passed. He took the book over to the candle and began to leaf through its pages.

'Where's the bit about Lazarus?' he asked suddenly.

Sonya was looking stubbornly at the floor, and did not answer. She was standing a little to one side of the table.

'Where's the bit about the raising of Lazarus? Find it for me, Sonya.'

She gave him a sideways look.

'You're looking in the wrong place . . . It's in the fourth Gospel . . .' she whispered severely, making no move towards him.

'Find it and read it to me,' he said. Then he sat down at the table, leaned on it with one elbow, propped his head on his hand, and stared gloomily to one side, preparing to listen.

'Come to the seventh verst* in three weeks' time, you'll be most welcome! I think I'll be there myself, if I'm not in an even worse place,' he muttered to himself.

Sonya stepped uncertainly over to the table, having listened with suspicion to Raskolnikov's strange request.

'Haven't you ever read it?' she asked, glancing at him across the table without much trust.

'A long time ago . . . When I was at school. Go on, read it!'

'Haven't you heard it in church?'

'I . . . don't go. Do you?'

'N-no,' Sonya whispered.

Raskolnikov gave her an ironic smile.

'I understand . . . I suppose that means you won't be at your father's funeral tomorrow?'

'Oh, I will. I went to church last week, as well . . . for another funeral.'

'Whose?'

'Lizaveta's. Someone murdered her with an axe.'

His nerves were growing more and more on edge. His head began to go round.

'You were friendly with Lizaveta?'

'Yes . . . She was a righteous woman . . . she used to come . . . seldom . . . it was difficult for her. She and I used to read . . . and talk. She will see God.'

These bookish words sounded strange to his ears, and here was another piece of news: there had been some sort of mysterious get-togethers with Lizaveta – holy fools, the two of them.

'I'll be turning into a holy fool myself soon, it's catching!' he thought. 'Go on, read it!' he exclaimed suddenly in a pressing, irritated voice.

Sonya was still wavering. Her heart was beating violently. For some reason she did not dare to read to him. In a state approaching agony he looked at the 'wretched madwoman'.

'What do you want me to read it for? I mean, you don't believe in God, do you? . . .' she whispered quietly, almost panting.

'Read it! I really want you to!' he insisted. 'You read it for Lizaveta, after all!'

Sonya opened the book and found the passage. Her hands were shaking, her voice was not up to it. Twice she began, yet could not articulate the first syllable.

'"Now a certain man was sick, named Lazarus, of Bethany . . ."' she got out, at last, with an effort, but suddenly, when she reached the fourth word, her voice twanged and then broke like a string that has been stretched too taut. Her breathing was cut off, and her chest was constricted.

Raskolnikov partly understood why Sonya could not prevail on herself to read to him, and the more he understood, the more bluntly and irritably he insisted that she do so. He could imagine only too well how hard it was now for her to give away and reveal everything that was *her*. He knew that these feelings really did constitute, as it were, her most genuine and possibly oldest *secret*, one that she might have nurtured from her girlhood, from the time when she had still been living with her family, in the presence of her luckless father and her grief-crazed stepmother, among the hungry children, the hideous shrieks and the reprimands. At the same time, however, he knew now, and knew for a fact, that even though she was miserably unhappy and horribly afraid of something as she now began to read, at the same time she had an agonizing desire to read to him, in spite of all her misery and fear, and that it was *him* she wanted to read to, to make sure that he heard it, and that she wanted it to be *now* – 'however things may turn out later on!' This he read in her eyes, deduced from her rapturous excitement . . . She mastered herself, suppressed the spasm in her throat which had cut off her voice at the beginning of the verse, and continued to read the eleventh chapter of the Gospel according to St John until she reached verse nineteen:

'"And many of the Jews came to Martha and Mary to comfort them concerning their brother.

'"Then Martha, as soon as she heard that Jesus was coming, went and met him: but Mary sat still in the house.

'"Then said Martha unto Jesus, Lord, if thou hadst been here, my brother had not died.

'"But I know, that even now, whatsoever thou wilt ask of God, God will give it thee."'

At this point she stopped again, sensing with embarrassment that her voice was going to tremble and break off again . . .

'"Jesus saith unto her, Thy brother shall rise again.

'"Martha saith unto him, I know that he shall rise again in the resurrection at the last day.

'"Jesus said unto her, *I am the resurrection, and the life*: he that believeth in me, though he were dead, yet shall he live:

'"And whosoever liveth and believeth in me, though he were dead, yet shall he live:

'"And whosoever liveth and believeth in me shall never die. Believest thou this?

'"She saith unto him"' (And, taking a new breath, apparently in pain, Sonya read distinctly and forcefully, as though she herself were confessing her creed for all to hear): '"Yea, Lord: I believe that thou art the Christ, the Son of God, which should come into the world."'

She made as if to stop, quickly raised her eyes to *him*, but soon mastered herself again and began to read on. Raskolnikov sat listening motionlessly, without turning round, propping his elbow on the table and looking to one side. They reached verse thirty-two.

'"Then when Mary was come where Jesus was, and saw him, she fell down at his feet, saying unto him, Lord, if thou hadst been here, my brother had not died.

'"When Jesus therefore saw her weeping, and the Jews also weeping which came with her, he groaned in the spirit, and was troubled.

'"And said, Where have ye laid him? They said unto him, Lord come and see.

'"Jesus wept.

'"Then said the Jews, Behold how he loved him!

'"And some of them said, Could not this man, which opened the eyes of the blind, have caused that even this man should not have died?"'

Raskolnikov turned round to face her and looked at her in excitement: yes, he had been right! She was shaking all over in a real, genuine fever. He had been expecting this. She was approaching the description of the great and unprecedented miracle, and a sense of immense triumph had taken hold of her. Her voice had become as resonant as metal; triumph and joy sounded in it, giving it strength. The lines swam before her, for her eyes were growing dim, but she knew by heart what she was reading. At the verse she had just read – 'Could not this man, which opened the eyes of the blind . . .' – lowering her voice, she ardently and passionately conveyed the doubt, reproaches and abuse of the unbelievers, the unseeing Jews, who presently, in a moment, would fall as though struck by a thunderbolt, sobbing, and attaining belief . . . 'And *he*, *he* – also blinded and unbelieving – he, too, will hear it in a moment, he too will come to believe, yes, yes! Now, this very minute,' she thought in her dream, and she shook with joyful expectation.

'"Jesus therefore again groaning in himself cometh to the grave. It was a cave, and a stone lay upon it.

'"Jesus said, Take ye away the stone. Martha, the sister of him that was dead, saith unto him, Lord, by this time he stinketh: for he hath been dead four days."'

She stressed the word 'four' with great energy.

'"Jesus saith unto her, Said I not unto thee, that, if thou wouldst believe, thou shouldst see the glory of God?

'"Then they took away the stone from the place where the dead was laid. And Jesus lifted up his eyes, and said, Father, I thank thee that thou hast heard me.

'"And I knew that thou hearest me always: but because of the people which stand by I said it, that they may believe that thou hast sent me.

'"And when he had thus spoken, he cried with a loud voice, Lazarus come forth.

'"*And he that was dead came forth*,"' (she read loudly and ecstatically, shaking and shivering, as though she were seeing it in real life) '"bound hand and foot with graveclothes: and his face was bound about with a napkin. Jesus saith unto them, Loose him, and let him go.

'"*Then many of the Jews which came to Mary, and had seen the things which Jesus did, believed on him.*"

Further she did not read, nor was she able to, closed the book and quickly got up from her chair.

'That's all there is about the raising of Lazarus,' she whispered sternly and abruptly, and stood unmoving, turned away to one side, not daring to raise her eyes to him, as though she were embarrassed. Her feverish shaking still continued. The stub of candle had long been guttering in its crooked candlestick within that wretched room, shedding its dim light on the murderer and the prostitute who had so strangely encountered each other in the reading of the eternal book. Some five minutes or more went by.

'I've come to talk about some business with you,' Raskolnikov suddenly said in a loud voice, frowning; he got up and went over to Sonya. Sonya raised her eyes to him without saying anything. His gaze was peculiarly stern, and it contained a kind of wild determination.

'I deserted my family today,' he said. 'My mother and sister. I shan't see them any more. I've severed my links with them.'

'Why?' Sonya asked, as though stunned. Her recent meeting with his mother and sister had left a deep impression on her, though it was one she could not define. She greeted this news of a severing of links with something approaching horror.

'You're all I've got now,' he added. 'Let's be off . . . I've come to you. We're cursed together, so let's take the road together!'

His eyes were glittering. 'Like a man insane!' Sonya thought, in her turn.

'Where to?' she asked, in fear, and took a step back in spite of herself.

'How should I know? All I know is that it must be the same road – towards the same goal!'

She looked at him in total incomprehension. All she could see was that he was horribly, infinitely unhappy.

'None of them would understand if you were to tell them,' he went on. 'But I've understood. You're necessary to me, and that's why I've come to you.'

'I don't understand . . .' Sonya whispered.

'You'll understand later on. You've done the same thing, after all, haven't you? You've also stepped across . . . found it in yourself to step across. You've committed moral suicide, you've wrecked a life . . . *your own*. (It's all the same!) You might have lived a life of reason and the spirit, but you'll end up in the Haymarket . . . But you won't be able to endure it, and if you remain *alone*, you'll go mad, like me. You're like a madwoman, even now; that means we must go together, along the same road! Let's be off!'

'Why? Why are you saying this?' Sonya said, made strangely and restlessly uneasy by his words.

'Why? Because you can't go on like this – that's why! You must finally confront things seriously and directly, and not weep and wail like a child about God not letting it happen. I mean, what would happen if you were to be carted off to hospital tomorrow? That mad, consumptive woman will die soon, and what will happen to the children? Do you think Polya won't go down the slippery slope? Haven't you seen the children on the street corners round here, those whose mothers have sent them out to beg for alms? I know the sort of places those mothers live in, and the sort of conditions they're surrounded by. In those places it's impossible for children to remain children. In those places a seven-year-old is a depraved thief. And yet children are the image of Christ: "for of such is the kingdom of heaven". He commanded us to revere them and love them, they're the humanity of the future . . .'

'But what then – what's to be done?' Sonya said, weeping hysterically and wringing her hands.

'What's to be done? To break what has to be broken, once and for always, that's all: and to take the suffering upon oneself! What? You don't understand? You will, later on . . . Liberty and power, but above all power! Over all trembling mortals and over the whole antheap!* . . . There's your goal! Remember that! That's my parting message! This may be the last time I shall ever speak to you again. If don't come back tomorrow, you'll hear about it all for yourself, and hen I want you to remember those words I spoke to you just now. And perhaps some day, later on, after years of experience, you'll understand what they mean. But if I do come back tomorrow, I'll tell you who murdered Lizaveta. Goodbye!'

Sonya shuddered with fright.

'You mean you *know* who murdered her?' she asked, going numb with horror and staring at him wildly.

'I know and I'll tell you . . . You I'll tell, and you alone! I've singled you out. I won't come to ask you to forgive me, I'll simply tell you. I singled you out a long time ago as the person to tell this to, I thought of it back at the time when your father spoke about you and when Lizaveta was still alive. Goodbye. Don't give me your hand. Until tomorrow!'

He went out. Sonya watched him go as though he were a man insane; but she herself was like a woman insane, and she knew it. Her head was spinning. 'Oh merciful Lord! How does he know who murdered Lizaveta? What was the meaning of those things he said? This is terrible!' But at the same time *the thought* never entered her head. Not on any, any account! . . . Oh, he must be terribly unhappy! . . . He'd deserted his mother and sister. Why? What had happened? And what plans were in his head? What had he said to her? He'd kissed her foot and said . . . said (yes, he'd said it quite distinctly) that he couldn't live without her . . . Oh, merciful Lord!

Sonya spent the entire night with a high temperature and delirium. From time to time she would leap up, weeping and wringing her hands, and then relapse into a feverish slumber in which she dreamt of Polya, Katerina Ivanovna, Lizaveta, her reading from the New Testament and him . . . him, with his pale face, his burning eyes . . . He was kissing her feet, weeping . . . Oh, merciful Lord!

Behind the door on the right, the very same door that divided Sonya's room from the apartment of Gertruda Karlovna Resslich, was an intermediate room which had long stood empty, belonged to Mrs Resslich's apartment and was up for rent, a fact attested to by notices on the front gate and stickers in the windows that gave on to the Canal. Sonya had long been used to thinking of this room as unoccupied. Yet all this time, by the door of the empty room, Mr Svidrigailov had been standing, keeping quiet and listening. When Raskolnikov went out, he stood for a moment, pondering, then tiptoed back to his own room, which adjoined the empty one, got a chair and carried it right up to the door that led into Sonya's room. The conversation had struck him as interesting and important, and he had enjoyed it very, very much – so much so, in fact, that he had brought in a chair, so that on any future occasion, such as tomorrow, for example, he would not have to sustain the rigours of standing up for a whole hour, but could make himself a little more comfortable, in order that his enjoyment might be complete in every respect.

V

When on the following morning, at eleven o'clock precisely, Raskolnikov entered the building of the — District Police Station, found his way up to the Criminal Investigation Department and requested that Porfiry Petrovich be informed of his arrival, he was rather surprised that it took so long for anyone to attend to him: at least ten minutes went by before his name was called. Somehow he had imagined that they would fall upon him instantly. Meanwhile, however, he stood in the waiting room, and people came and went, seeming not to take the slightest interest in him. In the next room, which resembled an office, a few scribes sat copying documents, and it was obvious that none of them had the slightest notion of who Raskolnikov might be. With a restless and suspicious gaze he looked around him to see if there might not be some guard, some secret eye being kept on him to see that he did not go away. But there was nothing of that sort: all he could see were office-workers going about their petty concerns, and a few other people of some description or other, and none of them could have cared less where he went. More and more resolutely the conviction formed in him that if that enigmatic man, that apparition who had yesterday materialized from nowhere, really had known and seen everything, then it was unlikely that he, Raskolnikov, would now be allowed to stand here like this, quietly waiting. It seemed unlikely, too, that they would have waited until eleven o'clock for him to roll up and tender his greetings. It could mean only one of two things: either that man had not yet made any statement to the police, or . . . the plain fact was that he, too, knew nothing and had not actually seen anything with his own eyes (as indeed how could he have?), and that consequently all that had happened to him, Raskolnikov, the day before, had been an apparition, exaggerated by his own sick and overstimulated imagination. This hunch had even begun to dawn on him the day before, at the time of his most intense anxiety and despair. Having weighed all this over as he prepared for fresh combat, he suddenly felt himself trembling – and a sense of positive indignation seethed up in him at the thought that he was trembling with fear of the hated Porfiry Petrovich. The most horrible prospect he could think of was to encounter that man again; he hated him beyond all measure, beyond all bounds, to the point where he was actually afraid of somehow giving himself away by his hatred. So intense was that indignation that his trembling stopped at once; he prepared to enter with an air of cold insolence and made a vow to himself to say as little as possible, to keep his eyes and ears open and, on this occasion at least, concentrate the utmost effort on keeping his morbidly overstimulated temperament in check.

Porfiry Petrovich turned out to be alone in his chambers just at that moment. His 'chambers' were a room, neither large nor small; it contained a large writing desk with an oilcloth-covered sofa in front of it, a secretaire, a book-case in one corner and a few chairs – government furniture, all of it, made of yellow, polished wood. In the corner of the rear wall was a closed door, or partition, rather: there must, it appeared, be other rooms beyond this one. When Raskolnikov came in Porfiry immediately closed the door by which he had made his entrance, and they were alone together. He greeted his visitor with an apparently cordial and welcoming air, and it was only after several minutes had passed that Raskolnikov observed in him what seemed to be signs of embarrassment, as though he had suddenly been caught off his guard or discovered doing something very secret and private.

'Ah, good sir! So here you are . . . in our neck of the woods . . .' Porfiry began, stretching out both arms to him. 'Well, sit down, my dear fellow! But perhaps you don't like to be called "good sir" and "my dear fellow" – as it were, *tout court*? Please don't think I'm being over-familiar, will you? . . . Yes, right here, on the sofa.'

Raskolnikov sat down, not taking his eyes off him.

Porfiry's phrase 'in our neck of the woods', his apologies and unduly familiar language, his use of the French expression *tout court*, and so on – all of this told him a great deal. 'I notice that he stretched out both arms to me, but didn't let me shake his hand, withdrew it in time,' flashed through his brain with suspicion. Both men were eyeing each other warily, but no sooner did their eyes meet than they would avert them with the swiftness of lightning.

'I've brought you that application . . . about the watch . . . look, here it is. Have I written it correctly, or will I need to copy it out again?'

'What? Oh, that letter . . . Yes, yes . . . have no fear, that will do perfectly,' Porfiry Petrovich said, as though he were in some kind of haste, and, having said it, took the letter of application and read it through. 'Yes, that will do perfectly, sir. No more than that is required,' he said in the same rapid voice, and put the letter on his desk. Later, after a minute or two, by which time he was talking about something else, he picked it up again and transferred it to his secretaire.

'I think you said yesterday that you wanted to ask me some . . . formal questions about how well I knew the woman who was murdered?' Raskolnikov began again. 'Oh, why did I say "I think"?' flashed through his head like lightning. 'And why am I so worried about having said it?' flashed through it like lightning a split second later.

And suddenly he had a feeling that his over-anxiety had, from the merest contact with Porfiry, from the very first words they had uttered, from their very first sight of each other, in one instant grown to monstrous proportions . . . and that this was extremely dangerous: his nerves were on edge, and his agitation was increasing. 'This is bad, bad! . . . I'm going to say the wrong thing again!'

'Yes, yes, yes, now please don't let me put you to any bother, everything's perfectly all right. We've all the time in the world, sir, all the time in the world,' Porfiry Petrovich muttered, waddling to and fro in the region of his desk, but seemingly without any aim, lurching now towards the window, now towards the secretaire, then back to the desk again, at one moment avoiding Raskolnikov's suspicious gaze, at the next suddenly coming to a halt and looking straight at him, steadily. He made a thoroughly strange spectacle, his small, rather fat and rotund figure for all the world like a little ball rolling off in various directions and instantly bouncing back from the room's walls and corners.

'There's no hurry sir, no hurry at all! I say, do you smoke? Got some of your own? Here, sir, have one of mine . . .' he continued, offering his visitor a cigarette. 'I'm seeing you in here, but you know, my own quarters are just through that partition there . . . they're provided for me by the government, but I'm living in privately owned accommodation just now, temporarily. They had to do some sort of repairs through there. They're nearly finished now . . . You know, if you ask me, government quarters are a famous thing – eh? What do you think?'

'Yes, they are,' Raskolnikov answered, looking at him almost mockingly.

'A famous thing, a famous thing . . .' Porfiry Petrovich said, as though he had suddenly thought of something quite different. 'Yes, a famous thing!' he almost shouted, at last, suddenly hurling his gaze at Raskolnikov and coming to a standstill only two paces from him. This somewhat inane pronouncement, many times repeated, that government quarters were a famous thing, was in its trite vulgarity too much at odds with the serious, calculating and enigmatic look he was now fixing on his visitor.

All this, however, merely set Raskolnikov's rage boiling even more fiercely, and by now he was quite unable to restrain himself from issuing a mocking and somewhat incautious challenge.

'I know what I want to ask you,' he said suddenly, looking at Porfiry with near-insolence, and almost taking pleasure in it. 'Why, there exists, I believe, a certain legal maxim, a kind of legal technique, if you like, which is used by all state investigators, and consists in starting the inquiry from some remote point, from some trivial matter, or even from a serious one, as long as it's wholly irrelevant, in order, as it were, to give the person being questioned a certain confidence or, rather, to make him feel at his ease, to allay his jumpiness, and then suddenly hit him bang on the head in a thoroughly unexpected way with the most fatal and dangerous question; is that so? I've heard that this technique is mentioned in all the textbooks and manuals to this very day.'

'Indeed, indeed . . . so you think that's why I began talking to you about government quarters, do you . . . eh?' And, having said this, Porfiry Petrovich narrowed his eyes to slits and gave a wink; a look of cheerful cunning fleeted across his face, the wrinkles on his forehead were smoothed out, his eyes contracted, his features distended, and he suddenly dissolved in a bout of prolonged, nervous laughter, rocking and swaying all over and looking Raskolnikov straight in the eye. Raskolnikov started to laugh, too, though it cost him a certain effort; but when Porfiry, observing that he, too, was laughing, went off into such peals of laughter that he almost turned purple, Raskolnikov's disgust suddenly got the better of all caution: he stopped laughing, frowned, and looked at Porfiry long and loathingly, never once taking his eyes off him throughout the entire duration of his extended and, it seemed, intentionally unceasing bout of mirth. A lack of caution was, however, observable on both sides: the effect of Porfiry Petrovich's outburst was to make it look as though he were laughing in the face of his visitor, who was viewing the whole business with loathing, and as though, moreover, he were very little put out by this circumstance. This latter insight told Raskolnikov a very great deal: he now saw that Porfiry Petrovich had probably not been at all embarrassed at their previous meeting, but that, on the contrary, it was he, Raskolnikov, who had in all likelihood fallen into a trap, that there was something going on here of which he had no knowledge, something with a special purpose; that it had all quite possibly been set up beforehand and in a moment would make its presence felt and come crashing down on top of him . . .

He came straight to the matter in hand, got to his feet and picked up his cap.

'Porfiry Petrovich,' he began resolutely, but rather too irritably. 'Yesterday you expressed the wish that I should come and see you in order that you might put certain questions to me.' (He placed special emphasis on the word *questions*.) 'I have come as you requested, and if there is anything you would like to ask me, then please do so – otherwise you must forgive me if I leave. I don't have much time, there is a matter I must see to . . . I have to attend the funeral of that civil servant who was run down in the street, about whom you . . . also know . . .' he added, immediately kicking himself for having added this, and then growing even more irritable. 'I'm sick of all this, do you hear, sir, and have been so for a long time now . . . It's partly this that made me ill . . . In fact, to put it bluntly,' he almost shouted, sensing that the reference to his being ill was even more out of place, 'to put it bluntly: be so good as either to ask your questions or let me go, this instant . . . and if you are going to question me, then do it according to the proper form, sir! I shall not cooperate unless you do; and so I shall now say goodbye to you, as there seems to be nothing more for the two of us to discuss together.'

'Great heavens above! What's all this you're going on about? What would I be doing questioning you?' Porfiry Petrovich clucked, at once altering his general manner and tone of voice, and ceasing his laughter instantly. 'Please, don't let me put you to any bother,' he fussed, now resuming his lurching walk in all directions, now suddenly trying to make Raskolnikov sit down. 'We've all the time in the world, sir, all the time in the world, and all this is nothing but a lot of nonsense! I'm actually very pleased that you've come to see us at last . . . I view you as my personal guest. And as for that accursed laughter, dear Rodion Romanovich, you'll have to forgive me. It is Rodion Romanovich, isn't it? I mean, Romanovich is your patronymic, I believe? . . . I live on my nerves a lot, you see, sir, and you entertained me greatly with the wittiness of your observation; sometimes I really begin to wobble like a piece of india-rubber, and it goes on for half an hour at a stretch . . . I laugh easily, you see, sir. Being built the way I am, I'm sometimes afraid I shall have an attack of palsy. Oh, do sit down, what's the matter? . . . Please, dear fellow, otherwise I shall think you're angry with me . . .'

Raskolnikov kept silent, listened and observed, still frowning wrathfully. He did, in fact, sit down, but kept a hold of his cap.

'I will tell you one thing about myself, dear Rodion Romanovich, in explanation of my character, as it were,' Porfiry Petrovich went on as he fussed about the room, trying as before, it seemed, to avoid meeting his visitor's eyes. 'I'm not married, you know – an unworldly, unfamiliar sort of fellow, and what's more one who has had his day, one who is set in his customs, sir, gone to seed and . . . and . . . and have you noticed, Rodion Romanovich, that among us, and by that I mean among us here in Russia, sir, and in particular among our St Petersburg circles, if two intelligent individuals, not necessarily well-acquainted but who, as it were, have a mutual respect for each other, like you and I just now, sir, come together, entire half-hours can pass without either of them being able to find the most trivial subject of conversation? They seize up on each other, sit there in mutual embarrassment. Everyone has a subject of conversation – ladies, for example . . . society men, say, men of high fashion – they never lack subjects of conversation, *c'est de rigueur*, and yet run-of-the-mill fellows – like us – are always embarrassed and stuck for anything to say . . . the thinking ones, that is. What's the reason for it, dear chap? Whether it's because we have no interest in what goes on in society, or whether it's just that we're terribly anxious not to deceive one another – I don't know. Eh? What do you think? Oh, I say, do put down that cap of yours, anyone would think you were just about to leave, it really makes me feel uncomfortable just to look at you . . . As I said, I'm really very pleased you're here . . .'

Raskolnikov put down his cap, but continued to say nothing, and went on listening, frowning and serious-faced, to Porfiry's empty and inconsistent chatter. 'What's his game – does he really think he'll distract my attention with this stupid chatter of his?'

'I can't give you coffee, there aren't the facilities for it here; but why not just sit with a friend for five minutes or so, to pass the time?' Porfiry babbled on, incessantly. 'And you know, all these judicial responsibilities of mine . . . and look, my dear fellow, don't take offence at my walking up and down like this; you'll have to forgive me, I'm really terribly afraid of offending you, but you see I simply must have physical exercise. I spend all my time sitting down, and it's such a relief to be able to walk about for five or ten minutes or so . . . I've got piles, you see . . . Actually, I'm thinking of taking up gymnastics; I'm told there's a place where real state councillors, no less, enjoy the use of skipping-ropes – there are even privy councillors among them; you see where science is taking us, in this century of ours? . . . Yes, sir . . . And as regards these responsibilities of mine here, these questionings and all the rest of that formal business . . . Why, you yourself were talking about being questioned just now, my dear fellow . . . Well, if you really want to know, dear Rodion Romanovich, these questionings sometimes confuse the questioner more than they do the person being questioned . . . as you yourself so wittily and correctly observed just now, my dear fellow.' (Raskolnikov had observed nothing of the kind.) 'One gets so mixed up! So mixed up! And it's always the same thing, over and over again, like someone beating a drum! Oh well, the reforms* are in progress now, and at least our official title is to be changed, hee-hee-hee! And as for our questioning techniques – as you so wittily called them – I'm in complete agreement with you, sir. I mean, I'd like to meet a defendant, even the most homespun of muzhiks, who didn't know that they're going to start off by showering him with irrelevant questions (to use your happy turn of phrase), and then suddenly hit him bang on the head, with the butt of the metal, tee-hee-hee! Bang on the head, to employ your happy expression! Ha, ha! So you really thought that I began talking about my quarters in order to make you . . . tee-hee! An ironical fellow, aren't you? Oh well, I shan't go on! Yes, actually, you know, one little word leads to another, one thought suggests another – I mean, you were talking about formal methods earlier, in connection with, you know, questioning procedures, sir . . . But what good are formal methods? You know, in many cases, formal methods are just rubbish. Sometimes one gains more from simply having a friendly chat. Oh, the formal methods will always be with us, sir, you may be assured of that; but what good are they, in the last analysis, I ask you? It's pointless trying to tie an investigator's hands with formal methods at every turn. The work of an investigator is, in its own way, one of the liberal arts, as it were, or something very near it . . . tee-hee-hee!'

Porfiry Petrovich stopped for a moment in order to get his breath back. He had been babbling on persistently, in a stream of empty and meaningless phrases into which he would suddenly insert a few enigmatic words, only to slip back at once into meaningless verbiage again. He had almost been running about the room, moving his fat little legs ever more swiftly, looking constantly at the floor, his right arm behind his back, while he waved his left arm ceaselessly in the air, performing various gestures which were invariably quite out of keeping with what he was saying. Raskolnikov suddenly noticed that, on a couple of occasions, as he raced about the room, he had seemed to pause beside the door for a moment, as though he were listening . . . 'What's he doing – waiting for something?'

'Why, you really are absolutely right, sir,' Porfiry said, cheerfully resuming his flow of talk and looking at Raskolnikov with extraordinary bonhomie (making the latter nearly jump out of his skin and prepare himself for the worst) – 'really absolutely right, sir, in poking fun at our legal formalities with such sharp-wittedness, hee-hee! These deep, psychological techniques of ours (well, some of them, at any rate) are thoroughly ridiculous, sir, yes, and even possibly futile, sir, especially when they're hemmed in by formalities. Yes, sir . . . there I am going on about formalities again: I mean, suppose I think, or suspect, rather, that this, that or the other person who is involved in some case that has been entrusted to me is guilty of having committed a crime . . . You're studying law, aren't you, Rodion Romanovich?'

'Yes, or rather I was . . .'

'Well, then, here's a little example for you, one that you might like to keep in mind for the future – oh, please don't think that I'd dream of trying to teach you anything: why, not in view of all these articles on crime you've been publishing! No, sir, but let me make so bold as to put before you just one small example, in the form of a case-study, as it were. For example, suppose I consider this, that or the other person to be guilty of having committed a crime, well, why, I ask, should I inconvenience the fellow before I need to, even though I've got evidence against him, sir? There are some chaps, of course, whom I have to arrest at once, but, I mean, there are others who are quite different in character, I do assure you, sir – so why shouldn't I let him run around town for a while, tee-hee! No, but I see you don't quite understand, so let me illustrate it for you a little more clearly: if, for example, I were to haul him in too soon, why, in so doing I might easily be giving him a certain moral support, as it were, tee-hee! That makes you laugh, does it, eh?' (Nothing could have been further from Raskolnikov's mind than laughter; he sat with his lips clamped together, never once removing his inflamed gaze from Porfiry Petrovich's eyes.) 'And yet, you see, that's the way it is with certain types, because people vary so much, yet we only have one practical method to apply to them all. You talked just now about evidence; but well, yes, one may very well have evidence, but you know, evidence is for the most part a matter of conjecture, my dear fellow, and I mean, after all, I'm only an investigator, and therefore as prone to weakness as the next man, and I swear to you: what I want is a case that can be presented with mathematical clarity, I want the kind of evidence that looks as straightforward as two times two! I want it to look like direct and irrefutable proof! And you see, if I haul him in before time – even though I'm convinced that *he*'s the one – well, you see, I may very well be depriving myself of the means of getting him to give the game away even further – why? Because I'll have given him a definite place in the whole business, I'll have, as it were, given him a sense of psychological security and put his fears at rest, and he'll go cold on me and withdraw into his shell: what he'll have realized is that he's a convict. They say that down there in Sebastopol, just after the Battle of the Alma,* the people in intelligence were very worried that the enemy was just about to launch an open attack and take the town in one go; but when they saw that the enemy preferred a straightforward siege and was digging his first line of trenches, it's said that those same people in intelligence were much relieved and felt their minds had been put at rest: it meant, you see, that the thing would drag on for at least two months, because that was how long a straightforward siege would take! I expect you're laughing again, you don't believe me, eh? Well, and of course you're right. You're right, sir, you're right! Those are all rather special cases, I agree with you, the one I've just cited is a very special case indeed! But you see, my dear, good Rodion Romanovich, what you need to observe in them is this: the general case, the one all our legal rules and formalities are designed for and the one on the basis of which they're all worked out and written into the legal textbooks, simply doesn't exist, for the very good reason that every case, every crime, if you like, as soon as it takes place in reality, turns into a thoroughly special case; I mean, sometimes it's even something that's never happened before. One sometimes encounters the most comical instances of this kind, sir. Say I leave a certain gentleman completely alone: I don't arrest him and I don't trouble him, but I make damn sure that every hour and every minute he knows, or at least suspects, that I know everything, the whole seamy story, and that I'm keeping an eye on him night and day, watching him unremittingly, and if he's conscious of the never-ending suspicion and terror in which I'm keeping him, I tell you, sir, he'll go off into a whirl, he'll come running of his own accord, and he may even do something that will look like two times two, and will, as it were, have a mathematical appearance – that's always most gratify-ing, sir. It may happen in the case of a clodhopping muzhik, or it may happen in the case of people such as ourselves, intelligent men of the contemporary world whose development has taken a certain direction – all the more so because of that! Because, my dear fellow, it's always very important to know the direction a person's development has taken. And what about nerves – nerves, sir? You've forgotten about them! I mean, all those thin, ill, nervous characters one sees around nowadays! . . . And all that spleen, all that spleen they've got inside them! Why, I tell you, sir, there are times when a fellow like that can be a kind of walking gold mine! And it's no skin off my nose if he goes walking about the town without any handcuffs on! Leave him alone, let him go gadding around for the time being if he wants to; I mean, I know that he's already on my plate and won't abscond! Where would be abscond to, hee-hee! Abroad? A Pole might run abroad, but *he* won't, especially since I've been keeping an eye on him and have taken certain precautions. Will he run into the depths of our fatherland, perhaps? But I mean, there are only muzhiks there,

real, Russian, homespun ones; why, a man of contemporary education and development would sooner go to jail than live among such
foreigners as those muzhiks of ours, tee-hee! But that's all nonsense,
mere circumstantial stuff. What, abscond? That's just a formal term
we use; no, the main thing is something else; it's not just that he
won't abscond because he has nowhere to run to: he won't abscond
psychologically, hee-hee! How do you like that as a way of expressing
it? A law of nature will prevent him from getting away from me, even
though he has somewhere to run to. Have you ever watched a moth
near a candle-flame? Well, that's the way he'll be with me, hovering,
circling around me like a moth at a lighted candle; he'll lose his taste
for freedom, he'll start to think, get tangled in his thoughts, ensnare
himself all round as though in some net or other, worry himself to
death! . . . And that's not all: he himself will serve me up a nice,
mathematical formula like two times two – if only I give him enough
latitude . . . And on he'll go, performing a circular orbit around me,
narrowing the radius further and further, until – pop! He'll fly straight
into my mouth and I'll swallow him whole! Most gratifying, sir, tee-
hee-hee! Do you believe me?'

Raskolnikov made no reply; he sat pale and motionless, staring into
Porfiry's face with the same look of tension.

'That was a lesson and no mistake!' he thought, growing cold. 'This
is more than the cat-and-mouse game he was playing yesterday. And
he's not just showing off his power for the sake of it, either, implying
it to me: he's far too clever for that . . . There's some other motive at
work here, but what is it? Oh, go to the devil, brother, you're trying
to frighten me and play a cunning dodge! You've no proof, and that
fellow yesterday didn't exist! You're just trying to put me off my
guard, make me lose my head prematurely, and then bang the lid on
me; but you're on the wrong track, you won't get anywhere! But why
would he imply all those things to me? . . . Does he think he can play
on my nerves? . . . No, brother, you're on the wrong track, you won't
get where you want to go, even if you have set something up in
advance . . . Well, let's see what it is you *have* set up.'

And with all his might he held himself in check, preparing himself
for a terrible and unknown catastrophe. At times he felt like rushing
at Porfiry and strangling him right there and then. Even as he had
entered this room, he had been afraid of his own violent rage. He
could feel that his mouth had dried up, his heart was beating like a

hammer, the foam had coagulated on his lips. But all the same he was determined to keep silent and not say one word prematurely. He realized that this was the best tactic to adopt in the position he was in, because not only would he avoid the risk of saying the wrong thing, he would also irritate his enemy with his silence, and possibly make him say something ill-advised. That, at least, was what he hoped.

'But I see that you don't believe me, sir; you think I'm still making harmless jokes at your expense,' Porfiry began again, growing more and more affable, keeping up an unceasing chuckle of pleasure, and resuming his gyrations around the room. 'And, of course, you're quite right, sir; why, even the shape of my body has been ordained by God in such a manner that it suggests only comic thoughts to others; I'm a clown, sir; but let me tell you this, and repeat it again, and that is that you, my dear Rodion Romanovich, forgive an old man for saying so, are a man still young, a man, as it were, in the prime of his youth, and accordingly you place a supreme value on the human intellect, as all young people do. You are tempted by the playful sharpness of the intellect and the abstract arguments of reason, sir. In fact, just like the Austrian *Hofkriegsrat** in the old days, so far as I am able to form any judgement on events of a military nature; on paper they had defeated Napoleon and taken him prisoner, and yet as they were sitting there in their study working it all out in the most sharp-witted manner, what did General Mack do but go and surrender with his entire army, hee-hee-hee! I can see, I can see, dear Rodion Romanovich, that you're laughing at me: here am I, a civilian state employee, picking all my examples from military history. But what am I to do, it's a weakness of mine, I'm fond of military matters, and I'm inordinately fond of reading all those military reports . . . I suppose I'm in the wrong career, really. I ought to have served in the military, sir, really I ought. I might not have become a Napoleon, but I'd have made the rank of major, sir, hee-hee-hee! Well, sir, but let me tell you, my dear fellow, the whole unvarnished truth about what we were discussing, those *special cases*, that is to say: reality and human nature, my dear sir, are not to be taken lightly, and my goodness, how they sometimes cut the ground from under the most sagacious estimates! Ah, listen to an old man . . . I'm serious, Rodion Romanovich.' (As he said this the barely thirty-five-year-old Porfiry Petrovich really did appear suddenly to become much older: even his

402

voice changed, and he seemed to grow hunched and stooped all over.) 'What's more, I'm a man who tells things the way they are, sir . . . Would you agree? What's your opinion? I don't think it can possibly be denied: the things I'm telling you for nothing! Why, I'm not even asking for a bonus, tee-hee! Well, so there we are, sir; let me continue: sharp-wittedness is, in my opinion, a wonderful thing, sir; it is, as it were, an embellishment of nature and a solace in life, and what conjuring tricks it can perform! Why, it can baffle the daylights out of a poor investigator, who has a hard enough time trying not to be carried away by his own imagination, something that invariably happens, for he's only human, sir! Yet it's human nature that gets the poor investigator out of his difficulty, sir, more's the pity! And that's just what those young fellows who're carried away by their own sharp-wittedness, "stepping across all obstacles" (as you expressed it with such wit and cunning), don't seem to take into account. We shall assume that he'll lie, this fellow, this *special case*, sir, this *incognito*, sir, and that he'll lie brilliantly, in the most cunning manner; one might well imagine that this is his moment of triumph, that now he can enjoy the fruits of his sharp-wittedness, but no – pop! Right at the most interesting moment, the moment when it's likely to cause the greatest degree of scandal, he falls down in a dead faint. We shall assume that it's caused by his illness, by the airlessness – rooms can sometimes be very airless – but even so, sir! Even so, he has given us an idea! He has lied splendidly, but he's left human nature out of his calculations. There's perfidy for you, sir! On another occasion, getting carried away by the playfulness of his sharp-wittedness, he'll start trying to make a fool of the person who suspects him, he'll turn pale *a little too naturally*, so that it seems a little too lifelike, and again he has given us an idea! Even though he hoodwinks the person the first time, the person will think it over during the night, if he's got any brains. And that's the way it goes every step of the way, sir! And it won't stop there: our special case will start trying to run ahead of the game, butt in where he's not been invited, he'll start talking ceaselessly about things he ought to keep quiet about, he'll start launching into allegories of various kinds, hee-hee! He'll come to the station himself and ask: "Why are they taking so long to arrest me?" Tee-hee-hee! And I mean, this sort of thing can happen to the most sharp-witted fellows one can think of, to psychologists and *littérateurs*, sir! Human nature is a mirror, sir, a mirror, of the most transparent kind!

Look in it and feast your eyes, sir! But why have you gone so pale, Rodion Romanovich, is the room too airless for you, shall I open a window?'

'Oh, please don't bother,' Raskolnikov shouted, and suddenly burst into loud laughter. 'Please don't bother!'

Porfiry came to a standstill opposite him, waited for a moment and suddenly burst out laughing himself, in his wake. Raskolnikov got up from the sofa, suddenly cutting short his own, by now almost epileptic, laughter.

'Porfiry Petrovich!' he said loudly and distinctly, though he could hardly stay upright on his trembling legs. 'It is clear to me now that you definitely suspect me of having murdered that old woman and her sister Lizaveta. For my part, I will tell you that I grew heartily sick of all this a long time ago. If you believe that you have the right to prosecute me, then please do so; if you are going to arrest me, arrest me. But I won't allow you to laugh in my face and torment me like this.'

Suddenly his lips began to quiver, his eyes burned with fury, and his voice, which until now had been restrained, began to boom.

'I won't allow it, sir!' he shouted, suddenly, bringing his fist down with all his might on the desk. 'Do you hear, Porfiry Petrovich? I won't allow it!'

'Oh heavens above, what's this, now?' Porfiry Petrovich exclaimed, apparently in utter alarm. 'My dear fellow! Rodion Romanovich! Old chap! Dear benefactor! What's the matter?'

'I won't allow it!' Raskolnikov shouted again.

'My dear fellow, keep your voice down! I mean, they'll hear, they'll come in! Well, what would we tell them, just think!' Porfiry Petrovich whispered in horror, bringing his face right up to Raskolnikov's.

'I won't allow it, I won't allow it,' he repeated mechanically, but now suddenly in a dead whisper.

Porfiry quickly turned away and ran to open the window.

'We must let some fresh air in! And you must have a glass of water, my dear man, you've had a fit, sir!' And he rushed to the door in order to send for some water, but there happened to be a decanter of water in the corner.

'My dear fellow, drink this,' he whispered, rushing towards him with the decanter. 'Perhaps it will help . . .' Porfiry Petrovich's alarm and sympathy were so natural that Raskolnikov fell silent and began to study him with wild curiosity. He declined, however, to accept the water.

'Rodion Romanovich! My dear chap! You know, you'll drive yourself crazy if you go on like this, I do assure you – a-ach! Dear me! Come on, drink this! Drink just a little of it!'

He made him take the glass into his hands. Raskolnikov raised it to his lips mechanically, but, remembering where he was, put it down on the table with disgust.

'Yes, sir, you've had a fit! If you go on like this you'll bring your old illness back again,' Porfiry Petrovich said with friendly sympathy, though with a slightly embarrassed look. 'Heavens above! I mean, why don't you look after yourself? Why, Dmitry Prokofich came to see me yesterday – oh, I admit, sir, I admit that I've a nasty, sarcastic nature, but the conclusions he drew from it! . . . Heavens above! He came to see me yesterday, after you'd been here, we had dinner together, he talked and talked, I simply threw up my hands in bewilderment; well, I thought . . . heavens above! Was it you who sent him? Oh, sit down, my dear fellow, in Christ's name sit down!'

'No, I didn't send him! But I knew he was going to see you and the reason for his visit,' Raskolnikov replied, acidly.

'You knew?'

'Yes. So what?'

'Simply, Rodion Romanovich, my dear fellow, that that's not the only exploit of yours I know about; I know about all of them, sir! Why, I know about your going off *to rent new lodgings in another apartment* late at night, after darkness had fallen, about your ringing the doorbell, asking about the blood, and fairly baffling the workmen and the yardkeepers no end. You see, I understand your state of mind, the state of mind you were in that day . . . But I'll say it again: if you go on like this you will drive yourself crazy – I mean it, you will, sir! You'll go off into a spin! You've an awful lot of indignation boiling inside you, sir, righteous indignation at the insults you've received, first from fate and then from the police, and you've been dashing hither and thither in order, as it were, to make everyone start talking and so have done with the whole thing at one go, because you're sick of this stupid nonsense and all these suspicions. That's right, isn't it? . . . I've fathomed your mood, haven't I? Only if you go on like this it's not just yourself you'll drive off into a spin, but my dear Razumikhin too; and I mean, he's too *good* for that kind of thing, you know it yourself. You have an illness and he has virtue, and your illness may be catching for him . . . My dear fellow, when you've calmed down I'll explain it to you . . . but sit down, my dear fellow, for Christ's sake sit down! Please, take a rest, you look dreadful; sit down.'

Raskolnikov sat down; his shivering had passed, and a hot fever broke out all over his body. In deep amazement he listened tensely to the alarmed Porfiry Petrovich, who was tending to him in such a friendly way. He did not, however, believe a single word he was saying, even though he felt a strange inclination to do so. Porfiry's unexpected remark about the apartment had come as a complete shock to him. 'Does that mean he knows about the apartment?' he thought suddenly. 'He told me about it himself!'

'Yes, sir, we had a case almost identical to this, a psychological one, in the course of our judicial work, a case of illness, sir,' Porfiry went on quickly. 'He also tried to hang a murder on himself, sir, and my, how he went about it: came up with a regular hallucination, provided us with evidence, described the circumstances, got everyone well and truly mixed up, and for what reason? He himself, quite without premeditation, had been the cause of a murder, but only in part, and when he discovered that he'd given the murderers their opportunity, he got depressed, went into a kind of trance, began imagining things, went right off the rails, and started telling everyone that *he* was the murderer! But the Supreme Senate finally got to the bottom of the case and the wretched fellow was acquitted and sent off to the poorhouse. Thank goodness for the Supreme Senate! Tut, tut, tut, dear, dear, dear! But if you go on like that what can you expect, dear fellow? If you go on like that you'll end up with brain-fever, and if you follow these impulses to overstimulate your own nerves, you'll be off ringing doorbells and asking questions about blood, sir! I mean, I've studied all this psychology stuff in the course of my work. People who go on like that sometimes have an urge to throw themselves out of windows or jump off church towers, and it's a tempting sort of sensation. It's the same with ringing doorbells, sir . . . It's an illness, Rodion Romanovich, an illness! You're neglecting your health, sir. You ought to consult an experienced medic, not that fat chap of yours! . . . What's wrong with you is delirium! The plain fact is that you're doing everything in a state of delirium!'

For a moment everything began to spin violently around Raskolnikov.

'Can it really be?' flashed through his head. 'Can it really be that he's lying even now? No, it's impossible, impossible!' he thought, repulsing this idea, feeling even before he had thought it to what heights of rabid fury and rage it was capable of leading him, feeling that he might even go mad with rage.

'That wasn't something that happened in a state of delirium, it was real!' he shouted, exerting all the powers of his reason in an attempt to fathom what Porfiry's game was. 'It was real, real! Do you hear?'

'Yes, sir, I understand, and I hear, too. You kept saying the same thing yesterday, that it had nothing to do with delirium – you were quite adamant about it! I understand everything that you can possibly tell me, sir! Dear, dear me! . . . But Rodion Romanovich, my dear young benefactor, please at least take account of this: I mean, for heaven's sake, if you were really guilty or in some way mixed up in that accursed business, would you be so adamant about insisting that you weren't delirious when you did all that, but were, on the contrary, in full possession of your faculties? Would you make a particular point of insisting on it, with your special form of stubbornness – would you? In my opinion the answer would have to be no. I mean, if you did have something on your conscience, you'd have insisted the contrary was true: that you had most certainly been delirious! Isn't that right? It is, isn't it?'

There was a note of slyness in this question. Raskolnikov shrank back hard against the back of the sofa, away from Porfiry, who was leaning towards him, and studied him in amazement, silently and fixedly.

'And what about Mr Razumikhin, and the question of whether he came to talk to me yesterday of his own accord, or whether it was your own idea? I mean, you'd have been bound to say that he came of his own accord, and conceal the fact that it was your own idea! But you haven't done that! You keep insisting that it was your own idea!'

Raskolnikov had never insisted anything of the kind. A cold shiver passed down his spine.

'You're lying,' he said slowly and weakly, his lips contorted in a painful smile. 'You're trying to show me again that you know my whole game, that you know all my answers in advance,' he said, half aware that he was not weighing his words as he ought to. 'You're trying to frighten me . . . or else you're just laughing at me . . .'

As he said this, he continued to stare fixedly at Porfiry, and suddenly a limitless and malicious hatred flashed in his eyes.

'You're lying!' he shouted. 'You yourself know very well that the best subterfuge for a criminal is to tell the truth as much as possible . . . and to do all he possibly can not to conceal anything that doesn't matter. I don't believe you!'

'You are a flighty fellow, aren't you?' Porfiry began to giggle. 'There's no bringing you round; some kind of monomania has taken hold of you. So you don't believe me? Well, I will tell you that you do believe me, at least a quarter of the way, and that I am going to see to it that you believe me the other three-quarters of the way, because I am genuinely fond of you and sincerely wish you well.'

Raskolnikov's lips began to tremble.

'Yes, sir, I wish you well, and let me tell you once and for all,' he went on, gently, in a friendly tone of voice, taking hold of Raskolnikov's arm slightly above the elbow. 'Let me tell you once and for all: look after your illness. Particularly since your family is here now; you must keep it in your thoughts. What you ought to be doing is putting them at ease and spoiling them a bit, but all you do is frighten them . . .'

'What business is it of yours? How do you know that? Why are you so interested? Does this mean that you've been following me around and are trying to demonstrate it to me?'

'My dear fellow! Why, it's from you, from you yourself that I've learned it all. You don't seem to notice that in your agitation you tell me and others everything. I also learned a great number of interesting details from Mr Razumikhin – Dmitry Prokofich – yesterday. Well, sir, but you've interrupted me; what I'm trying to say is that because of your over-anxiousness, for all your sharp-wittedness, you've really lost your ability to see things from a common-sense point of view. I mean look, for example, let's go back to what we were talking about, your ringing the doorbell; a priceless gem of information like that, a piece of evidence (a genuine piece of evidence, sir!), and I give it to you with both hands – I, the investigator! Doesn't that tell you anything? I mean, if I'd suspected you the least little bit, do you think I'd have done a thing like that? On the contrary, my job would have been first to lull your suspicions and not let on that I already knew about that fact, that piece of evidence; by doing so, to draw you off in the opposite direction and then suddenly bring the butt of the metal (to use your own expression) down on your head, and say: "What, sir, were you doing in the murdered woman's apartment at ten o'clock last night, or was it nearer to eleven? And why did you ring the doorbell? Why did you ask about the blood? Why did you try to bluff the yardkeepers and make them go down to the local police lieutenant's bureau with you?" That's what I'd have done if I'd had the merest grain of suspicion about you. I'd have taken a statement from you with all the formalities, we'd have searched your quarters, and you might even have been arrested . . . So that means, you see, that I don't suspect you – otherwise I'd have behaved differently! But I'll say it again, sir: you've lost your ability to see things from a common-sense point of view, and in fact you can't see anything at all.'

Raskolnikov made a convulsive jerk with his whole body, so violent that Porfiry Petrovich noted it only too well.

'You're lying!' he shouted. 'I don't know what your motives are, but you're lying . . . You weren't talking like this a moment ago, and it's impossible for me to be mistaken . . . You're lying!'

'Oh, so that's what you think, is it?' Porfiry said, obviously annoyed, but maintaining the most cheerful and sardonic air, apparently not at all concerned what opinion Mr Raskolnikov might have of him. 'You think I'm lying, do you? . . . After the way I treated you just now (I, a state investigator), supplying you with all the answers and giving you everything you need for your own defence, bringing in all the psychological stuff about it being due to your illness, your delirium, your having taken proper umbrage – to a mixture of melancholy and policemen, and all the rest of it? Eh? Tee-hee-hee! Though, as a matter of fact, I think it's only right to point out that all those psychological explanations, those dodges and excuses, really don't wear very well and are a matter of conjecture: "Illness," you say, "delirium, fantasies, it was all a hallucination, I don't remember." That's all very fine, sir, but why, my dear fellow, did you hallucinate those *particular* fantasies when you were sick and delirious, and not some others? I mean, you could have had others, sir, couldn't you? Eh? Tee-hee-hee-hee!'

Raskolnikov looked at him with proud contempt.

'Let's come to the point,' he said, loudly and earnestly, getting up and pushing Porfiry away from him slightly as he did so. 'Let's get to the point: what I want to know, once and for all, is: do you consider me free from suspicion or *do you not*? Come on, Porfiry Petrovich, give me a clear and final answer, and be quick about it, I want to hear it right now!'

'My goodness, what a job, what a job I'm having with you!' Porfiry exclaimed, looking thoroughly sly and cheerful, and not in the least concerned. 'What's the point in your knowing, what's the point in your knowing so much, when they haven't started bothering you at all, yet? Why, you're just like a child that wants to play with matches! And why are you so worried? Why are you thrusting yourself on us like this, for what reason? Eh? Tee-hee-hee!'

'I will say it again,' Raskolnikov shouted in fury. 'I can no longer endure . . .'

'What, sir? The uncertainty?' Porfiry said, interrupting.

'Stop tormenting me! I won't allow it . . . I tell you, I won't allow it! . . . I categorically refuse! . . . Do you hear? Do you hear?' he shouted, again slamming his fist down on the table.

'Keep your voice down, keep it down! They'll hear, you know. I warn you in all seriousness: watch out for yourself. I'm not joking, sir!' Porfiry said in a whisper, but this time his face lacked the expression of feminine good nature and alarm it had worn earlier; indeed, now he was quite simply *giving orders*, furrowing his brow and seeming in one go to sweep away all the mysteries and ambiguities there had been. This only lasted a moment, however. The bewildered Raskolnikov suddenly fell into a condition of genuine frenzy; but it was strange: he again obeyed the command to keep his voice down, even though he was in the most intense paroxysm of fury.

'I won't allow you to torment me like this,' he suddenly whispered in his earlier tone of voice, with pain and hatred, realizing for a second that he had no option but to obey the command, his fury intensifying even further at this thought. 'Arrest me, search my lodgings, do as you please, but do it according to the rule-book, and stop playing with me, sir! Do not dare to presume . . .'

'Oh, don't worry about the rule-book,' Porfiry said, interrupting with his earlier sly smile, feasting his eyes on Raskolnikov with positive pleasure. 'My dear fellow, I invited you here today, as it were, to my home – in a completely friendly fashion!'

'I don't want your friendship and I spit upon it! Do you hear? And look: I'm going to take my cap and leave, now. Well, what have you got to say to that, if you're going to arrest me?'

He snatched up his cap and walked towards the door.

'But don't you want to see my little surprise?' Porfiry giggled, again taking hold of him slightly above the elbow and coming to a halt beside the door. He was manifestly growing more and more cheerful and playful, and this finally drove Raskolnikov out of himself.

'What little surprise? What are you talking about?' he asked, suddenly stopping in his tracks and looking at Porfiry with fright.

'My little surprise, sir, look, over there, he's sitting on the other side of that door, hee-hee-hee!' (He pointed to the closed door of the partition which led into his government quarters.) 'I even locked him in so he wouldn't run away.'

'What on earth? Where? What? . . .' Raskolnikov went over to the door and tried to open it, but it was locked.

'It's locked, sir – look, here's the key!'

And true enough, he showed him the key, taking it out of his pocket.

'You're still lying!' Raskolnikov began to yell, now unable to control himself. 'You're lying, you damned Mr Punch!' And he hurled himself at Porfiry, who although he was retreating towards the door showed not the slightest sign of fear.

'I understand everything, everything!' Raskolnikov said as he leapt up to him. 'You're lying and teasing me, to make me give myself away . . .'

'You can't give yourself away any further, Rodion Romanovich, my dear fellow. Why, you're in a positive frenzy. Please stop shouting, sir, or I'll call in my assistants!'

'You're lying, it's all empty air! Go ahead, call them in, then! You knew I was ill, and you tried to overtax me to the point of hysteria in order to make me give myself away, that's what your motive was! Well, let's see your evidence! I see it all now! You haven't any evidence, all you've got is trashy, good-for-nothing guesses, the hunches of Mr Zamyotov! . . . You knew what sort of man I am, you wanted to drive me to frenzy, and then suddenly knock the wind out of me with priests and deputies . . . Is it them you're waiting for, eh? What are you waiting for? Where are they? Let's see them!'

'Oh, what deputies are you talking about, my dear fellow? The things a man will get into his head! The way you're carrying on we couldn't possibly do things according to the rule-book, as you call it – the fact is, my dear chap, you haven't the slightest idea of what you're talking about . . . But the rule-book won't go away, sir, you'll see for yourself! . . .' Porfiry muttered, putting his ear to the door.

Just then there was indeed a commotion on the other side of the door, in the next room.

'Ah, they're coming!' Raskolnikov shouted. 'You sent for them! . . . You've been waiting for them! You were expecting them . . . Well, let them all come in: deputies, witnesses, whoever you like . . . Let's see them! I'm ready! Ready! . . .'

But just at that point a strange incident took place, something so unlooked-for, given the general turn of events, that neither Raskolnikov nor Porfiry Petrovich could possibly have expected such a dénouement.

VI

Later on, whenever he remembered that moment, it presented itself to Raskolnikov in the following manner:

The commotion that had made itself heard on the other side of the door suddenly grew louder, and the door opened a little way.

'What on earth?' Porfiry Petrovich exclaimed in annoyance. 'Why, I gave specific instructions . . .'

For an instant no one replied, but it could be seen that there were several people on the other side of the door, apparently trying to push someone away.

'What on earth's going on out there?' Porfiry Petrovich said again, in alarm.

'They've brought the prisoner, Nikolai,' someone's voice said.

'I don't need him just now! Take him away, and tell him to wait! . . . What's he doing here? Damn it, what a shambles!' Porfiry shouted, as he rushed to the door.

'But, sir, he's . . .' the same voice began again, and was suddenly cut short.

For roughly two seconds, no more, there was a genuine struggle; then suddenly someone gave someone else a violent shove, and a very pale man walked straight into Porfiry Petrovich's chambers.

The outward appearance of this man was at first sight very strange. He was staring straight in front of him, but apparently without seeing anyone. There was a glitter of determination in his eyes, but at the same time his features were covered in a deathly pallor, as though he were being led to the scaffold. His lips, which had turned utterly white, were twitching slightly.

He was still very young, dressed like a plebeian, of average height, lean and thin, his hair cropped in a short circle, with delicate, rather dry-looking features. The man who had been so unexpectedly pushed aside by him was the first to rush into the room after him, and managed to grab him by the shoulder: this was one of the guards; but Nikolai jerked his arm free and got away from him a second time.

A group of inquisitive onlookers began to gather in the doorway. Some of them tried to come inside. The whole of what has just been described took place in little more than a single instant.

'Go away, you're too early! Wait until you're called! . . . Why has he been brought so soon?' Porfiry Petrovich muttered in extreme annoyance, as though all his calculations had been upset. But Nikolai suddenly got down on his knees.

'What are you doing?' Porfiry shouted, in amazement.

'I'm the guilty one! The sin is mine! I'm the murderer!' Nikolai finally got out, as though he were a little short of breath, but in rather a loud voice.

For about ten seconds there was a silence, as though they had all been stunned; even the guard staggered back and, instead of going up to Nikolai, beat an automatic retreat to the doorway and stood there, motionless.

'What on earth?' Porfiry Petrovich exclaimed, when he had recovered from his momentary state of numb shock.

'I'm . . . the murderer . . .' Nikolai repeated, after a slight pause.

'What . . . you . . . Whom have you murdered?'

Porfiry Petrovich looked as though he were at his wit's end.

Nikolai paused again slightly.

'Alyona Ivanovna and her sister, Lizaveta Ivanovna – I murdered them . . . with an axe. I had a black turn . . .' he added suddenly, and again fell silent. He was still on his knees.

413

Porfiry Petrovich stood motionless for a few seconds, as though he were reflecting, but then suddenly flew into motion again, waving his arms at the uninvited witnesses. In a trice they disappeared from view, and the door closed. Then he took a glance at Raskolnikov, who was standing in the corner, staring wildly at Nikolai, and began to move in his direction, but then stopped suddenly, looked at him, swiftly transferred his gaze to Nikolai, then back to Raskolnikov, then over to Nikolai again and then abruptly, as though with great interest, pounced on Nikolai.

'What do you mean, trying to run ahead of me with your black turns?' he shouted at him, with something approaching malice. 'I haven't asked you yet if you had a black turn . . . what I want to know is: have you committed a murder?'

'I'm the one that did it . . . I'll make a statement . . .' Nikolai said.

'Oh, for God's sake! What did you do it with?'

'An axe. One I had handy.'

'I say, the man's in a hurry! Just you alone?'

Nikolai did not understand the question.

'Was it just you who did it?'

'Yes. Mitka's innocent – he had no part in any of it.'

'Now take your time with Mitka, will you? Oh, my God! . . . But then why, why did you run down the stairs that time? I mean, the yardkeepers ran into you both!'

'I did it to throw them off the trail . . . running away with Mitka . . . that time,' Nikolai answered, hurrying his words as though he had prepared them in advance.

'Yes, I was right!' Porfiry exclaimed malevolently. 'He's simply repeating something he was told to say!' he muttered, as if to himself, and again he suddenly looked at Raskolnikov.

So taken up with Nikolai had he apparently been that for one second he had actually forgotten about Raskolnikov. Now he suddenly gathered his thoughts again, and looked positively embarrassed . . .

'Rodion Romanovich, my dear fellow! I'm terribly sorry, sir!' he said, rushing over to him. 'This simply won't do, sir; please . . . there's nothing for you to do here . . . I'm afraid I'm . . . you see what surprises there are! . . . Please be so good, sir! . . .'

And taking him by the arm, he showed him to the door.

'It looks as though you weren't expecting this,' Raskolnikov said.

As might have been expected, although he had not really taken everything in as yet, he had already cheered up considerably.

'You weren't expecting it either, dear fellow. Look at your hand – it's trembling, tee-hee!'

'You're trembling, too, Porfiry Petrovich.'

'So I am, sir, so I am; most unexpected . . .'

By now they were standing in the doorway. Porfiry was waiting in impatience for Raskolnikov to go out of it.

'So you're not going to show me your little surprise, then?' Raskolnikov said, suddenly.

'Listen to him talk, yet his teeth are chattering together in his head, tee-hee! You *are* an ironical fellow, aren't you? Well, sir, *au revoir*.'

'If you want my opinion, it's *goodbye*.'

'As God sees fit, sir, as God sees fit!' Porfiry muttered, with a sort of twisted smile.

As he passed through the office, Raskolnikov noticed that many of the people there gave him fixed stares. Among the crowd in the entrance hall he saw the two yardkeepers from *that* building, the ones he had tried to talk into going down to the police station with him that night. They were standing there, waiting for something. But no sooner was he out on the staircase than he suddenly heard the voice of Porfiry Petrovich behind him once again. Turning roumd, he saw that Porfiry was trying to catch him up, thoroughly out of breath.

'There's just one other thing, Rodion Romanovich, sir; as far as all that other stuff's concerned, it's as God sees fit, but even so I shall have to ask you a few formal questions . . . so we'll be seeing each other again, yes, we shall, sir.'

And Porfiry came to a standstill in front of him, smiling.

'Yes, we shall, sir,' he added, once more.

He looked as though there was something else he wanted to say, but was somehow unable to get it out.

'You really must forgive me for my behaviour just now . . . I was a little hasty,' Raskolnikov began, his spirits now completely restored, to a point where he could not resist a bit of a swagger.

'It's quite all right, sir, it's quite all right . . .' Porfiry chipped in, almost joyfully. 'I was hasty, too . . . I do have a poisonous tongue, I confess, I confess! So we'll be seeing each other, sir. If God sees fit, we'll be seeing a great, great deal of each other, sir! . . .'

'And shall we really get to know each other at last?' Raskolnikov asked.

'We shall, we shall,' Porfiry Petrovich said, affirmatively, and, screwing up his eyes, gave him a very serious look. 'Off to that name-day celebration, are you, sir?'

'It's a funeral, actually.'

'Ah yes, it's that funeral! Well, do look after your health, sir, do look after your health . . .'

'I must say I don't really know what I can wish you in return,' Raskolnikov said, already beginning to resume his descent of the staircase, but then turning round again to face Porfiry. 'I'd like to wish you every success, but I mean, you yourself are aware of what a comical job yours is!'

'Why is it comical, sir?' Porfiry Petrovich said, instantly pricking up his ears, and also on the point of turning to go.

'Well, I mean, look at the psychological torture you've been meting out to that poor Mikolka, in that way of yours you have, to the point where he confessed; you must have been hammering on at him day and night, telling him "you're the murderer, you're the murderer!" – Well, and yet now that he's confessed, you're picking him to little pieces again, telling him that he's lying, that he's not the murderer, that he couldn't possibly be the murderer, and that he's just repeating something he was told to say. Well, what sort of a job is that if it's not a comical one?'

'Tee-hee-hee! So you noticed when I told Nikolai just now that he was repeating something someone had told him to say?'

'How could I fail to?'

'Tee-hee! That was sharp-witted, sharp-witted of you, sir. You notice everything! You have a genuinely playful intellect, sir! And you fasten right on the most comical note . . . tee-hee! Is it the writer Gogol whom they say possessed that ability in the very highest degree?'

'Yes, that's right, Gogol . . .'

'Yes, sir, Gogol, sir . . . I look forward to our next meeting with the greatest of pleasure, sir.'

'I, too . . .'

Raskolnikov headed straight for home. So tired and confused was he that when he got back to his room he threw himself on the sofa and sat there for a quarter of an hour, merely resting and trying to do what he could to gather his thoughts. He did not even try to think about Nikolai: he felt he had been defeated; that in Nikolai's confession there had been something inexplicable, astonishing, something he could not fathom now for all the world. But Nikolai's confession was an established fact. The consequences of that fact at once became clear to him: his lie could not but be found out, and when it was he would be taken in hand again. But until then, at least, he was free; now he must do all he could in order to protect himself, for the danger was unavoidable.

The question was: how unavoidable? The situation was beginning to become clear. As he recalled, *in rough outline*, the overall implications of the scene that had taken place between Porfiry and himself, he could not help but shudder with horror again. Of course, he did not yet know all Porfiry's motives, had been unable to make out what it was he had been bargaining on just now. But a part of the game he was playing had been revealed, and of course, no one was more aware than he was of the risk to himself that this 'move' in Porfiry's game involved. A little longer and he *might* have given himself away completely, in such a manner that it could be regarded as evidence against him. Aware of his morbid temperament, having correctly sized him up and seen into him right from the very first glance, Porfiry had acted, if somewhat too vigorously, then none the less with almost unerring sureness. There was no question but that Raskolnikov had succeeded in compromising himself to the hilt just now, but so far he had not given Porfiry any *evidence*; as yet there was nothing positive. But did he have a proper grasp of the situation now? Was he not mistaken? What result had Porfiry been trying to achieve today? Had he really had something up his sleeve? What had it been? Had he really been waiting for something or not? What would their parting have been like today had it not been for the unexpected catastrophe brought about by Nikolai?

Porfiry had come very close to showing his entire hand; of course, he had taken a risk in doing so, but he had done it, and if he had really had something more up his sleeve, he would (so it seemed to Raskolnikov) have shown that, too. What had the 'surprise' been? Was it a joke of some kind? Had it meant anything, or not? Could there have been some piece of evidence concealed beneath it, something akin to a positive accusation? What about the man who had come to see him yesterday? Where had he vanished to? Where was he today? He was certain that if Porfiry really had anything on him, it had something to do with that man yesterday . . .

He was sitting on the sofa, his head slumped on his chest, leaning his elbows on his knees and covering his face with his hands. The nervous tremor still continued in every limb of his body. At last he got up, took his cap, thought for a moment and then walked towards the door.

He somehow felt that at least for the rest of today he could almost certainly consider himself out of danger. Suddenly his heart felt a sensation approaching joy: he wanted to go to Katerina Ivanovna's as soon as possible. He was too late for the funeral, of course, but he would still be in time for the *zakuski*, and there, in a moment or two, he would see Sonya.

He stopped, reflected, and a painful smile forced itself to his lips.

'Today! Today!' he said to himself. 'Yes, this very day! That's how it must be . . .'

At the instant he began to open the door it suddenly began to open of its own accord. He shivered and leapt back. The door was opening slowly and quietly, and suddenly a figure appeared – that of yesterday's man *from under the ground*.

The man paused in the doorway, looked at Raskolnikov without saying anything, and took a step into the room. He was exactly as he had been yesterday, the same figure, dressed in the same way, but in his gaze and features there was a marked alteration: now he looked somewhat down-in-the-mouth, and after a moment or two he exhaled a deep sigh. All that remained was for him to put his palm to his cheek and twist his head to one side, and he would have looked just like a woman.

'What do you want?' Raskolnikov asked, stiff with fright.

The man said nothing; then suddenly he bowed deeply to him, almost down to the floor. At any rate, he touched the floor with one finger of his right hand.

'What are you up to?' Raskolnikov shouted.

'I'm guilty,' the man articulated quietly.

'What of?'

'Evil thoughts.'

They both looked at each other.

'I got annoyed. When you arrived that time – maybe you were drunk or something – and tried to make the yardkeepers go down to the police station with you and asked questions about the blood, I got annoyed about them leaving you alone and thinking you were just drunk. I got so annoyed that I couldn't sleep. And since we remembered your address, we came here yesterday and asked for you . . .'

'Who did?' Raskolnikov interrupted, beginning to remember for an instant.

'I did. I mean, I insulted you.'

'So you live in that building?'

'In the same; why, I was standing with them in the gateway, or have you forgotten? We've had our workshop there from time immemorial. We're furriers, artisans, do our work at home . . . but what made me most annoyed of all was . . .'

And suddenly Raskolnikov had a clear memory of the entire scene that had taken place in the gateway two days earlier; he remembered that there had been, in addition to the yardkeepers, a few other men standing there; there had been women, too. He recalled one voice suggesting they take him straight to the police station. He could not remember what the man who had spoken had looked like, but he did have a memory of having said something to him in reply, of turning round towards him . . .

So this was what lay behind all yesterday's horrible events. Most horrible of all was the thought that he really had almost come to grief, had very nearly cooked his own goose because of a *trivial* occurrence like that. It meant that, apart from the story of his visit to the apartment as a prospective lodger and his asking about the blood, this man knew nothing worth telling. It meant that Porfiry, too, knew about nothing, nothing, apart from his *delirium*, had no other evidence than all this *psychology*, which was all *conjecture*, had nothing positive to go on. It meant that, unless more evidence turned up (and it must not turn up, must not, must not!) . . . there was nothing more they could do to him, was there? How could they convict him, even if they were to arrest him? It also meant that Porfiry had only now found out about the apartment, and had not known about it earlier.

'Was it you who told Porfiry today . . . that I went there?' he exclaimed, struck by a sudden idea.

'Which Porfiry would that be?'

'The state investigator.'

'Yes, I told him. The yardkeepers didn't go down to the station at the time, but I did.'

'Today?'

'I got there a minute before you. And I heard it all, the whole thing, the way he tortured you.'

'Where? How on earth? When?'

'I was sitting in there all the time, right behind that partition of his.'

'What? So you were the surprise, were you? But how could this possibly happen? For pity's sake!'

'When I saw,' the artisan began, 'that the yardkeepers weren't going to go down there just because I told them to, saying that it was too late, and that in any case he'd probably fly off the handle at them for not having come immediately, I got annoyed, I couldn't sleep, and I started finding a few things out. Well, I finished doing that yesterday, and today I went along there. The first time I went, he wasn't there. I went back about an hour later, but they wouldn't let me in to see him. The third time I went, I was allowed in. I began to give him all the information, just the way it happened, and he started leaping about the room and beating his breast: "What are you doing to me, you bandits?" he said. "If I'd known all this, I'd have had him brought here under armed escort!" Then he ran out, told someone to come and see him and stood talking to him in a corner, and then he came back to me again and started asking me questions and shouting at me. Read me a regular sermon, he did; I gave him all the information I had and told him you hadn't dared to make any reply to the things I said to you yesterday and that you hadn't recognized me. And he began running about again, beating his breast, flying off the handle and racing to and fro, and when they came in to tell him you were there, "All right," he said, "you go behind that partition, sit there and don't move, whatever you may hear," and he brought me a chair himself and locked me in; "I may question you, too," he said. But when Nikolai was brought in, as soon as you'd gone, he let me out and told me to go: "I'll require your presence again," he said, "and I'll want to ask you some more questions . . ."'

'Were you there when he questioned Nikolai?'

'After he'd let you go, he let me go as well, and then he started questioning Nikolai.'

The artisan paused and suddenly bowed again, touching the floor with one finger.

'Forgive me my slander and my hatred.'

'God will forgive you,' Raskolnikov answered, and as soon as he said this, the artisan bowed to him, not to the floor, this time, however, but only to the waist, turned slowly away and went out of the room. 'It's all conjecture, it's still all conjecture,' Raskolnikov kept saying to himself, and left the room in better spirits than ever.

'Now let's resume the struggle,' he said with a vicious, sarcastic smile, as he went down the stairs. The viciousness was aimed at himself; he remembered his 'faint-heartedness' with shame and contempt.

PART FIVE

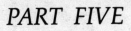

The morning that followed his fateful meeting with Dunya and Pulkheria Aleksandrovna had a sobering effect on Pyotr Petrovich. To his exceedingly great annoyance, he had little by little been compelled to accept as an unalterable *fait accompli* the very thing which only the previous day had seemed an event belonging almost to the realms of fantasy, and which, although it had taken place, still seemed impossible to him. All night a black serpent of wounded self-esteem had eaten at his heart. The first thing Pyotr Petrovich did upon getting out of bed was to take a look in the mirror. He was afraid he might have had an attack of jaundice overnight. From this point of view all was, however, still satisfactory for the moment and, having taken a look at his nobly virtuous, white and of late somewhat portly features, Pyotr Petrovich actually felt somewhat consoled for a moment, in the fullest conviction that he would be able to find himself a wife somewhere else, and perhaps a better one, too; but at once came to his senses and spat to one side with energy, bringing a silent but sarcastic smile to the face of his young friend and room-companion, Andrei Semyonovich Lebezyatnikov. Pyotr Petrovich noticed this smile, and he immediately put it down as a black mark against his young friend. He had been putting down a good many black marks against him recently. His rage grew doubly intense when he suddenly realized that he ought not to have told Andrei Semyonovich about the results of last night's meeting. That was the second mistake he had made yesterday, in the heat of the moment, under the sway of his own over-expansiveness and irritation . . . And then all throughout this morning, as if by special design, one disagreeable event had followed another. Even at the Senate a setback had awaited him in connection with the matter he was petitioning for there. He was particularly irritated by the owner of the apartment he had rented with a view to his impending marriage, and which had been brightened up at his own expense: this owner, a German craftsman who had made a lot of money, would not on any account agree to violate the terms of the contract that had just been signed and demanded the full forfeit prescribed therein, in spite of the fact that Pyotr Petrovich was returning the apartment to him in a state of virtual redecoration. Things were exactly the same in the furniture store, where the staff refused to give him back one single rouble of the deposit he had paid on the furniture that he had purchased, but had not yet been moved into the apartment. 'I'm not getting married just for the sake of the furniture!' Pyotr Petrovich said to himself, grinding his teeth, and at the same time a desperate hope fleeted through his mind once more: 'Is the whole situation really so irrevocably lost and hopeless? Can I really not have another try?' The thought of Dunya sent another seductive twinge to his heart. In agony he endured this moment and it was an undeniable fact that had it been possible for him to do away with Raskolnikov right there and then, by simply stating the desire, Pyotr Petrovich would have lost no time in stating it.

'I also went wrong in not giving them any money,' he thought as he returned in low spirits to Lebezyatnikov's closet of a room. 'Why was I such a Jew, the devil take it? It wasn't even a real saving! I planned to make their lives a misery and lead them to the point where they'd view me as their Providence, and see what they've gone and done! Confound it! No, if to cover this whole visit I'd given them, say, fifteen hundred roubles for the trousseau and the presents and all those various little boxes, toilet-cases, cornelians, dress-materials and all that frilly rubbish they could have bought at Knop's or the English Shop,* the whole thing would have been neater and . . . more secure! They wouldn't have been able to refuse me so easily then! They're the sort of people who would have thought it their duty to give back both presents and money in such a situation; and it would have been difficult for them to do that, it would have broken their hearts! And their consciences would have bothered them: "How can we drive away a man who's been so generous to us, and tactful about it, too?" Damn! I slipped up there!' And, beginning to grind his teeth again, Pyotr Petrovich admitted that he'd been a fool – but only to himself, of course.

Reaching this conclusion, he went home twice as irritated and enraged as he had been on setting out. The preparations for the funeral snacks in Katerina Ivanovna's room aroused a mild curiosity in him. The previous day he had heard a few things about this promised event; he even thought he remembered having been invited to it; but because of his own troubles nothing else had engaged his attention. Making haste to inquire about it from Mrs Lippewechsel, who was busying herself with the laying of the table in the absence of Katerina Ivanovna (who was at the cemetery), he had discovered that the event was to be a grand one, that nearly all the lodgers had been invited, even those whom the deceased had not known, that even Andrei Semyonovich Lebezyatnikov had been invited, in spite of his earlier quarrel with Katerina Ivanovna, and that to cap it all, he himself, Pyotr Petrovich, had not only been invited but was actually expected with the greatest of impatience, being very nearly the most important lodger and guest of them all. Amalia Ivanovna had also been invited as a guest of honour, in spite of all the earlier unpleasantness, and was now for that reason bustling about in her role of landlady, almost deriving pleasure from it; she was moreover dressed up to the nines, in mourning perhaps, but nevertheless in mourning that was new and made of silk, and taking pride in it. All this evidence and information had given Pyotr Petrovich a certain idea, and it was in a state of some reflection that he entered his room, or rather the room of Andrei Semyonovich Lebezyatnikov. The fact was, he had also discovered, that among those invited was Raskolnikov.

For some reason Andrei Semyonovich had been at home all that morning. To this gentleman Pyotr Petrovich had formed a strange, yet in part quite natural relation: Pyotr Petrovich despised and hated him beyond all measure, and had done so from the day he had moved in with him; yet at the same time he seemed a little apprehensive of him. On arriving in St Petersburg he had put up at his lodgings not merely out of stingy thrift – though that had probably been his main motive – there had been another motive, too. Back in the provinces he had heard of Andrei Semyonovich, his former pupil, as one of the foremost young progressives, who even played a significant role in certain curious and legendary circles. Pyotr Petrovich had been struck by this. For these powerful, omniscient circles with their contempt for everyone and accusations against all and sundry had long inspired Pyotr Petrovich with a peculiar, though wholly vague, sense of terror. It went without saying that, back there in the provinces, he had been unable to form even an approximate conception of *what it was all about*. He had heard, like everyone else, that particularly in St Petersburg there were to be found progressives, nihilists, public accusers, and so on, and so forth, but, like many people, he tended to exaggerate and distort the sense and significance of these labels to the point of the absurd. For several years now he had feared more than anything else being made the victim of a *public accusation*, and this was the principal reason for his constant, exaggerated sense of anxiety, especially when he had dreamt of moving his practice to St Petersburg. In this respect he was, as they say, 'affrit', in the way small children sometimes are. Some years earlier, in the provinces, when he had only just been beginning to organize his career, he had encountered two cases involving the merciless public accusation and exposure of rather important persons in local government to whom he had been attached and who had afforded him official protection. One of these cases had ended in a particularly scandalous manner for the man who had been accused, and the other had very nearly ended in outright disaster. This was why Pyotr Petrovich had made it his object to discover, as soon as he arrived in St Petersburg, 'what it was all about' and, if necessary, to get ahead of the game and curry favour with 'our younger generations'. In this matter he had placed his reliance upon Andrei Semyonovich and had, for his visit to Raskolnikov, for example, already learned how to roll off certain phrases parrot-fashion . . .

Of course, he had quickly perceived that Andrei Semyonovich was an extremely vulgar and simple-minded little man. But this in no way altered Pyotr Petrovich's opinion or made him feel any the more confident. Even had he gained the certainty that all progressives were the same little idiots, his anxiety would not have been laid to rest. If he were to be quite honest, none of these theories, ideas and systems (with which Andrei Semyonovich positively assailed him) was of the slightest interest to him. He had his own, personal motive. All he wished to do was to ascertain as quickly as possible *what was going on here*, whether *these people* had any power or not, and whether he personally had any reason to be afraid of them. If he were to undertake a certain project, would they accuse him or would they not? And if so, what would they accuse him of, and why particularly now? Nor was that all: might it not be possible for him to ingratiate himself with them and then pull a fast one on them, if they really were so powerful? Did he or did he not need to do this? Might he not, for example, further his career a little at their expense? In short, there were hundreds of questions waiting to be answered.

This Andrei Semyonovich was a wasted and scrofulous individual, small in stature, employed in some civil service department or other; he was blond to the point of strangeness, and sported a pair of mutton-chop whiskers of which he was very proud. On top of all this, he almost constantly suffered from an infection in both eyes. As for his heart, it was rather soft, but he spoke in a thoroughly self-confident and sometimes positively overbearing manner – which, when one compared it with his pathetic appearance, nearly always sounded ridiculous. At Amalia Ivanovna's he was, however, considered one of the more distinguished residents, that is to say, he did not indulge in drinking and always paid his rent on time. In spite of all these qualities, Andrei Semyonovich really was rather stupid. He adhered to the cause of progress and 'our younger generations' as a kind of enthusiastic pastime. He was one of that countless and multifarious legion of vulgar persons, sickly abortions and half-educated petty tyrants who like a flash attach themselves to those current ideas that are most fashionable in order, again like a flash, to vulgarize them, caricaturing the very cause they seek to serve, sometimes with great genuineness.

In spite of his being very good-natured, Lebezyatnikov was, however, also beginning to tire of his room-companion and former tutor Pyotr Petrovich. This state of affairs had come about mutually and seemingly by chance. Andrei Semyonovich might be rather simple-minded, but even so he had begun to realize that Pyotr Petrovich was deceiving him and viewed him with secret contempt, and that 'this fellow' 'was the wrong sort altogether'. He had attempted to explain to him the system of Fourier and the theory of Darwin, but Pyotr Petrovich had, especially of late, begun to listen with just a shade too much sarcasm, and had even, most recently, begun to respond with abuse. The truth of the matter was that his instincts had begun to tell him that Lebezyatnikov was not only a vulgar and stupid little man, but was also possibly a liar, and that he had no significant connections whatsoever even within his own circle, but had only heard a few things at third-hand; not only that: it was probable that he did not even have a decent grasp of his own 'propaganda', for he said far too many contradictory things, and what kind of a public accuser would he make? We should, incidentally, observe in passing that during the last week and a half Pyotr Petrovich had (particularly in the first few days) gladly accepted from Andrei Semyonovich some very strange items of praise; that is to say, he had made no objection and had remained silent when, for example, Andrei Semyonovich had ascribed to him a readiness to assist the founding of a new and soon-to-be-established 'commune'* somewhere in Meshchanskaya Street; or, for example, not to stand in Dunya's way if, right from the first month of their marriage, she decided to take a lover; or, not to have his children baptized, and so on and so forth – all of it along the same lines. Pyotr Petrovich, true to form, did not object to having such qualities ascribed to him and allowed himself to be praised even in this manner – so pleasant to him was any form of praise.

Pyotr Petrovich, who for certain reasons of his own had that morning cashed some five per cent bonds, was sitting at the table counting packets of credit and serial notes. Andrei Semyonovich, who practically never had any money, was pacing about the room and doing his best to eye all these packets indifferently and even with disdain. Pyotr Petrovich, for example, would never for one moment have believed that Andrei Semyonovich was really capable of viewing such a large amount of money with indifference; Andrei Semyonovich, for his part, reflected bitterly that Pyotr Petrovich really was in all probability capable of thinking about him in this light, and was possibly even glad of the chance to tease and tickle his young friend with these laid-out piles of banknotes, in order to remind him of his insignificance and the difference that existed between them.

On this occasion he found Pyotr Petrovich quite extraordinarily irritable and inattentive, in spite of the fact that he, Andrei Semyonovich, had just begun to expand on his favourite theme – the establishment of a new and special form of 'commune'. The brief retorts and observations that escaped from Pyotr Petrovich in the intervals between his clicking of the beads on the abacus were redolent of the most undisguised and intentionally discourteous mockery. But the 'humane' Andrei Semyonovich ascribed Pyotr Petrovich's mood to his break with Dunya of the evening before, and burned with eagerness to bring the conversation round to that subject as soon as possible: he had something progressive and propagandistic to say on that account, something that might console his estimable friend and would 'undoubtedly' be of benefit to his further development.

'What's this funeral banquet they're organizing at that . . . widow's place?' Pyotr Petrovich suddenly asked, interrupting Andrei Semyonovich just as he was coming to the most interesting part.

'You mean you don't know? But I spoke to you on that theme yesterday, developing my theory about all those rituals . . . And I mean, she invited you too, so I heard. You yourself spoke to her yesterday.'

'I certainly never expected that that destitute fool of a woman would spend all the money she got from that other fool, Raskolnikov, on a funeral banquet . . . I was positively astonished just now, as I walked past: such preparations are going on there – they even have wines! . . . People have been invited – the devil only knows what sort of an affair it's going to be!' Pyotr Petrovich continued, probing the matter and pursuing the conversation apparently with some ulterior motive. 'What? You say I've been invited, too?' he added suddenly, raising his head. 'When was that? I don't remember it. In any case, I shan't go. What business have I there? I talked with her only yesterday, in passing, about the possibility of her receiving a year's salary as the destitute widow of a civil servant, in the form of an extraordinary allowance. Perhaps that's why she's invited me, ha-ha!'

'I'm not going, either,' Lebezyatnikov said.

'I don't wonder! After dealing out a personal thrashing like that. I can imagine you might feel too ashamed, ha-ha-ha!'

'Who dealt out a thrashing? To whom?' Lebezyatnikov said, thrown suddenly into a flutter, and even blushing.

'Why, you did, to Katerina Ivanovna, about a month ago! I mean, I heard about it, sir, yesterday, sir . . . So that's the sort of thing those convictions of yours lead you to do! . . . And the woman question didn't fare very well, either, did it? Ha-ha-ha!'

'It's all nonsense and slander!' Lebezyatnikov said, flaring up; he was constantly afraid of anyone mentioning this episode. 'It wasn't like that at all! It was quite different . . . What you heard is wrong; it's just idle gossip! I was simply defending myself that time. It was she who attacked me, she used her fingernails . . . She pulled out the whole of one of my side-whiskers . . . I would hope that it is permissible for anyone to defend his or her person. Quite apart from the fact that I will not allow anyone to treat me with violence . . . on principle. Because it more or less amounts to despotism. What should I have done: just stood there and let her carry on? I merely pushed her away, that's all.'

'Ha-ha-ha!' Luzhin continued to mock, with angry malice.

'You're just picking on me because you're annoyed and angry . . . It's all nonsense, and it has not the slightest, not the slightest connection with the woman question. You've got hold of the wrong end of the stick; at first I thought that if it were accepted that a woman is a man's equal in everything, even in strength (which people are already claiming is so), then there ought to be equality in this case, too. Of course, I reasoned afterwards that such a question ought in essence never to arise, because fights ought never to arise, and because in the society of the future fighting will be unthinkable . . . and because, in the last analysis, it's a bit strange to look for equality in fighting. I'm not so stupid . . . though of course fighting does still exist . . . that's to say, it won't exist in the future, but for the present it does . . . oh, the devil confound it! You're getting me quite confused! That unpleasant incident has nothing to do with my not going to the funeral banquet. I'm staying away out of principle, so as to have no part in the vile superstition of funeral banquets, that's what! Actually, I might even have gone, just to laugh at the whole business . . . But there aren't going to be any priests there, worse luck. If there were to be priests, I'd most certainly have gone.'

'You mean you'd sit down to other people's hospitality and at the same time spit on it, and on those who've invited you? Is that what you're saying?'

'Oh, it has nothing to do with spitting; it's more a question of making a protest. I'd be doing it with the aim of being useful. I might indirectly assist the cause of education and propaganda. Everyone has a duty to spread education and propaganda, and the more bluntly the better, if you ask me. I might implant an idea, a seed . . . From that seed something real might grow. How would I be offending them? They might get offended initially, but then they would see for themselves that I'd done them a good turn. It's like what happened with Terebyeva (she's a member of our commune just now) recently, when she left her family and . . . gave herself to a fellow; they said she'd acted too crassly in writing to her mother, saying she didn't want to live among prejudice anymore and was entering into a citizens' marriage, and that she ought to have spared her parents' feelings, been more gentle with them in her letter. But in my opinion that's all rubbish, and being gentle would have been quite the wrong thing; on the contrary, on the contrary, in a case like that, too, what she needed to do was make a protest. Or look at Varents. She'd lived with her husband for seven years, but she abandoned her two children and severed her relations with her husband in one go, writing to him: "I have come to the realization that I cannot be happy with you. I will never forgive you for having kept me from the truth and concealing from me that there exists another ordering of society,

432

embodied in the commune. I have recently learned all this from a man of generous ideals, to whom I have given myself, and together with him I am settling down in a commune. I tell you this directly, as I consider it ignoble to deceive you. You may do as you think fit. Do not suppose you can make me come back, you are too late. I want to be happy." That's how to write a letter of that kind!'

'Is this the Terebyeva you told me the other day was in the middle of her third citizens' marriage?'

'It's only her second, if one takes a correct view of the matter! But even if it were her fourth, or her fifteenth, what does it matter? That's all just a lot of nonsense. I've never felt so sorry that my father and mother are dead as I do now. Sometimes I've even dreamt of how, if they'd been alive still, I'd have given them a thumping great protest to think about! I'd have let them down on purpose . . . And it wouldn't have just been a question of my being "self-supporting", confound it! I'd have shown them! I'd have surprised them, all right! It really is too bad I don't have anyone!'

'No one to surprise, eh? Ha-ha! Well, have it as you will,' Pyotr Petrovich said, interrupting. 'But tell me: I mean, you know the dead man's daughter, the skinny creature, don't you? Are they really true, the things people say about her?'

'What can I say? In my opinion, that is, in my own personal opinion, she's in the most normal situation a woman can find herself in. Why not? I mean to say – *distinguons*. In the way society is ordered at present, it is, of course, not quite a normal one, because it has been compelled upon her, but in the future order of society it will be completely normal, as it will be freely chosen. Why, even now she has been within her rights: she has suffered, and that has been her reserve, her capital, as it were, of which she has a perfect right to dispose as she pleases. Of course, in the society of the future those sort of reserves won't be necessary; but her role will be defined in a different sense, determined rationally and harmoniously. As for Sofya Semyonovna's personal actions, I regard them as an energetic and wholehearted protest against the arrangements of society, and I respect her profoundly for it; as I watch her, I even rejoice!'

'The way I heard it was that you were the person who got her kicked out of these rooms!'

Lebezyatnikov grew positively enraged.

'That's another piece of idle gossip!' he howled. 'That's not at all,

433

not at all the way it happened! I mean, it's simply not true! It was Katerina Ivanovna who made all that up, because she didn't understand! And I never tried to endear myself to Sofya Semyonovna! All I did was quite simply try to educate her, completely disinterestedly, trying to arouse her to protest . . . Protest was all I was after, and in any case Sofya Semyonovna couldn't have stayed in these rooms!'

'What did you do – ask her to go and live in that commune?'

'You're still trying to make a fool of me, and rather unsuccessfully, may I add. You don't understand. Roles like that don't exist in a commune. Communes are set up precisely in order to avoid there being roles like that. In a commune a role like that would entirely alter its current significance; things that seem stupid here become intelligent there, and what might seem unnatural here, the way things are currently, become entirely natural there. Everything depends on a man's surroundings and environment. Everything proceeds from the environment, and a man is nothing on his own. I'm still on good terms with Sofya Semyonovna even now, which may serve as proof to you that she has never considered me her enemy or molester. Yes! I am trying to coax her to join the commune now, but from quite, quite different motives! What do you find so amusing about it? We're trying to establish our own commune, which is of a special kind, and is based much more broadly than those that have existed previously. We have taken our convictions further. There is more that we reject! If Dobrolyubov were to come back from the grave, I'd have a few things to tell him. And if Belinsky were to, I'd roll right over him! But meanwhile I'm continuing to educate Sofya Semyonovna. What a noble, noble character she has!'

'Oh, so you're profiting from her noble character, too, eh? Ha-ha!'

'No, no! Absolutely not! On the contrary!'

'Aha, it's on the contrary, now, is it? Ha-ha-ha! Now you're talking!'

'But I assure you it's so! Why would I try to conceal it from you, be so good as to tell me? On the contrary, I even find it strange myself: she's so intensely, so timorously chaste and modest with me!'

'And you, of course, are trying to educate her . . . ha-ha! Trying to demonstrate to her that all that modesty is nonsense?'

'Absolutely not! Absolutely not! Oh, what a crass, what a downright stupid – if you will forgive me – conception you have of the word "education"! You d-don't understand! Oh, Lord, how . . . unready you are! We are seeking the liberation of woman, yet you can only

434

think of one thing . . . Leaving aside entirely the question of chastity and female modesty as things useless in themselves and even based on downright prejudice, I am perfectly, perfectly willing to tolerate her chaste behaviour with me, because it expresses the whole of her freedom, the whole of her right! Naturally, if she were to say to me: "I want to possess you," I would consider myself very fortunate, for I fancy the girl quite a lot; but for the present, for the present, at least, it goes without saying that no one has treated her more courteously and considerately, or with more respect for her dignity, than I . . . I wait and hope – that is all!'

'What you ought to do is give her some sort of present. I'll wager you've never even thought of doing that.'

'I told you, you d-don't understand! It's true that that's the sort of position she's in, but – that's another matter! Quite another matter! You simply have contempt for her. In apprehending a phenomenon that you mistakenly consider to be worthy of contempt, you deny a human creature a humane response. You don't know what a character she has! The only thing that vexes me is that she seems to have stopped reading altogether of late, and doesn't borrow books from me any more. She used to, you know. The other thing that's a pity is that for all her energy and her determination to register a protest – which she's demonstrated to me once – she still doesn't seem to have very much self-dependence, or independence, if you know what I mean, she's rather short on the kind of negation that's required if one is to throw off certain prejudices and . . . stupidities. But even in spite of that, she has an excellent grasp of certain questions. She's developed a marvellous grasp, for example, of the question concerning the kissing of hands,* that's to say, that a man insults a woman and doesn't treat her as an equal if he kisses her hand. That matter was the subject of debate among us, and I told her about it immediately. She was also very interested when I described to her the workers' cooperatives in France. Just now I'm telling her about the question concerning the free access to rooms* in the society of the future.'

'And what might that be?'

'We had a debate recently on the question of whether one member of the commune has a right to walk into the room of another member, whether it's a man or a woman, at any time of the day or night . . . well, and it was decided that they do . . .'

'Yes, and at the very moment when he or she is engaged in some pressing personal necessity, ha-ha!'

At this, Andrei Semyonovich really lost his temper.

'You're still going on about that! That's all you want to talk about, those damned "necessities"!' he shouted with hatred. 'Confound it, I shall never forgive myself for having mentioned those damned necessities, in the course of explaining the system to you, before you were ready for it. The devil take it! It's invariably a stumbling-block for your sort of person – and what's even worse, you make it into the subject of jokes before you have any idea of what it's all about. I mean, it's as though you were proud of it, or something! Confound it! I've said time and time again that the only way that that question can be explained to newcomers is right at the end, when they've been won over to the system, when they've completed their education and are on the right path. And what, tell me please, is so shameful and contemptible, even in cesspools? I'd be the first to go and clean out any cesspools you'd care to name! It doesn't even involve any self-sacrifice! It's simply work, a noble activity that is socially useful and is far and away superior to the activity of any Raphael or Pushkin,* for the simple reason that it's more useful!'

'And more noble, more noble – ha-ha-ha!'

'What do you mean, more noble? I don't understand expressions like that when they're used to describe human activity. "More noble", "more magnanimous" – all that's just absurd rubbish, old prejudice-ridden words which I reject! All that is *useful* to mankind is noble! That is the only word I understand: *useful*! Snigger all you like, but it is so!'

Pyotr Petrovich had not laughed so much for a long time. By now he had finished counting the money and had stuffed it away. For some reason, however, a portion of it remained on the table. This 'cesspool question' had, all its vulgarity notwithstanding, served on a number of occasions now as the pretext for strife and dissension between Pyotr Petrovich and his young friend. What was so stupid about the whole affair was that Andrei Semyonovich really was angry. As for Luzhin, he found it a convenient outlet for his frustration, and at the present moment felt a particular desire to make Lebezyatnikov angry.

'You're simply aggressive and in a bad temper because of the rebuff you received yesterday,' Lebezyatnikov burst out at last. Somehow, in spite of all his 'independence' and 'protest', he did not dare to oppose Pyotr Petrovich and in general treated him with a kind of habitual deference that was a hangover from former years.

'Look, I know what you can tell me,' Pyotr Petrovich said, interrupting with haughty irritation. 'Can you do this for me . . . or rather, tell me, sir: are you really on sufficiently intimate terms with this young female person that you could ask her, this very moment, to come in here, into this room? I think they've all come back from the cemetery, now . . . I can hear feet walking about . . . I need to see her . . . the young person.'

'But why do *you* need to see her?'

'Oh, because I do, sir, because I do. Today or tomorrow I shall be leaving here, and so I should like to tell her . . . But actually, you may as well stay here during our meeting. It'll probably be better that way. Otherwise God knows what you may get into your head.'

'I won't get anything into my head . . . I was merely asking, that's all, and if you have some business to discuss with her, there's nothing easier than to ask her to come in. I'll go along there now. And you may be assured that I won't interfere.'

True enough, some five minutes later Lebezyatnikov returned with Sonya. She came in looking thoroughly astonished and, as usual, abashed. She was always abashed on such occasions, and was very frightened of new people and new acquaintances, had been as a child, and was even more so now . . . Pyotr Petrovich greeted her 'kindly and politely', though with a slight touch of affable familiarity, suitable, in Pyotr Petrovich's view, to a man as respected and of such elevated social standing as himself, when talking to a female person as youthful and in a certain sense *interesting* as she. He hastened to 'put her at her ease' and asked her to sit down at the table opposite him. Sonya sat down and looked around – at Lebezyatnikov, at the money that was lying on the table, and then suddenly back at Pyotr Petrovich again, and after that she did not take her eyes off him, but kept staring at him as though she were riveted to him. Lebezyatnikov made off towards the door. Pyotr Petrovich stood up, motioned to Sonya to remain seated, and stopped Lebezyatnikov in the doorway.

'Is that Raskolnikov fellow there? Has he come too?' he asked him in a whisper.

'Raskolnikov? Yes. What of it? Yes, he's there . . . He's only just walked in, I saw him . . . What about it?'

'Well, in that case I must make a special plea to you to remain here with us, and not leave me alone with this . . . young lady. It's a trifling matter, but God knows what conclusions people may jump to. I don't want Raskolnikov to tell them about it *in there* . . . Do you understand what I'm talking about?'

'Ah, I've got it, I've got it! Lebezyatnikov said, suddenly seeing the point. 'Yes, you have a right . . . I must say that in my own personal opinion I think you're getting unduly worried, but . . . even so, you do have a right. Very well, I shall stay. I'll stand by the window here and won't interfere. In my opinion, you have a right . . .'

Pyotr Petrovich returned to the sofa, sat down opposite Sonya, gave her a close look and then suddenly assumed an air of extreme decorousness, which was even slightly stern, as if to say: 'Now don't go getting any ideas, madam.' Sonya's embarrassment was by now complete.

'In the first place, Sofya Semyonovna, you must tender my excuses to your much-esteemed mother . . . Please correct me if I am wrong – Katerina Ivanovna is your stepmother, isn't she?' Pyotr Petrovich began, very decorously, but kindly enough for all that. It was plain that his intentions were most cordial.

'That's right sir, yes, sir; she's my stepmother, sir,' Sonya replied quickly and fearfully.

'Well then, please tell her I am sorry that because of circumstances beyond my control I find myself unable to attend the *blinis* . . . the funeral banquet, that is to say, at your lodgings, in spite of your mother's kind invitation.'

'Yes, sir; I'll tell her, sir.' And Sonya hurriedly leapt up from her chair.

'That isn't all, my dear – there is *more*,' Pyotr Petrovich said, stopping her and smiling at her lack of sophistication and ignorance of social customs. 'Dear Sofya Semyonovna, you little know me if you suppose that I would trouble a young lady such as yourself in person and ask you to come and see me about such an insignificant matter which concerns myself alone. No, I have another reason for wishing to see you.'

Sonya hurriedly sat down. The grey-and-rainbow-coloured bank-notes, which had still not been cleared from the table, caught her attention again fleetingly, but she quickly averted her gaze from them and raised it to Pyotr Petrovich: she suddenly felt it was terribly improper for *her* in particular to look at someone else's money. She fixed her eyes on Pyotr Petrovich's gold lorgnette which he was holding in his left hand and at the large, massive, extremely handsome ring with its yellow stone that adorned the middle finger of that hand – but then suddenly she averted her gaze from it, too, and, no longer knowing where to look, ended up staring straight into Pyotr Petrovich's eyes once more. After a pause that was even more decorous than his previous one, Pyotr Petrovich said:

'I had occasion yesterday to exchange a few words with Katerina Ivanovna, poor lady. Those few words were enough to apprise me of the fact that the condition she currently finds herself in is one of – unnaturalness, if I may thus express it . . .'

'Yes, sir . . . one of unnaturalness, sir,' Sonya hurried to agree.

'Or, to put it more simply and straightforwardly – one of illness.'

'Yes, sir, more simply and straightforw . . . yes, sir, she's ill.'

'Quite so. And so it is that from a sense of humanity, and, and, and, how shall I put it, compassion, I should like to do something to help her, in view of the inevitably unfortunate lot that awaits her. It would appear that the whole of this most destitute family now depends on you alone.'

'There's something I want to ask,' Sonya said, standing up all of a sudden. 'What did you say to her yesterday about the chance of her receiving a pension? Because yesterday she told me that you'd undertaken to get her one. Is that true, sir?'

'Certainly not, my dear. It's actually rather a silly thing for her to have said. All I did was hint at the possibility of her receiving some temporary assistance as the widow of a government employee deceased while employed in the service – as long as she has someone to pull the right strings for her – but it seems that your deceased parent hadn't actually been doing any work at all of late. In short, though there might be some hope, it could only be of a most ephemeral nature, as in essence there is no entitlement to assistance in this case, and even possibly the reverse . . . Yet there she was, already thinking about a pension, ha-ha-ha! The lady has some spirit!'

'Yes, sir, she has been thinking about a pension . . . Because she's kind-hearted and easily taken in, and her kind-heartedness makes her believe all the things people tell her, and . . . and . . . and . . . that's just the way she thinks . . . Yes, sir . . . You must forgive her, sir,' Sonya said, and again got up in order to go.

'But you haven't let me finish what I was about to say, my dear.'

'No, sir, I haven't,' Sonya muttered.

'Then please sit down.'

Sonya became terribly confused and sat down again for a third time.

'In view of the position she is in, with unfortunate minors to look after, I should like – as I have already said – to do whatever I can, within the limit of my powers, in order to help her; but I must stress that it can only be within the limit of my powers, my dear – no more than that. It might, for example, be possible to organize a subscription fund for her, or, as it were, a lottery . . . or something of that nature – the sort of thing that is usually done by relatives or at any rate by those who wish to help. It was this that I was anxious to tell you. That sort of thing would be perfectly possible, my dear.'

'Yes, sir, very well, sir . . . God will thank you for this, sir . . .' Sonya babbled, staring fixedly at Pyotr Petrovich.

'Possible, but . . . We shall see about it later . . . Though we might make a start on it this very day. Let us meet this evening, my dear, talk it over and lay the groundwork, as it were. Come and see me at about seven. Andrei Semyonovich, I hope, will also join us . . . But . . . there is one thing I must make thoroughly clear in advance. It was in this connection that I troubled you, Sofya Semyonovna, in asking you to come here in person. You see, my dear, it is my opinion that it would be foolish and indeed dangerous to put money straight into Katerina Ivanovna's hands; as proof of this I would cite the funeral banquet she is holding today. Though she does not know where her next crust of bread is coming from, and . . . and she and her children do not even have proper shoes, or anything, she has today purchased Jamaican rum and even, it would appear, Madeira, and, and, and *coffee*! I saw it as I was passing. Tomorrow the whole burden will descend upon your shoulders again, all the way to the last crust of bread; that is absurd, my dear. And so it is my personal view that the subscription fund must be organized in such a manner that the unfortunate widow should, as it were, know nothing about the money, and that you should, perhaps, be the only person who does. Do you think that makes sense?'

'I don't know, sir. She's only doing this today, sir . . . it's once in her lifetime . . . she wanted so terribly to remember her husband, do something in his honour, as a kind of memorial . . . and she's very intelligent, sir. But then again, it's as you wish, sir, and I will be very, very, very grateful to you, sir . . . they all will be . . . and God will be, too, and the orphans, sir . . .'

Sonya left her sentence unfinished and burst into tears.

'Yes, my dear. Well, think about it; and now I should be glad if you would accept, in the interests of your mother, an initial sum from me personally – it is the best that I can do. I must earnestly request that my name not be mentioned in connection with any of this. Here you are, my dear – saddled as I am myself with worries, this is all that I can . . .'

And Pyotr Petrovich carefully unfolded a ten-rouble banknote and handed it to Sonya. Sonya took it, blushed scarlet, leapt to her feet, muttered something and quickly said goodbye. Pyotr Petrovich solemnly accompanied her to the door. At last she darted out of the room in a state of utter agitation and exhaustion, and returned to Katerina Ivanovna totally confused.

Throughout the whole of this scene Andrei Semyonovich had either been standing by the window or wandering about the room, anxious not to interrupt the conversation; but when Sonya had left, he suddenly went up to Pyotr Petrovich and held out his hand to him in · solemn greeting.

'I heard and *saw* it all,' he said, laying particular emphasis on the latter word. 'That was nobly – I mean to say, humanely – done. You were trying to avoid any scenes of gratitude, I could see that! And though I must confess to you that my principles forbid me to condone private charity, as not only does it fail radically to root out evil, but actually fuels it even more, even so I cannot help admitting that I viewed what you did with satisfaction – yes, yes, it appeals to me.'

'Oh, don't talk such nonsense!' Pyotr Petrovich muttered in some agitation, giving Lebezyatnikov a strange look.

'It isn't nonsense! A man who has been insulted and brought to the point of vexation as you were by yesterday's events, yet is still able to think of the misfortune of others – such a man, sir . . . even though by his actions he is committing an error against society – is none the less . . . worthy of respect! I must say I didn't expect it of you, Pyotr Petrovich, particularly in view of your way of seeing the world – oh, how your way of seeing the world stands in your path! How upset you are, for instance, by this rebuff you received yesterday,' exclaimed the soft-hearted Andrei Semyonovich, again experiencing a wave of intense sympathy for Pyotr Petrovich. 'Yet what use, what use would that marriage, that *legal* marriage have been to you, my good, my kind Pyotr Petrovich? What use would that marital *legality* have been to you? Well, chastise me if you wish, but I am glad, glad that it has not come about, and that you are free, that you are not yet lost to mankind, glad . . . There: I have told you my opinion!'

'Because sir, I do not wish to wear horns and raise other men's children in one of those citizens' marriages of yours – that is the reason why legal marriage is necessary to me,' Luzhin said, for want of a better reply. There was evidently something on his mind, something that was occupying all his attention.

'Children? You're on to the subject of children, are you?' Andrei Semyonovich said with a start, like a warhorse hearing the martial trumpet. 'The question of children is a social one, and of the first importance, I agree: but it is a question that will be resolved differently in future. There are some who reject children altogether, as they do all that suggests the family. We shall speak of children later, but for the present, let us get to grips with the horns! I will confess to you that I have a special weakness for this point. "Horns" – that loathsome, hussar-barrack-room, "Pushkinian" expression* – will be quite unthinkable in the dictionary of the future. For what are horns? Oh, what a delusion! What horns? Why are they called horns? Such nonsense! They certainly won't exist in any citizens' marriage! Horns are simply the natural consequence of legal marriage, a corrective to it, as it were, a protest against it, so that in that sense at least they are in no way degrading . . . And if I should ever – supposing the absurd to be possible – enter into a legal marriage, I would be positively glad of your damnable horns; then to my wife I would say: "My dear, until now I have merely loved you, but now I respect you, because you have succeeded in making a protest!"* You think that's funny, do you? That's because you're not strong enough to tear yourself away from your prejudices! The devil take it, of course I understand how unpleasant it can be when people play false in legal marriage: but I mean, that is simply the ignoble consequence of an ignoble institution, in which both partners are degraded. But when, on the other hand, horns are worn openly, as they are in a citizens' marriage, then they no longer exist, they are unthinkable and actually lose the appellation of horns altogether. On the contrary, your wife will merely be demonstrating to you how much she respects you, considering you incapable of opposing her happiness and so educated that you won't revenge yourself on her for taking a new husband. The devil take it, I sometimes imagine that if I were to be given away in marriage . . . Confound it! I mean, if I were to enter upon marriage (whether a legal or a citizens' one, it would make no difference), I think I myself would get my wife a lover if she took too long about finding one. "My dear," I'd say to her, "I love you, but in addition to that I want you to respect me – there!" Do you see, do you see what I'm saying?'

Pyotr Petrovich kept laughing, 'ha-ha', to himself as he listened, but without any special enthusiasm. Indeed, he was hardly listening to any of it. He really was thinking about something else, and even Lebezyatnikov finally noticed this. Pyotr Petrovich was in an undeniable state of agitation, rubbing his hands, thinking and pondering. Later on, Andrei Semyonovich recalled all this and succeeded in putting two and two together . . .

II

It would be hard to say what precisely the reasons were that had put the idea of this senseless funeral banquet into Katerina Ivanovna's muddled head. She really had squandered very nearly ten of the twenty or so roubles Raskolnikov had given her for the expenses of Marmeladov's funeral. It might have been that Katerina Ivanovna considered herself under an obligation to her dead husband to honour his memory 'in proper fashion', so that all the residents, and Amalia Ivanovna in particular, should know that he had been 'no worse than they were, and possibly even rather better', and that none of them was entitled to 'behave in that stuck-up manner' in his presence. It was possible that the decisive factor was that singular 'pride of the poor', in consequence of which, where certain social rituals are concerned, rituals obligatory and unavoidable for each and every participant in our mode of life, many poor people strain themselves to their last resources and spend every last copeck they have saved in order to be 'no worse than others' and in order that those others should not 'look down their noses' at them. It was highly probable,

443

too, that Katerina Ivanovna wished, precisely on this occasion, precisely at the moment when she appeared to have been abandoned by everyone in the whole world, to demonstrate to all those 'nasty, worthless tenants' that not only did she 'know how to do things properly and entertain in style', but that she had not been prepared by her upbringing for such a lot in life, having been reared 'in the noble, one might even say aristocratic, home of a colonel', and had certainly not been intended to sweep her own floor and wash the rags of her children at nights. These paroxysms of pride and vanity sometimes visit the very poorest and downtrodden people, among whom they occasionally acquire the character of an irritable, overwhelming need. But Katerina Ivanovna was not one of the downtrodden: while her circumstances might destroy her entirely, the prospect of her being mentally *trodden on*, that is to say of her being intimidated and deprived of her own will, was not in view. Then again, Sonya had with good reason said of her that her mind was growing confused. True, it could not yet have been maintained that this was so in any conclusive or definitive sense, but the fact remained that recently, throughout the whole of the past year, her poor head had been through such a great deal that some harm had been inevitable. As medical men have observed, the serious onset of consumption also tends to cause a derangement of the mental faculties.

Wines, in the plural, and of different varieties, there were none; neither was there any *madeira*. That had been an exaggeration. There was, however, drink. There were vodka, rum and Lisbon wine, all of the most inferior quality, but present in ample quantities. As for comestibles, there were, besides the traditional *kut'ya*,* some three or four dishes (one of which, incidentally, was *blinis*), all from Amalia Ivanovna's kitchen, and in addition two samovars had been set up for the tea and punch that was to follow the meal. Katerina Ivanovna herself had seen to the purchase of the provisions with the help of a wretched little Pole who lived at Mrs Lippewechsel's, heaven only knew for what reason, and who had immediately turned himself into Katerina Ivanovna's errand boy, having spent the whole of the previous day and the whole of that morning rushing about frantically at top speed, apparently making a particular effort to render this latter circumstance as noticeable as he could. Every moment or so he had come running to Katerina Ivanovna, had even gone out to look for her in the Gostiny Dvor, kept calling her *pani chorazyna*,* and ended by making her sick and tired of him, even though at first she had said that without this 'obliging and generous' man she would have been totally lost. It was typical of Katerina Ivanovna that she would hurry to deck out anyone and everyone in the brightest and most favourable colours, to praise them in such terms that would make people sometimes feel positively embarrassed, to ascribe to their credit various things that had never actually taken place, to believe quite sincerely and candidly that they had and then suddenly, overnight, grow disillusioned with them, snubbing, abusing and driving away with violent shoves the very person she had, only a few hours ago, quite literally worshipped. She was by nature cheerful, peaceable and fond of laughter, but her constant misfortunes and reverses had made her desire and demand so *fiercely* that everyone should live in peace and happiness and *not dare* to live in any other way that the very slightest dissonance in her life, the very slightest rebuff, would immediately send her into a state bordering upon frenzy, and in a single flash, after the most resplendent hopes and fantasies, she would begin to curse fate, raging at anything that was on hand and beating her head against the wall. Amalia Ivanovna had also suddenly acquired extraordinary importance in Katerina Ivanovna's eyes and had received from her an extraordinary degree of respect, probably for the sole reason that this funeral banquet was being held and that Amalia Ivanovna had decided to take a personal hand in all the preparations for it: she had undertaken to lay the table, to provide the tablecloth and napkins, the crockery and so on and to cook the food in her own kitchen. Katerina Ivanovna had left her in charge of everything and had gone off to the cemetery. And indeed, it had all been magnificently prepared: the table had actually been properly laid for once, and although all the crockery and cutlery, the forks, knives, glasses and cups, were a mixed assembly, of various styles and calibres, belonging to different tenants, everything was in place by the appointed hour, and Amalia Ivanovna, feeling that she had performed her task with distinction, greeted the returning guests with a certain pride, grandly attired in a black dress and a cap adorned with new mourning ribbons. For some reason this pride, though merited, did not appeal to Katerina Ivanovna: 'One might think the table might never have been laid were it not for Amalia Ivanovna!' She was likewise unimpressed by the cap with its new ribbons: for all she knew, this stupid German woman was simply proud of being the

445

landlady and of having consented out of charity to help her poor tenants. Out of charity! Thank you very much! In the home of Katerina Ivanovna's father, who had been a colonel and very nearly the governor of a province, the table had on occasion been laid for forty people, 'and Amalia Ivanovna, or, more correctly, Lyudvigovna, would not even have been allowed in the kitchen . . .' All the same, Katerina Ivanovna decided not to make her feelings known prematurely, though in her heart she had determined that Amalia Ivanovna must be taken down a peg or two and put in her proper place that very day, or otherwise heaven only knew what ideas she might get, and for the meantime simply treated her with coldness. Another unpleasant circumstance was also contributing to Katerina Ivanovna's irritation: of the tenants who had been invited to the funeral banquet, hardly any had arrived, with the exception of the little Pole, who had even managed to look in at the cemetery as well; the tenants who did show up for the actual snacks themselves were all the seediest and poorest ones, many of them not even sober, quite simply the riff-raff. All the more senior and respectable ones were absent, as if in accordance with some earlier plan. Pyotr Petrovich Luzhin, for example, who might have been said to be the most respectable of all the tenants, did not put in an appearance, and yet only the previous evening Katerina Ivanovna had told the whole wide world – in other words, Amalia Ivanovna, Polya, Sonya and the little Pole – that this was a most noble and magnanimous man, endowed with a vast range of connections and a private fortune, her first husband's former friend, who had been received in her father's house and who had promised to exercise every means possible to get her a sizeable pension. We should observe here that in boasting of anyone's connections and private fortune Katerina Ivanovna did so without any selfish aims or personal calculation whatsoever, from pure disinterest, out of the fullness of her heart, as it were, and the sheer satisfaction of giving praise and increasing even further the value of its object. In addition to Luzhin and doubtless 'following his example', 'that nasty villain Lebezyatnikov' had not appeared, either. Who did he think he was? He had only been invited out of charity, and because he lived in the same room as Pyotr Petrovich and was his friend, and so 'it would have been embarrassing not to invite him'. There was also a certain fine lady and her 'overripe spinster' of a daughter, who, although they had been living only for a couple of weeks in Amalia

Ivanovna's rented rooms, had already made several complaints about the noise and shouting that had come from the Marmeladovs' room, especially when the deceased had returned home drunk, complaints of which Katerina Ivanovna had naturally become aware from the lips of Amalia Ivanovna when the latter in the course of a row with her had threatened to evict the entire family, shouting at the top of her voice that they were disturbing 'respectable tenants', 'whose feet they were not worth'. Katerina Ivanovna had now made a special point of inviting this lady and her daughter, 'whose feet they were not worth', particularly since up until now, whenever they had met one another by chance, the lady had haughtily turned away – so now she would learn that here 'we think and feel on a rather higher level, and harbour no malice', and they would see that Katerina Ivanovna had not been accustomed to living in such circumstances. She had been planning to explain this to them at the meal-table, along with the fact of her deceased father's gubernatorial status, observing in passing as she did so that there was really no need for them to turn away upon meeting her, and that this was extremely stupid. Neither had the fat lieutenant-colonel (who was really a retired second-grade captain) shown up, but it turned out that he had been 'legless' since the morning of the previous day. In short, the only guests who put in an appearance were: the little Pole, a shabby office clerk with no conversation, dressed in a stained tail-coat, his face covered in blackheads, who gave off a repulsive smell; then there was a little, deaf old man who was almost completely blind, had once worked in a postal station somewhere and had for some obscure reason been living at Amalia Ivanovna's for longer than anyone could remember. A certain drunken retired army lieutenant, really just a supply clerk, also arrived; he had the loudest and most indecent laugh, and – 'can you imagine it?' – was not even wearing a waistcoat! There was one man who sat straight down at the table without even saying hallo to Katerina Ivanovna, and finally there was a certain individual who, for lack of any other clothing, arrived in his dressing-gown, but this was considered so improper that by dint of vigorous efforts Amalia Ivanovna and the little Pole managed to show him the door. The little Pole, however, had brought two other little Poles along with him, who had never lived at Amalia Ivanovna's and whom no one had ever seen at the rented rooms before. All of this irritated Katerina Ivanovna in the extreme. For whom had all these preparations been made, after all? In order to save space, the children had not been seated at the table, which as it was took up practically the whole room, but had had places laid for them on the travelling-box in the rear corner, the two younger ones being posted on the bench, while Polya, as eldest, had the task of keeping an eye on them, giving them their food and wiping their little noses 'like well-brought-up children'. In short, Katerina Ivanovna found herself with no alternative but to receive her guests with a redoubled grandness of manner and a positive *hauteur*. Of some of them she took a particularly dim view, eyeing them severely and requesting them to sit down at table with an air of lofty superiority. For some reason, convinced that Amalia Ivanovna must be to blame for all the non-arrivals, she suddenly began to address her in an extremely offhand way, which Amalia Ivanovna noticed at once and which offended her vanity no end. A beginning of this kind did not augur a felicitous conclusion. At last they were seated.

Raskolnikov had entered almost at the very moment of their return from the cemetery. Katerina Ivanovna had been delighted to see him, in the first instance because he was the only 'educated guest' of those she had invited and, as everyone knew, was 'getting ready for a professorship at St Petersburg University', and in the second instance because he had immediately and politely apologized to her for not having been able to attend the funeral, in spite of his earnest wish to do so. She had fairly pounced on him, had made him sit on her left at table (Amalia Ivanovna was seated on her right) and, in spite of her constant fussing and fretting about the food being properly passed round so that everyone got some of everything, in spite of her tormenting cough, which every few moments interrupted her speech and deprived her of air, and seemed to have become much worse during these past few days, she kept turning constantly to Raskolnikov and in a semi-whisper pouring out to him all her pent-up feelings and all her justified indignation about the disastrous funeral banquet; at the same time her indignation alternated with the most cheerful, the most unrestrained laughter directed at her assembled guests, and particularly at the landlady herself.

'It's that old cuckoo who is to blame for it all. You know who I mean; her, her!' and Katerina Ivanovna nodded his attention towards the landlady. 'Look at her: making those big eyes like that, she knows we're talking about her, but she can't understand what we're saying, and her eyes are popping out of her head. Phoo, the old owl, ha-ha-ha! . . . Cahuh-cahuh-cahuh! And what's she trying to prove with that cap? Have you noticed that she wants everyone to think she's making me a concession and doing me a favour by attending? I asked her, since she's a woman of social standing, to invite some of the better sort of people, and particularly those who knew my dead husband, and look who she's brought with her! Clowns! Chimney-sweeps! Look at that one with dirt all over his face: he's a walking nonentity! And those wretched little Poles! . . . ha-ha-ha! Cahuh-cahuh-cahuh! No one, no one has ever seen them here before, not even I have ever seen them; so why have they come, I ask you? There they sit, neatly in a row. *Panie, hej*!!' she suddenly shouted to one of them. 'Have you had a *blini*? Have some more! Drink the beer, the beer! Won't you have some vodka? Look: he's leapt to his feet, he's bowing, look, look: they must be starving, the poor wretches! Never mind, let them eat. At least they don't make any noise, although . . . although I must say I fear for the landlady's silver spoons! Amalia Ivanovna!' she said to her suddenly, almost out loud. 'If anyone steals your spoons I must warn you in advance that I can't be held responsible for them! Ha-ha-ha!' she laughed, turning back to Raskolnikov again suddenly, nodding his attention towards the landlady again and delighting in her own mischievous behaviour. 'She didn't understand, she didn't understand that time, either! She's sitting there with her mouth open, look: she's an owl, a real old owl, a brown owl wearing new ribbons, ha-ha-ha!'

At that point her laughter again turned into an unbearable coughing, which went on for all of five minutes. Some blood was left on her handkerchief, and drops of sweat stood out on her forehead. She showed the blood to Raskolnikov without saying anything and, as soon as she had recovered her breath, immediately whispered to him again in extreme animation, with a red spot on each cheek:

'You see, I gave her the most subtle task, one might say, of inviting that lady and her daughter – you know who I'm talking about, don't you? Well, she needed to do it in the most delicate manner possible, to employ all her tact and skill, but she went about it in such a way that that country goosecap, that overweening frump, that worthless provincial slattern, just because she's the widow of some major or other and has come to plead for a pension and wear out her skirt-hems on the doorsteps of the government offices, because at fifty-five she dyes her hair with antimony and uses powder and rouge (it's well-known!) . . . that even a frump like that did not see fit to come – not only that, but she didn't even send her excuses for not attending, as the most ordinary rules of politeness demand! Also, I simply can't understand why Pyotr Petrovich hasn't come, either! And where's Sonya? Where's she got to? Ah, here she is at last! Well, Sonya, where have you been? I find it strange that you should be late even for your father's funeral. Rodion Romanovich, please let her in at your side. There's a place for you, Sonya . . . have some of whatever you like. Have some of the jellied meat, it's the best thing there is on the table. They'll be bringing some more *blinis* in a minute. Have the children had some? Polya, have you something of everything over there? Cahuh-cahuh-cahuh! Well, that's all right, then. Now be a good girl, Lyonya, and Kolya, don't kick your legs; sit the way a well-brought-up boy ought to sit. What's that, Sonya?'

Sonya had at once launched into a hurried delivery of Pyotr Petrovich's excuses, trying to speak her words out loud, so that everyone could hear, and using the most carefully chosen and deferential expressions which she had specially made up on Pyotr Petrovich's behalf, with certain adornments of her own. She added that Pyotr Petrovich had particularly asked her to say that as soon as it was possible for him to come and see her he would do so in order to discuss certain business matters *confidentially*, and come to an agreement about what might be arranged for the future, and so on, and so forth.

Sonya knew that this would appease and quieten Katerina Ivanovna, flatter her vanity and, most importantly, satisfy her pride. She sat down beside Raskolnikov, hastily greeted him, and gave him an inquisitive look in passing. During all the time that remained, however, she seemed to avoid either looking at him or talking to him. Her mind seemed to be elsewhere, though this did not prevent her from looking Katerina Ivanovna in the face in order to play along with her wishes. Neither she nor Katerina Ivanovna were dressed in mourning, since they had no such garments; Sonya was wearing some dark brown affair, and Katerina Ivanovna had on her only dress, a dark cotton one with stripes. The tidings from Pyotr Petrovich had the desired effect. Having listened to Sonya gravely, Katerina Ivanovna inquired with continued gravity after Pyotr Petrovich's health.

Immediately after that, and almost out loud, she *whispered* to Raskolnikov that it really would have been a little strange for a man as respected and of such social standing as Pyotr Petrovich to fall in with such 'unusual company', in spite of all his devotion to her family and his earlier friendship with her father.

'That is why I am particularly grateful to you, Rodion Romanovich, for not having shunned my hospitality, even in surroundings such as these,' she added, almost so everyone could hear. 'However, I am certain that it was only your special friendship with my poor deceased husband that prompted you to keep your word.'

Then once more she surveyed her guests proudly and with dignity, and suddenly she inquired of the little deaf old man with particular solicitude whether he would like some more of the main course and whether he had been served with the Lisbon wine? The little old man made no reply, and it took him a long time to understand what the question was, even though his neighbours began to shake him out of his slumbers. All he did, however, was gaze around him with his mouth open, which fanned the general mirth still further.

'Look at that moon-calf! Look, look! What have they brought him along for? Now as far as Pyotr Petrovich is concerned, I have always had great faith in him,' Katerina Ivanovna went on in Raskolnikov's ear, 'and of course I need hardly say that he's not like . . .' – she turned to Amalia Ivanovna, loudly and abruptly, with an air of such extreme severity that Amalia Ivanovna grew positively frightened – 'not like those dressed-up draggle-tails whom Papa would never have even engaged as cooks in his kitchen, and whom my deceased husband would have been doing an honour in receiving, which he would only have done out of the inexhaustible kindness of his nature.'

'Yes, ma'am, he was certainly fond of a drink; that was what he used to like – a good drink, ma'am!' the retired supply clerk bawled suddenly, downing his twelfth glass of vodka.

'My deceased husband did indeed have that failing, and it's no secret to anyone,' Katerina Ivanovna said, battening on to him suddenly. 'But he was a kind and noble man who loved and respected his family; the only bad thing was that because of his kindness he put too much trust in all kinds of depraved people and heaven only knows who he used to drink with – men who were not worth the soles of his boots! Imagine, Rodion Romanovich, they found a honey-cake cockerel in one of his pockets: he'd come back dead drunk, yet he'd remembered the children.'

'A cock-er-el? Did you say: a cock-er-el?' bawled the gentleman from supplies.

Katerina Ivanovna did not favour him with an answer. She had fallen into a reverie, and uttered a sigh.

'I expect you're like all the rest, and think I was too strict with him,' she continued, turning to Raskolnikov. 'But you know, it's not true! He respected me, he respected me very, very much! The man had a good, kind soul! And how sorry I used to feel for him sometimes! He used to sit looking at me from a corner, and I'd feel so sorry for him, I'd want to put my arms round him, but then I'd think to myself: "If you do that, he'll go and get drunk again," and it was only by being strict that I could do anything to restrain him.'

'Yes, ma'am, much was the tugging of his locks, much was the tugging thereof,' the supply clerk roared again, emptying another glass of vodka into himself.

'There are some fools who could do with a taste of the broom handle, never mind the tugging of locks. And I don't mean the departed now, either!' Katerina Ivanovna snapped at the supply clerk.

The red spots on her cheeks were glowing brighter and brighter, her chest was heaving. She looked, given another moment or two, as though she might start a scandalous scene. Many of the guests were sniggering, and many of them evidently found this an agreeable prospect. People began to nudge the supply clerk and whisper things to him. It was obvious that they were trying to egg him on.

'Pe-e-ermit me to inquire what you are getting at, ma'am,' the supply clerk began. 'That is to say, on whose noble account . . . you were so good just now as to . . . But oh, never mind! It's just nonsense! A widow! A widow woman! I forgive her . . . *Passe!*' And he knocked back another glass of vodka.

Raskolnikov sat listening in silent disgust. He ate merely from politeness, picking at the titbits that Katerina Ivanovna kept putting on his plate every moment, and then only in order not to offend her. He kept giving Sonya fixed glances. But Sonya was becoming more and more anxious and concerned; she had also begun to sense that the funeral banquet was not going to end peacefully, and was watching Katerina Ivanovna's mounting irritation in terror. She was, it should be noted, aware that the principal reason for the two out-of-town ladies having greeted Katerina Ivanovna's invitation with such contempt was herself, Sonya. She had heard from Amalia Ivanovna that the mother had taken positive umbrage at the invitation and had advanced the question: 'How can I possibly ask my daughter to sit beside *that girl*?' Sonya had a foreboding that Katerina Ivanovna somehow already knew this, and that the insult to her, Sonya, meant more to Katerina Ivanovna than the insult to her personally, to her father and children; that it was, in short, a mortal insult; and Sonya knew that Katerina Ivanovna would not rest now until she had 'shown those draggle-tails that they're both . . .' and so on, and so forth. Just then, as though he had been waiting for precisely this moment, someone at the far end of the table sent Sonya a plate containing two hearts, shaped from black bread, pierced by an arrow made of the same substance. Katerina Ivanovna flushed crimson and at once observed in a very loud voice, the full length of the table, that the man who had sent it was a 'drunken ass'. Amalia Ivanovna, also sensing that something unpleasant was about to happen, and at the same time wounded to the depths of her soul by Katerina Ivanovna's haughty attitude towards her, suddenly began, for no particular reason other than to divert the unpleasant mood of the gathering in another direction and, while she was about it, raise herself in the general esteem, to relate the story of how 'Karl from the pharmacy', an acquaintance of hers, had been taking a cab somewhere one night and of how 'the cabman tried to kill him, and Karl begged him very, very much not to kill him, and cried, and begged with folded hands, and was so very, very frightened that his fear broke his heart'. Katerina Ivanovna, though she smiled, also observed that Amalia Ivanovna should not try to tell anecdotes in Russian. This offended Amalia Ivanovna even more, and she retorted that her '*Vater aus Berlin* was a very, very important man who went about with his hands in the pockets'. Being easily amused, Katerina Ivanovna could not restrain herself and went off into terrible fits of laughter, with the result that Amalia Ivanovna began to lose the last of her patience and very nearly lost it altogether.

'There's the brown owl for you!' Katerina Ivanovna immediately began whispering to Raskolnikov. 'What she was trying to say was that he used to keep his hands in his pockets, but the way she said it sounded as though he was a pickpocket, cahuh-cahuh! And have you noticed, Rodion Romanovich, that it really is true that all these St Petersburg foreigners, who are most of them Germans, and come to settle with us for some strange reason, are all more stupid than we are! I mean, you must admit, what sort of a story is that to tell, about "Karl from the pharmacy" getting his heart "broken with fright" and instead of tackling the cabman "folding his hands" – the milksop! – "and crying, and begging very, very much"? Oh, the big birdbrain! And I mean, she thinks it's very touching, and has no idea of how stupid she is! If you ask me, that drunken supply clerk's far more intelligent than she is; at least he doesn't try to hide the fact that he's a dissolute fellow who's drunk away the last remaining shreds of any sense he may have had – whereas these foreigners are all so sedate and serious . . . Look at her sitting there with her eyes popping out of her head. She's angry! Angry! Ha-ha-ha! Cahuh-cahuh-cahuh!'

Thus cheered and fortified, Katerina Ivanovna immediately launched into various details of this and that, and suddenly began to talk about how with the help of the pension she was going to receive she would most certainly open a boarding-school for daughters of the gentry in her native town of T . . . Katerina Ivanovna had not yet told Raskolnikov about this matter herself, and she lost no time in throwing herself into the most alluringly detailed description of her plans. By some mysterious magic there suddenly appeared in her hands the very same 'testimonial of good progress' that Marmeladov had told Raskolnikov about back in the drinking den, when he had explained to him that Katerina Ivanovna, his wife, at the ball that was held upon her graduation had danced with the shawl 'in the presence of the governor and other notables'. This testimonial was evidently now intended to serve as a proof of Katerina Ivanovna's right to establish a boarding-school in her own name; but had really been held in reserve with the aim of removing the shine from 'those two dressed-up draggle-tails' once and for all, if they should put in an appearance at the banquet, and of clearly demonstrating to them that Katerina Ivanovna came from a most well-born, 'one might even say aristocratic family', was 'a colonel's daughter and quite certainly better than those adventuresses of whom there seemed to have been such a proliferation just lately'. The testimonial at once passed from hand to hand among the drunken guests, something that Katerina Ivanovna did not try to stop, as it really did state *en toutes lettres* that she was the daughter of a court councillor and chevalier, and was consequently very nearly a colonel's daughter. Blazing with ardour now, Katerina Ivanovna immediately began to expand on all the details of her future bright and tranquil life in T . . .; she talked of the male teachers from the local gymnasium whom she would invite to give lessons in her boarding-school; of a certain venerable old man, a Frenchman by the name of Mangot, who had taught Katerina Ivanovna French at the institute she had attended and who even now was living out his days in T . . . and would certainly agree to teach for her in return for the most modest payment. At last she came to the subject of Sonya, who would 'go to T . . . together with Katerina Ivanovna and help her there in all things'. At that point, however, someone at the other end of the table gave a snort. Katerina Ivanovna, though she at once tried to pretend that in her scorn she had not even noticed the laughter that had broken out at the other end of the table, at once began, raising her voice on purpose, to talk with animation about Sofya Semyonovna's undoubted qualifications for serving as her assistant, about her 'meekness, patience, self-denial, good manners and education', while she patted Sonya on the cheek and, getting up slightly, implanted two hot kisses there as well. Sonya blushed scarlet, and Katerina Ivanovna suddenly began to cry, observing of herself as she did so that she was 'an idiot with weak nerves and upset beyond the limit', that it was 'time to bring the proceedings to an end' and, since the snacks had all been eaten, that tea should be served. At that very moment Amalia Ivanovna, who had by now taken thorough offence at the fact that she had not taken the slightest part in any of this conversation and that no one had even been listening to her, suddenly risked making one final attempt to join in and, with concealed sadness, ventured to communicate to Katerina Ivanovna a certain rather down-to-earth and well-considered observation to the effect that in the future boarding-school it would be necessary to pay particular attention to the cleanliness of the young ladies' linen ('*die Wäsche*') and that 'there would have to be one good lady ('*die Dame*') who would see that the laundry was done properly', and in the second place, 'that none of the young girls read novels on the sly at nights'. Katerina Ivanovna, who really was upset and very tired and who had by now had quite enough of the funeral banquet, immediately 'snapped' at Amalia Ivanovna that she was 'spouting nonsense' and did not know what she was talking about; that concerns about '*die Wäsche*' were the province of the matron, and had nothing to do with the directress of a high-class boarding-school; and that as for her remark about the reading of novels, it was simply improper, and she must ask her to be silent. Amalia Ivanovna flushed red and, losing her temper, observed that she had 'meant well', and had 'very much meant well already', and that Katerina Ivanovna had 'long not paid the debt for the apartment'. Katerina Ivanovna at once 'laid into her', saying she was not telling the truth when she said she had 'meant well', as the day before, when her departed husband had still been lying on the table, she had importuned her about the rent. In reply to this Amalia Ivanovna quite logically observed that she had 'invited those ladies', but that 'those ladies had not arrived', because 'those ladies' were 'high-class ladies' and could not come visiting 'low-class ladies'. Katerina Ivanovna immediately 'stressed' to her that in view of the fact that she was a slut, it ill became her to make judgements about what 'high-class' meant. Amalia Ivanovna would not put up with this, and declared in return that her *'Vater aus Berlin'* was 'a very important man who walked with both hands in the pockets and did everything like this: poof! poof!'; and in order to make the representation of her *'Vater'* more lifelike, Amalia Ivanovna leapt up from the chair, stuck both her hands in her pockets, blew out her cheeks and began to mouth incoherent sounds that resembled 'poof-poof', surrounded by the loud laughter of all the tenants, who had been purposely encouraging Amalia Ivanovna with their approval, sensing that a skirmish was near. But this was more than Katerina Ivanovna could endure, and she 'rapped out' for all to hear that more likely than not there was no *'Vater'*, and never had been, and that Amalia Ivanovna was simply a drunken St Petersburg Finn, and had probably worked as a cook earlier, or even as something worse. Amalia Ivanovna went as red as a lobster and shrieked that Katerina Ivanovna had probably 'never had a *Vater* at all'; but that she 'had a *Vater aus Berlin*' who 'wore a long frock-coat, and alvays went "poof, poof, poof!"' Katerina Ivanovna observed with scorn that her own origins were well-known to everyone and that in the testimonial it was stated in printed characters that her father had been a colonel; but that Amalia Ivanovna's father (if she had one) was probably some St Petersburg Finn who worked as a milkman; but that it was more likely she had no father at all, since nobody seemed to know whether Amalia Ivanovna's patronymic was Ivanovna, or whether it was Lyudvigovna. At that Amalia Ivanovna, flying at last into an all-out rage and banging her fist on the table, began to shriek that her name was 'Amal-Ivan', not 'Lyudvigovna', and that her *Vater*'s name was

'Johann' and that 'he was a *Bürgermeister*', and that Katerina Ivanovna's *Vater* had 'never ever been a *Bürgermeister*'. Katerina Ivanovna rose from her chair and sternly, in a voice that seemed calm (though she was deadly pale and her chest was heaving deeply), announced to her that if she dared to 'mention her rubbishy *Vater* in the same breath' as her 'beloved Papa' one more time, then she, Katerina Ivanovna, would 'tear off her cap and stamp on it with her heels'. At the sound of this, Amalia Ivanovna began to rush about the room, shouting for all she was worth that she was the landlady and that Katerina Ivanovna must 'get out of the apartments this minute'; then for some reason she ran to collect her silver spoons from the table. Noise and uproar followed; the children began to cry. Sonya rushed over to Katerina Ivanovna in an attempt to restrain her; but when Amalia Ivanovna suddenly shouted something about 'the yellow card', Katerina Ivanovna shoved Sonya aside and threw herself at Amalia Ivanovna in order to execute her threat in respect of the cap there and then. At that moment the door opened, and in the threshold Pyotr Petrovich Luzhin suddenly appeared. He stood surveying the entire company with a stern and attentive gaze. Katerina Ivanovna threw herself towards him.

III

'Pyotr Petrovich!' she shouted. 'At least you will protect us! Please get it into the head of this stupid creature that she has no right to talk like this to a well-born lady in distress, that there are laws about such things. I'll go to the governor-general himself . . . She must be made to answer . . . In memory of my father's hospitality, protect his orphans.'

'Now then, madam, now then . . . Now then, if you please,' Pyotr Petrovich said, fending her off. 'As you very well know, I never had the honour of making your father's acquaintance . . . now then, madam, if you *please*!' (Someone went off into loud laughter.) 'I am afraid I do not intend to become embroiled in your constant bickering with Amalia Ivanovna, madam . . . I am here on a pressing matter of my own . . . and wish to speak at once with your stepdaughter, Sofya . . . er . . . Ivanovna . . . That is correct, is it not? Now then, please will you let me through, madam . . .'

Katerina Ivanovna stayed transfixed to the spot, as though she had been struck by a thunderbolt. She was unable to comprehend how Pyotr Petrovich could thus repudiate her dear papa's hospitality. Having dreamed it up, she now believed in it devoutly. She was also shocked by Pyotr Petrovich's tone of voice, which was dry, business-like and full of a kind of contemptuous menace. All the others also gradually fell silent upon his entrance. For in addition to the fact that this 'serious and businesslike' man all too plainly failed to harmonize with the rest of the company, it was evident that he had arrived for some important reason, that only some extraordinarily pressing motive could have induced him to join such company, and that consequently in a moment something was going to happen, some event was going to take place. Raskolnikov, who was standing beside Sonya, moved aside to make way for him; Pyotr Petrovich seemed not to take the slightest notice of him. After a moment or two Lebezyatnikov also appeared on the threshold; he did not come into the room, but remained where he was, with a peculiar look of curiosity that was almost one of astonishment; he lent an ear to what was being said but for a long time seemed unable to comprehend any of it.

'Forgive me for possibly interrupting you, but this is a rather serious matter,' Pyotr Petrovich observed, somewhat generally and without turning to anyone in particular. 'I must say I am quite relieved that we have an audience. Amalia Ivanovna, I must ask you, as landlady of these apartments, to address particular attention to what I am now about to say to Sofya Ivanovna. Sofya Ivanovna,' he went on, turning directly to the thoroughly astonished and already frightened Sonya, 'immediately after your visit to me in the room of my friend, Andrei Semyonovich Lebezyatnikov, I discovered that a state credit bill, belonging to me and possessing a value of one hundred roubles, was missing from my table. If by any manner of means you know and are able to tell us where it now is, then I give you my word of honour, and summon those present as witnesses, that I shall let the matter end there. If such is not the case, then I shall have no option but to resort to measures of a thoroughly serious nature, and then . . . you will have only yourself to blame!'

Total silence reigned in the room. Even the crying children quietened down. Sonya stood in deathly pallor, staring at Luzhin and unable to find a reply. It was if she had not yet taken in what he had said. Several seconds went by.

'Well, mademoiselle, what have you to say for yourself?' Luzhin asked, looking fixedly at her.

'I don't know . . . I know nothing . . .' Sonya said, at last, in a feeble voice.

'You don't? You know nothing about it?' Luzhin asked, keeping up the pressure, and again said nothing for a few seconds. 'Think, mademoiselle,' he began sternly, but still as though he were trying to persuade her. 'Consider the matter. I am prepared to give you some more time for reflection. Let me put it to you like this: if I were not so firmly convinced I am right, I should never, in the light of the experience I possess, have risked accusing you so directly; for I should myself, in a certain manner of speaking, be held answerable for making a direct, vocal but false, or let us simply say mistaken, accusation of that kind. Of that I am aware. This morning I cashed, in order to meet certain personal expenses, a few five per cent bonds in the nominal sum of three thousand roubles. I have the receipt in my wallet. On arriving home – Andrei Semyonovich will testify to this – I began to count the money and, having counted 2,300 roubles of it, put it away in my wallet, which I keep in the inside pocket of my frock-coat. On the table there remained some five hundred roubles in credit bills, among them three banknotes with the value of a hundred roubles each. Just then you arrived (at my summons) – and during all the time you were in my quarters you were in a state of extreme embarrassment, so much so that three times in the course of our conversation you got up in a hurry to be off somewhere, even though we had not finished talking. Andrei Semyonovich is able to testify to all of this. I think, mademoiselle, you will probably not deny that I summoned you through the intermediacy of Andrei Semyonovich for the sole and exclusive purpose of discussing with you the orphaned and helpless condition of your relative, Katerina Ivanovna (whose funeral banquet I was unable to attend), and the advantage there would be in organizing for her benefit something in the nature of a subscription, lottery or similar means of raising money. You thanked me and even shed a few tears (I relate it all as it happened, in the first place in order to refresh your memory and in the second place in

459

order to demonstrate to you that not the slightest detail has been effaced from my own memory). Thereupon I took from the table a ten-rouble banknote and gave it to you on my own behalf for the protection of the interests of your relative, under the guise of first-aid. All of this was observed by Andrei Semyonovich. Then I accompanied you to the door – still in the same state of embarrassment – after which, having myself remained alone with Andrei Semyonovich and talked with him for some ten minutes or so, Andrei Semyonovich departed, I returned to the table where the money was still lying with the object of counting it and putting it aside for a special purpose, as I had originally planned. To my surprise one of the hundred-rouble notes was not there. Consider, if you will, my position: I could not possibly suspect Andrei Semyonovich; the very idea still makes me ashamed. Neither could I have been in error regarding the total, as a moment before you arrived, having finished the counting, I had found it to be correct. I think you will agree that, in view of your embarrassment, your hurry to be gone and the fact that you placed your hands on the table for a time; and, finally, taking into account your social position and the habits that are associated with it, I was, as it were, *compelled* with horror and against my will to form a suspicion – a cruel one, it is true, but one that is – just! I wish to add and to state again that, in spite of all my *self-evident* conviction that I am right, I realize that there is none the less present in the accusation I now make a certain risk for myself. But, as you see, I have not let the matter lie; I have risen in protest and will tell you the reason why: solely, solely because of your most flagrant ingratitude, madam! What? I invite you to visit me in the interests of your utterly impoverished relative, I give you ten roubles out of charity, the most that I can afford, and this is how you repay me for it! No, madam, that is wrong! You must be taught a lesson. Consider! Indeed, as your true friend I beg of you (for I am the best friend you can hope for at this moment) – come to your senses! Otherwise there will be no pleading with me. Well, then?'

'I stole nothing from you,' Sonya whispered in horror. 'You gave me ten roubles; here, have them back.' From her pocket Sonya produced a handkerchief, searched for the knot in it, untied it, took forth the ten-rouble bill and stretched out her hand towards Luzhin.

'And you won't own up to the remaining hundred roubles?' he said, insistently and reproachfully, refusing to accept the banknote.

Sonya gazed around her. Everyone was looking at her with such horrible, stern, mocking, hateful faces. She glanced at Raskolnikov . . . he was standing over by the wall, with his arms folded, and was watching her with a burning stare.

'O merciful Lord!' broke from Sonya.

'Amalia Ivanovna, we shall have to let the police know about this, and so I must kindly ask you to send for the yardkeeper now,' Luzhin said softly and even tenderly.

'*Gott der Barmherzige!** I always knew she was stealing!' Amalia Ivanovna exclaimed, clasping her hands together.

'Did you, indeed?' Luzhin said, following this up. 'So you must have had at least some sort of grounds for drawing such a conclusion. I beg you, my dearest Amalia Ivanovna, to remember those words of yours, which were uttered, I should add, in the presence of witnesses.'

A loud murmur of voices suddenly arose on all sides. Everyone stirred into action.

'Wha-a-t?' Katerina Ivanovna suddenly shouted, coming to her senses. As though she had broken loose from some impediment, she flew at Luzhin. 'What! Are you accusing her of theft? My Sonya? Oh, you villains, villains!' And rushing over to Sonya, she embraced her in her withered arms as in a vice.

'Sonya! How could you dare to accept ten roubles from him? Oh you silly idiot! Give it here! Give me those ten roubles this instant – there!'

And snatching the banknote out of Sonya's hands, Katerina Ivanovna crushed it into a ball and hurled it violently right in Luzhin's face. The paper pellet struck Luzhin on one eye and bounced back on to the floor. Amalia Ivanovna rushed to pick up the money. Pyotr Petrovich lost his temper.

'Restrain this madwoman!' he shouted.

Just then a few more people appeared in the doorway, at Lebezyatnikov's side, and peeping through among them were the two ladies from out of town.

'What? Madwoman? Are you calling me a madwoman? You fool!' Katerina Ivanovna shrieked. 'You're a fool, a canting, quibbling stuffgown, a despicable man! Sonya, Sonya take money from you? Sonya a thief? Why, she's the one who'd give it to *you*, you fool!' And Katerina Ivanovna burst into hysterical laughter. 'Look at the fool!'

she cried, rushing hither and thither, pointing everyone's attention towards Luzhin. 'What? You too?' she said, catching sight of the landlady. 'Have you come here, too, you sausage-maker's wife, to tell me that she "was stealing", you miserable Prussian chicken-leg in a crinoline? Oh you monsters, you monsters! Why, she's been in this room all the time; as soon as she came back from seeing you, you despicable villain, she came in here and sat down beside me – everyone saw her. Right here, next to Rodion Romanovich! . . . Why don't you search her? If she hasn't been anywhere else the money ought still to be on her! Go on, search her, search her! Only if you don't find anything, my dear, then I'm sorry, but you'll answer for it! I'll go to His Majesty, His Majesty, to the Tsar himself, I'll throw myself at his merciful feet, right now, today! I – an orphan! I'll be let in. You think I won't? You're wrong, I will, I wi-i-ll! Is it because she's so meek and mild, is that what you're counting on? Is that it? Well, I have a fiery temper! You'll come to grief! Go on, search her! Go on, search her, search her, why don't you – search her!!'

And in a frenzy Katerina Ivanovna tugged at Pyotr Petrovich, dragging him over to Sonya.

'I am prepared to assume complete responsibility . . . but you must calm yourself, calm yourself, madam! I can see only too well that you have a fiery temper! . . . This is . . . this is . . . what are you doing, madam?' Luzhin muttered. 'This ought to be done in the presence of the police . . . though actually there are now more than enough witnesses . . . I am prepared, madam . . . But in any case it is difficult for a man . . . on account of his sex . . . If perhaps Amalia Ivanovna were to lend her assistance . . . though, in fact, this is not the way to go about such matters . . . What are you doing, madam?'

'Let anyone you like do it! Let anyone who wants to search her!' Katerina Ivanovna shouted. 'Sonya, turn out your pockets and let them see! There! There! Look, you monster, it's empty, that's the pocket her handkerchief was in, and it's empty, see? There's the other pocket! There! There! You see? You see?'

And Katerina Ivanovna, attacking both pockets, tore rather than turned them inside out, first one and then the other, exposing their linings. From the second pocket, however, a piece of paper suddenly leapt out and, describing a parabola in the air, fell at Luzhin's feet. Everyone saw it; many exclaimed out loud. Pyotr Petrovich stooped down, retrieved it with two fingers from the floor, raised it for all to see and unfolded it. It was a hundred-rouble banknote, folded in eight. Pyort Petrovich moved his arm round, showing the note to everyone.

'Thief! Out of my apartments! Police, police!' Amalia Ivanovna began to howl. '*Nach Sibirien* with them!'

Exclamations flew on every side. Raskolnikov said nothing, still keeping his gaze on Sonya and occasionally, but quickly, transferring it to Luzhin. Sonya was still standing on the same spot, as though in a trance. She did not even seem to be particularly surprised. Suddenly the colour flooded the whole of her face; she uttered a shriek and covered her face with her hands.

'No, I didn't do it! I didn't take it! I don't know anything about it!' she exclaimed in a heart-rending wail and rushed over to Katerina Ivanovna. Katerina Ivanovna caught her to her bosom and pressed her tightly against it, as though with her chest she were trying to protect her from them all.

'Sonya! Sonya! I don't believe it! Look, you see – I don't believe it!' Katerina Ivanovna cried (in spite of all the manifest visibility with which she was confronted), shaking her in her arms like an infant, kissing her innumerable times, catching her hands and kissing them, too, almost sinking her teeth into them. 'As if you would have taken it! Why, how stupid can these people be? O merciful Lord! You're stupid, stupid!' she shouted, addressing them all. 'Why, you don't know, you don't know what a heart this girl has, what sort of a girl this is! She take the money, she? Why, she'd take off her last dress and sell it, go barefoot and give you the money if you needed it, that's the sort of girl she is! She took the yellow card because my children were dying of hunger, she sold herself for our sake! . . . Oh, departed, departed! Oh, departed, departed! Do you see? Do you see? A fine funeral banquet we're holding for you! O merciful Lord! But why are you all just standing there? Why don't you defend her? Rodion Romanovich! Why are you not interceding for her? Do you believe it, too? You're not one of you worth her little finger, not one, not one, not one of you! O good God! Defend her now, at last!'

The weeping of the poor, consumptive, lonely Katerina Ivanovna had, it appeared, had a powerful effect on the audience. Such wretchedness, such suffering was there in this face distorted by pain, withered and consumptive, in these parched, blood-clotted lips, in this hoarsely shouting voice, in this violent weeping that was like the weeping of a child, in this trusting, childish and at the same time despairing plea for someone to come to the defence, that everyone seemed to take pity on the unhappy woman. At any rate, Pyotr Petrovich at once 'took pity'.

'Madam! Madam!' he exclaimed in an imposing voice. 'The fact of this evidence has nothing to do with you! No one would venture to accuse you of complicity or prior intent, not least in view of the fact that it was you who brought it to light when you turned out her pockets: that means you did not surmise anything. I am most, most ready to take compassion if, as it were, desititution prompted Sofya Semyonovna to do what she did, but then why, why, mademoiselle, were you unwilling to own up? Were you afraid of the disgrace? Of taking the first step? Did you lose your nerve, perchance? An understandable reaction, mademoiselle, a very understandable reaction . . . But then why did you embark upon such misdeeds? Ladies and gentlemen!' he cried, addressing all who were present. 'Ladies and gentlemen! Out of a sense of compassion and, as it were, condolence, I am even how, in spite of the personal insults I have received, prepared to grant forgiveness. But may your present shame serve you as a lesson for the future, mademoiselle,' he said, turning to Sonya. 'That being said, I shall take the matter no further and, so be it, will drop the case. Enough!'

Pyotr Petrovich took a surreptitious glance at Raskolnikov. Their gazes met. Raskolnikov's burning stare was ready to incinerate him. Katerina Ivanovna, meanwhile, seemed no longer to be aware of anything: she was embracing and kissing Sonya like a woman who had lost her mind. The children had also put their little arms around Sonya from all sides, and Polya – who did not really quite understand what it was all about – seemed to have drowned in tears altogether, shaking with strained sobs and hiding her pretty little face, swollen with weeping, on Sonya's shoulder.

'How despicable this is!' a loud voice suddenly rang out in the doorway.

Pyotr Petrovich quickly looked round.

'What a despicable thing to do!' Lebezyatnikov said again, looking him fixedly in the eye.

Pyotr Petrovich actually jumped. Everyone noticed this. (They remembered it later on.) Lebezyatnikov strode into the room.

'And you dared to put me there as a witness?' he said, going up to Pyotr Petrovich.

'What is the meaning of this, Andrei Semyonovich? What are you talking about?' Luzhin muttered.

'The meaning of it is that you're . . . a slanderer, that's what I'm talking about!' Lebezyatnikov said heatedly, looking at him sternly with his weak-sighted eyes. He was horribly angry. Raskolnikov fairly glued his eyes to him, as if he were waiting to catch and weigh his every word. Once again silence reigned. Pyotr Petrovich almost seemed to lose his nerve, especially at that initial moment.

'If you are talking to me . . .' he began, with a hesitation in his speech. 'But what has got into you? Have you your wits about you?'

'Yes, I have, and the fact is you're a . . . twister! Oh, how despicable this is! I've listened to it all, I've waited on purpose in order to understand it all, though I must confess that even now it doesn't seem quite logical . . . But what I can't understand is – why you've done this.'

'But what have I done? Stop talking in these rubbishy riddles of yours! Or have you been drinking, possibly?'

'It's you, you despicable man, who drink, for all I know – not I! I never touch the stuff, because it's against my convictions! Can you imagine it, he himself gave that hundred-rouble note to Sofya Semyonovna with his own hands – I saw him, I'm a witness, I'm willing to take the oath! It was him, him!' Lebezyatnikov said, turning to each and every person in the room.

'Have you taken leave of your senses, you namby-pamby weakling?' Luzhin howled. 'She herself here, in your presence . . . she herself here, just now, in front of all these people stated that apart from those ten roubles she received nothing from me. In view of that fact, how could I possibly have given it to her?'

'I saw it, I saw it!' Lebezyatnikov shouted, in confirmation of his claim. 'And even though it's against my convictions, I would be prepared to swear to it on oath in any court of law you'd care to name, because I saw how you slipped it into her pocket on the sly! Only I, like the fool I was, thought you'd done it as a good deed! When you were saying goodbye to her in the doorway, as she was turning away and you were pressing her arm in one hand, with your other, your left one, you put that banknote into her pocket on the sly. I saw it! I saw it!'

Luzhin turned pale.

'You're talking rubbish!' he exclaimed, insolently. 'And in any case, how could you possibly have been able to see the banknote from where you were standing, over there by the window? You simply imagined it . . . with your weak-sighted eyes. You're raving!'

'No, I didn't imagine it! Even though I was standing far away I saw it all, all of it, and even though you're right, and it was difficult to see the banknote from over by the window, I knew because of the peculiar circumstances, knew for certain that it was a hundred-rouble note, because as you were giving Sofya Semyonovna the ten-rouble note – I saw it myself – you picked up a hundred-rouble note from the table. (I saw that because I was standing close to you at the time, and as a certain thought immediately occurred to me, I didn't forget about you holding that note.) You folded it and held it clutched in your hand throughout the whole conversation. After a while I forgot about it again, but when you got up you transferred it from your right hand into your left, and almost dropped it; at that point I remembered about it again, because the same thought came back to me, namely that you were trying to do a good deed for her without my noticing it. You may imagine how closely I began to follow your movements – well, and I saw you manage to slip the banknote into her pocket. I saw it, I saw it, and I would swear to it on oath!'

Lebezyatnikov was very nearly choking. From all sides various assorted exclamations began to resound, most of which denoted astonishment; one or two, however, assumed a threatening nature. Everyone came crowding over to Pyotr Petrovich. Katerina Ivanovna flung herself at Lebezyatnikov.

'Andrei Semyonovich! I have been mistaken in you! Defend her! You are the only one who is not against her! She's an orphan, and God has sent you to her! Andrei Semyonovich, my darling man, my dear, dear fellow!'

And Katerina Ivanovna, almost unaware of what she was doing, threw herself on her knees in front of him.

'Poppycock!' Luzhin howled, enraged to a pitch of fury. 'You talk nothing but poppycock, sir! "Forgot, remembered, remembered, forgot" – what sort of language is that? So I slipped it to her on purpose, did I? Why, I'd like to know? For what purpose? What could I possibly have in common with that . . .'

'For what purpose? That's what I myself would like to know, but if one thing is certain, it's that what I am describing is a true fact! I am so far from being mistaken, you loathsome, criminal man, that I even remember the question that occurred to me in this connection at the very time I was thanking you and shaking your hand. It was: why had you put your hand in her pocket on the sly? Or, to be more precise: why had it been on the sly? Was it really only because you wanted to conceal it from me, knowing that I hold convictions of an opposite nature and reject all forms of private philanthropy as bringing about no radical cure? Well, I decided that you really were ashamed to be giving away such a mint of wealth in front of me and also, perhaps, I thought, he wants to make it a surprise for her, give her a bit of a shock when she discovers a whole hundred-rouble note in her pocket. (Because some practitioners of philanthropy are very fond of spinning out their good deeds as much as they possibly can; I know from experience.) Then I also had the idea that your intention was to put her to the test, that is to say, wait and see if she'd come and thank you for the money when she discovered it! After that I had the notion that you wanted to avoid effusions of gratitude and, well, as the saying is, that the right hand should not know . . . something like that, to put it briefly . . . Yes, well, all sorts of ideas came into my head, and so I decided to think about it all properly later on, but even so I thought it untactful to let on to you that I knew your secret. But then another question came into my head all of a sudden, involving the possibility that Sofya Semyonovna might quite easily lose the money before she noticed she had it; that was why I decided to come here, to ask her to come outside and tell her that she'd had a hundred roubles put in her pocket. Well, on my way I looked in at the room of the Misses Kobylyatnikov, in order to give them a copy of *A General Treatise on the Positive Method** and particularly in order to introduce them to Piederit's article* (and also the one by Wagner); after that I came here, and what a to-do I found in progress! I mean, how could I possibly have all these thoughts and ideas if I hadn't seen you put the hundred roubles in her pocket?'

As Andrei Semyonovich brought his wordy arguments to an end with this most logical of conclusions he grew horribly fatigued, and the sweat even rolled down his face. Alas, he was unable to express himself properly in Russian (having no knowledge of any other language), with the result that he became completely drained of energy and even seemed to grow thinner after his feat of lawmanship.

All this notwithstanding, his oration produced an extremely marked effect. He had spoken with such heated conviction that everyone apparently believed him. Pyotr Petrovich sensed that things were not going well for him.

'What business is it of mine if you have some stupid questions stuck in your head?' he exclaimed. 'That is no proof, sir! You could have dreamt it all in your sleep, and that's the truth of it! Well I tell you that you're lying, sir! You're lying and defaming my character in public because of some malicious grudge you've got against me, and especially because you're annoyed that I wouldn't concur with your godless, free-thinking ideas about society, that's what!'

This eccentric flight was, however, of no benefit to Pyotr Petrovich. Indeed, a ripple of disapproval was heard on every side.

'Ah, so that's your tack now, is it?' Lebezyatnikov shouted. 'You're spouting rubbish! Go on, call the police, and I'll take the oath! There's just one thing I don't understand: why he risked his neck by doing something so despicable! Oh, base and wretched man!'

'I can explain why he did it, and if necessary I'll take the oath myself!' Raskolnikov said at last in a firm voice, and he strode forward.

He was, to all appearances, firm and composed. It was quite plain to everyone simply from one glance that he really did know what this was all about, and that the dénouement was at hand.

'It's all quite clear to me now,' Raskolnikov went on, addressing Lebezyatnikov directly. 'Right from the start of this episode I had my suspicions that there was some vile, dirty trick involved in all this; my suspicions were formed as a result of certain particular circumstances, known to me alone, which I shall explain to everyone in a moment: they are what all this is about. It is you, Andrei Semyonovich, who with your invaluable testimony have finally clarified the situation to me. I ask everyone, everyone to listen. This gentleman' (he pointed at Luzhin) 'was recently seeking to marry a certain young lady – my sister, in fact – Avdotya Romanovna Raskolnikova. Having arrived in St Petersburg, however, he quarrelled with me the day before yesterday, during our first interview, and I threw him out of my lodgings, as two people who were there will corroborate. This man is feeling very sorry for himself . . . I did not as yet know the day before yesterday that he was staying at these apartments, in your room, Andrei Semyonovich, and that consequently on the very day of our

468

quarrel, the day before yesterday, that is, he was a witness to my giving Katerina Ivanovna, the widow of the deceased, some money to help with the funeral expenses. He immediately wrote a letter to my mother informing her that I had given all my money not to Katerina Ivanovna but to Sofya Semyonovna, and expressing himself in the most ignoble terms about . . . about Sofya Semyonovna's character, making veiled allusions about my relationship with her. All this, you understand, was done with the aim of stirring up trouble between myself and my mother and sister, in order to give them the idea that I had squandered their last remaining money, which they had sent me to help me, for dishonourable ends. Yesterday evening, in the presence of my mother and sister, and when he was also there, I re-established the truth, proving that I had given the funeral money to Katerina Ivanovna and not to Sofya Semyonovna, and that when I met Sofya Semyonovna the day before yesterday I was not personally acquainted with her, nor had I ever even seen her before. To this I added that he, Pyotr Petrovich Luzhin, in spite of all his virtues, was not worth the little finger of Sofya Semyonovna, on whom he had cast such evil aspersions. In response to his question as to whether I would allow Sofya Semyonovna to sit next to my sister, I replied that I had already done so, that very day. Filled with spite because my mother and sister would not fall out with me on account of his slanderous remarks, he began, one by one, to say the most outrageously insulting things to them. A decisive rift took place, and he was dismissed from the premises. All this happened yesterday evening. Now, I request your particular attention: I think you will see that if he could prove that Sofya Semyonovna was a thief, he would also achieve his principal aim of demonstrating to my mother and sister that he had been more or less correct in his suspicions; that he had been right to lose his temper when I had put Sofya Semyonovna and my sister on the same level; that, consequently, by attacking me, he had been defending and preserving the honour of my sister and his wife-to-be. In short, by means of all this he could once again stir up trouble between me and my family, once again, of course, in the hope of entering their good graces. All this is quite apart from the fact that he was taking his personal revenge on me, as he had reason to suppose that the honour and happiness of Sofya Semyonovna are very valuable to me. That's all he was after! That's my understanding of this business. That was the only reason for it, and there can have been no other!'

Thus, or almost thus, did Raskolnikov conclude his address, frequently interrupted by the exclamations of his audience, who were, however, listening with close attention. But in spite of all the interruptions, he spoke calmly, incisively, clearly, precisely and firmly. His incisive voice, his tone of conviction and the stern expression on his face had an extremely powerful effect on all those present.

'Yes, yes, it's true!' Lebezyatnikov affirmed enthusiastically. 'It must be true, because he made a special point of asking me as soon as Sofya Semyonovna came into the room whether you were there and whether I had seen you among Katerina Ivanovna's guests. He made me go over to the window with him in order to ask the question, which he put to me in secret. That means that the very thing he wanted was for you to be here! It's true, it's all true!'

Luzhin said nothing and smiled contemptuously. He was, however, very pale. He seemed to be trying to think of how he could extricate himself from this predicament. However much he might have wanted to give the whole thing up for lost and go away, this was hardly possible at the present moment; it would have been tantamount to an open admission that the accusations that had been brought against him were justified, and that he really had been guilty of defaming Sonya Semyonovna's character. What was more, the audience, already quite drunken, was growing extremely restless. The supply clerk, though he had not entirely grasped what was going on, was shouting louder than any of them, proposing certain measures for Luzhin that were of a decidedly unpleasant nature. There were, however, some who were not drunk; people came crowding and gathering from all the rooms. All three Poles were terribly excited and kept showering him with cries of *'panie lajdak!'** which they accompanied with threats, Polish-style. Sonya had been listening with intense concentration, but she too seemed not to have grasped everything, as though she were wakening out of a trance. All she seemed set on was not to remove her eyes from Raskolnikov, sensing that in him lay her only protection. Katerina Ivanovna was breathing hoarsely and with difficulty, and was, it appeared, in a state of fearful exhaustion. The most uncomprehending of them all was Amalia Ivanovna who, mouth agape, had not been able to make anything of

470

this latest part of the talk whatsoever. All she could see was that Pyotr Petrovich had somehow been caught in a fix. Raskolnikov started to ask them all to listen again, but they would not let him finish; they were all shouting, crowding around Luzhin with oaths and threats. But Pyotr Petrovich was not abashed. Realizing that his attempt to incriminate Sonya had completely failed, he resorted to downright brazenness.

'Now then, ladies and gentlemen, now then; don't jostle me, let me past!' he said, as he made his way through the crowd. 'And kindly stop threatening me; I assure you that you will get nowhere that way, I am no coward. On the contrary, ladies and gentlemen, it is you who will have to answer for having obstructed a criminal process by means of force. The she-thief has been unmasked, and more than so, and I shall prosecute. The members of a court will not be so blind, or . . . drunken, and they will not believe the two died-in-the-wool God-haters, insurrectionists and free-thinkers who have accused me from motives of personal vengeance which they, in their stupidity, admit . . . Yes, now then, if you please!'

'I don't want to see you in my room again; please move out, and consider everything finished between us! Oh, when I think what efforts I've made to explain it all to him . . . for a whole two weeks!'

'Why, I myself told you earlier today that I was going, when you were trying to detain me; now, sir, I will merely add that you are a fool. I wish you success in curing your mental deficiency and your weak-sighted eyes. Now then, if you please, ladies and gentlemen!'

He squeezed his way through; but the supply clerk did not intend to let him get away so easily, with nothing but oaths; he snatched up a glass tumbler from the table, brandished it in the air and threw it at Pyotr Petrovich; but the tumbler went flying straight at Amalia Ivanovna, and struck her. She uttered a shriek, and the supply clerk, who had lost his balance while swinging his arm, fell heavily under the table. Pyotr Petrovich returned to his room, and a half an hour later he was gone. Sonya, being of a timid disposition, had been aware long before now that her good name could be more easily destroyed than most people's, and that anyone who cared to could wound her practically without fear of retribution. Yet even so, right up until this very moment, she had imagined that it might somehow be possible for her to avoid disaster – by being meek and cautious, and obedient to all and sundry. Great, therefore, was her disillusionment. She could, of course, have borne it all with patience and almost without a murmur – even this. Her initial suffering had, however, been too great. In spite of her sense of triumph and vindication, when her initial fear and shock had passed, when she had clearly understood and perceived the nature of the whole incident, her feeling of helplessness and personal mortification had constricted her heart with pain. She had begun to have a hysterical attack. At last, unable to endure any more, she had rushed out of the room and run off home. This had taken place almost immediately after Luzhin's departure. As for Amalia Ivanovna, when, amidst the loud laughter of those present, the glass had struck her, she too at last had enough of 'the hangover after someone else's feast', to quote the Russian proverb. With a shriek like a banshee, she hurled herself at Katerina Ivanovna, considering her to be to blame for everything:

'Out of these apartments! Now! *Marsch!*' And with these words she began to snatch up all the possessions of Katerina Ivanovna that fell within her grasp, throwing them on the floor. Almost crushed and defeated as it was, very nearly fainting, pale, and gasping for breath, Katerina Ivanovna leapt up from the bed (on which she had just collapsed in exhaustion) and rushed at Amalia Ivanovna. But the struggle was all too unequal: Amalia Ivanovna repulsed her as though she were a feather.

'What? Is it not enough that I've been godlessly slandered? Must this creature attack me as well? What? Am I to be driven from my lodgings on the day of my husband's funeral after offering you my hospitality, on to the street, with my orphans? And where will I go?' the poor woman wailed, sobbing and choking for breath. 'Oh God!' she shouted suddenly, her eyes flashing. 'Is there really no justice? Who are you supposed to look after, if not us orphans? But we shall see! There *are* justice and truth on earth, there are, I'll find them! Wait for a moment, you godless creature! Polya, wait here with the children, I'll be back. Wait for me, even if it's out on the street! We'll see if there's any justice upon earth!'

And, casting over her head the same green *drap-de-dames* shawl that Marmeladov had described in his narrative, Katerina Ivanovna squeezed her way through the drunk and disorderly crowd of tenants who were still crowding the room, and with a wail ran out into the street in tears – with the ill-defined object of somewhere finding justice without delay and at whatever cost. In terror, Polya hid with the children in the corner on the travelling-box, where, embracing the two little ones, trembling all over, she began to await her mother's return. Amalia Ivanovna rushed about the room, screeching, wailing, hurling everything that came within her grasp on to the floor, and generally making an infernal din. The tenants were bawling things in all directions, this way and that – some giving their frank opinion of what had taken place, others shouting and quarrelling, and others yet again starting to sing songs . . .

'And now it's my turn!' Raskolnikov thought. 'Very well, Sonya Semyonovna, let's see what you'll say to this!'

And he set off for Sonya's apartment.

IV

Raskolnikov had been a brisk and active defender of Sonya against Luzhin, in spite of the fact that he himself bore so much horror and suffering within his soul. Having endured so much that morning, it was as if he had been glad of this opportunity to vary his thoughts and feelings, which had become intolerable. This was quite apart from any element of personal sincerity in his striving to intercede for Sonya. Moreover, his approaching rendezvous with her was preying on his mind and causing him terrible anxiety: he *would have to* tell her who had killed Lizaveta, and he kept sensing in advance the fearsome torment that would cause him, a torment he was almost physically attempting to ward off. And thus it was that when, as he left Katerina Ivanovna's, he exclaimed: 'Very well, Sofya Semyonovna, let's see what you'll say to this?' He had still been in a state of visible excitement which was connected to the briskness of the challenge he had issued to Luzhin, and to his recent victory over him. But within him something strange took place. As he approached Kapernaumov's rented rooms, he felt a sudden sense of fear and helplessness. Outside Sonya's door he stopped, pondering to himself the strange question: 'Do I have to tell her who killed Lizaveta?' The question was a strange one because suddenly, at the same time, he felt that not only must he tell her – it was impossible for him to put off that moment, even temporarily. He had not yet managed to fathom why it was impossible; he simply *sensed* it, and this tormenting acknowledgement of his own helplessness in the face of necessity weighed him down. In order to stop thinking and worrying, he quickly opened the door and from the threshold looked at Sonya. She was sitting at the table, leaning her head on her hands, but when she became aware of Raskolnikov she immediately got up and came towards him as though she had been waiting for him.

'What would have happened to me if it hadn't been for you?' she said quickly, meeting him as he was only halfway across the room. It was clear that she had wanted to tell him this as soon as possible. This was why she had been waiting.

Raskolnikov went over to the table and sat down on the chair from which she had just risen. She stood two paces away from him, exactly as she had done the evening before.

'Well, Sonya?' he said, suddenly feeling his voice tremble. 'I mean, the whole business, it was all because of your "social position and the habits associated with it". Did you grasp that just now?'

A look of suffering came to her face.

'Oh, don't speak to me the way you did last night!' she said, interrupting him. 'Please, don't begin that again. I have enough torments as it is . . .'

She smiled quickly, afraid that he might find the reproach unpleasing.

'It was foolish of me to leave like that. What's going on there now? I was on the point of going back, but I kept thinking that you . . . might come here.'

He told her that Amalia Ivanovna was turning them out of the apartment and that Katerina Ivanovna had run off somewhere 'to search for justice'.

'Oh my God!' Sonya said, starting. 'We must go immediately!'

And she snatched up her little mantilla cape.

'It's always the same story!' Raskolnikov exclaimed in irritation. 'They are all you ever think of! I want you to stay here with me.'

'But what about . . . Katerina Ivanovna?'

'Oh, you can't possibly avoid her. She'll be round here to see you herself, now that she's left the apartment,' he added tetchily. 'And you know as well as I do that if she doesn't find you here, you'll be held to blame . . .'

Sonya cowered down on a chair in agonized indecision. Raskolnikov said nothing, looked at the floor and seemed to be thinking about something.

'Let's assume that Luzhin didn't feel like it just now,' he began, not looking at Sonya. 'Well, but if he *had* felt like it or if it had in any way been a part of his plans, he'd have tried to get you put in jail, and only Lebezyatnikov and I could have stopped him. He would, wouldn't he? Eh?'

'Yes,' she said, weakly. 'Yes!' she repeated, in a state of anxiety, her mind elsewhere.

'And, I mean, I might very well not have been there! And as for Lebezyatnikov, it was quite by chance that he happened to turn up.'

Sonya said nothing.

'Well, and if you had gone to jail, what then? Do you remember what I said to you last night?'

Again she made no reply. He waited until she was ready.

'And there was I thinking you were going to shout: "Oh stop it, don't say anything!" again,' Raskolnikov laughed, though with something of an effort. 'What – more silence?' he asked, after a moment. 'I mean, we have to talk about something, don't we? You know, I'd be quite interested now to learn how you'd deal with a certain "question", to use Lebezyatnikov's word.' (He seemed to be growing confused.) 'No, really, I'm serious. Imagine, Sonya, that you'd known in advance exactly what Luzhin had planned to do, and known (for a certainty, I mean) that it would cause the total ruin of Katerina Ivanovna and her children; and of yourself, too, into the bargain (since you don't attach any value to yourself, let it be *into the bargain*). Of Polya too . . . because she'll go down the same road. Well, then: if it were suddenly given to you to decide which one of them was to go on living in the world, that is to say, whether Luzhin was to continue his existence and go on doing loathsome things, or whether Katerina Ivanovna was to die, what would your decision be? Which of them would you have die? I ask you.'

Sonya looked at him nervously: she had sensed something peculiar in this unsteady monologue that seemed to be working towards something by a devious route.

'I had a feeling you were going to ask me something like that,' she said, giving him a searching look.

'Yes, all right; but what would you decide?'

'Why do you ask about something that's impossible?' Sonya said, with distaste.

'So you'd rather Luzhin continued his existence, doing loathsome things! Don't you even dare to decide that?'

'But I mean, I can't fathom Divine Providence . . . And why are you asking me a question that it's wrong to ask? Why such futile questions? How could that ever depend on my decision? And who am I to set myself up as a judge of who should live and who should not?'

'Well, if you're going to involve Divine Providence in it, you won't get anywhere,' Raskolnikov muttered, gloomily.

'You'd better come to the point and say what it is you want!' Sonya exclaimed with a look of suffering. 'There's something you're hinting at again . . . Have you really only come here in order to torment me?'

She could not hold out any longer, and suddenly broke into bitter weeping. He looked at her in weary gloom. Some five minutes went by.

'You know, you're right, Sonya,' he said quietly, at last. He had undergone a sudden change; his air of assumed insolence and impotent challenge had disappeared. Even his voice had suddenly become strained. 'I told you yesterday that I wouldn't come to ask for forgiveness, and yet very nearly the first thing I did was to ask you for forgiveness . . . That remark I made about Luzhin and Providence was meant for myself . . . It was me asking for forgiveness, Sonya . . .'

He attempted to smile, but his pale smile betrayed something helpless and unfinished. He inclined his head and covered his face with his hands.

And suddenly a strange, unexpected sensation approaching a caustic hatred of Sonya passed through his heart. As though in fear and wonder at this sensation, he suddenly raised his head and gave her a fixed look; but what he found was her own nervous gaze upon him, anxious to the point of torment; there was love in that gaze; his hatred vanished like a wraith. This was something else; he had mistaken one feeling for another. All this meant was that *that* moment had arrived.

476

Again he covered his face with his hands and inclined his head towards the floor. Suddenly he grew pale, got up from his chair, looked at Sonya and, without saying anything, like an automaton went over and sat down on her bed.

To him this moment felt horribly similar to the one when he had stood behind the old woman with the axe already freed from its loop, sensing that there was 'not another moment to be lost'.

'What's wrong with you?' Sonya asked, horribly frightened.

He was unable to say anything. He had never, never planned to *declare* it like this, and did not understand what was happening to him. Quietly she went over to him, sat down on the bed beside him and waited, not taking her eyes off him. Her heart was pounding and sinking. It grew unbearable: he turned his dead-pale face towards her; his lips twisted helplessly as he tried to say something. A wave of horror passed through Sonya's heart.

'What's wrong with you?' she said again, moving away from him slightly.

'It's all right, Sonya. Don't be frightened . . . it's just a lot of rubbish! In the end, it really is rubbish, if one gives it any thought,' he muttered like a man unconscious and in a fever. 'Only, why have I come to torment you?' he added suddenly, looking at her. 'In the end. Why? I keep asking myself that question, Sonya . . .'

It was probably true that he had indeed asked himself that question four hours earlier, but now he uttered it in total helplessness, hardly aware of what he was doing and feeling a constant tremor throughout his whole body.

'Oh, how you're torturing yourself!' she said with a look of suffering.

'It's all a lot of rubbish! . . . Listen, Sonya – this is what it is (for some reason he suddenly smiled, a pale and helpless smile, lasting a couple of seconds). 'Do you remember what I was trying to tell you last night?'

Sonya waited nervously.

'On my way out I said that I might be saying goodbye to you forever, but that if I came back today I would tell you . . . who killed Lizaveta.'

She suddenly began to quiver in every limb of her body.

'Well, and so I've come to tell you.'

'So you were in earnest yesterday . . .' she whispered with effort.

'How is it that you know?' she asked quickly, as though suddenly regaining consciousness.

Sonya had begun to breathe with difficulty. Her face was becoming paler and paler.

'I just know.'

For a moment she said nothing.

'Well, have they found *him*?' she asked timidly.

'No, they haven't.'

'Then how do you know about *that*?' she asked, barely audibly, and again after a silence that lasted almost a minute.

He turned round to face her and gave her a look of the utmost fixedness.

'Guess,' he said with his earlier crooked, helpless smile.

Convulsions seemed to pass throughout her entire body.

'But you're . . . why are you . . . trying to frighten me like this?' she said, smiling like a child.

'If I know . . . then I must be a close acquaintance of *his*,' Raskolnikov went on, went on relentlessly, continuing to look into her face as though he had not the help to draw his eyes away. 'He didn't mean . . . to kill Lizaveta . . . He . . . killed her . . . by accident. He meant to kill the old woman . . . when she was alone . . . and he went there . . . but then Lizaveta came in . . . So he killed her . . . too.'

Another terrible minute went by. They both stared at each other.

'So you can't guess, then?' he asked suddenly, with the sensation of a man throwing himself from a steeple.

'N-no,' Sonya whispered, barely audibly.

'Then have a proper look.'

And as soon as he said this, a certain earlier, familiar sensation suddenly turned his soul to ice: he looked at her, and suddenly in her face he saw the face of Lizaveta. He had a vivid memory of the expression on Lizaveta's features as he had approached her with the axe and she had backed away from him towards the wall with her hand held out in front of her and a look of utterly childish terror in her eyes, exactly as little children do when they begin to be frightened of something, stare motionlessly and apprehensively at the frightening object, move backwards and, stretching out one little hand, prepare to burst into tears. Almost the same thing took place now with Sonya: it was with the kind of helplessness and fear that she looked at him for a time and then suddenly, holding out her left

478

hand, rested her fingers slightly, the merest fraction, on his chest and began to get up from the bed, backing further and further away from him, as her gaze fastened on him ever more motionlessly. Her horror suddenly found its way to him, too: the same fear was displayed in his face, and he began to look at her in the same way, almost with the same *childish* smile.

'Have you guessed?' he whispered at last.

'O merciful Lord!' The words tore from her breast in a terrible wail. Helplessly she collapsed on to the bed, her face to the pillows. A moment later, however, she quickly got up, moved towards him, seized both his hands and, gripping them tightly with her slender fingers that were like a vice, again began to look into his face motionlessly, as though her eyes had been glued there. This last, desperate look was an attempt on her part to seek out and catch some last glimpse of hope. But there was no hope: there remained not the slightest shadow of doubt – it was all *true*! Even afterwards, later on, when she remembered that moment, she had a strange, uncanny feeling: how was it she had been able to perceive with such *immediacy* that there was no shadow of doubt? After all, she could not very well have said that she had had a premonition about something of that kind, could she? And yet now, when he had only just told her about it, she suddenly felt it was precisely *that* that she *had* had a premonition about.

'Enough, Sonya, enough! Don't torture me!' he begged her in a voice of martyred suffering.

He had never, never planned to reveal it to her like this, but *that was how it had happened*.

Almost unaware of what she was doing, she leapt up and, wringing her hands, got as far as the middle of the room; but she quickly came back and sat down beside him again, almost touching him shoulder to shoulder. Suddenly, as though she had been cut to the marrow, she shuddered, uttered a cry and, without knowing for what reason, fell on her knees in front of him.

'What is it, what have you gone and done to yourself?' she said despairingly and, jumping up from her knees, she threw herself on his neck, embracing him and gripping him as hard as she could in her arms.

Raskolnikov started back and looked at her with a sad smile: 'You're a strange one, Sonya,' he said. 'You put your arms round me and kiss me after I've told you a thing like *that*. You don't know what you're about.'

'There's no one, no one in the whole world more unhappy than you are now,' she exclaimed in a kind of frenzy, oblivious to his remarks, and suddenly burst into violent sobs, as if she were having a fit of hysteria.

A sensation he had not experienced for a long time came flooding into his soul like a wave and instantly softened it. He did not resist the sensation: two tears rolled from his eyes and hung on his lashes.

'So you're not going to leave me, Sonya?' he said, looking at her almost with hope.

'No, no; I'll never leave you, no matter where you go!' Sonya cried aloud. 'I'll follow you, I'll follow you everywhere! O merciful God! . . . Oh, how unlucky I am! . . . Why, why didn't I meet you earlier? Why didn't you come before? O merciful Lord!'

'Well, here I am.'

'But only now! Oh, what can we do now? . . . Together, together,' she repeated as though in a trance, embracing him again, 'we'll go and do penal servitude together!' A spasm ran through him, and his earlier, hate-filled and almost supercilious smile forced itself to his lips.

'I may not be willing to go and do penal servitude yet, Sonya,' he said.

Sonya gave him a quick look.

After her initial blazing and agonizing sense of compassion for the unhappy man the terrible idea of the murder struck her again. In his altered tone of voice she suddenly thought she could hear the murderer. She stared at him in amazement. As yet she knew nothing, neither why this thing had happened nor what its reason had been. And again she could not believe it. Him, him the murderer? Was it really possible?

'But what's happening? Where am I?' she said in deep bewilderment, as though she had not yet regained consciousness. 'How, how could you, *a man like you* . . . do a thing like this? . . . What's happening?'

'Oh, I did it so I could rob her. Stop it, Sonya!' he replied almost wearily, and even with a certain annoyance.

Sonya froze as though she had been stunned, but suddenly shouted:

'You were hungry! You did it . . . did you do it to help your mother? Was that it?'

'No, Sonya, no,' he muttered, turning away and lowering his head. 'I wasn't as hungry as that . . . I really did want to help my mother, but . . . even that's not quite correct . . . don't torment me, Sonya!'

Sonya clasped her hands in dismay.

'But is this all really, really true? Merciful Lord, what kind of truth is it? Who could ever bring himself to believe it? . . . And how, how could you give away the last copeck you had, yet murder someone in order to rob her? Ah! . . .' she cried suddenly, 'that money you gave Katerina Ivanovna . . . was that the money you . . . O merciful Lord, was it really *that* money?. . .'

'No, Sonya,' he hurriedly interrupted. 'It wasn't that money, put your mind at rest! That money had been sent to me by my mother through a certain merchant, and I was ill when I received it, the same day that I gave it away . . . Razumikhin saw it . . . he accepted it in my name . . . that money was my own, my own, really mine.'

Sonya was listening to him in bewilderment, doing her utmost to make some sense of it all.

'But as for *that* money . . . I actually don't even know whether there was any money there,' he added quietly and as though he were reflecting about something. 'I took her purse, the chamois-leather one, off her neck . . . it was a full purse, stuffed tight . . . but I didn't look inside it; I probably didn't have time . . . Well, and the objects, all those cufflinks and chains – I buried all those things the following morning together with the purse under a building-block in a backyard on V— Prospect . . . It'll all still be there now . . .'

With her whole attention, Sonya listened.

'Well, but then why . . . why did you say you did it in order to rob her, if you didn't take anything?' she asked quickly, clutching at a straw.

'I don't know . . . I haven't decided yet whether I'm going to take that money or not,' he said, again as though he were reflecting about something, and suddenly, coming back to himself again, gave a brief, quick, ironic smile. 'That was a stupid thing I blurted out just now, wasn't it?'

For a moment the thought flashed through Sonya's head: 'What if he's mad?' But she abandoned it instantly: no, this was something else. She could make nothing, nothing of it!

'Look, Sonya,' he said suddenly, with a kind of inspiration. 'Look, I'll tell you this: if the only reason I'd killed her was because I was hungry,' he went on, emphasizing each word and gazing at her in a way that was mysterious, but sincere, 'I'd be . . . *happy* now! That's what I want you to know! . . . And why, why should it mean so much to you?' he cried out a moment later with something almost akin to despair. 'Why should it mean so much to you that I confessed to having done something evil just now? I mean, why is this stupid victory over me so important to you? Oh, Sonya, do you think that's why I came to see you just now?'

Sonya again tried to say something, but no words came.

'I asked you to come with me yesterday because you're all I have left.'

'Come with you where?' Sonya asked, timidly.

'Oh, not in order to go stealing and murdering, you needn't be scared, that's not the purpose,' he said with a caustic smile. 'We're different sorts of people. And you know, Sonya, I've only just realized now *where* it was I was asking you to accompany me yesterday! When I asked you yesterday I still didn't know that. I asked you for one purpose, and it's for one purpose that I've come to see you: I want to ask you not to abandon me. You won't abandon me, Sonya?'

She gripped his hand tightly.

'Oh, why, why did I tell her?' he exclaimed in despair a moment later, looking at her in infinite torment. 'I mean, there you are, Sonya, sitting there, waiting for me to explain, I can see that; but what can I say to you? Why, you won't understand any of it, you'll just wear yourself away with suffering . . . all because of me! I mean, look: there you go crying and putting your arms round me again – well, why are you doing that? Because I couldn't hold out on my own and went running off to someone else in order to unburden myself: "You suffer, too, and then I'll feel better!" And you can love a villain like that?'

'But you *are* suffering, aren't you?' Sonya cried.

Again the feeling flooded into his soul like a wave and again for an instant softened it.

'Sonya, I have a spiteful heart, take note of that: that may explain a lot of things. I came here because I'm full of spite. There are some who would not have. But I'm a coward and . . . a villain! Anyway

. . . never mind that! All that's not important . . . I must speak now, yet I don't know how to begin . . .'

He paused and reflected.

'Damn it, we're too different from each other!' he exclaimed again. 'We'd never make a couple. Oh, why, why did I ever come here! I'll never forgive myself for this!'

'No, no, it's good that you came!' Sonya cried. 'It's better that I should know! Far better!'

He looked at her in pain.

'It really was that!' he said, as though he had made up his mind. 'I mean, it really happened! You see, I wanted to become a Napoleon, and that's why I killed . . . Well, now do you understand?'

'N-no,' Sonya whispered, naïvely and timidly. 'But . . . go on, go on! I *will* understand, I'll understand it all *in my own way*,' she said, imploring him.

'You will? Very well, then – we shall see!'

He fell silent and thought for a long time.

'It was like this: I once asked myself the question: what if Napoleon, for example, had been in my position, and instead of having a Toulon, and an Egypt, and a crossing of Mont Blanc to begin his career with, what if instead of all those beautiful and monumental things he had quite simply had nothing but an absurd old woman, a petty bureaucrat's widow, whom he was also going to have to murder, so he could steal all the money out of her chest (to help his career, do you see?) – well, would he have been able to bring himself to do it, if there had been no other way out? Would not the lack of monumentality in such an action have jarred upon him to such an extent that he would have viewed it as . . . positively sinful? Well, let me tell you that I spent a horribly long time agonizing over that question, and that I really felt horribly ashamed of myself when I finally realized (it came to me all of a sudden) that not only would the lack of monumentality not have jarred on him – it wouldn't even have entered his head: what was so jarring about it? And if there had been no other way out for him, he'd have strangled her without letting her utter a sound, without a moment's thought! . . . Well, that's what I did, too . . . I gave up my thinking . . . and strangled her . . . following the example of an authority on such matters . . . And that's how the whole thing came to happen! Don't you think that's amusing? Yes, Sonya, the most amusing thing of all is that that may really be how it came to happen . . .'

Sonya did not find it amusing at all.

'I'd rather you told me in a straightforward way . . . without examples,' she asked him, even more timidly and in a voice that was barely audible.

He turned to face her, looked at her sadly and took her hands.

'Once again, you're right, Sonya. Actually, all of what I've been telling you is nonsense, almost pure drivel! Look: you know, don't you, that my mother has almost nothing. My sister obtained an education of sorts, and was then condemned to go wandering about as a governess. I was the focus of all their hopes. I went to university, but I couldn't manage to support myself, and I had to give up my course. Even if I'd stuck at it, the most I could have hoped for would have been to have become some kind of teacher or civil servant on a salary of a thousand roubles a year (if things worked out favourably) . . .' (He was talking as though this were something he had learnt by rote.) 'And by then my mother would have wasted away with care and unhappiness, and I still wouldn't have been able to put her mind at rest, and my sister . . . well, my sister might suffer an even worse fate! And in any case, who wants to let life pass him by and turn away from everything, forget about his mother and endure the insults piled upon his sister in dutiful silence? Where's the point in it? Is the point to bury them and then acquire a new family – a wife and children, only to desert them, too, without a copeck or a crust of bread? Well . . . well, and so I decided that once I'd got my hands on the old woman's money I'd use it to meet my requirements during my first years at the university, without being a burden on my mother, and for my first steps after university – and do it all on a grand scale, in true radical style, in order to build a completely new career for myself and set out on a new and independent path . . . Well . . . well, and that's all. Of course, my killing the old woman was an evil thing to do . . . but enough of that!'

He dragged himself to the end of his story with a kind of helplessness, and lowered his head.

'No, that's wrong, that's wrong,' Sonya exclaimed in anguish. 'And in any case, people are not allowed to behave like that . . . No, it's wrong, wrong!'

'You can see for yourself that it is! . . . Yet I mean, I was quite sincere in what I told you, and it's the truth!'

'What kind of truth is that? O merciful Lord!'

'Look, Sonya, all I killed was a louse – a loathsome, useless, harmful louse!'

'But that louse was a human being!'

'Oh, I too know that she wasn't really a louse,' he replied, looking at her strangely. 'Actually, I'm talking nonsense, Sonya,' he added. 'I've been doing that for a long time now . . . All that's wrong; you're quite correct. The real reasons involved are quite, quite, quite different! . . . I haven't spoken to anyone for such a long time, Sonya . . . My head's aching very badly now.'

His eyes were burning with a feverish light. He was almost beginning to rave; a restless smile flickered on his lips. Through his excited state of mind a terrible helplessness could now be glimpsed. Sonya understood the agony he was in. Her head was also beginning to go round. What strange things he had said: she thought she had understood some of them, but . . . 'But how can it be? How can it be? O merciful Lord!' And she wrung her hands in despair.

'Yes, Sonya, it's wrong!' he began again, suddenly raising his head as though an unexpected turn of thought had occurred to him and roused him to excitement again. 'It's wrong! Yes, you'd do better to suppose (yes, this is really much better!) that I'm vain, envious, spiteful, nasty and vindictive, well . . . and, if you like, also with a leaning towards insanity. (You may as well have it all at once! People have spoken of insanity before now, I've observed!) Look, I told you just now that I was unable to support myself while I was at the university. But you know, I might very well have been able to. My mother would have sent me the money to pay the fees, and I could have earned enough by myself for boots, clothes and bread: I know I could have! There was private teaching to be had; they were offering fifty copecks an hour. Razumikhin works, you know. But I turned spiteful and refused. Yes, *spiteful* (that's the right word for it!). And then like a spider I crept away and hid in my corner. I mean, you've been in my rat-hole, you've seen it . . . And you know, Sonya, low ceilings and cramped rooms cramp the soul and the mind, too! Oh, how I hated that rat-hole! Yet even though I hated it, I didn't want to leave it. I made a special point of not wanting to! I stayed in it for days on end, unwilling to work, unwilling even to eat, just lying there. If Nastasya brought me food I'd eat it, if she didn't I'd let the day go by without eating; I wouldn't ask for anything out of spite! I had no light at night, I just lay there in the darkness, I refused to earn money to buy candles. I was supposed to be studying, but I'd sold all my books; there's a finger's thickness of dust lying on the papers and exercise-books on my table now. I preferred simply to lie there thinking. And I went on thinking and thinking . . . And what dreams I had, such strange and diverse dreams, there'd be no point in trying to tell you them! The thing was, though, that I also began to imagine . . . No, that's not right! I'm not telling you correctly again! You see, I kept asking myself: "Why am I so stupid? Why is it that if others are stupid and I know for a certain fact that they're stupid, I don't want to be cleverer?" Then, Sonya, I realized that if I were to wait until everyone else had grown cleverer, I'd have to wait for a very long time . . . Then I also realized that that was never going to happen, that people aren't going to change and that no one can make them any different from what they are, and that it's not worth the effort to try! Yes, that's how it is! That's the law they operate by . . . It's a law, Sonya! It really is true! . . . And now I know, Sonya, that whoever is strong and powerful in mind and spirit is their lord and master! Whoever takes a lot of liberties is right in their eyes. Whoever is able to spit on most things, they consider their law-giver, and the person who takes the most liberties of all is the one who is most in the right! That's how it's been in the past, and that's how it will always be! Only a blind person could fail to perceive it!'

Although he was looking at Sonya as he said this, Raskolnikov was no longer concerned about whether she understood what he was saying or not. His fever had completely taken hold of him. He was in a kind of black ecstasy. (It was true – he really had not spoken to anyone for a very long time!) Sonya realized that this black catechesis had become his creed and his law.

'And then it was, Sonya, that I understood,' he went on ecstatically, 'that power is given only to those who dare to lower themselves and pick it up. Only one thing matters, one thing: to be able to dare! It was then that I conceived a certain idea, for the first time in my life, an idea that has never occurred to anyone before me! Not anyone! I suddenly saw, as clearly as the sun, that in the past no one has ever dared, and still does not dare, quite simply to pick up all that absurd nonsense by the tail in passing and toss it to the devil! I . . . I wanted to *make the dare*, and so I killed someone . . . To make the dare – that was the only reason for it, Sonya!'

'Oh, stop it, stop it, don't say any more!' Sonya exclaimed, clasping her hands in dismay. 'You've strayed away from God, and God has laid His hand upon you and given you up to the Devil! . . .'

'Come to think of it, Sonya – when I was lying there in the darkness imagining all those things, was that the Devil stirring me up? Eh?'

'Stop it! Don't laugh, you blasphemer – you understand nothing, nothing! O merciful Lord! He'll never, never understand!'

'Be quiet, Sonya. I'm not laughing at all; I mean, I know it was the Devil who led me to do it. Be quiet, Sonya, be quiet!' he repeated blackly and insistently. 'I know it all. All of that passed through my mind, and I whispered it to myself as I lay there in the darkness . . . I argued it all through with myself, right down to the last, most insignificant detail, and I know it all, all of it! And I got so sick, so sick of all that drivel! I kept wanting to forget it all and make a fresh start, Sonya, to stop uttering drivel! Do you really think I went into it like a fool, head first? No, I went into it like a fellow with some brains, and that was my undoing. Do you really think I didn't know, for example, that the very fact that I'd started to search my conscience and ask myself whether I had any right to assume power over someone else like that meant that I didn't have any such right. Or that the fact I was asking myself the question: "Is man a louse?" meant that man wasn't a louse *for me*, but might very well be for someone to whom the question would never occur and who would go straight into action at once . . . Or, finally, that the fact I'd spent so many days agonizing over the question of whether I was a Napoleon or not meant that I knew beyond all shadow of doubt that I wasn't one . . . I endured the whole, the whole of the torment that drivel caused me, Sonya, and I tried to shake it off: I wanted to kill without casuistry, Sonya, to kill for my own sake, for no one but myself! I didn't want to lie about that even to myself! I didn't kill in order to help my mother – that's rubbish! I didn't kill in order to get money and power and thus be able to become a benefactor of mankind. That's rubbish, too! I simply killed; I killed for my own sake, for no one but myself, and the question of whether I'd become someone's benefactor or spend all my life like a spider, drawing people into my web and sucking the vital juices from them, was a matter of complete indifference to me at that moment! . . . And above all, it wasn't the money I wanted as a result of killing; at least, it wasn't so much the money as something else . . . I know all this now . . . You must understand me: in taking the path that I did, I might very well never have committed another murder again. It was something else I needed to find out, it was something else that was forcing my hand: what I needed to know, and know quickly, was whether I was a louse, like everyone else, or a man. Whether I could take the step across, or whether I couldn't. Whether I could dare to lower myself and pick up what was lying there, or not. Whether I was a quivering knave, or whether I had a *right* . . .'

'To kill? Whether you had a right to kill?' Sonya cried, her hands still clasped in dismay.

'Oh, for God's sake, Sonya!' he exclaimed in irritation, seemed on the point of delivering some retort, but then fell contemptuously silent. 'Stop interrupting me! I was simply trying to prove one thing to you: that the Devil led me to do what I did and only afterwards explained that I had no right to do it, because I'm just a louse like everyone else! He mocked at me, and so I came here to you! Receive your guest! If I weren't a louse, would I have come to you? Listen: when I went to see the old woman that day I only intended to conduct a *rehearsal* . . . You may as well be aware of that!'

'And you killed her! You killed her!'

'But I mean, what sort of killing was it? Is that the way people kill? Do they go about it as I did that day? Some time I'll tell you how I went about it . . . Did I really kill the old woman? No, it was myself I killed, not the old woman! I bumped myself off, in one go, for ever! . . . And as for the old woman, it was the Devil who killed her, not I . . . Enough, enough, Sonya, enough! Let me alone!' he cried suddenly in a convulsion of anguish. 'Let me alone!'

Placing his elbows on his knees, he jabbed the palms of his hands against his head like pincers.

'Oh, what suffering!' The words broke from Sonya in a tormented wail.

'Well, what should I do now? Tell me that!' he asked, lifting his head suddenly and looking at her with a face that was hideously distorted with despair.

'What should you do?' she exclaimed, leaping up from her chair, and her eyes, hitherto filled with tears, suddenly began to flash. 'Get up!' (She gripped him by the shoulder; slowly he began to get up, staring at her in near-amazement.) 'Go immediately, this very moment, go and stand at the crossroads, bow down, first kiss the ground that you've desecrated, and then bow to the whole world, to all four points of the compass and tell everyone, out loud: "I have killed!" Then God will send you life again. Will you go? Will you?' she demanded, quivering all over, as though she were in the throes of a seizure, gripping him by both hands, clenching them hard in her own and staring at him with a gaze of fire.

He was amazed and even shocked by her sudden ecstatic outburst.

'Is it penal servitude you mean, Sonya? Must I give myself up?' he asked, blackly.

'You must accept suffering and redeem yourself by it, that's what.'

'No! I won't go to them, Sonya.'

'But how will you live, how will you live? What will keep you alive?' Sonya exclaimed. 'How will life be possible for you now? I mean, what will you tell your mother? (Oh, what will happen to them now?) But what am I saying? Why, you've already deserted your mother and sister. Yes, you've deserted them, deserted them, O merciful Lord!' she exclaimed. 'Yes, he knows it all himself! But how can you live without anyone, without anyone at all? What will happen to you now?'

'Don't behave like a child, Sonya,' he said softly. 'In what way am I guilty in their regard? Why should I go to them? What would I tell them? All that's just ghosts . . . They themselves slaughter people in their millions, and they consider it a virtue, too. They're scoundrels and villains, Sonya! . . . I won't go to them. What would I say: that I'd killed her, but hadn't dared to take her money, had hidden it under a building-block?' he added with a caustic and ironic smile. 'I mean, they'd laugh at me, they'd say: you were a fool not to take it. A coward and a fool! They wouldn't understand any of it, Sonya, not any of it, and they're not worthy of attaining such understanding. Why should I go to them? I won't. Don't behave like a child, Sonya . . .'

'Oh, how you'll suffer, how you'll suffer!' she kept saying, stretching out her arms to him in a desperate act of imploring.

'Perhaps I haven't *yet* done myself justice,' he observed blackly, as though in reflection. 'Perhaps I'm still a human being, perhaps I'm not a louse *yet*, and have been in too much of a hurry to condemn myself . . . I'll struggle a bit more *yet*.'

An arrogant smile was forcing itself to his lips.

'To bear suffering like that! For your whole life, your whole life! . . .'

'I'll get accustomed to it . . .' he said, bleakly and reflectively. 'Look,' he began a moment later, 'you've done enough crying, it's time we got down to business: I came to tell you that they're on my trail now, trying to ensnare me . . .'

'No!' Sonya screamed in fear.

'What are you screaming for? I thought you wanted me to go and do penal servitude, yet now you're terrified! But look: I'm not going to let them get me. I'll struggle a bit more with them yet, and they won't be able to lay a finger on me. They have no real evidence. Yesterday I was in great danger and thought the game was up, but today things are better. All their evidence is mere conjecture, and that means I can turn their accusations to my advantage, don't you see? And turn them I shall, because now I've learnt a lesson or two . . . There's no way I can avoid them putting me in jail. If it hadn't been for a certain incident, they'd have put me in jail this very day, and it's still quite probable that they will do just *that* . . . But that's nothing, Sonya: I'll do a little time, and then they'll let me out again . . . because they haven't got one piece of genuine proof, and they're not going to get one, believe you me. With what they've got they could never put a man on trial. Well, that's enough of that . . . I just wanted you to know . . . I'll do what I can to reassure my mother and sister and not frighten them . . . In any case, I think my sister's all right for the future now . . . and if that's so, my mother is too. Well, that's all. But be careful. Will you come and visit me in jail when I'm there?'

'Oh, yes, yes!'

They both sat there together, sad and depressed, as though they had been thrown up on to some empty seashore after a tempest, alone. He looked at Sonya and felt how intensely her love was concentrated on him, and it was strange, but he suddenly experienced a sense of pain and aggrievement that anyone should love him as much as that. Yes, it was a strange and terrible sensation! As he had been walking to Sonya's, he had felt that in her lay his only hope and salvation; he had intended to unload at least a portion of his torments, and now suddenly, when the whole of her heart had directed itself towards him, he knew and felt that he was now inexpressibly more unhappy than he had been earlier.

'Sonya,' he said. 'I think it might be better if you don't come and visit me when I'm in jail.'

Instead of replying, Sonya wept. Several minutes went by.

'Are you wearing a crucifix?' she suddenly asked, unprompted, as though she had just remembered something.

At first the question did not register with him.

'You're not, are you? Well, here you are, take this one, it's made of cypress wood. I have another one, made of copper, it belonged to Lizaveta. Lizaveta and I swapped crucifixes, she gave me hers and I gave her mine, the one with the little icon on it. I shall wear Lizaveta's from now on, and this one's for you. Take it . . . I mean, it's my own! It's my own!' she implored him. 'We shall go and suffer together, and we shall bear our crosses together! . . .'

'All right then, give me it,' Raskolnikov said. He was reluctant to upset her. But suddenly he drew back his hand.

'Not now, Sonya. Later,' he added, in order to calm her.

'Yes, yes, later, later,' she agreed, enthusiastically. 'When you go to your sufferings, that's when you must put it on. You will come to me, I'll put it around your neck, and we'll pray and take the road together.'

Just then someone knocked at the door three times.

'Sofya Semyonovna, may I come in and see you?' a very familiar voice said in polite tones.

Sonya raced towards the door in alarm. The blond physiognomy of Lebezyatnikov peered into the room.

V

Lebezyatnikov had a look of alarmed concern.

'I must see you for a moment, Sofya Semyonovna. Please forgive me . . . I somehow thought I should find you here,' he said, turning to Raskolnikov suddenly. 'That's to say, I didn't think . . . in that sort of way . . . but I merely thought . . . Katerina Ivanovna has gone insane,' he blurted out suddenly to Sonya, transferring his attention away from Raskolnikov.

Sonya gave a little scream.

'At least, I think she has. Anyway . . . we don't know what to do with her, and that's a fact, miss! She came back, having apparently been thrown out of some house or other, and even possibly having been beaten . . . that's the way it looked, anyway . . . She'd gone to see Semyon Zakharych's boss, but he wasn't in; he was dining with some other general . . . Would you believe it – she went running off to where they were dining . . . to the house of this other general, and imagine – she really insisted on seeing Semyon Zakharych's boss, she actually had him called away from the dinner table. I expect you can picture what happened. She was thrown out of the house; and she says that she returned the abuse and threw something at him. That's not too hard to credit . . . How she wasn't arrested, I shall never understand! Now she's trying to describe it all to everyone, even Amalia Ivanovna, but you can't make out what she's saying, she keeps shouting and beating her head . . . Oh yes, and she keeps telling everyone and shouting it out loud that since everyone has abandoned her, she's going to take her children out to the street and be a street musician, and the children will sing and dance, and so will she, and they'll get money that way, and every day they'll go and perform under the general's window . . . "Let them see how the well-brought-up children of a high-ranking father have taken to the streets to beg!" She keeps hitting the children, and they cry. She's teaching Lyonya to sing "The Little Homestead", the boy to dance, and Polina Mikhailovna, too, and she's been tearing up her clothes; she's made little caps for them to wear, like actors; she says she'll carry a metal basin and bang it instead of playing the hurdy-gurdy . . . She won't listen to anyone . . . I mean, what kind of behaviour is that? It simply can't go on!'

Lebezyatnikov would have continued, but Sonya, who had been listening to him, scarcely able to draw breath, suddenly snatched up her mantilla and hat and rushed out of the room, putting them on as she went. Raskolnikov went out after her, and Lebezyatnikov followed.

'She really has gone insane!' he said to Raskolnikov, coming out into the street with him. 'I didn't want to frighten Sofya Semyonovna, so I said "I think she has", but there can be no possible doubt. There are these tubercles that grow on the brain in cases of consumption;

it's a pity I don't know any medicine.* Actually, I did try to reason with her, but she won't listen.'

'Did you tell her about the tubercles?'

'Oh, for heaven's sake, I said nothing about that. In any case, she wouldn't have been able to understand. No, what I mean is that if you can reason with a person logically and show him that he really has nothing to cry about, then he'll stop crying. It's simple. But I expect your view is that he won't?'

'Life would be too easy then,' Raskolnikov replied.

'As you please, as you please; of course, Katerina Ivanovna would have some difficulty in understanding; but are you aware that in Paris there have already been some serious experiments relating to the possibility of treating the insane by means of the simple influence of logical reasoning? There was a certain professor there who died not so long ago, a serious scientist who believed that such a treatment was possible. His basic idea was that there is nothing particularly wrong with the organism of the insane person, and that insanity is, as it were, a logical error, an error of judgement, a mistaken view of things. He would refute the arguments of his patient step by step and, would you believe it, it's said he achieved results that way! But in view of the fact that he accompanied this treatment with cold baths, those results should, of course, be viewed with some scepticism . . . At least, I think they should . . .'

Raskolnikov had stopped listening long ago. As he drew level with the building in which he lived he gave Lebezyatnikov a nod and turned in through the gateway. Lebezyatnikov snapped out of his reverie, looked around him and went running on his way.

Raskolnikov went into his closet of a room and stood in the centre of it. Why had he returned here? He looked at that yellowish, scraped wallpaper, at the dust, at his little couch . . . From the courtyard below there was a sharp, incessant banging sound; someone seemed to be driving something into some object somewhere, a nail, perhaps . . . He went over to the window, raised himself on tiptoe and for a long time, with an air of extreme and concentrated attention, searched the courtyard with his eyes. But the yard was deserted, and no hammerers could be seen. On the left, in the outhouse, a few open windows were visible; on their windowsills stood pots of straggling geraniums. Washing was hung up outside the windows . . . All this he knew by heart. He turned away and sat down on the sofa.

Never, never before had he felt so horribly alone!

He felt yet again that perhaps he really did hate Sonya, and particularly now that he had made her even more unhappy. Why had he gone to her to ask her for her tears? Why was it so essential for him to make her life a misery? Oh, what vileness!

'I shall stay as I am, on my own!' he said suddenly, in a decisive tone of voice. 'And she's not going to visit me in jail, either!'

About five minutes later he raised his head and gave a strange smile. He had had a strange thought. 'Life might really be better in penal servitude,' he suddenly reflected.

He could not remember how long he had sat in his room, with all those vague thoughts crowding his head. The door opened suddenly, and in walked Avdotya Romanovna. At first she stood still and looked at him from the threshold, as he had looked at Sonya earlier that day; then she came inside and sat down on the chair opposite him, in the place she had sat the day before. He looked at her in silence and somehow without any thought.

'Don't be angry, brother, I've only come to see you for a moment,' Dunya said. The expression on her face was one of thoughtfulness, but it contained no severity. Her gaze was clear and calm. He saw that this woman, too, had come to him with love.

'Brother, I know everything, *everything* now. Dmitry Prokofich has told me about the whole affair, and has explained it to me. You are being persecuted and tormented because of a stupid and infamous suspicion . . . Dmitry Prokofich has told me that you're not in any danger and that there's really no need for you to react to it all with such horror. I see the matter differently, and *fully understand* the anger you must feel, and the fact that this indignation may leave its mark on you for the rest of your life. That is what I'm afraid of. As for your having abandoned us, I do not condemn you for that and would not dare to do so, and please forgive me for having reproached you earlier. I can feel only, well, that if I had a great unhappiness like that, I too would want to go away from everyone. I will never tell mother *about this*, but I will mention you to her constantly and tell her on your behalf that you will be coming to see us very shortly. Please don't worry about her; *I* shall calm her down; but don't you be a source of worry to her, either – come and see us at least once; remember that she's your mother! But the reason I've come to you just now is simply to say' (Dunya began to get up from her chair) 'that if I can be of any help to you, if there is anything that you require, even if it's . . . my whole life, or something . . . then call to me, and I shall come to your side. Goodbye!'

She turned sharply and walked towards the door.

'Dunya!' Raskolnikov exclaimed, stopping her. He got up and went over to her. 'That Razumikhin fellow – Dmitry Prokofich, I mean – is a very good man.'

Dunya blushed the merest shade of pink.

'Well?' she said, waiting for a moment.

'He's a down-to-earth man, hard-working, honest and capable of intense love . . . Goodbye, Dunya.'

Dunya flushed all over, and then suddenly looked alarmed.

'But what's this, brother? The way you're . . . giving me advice like this . . . it's as if we were parting forever!'

'It doesn't matter . . . goodbye . . .'

He turned and walked away from her over to the window. She stood there for a moment, looking at him uneasily, and then left in a state of alarm.

No, he had not been cold towards her. There had been one moment (at the very end), when he had felt a terrible desire to embrace her tightly and *say farewell* to her, even *tell* her, but he had not even been able to bring himself to give her his hand:

'Later on she might shudder when she recollected that I'd embraced her; she might say that I'd stolen her kiss!'

'But will *that one* be able to hold out or won't she?' he added to himself a few moments later. 'No, she won't; *women like her* are never able to hold out . . .'

And he thought about Sonya.

From the window came a breath of fresh air. The light outside was less intense now. He suddenly took his cap and went out.

It was, of course, impossible that he should take any concern for his morbid condition, and indeed he would have rejected the idea of any such concern, even had it occurred to him. But all the constant anxiety, all the mental horror he had experienced could not but wreak its consequences. Though he was not yet prostrated by a full-blown fever, this was probably due to the fact that his constant inner anxiety was keeping him on his feet and in full consciousness, but in an artificial way, and only temporarily.

He wandered without aim. The sun was going down. A strange

anguish had begun to tell on him of late. In it there was nothing particularly searing or burning; but from it there emanated something constant, eternal, that gave a foretaste of unending years of this cold, numbing anguish, a foretaste of a kind of eternity in 'one arshin of space'. This sensation generally began to torment him even more fiercely during the hours of evening.

'It's these really stupid, purely physical ailments, which are linked to the sunset or something, that make a man do stupid things, no matter how hard he tries not to! Never mind Sonya – it'll be Dunya you go and see next!' he muttered with hatred.

Someone called his name. He looked round; Lebezyatnikov was rushing towards him.

'Would you believe it? I've been to your place, I've been looking for you. Would you believe it? She's carried out her threat and taken the children with her! Sofya Semyonovna and I had a terrible time finding her! She herself is beating a frying-pan, and she's making the children sing and dance. The children are crying. They stop whenever they come to a crossroads or a row of shops. There's a crowd of stupid people running after them. Come on!'

'What about Sonya? . . .' Raskolnikov asked in anxiety as he hurried off after Lebezyatnikov.

'Simply in a frenzy. Not Sofya Semyonovna, that is, but Katerina Ivanovna; though actually, Sofya Semyonovna's in a frenzy, too. But Katerina Ivanovna is *really* in a frenzy. I tell you, she's gone quite insane. They'll be hauled in by the police. Imagine what effect that will have . . . They're along by the Canal just now, at — Bridge, just a stone's throw from where Sofya Semyonovna lives. Very close by.'

Down by the Canal, very near the bridge and only two buildings along from the one in which Sonya lived, a little group of people had gathered. There was a notable concurrence of little street-urchins, boys and girls alike. The hoarse, hysterical laughter of Katerina Ivanovna could be heard even from the bridge. And indeed, this was a strange spectacle, capable of arousing the interest of a street audience. Katerina Ivanovna, in her old dress, her *drap-de-dames* shawl and battered straw hat, which had slanted over in an outrageous mass to one side, really was in the last stages of frenzy. She was tired and out of breath. Her exhausted, consumptive features looked even more martyred than ever (this, added to the fact that out in the street, in the sunshine, a consumptive person always looks more ill and deformed than when seen indoors); but her excited state had not grown any the less, and with every moment that passed she was becoming more and more overstimulated. She would rush at her children, shout at them, tell them what to do, instruct them right there in front of all the people in how to dance and what to sing, start explaining to them why it was necessary, then lapse into despair when they did not understand, and start hitting them . . . Then, without finishing, she would rush at the audience; if she saw anyone who was even slightly well-dressed and had stopped to take a look, she would at once launch into an explanation to the effect that this was what the children 'of a good, one might even say aristocratic family' had been reduced to. If she heard laughter in the throng or a cocky remark, she would instantly pounce upon the rude upstarts and start shouting at them. Some people really were laughing, while others shook their heads; everyone found the spectacle of the crazy woman with the frightened children an interesting one. Of the frying-pan Lebezyatnikov had described there was no evidence; instead of banging a frying-pan, however, Katerina Ivanovna had begun to clap out the time with her emaciated palms as she forced Polya to sing, and Lyonya and Kolya to dance; moreover, she herself had begun to sing, but each time she did so she would break off on the second note in fits of terrible coughing, which plunged her back into despair again, as she cursed her cough and wept bitterly. What infuriated her most of all was the weeping and terror of Kolya and Lyonya. She really had made an effort to dress the children up in costumes in the way in which street singers of both sexes dress. The little boy had had a turban made of some red-and-white material set upon his head to make him look like a Turk. There had not been enough to make a costume for Lyonya, too; on her head she wore the red knitted woollen cap (or rather nightcap) of the deceased Semyon Zakharych through which was run a piece of ostrich feather that had belonged to Katerina Ivanovna's grandmother and which she still kept in her travelling-box as a family curiosity. Polya was wearing her ordinary dress. She was looking at her mother in timid embarrassment, staying close by her, hiding her tears, realizing that her mother was not in her right mind, and staring around her with an uneasy gaze. The street and the crowd had frightened her horribly. Sonya kept persistently following Katerina Ivanovna around, weeping and imploring her to return home that very moment. But Katerina Ivanovna was not to be placated.

'Stop it, Sonya, stop it!' she kept shouting in a quick patter as she hurried to and fro, gasping and coughing. 'You have no idea what you're asking, like a little child! I've already told you that I won't go back to that drunken German woman's. Let everyone see, let all St Petersburg see them begging for alms, these children of a well-born father, who served justice and the faith all his life, and who, it may be said, died in the execution of his duty.' (Katerina Ivanovna had already managed to create this fantasy for herself and to believe in it blindly.) 'Let him see it, let that wretched villain of a general see it. Anyway, you're being stupid, Sonya; what are we going to eat now, tell me that? We've tormented you enough, I won't allow it any more! Ah, Rodion Romanych, it's you!' she exclaimed, catching sight of Raskolnikov and rushing towards him. 'Please explain to this silly idiot of a girl that this is the most sensible thing for us to do. Even street performers earn money, and everyone will be able to pick us out at once, will realize that we're an impoverished family of well-born orphans who have been reduced to penury, and then that general will lose his position, you'll see! We'll go and stand under his windows every day, and when the Tsar drives past I'll get down on my knees, push all these children in front of me and point to them, saying: "Protect them, Father!" He is the father of the orphans, he is merciful, he will protect them, and that wretched general . . . Lyonya! *Tenez-vous droite!* I want you to dance again in a moment, Kolya. What are you whimpering for? He's whimpering again! Well, what is it – what are you afraid of, you silly little idiot? Merciful Lord! What am I to do with them? Rodion Romanych! If you only knew what a muddle-headed lot they are! Oh, what can one do with children like these? . . .'

And, very nearly in tears (a circumstance that did not prevent her from keeping up a constant and unceasing patter of speech), she pointed to her whimpering children. Raskolnikov began to try to persuade her to go home, and even said, thinking that it might have an effect on her vanity, that it was not proper for her to wander about the streets like a common busker, as she was preparing to become the directress of a high-class girls' boarding-school . . .

'A boarding-school, ha, ha, ha! Green grows the grass far yonder!'

Katerina Ivanovna exclaimed, bursting into laughter which immediately turned into fits of coughing. 'No, Rodion Romanovich, that dream has faded! They've all turned their backs on us! . . . And that wretched general . . . Do you know, Rodion Romanych, I threw an inkwell at him! There was one right there on the table in the manservants' room beside the sheet of paper on which people signed their names, and I signed mine, too, threw the inkwell at him and ran away. Oh, the villains, the villains. But to hell with them; now I shall feed these children myself, without bowing to anyone! We've tortured her enough! (She pointed at Sonya.) Polechka, how much have you all collected, show me? What? Only two copecks? Oh, the scoundrels! They don't give us anything, just run after us sticking their tongues out! Now what's that dunce laughing at?' she said, pointing at a member of the crowd. 'It's all because Kolya's so slow-witted, he's nothing but trouble! What do you want, Polechka? Speak to me in French, *parlez-moi français*. After all, you do know a phrase or two, I taught you! . . . Otherwise how will people know that you're from a good family, well-brought-up children, quite different from the usual street performers; we're not performing some "Petrushka" out in the streets, we're going to sing an aristocratic romance . . . Yes, what shall we sing? You keep on interrupting me, but we . . . you see, Rodion Romanych, we stopped here in order to decide what to sing – something that even Kolya can dance to . . . because we're doing all this, as I think you can imagine, without the slightest preparation; we must come to an agreement so we can rehearse it all thoroughly, and then we shall go off to the Nevsky Prospect, where there will be far more people of good society, who will notice us instantly. Lyonya knows "The Little Homestead" . . . That's the only song she knows, but everyone sings it – no, we must find something much more aristocratic than that . . . Well, Polya, have you thought of anything? I do wish you'd help your mother! My memory, my memory must have gone, otherwise I'd remember something! No, not "The Hussar Leaned On His Sabre",* for heaven's sake! Oh, let's sing something in French, and then people will see at once that you're children of the gentry, and that will touch their feelings far more deeply . . . What about *"Marlborough s'en va-t-en guerre"*, since that's a children's song, a real children's song – it's used in all aristocratic families for lulling the children to sleep:

Marlborough s'en va-t-en guerre,
Ne sait quand reviendra. . .'

she began to sing . . . 'No, wait, "*Cinq sous*"* would be better! Now
then, Kolya, put your hands to your sides, quickly, and Lyonya, you
keep dodging away in the other direction, and Polechka and I will
sing and clap out the time!

Cinq sous, cinq sous
Pour monter notre ménage . . .

Cahuh-cahuh-cahuh!' (And she burst into fits of coughing.)
'Straighten your dress, Polechka, your shoulders are showing,' she
said through her cough, as she recovered her breath. 'It's very
important that you should behave decorously and with a bit of
refinement, so that everyone can see that you're children of the
gentry. I told you that your bodice ought to be cut longer and be two
widths thick, didn't I? That was you, Sonya, you and your advice:
"Make it shorter, shorter," you kept saying, and now you've made
the child look a complete mess . . . Oh, there you all go crying again!
What's wrong with you, you stupid children? Come along, Kolya, I
want you to start now, quick, quick, quick – oh, what a tiresome
boy! . . .

Cinq sous, cinq sous . . .

Another soldier! Well, what do you want?'

It was indeed so: a policeman was squeezing his way through the
crowd. But at the same time a gentleman in a uniform jacket and
overcoat, a sedate civil servant of about fifty with a medal round his
neck (this latter feature was especially gratifying to Katerina Ivanovna,
and made an impression on the policeman, too), came up to Katerina
Ivanovna and silently handed her a green three-rouble note. His face
expressed sincere compassion. Katerina Ivanovna took the banknote
and bowed to him politely, even ceremoniously.

'I thank you, my dear sir,' she began in a haughty manner. 'The
reasons that have prompted us . . . take the money, Polechka. You
see? There *are* well-born and magnanimous people who are instantly
ready to help a poor gentlewoman in her misfortune. As you can see,
my dear sir, these are well-born orphans, one might even say, with
the most aristocratic connections . . . But this general was sitting

eating his hazel-grouse . . . and he stamped his feet because I'd disturbed him . . . "Your Excellency," I said, "please protect these poor orphans, as you knew my deceased Semyon Zakharych very well, and as the most villainous of villains most cruelly slandered his very own daughter on the day of his death . . ." Here's that soldier again! Protect us!' she cried to the civil servant. 'What does this soldier want with me? We came here after running away from one of them on Meshchanskaya Street . . . Well, what errand brings you hence, fool?'

'You're not allowed to carry on like this in the street, ma'am! You're causing a disturbance.'

'Speak for yourself! It's just the same as if I were going around playing the hurdy-gurdy. What's it got to do with you?'

'As far as the hurdy-gurdy's concerned, ma'am, you have to have a licence to possess one of them, and in any case you're upsetting people just by the way you're carrying on. Where do you live, may I ask?'

'What do you mean, a licence?' Katerina Ivanovna wailed. 'I've only just buried my husband today, what licence do I need?'

'Madam, madam, please calm yourself,' the civil servant began. 'Come along, I'll take you home . . . It isn't right for you to be out here in this crowd . . . you aren't well . . .'

'My dear, dear sir, you don't know anything about it!' Katerina Ivanovna shouted. 'We're going to the Nevsky Prospect. Sonya! Sonya! She's crying, too! Oh, what's wrong with you all? . . . Kolya, Lyonya, where are you off to?' she suddenly exclaimed in a scared voice. 'Oh, stupid children! Kolya, Lyonya! Oh, where are they going? . . .'

What had happened was that Kolya and Lyonya, frightened beyond the limits of endurance by the street crowd and the behaviour of their mentally disturbed mother, and having, moreover, caught sight of a soldier who looked as though he was going to capture them and take them off somewhere, had suddenly, as if by some tacit agreement, seized each other by the hand and rushed off in flight. Sobbing and wailing, poor Katerina Ivanovna dashed off to catch them up. As she ran, weeping and gasping for breath, she made a pitiful spectacle. Sonya and Polya darted after her in pursuit.

'Get them back, get them back, Sonya! Oh, stupid, ungrateful children! . . . Polya! Catch them . . . It was for you children that I . . .'

As she ran at full speed she tripped and fell.

'She's cut and bleeding! O merciful Lord!' Sonya exclaimed, stooping over her.

Everyone came running, everyone crowded around. Raskolnikov and Lebezyatnikov were the first to arrive; the civil servant also hurried over, followed by the policeman, who was muttering '*Ekhma!*' the way peasants do, and making a hopeless gesture, sensing that the incident had taken a troublesome turn.

'Off you go now! Move along!' he shouted, trying to disperse the people who were crowding around.

'She's dying!' somebody cried.

'She's gone mad!' said someone else.

'May the Lord preserve us,' a woman said, crossing herself. 'Have they caught the little boy and girl? There they are, bringing them now, the eldest daughter's got hold of them . . . Look at them, the wild things!'

But when they had a proper look at Katerina Ivanovna, they saw that she had not cut herself on a stone, as Sonya had thought, and that the blood that was staining the pavement was welling up from inside her by way of her throat.

'I know what that is, I've seen it before,' the civil servant muttered to Raskolnikov and Lebezyatnikov. 'It's consumption; the blood comes welling up and chokes them. It happened to a female relative of mine, I witnessed it only recently, and it was the same with her, she coughed up a tumbler and a half, quite suddenly . . . But what ought we to do? I mean, she's going to die in a moment!'

'Bring her this way, this way, up to my room!' Sonya begged. 'This is where I live! . . . Look, it's this house here, the second one along . . . Bring her up to my room, quickly, quickly! . . .' she said, rushing from one person to the other. 'Send for a doctor . . . O merciful Lord!'

By dint of the civil servant's efforts this task was completed, and even the policeman helped to carry Katerina Ivanovna upstairs. She was brought into Sonya's room practically unconscious and placed on the bed. She was still bleeding from the mouth, but she seemed to be coming round. They all came into the room, one after the other – Sonya, Raskolnikov, Lebezyatnikov, the civil servant and the policeman, who had been chasing the crowd away, some members of which had accompanied them right up to the door. Polya brought Kolya and Lyonya in, holding them by the hands; they were both weeping and trembling. People even came through from the Kapernaumovs': Kapernaumov himself, lame and blind in one eye, a strange-looking man with hair and side-whiskers that bristled upright; his wife, who looked as though she had been frightened once too often, and a few of their children with faces that were frozen in expressions of constant surprise, their mouths open wide. Amidst all these spectators Svidrigailov, too, suddenly appeared. Raskolnikov stared at him in astonishment, unable to think where he could have come from, and failing to recollect him among the crowd.

People were talking about the need for a doctor and a priest. Although the civil servant whispered to Raskolnikov that in his opinion a doctor was now superfluous, he made arrangements to have one sent for all the same. Kapernaumov himself went on this errand.

In the meantime Katerina Ivanovna had got her breath back, and the blood had stopped flowing temporarily. She was looking with an unhealthy but fixed and penetrating gaze at the pale and trembling Sonya, who was wiping the drops of sweat from her brow with a handkerchief; at last she asked to be lifted up. She was raised into a sitting position on the bed, while hands supported her on both sides.

'Where are the children?' she asked in a faint voice. 'Have you brought them, Polya? Oh, you stupid things! . . . Why did you run off like that . . . ah?'

Blood still caked her dried-up lips. She let her gaze move round the room, taking everything in:

'So this is the kind of place you live in, Sonya! I've never been to see you here before . . . never had the occasion . . .'

She looked at her with suffering:

'We've sucked you dry, Sonya . . . Polya, Lyonya, Kolya, come here . . . Well, here they are, Sonya, all of them, take them . . . from one set of hands to another . . . but I've had enough! The ball is over! Gh-ha! . . . Lay me down again, let me at least die peacefully.'

And they lowered her back onto the pillow again.

'What? A priest? . . . There's no need . . . Where would you get the money for one? . . . I have no sins! . . . In any case, God will have to forgive me . . . he knows how much I've suffered! . . . And if he won't forgive me, there's even less need! . . .'

A restless fever was taking an ever-increasing hold of her. From time to time she would shudder, move her gaze round and recognize

503

everyone for a moment; but these brief glimpses of awareness would immediately give way to delirium once more. She was breathing hoarsely and with difficulty, and something seemed to be bubbling in her throat.

'"Your Excellency! . . ." I said to him,' she screamed out, taking a deep gulp of breath after every word. '"That Amalia Ivanovna . . ." Ah! Lyonya, Kolya! Hands at your sides, quick, quick, *glissez-glissez*, *pas-de-basque*! Tap your feet . . . Be a graceful child.

> Du hast Diamanten und Perlen . . .

How does it go after that? That's what we ought to sing . . .

> Du hast die schönsten Augen,
> Mädchen, was willst du mehr?*

Oh yes, of course! *Was willst du mehr* – he's contradicting her, the idiot! . . . Ah yes, and then there's another one:

> In heat of noon, in Dagestan's deep valley . . .*

Ah, how I used to love that song . . . I loved that romance to the point of adoration, Polechka! . . . you know, your father . . . used to sing it before we were married . . . Oh, vanished days! . . . That's the one, that's what we ought to sing! Now how does it go, how does it go . . . Oh, I've forgotten . . . But remind me – how does it go?' She was in a state of extreme agitation and was making efforts to get up. At last, in a hoarse, terrible, overstrained voice she began to recite, screaming and gasping at every word, with an air of obscurely mounting terror:

> In heat of noon! . . . in Dagestan's! . . . deep valley! . . .

'Your Excellency!' she suddenly cried in a heartrending wail, and dissolving in tears, 'protect these orphans! Since you've known the hospitality of the deceased Semyon Zakharych! . . . who was even almost an aristocrat! . . . Gh-ha!' she gasped, shuddering, suddenly regaining consciousness and gazing round at everyone with a kind of horror, but then recognizing Sonya. 'Sonya, Sonya!' she said meekly and affectionately, as though surprised at seeing her in front of her. 'Sonya, dearest, are you here, too?'

Once more they helped her to sit up.

'Enough! . . . It's time! . . . Farewell, my poor creature! . . . They've driven the jade to death! . . . I've overstrai-i-ned myself!' she cried, despairingly and full of hatred, and collapsed on the pillow with a thud.

Again she lost consciousness, but this final oblivion did not last long. Her withered, pale-yellow face jerked back, her mouth opened, and her legs stretched out convulsively. She gave a deep, deep sigh and died.

Sonya fell on her corpse, gripped her in her arms and froze there, her head fixed close to the dead woman's withered chest. Polya fell prostrate at her mother's feet, kissing them and sobbing violently. Kolya and Lyonya, who did not yet understand what had happened, but sensed that it must be something very dreadful, seized each other's little shoulders in an embrace and, fixing each other with their eyes, suddenly, both at the same time, opened their mouths wide and began to howl. They were both still wearing their fancy costumes: Kolya in his turban, and Lyonya in her skull-cap with its ostrich-feather.

And how was it that the 'testimonial of good progress' had suddenly turned up on the bed beside Katerina Ivanovna? It was lying right there, by her pillow; Raskolnikov could see it.

He withdrew to the window. Lebezyatnikov came running over to him.

'She's dead!' Lebezyatnikov said.

'Rodion Romanovich, I'd like to have a couple of words with you,' Svidrigailov said, approaching. Lebezyatnikov immediately made way for him and retired discreetly into the background. Svidrigailov led the surprised Raskolnikov even further into the corner.

'All this bother, I mean the funeral and so on – I shall take it all upon myself personally. You know, it all costs money, and as I told you, I have more than I need. I shall place the little Polya and those two little fledglings in some better category of orphanage and endow each of them with the capital sum of one and a half thousand roubles, to be paid on their maturity, in order that Sofya Semyonovna may not be troubled any more on their account. And while I'm about it, I shall pull her out of the cesspool, too, for she's a fine girl, don't you think? Well sir, and so you may tell Avdotya Romanovna that this is the use to which I have put her ten thousand.'

'What do you expect to gain by all this philanthropy?' Raskolnikov inquired.

'A-ah! A man of suspicion!' Svidrigailov laughed. 'Look, I told you: I don't need that money. Well, won't you let me simply do it out of humanity? I mean, after all, it's not as if she were a "louse"' (he poked a finger in the direction of the corner where the dead woman lay) 'like certain old female pawnbrokers we know, is she? Come now, I think you'll agree: "Is Luzhin to continue his existence and go on doing loathsome things, or is she to die?" And I mean, if I don't offer my assistance, why "Polya, for example, will go that way too, she'll go down the same road . . ."'

He said this with a kind of *winking*, jolly roguery, never taking his eyes off Raskolnikov. Raskolnikov turned pale and his blood ran cold as he heard the things he himself had said to Sonya. He instantly recoiled, staring wildly at Svidrigailov.

'H-how . . . do you know?' he whispered, scarcely breathing.

'Why, I live just through the wall from here, at Madam Resslich's. These are Kapernaumov's rooms, and through there lives Madam Resslich, my old and most devoted friend. I'm one of the neighbours, sir.'

'You?'

'The very same,' Svidrigailov continued, quaking with laughter. 'And I can assure you on my honour, my dear, dear Rodion Roman-ovich, that I found what you said of remarkable interest. Why, I told you we would come to be on closer terms with each other, I predicted it to you – well, and so it's come true. And you will see what an adaptable fellow I am. You'll see that I'm still not too much of a bore . . .'

PART SIX
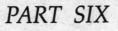

For Raskolnikov a strange time began: as though a mist had suddenly fallen before him, enclosing him in a gloomy and desperate solitude. When he remembered this time later on, long afterwards, he was able to perceive that his awareness must at times have been dimmed and that this must have gone on, with various intervals, right up until the final catastrophe. He was positively convinced that there were many things about those days concerning which he had been in error – the length of time that had elapsed between certain events, for example, and the dates at which they had occurred. At least, as he remembered it all subsequently and endeavoured to make sense of it all, there were many things he discovered about himself, going merely on the information he received from people who had happened to be present. He would, for example, confuse an event with one that bore no relation to it; another event he would view as the consequence of one that existed only in his imagination. At times he was seized by a morbid and tormenting anxiety, which had even transformed itself into panic terror. But he also recalled that there had been minutes, hours and even possibly days full of an apathy that had taken hold of him as though in contrast to his earlier terror – an apathy similar to the morbidly indifferent condition of certain people on their death-beds. In general, during those final days he tried more or less to flee from any clear and complete understanding of his position; certain vital facts that demanded instant clarification were a particular source of depression to him; there were, however, other worries from which he would have given anything to escape and shake himself free, because in the situation he was in to forget about them threatened him with total and inevitable disaster.

Svidrigailov caused him particular anxiety; one might even have said that he was, in a sense, fixated on Svidrigailov. From the time that Svidrigailov had spoken those threatening words, whose import was all too clear to him, in Sonya's lodgings at the moment of Katerina Ivanovna's death, the normal flow of his thoughts seemed to have been broken. But, in spite of being extremely worried by this new event, Raskolnikov seemed to delay in seeking an explanation for it. At times – as, for example, finding himself one day in some remote and secluded district of the city, alone at a table of some wretched inn, sunk in reflection and hardly conscious of how he had ended up there – he would suddenly remember Svidrigailov: he would suddenly become all too clearly and uneasily aware that he ought to come to some arrangement with that man and, as far as was possible, settle the matter once and for all. On one occasion, having wandered to some place beyond the city boundaries, he even fancied that he was waiting for Svidrigailov and that they had agreed to meet there. On another occasion he awoke before dawn to find himself somewhere on the ground, in the midst of some bushes, with almost no inkling of how he had strayed there. There was also the fact that during those two or three days that followed the death of Katerina Ivanovna he had actually met Svidrigailov a few times, almost invariably in Sonya's lodgings, where he would look in more or less without purpose, but always only for a moment. They would always bandy a few words, but never once spoke about the capital point, as though they had agreed to keep quiet about that for the time being. The body of Katerina Ivanovna still lay in its coffin. Svidrigailov dealt with the arrangements for the funeral, fussing around. Sonya was also very preoccupied. During their last meeting Svidrigailov had explained to Raskolnikov that he had managed to solve the problem of what to do about Katerina Ivanovna's children, and that the solution was a successful one; that, thanks to some connections he had, certain persons had been contacted with whose help all three orphans could be placed at once in institutions that were thoroughly suitable for them; that the money which had been put aside for them had also helped in many respects, as it was far easier to place orphans with capital than orphans who were destitute. He also said something about Sonya, promising to look in on Raskolnikov himself in a day or two's time, saying that he wanted to ask his advice, that it was essential that they had a word or two together, that there were certain matters . . . This conversation took place out in the passage, by the staircase. Svidrigailov looked fixedly into Raskolnikov's eyes and then suddenly, after a pause and with his voice lowered, inquired:

'But what's the matter with you, Rodion Romanovich? You don't seem at all yourself. You listen and look, yet you don't seem to take anything in. You must pull yourself together. Look, we'll have a talk; it's just a pity I have so much business to attend to, both my own and other people's . . . Ah, Rodion Romanovich, sir,' he added suddenly, 'all human beings need air, air, air . . . That above all else!'

He suddenly stepped aside in order to let a priest and a deacon pass up the stairs. They were going to perform the service for the dead. In accordance with the arrangements he had made, these services were being held punctually twice a day. Svidrigailov continued on his rounds. Raskolnikov stood for a while in reflection and then followed the priest into Sonya's lodgings.

He stood in the doorway. Quietly, decorously, mournfully, the service was beginning. In the consciousness of death and the sense of its presence there had always been for him something gloom-ridden and mystically horrible, ever since he had been a child; it was also a long time since he had heard a funeral mass sung. But here there was something else, too, something that contained an excess of horror and disquiet. He looked at the children: they were all on their knees beside the coffin, and Polya was crying. Behind them, weeping quietly and almost timidly, Sonya was praying. 'You know, she hasn't looked at me once during these last few days, and she hasn't said a word to me,' Raskolnikov suddenly thought. The sun was illuminating the room brightly; the smoke from the censer rose in clouds as the priest sang: 'Make their souls to rest, O Lord.' Raskolnikov stood throughout the entire service. As he performed the blessing and the parting, the priest seemed to look around him strangely. After the service, Raskolnikov went over to Sonya. She suddenly took him by both hands and leant her head against his shoulder. This brief gesture struck Raskolnikov with intense bewilderment; it was positively uncanny. What – did she feel not the slightest revulsion, not the slightest loathing for him, was there not the slightest tremor in her hand? This was some strange infinity of self-humiliation. That, at any rate, was how he read it. Sonya did not say anything. Raskolnikov gave her hand a squeeze and went out. He had begun to feel horribly gloomy. If it had been possible for him to go away somewhere just then and be completely alone, even though it were to be for the rest of his life, he would have counted himself a lucky man. The difficulty was that even though he had been almost constantly alone during these recent days, he had never once felt that he was alone. On occasion he had strolled into the suburbs, walked out along the high road, once even wandered into some wood or other; but the more secluded the location, the more powerfully he had seemed to sense someone's close and disturbing presence – not a particularly frightening one, but a very irritating one, with the result that he quickly went back to the town, mingled with the crowd, went into the inns and drinking dens, visited the secondhand stalls, the Haymarket. There he felt easier, even more secluded. There was one eating-house where, towards evening, people began singing songs; he sat for a whole hour, listening, and he recalled that he had really enjoyed himself very much. In the end, however, he had suddenly felt anxious again; it was as though his conscience had begun to bother him. 'Here I am, sitting listening to songs, when it's the last thing I ought to be doing!' he found himself thinking. What was more, he instantly realized that this was not the only thing that was bothering him; there was some problem that demanded an immediate solution, but what it was he could neither formulate in his mind nor give utterance to in words. Everything seemed to have wound itself into some kind of a ball. 'No, better to resume the struggle again! Better Porfiry again . . . or Svidrigailov . . . What I want is some kind of challenge again, an attack from someone to fend off . . . Yes! That's what I want!' he thought. He left the eating-house and very nearly broke into a run. For some reason, the thought of Dunya and his mother had suddenly filled him with panic terror. That night he had woken up before dawn in some bushes on Krestovsky Island, chilled to the very core, in a fever; he had set off home at once, arriving there in the early morning. After a few hours of sleep the fever had passed, but when he woke up it was late: two o'clock in the afternoon.

He remembered that today was the day of Katerina Ivanovna's funeral, and he felt relieved at having missed it. Nastasya brought him some food; he ate and drank with great appetite, almost with voracity. His head was clearer, and he felt calmer than he had done these last three days. He even had a fleeting sense of wonder when he remembered his earlier panic terror. The door opened and in walked Razumikhin.

'Aha! He's eating, so he can't be ill!' Razumikhin said, taking a chair and sitting down at the table facing Raskolnikov. He was worried, and made no attempt to conceal the fact. He spoke with visible annoyance, but without hurrying and without particularly raising his voice. One could suppose that some special resolve, exclusive of all else, had taken root in him. 'Listen,' he began, decisively. 'I don't give a damn about any of you, but the way I see this business now I'm quite clear about one thing and that's that I'm completely baffled; please don't think that I've come to interrogate

512

you. I couldn't care a spit about that! Nothing could be further from my mind! Even if you were to reveal everything to me, all your secrets, I probably wouldn't listen, I'd spit and leave. The only reason I've come here is in order to find out, once and for all, person to person, whether it's true that you're mad or not! You see, there's a conviction in certain quarters (oh, just somewhere around) that you may be a madman, or have a very decided leaning that way. I must confess to you that I myself have been strongly inclined to support that opinion, in the first place because of the stupid and rather vile things you've been doing (things that defy all explanation), and in the second place because of your recent behaviour towards your mother and sister. Only a monster and a villain, if not a madman, could have acted towards them as you have; and consequently, you're a madman . . .'

'When did you see them?'

'I've only just left them. And I suppose you haven't seen them since that day, have you? Where is it you go gadding around, tell me that, will you, please? I've already been here three times looking for you. Your mother has been seriously ill ever since yesterday. She wanted to come and see you; Avdotya Romanovna tried to stop her, but she wouldn't listen: "If he's ill," she said, "if his mind's disturbed, who's going to help him if not his own mother?" So we all came here – we couldn't just leave her on her own. We kept begging her to calm down all the way to your door. We came in, but you weren't here; she sat right there. She went on sitting for ten minutes, while we stood over her, not saying a word. Then she got up and said: "If he's gone out he must be all right, and he's forgotten about his mother, and in that case it's not at all the right thing for his mother to do, to stand on his threshold begging for kindness like alms – she ought to be ashamed." She went home and took to her bed; now she has a fever: "I can see he has time for *that girl of his*," she said. She thinks Sofya Semyonovna's your finacée or your mistress or something, I don't know. I immediately went off to see Sofya Semyonovna, because, brother, I wanted to find out the whole story – when I got there I looked: the coffin was there, the children were crying. Sofya Semyonovna was measuring them, making little mourning outfits for them. You weren't there. I took a glance round, made my excuses and left, and then went back and reported to Avdotya Romanovna. So all that was nonsense, and there was no *girl of yours*, and so the likeliest explanation was madness. But here you are wolfing boiled beef as though you hadn't eaten for three days. Oh, I know that madmen eat, too, but even though you haven't said a word to me yet, I know that you're . . . not mad! That I will swear! Anything else, but not mad. And so I say the devil take you all, because there's some sort of mystery here, some sort of secret; and I don't intend to cudgel my brains over your secrets. I've simply come in order to shout at you,' he concluded, getting up, 'to let off steam – and I know what I'm going to do now!'

'What are you going to do?'

'What business is it of yours?'

'You'd better be careful – you're going out to get drunk!'

'How . . . how did you know?'

'There, I was right, wasn't I?'

Razumikhin said nothing for a moment.

'You've always been a very cool-headed chap and you've never ever been mad,' he said suddenly, with heat. 'You're right: I *am* going out to get drunk! Goodbye!' And he started to go.

'I was talking about you to my sister, Razumikhin – the day before yesterday, I think it was.'

'About me? But . . . where could you have seen her the day before yesterday?' Razumikhin said, coming to a sudden halt and even turning a little pale. One could guess that his heart was beating slowly and violently within him.

'She came here on her own, sat here and talked to me.'

'She did?'

'Yes, she did.'

'What did you tell her . . . about me, I mean?'

'I told her that you were a very good, honest and hard-working man. I didn't tell her that you love her, because she knows that already.'

'She does?'

'There I go, right again! Wherever I go, whatever happens to me, you must remain their Providence. I'm going to hand them over to you, as it were, Razumikhin. I say that because I'm fully aware how much you love her, and I'm convinced of the purity of your heart. I also know that she might be able to love you, and may even do so already. Now make your decision as you think fit – whether you should go out and get drunk or not.'

'Rodya, old chap . . . Look . . . I mean . . . Oh, the devil! But where are you going? Look: if all this is a secret, then forget it! But I . . . I'll find out your secret . . . And I'm absolutely certain it's a lot of nonsense and pernicious nonsense at that, and that you dreamed it all up yourself. The fact is that in spite of it all, you're really an excellent chap! A most excellent chap . . .!'

'What I was going to add, before you interrupted me, was that you made a very sensible choice just now in saying that you didn't intend to find out what these mysteries and secrets are. Leave it for the time being, don't trouble your head about it. You'll find out everything in good time, when it's right for you to know. Yesterday a man told me that what human beings need is air, air! I intend to go and see him now and ask him what he meant by that.'

Razumikhin stood in agitated reflection, trying to make sense of it all.

'He's mixed up in a political conspiracy! He must be! And he's on the point of taking some decisive step – it's for certain! There can be no other explanation and . . . and Dunya knows . . .' he suddenly thought to himself.

'So Avdotya Romanovna comes to see you,' he said, making the words scan in rhythm, 'and you want to go and see a man who says that what's needed is more air, more air and . . . and I suppose that letter . . . is also part of it,' he concluded, almost to himself.

'What letter?'

'She had a letter today, it upset her terribly, terribly. You have no idea. I started talking about you – she asked me to be quiet. Then . . . then she said that we might soon be saying goodbye to each other, and then she began to thank me for something in an effusive sort of way; then she went back to her room and wouldn't talk to me any more.'

'She had a letter?' Raskolnikov asked, reflectively.

'Yes, that's right; didn't you know? Hm.'

They both said nothing.

'Goodbye, Rodion. You know, brother . . . there was a time when I . . . but it doesn't matter; goodbye. You see, there was a time . . . Well, goodbye! I must be going, too. I shan't do any drinking. I don't need to now . . . Oh, you're making it all up!'

He began to hurry; as he was on his way out, however, and having

515

almost closed the door behind him, he suddenly opened it again and said, looking rather to one side:

'Oh, by the way, you remember that murder, the one Porfiry was talking about: you know, the old woman? Well, listen, they've found the murderer, he turned himself in and provided all the evidence himself. It was one of those workmen, the decorators, just imagine – you remember how I was defending them? Would you believe it – he purposely arranged that whole scene on the stairs, laughing and fighting with his mate as the others, the yardkeeper and the two other witnesses were going up, it was meant to create a diversion. What cunning, what presence of mind in such a young puppy! It's hard to credit; yet he showed persistence, confessed to the whole thing! And how I went and fell for it! Oh well, in my opinion that fellow's nothing more nor less than a genius of dissimulation and inventiveness, a genius of the juridical ploy – and so I suppose there's nothing particularly astonishing about it! Are there really people like that? What gives him even more credibility in my eyes is the fact that he became a victim of his own temperament and confessed. That makes it all the more plausible . . . But oh, how I put my foot in it that time! I was practically climbing up and down the walls in my zeal to defend them!'

'I say, I wonder if you'd mind telling me where you found out about this and why it interests you so much?' Raskolnikov asked, visibly perturbed.

'Now there's a question! Why does it interest me? You can seriously ask that? . . . Why, I found out from Porfiry, among other people. Actually, I found out nearly all of it from him.'

'From Porfiry?'

'That's right.'

'What . . . what did he say?' Raskolnikov asked, in a frightened voice.

'He cleared it all up for me in the most excellent manner. Gave me a psychological elucidation, after his own method.'

'He did? *He* cleared it up for you?'

'Yes, he himself. But look, goodbye for now, I must be off. I'll tell you all about it later, but right now I've business to attend to. I must say there was . . . one moment when I thought . . . Oh, but never mind – later! I've no need to go off bingeing now. You've made me drunk without my ever going near the stuff. I mean, I'm drunk,

Rodka! I'm drunk without vodka. Well, goodbye; I'll look in again, very soon.'

He went out.

'He's mixed up in a political conspiracy, it's the only, only possible explanation!' Razumikhin said to himself with decisive finality, as he slowly went down the stairs. 'And he's drawn his sister into it, too; that may very, very easily be in keeping with Avdotya Romanovna's character. They've been having secret meetings . . . Why, she's hinted as much to me herself. If one pieces together some of the things she's said . . . and half said . . . and hinted . . . it all falls into place quite neatly! How else is one to throw any light on this tangled business? Hm . . . And yet I thought . . . Oh, merciful God, what didn't I think? No, that was some kind of a brainstorm, and I'm guilty before him! It was he who brought it on, that brainstorm, when we were standing under the lamp in the corridor that time. Ugh! What a base, vulgar, loathsome thought on my part! Good for you, Mikolka, coming clean like that . . . It explains so many other things that have happened! His illness that time, that strange behaviour of his, even earlier, when he was still at the university – how gloomy and morose he always was . . . But what's the meaning of this letter now? It may very well have something to do with the whole business, too. Who is it from? It makes me suspicious . . . Hm. No, I'm going to find out everything.'

He suddenly remembered all the things he had observed and deduced about Dunya, and his heart sank within him. He dashed out of the building and set off at a run.

No sooner had Razumikhin left than Raskolnikov got up, turned towards the window, slouched over to one corner, then to another, as though he had forgotten how narrow his room was, and . . . sat down on the sofa again. He seemed an entirely new man; once again, the struggle – that meant there was still a way out!

'Yes, it means there's still a way out! Everything's been far too closed in and confined, it's getting so I can hardly breathe, as though I were in some kind of a trance.' Ever since that scene with Mikolka in Porfiry's chambers he had begun to choke without any outlet, in narrow constriction. After his encounter with Mikolka, that same day, there had been the scene with Sonya; its development and conclusion had been not at all the way he had imagined beforehand . . . that meant he had lost his strength, momentarily and radically! In a single flash! And yet he had concurred with Sonya that day, concurred with all his heart in her assertion that he would not be able to live alone with a deed like that on his soul! And Svidrigailov? Svidrigailov was a mystery . . . Svidrigailov caused him anxiety, it was true, but somehow not in that particular connection. He thought there might also be a possibility of a further struggle with Svidrigailov ahead. Svidrigailov might also be a way out; but Porfiry was another matter.

So Porfiry had cleared it all up for Razumikhin, explained it all to him in *psychological* terms! He'd dragged in that accursed psychology of his again! Porfiry? How could Porfiry believe even for one moment that Mikolka was guilty after what had taken place between them that day, after that scene, face to face, before Mikolka had made his confession, and which was only open to *one* possible interpretation? (In these last few days Raskolnikov had several times remembered the whole of that scene with Porfiry in fleeting fragments; he was unable to endure the memory of it as a totality.) The words that had passed between them, the movements and gestures there had been, the looks they had exchanged, the tones of voice they had used, all of that had reached a point where no Mikolka (whom Porfiry had seen through right from his very first word and gesture), no Mikolka could have shaken the bedrock of his conviction.

What was he to think? Even Razumikhin had begun to have his suspicions! The scene under the lamp in the corridor had not taken place without reason. Razumikhin had gone rushing off to Porfiry . . . But what had the latter's purpose been in pulling the wool over his eyes like this? What did he hope to gain by diverting Razumikhin's attention towards Mikolka? Yes, he must be up to something; there was some plan here, but what was it? It was true that much time had passed since that morning – far too much time, and during all of it there had been no sign of Porfiry whatsoever. And that, of course, could only be for the worse . . .

Raskolnikov took his cap and, after some reflection, walked out of the room. This was the first day in all that time that he had at least felt in control of his reason. 'I must have done with Svidrigailov,' he thought, 'and at whatever cost, as soon as possible; I think he's also waiting for me to come to him of my own accord.' And at that moment there was such a burst of sudden hatred from his tired heart that he might very well have killed one of them: either Svidrigailov or Porfiry. At any rate, he felt that even if he was unable to do it now, he would be in the future. 'We shall see, we shall see,' he kept saying to himself.

But no sooner had he opened the door on to the stairs than he suddenly collided with Porfiry himself. Porfiry had come to see him. For a single moment Raskolnikov froze, petrified – but only for that single moment. It was strange: he was not particularly surprised to see Porfiry and was not even all that afraid of him. He merely shuddered, but then quickly and instantaneously gathered his wits in preparation. 'Perhaps this is the dénouement! But why has he crept up on the sly, like a cat, without my being aware of it? Did he overhear what we were saying?'

'An unexpected visitor for you, Rodion Romanovich!' Porfiry Petrovich shouted, laughing. 'I've long been meaning to drop in on you, and as I was passing this way I thought – why not look in for five minutes and pay you a visit? Are you off somewhere? I shan't detain you. I'll just have one cigarette, if you'll be so good.'

'Very well, Porfiry Petrovich – sit down, sit down,' Raskolnikov said, finding his visitor a chair with such an obviously pleased and friendly look that he would have been struck with wonder had he been able to see himself. The leavings, the dregs were being scraped out! Sometimes, in similar fashion, a man will endure half an hour of mortal terror at the hands of a brigand, yet when the knife is finally put to his throat, even his terror passes. He sat right down in front of Porfiry and, without so much as a blink, gazed at him. Porfiry narrowed his eyes and began to light his cigarette.

'Well, go on then, go on.' The words seemed to be on the point of leaping out of Raskolnikov's heart. 'Go on, why don't you tell me what it is you've got to say?'

II

'I mean, look at these cigarettes,' Porfiry Petrovich said at last, having lit one, his breath recovered. 'They do me harm, nothing but harm, yet I can't give them up! I cough, sir, I've begun to get a tickling in my throat, and I'm short of breath. I'm a coward, you know; I went to see B—* for a consultation the other day – he spends half an hour at an absolute *minimum* examining each patient; he actually burst out laughing just at the sight of me: tapped my chest and auscultated me. "By the way," he said, "you ought to avoid tobacco; your lungs are dilated." But I mean, how can I give it up? What am I going to use as a substitute? I don't drink, sir, and that's what's really wrong with me, hee-hee-hee, my not drinking's the real trouble I suffer from! All is relative, Rodion Romanych, all is relative!'

'What's he up to now?' Raskolnikov thought with distaste. 'Is he starting his old routine again?' The whole of the recent scene that had taken place at their last meeting suddenly came back to him, and the feeling he had had then surged towards his heart in a wave.

'You know, I came to see you a couple of evenings ago; perhaps you weren't aware of it?' Porfiry Petrovich went on, studying the room. 'I came into this very room. I happened to be passing, just as I was today – "Why don't I pay him a little visit?" I thought. I came up here, and the door to your room was wide open; I took a look round, waited for a bit, didn't bother reporting my presence to your serving-maid – and left. Don't you have a lock on your door?'

Raskolnikov's face was growing darker and darker. It was as if Porfiry had guessed what he was thinking.

'I've come to explain myself to you, dear Rodion Romanovich, to explain myself to you, sir! I owe you an explanation, and am indeed obliged to offer you one!' he continued with a little smile, even patting Raskolnikov on the knee with the palm of his hand. At almost the same instant, however, his face suddenly assumed a serious and troubled expression; to Raskolnikov's surprise, it even seemed to twitch with sadness. He had never so far seen such an expression on Porfiry's face, and had not suspected him to be capable of it. 'That was a strange scene that occurred between us last time, Rodion Romanych. I suppose a strange scene also occurred between us at our first meeting; but at the time . . . Well, but that's now just one thing among others. What I want to say to you, sir, is this: it may very well be that I am very guilty in your regard; I feel that to be the case, sir. I mean, just remember the way we parted: your nerves were screaming and your knees were trembling, and so were mine. And you know, the way the situation between us developed, it really wasn't decent – certainly not the way two gentlemen ought to behave. For we are, after all, gentlemen, are we not? That is to say, in all situations we are first and foremost gentlemen; that needs to be borne in mind, sir. I mean, remember the point it came to . . . simply quite indecent, sir.'

'What game is he playing, what does he take me for?' Raskolnikov wondered in amazement, raising his head and staring at Porfiry for all he was worth.

'After some thought I have reached the conclusion that it is better for us to be candid with each other,' Porfiry Petrovich went on, throwing his head back slightly and lowering his eyes, as though not wishing to embarrass his former victim any more and as though he were looking askance at his earlier tricks and ploys. 'No sir, suspicions and scenes of that kind cannot continue for long. Mikolka put us out of our misery that time, otherwise I really don't know what might have transpired between us. That wretched little weasel of an artisan was sitting behind the partition of my chambers – can you imagine it? Of course, you know that already; and I, for my part, know that he went to see you later on; but the things you supposed at the time weren't true: I hadn't sent for anyone, and I hadn't yet given any kind of instructions. I expect you're wondering why? What can I say: you see, the whole thing had fairly flabbergasted me, too. I only just managed to have the yardkeepers sent for. (I expect you noticed them on your way out.) A certain thought passed through my mind at the time, swiftly, with the speed of lightning; you see, Rodion Romanych, I was rather sure of what I thought I knew. All right, I thought, even if I let this one go, I'll catch the next one by the tail – and I shan't let go of that, at least, because it'll be mine, all mine. You know, Rodion Romanych, sir, you have a very irritable nature; I would even venture to say that it's excessively so, when viewed against the other basic features of your character and heart, which I flatter myself in the hope of having partially understood. Well, but of course, even then I should have realized that it doesn't always happen that a man will get up and blurt out his most cherished secrets to you. Even though it does happen, especially if one drives a man beyond the limit of his endurance, it is, I must admit, a rare occurrence. That I should have realized. No, I thought, just give me one little detail! Just the smallest detail, just one, as long as it's something I can take in my hands, as long as it's something concrete, and not this psychology stuff. Because, I thought, if a man is guilty, then one should at least expect to get something tangible out of him; and it's even permissible to look for the most unexpected result. At the time I was relying on your character, Rodion Romanych, on your character more than anything else, sir! I really had the highest hopes of you!'

'But you . . . why are you talking like this now?' Raskolnikov muttered at last, without even giving the question any proper thought. 'What's he talking about?' he mused to himself. 'Does he really think I'm innocent?'

'Why am I talking like this? Why, I've come to explain myself to you, sir, considering it, as it were, my sacred duty to do so. I want to put it all before you with perfect completeness, exactly as it happened, the whole episode of that brainstorm of mine. I've made you put up with an awful lot, Rodion Romanych. I'm not a monster, sir. I mean, I understand how hard it must be for a man to carry all this on his shoulders when he's depressed, but also proud, masterful and impatient, above all impatient! I, at any rate, consider you as a man of the most noble character, sir, with even the beginnings of true greatness of soul, though I don't agree with you in all your convictions, something I view it as my duty to declare to you in advance, openly and with complete sincerity, for above all I do not wish to deceive. When I made your acquaintance, I felt an attachment to you. Perhaps my way of putting it makes you want to laugh? You have a right to, sir. I know that you didn't like me from the very first sight of me, and there's really no reason at all why you should. Consider me how you will, but what I want to do now is employ every means at my disposal to wipe out the impression I made, and prove to you that I, too, am a man with a heart and a conscience. I speak sincerely, sir.'

Porfiry Petrovich observed a dignified silence. Raskolnikov felt an onrush of some new fear. The thought that Porfiry believed him to be innocent had suddenly begun to frighten him.

'I don't really think it's necessary for me to tell it all in sequence, the way it suddenly began,' Porfiry Petrovich went on. 'Indeed, I think that would be superfluous. And in any case, I doubt whether I'd be able to, sir. Because how is it to be properly explained? First of all, there were rumours going about. Now, as to what kind of rumours they were, from whom I heard them and when . . . and in what connection they came to concern yourself – all that is also, I believe, superfluous. For me personally it began by chance, an event of pure chance of which one could say in the highest degree that it might or might not have happened. What was it? Hm, I don't think we need go into that, either. All those things, those rumours and chance events, formed themselves into a single thought inside my head. I will confess to you openly, because if one is to confess, then it must be to everything – I was the first to pounce on you at the time. All that business about the markings the old woman made on her pledges and so on, and so forth – all that was a lot of rubbish, sir. One could count hundreds of such instances. I also had occasion to learn about the scene at the local police bureau, also by chance, sir, and not simply in passing but from the lips of a remarkable and capital story-teller who, without really being aware of it, gave a masterly account of the whole thing. It was all just one thing among so many others, Rodion Romanych, my dear chap! I mean, how could I have failed to start looking in a certain direction? A hundred rabbits will never make a horse, a hundred suspicions will never make a case, as a certain English proverb says, and I mean that's only common wisdom, sir, but you see one also has to deal with the passions, the passions, sir, for an investigator is only human. At that point, too, I recalled your article, the one in that old journal, you remember, you talked about it in some detail during your first visit. I poured a bit of scorn on it at the time, but that was in order to stir you up for later on. I shall say it again: you're a very impatient and over-sensitive fellow, Rodion Romanych. That you're bold, pushing, serious and . . . have felt, have felt a great deal, all that I've known for a long time, sir. I am familiar with all those sensations of yours, and I read your article as though it had been written by someone I knew. It had been thought up in a state of frenzy, during sleepless nights, with much surging and beating of the heart, with frustrated enthusiasm! Oh, that proud, frustrated, enthusiasm is a dangerous thing in youth! At the time I poured scorn on it, but now I will tell you that I'm really terribly fond – in an amateur capacity – of those first, youthful, impassioned essays of the pen. "Smoke, mist, a string vibrating in the mist."* Your article is absurd and fantastic, but it contains a gleam of sincerity, a youthful, uncorrupted pride, the boldness of despair; it's a gloomy piece of work, sir, but that's the good thing about it. I read your article through, and then put it aside, and . . . as I was doing so, I thought: "Well, that chap's going to have some problems!" So, I ask you, after an introduction like that, how could I fail to be engrossed by the sequel? Oh, good heavens, was I going to say anything? Was I going to put my finger on anything in particular? All I did at the time was observe. "What's going on here?" I thought. But nothing was going on, absolutely nothing, and even perhaps the highest degree of nothing. And in any case, for me, an investigator, to get so engrossed like that was actually quite improper: I had Mikolka on my hands, and there was evidence, too – whatever you say, it was evidence! And he, too, dragged in a psychological angle of his own; it was necessary to spend some time on him because, after all, this was a matter of life and death. Why am I telling you all this? So that you know, and so that, possessing the mind and the heart that you do, you won't blame me for my aggressive behaviour that time. It wasn't really aggressive, sir, I tell you that in all sincerity, hee-hee! What do you suppose: that I didn't search your room that time? Oh but I did, sir, I did, hee-hee, I did, while you were lying here ill in bed. Unofficially and incognito, but I did conduct a search. Your room was examined right down to the last stray hair, when the clues we had were fresh; but – *umsonst*!* I thought: this fellow's going to show up, he's going to show his face, and pretty quick, too; if he's guilty, he'll show his face. Another man might not, but this one will. And do you remember the way Mr Razumikhin began spilling the beans to you? We arranged that in order to get you worried, and so we let that rumour out on purpose, so he'd spill the beans to you, and Mr Razumikhin is not the kind of man who restrains his indignation. Mr Zamyotov was the one who first noticed your anger and your undisguised boldness: I mean, what kind of behaviour was that to go blurting out in an inn: "I killed her!" Such boldness, such daring, sir! "If he *is* guilty, he's a real fighter," I thought. So then I had a bit of a think, sir. I would wait! Wait for you with all my might, but meanwhile you'd quite simply wiped the floor with Zamyotov and . . . well, actually, the trouble with all that accursed psychology stuff is that it cuts two ways! Well, so I waited for you, I looked, and God gave you to me – you showed your face! My heart was fairly thumping, I can tell you. Ha! I mean, why did you come to see me that morning? The way you laughed, the way you laughed as you came in that time, do you remember? I mean, I saw through it all as though through a pane of glass, and if I hadn't been waiting for you in such a peculiar fashion I'd never have even have noticed anything in your laughter. That's what it means to "be in the right mood". And Mr Razumikhin that day – oh, the stone, the stone, do you remember, the one under which certain objects were hidden? Well, it was just as if I could see it, in a kitchen garden somewhere – that's what you told

Zamyotov, and you said the same thing when you came to see me the second time? And the way you began to go over your article that time, the way you started to expound the ideas in it – so that one construed your each and every word in a double sense, as though there were another sitting under it! Well you see, Rodion Romanych, it was in that manner that I reached the pillars of Hercules, and as soon as I knocked my forehead against them, I came to. "No," I said to myself, "what am I doing? I mean, all this can quite easily be explained in a different way, that will make it seem even more natural." Torment, sir! "No," I thought, "I'd do better getting hold of a little detail! . . ." And when I heard you talking about those doorbells, I fairly froze – I even got the shakes. "Well," I thought, "there it is, my little detail! The very one!" I wasn't even thinking any more, I simply couldn't bring myself to. I'd have given a thousand roubles of my own money at that moment just to have seen you *with my own eyes*: seen you walking that hundred yards side by side with that wretched little artisan, after he'd called you a murderer to your face, and not daring to ask him a single question the whole way! . . . Well, and the chill in your spinal cord? Those doorbells, when you were ill and half-delirious? After that, is it any wonder, Rodion Romanych, that I played such jokes on you? And why did you show your face just at that very moment? I mean, it was just as if someone had pushed you in, I swear to God it was, and if Mikolka hadn't pulled us apart, then . . . but do you remember Mikolka? Have you got him well in your memory? I mean, that was thunder, sir! It was thunder booming from a thundercloud, an arrow from the gods! Well, and how did I greet it? I didn't believe it, not one little word of it, you yourself saw how I was! But that's not all. Later, after you'd gone, when he began to give the most, most coherent replies to certain points I raised, so that I was struck with wonder, even then I didn't believe one brass copeck's worth of it! That's what they mean when they say a man's made himself as hard as a diamond. No, I thought, never! What's Mikolka got to do with it?'

'Razumikhin told me just now that you're still pressing the charge against Nikolai, and that you assured him of that fact . . .'

He ran out of breath, nearly choking, and did not finish his sentence. He listened in a state of agitation that was beyond all words as the man who had seen right through him disavowed his own perceptions. In his ambiguous words he was greedily searching and feeling for something more final and precise.

'Mr Razumikhin!' Porfiry Petrovich exclaimed, as though he were relieved at having been put a question by the hitherto silent Raskolnikov. 'Hee-hee-hee! Oh, Mr Razumikhin simply had to be got out of the way: two's company, three's a crowd. Mr Razumikhin's not your man, sir, he's just an innocent bystander; why, he came running to me with such a pale, pale face . . . Well, never mind about him, why get him mixed up in this? Now, as regards Mikolka, would you like to know what sort of a character he is – according to my understanding, that is? The first thing to be said is that he's still an ungrown child, and not so much a coward as a sort of artist. It's true, sir, don't laugh at my explaining him that way. He's harmless and susceptible to every influence. He has a heart; he has imagination. He likes to dance and sing, they say he tells stories in such a way that people come flocking from other parts to listen to him. He attends the school, he'll laugh to the point of collapse if you so much as show him a finger, and he drinks himself senseless, not so much from debauchery as from sheer occasion, now and then, the way a child might, when people ply him with vodka. Then there's the way he went stealing that time, yet he wasn't really aware he'd done anything wrong; because "if I picked them up off the pavement, what kind of stealing was that?" And did you know that he's a Raskolnik – or rather, not so much a Raskolnik as simply a sectarian; there were "Runners"* in his family, and it's not so long ago since he himself spent two whole years in the country under the spiritual guidance of some elder or other. All this I learned from Mikolka and his Zaraisk chums. And that's not the half of it! He actually intended to run away to a hermitage! He got the holy fever, used to stay up all night praying, reading the old, "true" books, and lost all sense of reality. St Petersburg had a powerful effect on him, especially the fair sex, and, of course, the vodka. He's a susceptible fellow, sir, and he forgot his elder and everything else as well. I have information that a certain artist here in town took a liking to him, began paying him visits, but then this incident blew up! Well, he was scared – could only think of hanging himself, or running away. What are we going to do about the image of our legal system that's developed among the common people? I mean, some of them are absolutely terrified by the word "trial"! Who's to blame for it? Well, perhaps these new courts will have some effect. My God, I do hope so. Well, sir: while he's been in gaol he's evidently remembered his honourable elder again; the Bible's come out again, too. Have you any conception, Rodion Romanovich, of what the word "suffering" means to some of them? They don't do it for the sake of anyone in particular, but just for its own sake, purely and simply as "suffering"; all that matters is to accept suffering, and if it's from the powers-that-be, that's all to the good. I once had a case of an incredibly docile prisoner who spent a whole year in gaol, he used to read his Bible on top of the stove at nights, well, and he read and he read to the point where he suddenly, for no apparent reason, snatched up a brick and threw it at the head gaoler, who'd done nothing to arouse the man's anger. And the way he threw it: he purposely aimed it an *arshin* too wide, so as not to cause the man any injury! Well, we all know what happens to a prisoner who attacks an officer with an offensive weapon: and he "accepted his suffering". So you see, I now suspect that Mikolka wants to "accept his suffering", or something of that sort. I know that to be true, sir; I even have evidence. It's just that he doesn't know that I know. Don't you think it's amazing that a bunch of peasants like that can throw up people with such imagination? One finds them everywhere. The elder's begun to have an influence on him again, particularly after the episode with the noose – that jogged his memory. But in any case, he'll tell me everything himself, he'll show his face. Do you suppose he'll be able to keep it up? Just you wait – he'll deny it all. I'm waiting for him to show up any moment now and go back on his testimony. I've taken a liking to this Mikolka, and I'm investigating him thoroughly. And what do you think? Tee-hee! To some of the points I put to him he gave me really coherent answers – he's obviously got hold of the necessary information and cleverly prepared himself; well, but with some of the other points he got himself into a fair old mess, didn't know a single thing, hadn't the foggiest, and didn't even suspect as much! No, Rodion Romanych old chap, Mikolka's not our man! This is a murky, fantastic case, a contemporary one, an incident that belongs to our own age, an age in which the heart of man has grown dark and muddied; in which one hears the saying quoted that "blood reinvigorates"; in which material comfort is preached as life's only aim. It's a case that involves dreams derived from books, sir, a heart that has been overstimulated by theories; in it we see a determination to take the first step, but it's a determination of a peculiar kind – the man's taken his resolve, but it's as if he'd fallen off a cliff or jumped from a steeple, as if he'd blundered into the crime like some clockwork automaton. He forgot to close the door behind him, and he killed, killed two people, because of a theory. He killed, and he didn't even bother to take the money that was there, and the things he did take he hid under a stone. It wasn't enough for him to go through torment as he stood behind the door as people were hammering at the door and ringing the bell – no, after that he had to go back to the empty apartment in a state of semi-delirium in order to remind himself of that bell, he needed to feel the chill down his spine once again . . . Well, that was probably caused by his illness, but what about this? He's committed a murder, yet he considers himself an honourable fellow, he has contempt for other people, goes around like some pallid angel – no, Mikolka's not our man, my dear Rodion Romanovich, Mikolka's not our man!'

These last words, following as they did on all that had gone before and had seemed like a disavowal, were wholly unexpected. Raskolnikov shuddered as though he had been run through by a blade.

'Then . . . who . . . is the murderer?' he asked, unable to restrain himself, in a gasping voice. Porfiry Petrovich fairly reeled back in his chair, as though this question was so unexpected that he was amazed by it.

'Who is the murderer? . . .' he said, as though unable to believe his ears. 'Why, *you* are the murderer, Rodion Romanovich! You are, sir . . .' he added almost in a whisper, in a voice of total conviction.

Raskolnikov leapt from the sofa, stood there for a few seconds and sat down again, without saying a word. Faint convulsions suddenly passed across his whole face.

'That lip of yours is quivering again, the way it did that time,' Porfiry Petrovich muttered, almost with sympathy. 'I don't think you've quite understood me, Rodion Romanych,' he added, after a slight pause, 'and that's why you're so dumbfounded. I came here with the specific purpose of saying everything and bringing the matter out into the open.'

'It wasn't me, I didn't do it,' Raskolnikov whispered, the way little children do when they are caught redhanded.

'Yes, Rodion Romanych, sir, it was you and no one else, sir,' Porfiry whispered sternly and with conviction.

They both fell silent, and their silence lasted a strangely long time, some ten minutes. Raskolnikov leaned his elbows on the table and ran his fingers through his hair, not saying anything. Porfiry Petrovich sat quietly waiting. Suddenly Raskolnikov gave Porfiry a contemptuous look.

'Up to your old capers again, Porfiry Petrovich? Still pursuing those methods of yours? I really wonder you're not sick of them by now!'

'Hah! That will do! What methods do I need now? It would be different if there were witnesses here; as it is, we're whispering in private. You can see for yourself that I haven't come here in order to hunt you down and trap you like a hare. Whether you confess or not is a matter of indifference to me right at this moment. In my own mind I'm convinced, and I don't need you to help me.'

'If that's so, why did you come here?' Raskolnikov asked, irritably. 'I'll put the question again: if you think I'm guilty, why don't you put me in prison?'

'Well now, there's a question! I'll answer it in stages: in the first place, it wouldn't do me any good to place you directly under arrest.'

'What do you mean, it wouldn't do you any good? If you're convinced, then you must . . .'

'Oh, what does it matter that I'm convinced? I mean, all this is still just a dream of mine, sir. Why should I put you *into retirement* like that? You yourself must know that's what it would be tantamount to, since you're asking me to do it. Say, for example, I were to bring you face to face with that wretched little artisan, and you said to him: "Are you drunk, or something? Who saw you with me? I simply thought you were a drunk, and you *were* drunk, in any case" – well, what would I be able to say to that, particularly since your version of events is more probable than his, because his testimony consists of nothing but psychology – which is almost an insult to his ugly mug – and you've hit the nail on the head, because the villain drinks like a fish and everyone knows it. And then there's the fact that I myself have already several times openly confessed to you that this psychology stuff is a two-edged weapon, that its other edge is always going to be larger and more plausible, and that apart from it, I haven't so far got anything on you. And even though I'm going to put you inside in any case, and have actually come here (though it's not official etiquette) in order to caution you about it in advance, I will tell you straight out (though again it's not official etiquette) that it won't do me any good. Well sir, and in the second place, I've come to see you . . .'

'Yes, and in the second place?' (Raskolnikov was still gasping.)

'Because, as I told you just now, I consider it my duty to offer you an explanation. I don't want you to see me as a monster, particularly as I'm sincerely fond of you, believe it or not. In consequence of which, in the third place, I've come to you with an open and straightforward proposition – that you should file a plea of guilty. That would be countless times better for you, and better for me, too – because then it would be over and done with. Well, what do you say – am I making sense to you?'

Raskolnikov thought for a moment.

'What I say is this, Porfiry Petrovich: I mean, you've been telling me yourself that it's all just psychology, yet here you are wandering over into mathematics. What if you're simply mistaken?'

'No, Rodion Romanych, I'm not mistaken. I am in possession of a certain little detail. You see, it was something I found at the time, sir; the Lord sent it to me!'

'What little detail?'

'I'm not going to tell you, Rodion Romanych. And in any case I don't have the right to delay any longer; I'm going to put you inside, sir. So reflect on it: *right now* it's all the same to me, and consequently, consequently I'm only thinking of you. I swear to God, it will be better for you, Rodion Romanych!'

Raskolnikov smiled an ironic, malevolent smile.

'Why, this is not only ridiculous, it's downright shameless. I mean, even if I were guilty (which I don't for one moment admit), why should I file a plea of guilty with you when you yourself say that when you put me inside it'll be as if I'd been put *into retirement*?'

'Ah, Rodion Romanych, don't place too much credence in words; it may be no sort of *retirement* at all! I mean, that's only a theory, and my own, to boot, and what kind of an authority am I to you? It's quite possible that I'm concealing something from you even now, sir. I'm not just going to produce everything and suddenly lay it all before you, hee-hee! And there's another thing: how can you ask why you should file a plea of guilty? Have you any idea what a reduction in your sentence that would mean? I mean, when would you be doing it, at what kind of a moment? Just think about that! When another man's already accepted responsibility for the crime and got the whole

530

case in a mess? And I swear to God himself that I'll fabricate a thing or two and arrange it with the authorities so that your plea will come as something totally unexpected. We'll completely demolish all that psychology, I'll convert all those suspicions about you into thin air, so that your crime will look like some kind of a brainstorm, because, in all conscience, a brainstorm is what it was. I'm a decent man, Rodion Romanych, and I'll keep my word.'

Raskolnikov fell sadly silent and let his head droop; he thought for a long time and at length smiled his ironic smile once more: this time, however, it was meek and mournful.

'No, I don't want it!' he said, as though he had completely given up trying to hide anything from Porfiry. 'It isn't worth it! I really don't want your reduction!'

'Ah! That was what I was afraid of!' Porfiry Petrovich exclaimed heatedly and almost in spite of himself. 'That was what I was afraid of: that you wouldn't want our reduction.'

Raskolnikov looked at him sadly and reprovingly.

'I say, don't turn your nose up at life!' Porfiry went on. 'You've still a great deal ahead of you. What do you mean, you don't want a reduction, what do you mean? You impatient man!'

'A lot of what ahead of me?'

'Life! What are you, a prophet? What do you know? Seek and ye shall find. Perhaps God's been waiting for you in all this. And you won't wear them forever, the fetters . . .'

'No, I'll get a reduction,' Raskolnikov laughed.

'What is it that you're scared of – the bourgeois shame? It may be that you're scared of it without realizing it – because you're young! Yet you know, you shouldn't feel any fear or shame at filing a plea of guilty.'

'Ha-ah! I don't give a spit for all that!' Raskolnikov whispered contemptuously and with revulsion, as though he did not even want to speak. He started to get up, as though he were about to go off somewhere, but then sat down again in visible despair.

'So that's what it is, is it? You've lost your confidence and think I'm indulging in gross flattery towards you; but have you really lived all that much? Are there really all that many things that you understand? You concocted a theory, and were then ashamed that it didn't hold water, that it turned out to be most unoriginal! And indeed, it turned out vile, there's no denying that, but even so you're not a hopeless

531

villain. Not such a villain at all! At any rate, you haven't fooled yourself for long, you've reached the pillars of Hercules in one go. I mean, what sort of man do you suppose I think you are? I think you're one of the kind who even if his intestines were being cut out would stand looking at his torturers with a smile – as long as he'd found a God, or a faith. Well, find those, and you'll live. You ought to have had a change of air long ago – one can see that a mile off. For heaven's sake – suffering's not such a very terrible thing. Go and suffer for a bit. That Mikolka fellow may well be right in wanting to suffer. I know you don't believe it – but don't try to be too clever, either; surrender yourself directly to life, without circumspection; don't worry – it will carry you straight to the shore and put you on your feet. What shore? How should I know? I simply believe that you still have a lot of living to do yet. I know that you're listening to my words just now as if they were some sermon learnt by rote; perhaps later on you'll remember them, perhaps they'll be useful to you some day; that's why I'm saying them. It's also a good thing that it was only an old woman you murdered. If you'd thought up another theory you might have committed some deed a hundred million times more horrible! It may be that you still ought to thank God; why, for all you know he may be preserving you for something. Be of great heart, and fear less. Are you afraid of the great discharge of duty that lies ahead of you? No, at the point you have reached, such fear is shameful. Since you have taken such a step, you must stand firm. You have reached the moment of justice. So discharge the duty that justice requires of you. I know you don't believe it, but I promise you, life will carry you through. You'll even get to like each other afterwards. What you need now, though, is simply air, air, air!'

Raskolnikov gave a terrible shudder.

'Who are you, anyway?' he exclaimed. 'What sort of a prophet are you? What's this majestic tranquillity from whose heights you're uttering these wise prophecies to me?'

'Who am I? Oh, I'm just a man who's had his day. A man who may have feelings and be capable of sympathy, who may even know a few things, but one who has quite definitely had his day. But you're a different kettle of fish: God has a life in store for you (though who knows, perhaps yours too will pass away like smoke and come to nothing). So what if you *will* end up with another class of person? You're not going to miss your creature comforts, are you? Not with a heart and feelings like yours! What does it matter that no one may see you for an awfully long time? Time's not what matters – it's you that does. Become a sun, and then everyone will see you. A sun must first and foremost be a sun. Why are you smiling again? Because I'm such a Schiller? And I bet you're thinking that I'm trying to ingratiate myself with you now! So what if I am? Tee-hee-hee! You know, Rodion Romanych, sir, I don't think you ought to believe everything I say – this is just the way I'm used to carrying on, I'll admit that; though I'd add just one thing: as to the question of to what extent I'm a villain and to what extent I'm a decent man you may judge for yourself!'

'When are you planning to arrest me?'

'Oh, I may allow you to wander around for another day and a half, or possibly two. Think about it, my dear chap, and say your prayers. It will be better for you, I swear to God it will, I promise you.'

'And what if I run away?' Raskolnikov asked, with a strange, ironic smile.

'No, you won't run away. A muzhik might run away, a fashionable sectarian* might run away – the lackey of other men's thoughts – because you've only to show him the tip of your finger, like Warrant Officer Dyrka,* and he'll believe anything you tell him for the rest of his life. And after all, you don't believe in your theory now – so what would you run away with? And what good would running away do you? Being on the run is an unpleasant, arduous business, and what you need above all else is to live and to be in a clearly defined situation with its own clearly defined air, and I mean, what kind of air would you find on the run? You'd run away and come back again of your own accord. *You can't get along without us*. And if I lock you up in a cell – you'll stay there for a month, or two, or three, and then suddenly, remember this, you'll turn yourself in in such a way that even you will be surprised. You won't know that you're going to do it until you do. I'm even certain that you'll decide to "accept suffering"; you don't believe what I'm saying now, but you'll think it over to yourself. Because suffering, Rodion Romanych, is a great thing; don't go looking at how fat I've got, there's no need; and yet, and yet I know – don't laugh – that suffering has a purpose. Mikolka's right. No, you won't run away, Rodion Romanych.'

Raskolnikov got up from where he had been sitting and took his cap. Porfiry Petrovich also got up.

'Going out for a walk? It should be a fine evening, as long as there isn't a thunderstorm. Though actually, it might be better if we were to have one, it might clear the air . . .'

He also took up his cap.

'Look here, Porfiry Petrovich,' Raskolnikov said with grim persistence, 'please don't get it into your head that I've made any kind of confession to you today. You're a strange man, and I've listened to you out of sheer curiosity. I've made no kind of confession to you at all . . . Bear that in mind.'

'Oh, I know, I'll bear it in mind – but I mean, look at you, you're positively trembling. Have no fear, my good chap; we shall do things your way. Go out and take a bit of a walk; only don't go too far, that's all. Oh, and just to be on the safe side, I have one little favour to ask you,' he added, lowering his voice. 'It's rather a tricky one, this, but important: if it should, er, possibly transpire (I personally don't believe that it will and consider you quite incapable of doing such a thing), if it should transpire – oh, just by some chance – that you should during the course of the next forty-eight hours conceive a desire to bring this business to an end in some different, imaginative way – by, for example, taking your own life (an absurd supposition, and you really must forgive me for mentioning it), then please leave a short but detailed note. You know, just a couple of lines, two lines will do, and don't forget to mention the building block: that would be the decent thing to do, sir. Well, sir, goodbye . . . I wish you good thoughts and happy undertakings!'

Porfiry went out looking somehow hunched, and as if he were trying to avoid looking at Raskolnikov. Raskolnikov went over to the window and waited with irritable impatience for the moment when, according to his estimate, Porfiry would emerge on to the street and proceed on his way. Then he, too, went quickly out of the room.

He was hurrying to see Svidrigailov. What he hoped to obtain from that man he himself did not know. But in that man there was concealed some hidden power that held sway over him. Having once perceived this, he had been unable to rest, and now, moreover, the time was at hand.

As he made his way along there was one question that particularly tormented him: had Svidrigailov been to see Porfiry?

So far as he could judge, he was ready to swear that he had not. Thinking about it more and more, remembering all that had happened during Porfiry's visit, he put two and two together: no, he had not, of course he had not!

But if he had not been to see Porfiry yet, would he or would he not do so eventually?

For the moment it seemed to him unlikely. Why was that? He could not have explained this either, but even if he had been able to, he would not have spent too much time worrying his head about this in particular. All of these things tormented him, yet at the same time left him somehow indifferent. The strange thing, which possibly no one would have believed, was that the question of his present, immediate destiny left him only faintly and somewhat absent-mindedly preoccupied. He was being tormented by something else, something of a far more important and ultimate nature – something that concerned himself and no one else, but that was different from all this, something essential. Furthermore, he was experiencing a sense of infinite moral weariness, even though his reason was functioning better than it had during all these recent days.

And was it really worth it now, after all that had taken place, to attempt to master all these newly arisen, trivial embarrassments? Was it, for example, really worth trying to hatch some intrigue in order to stop Svidrigailov going to see Porfiry; to study the behaviour of a man such as Svidrigailov, to make inquiries about him, waste time on him?

Oh, how tired he was of all that!

Yet here he was hurrying to see Svidrigailov; might it not be that he was hoping for something *new* from him, some hint, some way out? Like a man clutching at straws? Might it not be that fate and instinct were drawing them together? Perhaps it was merely the effect of weariness and despair; perhaps the person he needed was not Svidrigailov but someone else, and Svidrigailov merely happened to have turned up. Was it Sonya? But why would he go and see Sonya now? In order to ask for her tears again? And in any case Sonya frightened him. Sonya represented an inexorable judgement, a decision that could not be altered. Now it was either his way or hers. Particularly at this moment he did not feel up to going to see her. No, he would rather go and put Svidrigailov to the test! What was happening to him? He could not escape the inward feeling that it was precisely Svidrigailov who had for a long time now been the person he needed for some especial purpose.

That was all very well, but what could they possibly have in common? Even the wrongdoing each had committed could not be viewed on an equal level. Furthermore, this man was highly unpleasant, obviously a lecher, sly and deceitful beyond all doubt, and probably quite vicious. The stories about him tended to confirm that. He had, it was true, gone to some trouble for the sake of Katerina Ivanovna's children; but who could tell for what purpose, and in what lay the significance of his concern? This man was forever engaged in plans and projects of various kinds.

During all these days there was another thought that had kept constantly flickering through Raskolnikov's mind, causing him abominable torment, though he had made the most persistent efforts to banish it, so painful was it to him. He had sometimes fancied that Svidrigailov had been spying on him, was indeed doing so even now; that Svidrigailov had found out his secret; that Svidrigailov had designs on Dunya. What if he had them even now? The answer to this question was almost certainly that *he had*. And what if now, having learned his secret and thus gained power over him, he were to decide to use it as a weapon against Dunya?

This notion had sometimes tormented him even in his sleep, but only now, as he made his way to Svidrigailov's lodgings, did it appear to him with conscious vividness. This thought reduced him to black fury. For one thing, if it were true, then everything would be altered, even his own situation: he would have to disclose his secret to Dunya immediately. He would perhaps have to betray himself in order to prevent Dunya from taking some incautious step. What about the letter? That morning Dunya had received some letter or other! From whom in St Petersburg could she have had a letter? (Not Luzhin, surely?) It was true that Razumikhin was on guard there; but Razumikhin did not know anything. Perhaps he ought to tell it all to Razumikhin? Raskolnikov considered this prospect with loathing.

Whatever happened, he must see Svidrigailov as soon as possible, he decided to himself, conclusively. The important thing now, thank God, was not so much the details as the essence of the matter; but if, if he was capable of it, if Svidrigailov was pursuing some intrigue against Dunya, then . . .

So tired had Raskolnikov become after all this time, this long month, that he was by now unable to resolve such questions other than by one simple decision: 'Then I shall kill him,' he thought in cold despair. A feeling of heaviness constricted his heart; he came to a standstill in the middle of the street and began to look around him: which way was he going, and where had he reached? He was on — Prospect, some thirty or forty yards from the Haymarket, which he had just crossed. The whole of the second floor of the building on his left was taken up by an inn and eating-house. All the windows were wide open; the inn, to judge by the moving figures at the windows, was packed full of people. The saloon was overflowing with the sound of choral singing, the rasp of a clarinet and a violin, and the loud beat of a Turkish drum. Female shrieks could be heard. He was on the point of going back, puzzled as to why he had turned on to — Prospect, when suddenly, in one of the open windows at the far end, sitting right by the sill, at a tea-table, pipe in mouth, he caught sight of Svidrigailov. This gave him a terrible shock, amounting almost to terror. Svidrigailov was watching him and studying him in silence; what also caused Raskolnikov an instantaneous shock was the fact that Svidrigailov seemed to be on the point of getting up in order to slip away while still unnoticed. Raskolnikov immediately tried to make it look as though he had not spotted him, gazing reflectively to one side while all the time continuing to observe him out of the corner of his eye. His heart was beating anxiously. It was true: Svidrigailov evidently did not want anyone to see him. He had taken his pipe out of his mouth and had been about to move off with the intention of making himself scarce; having stood up and moved the table away, however, he had no doubt suddenly noticed that Raskolnikov had seen him and was watching him. Between them there now took place something that resembled the scene of their first meeting at Raskolnikov's lodgings, when he had been asleep. A crafty smile appeared on

Svidrigailov's face, and began to spread and spread. Both men knew that they had seen and had been watching each other. At last Svidrigailov broke into a loud laugh.

'Well, well, come up if you want; I'm in here!' he shouted out of the window.

Raskolnikov went upstairs to the inn.

He found Svidrigailov in a very small room at the back of the establishment; the room had one window and adjoined the main saloon, where at twenty small tables, amidst the desperate shouting of the *pesenniki*,* some merchants, civil servants and a large number of all kinds of townsfolk sat drinking tea. The sound of billiard balls was coming from somewhere. On Svidrigailov's table, facing him, stood an uncorked bottle of champagne and a glass that was half full. In the little room there was also a boy with a small hand-organ, and a healthy, red-cheeked girl in a tucked-up striped skirt and a Tyrolean bonnet with ribbons, a street singer of about eighteen who, in spite of the choral performance in the other room, was singing to the organ-player's accompaniment, in a rather hoarse contralto, some kind of manservants' ditty . . .

'That'll be enough,' Svidrigailov said, breaking her off as Raskolnikov entered.

The girl immediately cut short her performance and stood still in submissive expectancy. She had also sung her rhymed and somewhat dubious manservants' ditty* with a kind of earnest and submissive look on her face.

'Hey – Filipp, a glass!' Svidrigailov shouted.

'I haven't come here for champagne,' Raskolnikov said.

'As you wish, I didn't buy it for you. Here, Katya, you have some! That's all I want for today, now off you go!' He poured her a whole glass of the wine and placed one yellow paper rouble on the table. Katya drank the glass down in one, the way women do, that is to say in a dozen swallows, took the banknote, kissed the hand of Svidrigailov, who with the utmost gravity permitted her to do so, and left the room, the boy with the hand-organ trailing out after her. They had both been summoned up from the street. Svidrigailov had hardly yet spent a week in St Petersburg, but already everything around him was on some sort of patriarchal footing. The inn's manservant, Filipp, was by now a 'friend', and grovelled in servility. The door that led through to the saloon could be bolted; in this little room Svidrigailov was quite at home, and the likelihood was that he spent whole days in it. The inn was dirty, wretched and not even of average quality.

'I was on my way to see you, you're the very person I'm looking for,' Raskolnikov began. 'But why on earth did I suddenly take the turning on to — Prospect after I'd crossed the Haymarket? I never come along this way, and I never look in here. I always turn right after the Haymarket. And this street doesn't even lead to where you live. Yet I'd just turned the corner, and there you were! It's strange!'

'Why don't you just say it's a miracle?'

'Because it may only be an accident.'

'Oh, what's the matter with all these people?' Svidrigailov said, breaking into laughter. 'They won't admit the existence of miracles, even though they secretly believe in them! I mean, you say yourself that it "may be" only an accident. You have no idea how many wretched little cowards there are in this town on the question of having one's own opinion, Rodion Romanych! I don't mean you. You have your own opinion and have not been afraid to have it. It's for that very reason that you drew my curiosity.'

'Was that the only reason?'

'Why, it's sufficient, isn't it?'

Svidrigailov was evidently in a stimulated condition, but only slightly so; he had drunk only half a glass of the champagne.

'I seem to remember you came to see me before you'd found out that I was capable of having what you call my own opinion,' Raskolnikov commented.

'Oh, things were different then. A man's footsteps lead him to all sorts of places. But as far as the miracle's concerned I would say to you that I think you've spent the last two or three days asleep. It was I who suggested this inn, and it was no miracle that you came straight here; I myself explained to you how to get here, told you what street it was on, and the times at which you could find me here. Remember?'

'No, I've forgotten,' Raskolnikov answered with some surprise.

'I can believe it. Twice I told you. The address must have imprinted itself on your memory automatically. You also took the turning along here automatically, and you went straight to the right address without being conscious of it. Even as I was telling you I didn't have much faith that you'd taken it in. You certainly give yourself away, Rodion Romanych. And there's another thing: I'm convinced that there are many people in St Petersburg who talk to themselves as they go about. This is a town of semi-lunatics. If we had any seats of learning in this place, the medical men, the jurists and the philosophers would be able to conduct the most valuable investigations into St Petersburg, each according to their speciality. There aren't many places where there are as many gloomy, harsh and strange influences on the soul of man as there are in St Petersburg. Think what the climatic influences alone are worth! Yet this is the administrative centre of all Russia, and its character must have an effect on everything. But that's not what matters now; what matters now is that on several past occasions I've watched you from the wings. You come out of that building of yours – still holding your head up straight. By the time you've gone twenty paces you've begun to lower it and you're folding your hands behind your back. You look, but you evidently no longer see anyone either in front of you or to either side. Finally you begin to move your lips and talk to yourself, and sometimes you free one of your hands and declaim something out loud, and then you stand still for a long time in the middle of the road. That's very bad, sir. Someone apart from myself might see you, and it wouldn't do you much good. It's all really much of a muchness to me, and I'm not going to try to cure you, but I think you know what I mean.'

'So you know I'm being followed?' Raskolnikov asked, studying him keenly.

'No, I know nothing of the kind,' Svidrigailov replied in astonishment.

'Well then, let's leave the subject of me alone,' Raskolnikov muttered, frowning.

'Very well, let's do that.'

'I'd rather you told me, if it's true that you come here drinking regularly and told me to meet you here twice, why it was that when I looked up at this window from the street you hid and tried to slip away? I saw that very plainly.'

'Hee-hee! And why that day, when I stood on your threshold, did you go on lying on your sofa with your eyes closed pretending to be asleep, when you weren't asleep at all? I saw *that* very plainly.'

'I might have had . . . reasons . . . you know that yourself.'

'And I, too, might have had reasons, even though you're not going to find out what they were.'

Raskolnikov lowered his right elbow on to the table, supported his chin from below with the fingers of his right hand and stared fixedly at Svidrigailov. For about a minute he studied Svidrigailov's face, which even on earlier occasions he had always found startling. It was a strange face, and almost resembled a mask: white and rubicund, with rubicund, scarlet lips, a light-blond beard and blond hair that was still quite thick. His eyes were somehow excessively blue, their gaze excessively heavy and immobile. There was something terribly unpleasant about this handsome and extremely youthful – if years were anything to go by – face. Svidrigailov's clothes were fashionable, summer-styled and lightweight, his shirt and cuffs particularly smart. On one finger he wore an enormous ring studded with an expensive precious stone.

'Do I really have to waste time playing with you as well?' Raskolnikov said suddenly, coming straight to the point with a kind of convulsive impatience. 'Even though you may be the most dangerous man if you take it into your head to harm anyone, I personally don't intend to fool about any longer. I'll demonstrate to you now that I don't attach as much importance to myself as you no doubt think I do. You may as well know: I've come to tell you that if you maintain your former designs on my sister and if towards that end you plan to take advantage in any way of the things that have been revealed of late, then I will kill you before you put me in gaol. My word is my bond: you know that I am able to keep it. The second point is this: if there is anything you want to tell me – because during all this time I've had a feeling that there is – then tell me it quickly, because time is short and it may very well soon be too late.'

'I say, what's all the hurry?' Svidrigailov asked, studying him inquisitively.

'A man's footsteps lead him to all sorts of places,' Raskolnikov said, in black impatience.

'Only just now you were challenging me to be open with you, yet at the first question I put to you you refuse to answer,' Svidrigailov commented with a smile. 'You still think I have some kind of purpose up my sleeve, and so you view me with suspicion. Oh well, that's perfectly understandable on your part. But however much I'd like to be on closer terms with you, I shan't make the effort to persuade you that the contrary is true. Quite honestly, the game's not worth the candle, and in any case I had no plans to talk to you about anything in particular.'

'Then why was I so important to you the other day? I mean, you were looking after me, weren't you?'

'Oh, simply because you were an interesting subject for observation. The unreality of your situation appealed to me – that's all! That, and the fact that you happen to be the brother of a certain young lady who interested me greatly, that on frequent occasions I had heard a great deal about you from that very same young lady, and that consequently I decided you must have a great influence on her; that's not too little by way of explanation, is it? Hee-hee-hee! Though actually, I will admit that I find your question rather complicated, and it's hard for me to answer it. I mean, take just now, for example – I don't mind betting that you haven't come just to see me about that matter but about something new as well? I'm right, am I not? Yes?' Svidrigailov insisted with a crafty smile. 'Well, that being said, will you believe it if I tell you that even as I was on my way here in the train I was counting on the prospect of you also telling me something *new* and on my being able to borrow something from you! That's the kind of wealthy men we are!'

'What do you mean, borrow something from me?'

'Oh, how can I explain it to you? Do I myself really know? You see the sort of miserable little inn I spend all my days sitting in, and I quite enjoy it, actually, or rather it's not so much that I enjoy it as that one must have somewhere to sit. I mean, take that poor Katya girl – did you see her? . . . I mean, I wish I were a gourmand or a club gastronomer, but, well, you see the sort of meals I get!' (He jabbed a finger into the corner, where on a little table a small tin plate contained the remnants of a horrible dish of beefsteak and potatoes.) 'Incidentally, have you had anything to eat? I've had a bite or two and I don't want any more. I don't touch alcohol at all, hardly. Except for champagne – I only have one glass to last me the whole evening, and even then it gives me a headache. I asked them to bring me a bottle to set me up, because I'm about to go somewhere and you behold me in a singular frame of mind. That was why I attempted to hide just now like a schoolboy, thinking you'd slow me up; but it seems (he took out his watch) I can be with you for an hour; it's half past four now. You know, I sometimes wish I *were* something – oh, a landowner, or a father, or an Uhlan, a photographer, a journalist . . . but I'm nothing, I have no specialism! Sometimes I get very bored. Actually, I really did think you might have something new to tell me.'

'What sort of man are you? Why have you come to town?'

'What sort of man am I? You know the story: a member of the gentry, served two years in the cavalry, then loafed around here in St Petersburg for another two, then got married to Marfa Petrovna and went to live in the country. That's my biography!'

'They say you're a gambler.'

'No, what sort of gambler am I? I cheat at cards – I don't gamble.'

'So you were a cardsharper when you lived here before?'

'Yes, that's right.'

'Well, did you get horsewhipped?'

'It happened. Why?'

'Well, in that case you must have had the opportunity of challenging people to duels . . . as a rule that makes one's life more interesting.'

'I shan't contradict you, but I'm afraid I'm not given to philosophizing. To be perfectly honest with you, I came here more on account of the women.'

'Even though you've only just buried Marfa Petrovna?'

'That's right,' Svidrigailov smiled with disarming candour. 'So what? You seem to think there's something wrong about my mentioning women in that way!'

'You mean, do I or don't I think there's anything wrong about lechery?'

'Lechery? So that's where you're leading! Well, actually, for the sake of order I shall begin by answering your question about women in general terms; you see, I have a weakness for idle chatter. Tell me, why should I restrain myself? Why should I give up women, since at least they're something I care about? It's a pastime, at any rate.'

'So the only thing you're sure of finding here is lechery!'

'So what if it is? I think you've got lechery on the brain. Though I must admit I do like a straightforward question. In lechery there is at least something permanent, something that is truly founded upon nature and is not subject to the imagination, something that is present like a constantly live coal in the blood, forever setting one on fire, a coal it will take a long time, possibly into one's old age, to put out. I think you will agree that it's an occupation of a sort?'

'What are you so glad about? It's an illness, and a dangerous one.'

'Ah, so that's where you're leading! I agree that it's an illness, like everything that passes the bounds of moderation – and here it's essential to pass the bounds of moderation – but I mean, in the first place, it takes one man this way and another man that way, and in the second place, of course, one ought to observe moderation, prudence, even of a villainous kind, in all things, but you see, what am I to do? If I didn't have that, I'd probably just have to shoot myself. I agree that a man with any decency ought to put up with the frustration, but you see, I just . . .'

'And would you be able to shoot yourself?'

'That's enough!' Svidrigailov countered, with revulsion. 'Please do me the favour of not talking about that,' he added hurriedly, and without any of the bravado that had manifested itself in all his words so far. Even his face seemed to have altered. 'I admit it's an unforgivable weakness, but what am I to do? I'm afraid of death and I don't like it when people talk about it. Do you know that I'm a sort of mystic?'

'Aha, the ghost of Marfa Petrovna! Well, does she still keep on coming to see you?'

'Oh that – don't mention that either! It hasn't happened so far while I've been in St Petersburg; in any case, to the devil with it!' he exclaimed with an air of irritation. 'Let's rather talk about this . . . though actually . . . Hm . . . Damn! What a pity there's so little time, and I can't stay with you long. There's something I'd like to tell you.'

'Who do you have to go and see, a woman?'

'Yes, a woman, that's right, an unexpected encounter . . . but no, that's not what I want to tell you about.'

'But doesn't the loathsomeness, the sheer loathsomeness of this whole environment have any effect on you? Have you lost the strength to stop?'

'So you claim to have strength, do you? Hee-hee-hee! You surprised me just now, Rodion Romanych, even though I knew in advance it was going to be like this. You keep harping on to me about lechery and aesthetics! You're a Schiller, you're an idealist! All that, of course, is just as it should be, and one would indeed be surprised if it were any different, but I must say that even so it's a strange phenomenon when one comes across it in reality . . . Oh, what a pity there's so little time, because you really are a most intriguing subject! Incidentally, do you like Schiller? I think the world of him.'

'What a show-off you are!' Raskolnikov said with some disgust.

'Oh, my goodness!' Svidrigailov replied, bursting into laughter.

'Though actually I won't argue, I may very well be one; but why shouldn't I do a bit of showing off, if it doesn't do anyone any harm? I've been living in Marfa Petróvna's country house for seven years, and so now, having greedily pounced upon as intelligent a man as yourself – not only intelligent, but in the highest degree intriguing – I'm simply glad of the chance to loosen my tongue, and there's also the fact that I've been drinking these half-glasses of champagne and they've gone to my head a bit. No, the point is that there exists a certain circumstance which has bucked me up enormously, but about which I shall . . . remain silent. Where are you off to?' he asked suddenly, in alarm.

Raskolnikov had begun to get up. He had started to experience the room as heavy and stuffy, and felt uncomfortable about having come here. His suspicions of Svidrigailov had been confirmed: he saw him as the most empty and worthless villain in all the world.

'For heaven's sake sit down, don't go yet,' Svidrigailov implored him. 'Why don't you order yourself some tea? Come along, sit down, and I promise not to talk nonsense, about myself, at least. I shall tell you a story. If you'll let me, I shall tell you the story of how a woman, to use your style of language, "saved" me. It will also be a reply to your first question, as the young lady concerned is – your sister. May I tell you it? That way we shall kill time, too.'

'Go on then, but I hope you . . .'

'Oh, have no fear! What is more, even in such an unpleasant and empty character as myself, Avdotya Romanovna is capable only of implanting the most profound respect.'

IV

'You may perhaps know (actually, I've already told you about it),' Svidrigailov began, 'that I was locked up in the debtors' prison here, owing a tremendous sum of money, and without the slightest means in prospect for paying it. There's no point in going into all the details of how Marfa Petrovna bought me out when she did; have you any idea of the degree of moral insensibility to which a woman is sometimes capable of loving? She was a decent woman, not at all unintelligent (though completely lacking in education). Can you imagine? This same decent and jealously possessive woman took the step of condescending, after the most horrible scenes of frenzy and reproach, to a form of contract with me, one to which she adhered throughout the entire period of our marriage! The fact is that she was considerably older than me, and she constantly went around with some kind of clove in her mouth. I had enough brutishness in my soul and enough of my own form of decency to tell her right from the word go that it was quite out of the question for me to be faithful to her. That confession sent her into another frenzy, but I think that my crude candour actually appealed to her in a strange kind of way. It was as if she said to herself: "He mustn't really want to deceive me, if he's telling me about it in advance" – well, and to a possessive woman that's the thing that counts most of all. After lengthy bouts of tears a kind of verbal contract came into being between us; its stipulations were that firstly, I would never leave Marfa Petrovna and would always remain her husband; secondly, I would never absent myself without her permission; thirdly, that I would never retain a permanent mistress; fourthly, that in return for this Marfa Petrovna would occasionally allow me to cast an eye in the direction of the servant girls, but only with her confidential knowledge; fifthly, that woe betide me if I were ever to fall in love with a woman of our own social class; and sixthly, that in the event (which God forbid) of my ever being visited by some grand and serious passion, I must confide everything to Marfa Petrovna. As a matter of fact, with regard to this last point Marfa Petrovna was not particularly anxious; she was an intelligent woman, and consequently she was unable to look on me as other than a lecher and a libertine, for whom a serious love affair was an impossibility. But an intelligent woman and a possessive woman are two different things, and that was the trouble. Actually, if one is to form a dispassionate judgement about certain people, one must first of all jettison certain prejudices one may have, and also one's customary manner of dealing with the persons and objects that surround us. I think, therefore, that I am justified in relying on your judgement more than anyone's. You may already have heard many absurd and ridiculous things about Marfa Petrovna. It's true that she really did have certain utterly ridiculous habits; but I will tell you straight out that I sincerely regret the innumerable unhappinesses of

which I was the cause. Well, I think that will do by way of a
thoroughly proper *oraison funèbre* delivered by a loving husband over
his loving wife. On the occasions when we quarrelled I would, for the
most part, say nothing and refuse to be provoked, and as a rule this
gentlemanly behaviour paid its own dividends: it had its effect on
her, and she even found it appealing; there were times when she was
even proud of me. But all the same she couldn't stand your sister.
And how on earth did she ever come to take the risky step of
employing a raging beauty like that as a governess in her own home?
I can only explain it by the fact that Marfa Petrovna was a passionate
and susceptible woman and that she had quite simply fallen in love –
literally fallen in love – with your sister. Well, and so there was
Avdotya Romanovna! I realized perfectly well, right from the first
glance, that this was a bad business and I determined – what do you
suppose? – not even to look at her. But Avdotya Romanovna herself
took the first step – can you believe it? Can you believe, moreover,
that Marfa Petrovna even went so far as to lose her temper with me
for my constant silence on the topic of your sister, and for being so
unmoved by her ceaseless and enamoured outpourings about Avdotya Romanovna? I really still have no idea what it was she wanted!
Well, and of course Marfa Petrovna told Avdotya Romanovna all
about me, right down to the last detail. She had an unfortunate
character trait that drove her to tell every single person our family
secrets and she used to complain to them incessantly about me; so
why should she make any exception of her new and beautiful friend?
I assume that they talked of nothing but myself, and there can be no
doubt that Avdotya Romanovna became acquainted with all those
murky and mysterious legendary deeds that are ascribed to me . . . I
would venture to bet that you have also heard certain things of that
kind?'

'Yes, I have. Luzhin was accusing you of having caused the death
of a child. Is that true?'

'Please do me the favour of leaving those banal little stories alone,'
Svidrigailov said, turning away peevishly and with disgust. 'If you
really must know about all that nonsense, I shall tell you about it
separately sometime, but now . . .'

'People have also told me things about some manservant you had
on your estate and said that you were the cause of that, too.'

'*If* you don't mind – that's enough!' Svidrigailov broke in again with manifest impatience.

'Was that the same manservant who used to come and fill your pipe after he'd died ... the one you told me about yourself?' Raskolnikov asked, growing more and more irritated.

Svidrigailov gave Raskolnikov a close look, and to Raskolnikov it seemed for a moment as though in that look there flashed, like lightning, a malicious smile; but Svidrigailov restrained himself and answered with the utmost politeness:

'The very one. I perceive that all this is of extreme interest to you, and I shall consider it my duty to satisfy your inquisitiveness on all these points at the earliest convenient opportunity. The devil take it! I see that it really is possible for me to appear as a romantic personage to certain people. Well then, I think you can judge for yourself the degree to which I am obliged to my deceased Marfa Petrovna for having told your sister so many mysterious and interesting things about me. I do not presume to know what impression it all made on her; but at any rate it did me no harm. For all Avdotya Romanovna's natural aversion towards me, and in spite of my perpetually gloomy and off-putting air, she ended up feeling sorry for me – sorry for a hopeless case. And when a girl's heart starts to feel *sorry*, that is, of course, the most dangerous thing that can happen to her. She immediately wants to "rescue" him, bring him to reason, reanimate him, exhort him to more noble aims, and breathe into him new life and new activity – well, you know the sort of dreams they have along that line. I at once realized that the bird was going to fly into the net of its own accord, and I, in my turn, made myself ready. You seem to be frowning, Rodion Romanych? Never fear, sir – the whole business ended in nonsense. (The devil confound it, what a lot I seem to be drinking!) You know, I always regretted the fact that destiny had not seen fit to bring your sister into the world in the second or third century AD, as the daughter of some small-time sovereign prince somewhere, or some ruler or proconsul in Asia Minor. She would, without any doubt, have been one of those who suffered martyrdom, and she would of course have smiled as her bosom was seared by the red-hot pincers. She would have walked into it all on purpose, and in the fourth or fifth century she'd have gone off to the Egyptian desert and lived there for thirty years, nourishing herself on roots, visions and ecstasies. All that she's thirsting for, all that she demands is to accept torment for someone else's sake as quickly as possible, and if she doesn't get it, she'll probably jump out of the window. I've heard various things about a certain Mr Razumikhin. They say he's a sober-minded fellow (something his name suggests, he must be a seminarist); well, let him look after your sister. In a word, I think I've understood her, something I consider to my credit. But back then, back at the beginning of our acquaintance . . . you know how it is, one's always more stupid and frivolous, one sees things the wrong way, not as they really are. The devil take it, why is she so good-looking? It's not my fault! In a word, I got into all this because of a most uncontrollable surge of physical desire. Avdotya Romanovna is quite horribly, incredibly, unimaginably chaste. (Please observe that I tell you this about your sister as a matter of fact. She is chaste to a point where it may be considered an illness, in spite of all her lofty intellect, and it will harm her.) At the time there happened to be a girl with us, called Parasha, "dark-eyed Parasha",* who had just been brought in from another village, a serving-maid, and one whom I'd never set eyes on before – very pretty, but unbelievably stupid: she burst into tears, raised a howl that could be heard all over the estate, and there was a scandal. One afternoon, Avdotya Romanovna came specially to see me when I was on my own in an avenue of the orchard and, her eyes flashing, *demanded* that I leave poor Parasha alone. This was almost the first time we had ever spoken to each other *tête-à-tête*. I naturally considered it an honour to satisfy her wish, did my best to pretend shock and embarrassment, and in actual fact played the role rather well. There began to-ings and fro-ings, mysterious conversations, moral admonitions, beggings, beseechings, even tears – can you believe it, even tears! That's how intense the passion for propaganda gets in some of these girls! Well, of course, I blamed the whole thing on my unhappy lot, pretended to be avid and thirsting for the light and finally set in motion the principal and most unshakeable technique there exists for the subjugation of the female heart, a technique that has never yet failed any man and has the desired effect on every single woman without exception. This technique is the familiar one of flattery. There is nothing in the world more difficult than plain speaking, and nothing easier than flattery. If when a man is trying to speak plainly one-hundredth part of a false note creeps into what he is saying, the result is an instant dissonance, and following it – a scandal. In the case of flattery, however, even if everything in it, right down to the very last note, is false, it sounds agreeable and is received not without pleasure; even though it's a crude sort of pleasure, it's pleasure nevertheless. And no matter how crude the flattery may be, at least half of it always seems genuine. And that's how it is with people of all levels of education and from all layers of society. Even a vestal virgin could be seduced with flattery. And where ordinary people are concerned it's a positive walkover. I can never remember without laughing the time when I seduced a certain lady who was devoted to her husband, her children and her virtue. How enjoyable it was, and how little work it involved! The lady really was virtuous – in her own way, at any rate. My entire tactical method consisted simply in being perpetually overwhelmed by her chastity and in abasing myself before it. I flattered her outrageously, and no sooner had I obtained so much as a squeeze of her hand or even just a look from her than I would reproach myself for having wrenched it from her by force, for the fact that she had resisted me, resisted so violently that I would very likely never have obtained anything at all if I weren't so depraved; that she, in her innocence, had not foreseen the insidious nature of my tactics and had submitted inadvertently, without even knowing it or being aware of it, and so on, and so forth. In a word, I got what I was after, and my lady remained in the highest degree certain that she was innocent and chaste, had fulfilled all her duties and obligations, and had only suffered this lapse quite by accident. Oh, how angry she was with me when I finally told her that, in my own sincere conviction, she had been just as much in search of pleasure as I! Poor Marfa Petrovna was also horribly susceptible to flattery, and if I had felt so inclined I could have had her whole estate transferred to my name while she was still alive. (I say, I really am drinking far too much and talking my head off.) I hope you won't lose your temper if I mention now that the same effect had begun to make itself felt on Avdotya Romanovna. But I was stupid and impatient and I spoiled the whole affair. On several previous occasions (and on one of them quite decidedly) Avdotya Romanovna had told me that she thoroughly abominated the look in my eyes – can you believe it? She said, in so many words, that they contained a light that flared up ever more powerfully and recklessly, that frightened her and had at last become hateful to her. There's no need to go into all the details – the fact is that we parted. At that point I did another stupid thing. I launched myself into the crudest, most

550

jeering tirade against all that propaganda and those attempts to convert me; Parasha reappeared on the scene, and not only her – in a word, there was chaos. Oh, Rodion Romanych, if only once in your life you could see the way your sister's eyes are sometimes capable of flashing! Never mind that I'm drunk now and have just downed a whole glass of wine – I'm telling you the truth; I swear to you that I dreamt about those eyes; in the end I couldn't even stand the rustle of her dress. I really thought I was going to have an attack of epilepsy; I'd never imagined that I might end up in such a frenzy. In a word, what I needed to do was to make it up with your sister; but that was out of the question. And just fancy – what do you think I did then? The degree of stupefaction to which rage can drive a man! Never undertake anything when you're in a state of rage, Rodion Romanych. Reckoning that Avdotya Romanovna was after all not much more than a pauper (oh, please forgive me, I didn't mean to . . . but I mean, one word is as good as another, isn't it, as long as it gets the sense across?), that, in a word, she lived by the toil of her hands, that she had both your mother and yourself to maintain (oh, damn, you're frowning again . . .), I decided to offer her all my money (at the time I could realize up to thirty thousand) so that she'd run away with me, preferably here, to St Petersburg. It goes without saying that I'd have instantly sworn eternal love to her, bliss and all the rest of it. Can you believe it, I was so smitten that if she'd said to me: "Cut Marfa Petrovna's throat or poison her and marry me" – I'd have done it like a flash! But it all ended in the disaster you are already familiar with, and you can judge for yourself the pitch my rage attained when I learned that Marfa Petrovna had got hold of that scoundrelly scribe Luzhin and had practically arranged the wedding, which was, in essence, the same thing I would have proposed. Have I got it right? Have I? Eh? I notice you've started to listen to me very attentively . . . interesting young man . . .'

Svidrigailov struck his fist on the table in impatience. He had gone red in the face. Raskolnikov perceived beyond any doubt that the glass or glass and a half of champagne he had drunk, sipping it unnoticeably, in little swallows, had had a malignant effect on him – and he decided to take advantage of the opportunity. He regarded Svidrigailov with great suspicion.

'Well, after all that I'm quite convinced that you came to St Petersburg with my sister in view,' he said to Svidrigailov directly and without any attempt at concealment, in order to irritate him even further.

'I say – that's enough,' Svidrigailov said quickly, as though he had suddenly gathered his wits. 'Look, I told you . . . and in any case, your sister can't stand me.'

'Oh, I'm convinced of that, too; but that's not the point at issue now.'

'Convinced, are you? (Svidrigailov narrowed his eyes and smiled a mocking smile.) You're right, she doesn't love me; but never be too sure about the things that go on between a husband and a wife or a lover and his mistress. There will always be one little corner that will remain obscure to the rest of the world and which will only be known to the two of them. Are you so certain that Avdotya Romanovna looked on me with revulsion?'

'From certain things you've said during the course of our conversation I can see that even now you have your own ends in view, and that you have quite pressing designs on Dunya, which are of course villainous ones.'

'What? Did I say things like that?' Svidrigailov asked in utterly naïve alarm, paying not the slightest attention to the epithet attributed to his designs.

'Yes, and you're saying them now. Well, what are you so afraid of? Why have you taken fright all of a sudden?'

'Me? Afraid? Frightened? Frightened of you? It's rather you who ought to be afraid of me, *cher ami*. And in any case, what rubbish . . . Actually, though, I'm a bit tipsy, I can feel it; I nearly said something I shouldn't have again. To the Devil with this wine! Hey, bring me some water!'

He grabbed hold of the bottle and hurled it without ceremony out of the window. Filipp brought some water.

'That's a lot of nonsense,' Svidrigailov said, wetting a towel and putting it to his forehead. 'I can put paid to you with a single word, and reduce all your suspicions to nothing. Are you aware, for example, that I'm about to get married?'

'You already told me that before.'

'Told you, did I? I've forgotten. Well, if I did it can't have been very definite, as I hadn't even set eyes on my fiancée then; it was all just plans. However, now I do have a proper fiancée, and the deed is done, and if only I didn't have such urgent business to see to I'd most certainly take you off to see her – because I want to ask your advice. The Devil! I've only got ten minutes left! You see, look at the time; but I'll tell you about it anyway, because it's an interesting little knick-knack, my marriage, in its own way – where are you off to? Going again?'

'No, I'm not going anywhere now.'

'Not going anywhere? We'll see about that! Oh, it's true that I'll take you over there and show you my fiancée, only not just now, as now it will soon be time for you to go. You to the right and I to the left. Do you know that Resslich woman? The Resslich woman whose apartment I'm staying in just now – eh? Are you listening? Come on, you know, the one they say was involved in the drowning of that slip of a girl, in winter; come on, are you listening? Are you listening? Well, it was she who cooked all this together for me; you look sort of dreary, she said, it's time you had some fun. Well, I mean, it's true: I'm a gloomy, dreary sort of fellow. Perhaps you think I'm the cheerful type? Not a bit of it, I'm a gloomy chap: I don't bother anyone, just stay in my room all the time; sometimes I don't talk to anyone for three days. But that Resslich woman is a rogue, I don't mind telling you, I mean, God knows the things she's got in her head: she thinks I'll get bored with my wife, desert her and go off somewhere, and she'll be able to get her hands on her, put her into circulation; in our social set, that is to say, only a bit higher. She says the father's some kind of enfeebled civil servant who's retired now, spends all his days in an armchair and hasn't used his legs for three years. She says there's a mother, too, the kind of woman who knows which side her bread's buttered on, the mother is. There's a son who's working in the service out in the provinces somewhere, doesn't lift a finger to help them. One daughter's married and doesn't go to visit them, they have two little nephews to look after (as though their own kids weren't enough), and they've taken their younger daughter out of high school – she'll be just sixteen in a month's time, and that means they can marry her off to someone. That someone is me. We went to see them; what a comical set-up they have! I introduce myself: a landowner, a widower from a well-known family, with certain connections, with capital – well, so what if I *am* fifty, and she's only sixteen? Who's going to take any notice? I mean, it's tempting, eh? Ha-ha! It's tempting! You ought to have seen me talking to her Mama and Papa! It would have been worth paying just to watch me. She came in, dropped a curtsy, I mean, can you imagine it, she was still in short skirts, an unopened budlet, blushing and blazing like a sunrise (they had told her, of course). I don't know what your preferences are concerning the female physiognomy, but if you ask me, those sixteen years, those still-childish eyes, that shyness and those tears of embarrassment – if you ask me, those are preferable to any beauty, and she's a picture even as it is. She has this flaxen head of hair frizzed up into little lamblike curls, scarlet, bee-stung lips, legs that are really something! . . . Well, we introduced ourselves, I said I was in a hurry because of family business, and the following day – the day before yesterday, that is – we took the blessing. With that out of the way, whenever I go there now I immediately set her on my knee and won't let her down . . . Up she blushes like a sunrise again, and I cover her in kisses; her mother naturally tells her this is the man you're going to marry and that's what you're required to do, in a word, it's a real pot of honey! Quite honestly, the status of fiancé I occupy at the moment may even be preferable to that of husband. It involves what they call *la nature et la vérité*! Ha-ha! I've exchanged intimacies with her a couple of times – the little thing's not at all unintelligent; sometimes she gives me a secret glance – God, it burns right through me. You know, she has a little face like Raphael's Madonna. The Sistine Madonna has a fantastic face, the face of a sorrowful holy fool, didn't that leap to your eyes the first time you saw it? Well, it's something in that genre. The very next day after we'd taken the blessing I brought her about one and a half thousand roubles' worth of stuff: a diamond gew-gaw and a pearl one, and a silver ladies' toilet-box – about this size, full of all kinds of things, so that the little madonna's face fairly coloured up. I put her on my knee yesterday, and I must have done it with too little ceremony, for she blushed up all over and the tears came flooding, though she didn't want me to see them, and she was all on fire. Everyone had gone out for a moment, she and I were left there alone, and she suddenly flung herself on my neck (the first time she'd done it without prompting), embraced me with both her little arms, kissed me and swore she would be an obedient, faithful and loving wife, that she'd make me happy, that she'd throw her whole life into it, every single minute of her life, that she'd sacrifice everything, everything, and that all she wanted to possess in return for all this was *my respect*, and "other than that", she said, "I want nothing, no presents, nothing at all!" I think you'll agree that to hear a confession like that alone with a little sixteen-year-old angel like that, in a little tulle dress, with her frizzed-up curls, a blush of maidenly modesty on her cheeks and the tears of enthusiasm in her eyes – I think you'll agree that all that is just ever so slightly tempting. Don't you think so? I mean, it's worth something, eh? Come on, it is, isn't it? Well . . . well, listen . . . we shall go and see my fiancée . . . only not right now!'

'In a word, what you're saying is that this monstrous difference in years and development also arouses your lust! And yet you're still going ahead with this marriage?'

'What? But of course! Everyone must look out for himself, and the best time is had by those who're best able to deceive themselves. Ha-ha! I say, you've really plunged into virtue up to your neck all of a sudden, haven't you? Have a heart, old chap, I'm a sinful man. Hee-hee-hee!'

'You don't say so! Though you did find a home for Katerina Ivanovna's children. But . . . but you had your own reasons for doing that . . . I understand it all now.'

'On the whole I'm fond of children, I'm very fond of children,' Svidrigailov chortled. 'On that account I can even relate to you a certain very curious episode that is actually still taking place. On the first day after my arrival here I called in at one or two of those dives, well, after seven years away from the town I fairly pounced on them. You've probably observed that I'm not in any hurry to get together with my cronies, my former friends and acquaintances. Indeed, I'm trying to hold out for as long as possible without seeing them. You know, all the time I was living out there on Marfa Petrovna's country estate I kept being tormented by memories of all those mysterious locales and little snuggeries where a man who knows his way around can find a great many things. The devil take it! The common folk are drunk all the time, the educated youth is burning itself out in vain dreams and fantasies, crippling itself on theories; Jews have come flocking in from somewhere, hiding money away, and everyone else is indulging in sexual licence. Within hours of my arrival I'd fairly got the reek of this city, the old, familiar reek. I ended up at a certain *soirée dansante*, so-called – a terrible dive (I like my dives with a bit of filth in them), well, and of course, there was a cancan, of a kind there never was in my time. Yes, sir, there's been some progress in such matters. Suddenly I looked, and saw a little girl of about thirteen, dressed in the most charming way, dancing with a certain virtuoso; there was another right in front of her, *vis-à-vis*. On a chair over by the wall sat her mother. Well, it was quite some cancan! The girl got embarrassed, turned red in the face, finally took offence and began to cry. The virtuoso plucked her off her feet, began whirling her round and showing off in front of her, everyone roared with laughter and – I'm rather fond of our Russian audiences, even cancan ones, at such moments – they all cackled and shouted: "Now you're talking, that's the way! And don't give us children next time!" Well, I didn't give a spit, and anyway it was no business of mine whether they were entertaining themselves in a logical or illogical manner! I at once saw my opening, sat down beside the mother and began by telling her I was also from out of town, that these people were ignoramuses, that they were incapable of discerning true merit and treating it with the respect it deserved; I let her know that I had a lot of money; offered to take them home in my carriage; did so, made their acquaintance (they're living in some little closet of a room that they rent from tenants, they've only just arrived). She told me that she and her daughter could not view my acquaintance as other than an honour; I learned that they were absolutely destitute, and had come to press their case in some government office or other; I offered them my services, money; I learned that they had gone to the *soirée* by mistake, thinking that it was some kind of dancing-school; I offered to assist in the young lady's education, and give her lessons in French and dancing. They accepted with rapture, considered it an honour, and I'm still friendly with them . . . If you like, we can go there – only not right now.'

'Enough, enough of your vile, base anecdotes, you lecherous, base, lustful man!'

'A Schiller, a Russian Schiller, a Schiller, no less! *Où va-t-elle la vertu se nicher?** You know, I shall continue to tell you things like that on purpose, just in order to hear your screams. It's a real pleasure!'

'I bet it is; don't you think I feel absurd at this moment?' Raskolnikov muttered in rage.

Svidrigailov roared at the top of his voice with laughter; at last he summoned Filipp, settled his bill and began to get up.

'Well, I'm drunk, and *assez causé!*' he said. 'A real pleasure!'

'I don't wonder that you feel pleasure,' Raskolnikov screamed, also getting up. 'Of course it's a pleasure for a shabby old lecher to narrate his exploits – with another monstrous design of the same type in view – particularly in circumstances like these and to a person like me . . . It gets you aroused!'

'Well, if that's how you see it,' Svidrigailov replied, with a certain astonishment now, studying Raskolnikov, 'if that's how you see it, then you yourself are a cynic to be reckoned with. At least, you've got the material for one inside you in abundance. You're able to perceive a lot of things . . . well, and that means you can do a lot of things, too. But anyway, that's enough. I sincerely regret not having had longer to talk to you, and you're not going to get away from me . . . Just wait a little, that's all . . .'

Svidrigailov walked out of the inn. Raskolnikov followed him. Svidrigailov was not really very drunk; the wine had gone to his head momentarily, but the intoxication was growing less every moment. He was very preoccupied with something, something intensely important, and he was frowning. It was evident that some kind of anticipation was agitating and worrying him. During the last few moments his attitude towards Raskolnikov had undergone a change and with each moment that passed was becoming coarser and more mocking. Raskolnikov had taken note of all this and was also in a state of anxiety. Svidrigailov had become highly suspicious to him; he decided to follow him.

They emerged on to the pavement.

'You to the right, and I to the left, or, if you like, let's make it the other way round, only – *adieu, mon plaisir, au rendez-vous joyeux!*' And he set off rightwards, in the direction of the Haymarket.

V

Raskolnikov went after him.

'What is the meaning of this?' Svidrigailov exclaimed, turning round. 'Why, I thought I told you . . .'

'The meaning of it is that I'm going to stay close on your heels.'

'Wha-a-at?'

They both came to a halt, and for a moment they exchanged looks as though they were sizing each other up.

'From all your semi-drunken stories,' Raskolnikov snapped abruptly, 'I've concluded quite *definitely* that not only have you not given up your thoroughly vile intentions concerning my sister, but are actually brooding on them more than ever. It has come to my ears that my sister received some kind of letter this morning. All the time we were talking you could hardly keep still . . . All right, so you've managed to produce a wife from somewhere on the way; but that doesn't mean anything. I want to make sure for myself . . .'

It was doubtful whether Raskolnikov could have said with any clarity what he wanted now, or what it was he wanted to make sure of for himself.

'So it's like that, is it? Do you want me to call the police?'

'Go ahead!'

For a moment they stood facing each other. At last the expression on Svidrigailov's face underwent a change. Having satisfied himself that Raskolnikov had not been intimidated by his threat, he suddenly assumed the most cheerful and friendly air.

'I say, you are a strange fellow! I purposely didn't mention that business of yours, even though I'm naturally alive with curiosity. It's a fantastic business. I was going to put it off until another time, but you'd whet the appetite of a corpse . . . All right, come on then, only let me warn you in advance that I'm only going back to my place for a second in order to pick up some money; then I shall lock up, take a cab and spend the whole evening at the Islands. So what's the point in you coming with me?'

'I want to look in at the apartment, not to see you but to have a word with Sofya Semyonovna, and tender my excuses for not having attended the funeral.'

'As you like, but Sofya Semyonovna isn't there. She's taken all the children to the home of a certain lady, an old aristocratic woman who's a long-time friend of mine and runs some orphanages. I charmed her by taking her the money for all three of Katerina Ivanovna's fledglings, and I donated some more money of my own; I ended by telling the story of Sofya Semyonovna, with all the stops pulled out, not concealing a thing. It produced an incredible effect. That's why Sofya Semyonovna has an appointment today at the — Hotel, where my lady is spending some time away from her dacha.'

'Never mind, I'll call in all the same.'

'As you wish, only I shan't be your crony; anyway, what business is it of mine? All right, we're nearly there. You know, I'm convinced that the reason you view me with suspicion is because I've had the tact until now not to trouble you with awkward questions . . . know what I mean? You thought it was a bit strange; I bet that's what it is, isn't it? Well, I suppose that's what one gets for being tactful!'

'And for eavesdropping at doors!'

'Aha, so that's what you're getting at!' Svidrigailov laughed. 'Yes, I'd have been surprised if, after all that's taken place, you'd let that pass without comment. Ha-ha! I understood at least a part of the tricks you'd got up to . . . there . . . that time . . . and were describing to Sofya Semyonovna, but I mean, what was it really all about? Perhaps I'm just behind the times and incapable of understanding any of it. For heaven's sake, explain it to me, old chap! Enlighten me with the latest ideas!'

'You couldn't possibly have heard anything, you're just lying!'

'Oh, but I don't mean that, I don't mean that (though actually I did hear one or two things), no, I'm referring to the way you keep sighing and moaning all the time. Every few moments that Schiller in you keeps getting into a tizzy. And now it's "Don't eavesdrop at doors!" If that's the way you see it, why don't you just go and tell the authorities: "Do you know what's happened to me? There's turned out to be a small flaw in one of my theories!" If, on the other hand, you're convinced that it's· wrong to eavesdrop at doors, but it's perfectly all right to crack the skulls of old women, then off you go to America at the double! Run for it, young man! You may still have time. I speak in all sincerity. You don't have the money? I'll give you enough for the journey.'

'I've absolutely no plans of that kind,' Raskolnikov said, cutting him off with revulsion.

'I understand (by the way, please don't put yourself to any trouble; if you like, you needn't say much); I understand the kind of problems that are currently on your mind: they're moral ones, aren't they? Problems to do with man as a citizen? Oh, put them to one side; why should you bother with them now? Hee, hee! Because you're still a man and a citizen? Well, if that's so, then you shouldn't have poked your nose into all that in the first place; it's no good if you don't know

559

your own job. Well, you'll just have to shoot yourself; but perhaps you don't feel inclined to?'

'I think you're trying to irritate me on purpose, so I'll stop following you around . . .'

'You *are* a funny fellow; well, we're here now; let me welcome you to the staircase. You see, there's the entrance to Sofya Semyonovna's room – look, there's no one there! You don't believe me? Ask at Kapernaumov's; she hands her key in at his place. Look, here she is, the lady herself, Madame de Kapernaumov. Eh? What? (She's a bit deaf.) She's gone out? Where to? Well there you are, did you hear? She's not in and may not be back until late tonight. Well, now let's go along to my rooms. I mean, you did want to come in, didn't you? Well, here we are. Madame Resslich's not at home. That woman's forever on the go, but she's a good soul, I do assure you . . . She might have suited for you if you'd had a bit more sense. All right, watch: I'm going to take this five per cent bond out of the writing-desk (what a lot of them I still have left!), and it will go to the money-changer's today. All right, seen all you want? I can't spare any more time. The writing-desk is locked up, the rooms are locked up, and here we are on the staircase again. I say, if you like we can take that cab out there: I mean, I'm bound for the Islands. What do you say to a lift? Look, I'll be taking this cab all the way to Yelagin. What, you don't want to? Had enough? Come on, let's drive together, it's all right. I think it may be coming on to rain, but never mind, we'll lower the hood . . .'

Svidrigailov was already inside the cab. Raskolnikov concluded that his suspicions, for this moment at least, were baseless. Without a word of reply he turned and walked off back in the direction of the Haymarket. If he had turned round even once on his way, he would have seen Svidrigailov, having travelled no more than a hundred yards, pay the driver and dismount on to the pavement again. But by now he could see nothing, and he had turned the corner. A deep revulsion had drawn him away from Svidrigailov. 'And to think that I could for one moment have expected anything from that coarse evil-doer, that lustful villain and lecher!' he found himself exclaiming in spite of himself. It must be admitted that Raskolnikov uttered this judgement rather too hastily and without proper consideration. There was something about Svidrigailov's whole aura that lent him a certain originality, even mystery. As for his sister's place in all this, Raskol-nikov was still, however, firmly convinced that Svidrigailov was not going to leave her alone. But now it was becoming too unendurably painful to think and brood about all that!

In accordance with his habit, being left on his own, after a couple of dozen paces he fell into deep reflection. Going up on to the bridge, he stopped over by the railings and began to look at the water. Yet all the while Avdotya Romanovna was standing above him.

He had run into her at the entrance to the bridge, but had walked past, not recognizing her. Dunya had never encountered him in the street like this before and had been shocked and alarmed. She had stopped and wondered whether to call out to him or not. Suddenly she saw Svidrigailov coming hurriedly along from the Haymarket side.

He seemed, however, to be making his approach in a mysterious, cautious manner. He did not come up on to the bridge, but stopped at one side, on the pavement, doing his utmost to make sure that Raskolnikov did not see him. He had spotted Dunya long ago and had begun to make signs to her. She took the signs to mean that he wanted her not to call to her brother, but to leave him in peace, and that he was beckoning to her.

Dunya obeyed. She quietly slipped past her brother and went over to Svidrigailov.

'Let's get away from here quickly,' Svidrigailov whispered to her. 'I don't want Rodion Romanych to know about our meeting. I think I should tell you that I've been sitting with him in an inn not far from here, where he tracked me down of his own accord, and I only managed to get away from him with difficulty. He's somehow found out about the letter I sent you and he suspects something. I mean, you wouldn't have told him, would you? But if you didn't, then who did?'

'There, we've turned the corner,' Dunya said, interrupting him. 'My brother won't see us now. I want to make it clear that I won't go any further with you. Tell me it all here; it can all just as well be said out in the street.'

'Look, in the first place, this isn't the sort of thing that can possibly be talked about out in the street; in the second place, you must also hear what Sofya Semyonovna has to say; in the third place, I want to show you certain documents . . . Very well, then, if you won't agree to come up to my rooms I shall refuse to give you any explanation and shall go away at once. At the same time, I ask you not to forget that your beloved brother's most intriguing secret lies entirely in my hands.'

Dunya paused in indecision and fixed Svidrigailov with a piercing gaze.

'What are you afraid of?' Svidrigailov said calmly. 'We're not in the country here. Even in the country you did me more harm that I did you, but here . . .'

'Does Sofya Semyonovna know we're coming?'

'No, I haven't said a word about it to her and I'm not even sure whether she's there just now. Though she probably is. She buried her stepmother today: not the sort of day to go out visiting. I don't want to talk about this to anyone before the time is right, and I'm even slightly sorry I told you. In this case the slightest indiscretion will be equivalent to informing the police. I live right here, in this building, here we come to it now. There's our yardkeeper; the yardkeeper knows me very well; look, he's bowing; he's seen I'm walking with a lady, and of course he'll have taken note of your features, and that will stand you in good stead if you're very afraid of me and view me with suspicion. Please forgive me for putting it so crudely. I rent rooms from some tenants. Sofya Semyonovna lives through the wall from me, her place is also rented from some tenants. The whole floor is in the hands of tenants. Why are you so frightened, like a child? Am I really so very terrible?'

Svidrigailov's face distorted itself into a condescending smile; but now he was in no smiling mood. His heart was thumping and the breath caught in his chest. He was making a conscious effort to speak louder, in order to hide his growing excitement; but Dunya had not noticed this peculiar excitement; she was still too irritated by his remark that she was as frightened as a child and that he was an object of terror to her.

'Though I'm quite aware that you're a man . . . without honour, I'm not afraid of you in the slightest. Please lead the way,' she said, with a show of calm, though her face was very pale.

Svidrigailov stopped outside Sonya's room.

'Let me just find out if she's in or not. No, she isn't. We're out of luck! But I know she's likely to get back very soon. If she's gone out, it can only have been to see a certain lady about her orphaned siblings. Their mother has died. I also took a hand in the matter and made certain arrangements. If Sofya Semyonovna hasn't come back within ten minutes, I shall send her to see you, today if you like; well, and here are my lodgings. These are my two rooms. Through that door lies the apartment of my landlady, Mrs Resslich. Now if you'll just glance over here I'll show you my principal documents; this door here leads from my bedroom into two completely empty rooms, which are up for rent. Here they are . . . I'd give them a rather close look, if I were you.'

Svidrigailov occupied two rather spacious furnished rooms. Dunya gazed around her mistrustfully, but could observe nothing out of place either in the contents or the arrangement of the rooms, even though another observer might have noticed, for example, that Svidrigailov's apartment happened to lie more or less in between two almost uninhabited ones. The entrance to his quarters did not lead straight in from the outside passage, but through two of the landlady's rooms, which were almost empty. Unlocking his bedroom door, which had a proper lock and key, Svidrigailov showed Dunya another empty apartment, the one that was up for rent. Dunya paused on the threshold, not comprehending why she was being asked to look, but Svidrigailov was quick to explain:

'Look over here, towards this second large room. Observe this door – it's locked with a key. Beside the door stands a chair; there's only one chair in the two rooms. I brought it through from my quarters, so as to be able to listen in more comfort. Right behind that door is Sofya Semyonovna's table; that's where she sat talking to Rodion Roman-ych. And I overheard it all in here, sitting on that chair, for two evenings in a row, each occasion lasting a couple of hours – so I think you won't be surprised if I tell you I learned a few things.'

'You mean you were eavesdropping?'

'That's correct; now let's go back to my rooms; there's nowhere to sit down here.'

He led Avdotya Romanovna back into the first of his chambers, which served him as a reception room, and invited her to sit down on a chair. He himself sat down at the other end of the table, a good sagene* away from her, at any rate, though his eyes must already have been glittering with the flame that had so alarmed Dunya on earlier occasions, for she shuddered and gazed around her mistrust-fully again. Her gesture was an involuntary one; she clearly did not want to show her suspicion. But the secluded location of Svidrigailov's quarters had finally made its impression on her. She felt like asking whether at least his landlady was in, but she refrained from doing so . . . out of pride. There was, moreover, another suffering within her heart that was incomparably greater than any fear for her own safety. She was in the grip of an unendurable torment.

'Here is your letter,' she began, putting it on the table. 'Is it really permissible to write the sort of things that are in it? You allude to some crime that my brother is supposed to have committed. Your allusion is all too plain, you dare not try talk your way out of it now. I may as well tell you that I had already heard about this stupid tale before you wrote to me, and I don't believe a single word of it. It is an infamous and absurd suspicion. I know the story and how for what reason it was dreamed up. You cannot possibly have any evidence. You have promised to supply that evidence: go ahead, then, speak! But let me tell you in advance that I don't believe you! I don't believe you! . . .'

Dunya said this in a rapid patter, hurriedly, and for a moment a flush broke out on her face.

'If you hadn't believed me I don't really think you'd have risked coming to see me alone, would you? Why have you come here? Out of sheer curiosity?'

'Stop tormenting me – speak, speak!'

'One certainly can't deny that you're a girl with some pluck. To be quite honest, I thought you'd prevail upon Mr Razumikhin to accompany you here. But there was no sign of him, either with you or anywhere around you; I had a good look; that's courageous, it means you wanted to go easy on Rodion Romanych. And in fact, everything about you is divine . . . As regards your brother, what can I say? You saw him yourself just now. How did he strike you?'

'You're surely not basing your case on that alone, are you?'

'No, not simply on that, but on what he himself said. You see, he came here two evenings in a row to see Sofya Semyonovna. I showed you where they sat. He made a complete confession to her. He's a murderer. It was he who murdered the old pawnbroker woman, the civil servant's widow, with whom he himself had pawned certain items; he also murdered her sister, a market-woman by the name of Lizaveta, who happened to walk in as the widow was being murdered. He murdered them both with an axe he'd brought with him.

564

He murdered them in order to steal from them, and he stole: he took money and some sort of valuables . . . He communicated all this, word for word, to Sofya Semyonovna, who is the only person who is in on his secret, though she took part in the murder neither in word nor deed; on the contrary, she was as horrified as you are now. You needn't worry – she won't give him away.'

'It isn't possible!' Dunya muttered, her lips pale and rigid; she was gasping. 'It isn't possible, he had not the slightest reason, not the slightest motive . . . It's a lie! A lie!'

'It was a robbery – that's what the reason was. He took money and valuables. Oh, to be sure, because of his own qualms of conscience he didn't avail himself of either the money or the valuables, but hid them under some stone somewhere, and they're still there now. But that was because he didn't dare to avail himself of them.'

'But is it really likely that he'd go breaking in and stealing? That he could even think of doing such a thing?' Dunya exclaimed, leaping up from her chair. 'I mean, you know him, you've seen him! Do you think he could possibly be a thief?'

It was as if she were entreating with Svidrigailov; all her fear was forgotten.

'In cases like this, Avdotya Romanovna, there are thousands and millions of combinations and categories. A thief goes thieving, but he's well aware that he's a villain; yet I've heard of one man of good background who robbed the mail – who can tell, he may really have thought he was doing something perfectly respectable! It goes without saying that I, like you, would never have believed it if I'd been told about it by someone else. But I believed my own ears. He explained to Sofya Semyonovna all his reasons for doing it; at first she couldn't believe her ears either, but she ended by believing her eyes, her very own eyes. After all, he told her all about it personally.'

'What were the . . . reasons?'

'It's a long story, Avdotya Romanovna. In this case what's involved is – how can I put it to you? – a kind of theory, the sort of argument that says that a single villainous act is allowable if the central aim is good. One bad action and a hundred good deeds! It is, of course, galling for a young man of merit and inordinate self-esteem to be conscious that if, for example, he only had somewhere in the region of three thousand roubles, his whole career, the whole of his future development would take quite a different course, and yet he does not

565

have that three thousand. Add to that the irritation caused by hunger, cramped living quarters, ragged clothing, a vivid awareness of the splendour of his social position, and of the situation of his mother and sister. Worse than all of that, vanity, pride and vanity, though heaven knows, they may co-exist alongside positive tendencies . . . I mean, I'm not blaming him, please don't go away with that idea; and anyway, it's not my business. In this case there was also a little private sub-theory – a reasonable sort of theory – according to which people are divided, don't you know, into raw material and extraordinary individuals, that's to say, the sort of individuals for whom, because of their exalted position, there is no law, but who themselves create the laws for the rest of mankind, the raw material, the sweepings. Well, it's all right, it's a perfectly reasonable theory, *une théorie comme une autre*. Napoleon fascinated him dreadfully, or rather what really fascinated him was that a great many men of genius have turned a blind eye to isolated acts of wrongdoing in order to stride onwards and across, without reflecting. It appears that he, too, thought he was a man of genius – or at least was convinced of it for a certain period of time. He suffered greatly, and is still suffering, from the notion that while he was able to construct a theory, he wasn't able to do the stepping across without reflection, and so consequently is not a man of genius. Well, for a young man with any self-esteem that's positively degrading, especially in a time like ours . . .'

'What about pangs of conscience? Do you maintain that he lacks all moral feeling? Do you really think that's the kind of person he is?'

'Oh, Avdotya Romanovna, the waters have grown rather muddy now – not that they were ever particularly clear. Russians are on the whole a roomy-natured lot, as roomy as the land they inhabit, and they have an extremely marked penchant for the fantastic and the chaotic; but it's not much good having all that room if one is not particularly gifted. Do you remember all the things we used to say to each other about that as we sat, just the two of us, alone on the terrace in the garden, every evening after supper? I can remember you telling me off for just that kind of roominess. Who knows, perhaps at the very moment you uttered those words he was lying here in St Petersburg pondering those thoughts of his. After all, Avdotya Romanovna, it's not as if there were really any sacred traditions in our educated social circles these days: what people do is piece something together for themselves out of books . . . or fish something out of the chronicles. But, I mean, those are mostly scholars, and you know they're really just a bunch of old duffers, so that a man of society would feel it almost insulting to mimic them. In any case, you know my opinions by and large; I definitely don't blame anyone. I'm just a lily-fingered bystander, and that's the role I adhere to. We've already discussed this together several times, you and I. I've even had the good fortune to awaken your interest with my ideas . . . You're very pale, Avdotya Romanovna!'

'I know that theory of his. I read his article in that journal, the one about people to whom everything is permitted . . . Razumikhin brought it to me.'

'Mr Razumikhin? He brought you an article by your brother? In a journal? Is there such an article? I didn't know. I say, it must make interesting reading! But where are you off to, Avdotya Romanovna?'

'I want to see Sofya Semyonovna,' Dunya said, faintly. 'How do I get through to her room? She may have come back by now; I must see her now. It may be that she . . .'

Avdotya Romanovna was unable to finish her sentence; her breathing was quite literally cut off.

'Sofya Semyonovna won't be back until tonight. Something tells me that is the case. She would have come back very soon, but as she hasn't, it won't be till very late . . .'

'Oh, so you're lying! I see, you lied to me . . . you were lying all the time! . . . I don't believe you, don't believe you, don't believe you!' Dunya shouted in a complete frenzy, totally losing her head.

Almost in a faint she collapsed on to the chair Svidrigailov hurried to supply for her.

'Avdotya Romanovna, what's wrong with you, wake up! Here's some water. Just take one sip . . .'

He sprinkled some of the water on to her face. Dunya shuddered and woke up.

'That had a powerful effect on her!' Svidrigailov muttered to himself, frowning. 'Avdotya Romanovna, please put your mind at rest! You mustn't forget that he has friends. We'll save him, get him out of this. Would you like me to take him abroad? I have money; I can have a ticket for him in three days. And as for the fact of the murder, he'll accomplish a lot of good works yet, and all this will be wiped from the slate; please put your mind at rest. He may yet be a great man. I say, what has got into you? How do you feel now?'

'Evil man! He's even mocking at me! Let me go . . .'

'Where are you off to? I say, where are you going?'

'To find him. Where is he? Do you know? Why is this door locked? We came in through this door, but now it's locked. When did you lock it?'

'I didn't want all the neighbours to hear what we've been talking, or rather shouting, about. I'm not mocking at you at all; it's merely that I'm fed up talking in this language. Well, where do you plan to go in a state like that? Or do you intend to betray him? You'll just drive him into a rabid fury, and he'll betray himself. I think you ought to realize that he's already being followed, they're on his trail. You'll merely give him away. Please wait: I've just seen him, spoken to him; there's still a chance he can be saved. Please wait, sit down, let's consider it together. That's why I asked you to come here, in order to discuss this with you alone and give it proper consideration. Look, please sit down!'

'How can you possibly save him? Surely he's beyond saving now?'

Dunya sat down. Svidrigailov sat down at her side.

'The whole thing now depends on you, on you, on you alone,' he began with glittering eyes, almost in a whisper, losing the thread of his thoughts and even failing to articulate certain words in his excitement.

Dunya shrank further away from him in fear. He, too, was trembling all over.

'You . . . one word from you, and he is saved! I . . . I will save him. I have money and friends. I'll send him abroad immediately, I'll get him the passport he needs, I'll get two passports. One will be his, the other mine. I have friends; I have professional assistants . . . Would you like that? I'll get you a passport too . . . and one for your mother . . . Why should you end up with Razumikhin? I also love you . . . I love you infinitely. Let me kiss the hem of your dress, please, let me, let me! I can hardly bear the sound it makes as it rustles. Whatever you tell me to do, I will do it! I will do anything. I will do the impossible. Whatever you believe in, I will believe in it, too. I'll do anything, anything! Don't look at me, don't look at me like that! Do you realize that you're killing me?'

He was almost beginning to rave. Something had suddenly happened to him, as though the blood had rushed to his head. Dunya leapt up and hurled herself at the door.

'Open up! Open up!' she shouted through the door, in the hope of attracting someone's attention, and shaking it with her hands. 'Open up! Is there really no one there?'

Svidrigailov stood up and recollected himself. A hostile, derisive smile was slowly finding its way across his still trembling lips.

'There's no one in,' he said softly, spacing the words out. 'The landlady's gone out, and you're wasting your energy shouting like that; you're just working yourself up in vain.'

'Where is the key? Open the door this instant, you worthless man!'

'I have lost it, and I cannot find it.'

'Oh? So you intend coercion, do you?' Dunya exclaimed, turning as pale as death and rushing over to one corner, where she shielded herself behind a small table that chanced to be to hand. She did not scream, but fixed her tormentor with her gaze and keenly followed his each and every movement. Svidrigailov did not move from the spot either and stood at the other end of the room, facing her. He had even managed to regain his self-control, externally at least. His features were, however, still as pale as before. The derisive smile had not left his lips.

'You mentioned the word "coercion" just now, Avdotya Romanovna. If it were to come to that, I think I need hardly tell you that I have taken the necessary precautions. Sofya Semyonovna isn't here; the Kapernaumovs' apartment is a very long way away, through five locked rooms. Lastly, I am at least twice as strong as you and, what's more, have nothing to fear, as you wouldn't dare to complain to anyone afterwards: I mean, you wouldn't really want to betray your brother, would you? In any case, no one would believe you: why would a girl go on her own to see a single man in his lodgings? So that even if you were to sacrifice your brother, you wouldn't be able to prove anything: coercion is very difficult to prove, Avdotya Romanovna.'

'You villain!' Dunya whispered in indignation.

'As you wish, but please observe that I was speaking of the matter simply in the form of a hypothesis. In my personal opinion you are entirely right: coercion is an abominable thing. I brought it up merely in order to show you that you would have absolutely nothing on your conscience even if . . . even if you were to decide to save your brother voluntarily, in the manner I am proposing to you. You will merely be seen to have given way to force of circumstances, or rather to force point blank, if we must use that word. Think about it: the fate of your brother and your mother is in your hands. As for myself, I will be your slave . . . all my life . . . I shall wait over here . . .'

Svidrigailov sat down on the sofa, about eight paces away from Dunya. She now had not the slightest doubt as to his steadfast resolution. What was more, she knew the man . . .

Suddenly she took a revolver from her pocket, set it on its catch and lowered her hand with the revolver in it on to the small table. Svidrigailov leapt up from where he was sitting.

'Aha! So that's it!' he exclaimed in surprise, still with his ironic leer. 'Well, that completely alters the course of the matter! You're making it extremely easy for me, Avdotya Romanovna! And where did you get that revolver? Not from Mr Razumikhin, I'll warrant! Pah! Why, that's my own revolver! My old friend! And there was I looking high and low for it! . . . The shooting lessons I had the honour to give you back on the estate were not wasted, then.'

'It's not your revolver, it belonged to Marfa Petrovna, whom you murdered, villain! None of the things in her house were yours. I took it when I began to suspect what you might be capable of. Dare to take one step towards me and I promise I shall kill you!'

Dunya was in a frenzy of excitement. She levelled the revolver.

'Well, and what about your brother? I ask from curiosity,' Svidrigailov said, still without moving from the spot.

'Report him to the police, if you like! Don't move! Not one step! I'll shoot! You poisoned your wife, I know that now, you yourself are a murderer! . . .'

'So you're firmly convinced I poisoned Marfa Petrovna, are you?'

'Yes, it was you! You hinted at it to me yourself: you spoke to me of poison . . . I know you made a trip to town in order to get it . . . you'd been keeping it . . . It was you, it was most certainly you, you . . . bastard!'

'Even if it were true, I'd have done it because of you . . . you'd have been the motive all the same.'

'That's a lie! I've always hated you, always!'

'Aha, Avdotya Romanovna! You've evidently forgotten how in the heat of propaganda you yielded and thrilled . . . I saw it in your little eyes; don't you remember that evening, in the moonlight, as the nightingale was still singing?'

'That's a lie!' There was now a glint of fury in Dunya's eyes. 'It's a lie, you slanderer!'

'Is it? Well, perhaps it is. I told a lie. One shouldn't remind women of these little things.' He smiled his ironic smile. 'I know you're going to shoot me, my pretty little wild creature. Well then, shoot away!'

Dunya brought the revolver up and, deathly pale, her lower lip ashen and trembling, her large, black eyes glittering like fire, looked at him, her resolve now steady, taking aim and waiting for the first movement on his part. Never had he seen her so beautiful. The fire that glittered from her eyes at the moment she had raised the revolver had almost physically scorched him, and his heart contracted with pain. He took a step forward, and the shot rang out. The bullet slipped through his hair and struck the wall behind him. He paused and gave a quiet laugh:

'The wasp has stung me. She aimed straight at my head . . . What's this? Blood!' He produced a handkerchief in order to wipe away the blood that was flowing in a slender rivulet down his right temple; the bullet must have barely grazed the skin of the top of his head. Dunya lowered the revolver and gazed at Svidrigailov, less in terror than in a kind of wild bewilderment. It was as though she herself did not know what she had done, or what was taking place.

'Oh well, too bad – you missed! Try again, I'm waiting,' Svidrigailov said quietly, still smiling his ironic smile, though there was a black tinge to it now. 'Otherwise I'll get my hands on you before you have time to reload!'

Dunya shuddered, quickly reloaded, and again brought the revolver up.

'Leave me alone!' she said in despair. 'I promise you, I'll fire again . . . I'll . . . kill you! . . .'

'Oh well . . . at three paces you can't really fail to. But in that case . . . you won't do it . . .' His eyes had begun to glitter, and he took another two paces forward.

Dunya pressed the trigger – the gun misfired.

'You didn't load it properly. Never mind! You have one cap left. Set the chamber right, I'll wait.'

He stood two paces in front of her, waiting and looking at her with a gaze of wild determination that was inflamed and passionate, and heavy with pain. Dunya understood that he would sooner die than let her go. And . . . and of course, she would kill him now, at two paces! . . .

571

Suddenly she flung the revolver aside.

'She's given up the idea!' Svidrigailov said in astonishment, and heaved a deep breath. Something seemed to have instantly lifted from his heart, and it was possibly something other than the mere weight of mortal fear; though he could hardly have been aware of it at that moment. This had come as a deliverance from another, blacker and more wounding emotion which he himself could not have defined in all its force.

He approached Dunya and quietly put his arm round her waist. She offered no resistance, but, trembling all over like a leaf, looked at him with imploring eyes. He tried to say something, but his lips merely grimaced, and no words came out.

'Let me go!' Dunya said, imploringly, using the 'thou' form.

Svidrigailov started: she had spoken that 'thou' somehow differently from the way she had earlier.

'So you don't love me?' he asked quietly.

Dunya made a negative sign with her head.

'And . . . you can't? . . . Not ever?' he whispered with despair.

'Never!' Dunya whispered.

There ensued a moment of terrible, dumb conflict within Svidrigailov's soul. With an inexpressible gaze he looked at her. Suddenly he removed his hand from her waist, turned away, walked quickly over to the window and stood in front of it.

Another moment went by.

'Here is the key!' (He took it out of the left pocket of his topcoat and placed it behind him on the table without looking at Dunya and without turning round to look at her.) 'Take it; go, quickly! . . .'

He gazed stubbornly out of the window.

Dunya went over to the table to fetch the key.

'Quickly! Quickly!' Svidrigailov said, still without moving and still without turning round. But in that 'quickly' there was, undisguised, an obscure yet terrifying note.

Dunya caught it, snatched up the key, rushed to the door, opened it quickly and tore from the room. Within a moment, like a madwoman, hardly conscious of her actions, she had run down to the Canal and was off along it in the direction of — Bridge.

Svidrigailov continued to stand at the window for about another three minutes; at last he slowly turned round, looked about him and quietly passed the palm of his hand across his brow. A strange smile had distorted his face, a pathetic, sad, enfeebled smile, a smile of despair. The blood, which had dried by now, had left a stain on his palm: he looked at the blood with hatred; then he wetted a towel and washed his temple. The revolver which Dunya had thrown down and had slid over to the door suddenly caught his gaze. He picked it up and examined it. It was a small, three-chambered pocket revolver of an old make; it still contained two charges and a cap. It could be fired once more. He pondered for a moment, stuffed the revolver in his pocket, took his hat and went out.

VI

All that evening until ten o'clock he spent in various inns and dives, going from one to the other. Somewhere along his way Katya had appeared again, singing another manservants' ditty about how someone, 'a villain and a tyrant', had

Begun to kiss Katya . . .

Svidrigailov had been buying drinks for Katya, the boy organ-player, the male singers and the serving staff, as well as for two wretched little government scribes. The real reason he had had anything to do with these scribes was that they both had crooked noses: the nose of one was bent to the right, while that of the other was bent to the left. This had impressed Svidrigailov. They had finally lured him into some kind of pleasure garden, where he had paid for their drinks as well as supplying the money for the entrance fee. The garden contained one scraggy fir tree of some three years' growth and three shrubs. In addition to this, a 'Vauxhall'* had been built – really just an open-air drinking den, but there it was also possible to obtain tea, and there were, moreover, one or two green tables and chairs. A chorus of inferior singers and some sort of inebriated Munich German who looked like a circus clown, with a red nose, but somehow extremely sad, were trying to entertain the audience. The scribes got into a quarrel with some other scribes, and had been on the point of fighting. Svidrigailov was chosen to be their judge. This function he had carried out for a quarter of an hour, but they shouted so much that there had not been the slightest chance of making any sense of the matter. The only certainty that transpired was that one of them had stolen something and had actually sold whatever it was to some Jew who had turned up; but, having sold it, would not share the proceeds with his companion. The stolen object finally proved to be a teaspoon belonging to the Vauxhall. Its absence was noted in the Vauxhall, and the matter began to assume troublesome proportions. Svidrigailov had paid for the spoon, got up and left the garden. By that time it was about six o'clock. He himself had not drunk one drop of alcohol during all this time and while they had been in the Vauxhall had ordered only tea, and that more for reasons of propriety than anything else. Meanwhile a murky, oppressive evening wore on. Towards ten o'clock fearsome thunderclouds moved in from all sides; there was a crack of thunder and the rain came sluicing down like a waterfall. The water did not fall in drops, but lashed the earth in cascading spurts. Every moment or so there were flashes of lightning, and one could count up to five in each of them. Wet to the skin, he went back to his rooms, locked himself in, opened the writing-desk, took out all his money and tore up two or three documents. Then, stuffing the money in his pocket, he began to change his clothes, but, looking out of the window and listening to the rain and thunder, took his hat and went out, leaving his rooms unlocked. He went straight along to Sonya's. She was back.

She was not alone; around her were the four small children of Kapernaumov. Sofya Semyonovna was giving them tea. She greeted Svidrigailov in deferential silence, eyed his drenched clothing with surprise, but said not a word. The children all instantly ran away in indescribable terror.

Svidrigailov took a seat at the table and asked Sonya to sit down beside him. She timidly made ready to listen.

'Sofya Semyonovna, it's possible that I may be leaving for America,' Svidrigailov said, 'and since this is probably the last time we shall see each other, I have come to make certain arrangements. Well, so you saw that lady today? I know what she said to you, there's no need to repeat it.' (Sonya began to make a motion, and blushed.) 'These people have a certain cast of mind. As regards your small sisters and brother, they really have been provided for, and the money that is due to them has been entrusted for each of them, under signature, into safe hands in the proper quarters. Actually, I think you ought to take these signed receipts and keep them, just in case. Here, take them! Well then, that's that. Here are three five per cent bonds, worth three thousand roubles in all. I want you to take these for yourself, solely for yourself, and let it be agreed between us that no one shall know of it, whatever may come to your ears later on. This money will be necessary to you, because, Sofya Semyonovna, to live as you have been living is not seemly, and in any case now you have no need to do so.'

'I'm so much in your debt, sir, and so are my orphans and my dead stepmother,' Sonya said, hurriedly, 'that if I haven't yet thanked you properly, you . . . mustn't think . . .'

'Oh, there, there, that will do!'

'But you know, Arkady Ivanovich, this money – I'm very grateful to you, of course, but I really don't need it now. If I've only myself to support, I can always do that, please don't think me ungrateful: if you want to be really generous, then you should use this money to . . .'

'To give to you, to you, Sofya Semyonovna, and please take it without too many words, because I really haven't the time. You're going to need it. Rodion Romanovich has two roads open to him: either a bullet in the forehead or Vladimirka.'* (Sonya gave him a wild look and began to tremble.) 'Don't worry, I know it all, I've heard it from his own lips, and I'm not a gossip; I shan't tell anyone. That was sensible advice you gave him that time, when you told him to go and give himself up. It would be far more advantageous to him. Well, if it turns out to be Vladimirka – he'll go off there, and you'll follow him, I expect? That's right, isn't it? Isn't it? Well, and if that's the case, then you really will need the money. You'll need it for him – do you see what I mean? In giving it to you, I'll also be giving it to him. What's more, you've promised Amalia Ivanovna to pay her the money she's owed; I mean, I heard you say you would. Why do you take all these contracts and obligations onto your shoulders in such an ill-considered manner, Sofya Semyonovna? After all, it was Katerina Ivanovna who owed the money to that German woman, not you, so you oughtn't to give a spit for the German woman. You won't make your way in the world if you carry on like that. Well, if anyone should ask you – oh, tomorrow or the day after tomorrow – if you've seen me or have any information about me (and ask you they will), then please don't mention that I paid this visit to you, and under no circumstances show the money to anyone or tell them I gave it you.

Well, goodbye now.' (He got up from his chair.) 'Give my greetings to Rodion Romanych. Oh, and by the way: if I were you, I'd give that money to Mr Razumikhin to look after for the time being. You know Mr Razumikhin, don't you? Of course you do. He's not a bad sort of fellow. So take it to him, tomorrow or . . . when the time comes. And until then hide it somewhere far from prying eyes.'

Sonya also leapt up from her chair, and she looked at him in fear. She wanted very much to say something, ask a certain question, but in those first few moments did not dare to begin it, and indeed, did not know how to.

'You're not . . . you're not going out in rain like that, are you, sir?'

'I say, it's not much good a chap setting off for America if he's afraid of the rain, hee-hee-hee! Goodbye, Sofya Semyonovna, my dear! Live and live long, you'll stand others in good stead. And before I forget . . . please tell Mr Razumikhin that I bow to him. Put it in just those words: say, "Arkady Ivanovich Svidrigailov bows to you." Be sure you get it right.'

He went out, leaving Sonya in a state of bewilderment, fear and a kind of dark, vague suspicion.

It turned out later that on this same evening, at about midnight, he had made yet another highly eccentric and unexpected visit. The rain had still not stopped. At twenty minutes to twelve, wet all over, he had gone on foot to the cramped little apartment that belonged to the parents of his fiancée and was situated on Vasily Island, in the Third Line, on Maly Prospect. He had to do a great deal of knocking before they opened up, and was initially the cause of a major commotion; but Arkady Ivanovich could, when he wanted to, be a man of the most charming manners, with the result that the original (though, it must be confessed, thoroughly astute) supposition of the fiancée's parents, that Arkady Ivanovich must somewhere on his route have drunk himself into a condition of such intoxication that he no longer knew what he was doing, was instantly confounded. The enfeebled progenitor was wheeled through in his armchair to see Arkady Ivanovich by the fiancée's wise and soft-hearted mother who, following her custom, immediately began to ask all sorts of round-about questions. (This woman never asked her questions in a straight-forward manner, but would invariably start the ball rolling first with smiles and the rubbing of hands, and then, if it was really quite essential to ascertain something in definite, unambiguous terms – for example: when was Arkady Ivanovich going to fix a date for the wedding? – would begin with the most inquisitive and almost avid questions about Paris and the court life there and only then arrive, in accordance with procedure, at the Third Line of Vasily Island.) At any other time all this would, of course, have aroused great respect, but on the present occasion Arkady Ivanovich appeared for some reason to be exceptionally impatient, curtly demanding to see his fiancée, even though he had already been informed at the very outset that his fiancée had gone to bed. It need hardly be said that the fiancée made her appearance; Arkady Ivanovich told her straight out that because of something extremely important that had come up, he was compelled to travel away from St Petersburg for a time, and had therefore brought her fifteen thousand silver roubles in bonds and credit notes of various kinds, asking her to accept them from him as a present, and saying that he had long intended to give her this trifle before the wedding. These explanations in no way manifested any particular logical connection between his imminent departure and the gift or the urgent necessity of his coming to present it to them at midnight in the pouring rain, but even so, the whole thing went off quite smoothly. Even the indispensable sighs and exclamations, the questions and expressions of surprise, suddenly became unusually muted and restrained; on the other hand, however, gratitude of the most ardent kind was displayed and was also lent force by the tears of that wisest of mothers. Arkady Ivanovich got up, laughed, kissed his fiancée, patted her on the cheek, assured her he would be back soon and, noticing in her eyes not only a certain childish curiosity but also a very earnest, unspoken question, thought for a moment, gave her another kiss and as he did so experienced a pang of sincere regret within his soul that the gift would immediately be placed under lock and key for safekeeping by that wisest of mothers. He went out, leaving them all in a thoroughly excited condition. But the soft-hearted mama instantly, in a semi-whispered patter, solved some of the more taxing riddles by declaring that Arkady Ivanovich was an important man, a man of business and connections, a wealthy man – heaven only knew what was on his mind, he had decided something and set off, his decision had led him to part with all that money, and consequently there was no cause for wonder. It was, of course, strange his being so wet, but if one considered the English, for example, they were even more eccentric, and in any case none of these society people paid any attention to what was said about them. It was even possible that he went around like that on purpose in order to show that he was not afraid of anyone. The main thing was, however, that they should not tell anyone about all this, because heaven only knew what might happen then, and the money must be immediately placed under lock and key; and, of course, the best thing about it all was that Fedosya had been sitting in the kitchen, and not on any, any, any account must they breathe a word of it to that old vixen Resslich, and so on, and so forth. They sat up whispering until about two o'clock. The fiancée, however, went back to bed much earlier, astonished and a little sad.

Svidrigailov meanwhile was, on the very stroke of midnight, crossing —chkov Bridge* towards the St Petersburg Side. The rain had stopped, but there was a roaring wind. He was beginning to shiver, and for a single moment he looked at the black water of the Little Neva with a kind of especial curiosity. Standing there above the water, however, he soon began to feel very cold; he turned round and walked over to —oy Prospect.* He strode along the endless —oy Prospect for a very long time, almost half an hour, several times losing his foothold in the darkness on the wooden paving-slabs, but never once giving up his search for something on the right-hand side of the street. Somewhere along here, at the end of the street, he had while passing recently noticed a hotel which although built of wood was quite a large one; its name, as far as he could remember, was something like The Adrianopolis. He had not been out in his reckonings: in a godforsaken district like this the hotel was such an evident landmark that it was quite impossible not to see it, even in the darkness. It was a long, blackened wooden building in which, the late hour notwithstanding, lights were still burning; the place appeared to be quite busy. He went inside and asked the ragamuffin who met him in the passage for a room. After giving Svidrigailov a quick look up and down, the ragamuffin shook himself into life and instantly led him off to a distant room, stuffy and narrow, somewhere right at the end of the passage, in a corner, under the staircase. This was the only room to be had; all the others were occupied. The ragamuffin gave him an inquiring look.

'Do you serve tea?'

'Yes, sir.'

'What food have you got?'

'There's veal, sir, vodka, sir, *zakuski*, sir.'

'Bring me tea and some veal.'

'And you don't want anything else?' the ragamuffin asked in positive bewilderment.

'No, that's all, that's all.'

The ragamuffin went off, thoroughly disappointed.

'This must be a good place,' Svidrigailov thought. 'How is it I didn't know about it? I probably also look like someone who was on his way back from a *café chantant* but got involved in some episode *en route*. In any case, it would be interesting to find out who's staying here and spending the night.'

He lit a candle and examined the room in more detail. It was a little cell, so tiny that Svidrigailov almost had to stoop in it, with one window; the bed was very dirty; a simple painted chair and table took up almost all the remaining space. The walls looked as though they had been knocked together out of boards, covered in shabby wallpaper so dusty and tattered that while it was still possible to guess its colour (yellow), none of the pattern could be deciphered at all. One portion of the wall and the ceiling had been cut obliquely, as is usually done in attic rooms, but above this sloping portion ran the staircase. Svidrigailov put the candle down, seated himself on the bed and began to ponder. But a strange and ceaseless whisper, which was coming from the cell next door and sometimes rose almost to a cry, at last drew his attention. This whisper had been going on incessantly ever since he had come in. He listened: someone was shouting at someone else, and reproaching whoever it was almost in tears, but only one voice was audible. Svidrigailov got up, shielded the candle with his hand, and in the wall a chink of light instantly appeared: he stepped over to it and began to look. In a room that was slightly larger than his own, there were two male guests. One of them, in his shirtsleeves, his head covered in abundant curls and his face red and inflamed stood in the pose of an orator, his legs splayed apart in order to keep his balance; beating his breast, he was reproaching the other in emotional tones for the fact that he was destitute and did not even possess a civil service rank, that he had dragged him out of the mire and could tell him to go any time he felt like it, and that all this was being witnessed by none but the finger of the Almighty. The companion who was the object of these reproaches was sitting on a chair and had the look of a man who badly wanted to sneeze, but could not for the life of him do so. From time to time he gazed at the orator with a sheeplike and lacklustre stare, but he evidently had not the slightest conception of what it was all about, and it was doubtful whether he could even hear any of it. A guttering candle stood on the table, together with an almost empty decanter of vodka, vodka-glasses, a loaf of bread, tumblers, cucumbers and a tea-service the tea in which had long ago been drunk. Having given this scene his careful scrutiny, Svidrigailov indifferently moved away from the chink and sat down again on the bed.

The ragamuffin, who had returned with the tea and veal, could not resist asking once more whether he 'wanted anything else', and, on again receiving a negative reply, beat a definitive retreat. Svidrigailov fell upon the tea in eagerness, anxious to warm himself, and drank a glass of it, but was unable to eat a single morsel, as he had completely lost his appetite. He was showing clear signs of incipient feverishness. He took off his overcoat and jacket, wrapped himself up in a blanket and lay down on the bed. He was annoyed: 'It would have been better not to be ill on this occasion at least,' he thought, and smiled a sardonic smile. The room was airless, the candle was burning dimly, the wind roared outside, somewhere in a corner a mouse was scrabbling, and the whole place seemed to have a reek of mice and of something leathery. He lay and seemed to lose himself in reverie: thought followed thought. It seemed to him that he would very much like to have been able to fix his imaginings on some one thing in particular. 'There must be some sort of garden under this window,' he thought. 'It's the trees that are making that roaring noise; how I detest the roaring of trees at night, in darkness and storm – a horrible sound!' And he remembered how, as he had made his way earlier past Petrovsky Park he had thought about it with positive loathing. That reminded him of —kov Bridge and the little Neva, and again he found himself feeling cold, as he had done earlier, standing above the water. 'I've never ever cared for water, not even in landscapes,' he thought, and he suddenly smiled his sardonic smile again as a certain curious thought occurred to him: 'I mean, all those questions of aesthetics and comfort oughtn't to matter a damn to me now, yet lo and behold, I'm as choosey as a wild animal selecting a place for itself . . . in a similar situation. I should have taken the turning into Petrovsky Park back earlier! It must have seemed too dark and cold at the time, hee-hee! I was hardly in need of agreeable sensations! . . .

Speaking of which, why don't I douse the candle?' (He blew it out.) 'Those characters next door have gone to bed,' he thought, no longer seeing any light in the chink he had peeped through just now. 'You know, Marfa Petrovna, this would be a good time for you to come visit me – it's dark, the place is eminently suitable, and the moment quite inspired. And yet you won't do it . . .'

For some reason he suddenly recalled how earlier that day, an hour before carrying out his plan concerning Dunya, he had told Raskolnikov he thought it would be a good thing if he were to entrust her to the care of Razumikhin. 'I probably said that just to give myself a cheap thrill, as Raskolnikov guessed. But that Raskolnikov's a scoundrel. He's got a lot on his conscience. He may eventually become a proper scoundrel, when he's put all the nonsense behind him, but for the present he's *far too fond of life*! As far as that point's concerned that crowd are bastards. Well, let the devil do with them as he pleases, it's no business of mine.'

He was still unable to get to sleep. Little by little the image of Dunya as he had seen her earlier began to rise up before him, and suddenly a shiver passed through his body. 'No, I must forget about that now,' he thought, regaining clarity for a moment. 'I must think about something else. It's a strange and ludicrous fact that I've never felt any great hatred for anyone, never even wanted to take my revenge, and I mean, that's a bad sign, a bad sign! Neither have I ever been given to argument or losing my temper – that's another bad sign! All those things I was promising her earlier, the devil take it! But after all, perhaps she'd have made a new man of me somehow . . .' He fell silent again and gritted his teeth: again the image of Dunya appeared before him exactly as she had been when, having fired her first shot, she had suddenly been horribly afraid, had lowered the revolver and looked at him in such numb immobility that he would have had time to assault her twice without her so much as raising a hand in her own defence, had he not suggested it to her himself. He remembered how in that instant he had felt sorry for her, felt as though his heart would break . . . 'Ach! To the devil! The same thoughts again! I must forget, forget all that! . . .'

By now he was beginning to lose consciousness: the fevered shivering had subsided; suddenly he felt something run under the blanket and cross his arm and leg. He gave a violent shudder: 'The devil damn me if that's not a mouse!' he thought. 'I've left the veal out on the table . . .' The last thing he wanted was to take off the blanket, get up and feel cold, but again something unpleasant suddenly fluttered across his leg; he tore the blanket from him and lit the candle. Shaking with feverish cold, he stooped down to examine the bed – there was nothing; he gave the blanket a shake, and suddenly a mouse leapt out of it on to the sheet. He lunged at it in an attempt to catch it, but the mouse did not leave the bed, flickered zigzags in all directions, slipped from under his fingers, ran across his hand and suddenly ducked away under the pillow; he turfed the pillow off, but instantly felt something slither on to his chest and then flit across his midriff and down his back, under his shirt. He gave a nervous spasm and woke up. The room was in darkness, he was lying on the bed, still huddled in the blanket as he had been before, and the wind was howling outside the window. 'What a revolting business!' he thought with annoyance.

He got up and sat himself on the edge of the bed with his back to the window. 'It's better if I don't try to sleep at all,' he decided. A cold damp stream of air was coming from the window, however; without raising himself from the spot, he drew the blanket over him and swathed himself in it. As for the candle, he did not light it. He was not thinking about anything, nor did he want to think; but waking dreams rose up one after the other, fragments of thought went flickering past, without beginning, end, or anything to connect them. He seemed to fall into a semi-slumber. It might have been the cold, the gloom, the dampness, the wind that was howling outside the window and making the trees sway, all of these combined, evoking in him an intense predisposition towards the fantastic, and a desire for it – but whatever the reason was, he kept seeing flowers. He imagined a charming landscape; a bright, warm, almost hot day, a feast day, Whit Sunday. A splendid, luxurious rural cottage, in the English style, grown all around with fragrant banks of flowers, planted with flowerbeds that passed right round the whole building; a porch, wound round with climbing creepers and crammed on every side with beds of roses; a bright, cool staircase, covered with a splendid carpet and bedecked with rare flowers in Chinese vases. He took particular notice of the vases in the windows containing water and bunches of white and tender narcissi, inclining on their long, bright-green, succulent stems, giving off a strong aromatic odour. He felt positively reluctant to leave them, but he climbed the staircase and entered a large, high-ceilinged reception room, and here again everywhere – by the windows, near the doors that were opened on to the terrace, on the terrace itself – everywhere there were flowers. The floors had been strewn with freshly scythed fragrant grasses, the windows were open, fresh, cool, light air filtered into the room, birds chirruped outside the windows, and in the middle of the room, on some tables covered with white satin shrouds, stood a coffin. This coffin was wrapped in white gros-de-Naples and trimmed with a thick white ruche. Garlands of flowers entwined it from every side. Covered in flowers, a young girl lay in it, dressed in a white tulle dress, her arms folded together and pressed to her bosom, as though they had been sculpted from marble. But her unbanded hair, the hair of a light blonde, was wet; a wreath of roses entwined her head. The unyielding and already stiffened profile of her face also seemed sculpted from marble, but the smile on her pallid lips was full of an unchildlike and limitless sorrow and a great, complaining lament. Svidrigailov knew what this girl was: there were no icons or lighted candles beside this coffin. This girl was a suicide – she had drowned herself. She was only fourteen years old, but this was a heart already broken, and it had destroyed itself, insulted by a humiliation that had terrified and astonished this young child's consciousness and had flooded her angelically pure soul with shame, tearing from her a last, final shriek of despair that was not heeded but brazenly cursed on a dark night, in the murk, in the cold, in the damp thaw weather, when the wind was howling . . .

Svidrigailov recovered his wits, got up from the bed and strode over to the window. He found the bolt by feel and opened the window. The wind lashed violently into his cramped little closet and covered his face and his chest, which was protected by nothing more than his shirt, with something that felt like hoar frost. There must really be something resembling a garden outside the window, and it was probably a pleasure-garden, at that; there too the *pesenniki* sang and tea was served around the tables. Now, however, droplets of rain were being whirled off the trees and bushes, it was as dark as a vault, so dark that one could only make out a few dim patches that denoted objects. Svidrigailov, leaning down and propping his elbows on the windowsill, continued to stare into this gloom for about another five minutes, without interruption. In the midst of the blackness and night a cannon-shot detonated, followed by another.

'Aha, the flood-warning! The water's rising,' he thought. 'By morning it will be rushing through the streets in the lower-lying parts of town, it will wash into basements and cellars, the cellar rats will come floating up, and out in the wind and rain people will start, cursing and wet, to drag what remains of their possessions up to the higher storeys . . . But what time is it now?' No sooner had he thought this than somewhere near to hand, ticking and seeming to hurry with all its might, a wall-clock struck three. 'My God, it will be light in an hour! What's the point in waiting? I'll go now, straight to Petrovsky Park: I'll pick out a large bush somewhere in there, one that's completely saturated in rain, so that one only has to brush it the merest bit with one's shoulder to send a million droplets pouring all over one's head . . .' He stepped away from the window, bolted it, lit the candle, pulled on his waistcoat and overcoat, put on his hat and went out, holding the candle, into the passage in order to track down the ragamuffin, who would be asleep in some little closet somewhere amidst all kinds of old junk and candle-ends, to pay him for the room and to leave the hotel. 'It's the best moment one could imagine, none better could exist!'

For what seemed an age he made his way through the long, narrow passage without finding anyone, and was on the point of giving a loud shout when suddenly in a dark corner, between an old cupboard and a door, he made out a strange object that appeared to be alive. He stooped down with the candle and saw a child – a little girl of about five, no more, in a little dress that was sopping wet as a floor-rag, shivering and weeping. She did not appear to be afraid of Svidrigailov, but was looking at him with dull astonishment in her large, black eyes, uttering a sob now and then the way children do when they have been crying for a long time, but have now stopped and are almost consoled, though the slightest little thing will suddenly make them sob again. The girl's little face was pale and exhausted; she was stiff with cold – how had she got here? She must have been hiding here, and had not been to bed all night. He began to ask her questions. The little girl suddenly livened up and babbled something to him very fast in her child's language. There was something about 'mumsie' and that 'mumsie come and smack me', about some cup that had been 'sashed' ('smashed'). The little girl went on talking incessantly; little by little it was possible to deduce from all her stories that this was an unloved child whose mother, doubtless some perpetually drunken cook from this very same hotel, had given a drubbing and frightened out of her wits; that the little girl had broken a cup of her mother's and been so frightened that she had run away the previous evening; she had probably hidden out in the yard, in the pouring rain, and finally found her way in here, concealed herself behind the cupboard and remained sitting in this corner all night, weeping, shivering with damp, darkness, and the fear that she would now be sorely beaten for all this. He picked her up, carried her back to his room, put her on the bed and began to take her clothes off. Her tattered shoes, which she was wearing on bare feet, were as wet as though they had lain all night in a puddle. Having undressed her, he put her inside the sheets, covered her and tucked her up in the blanket so that not even her head was visible. She fell asleep instantly. This accomplished, he again fell into gloomy thought.

'What on earth am I getting myself mixed up in?' he decided suddenly with a leaden sense of rancour. 'Just a lot of nonsense!' Irritably he picked up the candle in order to go out and this time track down the ragamuffin no matter what and get out of this place as soon as possible. 'Ah, but the kid!' he thought with an oath, as he was opening the door, and went back to look at the little girl again and see whether she was asleep and if so how soundly. Cautiously he raised the blanket a small way. The little girl was soundly and blissfully asleep. The blanket had made her warm, and the colour had spread across her pale cheeks. But there was something strange: this colour was more livid and more powerful than any ordinary child's flush. 'It must be a feverish flush,' Svidrigailov thought. 'It's like the way they look when they've been given a whole glass of wine to drink. Her little scarlet lips seem to be burning, blazing – but what's this?' He suddenly fancied that the long, black lashes of one of her eyes were quivering and blinking, that they were being raised and that from under them a sly, sharp little eye was peeping out, winking in a most unchildlike fashion, as though the little girl were not asleep but only pretending. Yes, he was right: her lips were parting in a smile; the corners of them were twitching, as though she were trying to restrain herself. But now she had abandoned all restraint; this was laughter, open laughter; something insolent and provocative shone in that not-at-all childlike face; this was lust, this was the face of a *dame*, the insolent face of a *dame aux camélias*. There – without any attempt at concealment now, both eyes had opened: they were studying him up and down with a burning and shameless gaze, they were inviting him, laughing . . . There was something infinitely monstrous and outrageous in that laughter, in those eyes, in all this filth in the countenance of a child. 'What? A five-year-old?' Svidrigailov whispered in genuine horror. 'What . . . what on earth is this?' But there she was, turning her scarlet-burning gaze full on him now, stretching her arms out . . . 'Hah! Cursed one!' Svidrigailov exclaimed in horror, raising his hand above her . . . But at that very same moment he woke up.

He was still in the same bed, still swathed in the blanket; the candle was out, and full daylight showed white in the window.

'Nightmares all night!' He sat up with resentment, feeling totally shattered; his limbs ached. Outside there was a very thick mist, and nothing could be seen. It was about six o'clock; he had slept too long! He got up and put on his jacket and overcoat, which were still damp. Feeling in his pocket for the revolver, he took it out and adjusted the remaining cap; then he sat down, took a notebook from his pocket and on its first page, where they would be most noticeable, wrote a few lines in large characters. When he had read them over, he began to ponder, leaning his elbow on the table. The revolver and the notebook lay there, by his elbow. The flies, disturbed from their slumber, crawled slowly over the untouched portion of veal that also lay on the table. For a long time he gazed at them and then finally began the attempt to catch one of them with his right hand. Again for a long time, he exhausted himself in these efforts, but could not catch it for the life of him. At last, catching himself at this interesting occupation, he recovered his wits, shuddered, stood up and walked decisively out of the room. A moment later he was out in the street.

A thick, milky fog lay over the city. Svidrigailov made his way along the dirty, slippery wooden pavement in the direction of the Little Neva. In his mind he saw the waters of the Little Neva, swollen overnight, Petrovsky Island, the wet pathways, wet grass, wet trees and bushes and, at last, the very bush . . . In his irritation he began to study the buildings in order to have something else to think about. As he walked along the Prospect he encountered neither pedestrians nor cabs. Dirty and forlorn, the bright-yellow wooden houses stared with their closed shutters. The cold and damp had chilled his body, and he began to feel feverish. Every so often he would come across the signs of small stores and greengrocers' shops and he would read each one attentively. Now he had come to the end of the wooden pavement. He was drawing level with a large stone building. A dirty little dog, trembling with cold, its tail between its legs, ran across his tracks. Some man in an overcoat, dead-drunk, lay face down across the pavement. Svidrigailov gave him a glance and walked on. A tall watchtower* caught his gaze on the left. 'Hah!' he thought. 'This place will do, why go to Petrovsky Park? At least I'll have an official witness . . .' He nearly smiled an ironic smile at this new thought and took the turning into —skaya Street. Here was the large building with the watchtower. Outside the building's large gateway, leaning his shoulder against it, stood a short little man who was muffled up in a grey fireman's overcoat and a brass 'Achilles' helmet.* Dozily he cast a cold and disapproving glance at the approaching Svidrigailov. Manifest on his features was that age-old look of querulous sorrow that is so acerbicly imprinted on the faces of each member of the Hebrew tribe without exception. For a while the two of them, Svidrigailov and Achilles, studied each other in silence. At last Achilles decided that there was something not quite right about a man who although not drunk was standing three paces from him, looking steadily at him, and saying nothing at all.

'Vy you here, vat-z you va-a-ant?' he said, still without moving a limb or altering his position.

'Oh, nothing, thanks, old chap,' Svidrigailov replied.

'Here is not ze place.'

'Actually, old chap, I'm off to foreign parts.'

'Foreign parts?'

'America.'

'America?'

Svidrigailov took out the revolver and set the trigger. Achilles raised his eyebrows.

'Vy you here, vat-z you doing, here is not ze place for zese chokes [jokes].'

'Why is it not the place?'

'Because z-is not ze place.'

'Well, brother, this is all the same. The place is a good one; if they ask questions, reply that I said I was going to America.'

He put the revolver to his right temple.

'Vat-z-you doing, here is impossible, here is not ze place!' Achilles said, rousing himself and dilating his pupils wider and wider.

Svidrigailov pulled the trigger.

VII

That same day, but in the evening now, at around seven o'clock, Raskolnikov approached the lodgings of his mother and sister – those same lodgings in Bakaleyev's Tenements that Razumikhin had arranged for them. The entrance to the staircase led in from the street. Raskolnikov slowed his step as he approached, as though he were unsure whether to go inside or not. Not for any reason would he have gone back, however; his decision had been made. 'In any case it doesn't matter, they don't know anything as yet,' he thought, 'and they're accustomed to thinking me a bit strange . . .' His clothes were in a terrible state: covered in dirt, having spent all night out in the rain, they were ripped and torn to rags. His face was almost disfigured with weariness, the effects of the weather, physical exhaustion and his almost round-the-clock struggle with himself. All that night he had spent alone, God only knew where. But at least he had made his decision.

He knocked at the door; it was opened to him by his mother. Dunya was not there. Not even the servant-girl happened to be around at that moment. Pulkheria Aleksandrovna was at first speechless with joy and bewilderment; then she seized him by the hand and dragged him into the room.

'Well, here you are!' she began, stammering with joy. 'Rodya, you mustn't be angry at me for greeting you in this stupid fashion, with tears: I'm laughing, not crying. Did you think I was crying? No, I'm overjoyed, but I have this bad habit of getting tears in my eyes. It's ever since your father died, the slightest thing makes me cry. Sit down, my dear, you must be tired, I can see it. Oh, how muddy you've got yourself.'

'I was out in the rain last night, mother . . .' Raskolnikov began.

'No, oh no!' Pulkheria Aleksandrovna exclaimed, flinging herself towards him and breaking him off. 'You thought I was going to start asking you questions in that old mother's way of mine; there's no need to worry. I mean, I understand, I understand everything, I've already learned to see things the way people here do, and I really do think it's more sensible. I've decided once and for all that it's not for me to try to understand all your reasons for doing what you do, or to bring you to account for them. God knows what deeds and plans you may have in your head, or what thoughts may be taking shape there; is it for me to nudge your elbow and ask you what you're thinking about? I mean I . . . Oh, merciful Lord! Why am I rushing about like a scalded cat? . . . Look, Rodya, I've been reading your article, the one you had in the journal, for the third time now, Dmitry Prokofich brought me it. I fairly gasped aloud when I saw it; what a fool I am, I thought to myself, that's what he's doing with his time, that's the answer to the riddle! Men of learning are always like that. It's quite probable that he has some new ideas in his head just now; he's thinking them over, and I'm just bothering him and distracting him. I've been reading it, my dear, and of course I don't understand much of it; but that's how it's bound to be, really: how could I expect to?'

'Show me it, mother.'

Raskolnikov took the periodical and gave his article a cursory glance. However much counter it ran to his present situation and state of mind, he experienced none the less that strange and mordant sensation an author feels upon seeing himself in print for the first time; in addition, his twenty-three years were not without effect. This lasted one single moment. Having read a few lines, he frowned, and a terrible anguish clawed at his heart. The whole of his mental and emotional struggle of the last few months suddenly came back to him in a flood. With revulsion and annoyance he threw the article on to the table.

'All I know is, Rodya, that stupid though I may be, I can still see that very soon you're going to be one of the leading lights, if not *the* leading light in our intellectual world. And they dared to suppose you were mad. Ha-ha-ha! Don't you know? I mean, that's what they thought! Oh, the miserable worms, how could they ever recognize intellect? And I mean Dunya, Dunya also nearly believed them – what a terrible thing! Your dead father sent two submissions to journals – first some poems (I still have the notebook, I'll show it you some time), and then a whole novella (I'd asked him to let me copy it out for him), and then how we both prayed they'd be accepted – but they weren't! You know, Rodya, six or seven days ago I felt simply destroyed as I looked at your clothes, at the way you were living, at what you were eating and what you were going around in. But now I can see how silly that was of me, because whatever you want you'll now be able to get for yourself by virtue of your intelligence and talent. The explanation of all this is simply that for the time being you don't want it, because you're preoccupied with far more important matters . . .'

'Isn't Dunya here, mother?'

'No, Rodya. It's not very often that she is, she leaves me here on my own. Dmitry Prokofich, and I'm grateful to him for it, looks in to sit with me for a while now and then – he's forever talking about you. He's truly fond of you, my dear, and he has such respect for you. As far as your sister's concerned, I don't want to imply that she's being really inconsiderate to me, or anything like that. I mean, I'm not complaining. She has her temperament, and I have mine; now she's got some secrets she wants to keep; well, I don't have any secrets from either of you. Of course, I'm firmly convinced that Dunya's extremely clever and that, what's more, she loves both you and me . . . but I really don't know what all this is going to lead to. I mean, look how happy you've made me by coming to see me just now; yet off she's gone on some rounds or other; when she gets back I'll say to her: your brother was here while you were out – where have you been passing the time? Now you mustn't spoil me, Rodya: if you can, come and see me, but if you can't, there's nothing to be done, and I'll wait. For you see, I'll know all the same that you love me, and that will be enough for me. I shall read these literary works of yours, I shall hear everyone talking about you, and after a bit you'll come and see me yourself – what could be better? Why I do believe you've looked in just now in order to console your mother, yes, I can see it . . .'

At this point Pulkheria Aleksandrovna suddenly burst into tears.

'Oh, it's just me again! Don't pay any attention to me, silly woman that I am! Oh, for heaven's sake, what am I doing sitting around like this,' she exclaimed, 'after all, I've made coffee, yet I haven't given you any! That's what they mean when they talk about old women's selfishness. It'll be ready in a moment, in a moment!'

'Mother, please stop it, I'm going in a moment. I didn't come here for that. Please listen to what I have to say.'

Pulkheria Aleksandrovna timidly went over to him.

'Mother, whatever may happen, whatever you may hear about me, whatever people may tell you about me, will you go on loving me as you do now?' he asked suddenly out of the fullness of his heart, almost without thinking what he was saying or weighing it over.

'Rodya, Rodya, what's got into you? How can you ask such a thing?

And who's going to tell me things about you? Why, I shan't listen to anyone, no matter who they are, I shall just chase them away.'

'I've come to make it clear to you that I've always loved you, and that I'm glad we're alone now, even glad that Dunya's not here,' he continued with the same impetuosity. 'I've come to tell you straight out that even though you're going to be unhappy, you must always remember that your son now loves you more than himself and that all the things you've thought about me, that I'm cruel and don't love you, all those things are false. I'll never ever stop loving you . . . Well, I've said enough; I thought it was the right thing to do, to begin with that . . .'

Pulkheria Aleksandrovna put her arms round him without saying anything, pressed him to her bosom and quietly wept.

'Whatever's the matter with you, Rodya, I don't know what it is,' she said, at last. 'All this time I've thought it was just that we were making you bored, but now all the signs tell me that you've some great trouble ahead of you, and that's why you're so miserable. I've seen this coming for a long time, Rodya. Please forgive me for mentioning it; I think about nothing else, and I can't sleep at nights because of it. All last night your sister, too, lay in a delirium, and it was you she kept talking about. I managed to pick out some of it, but I couldn't make any sense of it. I spent all morning walking around as though I was going to my execution, waiting for something, and now here it is. Rodya, Rodya, where is it you're going? Are you going to make a journey somewhere?'

'Yes, I am.'

'It's as I thought! But look, I mean, I can come with you, if you need me to. So can Dunya; she loves you, she loves you very much, and Sonya Semyonovna could easily come with us too if necessary; I'd be glad to take her under my wing as though she were my own daughter. Dmitry Prokofich will help us to make the necessary preparations together . . . but . . . where is it you're . . . going?'

'Goodbye, mother.'

'What? Today?' she exclaimed, as though she were about to lose him forever.

'I can't remain here, I've no time, it's very urgent . . .'

'And I can't go with you?'

'No, but you can get down on your knees and say a prayer for me. Perhaps your prayer will be heeded.'

'Let me make the sign of the cross over you, and bless you! There, like that, like that. O God, what are we doing?'

Yes, he was glad, he was very glad that there was no one else there, that he and his mother were alone together. It was as though after all this horrible time his heart had suddenly softened. He fell down before her, he kissed her feet, and both of them, clasping each other in their arms, wept. On this occasion she was not even surprised, nor did she ask him any questions. She had known for a long time that something terrible was happening to her son, and that now some fearsome moment had ripened for him.

'Rodya, my dear boy, my first-born,' she said, sobbing. 'Now you're just the way you were when you were little, that's how you used to hug me and kiss me; back in the days when your father was still alive and we were struggling by you used to console us by the mere fact of being with us, and after I'd buried your father how many times we used to weep over his grave, with our arms about each other the way they are now. All this crying I've been doing is just because my mother's heart was able to sense trouble in advance. The first time I saw you that evening, do you remember, when we'd only just got here, I fathomed everything by the look in your eyes, and my heart fairly missed a beat; and today, when I opened the door to you, I looked and thought, yes, it's obvious, his hour of destiny is here. Rodya, Rodya, I mean, you're not going away right this very moment, are you?'

'No.'

'Will you come again?'

'Yes . . . I will.'

'Rodya, please don't be angry with me, I don't even dare to ask you any questions. I know I don't have any right to, but even so, can't you just tell me in a couple of words – is it far away you're going?'

'Very far away.'

'What is it that's taking you there – a job, your career, or what?'

'Whatever God will send . . . Only you must pray for me . . .'

Raskolnikov walked to the door, but she caught hold of him and looked into his eyes with a desperate gaze. Her face was contorted with horror.

'That's enough, mother,' Raskolnikov said, deeply regretting that he had ever had the idea of coming here.

'It's not forever? Say it's not forever? Say you'll come again, come tomorrow?'

'Yes, yes, I will – now goodbye.'

He finally managed to tear himself free.

The evening was fresh, warm and clear; the weather had brightened up since morning. Raskolnikov set off for his lodgings; he was in a hurry. He wanted to get it all over with by sunset. Until that time he was anxious to avoid meeting anyone. As he climbed the staircase to his lodgings he observed that Nastasya, having torn herself away from the samovar, was watching him closely and following him with her eyes. 'I wonder if there's someone up in my room?' he thought. In his mind's eye he saw with loathing an image of Porfiry. When, however, he arrived at his room and opened the door, he saw Dunya there. She was sitting utterly alone, in deep reflection, and had apparently been waiting for him for a long time. He paused on the threshold. She raised herself from the sofa in alarm and stood erect before him. Her gaze, motionlessly fixed upon him, displayed horror and inconsolable grief. By this gaze alone he could tell at once that she knew everything.

'What do you want me to do, come in or go away?' he asked her, uncertainly.

'I've spent the whole day at Sofya Semyonovna's; we were both waiting for you. We thought you'd be sure to go there.'

Raskolnikov entered the room and sat down on a chair in a state of exhaustion.

'I don't feel all that strong, Dunya; I'm very tired; but at this moment at least I'd like to regain complete control of myself.' He looked up at her with distrust in his eyes.

'Where were you all night?'

'I don't really remember; you see, sister, I wanted to make a clean break and kept going down to the Neva time after time; that I remember. I wanted to end it all there, but . . . I couldn't bring myself to do it . . .' he whispered, again casting a distrustful glance at Dunya.

'God be praised! That was the very thing we were afraid of, Sofya Semyonovna and I! That means you still believe in life; God be praised, God be praised!'

Raskolnikov smiled a bitter, ironic smile.

'I've never been a believer, yet just now as mother and I had our arms around each other, we wept; I have no faith, yet I asked her to pray for me. God knows how that can happen, Dunya, I don't understand it at all.'

'You went to see mother? You told her?' Dunya exclaimed in horror. 'Surely you can't have done that?'

'No, I didn't tell her . . . not in words; but she sensed a lot of it. She'd heard the things you said in your sleep when you were delirious. I'm convinced she already half understands. It may have been a mistake on my part to go and see her. I really don't know why I did it. I'm a rotten person, Dunya.'

'A rotten person, yet you're ready to go and take your suffering! I mean, you are going to do that, aren't you?'

'Yes, I am. Right now. Yes, in order to avoid this shame I wanted to drown myself, Dunya, but as I stood looking down at the water it occurred to me that if I really still believed I was strong, then I oughtn't to be afraid of shame either,' he said, forestalling her. 'Is that pride, Dunya?'

'Yes, Rodya, it's pride.'

A light seemed to flash in his deadened eyes; it was as though he took pleasure in still being proud.

'And you don't think it's simply because I was scared of the water?' he asked with an ugly, ironic smile, peering into her face.

'Oh, Rodya, that's enough!' Dunya exclaimed bitterly.

For about two minutes there was silence between them. He sat with his head lowered, looking at the floor; Dunya stood at the other end of the table, watching him in torment. Suddenly he rose:

'It's late, it's time. I'm going to turn myself in now. But I don't know why I'm going to do it.'

Large tears were flowing down her cheeks.

'You're crying, sister, but will you give me your hand?'

'Did you doubt that I would?'

She embraced him tightly.

'After all, by going to take your suffering you're wiping out half of your crime, aren't you?' she cried, squeezing him in her arms and kissing him.

'Crime? What crime?' he exclaimed in a sudden fit of fury. 'My killing a loathsome, harmful louse, a filthy old moneylender woman who brought no good to anyone, to murder whom would pardon forty sins, who sucked the lifeblood of the poor, and you call that a

594

crime? I don't think about it and I have no plans to wipe it out. And why do they keep poking me from all sides with their "Crime, crime!"? Only now do I see clearly the whole absurdity of my cowardice, now, when I've already taken the resolve to go to this needless shame! It's merely because of my own baseness and mediocrity that I'm taking this step, and possibly also because it may do me some good, as he suggested, that . . . Porfiry! . . .'

'Brother, brother, what are you saying? I mean, you have blood on your hands!' Dunya cried in despair.

'The blood that's on everyone's hands,' he caught her up, almost in a frenzy now, 'that flows and has always flowed through the world like a waterfall, that is poured like champagne and for the sake of which men are crowned in the Capitol and then called the benefactors of mankind. Well, just take a closer look and see what's really what! I wanted to do good to people and I'd have done hundreds, thousands of good deeds instead of this one stupid action, which wasn't even stupid, really, but just clumsy, as the whole idea wasn't nearly as stupid as it appears now, in the light of failure . . . (In the light of failure everything appears stupid!) By means of that stupid action I hoped to put myself in a position of independence, to take the first step, to obtain funds, and then the whole thing would have been wiped out by the measureless benefits (relatively speaking) that would have been achieved . . . But look at me, I couldn't even manage the first step, because I'm a – bastard! That's the long and the short of it! But even so I won't see it the way you do: if I hadn't failed, they'd have crowned me, but as it is, it's into the can with me!'

'But that's wrong, that's utterly wrong! Brother, what are you saying?'

'Aha! so I've put it in the wrong form, have I, not in the correct aesthetic form! Well, I must say I don't understand: why is it considered more respectable to hurl bombs at people in a regular siege? The fear of aesthetics is the first symptom of powerlessness! . . . Never, never have I seen that so clearly as now, and I understand my crime even less than ever! Never, never have I been stronger and more full of conviction than I am now! . . .'

The colour had fairly leapt to his pale, exhausted features. But, as he uttered this last exclamation, he chanced to meet the eyes of Dunya, and such, such was the agony for his sake he met in that gaze that he snapped out of his trance in spite of himself. He sensed that whatever else he had done, he had made these two poor women unhappy. There was no denying that he was the cause of their woes . . .

'Dunya, dear one! If I'm guilty of a crime, then please forgive me (though if I'm guilty, it's out of the question for me to be forgiven). Farewell! Don't let's argue! It's time, and more than time. Don't try to follow me, I beg you, I've another call to make . . . Just go now and sit with mother. I beg you to do that! It's the last and greatest request I shall make of you. You must stay beside her all the time; I left her in such a state of anxiety that she may not be able to endure it: she may either die or go mad. So stay with her! Razumikhin will be with you; I've told him . . . Don't shed any tears for me: I shall try to be brave, and honest, all the rest of my life, even though I am a murderer. Perhaps some day you'll hear my name. I won't bring shame on you, you'll see; I'll show you yet . . . but for now goodbye, until we meet again,' he concluded hurriedly, again noticing the strange look that had appeared in Dunya's eyes at these last words and promises of his. 'What are you crying like that for? Don't cry, don't cry; I mean, we're not parting for ever! . . . Oh yes! Wait, I forgot! . . .'

He went over to the table, picked up a fat, dusty volume, opened it and took out a small portrait, a watercolour on ivory that had been tucked way between its leaves. It was a portrait of his landlady's daughter, his one-time fiancée, the girl who had died of a fever, the strange one who had wanted to go and join a nunnery. For a moment he scrutinized her expressive and delicate little face, kissed the portrait and handed it to Dunya.

'You know, I also used to talk a lot *about that* to her, and only to her,' he said reflectively. 'It was to her heart that I confided much of what subsequently came to pass in such an ugly manner. You needn't worry,' he said, turning to Dunya. 'She no more agreed with me than you do, and I'm glad she's no longer alive. The main thing, the main thing is that now everything is going to take a new turn, is going to be broken in two,' he cried suddenly, falling back into his leaden anguish again. 'Everything, everything, and am I ready for it? Do I even really want it? They say it's necessary for me as a trial by ordeal! But what purpose, what purpose do all these senseless ordeals serve? What purpose do they serve, and will I be any nearer the answer to that question later on, when I've been crushed by sufferings, by idiocy, in senile helplessness, after twenty years' hard labour, than I am now, and what purpose will there be in my continuing to live? Why am I giving my assent to that kind of life for myself now? Oh, as I stood above the Neva this morning at dawn I knew I was a villain.'

At last they both stepped outside. Dunya found it hard, but she loved him! She went on her way, but, having gone some fifty paces, turned round again to look at him. He was still visible. But, when he reached the corner, he also turned round; for the last time their gazes met; but, having observed that she was looking at him, he made an impatient and even annoyed gesture with his hand, telling her to go, and abruptly turned the corner.

'That was a nasty thing for me to do, I realize that,' he thought to himself, feeling shame a moment later at the gesture of annoyance he had made to Dunya. 'But why do they love me so much, if I don't deserve it? Oh, if I were alone and no one loved me and I had never loved anyone! *All this would never have taken place!* But the interesting thing to know is whether in the course of the next fifteen to twenty years my soul will acquire such humility that I shall whimper in reverence before other people, ready to call myself a brigand at the first opportunity! Yes, that's it, that's it! That's why they're sending me into exile now, it's that that they want . . . There they all are, scurrying back and forth along the street, and I mean, every one of them is a brigand and a bastard at heart; worse than that – an idiot! But just try to get me out of my exile, and they'd all start foaming at the mouth with righteous indignation! Oh, how I hate them all!'

He began to think deeply about the process by which it might happen that he would finally, beyond all dispute, submit to them with the humility born of conviction. 'All right, why not? Of course, that's how it's got to be. Twenty years of incessant hardship ought to be enough to finish me off, oughtn't they? Constant dripping wears away the stone. And what's the point, what's the point of living after this, why am I going there now when I know perfectly well that it's all going to go according to the book, and not otherwise?'

This must have been the hundredth time he had asked himself that question since the night before, but even so he went.

VIII

When he went in to see Sonya dusk was beginning to fall. All day Sonya had been waiting for him in a state of terrible excitement. She and Dunya had waited together. Dunya had come to her that morning, having remembered Svidrigailov's remark of the day before that Sonya 'knew about it'. We shall not convey to the reader the details of the conversation, or the tears of both women, or how intimate they became. From that rendezvous Dunya had carried away at least one consolation, and that was that her brother would not be alone: it was to her, Sonya, he had gone first with his confession; it was in her that he had sought a human being, when he had needed one; as for Sonya she would follow him wherever fate might send him. Dunya had not asked, but had known that was how it would be. She had even looked at Sonya with a kind of reverence, at first almost embarrassing her with this feeling of reverence with which she approached her. Sonya had been almost on the point of tears: she considered herself unworthy even to glance at Dunya. Dunya's fair image, as she had bowed to her with such courtesy and respect at the time of their first meeting in Raskolnikov's lodgings, had remained in her soul forever as one of the most beautiful and ineffable visions of her life.

At last Dunya had run out of patience and had left Sonya in order to await her brother in his lodgings; she kept thinking that that was where he would make for first. Left alone, Sonya at once began to torment herself with fear at the thought that perhaps he might really commit suicide. The same fear haunted Dunya. All day long, however, they had used all kinds of arguments to reassure each other that that could not possibly be, and for the time they had spent together had been calmer. But now, no sooner had they parted than both the one and the other had begun to think only of that. Sonya kept remembering how Svidrigailov had told her the day before that there were two roads open to Raskolnikov – Vladimirka or . . . She was also familiar with his vanity, his arrogance, his self-pride and unbelief. 'Is it really only cowardice and the fear of death that are keeping him alive?' she thought at last, in despair. Meanwhile the sun was going down. She stood sadly at the window, staring out of it fixedly – but from this window all that was visible was the brown main wall of the neighbouring building. At last, when she had arrived at a complete conviction that the unhappy man was dead – he walked into her room.

A cry of joy burst from within her. Taking a close look at his face, however, she suddenly went pale.

'Yes, that's right,' Raskolnikov said with an ironic smile. 'I've come for your crosses, Sonya. After all, it was you who told me to go to the crossroads; what's the matter? Now that it's come to the point, have you got cold feet?'

Sonya was staring at him in consternation. This tone of voice seemed strange to her; a cold shiver passed throughout her body, but a moment later she realized that both tone and words were something he was affecting. There was also the way he was talking to her: looking away at an angle, as though he were trying to avoid gazing her straight in the eye.

'You see, Sonya, I've decided that it may be for my own good to do it this way. There's a certain circumstance involved in all this . . . Oh, it would take me too long to tell you about it, and in any case there's no point. Do you know the only thing that makes me angry? It's that all those stupid brutes will immediately surround me with their ugly mugs, gawp right at me, ask me their stupid questions, which I'll have to answer – they'll point their fingers at me . . . Pah! But you know, I shan't go to Porfiry; I'm fed up with him. No, I'd rather go and see my friend Gunpowder, I'll give him a real surprise, make a bit of a stir in my own way. But I must have some *sang froid*; I've grown far too acrimonious of late. Would you believe it: I nearly took my fist to my sister just now for turning round to look at me one last time. This state of mind's enough to make a swine of one! Ah, what's become of me? Well, then, where are they, your crosses?'

It was as if he were not his own man. He was not even able to stay in the same place for a single moment, nor could he concentrate his attention on a single object; his thoughts kept leaping ahead, one after the other, his speech wandered, and his hands were trembling slightly.

Without saying anything, Sonya produced two crucifixes from a drawer, a cypress one and a copper one, crossed herself, crossed him, and hung the cypress crucifix around his neck.

'I see, this is meant to symbolize my taking up the cross, hee, hee! As though I hadn't done enough suffering already! I get the cypress one, as befits a member of the common people; you get the copper one – it's Lizaveta's, isn't it? Let's see it – is that the one she was wearing . . . at the moment in question? I know of another two crosses, a silver one and one with an icon. I threw them on to the old woman's corpse that day. They're really the ones I ought to have now, they're the ones I ought to put on . . . But actually, I'm talking a lot of nonsense, I'm forgetting the matter in hand; for some reason my mind's grown distracted . . . You see, Sonya – I really came in order to warn you, so you'd know . . . Well, that's all . . . Yes, that's the only reason I came. (Hm, though actually I thought I'd say more.) After all, you yourself wanted me to go and give myself up, so now I shall, I'll go to jail, and your desire will be fulfilled; so why are you crying? You as well? Stop it, that's enough; oh, how tedious all this is!'

An emotion had, however, taken root in him; he felt a pang at his heart as he looked at her. 'Why this girl? Why is she crying?' he wondered. 'What am I to her? What's she crying for, why is she getting me ready for the journey, like mother, or Dunya? She wants to be my nanny!'

'Please make the sign of the cross over yourself, please say at least one prayer,' Sonya asked him in a trembling, timid voice.

'Oh, very well, certainly, as you please! And it comes straight from the heart, Sonya, straight from the heart . . .'

Though really he wanted to say something quite different.

He crossed himself several times. Sonya caught up her shawl and slipped it over her head. It was a green *drap-de-dames* shawl, probably the one Marmeladov had mentioned that time, the 'family' one. The thought occurred to Raskolnikov for a moment, but he did not ask about it. He really had begun to feel that his mind was growing alarmingly distracted and almost indecently anxious. This frightened him. He also suddenly found shocking the realization that Sonya intended to go with him.

'What are you doing? What business do you have going there? Stay here, stay! I'll go alone!' he snapped, irritable with apprehension; almost wild with anger, he strode towards the door. 'We can't have a whole retinue down there!' he muttered as he went out.

Sonya remained in the middle of the room. He had not even said goodbye to her, he had already forgotten her; a single gnawing and rebellious doubt seethed within his soul.

'But is this really right, is this the right thing to do?' he found himself thinking as he went down the stairs. 'Can I really not still call it all off and make amends for everything . . . and not go?'

But even so, he went. He had suddenly felt once and for all that there was no point in asking any questions. As he emerged on to the street, he remembered that he had not said goodbye to Sonya, that she was still standing in the middle of the room wearing her green shawl, not daring to move a limb because of the way he had shouted; and he paused for an instant. In that split second a certain thought flooded him with brilliant light – as though it had been waiting to finally overwhelm him.

'Why, why did I come and see her just now? I told her it was on business; what business? There was no business involved whatsoever! To tell her I was *going*; what of it? A fine sort of pretext that was! What was it then – do I love her? I don't really, do I? I mean, I chased her away just now as if she were a dog. What about those crucifixes – did I really want them from her? Oh, how low I've fallen! No – it was her tears I wanted, I wanted to see her fright, to watch her heart ache and torment itself! I needed to have something to catch on to, I wanted to play for time, to watch another human being! And I dared to have that kind of self-confidence, those kind of dreams about myself, beggar that I am, nonentity that I am, villain, villain!'

He was walking along the embankment of the Canal, and had not much further to go. When he reached the bridge, however, he paused and suddenly set off across it, breaking his route, and made his way up to the Haymarket.

Greedily he looked around him, to right and to left, scrutinizing each object intensely and unable to focus his attention on anything; it was all slipping away. 'In just a week or a month I'll be carted off somewhere on one of those convict transports, and how will I see this canal then – will I remember this?' flashed through his head. 'Take this sign here, how will I read these same letters then? Look, they've spelt it "Campany", well, let me remember that *a*, that letter *a*, and look at it in a month's time, that very same *a*; how will I look at it then? What will I be feeling and thinking? . . . Oh God, how base they will all seem, all these present . . . concerns of mine! Of course they'll seem curious . . . in their own way . . . (ha-ha-ha! what am I thinking of?) I'm turning into a child, boasting to myself; but why am I telling myself off? Ugh, how they shove! Look at that fat fellow – he must be a German – who shoved me just now; well, does he know whom he shoved? There's a woman with a baby, begging for alms, it's interesting that she should think I'm more fortunate than herself. All right then, I'll give her something, just for amusement's sake. I say, I still have a five-copeck piece in my pocket, where did that come from? Here you are, here you are . . . take that, little mother!'

'May God preserve you, sir!' the voice of the beggarwoman said in the tone of a lament.

He entered the Haymarket. He found it unpleasant, very unpleasant to rub shoulders with people, but he had purposely gone to the place where he would see the greatest number of them. He would have given the whole world to be alone; but he himself sensed that not for one moment would he be on his own. In the crowd a drunk man was causing a disturbance: he kept trying to dance, but collapsed to the ground. He was surrounded by a ring of people. Raskolnikov forced his way through the crowd, looked at the drunk man for a few moments and then suddenly gave a curt and abrupt laugh. A moment later he had already forgotten about him, did not even see him, even though he was looking at him. At last he moved away, not even conscious of where he was; but when he reached the centre of the square he was suddenly overtaken by a spasm, a single sensation that mastered him straight away, seized hold of him entirely – both in mind and in body.

He had suddenly recalled Sonya's words: 'Go up to the crossroads, bow to the people, kiss the earth, because you have sinned against it too, and tell the whole world out loud: "I'm a murderer!"' In remembering them, he had begun to tremble all over. And such a crushing weight did he now carry from the hopeless despair and anxiety of all this recent time, and especially of the last few hours, that he fairly leapt at the chance of this pure, new, complete sensation. It suddenly hit him like an epileptic seizure: a single spark began to glow within his soul, and suddenly it engulfed everything, like fire. Everything in him instantly grew soft, and the tears came spurting out. He fell to the ground where he stood . . .

He kneeled in the middle of the square, bowed down to the earth and kissed that dirty earth, with pleasure and happiness. He got up and bowed down a second time.

'My God, that chap's had a few!' a young lad beside him observed.

There was a burst of laughter.

'What it is, lads, is that he's off to Jerusalem with all his kids, and he's saying goodbye to his motherland, bowing to one and all, kissing the capital city of St Petersburg and its foundations,' a slightly drunken artisan supplied.

'He's still a young lad, too!'

'A gent by the looks of it!' someone observed in a sagacious voice.

'You don't know who's a gent and who isn't these days.'

All these comments and arguments had an inhibiting effect on Raskolnikov, and the words 'I've committed a murder', which had possibly been about to escape from his lips, died within him. He calmly endured all these shouts, however, and, without looking round, walked straight down the lane in the direction of the police bureau. A certain vision floated before him as he went, but it caused him no astonishment; he had already had a premonition that this was how it was going to be. As, on the Haymarket, he had bowed to the ground for the second time, turning round to the left, some fifty paces away from him, he had seen Sonya. She had been hiding from him behind one of the wooden huts on the square; so she had observed the whole of his *via dolorosa*! Raskolnikov felt and understood at that moment, once and for all, that Sonya was now with him forever and would follow him even to the ends of the earth, wherever his fate might decree. His heart turned over . . . but – here he was, he had reached the fateful spot . . .

He entered the courtyard in fairly good spirits. It was necessary to go up to the third floor. 'It'll take me a while to get up there,' he thought. On the whole it seemed to him that the fateful moment was still a long way off, that he still had a lot of time left, that there was still plenty of room for reflection.

Again the same sweepings, the same eggshells on the spiral staircase, again the doors of the apartments wide open, again the same kitchens from which came fumes and stink. Raskolnikov had not been here since that day. His legs lost sensation and sagged under him, but they moved. He paused for a moment in order to regain his breath, in order to recover himself, in order to go in 'like a human being'. 'Oh, what's the point? Why bother?' he thought suddenly, realizing what he was doing. 'If I must drain this cup, then surely nothing will make any difference? The more loathsome, the better.' Through his mind at that moment passed the figure of Ilya Petrovich – 'Gunpowder'. 'Do I really have to go and see him? Can't it be someone else? Can't I go and see Nikodim Fomich? Turn back right now and go and see the superintendent himself at his apartment? At least it would all go off in less official surroundings . . . No, no! Let it be Gunpowder, let it be Gunpowder! If I'm to drain it, then let me drain it all in one go . . .'

Growing cold, and only just aware of what he was doing, he opened the door of the bureau. On this occasion the place was practically deserted apart from a yardkeeper and some plebeian-looking fellow. The security attendant did not even bother to peer out from behind his partition. Raskolnikov walked into the next room. 'Perhaps I can still get away without telling them,' flashed through his head. Here a certain personage from among the scribes, dressed in an ordinary frock-coat, was getting ready to write something at his desk. In the corner another scribe was also setting to work. Of Zamyotov there was no sign. Needless to say, here was no sign of Nikodim Fomich, either.

'Isn't there anyone here?' Raskolnikov asked, addressing the personage at the writing desk.

'Who are you looking for?'

'Ah-h-h! By the ear unheard, by the eye unseen, but the Russian spirit . . . how does it go on in that fairy tale . . . I've forgotten! M-my c-compliments, sir!' a familiar voice suddenly exclaimed.

Raskolnikov gave a shudder. Before him stood Gunpowder; he had suddenly come out of the third room. 'This is fate personified,' Raskolnikov thought. 'What's he doing here?'

'Come to see us? What about?' yelped Ilya Petrovich. (He was by the look of it in a most excellent and even slightly stimulated mental condition.) 'If it's on business, you're too early. I myself am simply here by chance . . . However, I shall do what I can. I will confess to you, Mr – er – er . . . I'm sorry . . .'

'Raskolnikov.'

'Ah, of course: Raskolnikov! Could you really suppose I'd forgotten? Please, you mustn't think I'm such a . . . Rodion Ro . . . Ro . . . Rodionych, isn't it?'

'Rodion Romanych.'

'Yes, yes-yes! Rodion Romanych, Rodion Romanych! It was on the tip of my tongue. You know, I've been trying to get in touch with you for ages. I will confess to you that I was genuinely sorry we . . . dealt with you the way we did that time . . . it was explained to me afterwards, I learned that you are a young *littérateur* and even a scholar . . . and that, as it were, your first steps . . . Oh, good heavens! Which of our *littérateurs* and scholars did not begin with some eccentric first steps? My wife and I both have a deep respect for literature, and with my wife it even takes the form of a passion! . . . Literature and the arts! As long as the fellow's a gentleman, all the rest can be acquired by means of talent, knowledge, intellect, genius! A hat – well, what does a hat signify, for example? A hat is as plain as a pancake, I can buy it at Zimmerman's; but what lies under the hat and is covered by the hat, that I cannot buy, sir! . . . I will confess to you that I even wanted to come and have the whole matter out with you, but I thought perhaps you . . . But I'm neglecting to ask: is there something you want? They say your family has arrived in town?'

'Yes, my mother and sister.'

'I've actually had the honour and good fortune of meeting your sister – a charming and educated person. I will confess, I was sorry you and I got so angry with each other that day. A curious incident! And as for my viewing your fainting-fit that day in a certain light – it all became quite dazzlingly clear afterwards! Blind cruelty and fanaticism! I understand your indignation. Is it perhaps that you're moving your lodgings in connection with the arrival of your family?'

'N-no, I simply dropped by . . . I came to inquire . . . I thought I would find Zamyotov here.'

'Ah, yes! You and he have made friends; I heard about it, sir. But I'm afraid Zamyotov isn't here – you've missed him. Yes, sir, we've lost Aleksandr Grigoryevich! He left yesterday; he got a transfer . . . and, in the process of being transferred, he fairly quarrelled with us all . . . in a most impolite manner. He's an empty-headed young whippersnapper, and that's all there is to it; one might have thought he'd have come to something; but I mean, there you have it, our resplendent youth! He says he's going to take some examination or other, but I mean it's only so he can tell us about it and boast to us, that's how far *that* examination will go. I mean, he's not like you, or your friend there, Mr Razumikhin! Your career lies in the field of scholarship, and you won't be brought down by failure! For you all those charms of life, one might say – *nihil est*, you're an ascetic, a monk, a recluse! . . . what matters to you is the book, the pen behind the ear, your scholarly research – that's where your spirit soars! I myself do a little . . . have you by any chance read Livingstone's *Travels*?'

'No.'

'I must admit I have. Actually, you know, there's an awful lot of nihilists around these days; well, I mean, it's understandable; what kind of times are these, I ask you? But you see, I thought that perhaps with you I could . . . I mean, *you* can't possibly be a nihilist! Answer me truthfully now, truthfully!'

'N-no . . .'

'Now come along, you can be quite open with me, you needn't feel embarrassed, it's just as though we were alone, and not in here at all! "One thing that duty sends, another among . . ." – did you think I was going to say "friends"? No, sir, you guess wrongly! Not friendship, but a sense of being a citizen and a human being, a sense of humaneness and love of the Almighty. I may be an official, serving at my post, but I am forever obliged to be aware of the citizen and the human being in myself,* and to render account . . . You mentioned Zamyotov just now. Zamyotov will be off causing some scandal in the French manner inside some sleazy establishment over a glass of champagne or Don wine – that's your Zamyotov for you! While I, it may perhaps be said, as it were, have burned with devotion and lofty feelings, and what is more possess importance, rank, occupy a position! I'm married and have children. Fulfil my duty as a citizen and a human being – but what is he, may I ask? I address you as a man who has been ennobled by education. And then again, there are far too many of these midwives around, if you want my opinion.'

Raskolnikov raised his eyebrows interrogatively. The things Ilya Petrovich, who had plainly not long risen from table, was saying had been raining and rattling down before him for the most part like so many empty sounds. He had, however, absorbed the gist of some of them; he gazed with a question in his eyes, uncertain how all this was going to end.

'It's these girls with their hair cut short I'm talking about,' the loquacious Ilya Petrovich continued. '"Midwives" is the name I've invented for them, and I think it's a perfectly good one. Hee-hee! They get themselves into the Academy and learn anatomy; well, I ask you: if I fall ill am I going to summon a young girl to cure me? Hee-hee!'

606

Ilya Petrovich chortled away, thoroughly content with his own witticisms.

'Let us assume it's caused by an immoderate thirst for enlightenment; but I mean, once a person is enlightened, that's enough. But why abuse it? Why offend decent people, the way that blackguard Zamyotov does? Why did he insult me, I ask you? And then again there've been so many of these suicides of late – you simply have no idea. People spending the last of their money and killing themselves. Young girls and lads, old men . . . Even today there's been a report about some gentleman who arrived in town recently. Nil Pavlych, I say, Nil Pavlych! What's the name of that gent they say shot himself over on the St Petersburg Side this morning?'

'Svidrigailov,' someone replied from the other room with hoarse indifference.

Raskolnikov shuddered.

'Svidrigailov! Svidrigailov's shot himself!' he exclaimed.

'What! You know the man?'

'Yes . . . I do . . . He arrived in town recently . . .'

'That's right, he did, after he lost his wife; a man of dissolute behaviour, and he suddenly went and shot himself, in such a scandalous fashion, you simply have no idea . . . he left a few words in his notebook to the effect that he was dying in full possession of his faculties and requested that no one be blamed for his death. It's said he had money. How is it you know him?'

'He was a . . . friend of mine . . . My sister worked in their house as a governess . . .'

'My, my, my . . . Then you ought to be able to tell us about him. Didn't you suspect anything?'

'I saw him yesterday . . . he was . . . drinking . . . I knew nothing of this.'

Raskolnikov felt that something had fallen on top of him and was weighing him down.

'You're looking rather pale again. We have such stuffy offices up here . . .'

'Yes, it's time I was going,' Raskolnikov muttered. 'Forgive me for troubling you . . .'

'Oh, don't mention it, you're most welcome! It's been a pleasure, and I'm glad to say it . . .'

Ilya Petrovich even stretched out his hand.

'I simply wanted . . . to see Zamyotov . . .'

'I understand, I understand, and it's been a pleasure.'

'I'm . . . most glad . . . Goodbye, now . . .' Raskolnikov smiled.

He stepped outside; he was swaying. His head was going round. He could hardly tell whether he was standing upright. He began to descend the staircase, supporting himself with his right hand against the wall. He had a vague impression of some yardkeeper, housebook in hand, giving him a shove as he made his way past him upstairs to the bureau; of some wretched little dog barking and barking somewhere on the ground floor, and of some woman throwing a rolling-pin at it and shouting. He went down to the bottom and emerged into the courtyard. There in the yard, not far from the exit, stood the pale, utterly rigid figure of Sonya, looking at him with wild, wild eyes. He came to a halt in front of her. There was an expression of pain and exhaustion on her face, something akin to despair. She clasped her hands together. A lost, ugly smile forced its way to his lips. He stood there for a moment, smiled ironically, then turned back and began to ascend the stairs to the bureau again.

Ilya Petrovich had sat down and was rummaging through some documents. In front of him stood the muzhik who had shoved against Raskolnikov on his way up the staircase.

'Ah-h-h? You again! Left something? . . . But what's the matter with you?'

With lips turned pale, his gaze motionless, Raskolnikov quietly walked up to him, went right up to the desk, rested one arm on it, and tried to say something, but was unable to; all that came out were some incoherent sounds.

'You're feeling faint, a chair! Here, sit on this chair, sit down! Water!'

Raskolnikov lowered himself onto the chair, without, however, taking his eyes off the face of the disagreeably astonished Ilya Petrovich. For a moment they both looked at each other, waiting. Water was brought.

'I'm the person . . .' Raskolnikov began.

'Take a drink of water.'

Raskolnikov brushed the water aside and quietly, in measured tones, but distinctly, said:

'I'm the person who murdered the old civil servant's widow and her sister Lizaveta that day, I did it with an axe, and I robbed them.'

Ilya Petrovich opened his mouth. People came running from every quarter.

Raskolnikov repeated his deposition.

* * *

EPILOGUE

Siberia. On the bank of a wide, lonely river there is a town, one of Russia's administrative centres; in the town there is a fortress, in the fortress a prison. In the prison there is a penal exile of the second category, Rodion Raskolnikov. Since the day he committed his crime almost one and a half years have passed.

The legal processing of this case went through without much difficulty. The criminal backed up his deposition with firmness, precision and clarity, neither confusing any of the circumstances nor making any attempt to soften them in his favour, distorting no facts and leaving out not the slightest detail. He described the entire plan of the murder right down to the smallest minutiae: cleared up the mystery of the 'pledge' (the small flat piece of wood with the metal flange) that was found in the hands of the murdered old woman; narrated in detail how he had removed the keys from the dead woman's person, described those keys, described the trunk and what had filled it; even enumerated some of the individual items it had contained; cleared up the riddle of Lizaveta's murder; recounted how Koch had come up the stairs and knocked, followed by the student, describing everything they had said to each other; how he, the criminal, had then run down the stairs and heard the shouting of Mikolka and Mitka; how he had hidden in the empty apartment and then gone back to his own lodgings, and in conclusion gave the whereabouts of the block near the gate in the yard on Voznesensky Prospect, under which the goods and the purse were found. In short, the case was cut and dried. The investigators and the judges were, it must be said, very surprised that he should have hidden the purse and the goods under the block without availing himself of them, and even more so that not only was he unable to remember the details of any of the goods he had stolen, but was even mistaken as to their number. In particular, the fact that he had never once opened the purse and did not even know how much money it contained, seemed difficult to believe (the purse had turned out to contain 317 silver roubles and three twenty-copeck pieces; because of the long time they had spent under the block some of the banknotes on top, which bore the largest denominations, had suffered severe water damage). Much time was spent in attempting to discover why it was that the defendant should be lying about this one thing, while he had voluntarily and truthfully confessed to everything else. At last one or two members of the panel (especially the psychologists) actually admitted the possibility that he really had never looked inside the purse, and so had not known what it contained, and that in this state of ignorance he had put it under the block, but at that point it was concluded that the crime itself could only have been committed in a state of some temporary disturbance of the mind, as it were, under the influence of some dangerous monomania involving murder and robbery for murder and robbery's sake, without ulterior motive or thought of gain. This decision happened to coincide with the arrival of the latest fashionable theory of temporary insanity, the application of which to certain criminals is so frequently the object of such effort in our time. What was more, precise testimony to Raskolnikov's inveterate hypochondria was adduced by many of the witnesses, among them Dr Zosimov, Raskolnikov's ex-student colleagues, his landlady and serving-maid. All this did much to reinforce the conclusion that Raskolnikov was not at all the usual kind of murderer, brigand and robber, and that here they were faced with something rather different. To the great annoyance of those who supported this opinion, the criminal made practically no attempt to defend himself; in response to the final and deciding questions as to what had induced him to murder and what had made him commit robbery, he replied quite succinctly, with the most brutal precision, that the cause of the whole thing had been his rotten social position, his poverty and helplessness, and his desire to secure the first steps of his career with the help of at least three thousand roubles, which he had counted on finding in the home of the murdered woman. As for the murder, he had embarked upon it as a result of his frivolous and cowardly nature, which had, moreover, been overwrought by deprivation and failure. To the question as to what had prompted him to turn himself in, he replied bluntly that it had been genuine remorse. All this was almost indecent . . .

The sentence, however, turned out to be more lenient than might have been supposed, given the crime that had been committed, and this may have been for the reason that not only did the criminal make no attempt to justify himself – he seemed even to display a wish to incriminate himself further. All the strange and unusual circumstances of the case were taken into account. As to the criminal's ill and impoverished condition before he had committed his crime there was not the slightest doubt. The fact that he had not availed himself of the proceeds of the robbery was put down in part to the influence of awakening remorse, and in part to an impaired condition of his mental faculties during the enactment of the crime. The fact of Lizaveta's unexpected murder merely served as an example to reinforce this latter supposition: a man commits two murders yet forgets the door is open! And to cap it all, he turns himself in at the very point when the case has grown extraordinarily complicated as a result of the false self-incrimination of a depressed fanatic (Nikolai), and this at a time when not only is there no clear evidence against the real criminal, but there is hardly any suspicion of his guilt (Porfiry Petrovich fully kept his promise). All of this played a decisive role in softening the fate of the accused man.

In addition to this, there also appeared, quite unexpectedly, certain other circumstances that acted powerfully in the defendant's favour. The former student Razumikhin dug up from somewhere the information, supporting it with proof, that the criminal Raskolnikov had, during the period of his attendance at the university, helped with the last of his resources a certain poor and consumptive student colleague of his acquaintance, having more or less kept him alive for a six-month spell. Not only that, but following his death he had looked after the old and enfeebled father – now left among the living – of his deceased colleague (who had supported and sustained his father by his own labour very nearly from the age of thirteen), had, what was more, found the old man a place in a hospital, and when he too had died had arranged his funeral. All this information exercised a certain favourable influence on the decision of Raskolnikov's fate. Then again, no less a person than his former landlady the widow Zarnitsyna, the mother of his deceased fiancée, testified that when he had been living in another building at Five Corners Raskolnikov had, during a fire in the middle of the night, dragged two small children to safety from one of the apartments that was already in flames, and had suffered burns as a result. This piece of evidence was thoroughly investigated and rather well supported by the testimony of many of the witnesses. In short, the upshot was that the criminal was sentenced to penal servitude of the second category for a period of only eight years in all, in recognition of his having turned himself in and in view of certain circumstances that had reduced his guilt.

Right at the start of the trial Raskolnikov's mother became ill. Dunya and Razumikhin found a means of getting her out of St Petersburg for the entire duration of the trial. Razumikhin selected a town situated on the railway and within easy reach of St Petersburg, so he would have an opportunity of keeping a proper eye on all the details of the trial and at the same time be able to see Avdotya Romanovna as frequently as possible. Pulkheria Aleksandrovna's illness was of some strange, nervous kind and was accompanied by something close to insanity – if not complete, then at least partial. Dunya, on returning from her last meeting with her brother, had found her mother thoroughly ill, with a fever and delirium. That very evening she had come to an agreement with Razumikhin as to what they should tell her mother in response to her questions about her brother, and had even invented with him a whole story about Raskolnikov's departure for some distant spot on the frontiers of Russia on a certain private errand that would eventually bring him both money and fame. They were, however, struck by the fact that neither on that occasion nor on subsequent ones did Pulkheria Aleksandrovna ask any questions at all. Quite the reverse: she herself was full of some story about her son's sudden departure; with tears she described to them how he had come to say farewell to her; let it be known as she did so, by means of hints, that she alone was privy to a great number of very important and mysterious circumstances and that Rodya had a great many powerful enemies, making it positively essential for him to go into hiding. With regard to his future career, it seemed to her it would be brilliant and assured, once certain hostile circumstances had been got out of the way; she made it quite plain to Razumikhin that she considered her son would in time become a statesman, something that was proven by his article and his dazzling literary talent. This article was something that she read constantly, sometimes even reading it out loud, very nearly sleeping with it at her side; yet for all that she almost never asked where exactly Rodya was now, even in spite of the fact that they all too obviously avoided mentioning the subject to her – which alone ought to have alerted her suspicion. In the end they began to be frightened by the strange silence of Pulkheria Aleksandrovna on certain points. For example, she never even complained about not getting any letters from him, while earlier, when living in her little town, she had done nothing but live in the hope and expectation of the speedy receipt of a letter from her adored Rodya. This latter circumstance really seemed to defy explanation and caused Dunya no end of worry; she had been visited by the idea that her mother must have had a premonition of something dreadful that awaited her son and was afraid to ask any questions, lest she should discover something even more dreadful. Whatever the truth of the matter, Dunya clearly perceived that Pulkheria Aleksandrovna was not in a sound condition of mind.

On one or two occasions, however, it chanced that Pulkheria Aleksandrovna herself steered the conversation in such a manner that it would have been impossible in replying to her not to mention the place where Rodya now found himself; and when the replies could not help coming out, like it or not, with a hollow, suspicious ring to them, she suddenly grew thoroughly mournful, silent and downcast, a state of affairs that continued for a very long time. In the end Dunya saw that all this lying and invention was more trouble than it was worth, and she came to the inevitable conclusion that it would on certain points be better for her to remain completely silent; it was, however, growing transparently clear that her poor mother suspected some dreadful thing. Among much else, Dunya recalled her brother's remark that Pulkheria Aleksandrovna had overheard the words she had uttered in her delirium the night before that last, fateful day, following her scene with Svidrigailov; what if she had been able to make some of them out? Frequently, sometimes after several days and even weeks of downcast, gloomy silence and speechless tears, the sick woman would spring into a kind of hysterical life and suddenly begin to talk out loud, almost incessantly, about her son, her hopes, the future . . . Her imaginings were sometimes very strange. They played along with her, said yes to her in everything (it was probable that she saw all too clearly that this was what they were doing), yet still she went on talking.

Five months after the criminal had turned himself in, his sentence was delivered. Razumikhin went to see him in prison whenever this was possible. So also did Sonya. At last the hour of parting drew near; Dunya swore to her brother that this parting was not forever; so also did Razumikhin. In Razumikhin's young and excitable head there firmly took root the project of creating in the course of the next three to four years at least the beginnings of an eventual fortune, of scraping together some money and moving to Siberia, where the soil was rich in every respect but there was a shortage of workmen, farmhands

617

and capital; of settling in the same town where Rodya would be, and . . . of them all beginning a new life together. As they said farewell, they all wept. During those very last days Raskolnikov was extremely broody, asked frequent questions about his mother and constantly worried about her. In fact, he positively tormented himself about her, a fact which made Dunya anxious. Having learned in detail of his mother's disturbed state of mind, he became very gloomy. For some reason during all this time he had been particularly unforthcoming in the presence of Sonya. With the help of the money that had been left to her by Svidrigailov, Sonya had long ago made up her mind and got herself ready to follow the gang of convicts with which he too was to be dispatched. Not a word concerning this had ever been mentioned between her and Raskolnikov; both knew, however, that this was how it was going to be. At the time of their last farewell he had smiled strangely at the fervent assurances of his sister and of Razumikhin about the happy future they would have together when he had finished his penal servitude, and had prophesied that his mother's unhealthy condition would soon end in calamity. At last he and Sonya set off.

Two months later Dunya and Razumikhin were married. The wedding was a sad and quiet affair. Among the guests, it may as well be said, were Porfiry Petrovich and Zosimov. Throughout all this latter period Razumikhin wore the air of a man who has taken a firm resolve. Dunya had a blind faith that he would realize all his intentions, and it would have been hard for her to see him otherwise: this man displayed an iron will. Among other things, he began to attend university lectures again in order to be able to complete his course. Both of them spent practically every moment putting together plans for the future; both firmly intended to move to Siberia in five years' time. Until that day they were relying on Sonya's being there . . .

Pulkheria Aleksandrovna gave her blessing to the marriage with joy; after it, however, she seemed to grow even sadder and more worried. In order to afford her a pleasant moment, Razumikhin informed her, among other things, of the episode concerning the student and his senile father and of the fact that Rodya had sustained burns and even fallen ill after rescuing two little children from certain death the year before. Both pieces of news had the effect of sending

the already unbalanced Pulkheria Aleksandrovna into a state bordering upon frenzy. She talked about this ceaselessly, would even engage
passers-by in the street to tell them about it (though Dunya never left
her side). In public carriages, in shops, wherever she could capture a
listener of whatever kind, she would lead the conversation to the
subject of her son, to the article he had published, to his having
helped a student and suffered burns in a fire, and so on and so forth.
Poor Dunya did not know how to stop her. In addition to the danger
inherent in this morbid and frenetic mood, there was also the threat
of disaster involved in the possibility that someone might recall the
name Raskolnikov in connection with the recent court case and begin
talking about it. Pulkheria Aleksandrovna even discovered the
address of the mother of the two little children who had been saved
from the fire and wanted to go and visit her without fail. At last her
agitation reached extreme proportions. She would on occasion begin
to weep, was frequently ill and talked wildly in her fever. One
morning she announced straight out that according to her estimates
Rodya would soon be back again, that she remembered him telling
her as he had said goodbye to her that she should expect him at the
end of nine months. She began to tidy the apartment and made ready
to greet him, began to make some finishing touches to the room she
had designated for him (her own), clean the furniture, wash new
curtains and hang them up, and so on. Dunya grew alarmed, but did
not say anything and even helped her set the room up ready to
receive her brother. After a troubled day spent in constant imaginings,
in joyful daydreams and tears, at night she fell ill and by morning
already had a high temperature and delirium. A dangerous fever had
set in. Two weeks later she died. The words that escaped her lips
during her delirium made it clear beyond any doubt that she suspected far more concerning the terrible fate of her son than anyone
had supposed.

It was a long time before Raskolnikov found out that his mother
had died, even though he established a correspondence with St
Petersburg right at the very beginning of his life in Siberia. This
correspondence was arranged by Sonya, who punctually each month
sent a letter to St Petersburg in Razumikhin's name, and punctually
each month received an answer back. Dunya and Razumikhin had
initially found Sonya's letters rather dry and unsatisfactory; but they
eventually arrived at the conviction that no better account could be

desired, because as a result of these letters they obtained a most complete and precise idea of the fate of their unhappy brother. Sonya's letters were full of the most ordinary, everyday details and gave a most simple and clear description of Raskolnikov's life in penal servitude. They contained no statement of her own hopes, nor any suppositions about the future or descriptions of her own feelings. In place of attempts to throw light on his mental condition and inner life in general, there were nothing but facts – his own words, that is, in the form of news concerning the state of his health, what he had asked for at such-and-such a meeting, what he had requested from her, what he had asked her to do for him, and the like. All this news was imparted in extremely thorough detail. Eventually the image of their unhappy brother emerged of its own accord, in a precise and vivid silhouette; here there could be no error, for it was all true fact.

There was, however, little comfort to be extracted by Dunya and her husband from this news, particularly at the outset. Sonya constantly reported that he was in a state of unbroken gloom, had hardly anything to say for himself and showed an almost complete lack of interest in the news she brought him, fresh each time from the letters she had received; that he sometimes asked about his mother; and when at last, realizing that he had already guessed the truth, she told him of his mother's death, much to her surprise not even that piece of news seemed to have any particular effect on him, or at least that was the way it appeared to her on the outside. She related, among other things, that even though he was so plainly absorbed in himself and seemed to have closed himself off from everyone, he viewed his new life in a very simple and straightforward manner, that he had a clear understanding of his position, expected nothing better near to hand, had no frivolous hopes (something very common among people in his situation) and was more or less unastonished by his new surroundings, which were so little similar to anything he had known previously. She told them that his health was satisfactory. He performed the work he was required to do, neither trying to evade it nor approaching it with undue eagerness. That as to the food, he was more or less indifferent to it, but that this food, except on Sundays and feast days, was so abominable that in the end he had gladly accepted a small sum of money from her in order to be able to brew tea for himself each day; but that as far as everything else was concerned he had asked her not to trouble herself, assuring her that all these worries on his behalf were merely a source of annoyance to him. Sonya went on to relate that he shared living quarters with all the rest, that she had not seen the interior of their barracks, but assumed they were cramped, nasty and insanitary; that he slept on a plank bed with a piece of felt underneath him and did not intend to seek any other accommodation. But that the life he was leading was so crude and impoverished not because of any preconceived plan or intention, but simply because of his lack of engagement and his apparent indifference to his fate. Sonya made no bones about the fact that, particularly at the outset, he had not only showed little interest in her visits, but had almost lost his temper with her, had refused to say very much and had even crudely insulted her, but that eventually these meetings had become a habit for him and even a necessity, with the result that he was plunged into gloom when for several days she was ill and unable to visit him. She wrote that her meetings with him on Sundays and feast days took place by the prison gate or in the guardroom, whither he was summoned into her presence for a few minutes; but that on the other days of the week she visited him at his work, either in the workshops, at the brick factory or in the alabaster sheds on the bank of the Irtysh. For herself, Sonya informed them that she had actually managed to acquire a few contacts and patrons in the town; that she worked as a seamstress, and since the town was practically deficient in milliners, she had in many households become a positive necessity; the only thing she omitted to mention was that through her Raskolnikov had also received a certain degree of patronage from the authorities, that he had been given a reduced workload, and so on. Eventually the news came (Dunya noted a particular agitation and uneasiness in her letters), that he was estranged from everyone, that the other convicts in the prison did not like him; that for days on end he said nothing and was growing very pale. Suddenly, in her final letter, Sonya wrote that he had been taken very seriously ill and was in hospital, in the convicts' ward there . . .

He had been ill for a long time; but it was not the horrors of life in penal servitude, not the work, not the food, not his shaven head nor his ragged clothing that had worn him down: oh, what cared he about all those sufferings and tortures! On the contrary, he had been positively glad of the work: having physically exhausted himself by it, he was at least able to obtain for himself a few hours of peaceful sleep. And of what importance was the food to him – that watery shchi* with cockroaches in it? In his previous life as a student he had frequently not had even that. His clothing kept him warm and was well adapted to the way of life he led. As for the fetters on his legs, he did not even feel them. Ought he to be ashamed of his shaven head and grey-and-brown jacket? Ashamed in front of whom? In front of Sonya? Sonya who feared him, and he was to be ashamed in front of her?

Yet who would have believed it? He was indeed thoroughly ashamed in front of Sonya, whom in return he had tormented by his scornful and crudely insulting behaviour. But it was not his shaven head or his fetters he was ashamed of; his pride had been violently wounded; it was wounded pride that had made him fall ill. Oh, how happy he would have been if he could have heaped blame upon himself! Then he would have been able to endure anything, even shame and disgrace. But he was his own severest judge, and his embittered conscience could find no particularly dreadful guilt in his past, except perhaps for a simple *blunder* which might have happened to anyone. What really made him ashamed was that he, Raskolnikov, had gone to his doom so blindly, hopelessly, in deaf-and-dumb stupidity, following the edict of blind fate, and must submit and resign himself to the 'nonsense' of a similar edict if he were ever to know any rest.

An anxiety with no object or purpose in the present, and in the future nothing but endless sacrifice, by means of which he would attain nothing – that was what his days on earth held in store for him. And what of the fact that in eight years' time he would only be thirty-two and would be able to resume his life again? What good was life to him? What prospects did he have? What did he have to strive for? Was he to live merely in order to exist? But a thousand times before he had been ready to give up his existence for an idea, for a hope, even for an imagining. Existence on its own had never been enough for him; he had always wanted more than that. Perhaps it had been merely the strength of his own desires that made him believe he was a person to whom more was allowed than others.

And even if fate had sent him no more than remorse – burning remorse that destroyed the heart, driving away sleep, the kind of remorse to escape whose fearsome torments the mind clutches at the noose and the well, oh, how glad he would have been! Torment and tears – after all, that is life, too. But he felt no remorse for his crime.

At the very least he would have been able to feel anger at his stupidity, just as he had earlier felt anger at the stupid and outrageous actions that had brought him to the prison. But now, in prison, *in freedom*, he had once again considered and gone over all the things he had done and had found them to be not nearly as stupid and outrageous as they had seemed to him earlier, during that fateful time.

'In what way,' he thought, 'in what way was my idea any more stupid than the other ideas and theories that have swarmed in conflict with one another ever since this world was born? All one needs to do is take a broad, entirely independent view of the matter, a view that is shorn of ordinary prejudices, and then my idea will not seem half so . . . strange. Oh gainsayers and five-copeck sages, why do you stop half way?

'After all, why does what I did seem so outrageous to them?' he said to himself. 'Because it was an act of wickedness? But what do they mean, those words: "an act of wickedness"? My conscience is easy. Of course, from a legal point of view a crime was committed; of course, the letter of the law was violated and blood was spilt, well then, here is my head, take it in exchange for the letter of the law . . . and let that be that! Though of course in that case a great many of mankind's benefactors who did not inherit power but took it for themselves ought to have been executed at their very first steps. But those people had the courage of their convictions, and so *they were right*, while I didn't, and consequently had no right to take the step I did.'

This was the one respect in which he admitted to any crime: in not having had the courage of his convictions and in having turned himself in.

He also suffered from the thought of why he had not killed himself that day. Why had he stood gazing down at the river and decided that he would prefer to turn himself in? Did this desire for life really have such power, and was it really so hard to overcome it? Svidrigailov had overcome it, had he not, he who was so afraid of death?

He kept tormenting himself with this question and was unable to grasp that even that day, as he had stood looking down at the river, he had quite possibly sensed in himself and in his convictions a profound lie. He did not understand that this sense might have been the harbinger of the future crisis in his life, of his future recovery, his new vision of life.

He preferred to admit only to a certain blunting of his instincts, something he had been unable to break with or step across (out of weakness and personal insignificance). He looked at his companions in penal servitude and marvelled: how much all they, too, loved life, how they treasured it! It seemed to him that in prison it was loved and valued and treasured more than in freedom. What terrible sufferings and tortures some of them had endured – the vagrants, for example! Was it really possible that there could be such significance for them in a mere ray of sunlight, a dense forest, a cold spring somewhere in the mysterious depths of the woods, noticed some three years ago, and of the rendezvous which the vagrant dreamed as of a tryst with his beloved, seeing it in his dreams, the green grass around it, a bird singing in a bush? Observing further, he saw examples even more unfathomable.

In the prison, in the environment that surrounded him, there was of course much that he did not observe and did not at all wish to observe. It was as if he lived with his eyes forever lowered; what there was to see he found loathsome and unendurable. Eventually, however, many things began to fill him with wonder, and almost in spite of himself he began to observe things that before he had not suspected. His most general and inescapable wonder was, however, occasioned by the terrible and impassable abyss that lay between himself and all these people. He and they seemed to belong to quite different nations. He and they viewed one another with suspicion and hostility. He knew and understood the general causes of this separation; but never before had he believed it possible that those causes could be so deep-rooted and powerful. In the prison there were also some exiled Poles, political criminals. They simply viewed all these people as ignoramuses and peasants and looked down on them from above; but Raskolnikov was unable to do the same: he clearly perceived that these ignoramuses were in many respects more intelligent than those very Poles. There were also Russians who thoroughly despised the common prisoners – one former officer and two seminarists; Raskolnikov clearly observed their error, too.

As for himself, all the other convicts disliked him and avoided him. Eventually they even grew to hate him – why? He could not find the answer. He was despised and laughed at, laughed at for his crime by men who had done far worse things than he.

'You're a toff!' they would say to him. 'What business did you have going around with an axe? That's not the sort of thing toffs do.'

In the second week of Lent his turn arrived to fast and attend holy communion together with the other men from his barrack. He entered the church and prayed together with the others. On one occasion, he himself did not know the reason, there was a quarrel; all the men attacked him in a frenzy of rage.

'You're an unbeliever! You don't believe in God!' they shouted at him. 'We ought to kill you.'

Never once had he mentioned the subject of God and faith in their company, yet they wanted to kill him as an unbeliever; he said nothing and did not try to protest. One of the convicts prepared to hurl himself at him in a state of rabid fury; Raskolnikov awaited his attack in silent calm: he did not turn a hair, not a single feature of his face quivered. The guard managed to interpose himself between him and his would-be murderer – if he had not done so, blood would have been spilt.

There was one more question that remained unsolved by him: why had they all taken such a liking to Sonya? She had not tried to ingratiate herself with them; they encountered her seldom, only sometimes they were at their work when she would come out to them for a moment in order to see him. Yet all of them knew her, knew that she had *followed him*, knew how and where she lived. It was not as if she had given them money or performed any special services for them. Only on one occasion, at Christmas, had she brought alms for every man in the prison: pies and kalatches.* Little by little, however, they came to be on rather closer terms with Sonya: she would write letters for them to their families and post the letters at the post-office. Their kinsfolk, male and female, who visited the town, would leave, according to their instructions, items of personal use and even money for them, which they entrusted to Sonya's hands. Their wives and girlfriends knew her and would go to visit her. And when she appeared at their workplace in order to see Raskolnikov, or met a gang of convicts going to work – they would all take off their caps, and all would greet her: 'Little mother, Sofya Semyonovna, you're our mother, our kind, soft-hearted one!' they would say, those branded convicts to that small, thin creature. She would smile and greet them back, and they all loved it when she smiled at them. They were even fond of her manner of walking, and would turn round to look after her as she went on her way, passing appreciative comments about her; they often made such comments in connection with her being so small, and indeed could not find enough good things to say about her. They went to see her when they were ill, and she would tend to them.

He remained in hospital throughout all the end of Lent and Holy Week. As he got better, he remembered the dreams he had had as he lay there in fever and delirium. In his illness he had dreamt that the entire world had fallen victim to some strange, unheard of and unprecedented plague that was spreading from the depths of Asia into Europe. Everyone was to perish, apart from a chosen few, a very few. Some new kind of trichinae had appeared, microscopic creatures that lodged themselves in people's bodies. But these creatures were spirits, gifted with will and intelligence. People who absorbed them into their systems instantly became rabid and insane. But never, never had people considered themselves so intelligent and in unswerving possession of the truth as did those who became infected. Never had they believed so unswervingly in the correctness of their judgements, their scientific deductions, their moral convictions and beliefs. Entire centres of population, entire cities and peoples became smitten and went mad. All were in a state of anxiety and no one could understand anyone else, each person thought that he alone possessed the truth and suffered agony as he looked at the others, beating his breast, weeping and wringing his hands. No one knew who to make the subject of judgement, or how to go about it, no one could agree about what should be considered evil and what good. No one knew who to blame or who to acquit. People killed one another in a kind of senseless anger. Whole armies were ranged against one another, but no sooner had these armies been mobilized than they suddenly began to tear themselves to pieces, their ranks falling apart and their soldiers hurling themselves at one another, gashing and stabbing, biting and eating one another. All day in the cities the alarm was sounded: everyone was being summoned together, but who was calling them and for what reason no one knew, but all were in a state of anxiety. They abandoned the most common trades, because each person wanted to offer his ideas, his improvements, and no agreement could be reached; agriculture came to a halt. In this place and that people would gather into groups, agree on something together, swear to stick together – but would instantly begin doing something completely different from what had been proposed, start blaming one another, fighting and murdering. Fires began, a famine broke out. Everyone and everything perished. The plague grew worse, spreading further and further. Only a few people in the whole world managed to escape: they were the pure and chosen, who had been predestined to begin a new species of mankind and usher in a new life, to renew the earth and render it pure, but no one had seen these people anywhere, no one had heard their words and voices.

Raskolnikov was tormented by the fact that this senseless delirium should linger so sadly and so agonizingly in his memories, that the aftermath of those fevered dreams should be taking so long to clear. They were already in the second week after Holy Week; the days were warm, clear and springlike; the windows of the convicts' ward had been opened (they were covered by an iron grille and a sentry patrolled the ground beneath them). Throughout the whole duration of his illness Sonya had been able to visit him in the ward only twice; each time she had had to obtain permission, and this had been difficult. But she had often come into the courtyard of the hospital and stood under the windows, especially towards evening, and sometimes merely in order to stand in the yard for a moment and look at the windows of the ward from afar. One afternoon, towards evening, the now almost completely recovered Raskolnikov fell asleep; on waking up he chanced to go over to the window and suddenly saw in the distance, by the hospital gate, Sonya. She was standing there, looking as though she were waiting for something. In that moment something seemed to transfix his heart; he shuddered and quickly drew away from the window. On the following day Sonya did not come, nor did she on the day after; he noticed that he was waiting for her with anxious concern. At last he was discharged.

Arriving back at the prison, he discovered from the convicts that Sofya Semyonovna had fallen ill and was lying in bed in her quarters, unable to go anywhere.

He was very concerned, and sent someone over to find out how she was. Soon he found out that her illness was not a dangerous one. Having learned, in her turn, that he was so dejected and worried for her sake, Sonya sent him a note written in pencil, informing him that she was much better and that soon, very soon, she would come and see him at his work again. As he read this note his heart beat violently and painfully.

It was another clear, warm day. Early that morning, at about six o'clock, he set off for his work on the bank of the river, where a kiln for the baking of alabaster had been set up in a shed, and where they pounded it. Only three men had been sent there to work. One of the convicts went off with the guard to the fortress for some implement or other; the other man began to chop firewood and put it in the kiln. Raskolnikov went out of the shed right down to the bank, sat down on the logs that were piled near the shed and began to look out at the wide, lonely river. From the high river-bank a broad panorama opened out. From the far-off opposite bank he could just make out the sound of someone singing. Over there, in the boundless steppe awash with sunlight, he could see the yurts of the nomad tribesmen like barely perceptible black dots. Over there was freedom, over there lived other people, quite different from those who lived here, over there time itself seemed to have stopped, as though the days of Abraham and his flocks had never passed. Raskolnikov sat gazing motionlessly, without cease; his thoughts moved away into dreams, into contemplation; he had not a thought in his head, but a sense of weariness disturbed him and tormented him.

All of a sudden, Sonya was next to him. She had made her approach almost inaudibly and had sat down beside him. It was still very early, the chill of morning had not yet relented. She was wearing her old, threadbare 'burnous' cape and her green shawl. Her face still bore the signs of her illness, it had grown thin and pale and sunken. She gave him a pleased, friendly smile, but, following her habit, extended her hand to him timidly.

This was the way she had always proffered her hand to him – timidly, sometimes not even proffering it at all, as though she were afraid he would refuse it. He had invariably taken her hand with a kind of revulsion, invariably greeted her with something akin to annoyance, on occasion remaining stubbornly silent throughout the entire duration of her visit. Sometimes she had feared him, and had gone away in deep sorrow. But now their hands were not disjoined; he gave her a quick, fleeting glance, uttered no word and lowered his gaze to the ground. They were alone; no one could see them. At this moment the guard had his back turned.

How it came to pass he himself did not know, but suddenly it was as though something had snatched at him, and he was hurled to her feet. He wept, and hugged her knees. In that first split second she was afraid, and her whole face froze. She leapt up from where she was sitting and stared at him, trembling. But immediately, in that same instant, she understood everything. Her eyes began to shine with an infinite happiness; she had understood, and now she was in no doubt that he loved her, loved her infinitely, and that at last it had arrived, that moment . . .

They tried to speak, but were unable to. There were tears in their eyes. Both of them looked pale and thin; but in these ill, pale faces there now gleamed the dawn of a renewed future, a complete recovery to a new life. What had revived them was love, the heart of the one containing an infinite source of life for the heart of the other.

They determined to wait and endure. There were still seven years to go, and until that time was over how much unendurable torment and how much infinite happiness they would experience! But he had recovered, and he knew it, felt it completely with the whole of his renewed being, while she – she, after all, lived only in his life!

That same evening, when the barracks had been locked for the night, Raskolnikov lay on the plank-bed, thinking about her. Throughout that day he had even felt that all the convicts, his former enemies, now looked upon him differently. He had actually begun to talk to them, and they had replied to him in kindly tones. Now this came back to him; but after all, this was the only way it could be: surely everything now must change?

He thought about her. He recalled the way he had constantly tormented her, preying upon the emotions of her heart; he remembered her pale, thin little face, but now these memories caused him hardly any pain: he was aware of the infinite love with which he would make up for those sufferings now.

In any case, what were they, all those torments of the past, *all* of them? The whole thing, even his crime, even his sentence and exile, now seemed to him, on this first impulse, now seemed to him something alien and external, as though none of it had ever happened to him. He was, however, unable to give much prolonged or continuous thought to anything that evening, or to concentrate on any one idea; and anyway, even if he had been able to, he would not have found his way to a solution of these questions in a conscious manner; now he could only feel. In place of dialectics life had arrived, and in his consciousness something of a wholly different nature must now work towards fruition.

Under his pillow there was a copy of the New Testament. Mechanically, he took it out. This book was hers, was the same one from which she had read to him of the raising of Lazarus. At the outset of his penal servitude he had thought she would torment him with religion, talk about the New Testament and press books on him. Much to his great surprise, however, she never once even offered him a New Testament. He himself had asked for it not long before he had fallen ill, and she had brought him her copy in silence. Until now, he had never opened it.

Even now he did not open it, but a certain thought flickered through his mind: 'What if her convictions can now be mine, too? Her feelings, her strivings, at least . . .'

All that day she too had been in a state of excitement, and at night even suffered a return of her illness. So happy was she, however, so unexpectedly happy that her happiness almost made her afraid. Seven years, *only* seven years! At certain moments during the initial period of their happiness they both viewed those seven years as if they had been seven days. He did not even know yet that his new life had not been given him gratis, that he would have to purchase it dearly, pay for it by a great heroic deed that still lay in the future . . .

But at this point a new story begins, the story of a man's gradual renewal, his gradual rebirth, his gradual transition from one world to another, of his growing acquaintance with a new, hitherto completely unknown reality. This might constitute the theme of a new narrative – our present narrative is, however, at an end.

NOTES

p. 33 *At the beginning of July . . . weather:* the action of *Crime and Punishment* takes place in the summer of 1865, which in St Petersburg was a particularly hot one. 'Unbearable heat and humidity!' a contemporary newspaper account read. 'When one looks at the thermometer it reads 24 – 25 – 26 degrees Réaumur in the shade! At one, at two o'clock in the morning it is scarcely possible to breathe.'

p. 33 *S— Lane . . . K—n Bridge:* Stolyarny Lane and Kokushkin Bridge.

p. 33 *a tall, five-storey tenement:* throughout, 'tenement' and 'tenements' translate the Russian word *dom* (literally 'house'). These were large stone buildings in St Petersburg acquired in the eighteenth and nineteenth centuries by private landlords and divided up into separate apartments which were offered for rent. The tenants of the apartments frequently sublet rooms to people even poorer than themselves. Notices advertising vacant rooms and lodgings were posted at the gateways of the tenements, which were usually known and referred to by the owner's name.

p. 35 *Zimmerman's:* Zimmerman was a well-known St Petersburg hat manufacturer in whose shop Dostoyevsky himself once bought a hat.

p. 36 *the Canal:* Dostoyevsky refers to the Yekaterininsky (Catherine, now Griboyedov) Canal as *kanava* – literally 'the ditch', or open sewer. For clarity's sake I have opted for the 'the Canal', but the reader should bear in mind the negative associations.

p. 40 sukhar': a kind of rusk.

p. 42 poddyovka: a man's long-waisted coat.

p. 44 *have you ever . . . on the hay barges?:* the hay barges on the Neva were a favourite overnight resting-place for St Petersburg's tramps and down-and-outs.

p. 45 *Mr Lebezyatnikov, who follows the latest ideas:* Dostoyevsky discussed the connotations of this name in his draft sketches of the novel: 'Lebezyatnikov, cringing, acquiescence . . . the epitome of fawning.' Later he noted: 'Nihilism – the lackeydom of thought.' Lebezyatnikov also makes an appearance in Dostoyevsky's short story 'Bobok' (1873).

p. 45 *yellow card:* a reference to the system of licensed prostitution that existed in St Petersburg. Prostitutes carried a special yellow-coloured passport.

p. 45 *now revealed:* an allusion to Matthew 10:26: 'for there is nothing covered, that shall not be revealed; and hid, that shall not be known'.

p. 47 *danced with the shawl:* a privilege awarded for distinction in private boarding-schools for girls.

p. 48 *half-*shtof *of vodka:* a *shtof,* or 'shtoff', measured approximately 1.2 litres.

p. 49 *Lewes'* Physiology: *Physiology of Common Life* by George Henry Lewes. Dostoyevsky owned the second edition of the Russian translation of this work (1876), which enjoyed great popularity among female nihilists during the 1860s, along with the writings of Buckle, Darwin, Moleshott, Focht, Büchner and other positivist and/or materialist philosophers.

p. 49 *can a poor but honest . . . by honest work?:* the question of female labour was much discussed in Russian intellectual circles during the 1860s. In particular, see N. G. Chernyshevsky's novel *What Is To Be Done?* (1863).

p. 50 drap-de-dames *shawl: drap-de-dames* was a fine cloth used by ladies. Anna Grigoryevna Dostoyevskaya, the writer's second wife, describing her first visit to his apartment in 1866, recalled: 'I rang the bell and the door was immediately opened by an old servant-woman with a green checked shawl thrown about her shoulders. So recently had I read *Crime and Punishment* that I found myself wondering whether this shawl might have been the prototype of the *drap-de-dames* shawl that played such an important role in the Marmeladov household.'

p. 50 *Kapernaumov:* Kapernaumov's name has ambiguous connotations: 'Mr Capernaum' might seem a fitting name for Sonya's landlord

– but the word *kapernaum* was also nineteenth-century St Petersburg slang for a brothel.

p. 51   *'The Little Homestead': Khutorok*, a popular setting by Klimovsky of a ballad by Koltsov.

p. 63   *two lots in weight:* a *lot* was a Russian weight equivalent to 12.797 grams.

p. 72   *the* gospozhinki: in Orthodox Russia weddings are usually held in the period from Christmas to Shrovetide (*myasoyed*), when meat can be eaten. The *gospozhinki* are days of fasting, the duration of which are 1–15 August, and are followed by the Feast of the Assumption and another meat-eating period (*osenniy myasoyed*) that lasts until 14 November.

p. 73   *V— Prospect:* Voznesensky Prospect (now Prospekt Mayorova).

p. 76   Schöne Seelen: literally, 'beautiful souls'. A translation from the French *'belles âmes'*.

p. 76   *St Anne's Ribbon:* the Order of St Anne, awarded for prowess in state service. There were four grades of the award – Luzhin has the fourth and lowest.

p. 80   *K— Boulevard:* Konnogvardeysky (Horseguards) Boulevard, now Bul'var Profsoyuzov (Trades-Union Boulevard).

p. 81   *Svidrigailov!:* the name 'Svidrigailov' was already familiar to Dostoyevsky's contemporaries of the 1860s. In 1861, for example, the newspaper *Iskra* ran a column on 'fops up to no good in the provinces': Borodavkin ('a fop in the pedigree of Pushkin's Count Nulin') and 'his levrette Svidrigailov'. The latter was characterized as follows: '. . . Svidrigailov is a functionary of *certain*, or, as is said, *particular*, or, as is again the expression, *multifarious* errands . . . He is, if you like, a fixer . . . a man of obscure origins, with a sordid past; a repulsive individual, loathsome to the fresh, honest gaze, insidious, creeping into the soul . . . Svidrigailov has a finger in every pie: he is the president of some new committee, brought into being especially for him, he is involved in the produce fair business, he knows a trick or two in the horse trade, he is everywhere . . . if it is necessary to dream up some piece of chicanery, to transmit some piece of gossip to the right quarters, to play some dirty trick . . . to that purpose there is available a certain talented man – Svidrigailov; if in return for a post or a business favour one needs to extort a large friendly bribe from someone; if one needs to acquire a pretty governess . . . Hm! For such ends there exists the most keen-witted factotum, the most efficient intermediary – Svidrigailov . . . And this base, creeping, eternally grovelling individual, who offends against every kind of human dignity, flourishes: builds house after house, acquires horses and carriages, throws poisonous dust in the face of society, at the expense of which he grows fat, swells up like a sponge in soapy water . . .'

p. 82 *a cigarette:* the smoking of cigarettes in the street was made legal in St Petersburg on 4 July 1865; before then it had been prohibited by public statute.

p. 85 *a certain percentage has to go off down that road:* a reference to the essays in 'social statistics' (based on the ideas of the Belgian astronomer and statistician Adolphe Quetelet) by the popular economist A. Wagner, which had been appearing in the Russian press.

p. 88 *his tired eyes found the leafy coolness agreeable:* Raskolnikov has crossed the Little Neva by way of the Tuchkov Bridge. This was one of Dostoyevsky's own favourite walking-places in summer.

p. 90 kut'ya: a kind of sweet-rice gruel eaten at funeral meals.

p. 91 armyaks: an *armyak* (or 'armiak') is a peasant cloth coat.

p. 92 a kichka . . . koty on her feet: a *kichka* was a Russian festive headdress worn by married women. *Koty* are warm fur slippers.

p. 96 *K— Lane:* Konny Lane, now Grivtsov Lane.

p. 110 *Yusupov Park:* on Sadovaya Street, opposite Catherinehof Prospect (now Rimsky-Korsakov Prospect). The only park in Spasskaya, one of the most densely inhabited quarters of the town, and possessing a handsome fountain; during the daytime in summer it was usually full of artisans and members of the lower middle classes.

p. 110 *men who are being led to the scaffold . . . along the way:* there is an echo here of Victor Hugo's *Le Dernier Jour d'un Condamné* (1829), one of Dostoyevsky's favourite stories – and, of course, of the writer's own experience of death-sentence and reprieve.

p. 121 *the Gambrinus:* the Gambrinus beer-parlour was situated on Vasily Island. It was owned by a brewing company of the same name, which was derived from the legendary Flemish king and patron of brewers, who was supposed to have invented beer.

p. 141 *get it in all the newspapers:* sein Rock: his coat; gedruckt: printed. One contemporary feuilletonist wrote: 'The morals and manners of our literary backyard are becoming less and less civilized. One has occasion to hear the most outrageous things concerning the public accusers of various inns, restaurants and the like. They pop up everywhere, eating, drinking, receiving gifts and boasting that if everything is not to their taste they will deliver a public accusation forthwith – if, that is to say, they are not given the bribes they request or are asked for money in exchange for the wine they have imbibed and the food they have consumed.'

p. 141 *I'll give you the* zu Hundert *treatment:* a military expression, meaning 'I'll make you run the gauntlet'.

p. 141 *Nikodim Fomich himself:* in June 1865, pursued by his publisher Stellovsky, Dostoyevsky had received a summons to report to the police bureau in Stolyarny Lane in connection with the inventory of his property for non-payment of promissory notes. It seems probable that the district police official who was placed in charge of Dostoyevsky's case served as the prototype for Nikodim Fomich.

p. 149 *V— Prospect on to the square:* the location is Voznesensky Prospect. Anna Grigoryevna recalled that 'during the first weeks of our married life, out for a walk with me one day, Fyodor Mikhailovich led me into the courtyard of a certain building and showed me the stone block beneath which his Raskolnikov had hidden the goods he stole from the old woman. This courtyard is situated on Voznesensky Prospect, the second along from Maksimilianov Lane; on its site an enormous building has now been constructed, which at present houses the editorial offices of a German newspaper. When I asked him: "Why did you stray into this deserted courtyard?" Fyodor Mikhailovich replied: "For the purpose that passers-by usually go to secluded spots."'

p. 154 *whether a woman is a human being or not:* the 'woman question' was a topic of keen debate in Russia during the 1860s, which saw the publication of articles by Chernyshevsky on the subject ('Women, their Education and Social Significance' and 'John Stuart Mill on the Emanicipation of Woman' [1860]), as well as works by less well-known foreign authors with titles such as 'Woman in the Physiological, Pathological and Moral Respect; a Medical, Philosophical and Literary Treatise'.

p. 154 *Radishchev:* Aleksandr Nikolayevich Radishchev (1749–1802), the eighteenth-century Russian radical and social thinker and father of the Decembrists. In his article 'The Anthropological Principle in Philosophy' (1860), Chernyshevsky had called Rousseau a 'revolutionary democrat'.

p. 155 *First Line:* the 'Lines' were streets on Vasily Island, running perpendicular to the main thoroughfares. Also, the Third Line, p. 576.

p. 155 golovka: a headband.

p. 161 *not Razumikhin, as everyone calls me: razum* in Russian means 'reason' – to Dostoyevsky's readers of the 1860s the name would have had curiously mixed associations, suggesting a grotesque 'radicalization' of the aristocratic name 'Razumovsky' into something more consonant with 'Rakhmetov', the name of the politically committed hero of Chernyshevsky's *What Is To Be Done?* 'Vrazumikhin', on the other hand, has a more conventionally aristocratic ring.

p. 162 *the merchant Vakhrushin:* the name of the real-life merchant Bakhrushin was known all over Moscow.

p. 165 *Kharlamov's Tenements . . . the Buch ones:* Kharlamov's Tenements were situated near the Haymarket, in Konny Lane, while Buch's Tenements, on the Yekaterininsky Canal embankment, housed a bailiff's office.

p. 167 *Mr Chebarov:* an altered version of 'Bocharov', the name of Stellovsky's attorney.

p. 174 *Sharmer's:* the firm of I. G. Sharmer, a well-known St Petersburg tailor from whom Dostoyevsky bought his clothes.

p. 176 *'Palais de Cristal'*: the name of a hotel-cum-restaurant opened on the corner of Bolshaya Sadovaya Street and Voznesensky Prospect in 1862; it seems, however, that Dostoyevsky had in mind another establishment with this name, an inn situated on Zabalkansky Prospect. For the radical utopian socialists in Russia the real Crystal Palace was a symbol of the new social and economic order of which they dreamed (see Dostoyevsky's polemic with Chernyshevsky on this subject in *Notes from Underground* and *Winter Notes on Summer Impressions*). There is a note of irony in the name 'Crystal Palace' being applied to the seedy inn in which the nihilist Raskolnikov makes his confession to Zamyotov.

p. 179 *Mikolai*: in the passage that follows, Dostoyevsky uses the demotic forms of the names 'Nikolai' and 'Dmitry'.

p. 180 *. . . Mitrei*: see note to p. 179, above.

p. 190 *Jouvain manufacture*: a reference to the French glove-maker Xavier Jouvain of Grenoble, who invented a special last that gave his gloves their shape.

p. 191 *That's on Voznesensky . . . Yushin*: according to Anna Grigory-evna, the tenements were situated on the corner of Voznesensky Prospect and Kazan Street (now Plekhanov Street).

p. 193 *Go in pursuit . . . one*: Luzhin quotes, inexactly, a Russian proverb: 'Chase two hares, and you'll catch neither' (*Za dvumya zaytsami pogonish'sya, ni odnogo ne poymayesh*'). In his version it sounds most un-Russian, as though it had been translated from French or English.

p. 193 *founded upon self-interest*: a reference to the ideas of Jeremy Bentham.

p. 196 *some obscure, financial reason*: a reference to the case of A. Nikitenko, an official at the Russian Embassy in Paris who was murdered by a retired Russian army lieutenant who had been refused financial assistance to enable him to return home.

p. 201 *a flour-dealer's shop*: in the so-called 'Raspberry Patch' (Malin-nik) on the Haymarket, not far from Konny Lane (now No. 3,

Ploshchad' Mira), were housed the establishments of Gusarsky (flour-dealer), Konstantinova (public house), Petrova (inn–restaurant) and several brothels.

p. 202 *a side lane . . .* : Tairov Lane, now Brinko Lane. At No. 4 was housed the printing-press of Zhernakov, which published the journal in Nos. 6–7 of which Dostoyevsky's translation of Balzac's *Eugénie Grandet* appeared.

p. 204 *a man . . . sentenced to die:* the reference is to a passage from Victor Hugo's novel *Notre-Dame de Paris* (1831).

p. 205 *Izler:* Ivan Ivanovich Izler was the owner of a St Petersburg out-of-town artificial spa called 'Mineral Waters'. During the 1860s the newspapers printed a great many accounts of the comings and goings at his establishment.

p. 205 *Bartola . . . Massimo . . . Aztecs:* in 1865 the St Petersburg newspapers printed numerous stories about the arrival in the capital of a pair of midgets named Massimo (male, aged twenty-six) and Bartola (female, aged twenty-one), who were supposed to be descended from the ancient inhabitants of Mexico, the Aztecs. In St Petersburg they were exhibited by the entrepreneur Moris at No. 16, Malaya Morskaya Street.

p. 205 *fire at Peski . . . fire at St Petersburg Side:* Peski was the name of one of the more remote, outlying districts of St Petersburg, situated on Suvorov Prospect. The St Petersburg Side (now called the Petro-grad Side) was also a district of the capital separated from the rest of the town by the River Neva. Revolutionary students were suspected of starting the fires, which caused widespread death and destruction.

p. 212 Assez causé: one of Dostoyevsky's favourite expressions. The words are those of Balzac's Vautrin.

p. 218 *an-orangeing-and-a-lemoning:* this expression, like several others in the original Russian text of this passage, is taken from Dostoyevsky's *Siberian Notebook*, in which he recorded the idioms he heard in use among the convicts with whom he had lived during his term of penal servitude at Omsk.

p. 220 *Schiel's Tenements:* there were several 'Schiel's Tenements' in St Petersburg – these were probably the ones on the corner of Malaya

Morskaya Street and Voznesensky Prospect, where Dostoyevsky had lived from 1847 to 1849.

p. 258 *a Rubinstein:* the Russian composer and pianist Anton Grigoryevich Rubinstein (1829–94).

p. 259 kulebiakis: pies with meat, fish or cabbage stuffing.

p. 270 *the queen who mended her stockings in prison . . . triumphs and entrances:* a reference to Marie Antoinette, wife of Louis XVI of France.

p. 288 *the Mitrofaniyev Cemetery:* the Mitrofaniyev Cemetery in St Petersburg was opened in 1831 during a cholera epidemic. Poor civil service clerks, soldiers, tradespeople and artisans were buried there.

p. 300 *I say . . . on the exchequer:* a quotation from Gogol's *The Government Inspector*, Act I, scene i.

p. 308 *a prey to one's surroundings:* this phrase (R. *sreda zayela*) was much in vogue among Russian liberal intellectual circles during the late 1850s and early 1860s, as an explanation of the phenomenon of the 'superfluous man', as described by I. S. Turgenev in many of his stories and novellas.

p. 309 *phalanstery:* phalansteries were the communal palaces dreamed of by the French utopian socialist Charles Fourier (1772–1837).

p. 309 *sagenes:* a sagene, or *sazhen'*, was equivalent to 2.134 metres.

p. 312 *to step across:* the Russian word is *pereshagnut'*, closely related to *perestupat'* ('to step over', 'to transgress'), which in turn is related to the Russian word for 'crime' – *prestuplenie*. To a Russian reader the connection is immediately clear.

p. 314 *the New Jerusalem:* the origins of the expression 'New Jerusalem' are in Revelation 21:1–3:

> And I saw a new heaven and a new earth: for the first heaven and the first earth were passed away; and there was no more sea.
> And I John saw the holy city, new Jerusalem, coming down from God out of heaven, prepared as a bride adorned for her husband.
> And I heard a great voice out of heaven saying, Behold, the tabernacle of God is with men, and he will dwell with them, and

they shall be his people, and God himself shall be with them, and be their God.

The Saint-Simonists and other Utopian socialists of the early nineteenth century interpreted this vision as the coming of an earthly paradise or new Golden Age. It was one of the articles of faith of the Petrashevist movement to which Dostoyevsky had belonged in the 1840s.

p. 317 *The truly great . . . time upon earth:* this sentence is a paraphrase of a remark by Fourier concerning Julius Caesar.

p. 328 *J'apporte ma pierre à l'édifice nouveau:* the expression *'apporter sa pierre à l'édifice nouveau'* is frequently encountered in the writings of Fourier's pupil V. Considérant (1808–93).

p. 329 *how well I understand . . . 'trembling' mortals must obey:* the allusion is to the Koran and in particular Pushkin's lines from the cycle 'Imitations of the Koran' (1824):

> Take courage and, scorning deception,
> Cheerfully follow the path of truth,
> Love orphans and preach
> My Koran to trembling mortals . . .

Dostoyevsky owned a copy of M. Kasimirski's French translation of the Koran (1847) from which K. Nikolayev made his Russian translation (1864–5).

p. 339 *beneficent glasnost: glasnost* or 'public accountability' is not a new phenomenon in Russia. It was on occasion favoured by the Tsars as a way of attempting to defuse public discontent. The 'era' referred to by Svidrigailov lasted for a short time some five years before the writing of *Crime and Punishment*, when Alexander II relaxed the grip of the censor sufficiently to allow gentle criticism of those with power and authority.

p. 339 *The Indecent Act of* The Age: this was the title of a controversial article by M. L. Mikhailov, an ardent supporter of women's emancipation, in which he condemned a feuilleton that had appeared in the journal *The Age* under the signature of the poet and translator I. I. Veynberg, attacking the wife of a provincial civil service official for having taken part in a literary–musical soirée in Perm which had involved the reading of an 'immoral' episode from Pushkin's *Egyptian Nights*.

p. 341 *Dussot's:* Dussot's was a fashionable restaurant on Bolshaya Morskaya Street (now Herzen Street).

p. 341 *the* pointe: a reference to the fête ground on Yelagin Island. The newspapers often carried reports of the fêtes at the 'Château des Fleurs'.

p. 342 *the North Pole now:* in 1865 the St Petersburg newspapers announced an expedition 'for the Attainment and Investigation of the North Pole of the Terrestrial Globe'.

p. 342 *Berg:* a well-known St Petersburg entrepreneur who ran amusements and side-shows in the city's parks.

p. 344 *the* litiya: a Russian Orthodox liturgical term. In this context, it means a short requiem mass.

p. 350 *the Vyazemsky:* the 'Dom Vyazemskogo' or 'Vyazemsky Laura' near the Haymarket, a large building that served as an overnight resting-place for the city's down-and-outs, and was also used as a place of lodging by men who worked in the inns and drinking establishments.

p. 369 *at the same time:* Razumikhin's publishing plans are reminiscent of those entertained by Dostoyevsky himself in the 1840s, when together with his brother Mikhail he planned to issue a Russian translation of the complete works of Schiller.

p. 373 *where Sonya lived:* this is now No. 63, Griboyedov Canal.

p. 377 *the Row:* a special St Petersburg building containing a row of goods stores.

p. 384 *the seventh verst:* a reference to a lunatic asylum situated seven versts from the capital. To send someone 'to the seventh verst' was a familiar euphemism.

p. 389 *the whole antheap:* Dostoyevsky had already used the image of the 'antheap' – derived from Lessing and Voltaire, and also from the writings of the French novelist Charles Naudier – to describe mass society in *Winter Notes on Summer Impressions* and *Notes from Underground.*

p. 399   *the reforms:* the judicial reforms undertaken in Russia after 1864. These had the effect of limiting the powers of the police, encouraging a less formal interpretation of the criminal law and opening the courts to the public. Porfiry is a representative of the 'new order'.

p. 399   *the Battle of the Alma:* it was after the defeat of the Russian armed forces at the River Alma on 8 September 1854 that the Anglo-French troops began the siege of Sebastopol.

p. 402   *the Austrian* Hofkriegsrat: a reference to the surrender of General Mack to Napoleon at Ulm in 1805. The first part of Tolstoy's *War and Peace* ('1805'), which deals with this event, among others, had begun to appear in the Russian press in 1865. (The chapter concerned appeared in the *Russian Messenger*, 1866, No. 2, in between the first two parts of *Crime and Punishment.*)

p. 426   *Knop's:* a haberdasher's on Nevsky Prospect. *the English Shop:* this was situated on Malaya Millionnaya Street, and sold various items of foreign-made haberdashery.

p. 429   *a new and soon-to-be-established 'commune':* communes inspired by the ideas of Fourier and Chernyshevsky had begun to spring up in St Petersburg.

p. 435   *the kissing of hands:* a reference to the words of Vera Pavlovna in Chapter 2, XVIII of Chernyshevsky's *What Is To Be Done?*: 'Men should not kiss women's hands. My dear sir, it cannot but be offensive to women; it means that men do not consider them the same as themselves.'

p. 435   *the free access to rooms:* 'We shall have two rooms, one yours and one mine, and a third in which we shall drink tea, dine, receive guests . . . I shall not dare to go into your room, lest I disturb you . . . and you will not likewise enter mine . . .' (*What Is To Be Done?*, Chapter 2, XVIII).

p. 436   *Raphael or Pushkin:* a reference to the utilitarian arguments of the nihilist D. I. Pisarev, who considered that a pair of boots was preferable to the poetry of Pushkin.

p. 442 'Horns' – that . . . 'Pushkinian' expression: a reference to some lines from Pushkin's *Eugene Onegin*:

> And the majestic wearer of horns,
> Forever pleased with himself,
> His dinner and his wife.
> (Chapter I, Stanza XII)

p. 442 *My dear . . . making a protest:* a parody on Lopukhov's words to Vera Pavlovna when he discovers she has been having an affair with Kirsanov: 'After all, you won't stop respecting me, will you? . . . don't feel sorry for me: my fate will by no means be made pitiable by the fact that you have not deprived yourself of your happiness because of me' (*What Is To Be Done?*, Chapter 3, XXV).

p. 444 kut'ya: see note to p. 90.

p. 444 pani chorazyna: Madame Ensign (Polish).

p. 461 Gott der Barmherzige: German: Merciful God.

p. 467 A General Treatise on the Positive Method: a symposium of articles on psychology and social statistics that appeared in 1866, edited and translated by N. N. Neklyudov.

p. 467 *Piederit's article:* 'The Brain and its Functioning, A Popular Outline of Physiological Psychology' by the German physiologist Theodor Piederit (1826–82). See note on A. Wagner on p. 718.

p. 470 panie lajdak: 'the gentleman is a scoundrel' (Polish).

p. 493 *there are these tubercles . . . medicine:* according to Dostoyevsky's physician, Dr S. D. Yanovsky, the writer had during his youth been interested in diseases of the brain and the nervous system, and had read a good deal of scientific literature on the subject, including the work of the Austrian anatomist Franz Josef Gall (1758–1828). The theory of the 'tubercles' is, however, probably derived from the writings of a later researcher, the French physiologist Claude Bernard (1813–79).

p. 499 *The Hussar Leaned On His Sabre:* a well-known song ascribed to Vielgorsky, set to words by Batyushkov (his poem 'Parting', *Razluka*).

p. 500   Cinq sous: the beggars' aria from *Grâce de Dieu*, a well-known play by Gustave Dennery and A. P. Lemoine, which enjoyed a huge success in Russia.

p. 504   *Du hast Diamanten und Perlen . . . was willst du mehr:* lines from the poem by Heine, in Schubert's setting.

p. 504   *In heat of noon, in Dagestan's deep valley:* the poem 'Dream' by Mikhail Lermontov, probably in the setting by Paufler.

p. 520   *I went to see B——:* this is most probably Dr S. P. Botkin, a St Petersburg physician who treated Dostoyevsky himself.

p. 523   *'Smoke . . . in the mist':* an inexact quotation from Gogol's *Diary of a Madman.*

p. 524   umsonst: German: in vain, for nothing.

p. 526   *a Raskolnik . . . there were 'Runners':* 'Raskolnik' is a name for a religious dissenter, one of those involved in the schism (*raskol*) that took place in the Russian Orthodox Church in the mid-seventeenth century (see the Introduction). The 'Runners' (*beguny*), most of whom were peasants, artisans or runaway soldiers, were a sect that came into being at the end of the eighteenth century. They regarded the established Russian Church as a representative of the Antichrist and refused to be considered subjects of the Tsar. For them, the only salvation was in 'running', or fleeing from society, authority, the family and civil laws. They spent their lives on the road, wandering and begging.

p. 533   *a fashionable sectarian:* Dostoyevsky probably has in mind V. I. Kelsiyev, who in 1862 declared himself an *émigré* and went to London, where he began to publish material about the *raskol.*

p. 533   *Warrant Officer Dyrka:* someone of this name is mentioned in Gogol's play *The Marriage* (Act I, Scene 16), but Dostoyevsky seems to have confused him with Warrant Officer Petukhov in the same play (Act II, Scene 8).

p. 538   *the* pesenniki: *pesenniki* were male peasant choral singers.

p. 538   *manservants' ditty':* in Russian, *lakeyskaya pesnya* (literally 'lackeys' song') is a vulgar, hybrid blend of folk-song and drawing-room romance, often with somewhat 'dubious' words, usually sung by a falsetto male voice to the accompaniment of a guitar (the manservant Smerdyakov sings one in *The Brothers Karamazov*, Book Five, Chapter 2). Sung here by a woman, such a song acquires an added dimension of moral impropriety.

p. 549   *dark-eyed Parasha:* a paraphrase of the beginning of Derzhavin's poem 'To Parasha': 'Fair-haired Parasha, silver-pink of face . . .'

p. 556   Où va-t-elle . . . ?: a remark ascribed to Molière, in reply to a beggar, who thought Molière had given him a gold coin by mistake.

p. 563   *a good sagene:* see note to p. 309.

p. 573   *a 'Vauxhall': vakzal* – from the English 'Vauxhall Gardens'. The Russian word *vokzal* now means a railway station.

p. 575   *Vladimirka:* the region surrounding the town of Vladimir, through which the gangs of convicts bound for Siberia were dispatched.

p. 580   *—chkov Bridge:* Tuchkov Bridge, across the Little Neva from Vasily Island.

p. 580   *—oy Prospect:* Bolshoy Prospect, on the St Petersburg Side.

p. 587   *a tall watchtower:* the watchtower of the St Petersburg Side Fire Station.

p. 587   *a brass 'Achilles' helmet:* Russian firemen's helmets usually bore a representation of Achilles.

p. 606   *to be aware . . . in myself:* an echo of 'Nekrasovian' civic and public sentiment – by now alien to Dostoyevsky.

p. 622   shchi: Russian: cabbage soup.

p. 625   *kalatches:* Russian: white bread rolls.

READ MORE IN PENGUIN

In every corner of the world, on every subject under the sun, Penguin represents quality and variety – the very best in publishing today.

For complete information about books available from Penguin – including Puffins, Penguin Classics and Arkana – and how to order them, write to us at the appropriate address below. Please note that for copyright reasons the selection of books varies from country to country.

In the United Kingdom: Please write to *Dept. EP, Penguin Books Ltd, Bath Road, Harmondsworth, West Drayton, Middlesex UB7 ODA*

In the United States: Please write to *Consumer Sales, Penguin Putnam Inc., P.O. Box 12289 Dept. B, Newark, New Jersey 07101-5289.* VISA and MasterCard holders call 1-800-788-6262 to order Penguin titles

In Canada: Please write to *Penguin Books Canada Ltd, 10 Alcorn Avenue, Suite 300, Toronto, Ontario M4V 3B2*

In Australia: Please write to *Penguin Books Australia Ltd, P.O. Box 257, Ringwood, Victoria 3134*

In New Zealand: Please write to *Penguin Books (NZ) Ltd, Private Bag 102902, North Shore Mail Centre, Auckland 10*

In India: Please write to *Penguin Books India Pvt Ltd, 11 Community Centre, Panchsheel Park, New Delhi 110017*

In the Netherlands: Please write to *Penguin Books Netherlands bv, Postbus 3507, NL-1001 AH Amsterdam*

In Germany: Please write to *Penguin Books Deutschland GmbH, Metzlerstrasse 26, 60594 Frankfurt am Main*

In Spain: Please write to *Penguin Books S. A., Bravo Murillo 19, 1° B, 28015 Madrid*

In Italy: Please write to *Penguin Italia s.r.l., Via Benedetto Croce 2, 20094 Corsico, Milano*

In France: Please write to *Penguin France, Le Carré Wilson, 62 rue Benjamin Baillaud, 31500 Toulouse*

In Japan: Please write to *Penguin Books Japan Ltd, Kaneko Building, 2-3-25 Koraku, Bunkyo-Ku, Tokyo 112*

In South Africa: Please write to *Penguin Books South Africa (Pty) Ltd, Private Bag X14, Parkview, 2122 Johannesburg*

PENGUIN AUDIOBOOKS

A Quality of Writing That Speaks for Itself

Penguin Books has always led the field in quality publishing. Now you can listen at leisure to your favourite books, read to you by familiar voices from radio, stage and screen. Penguin Audiobooks are produced to an excellent standard, and abridgements are always faithful to the original texts. From thrillers to classic literature, biography to humour, with a wealth of titles in between, Penguin Audiobooks offer you quality, entertainment and the chance to rediscover the pleasure of listening.

You can order Penguin Audiobooks through Penguin Direct by telephoning (0181) 899 4036. The lines are open 24 hours every day. Ask for Penguin Direct, quoting your credit card details.

A selection of Penguin Audiobooks, published or forthcoming:

Little Women by Louisa May Alcott, read by Kate Harper

Emma by Jane Austen, read by Fiona Shaw

Pride and Prejudice by Jane Austen, read by Geraldine McEwan

Beowulf translated by Michael Alexander, read by David Rintoul

Agnes Grey by Anne Brontë, read by Juliet Stevenson

Jane Eyre by Charlotte Brontë, read by Juliet Stevenson

The Professor by Charlotte Brontë, read by Juliet Stevenson

Wuthering Heights by Emily Brontë, read by Juliet Stevenson

The Woman in White by Wilkie Collins, read by Nigel Anthony and Susan Jameson

Nostromo by Joseph Conrad, read by Michael Pennington

Tales from the Thousand and One Nights, read by Souad Faress and Raad Rawi

Robinson Crusoe by Daniel Defoe, read by Tom Baker

David Copperfield by Charles Dickens, read by Nathaniel Parker

The Pickwick Papers by Charles Dickens, read by Dinsdale Landen

Bleak House by Charles Dickens, read by Beatie Edney and Ronald Pickup

PENGUIN AUDIOBOOKS

The Hound of the Baskervilles by Sir Arthur Conan Doyle, read by Freddie Jones

Middlemarch by George Eliot, read by Harriet Walter

Tom Jones by Henry Fielding, read by Robert Lindsay

The Great Gatsby by F. Scott Fitzgerald, read by Marcus D'Amico

Madame Bovary by Gustave Flaubert, read by Claire Bloom

Mary Barton by Elizabeth Gaskell, read by Clare Higgins

Jude the Obscure by Thomas Hardy, read by Samuel West

Far from the Madding Crowd by Thomas Hardy, read by Julie Christie

The Scarlet Letter by Nathaniel Hawthorne, read by Bob Sessions

Les Misérables by Victor Hugo, read by Nigel Anthony

A Passage to India by E. M. Forster, read by Tim Pigott-Smith

The Iliad by Homer, read by Derek Jacobi

The Dead and Other Stories by James Joyce, read by Gerard McSorley

On the Road by Jack Kerouac, read by David Carradine

Sons and Lovers by D. H. Lawrence, read by Paul Copley

The Prince by Niccolò Machiavelli, read by Fritz Weaver

Animal Farm by George Orwell, read by Timothy West

Rob Roy by Sir Walter Scott, read by Robbie Coltrane

Frankenstein by Mary Shelley, read by Richard Pasco

Of Mice and Men by John Steinbeck, read by Gary Sinise

Kidnapped by Robert Louis Stevenson, read by Robbie Coltrane

Dracula by Bram Stoker, read by Richard E. Grant

Gulliver's Travels by Jonathan Swift, read by Hugh Laurie

Vanity Fair by William Makepeace Thackeray, read by Robert Hardy

Lark Rise to Candleford by Flora Thompson, read by Judi Dench

The Invisible Man by H. G. Wells, read by Paul Shelley

Ethan Frome by Edith Wharton, read by Nathan Osgood

The Picture of Dorian Gray by Oscar Wilde, read by John Moffatt

Orlando by Virginia Woolf, read by Tilda Swinton

READ MORE IN PENGUIN

A CHOICE OF CLASSICS

Armadale   Wilkie Collins

Victorian critics were horrified by Lydia Gwilt, the bigamist, husband-poisoner and laudanum addict whose intrigues spur the plot of this most sensational of melodramas.

Aurora Leigh and Other Poems   Elizabeth Barrett Browning

Aurora Leigh (1856), Elizabeth Barrett Browning's epic novel in blank verse, tells the story of the making of a woman poet, exploring 'the woman question', art and its relation to politics and social oppression.

Personal Narrative of a Journey to the Equinoctial Regions of the New Continent   Alexander von Humboldt

Alexander von Humboldt became a wholly new kind of nineteenth-century hero – the scientist–explorer – and in *Personal Narrative* he invented a new literary genre: the travelogue.

The Pancatantra   Visnu Sarma

The Pancatantra is one of the earliest books of fables and its influence can be seen in the *Arabian Nights*, the *Decameron*, the *Canterbury Tales* and most notably in the *Fables* of La Fontaine.

A Laodicean   Thomas Hardy

The Laodicean of Hardy's title is Paula Power, a thoroughly modern young woman who, despite her wealth and independence, cannot make up her mind.

Brand   Henrik Ibsen

The unsparing vision of a priest driven by faith to risk and witness the deaths of his wife and child gives *Brand* its icy ferocity. It was Ibsen's first masterpiece, a poetic drama composed in 1865 and published to tremendous critical and popular acclaim.

READ MORE IN PENGUIN

A CHOICE OF CLASSICS

Sylvia's Lovers Elizabeth Gaskell

In an atmosphere of unease the rivalries of two men, the sober tradesman Philip Hepburn, who has been devoted to his cousin Sylvia since her childhood, and the gallant, charming whaleship harpooner Charley Kinraid, are played out.

The Republic Plato

The best-known of Plato's dialogues, *The Republic* is also one of the supreme masterpieces of Western philosophy, whose influence cannot be overestimated.

Ethics Benedict de Spinoza

'Spinoza (1632–77),' wrote Bertrand Russell, 'is the noblest and most lovable of the great philosophers. Intellectually, some others have surpassed him, but ethically he is supreme.'

Virgil in English

From Chaucer to Auden, Virgil is a defining presence in English poetry. Penguin Classics' new series, Poets in Translation, offers the best translations in English, through the centuries, of the major Classical and European poets.

What is Art? Leo Tolstoy

Tolstoy wrote prolifically in a series of essays and polemics on issues of morality, social justice and religion. These culminated in *What is Art?*, published in 1898, in which he rejects the idea that art reveals and reinvents through beauty.

An Autobiography Anthony Trollope

A fascinating insight into a writer's life, in which Trollope also recorded his unhappy youth and his progress to prosperity and social recognition.

READ MORE IN PENGUIN

A CHOICE OF CLASSICS

Anton Chekhov	**The Duel and Other Stories**
	The Kiss and Other Stories
	The Fiancée and Other Stories
	Lady with Lapdog and Other Stories
	The Party and Other Stories
	Plays (The Cherry Orchard/Ivanov/The Seagull/Uncle Vania/The Bear/The Proposal/A Jubilee/Three Sisters)
Fyodor Dostoyevsky	**The Brothers Karamazov**
	Crime and Punishment
	The Devils
	The Gambler/Bobok/A Nasty Story
	The House of the Dead
	The Idiot
	Netochka Nezvanova
	The Village of Stepanchikovo
	Notes from Underground/The Double
Nikolai Gogol	**Dead Souls**
	Diary of a Madman and Other Stories
Mikhail Lermontov	**A Hero of Our Time**
Alexander Pushkin	**Eugene Onegin**
	The Queen of Spades and Other Stories
Leo Tolstoy	**Anna Karenin**
	Childhood, Boyhood, Youth
	How Much Land Does a Man Need?
	The Kreutzer Sonata and Other Stories
	Master and Man and Other Stories
	Resurrection
	The Sebastopol Sketches
	What is Art?
	War and Peace
Ivan Turgenev	**Fathers and Sons**
	First Love
	A Month in the Country
	On the Eve
	Rudin
	Sketches from a Hunter's Album